SHIRTALOON

HE WHO FIGHTS WITH MONSTERS

BOOK TWO

www.aethonbooks.com

Aethon Books
www.aethonbooks.com

Print and eBook formatting by Steve Beaulieu.

Published by Aethon Books LLC.

ALSO IN SERIES

HE WHO FIGHTS WITH MONSTERS

BOOK ONE

BOOK TWO

BOOK THREE

1
CLIMBING MOUNTAINS

Jason Asano walked through the halls of the cloud palace belonging to Emir Bahadir the powerful adventurer who had arrived in the city with such fanfare. The cloud palace was far from just white cloud-stuff, with the walls, floors and ceilings cast in sunset shades of blue, purple, orange and gold. In some areas the colour was startlingly vibrant; in others, soft and subdued. Everything glowed with its own light; Emir had told Jason it was absorbed sunlight the palace could store-up and distribute as needed. The floors underfoot had a springiness that was still stable, as if an overly sensible engineer had been forced to design a bouncy castle. The total effect was like walking through a fairy tale.

A full wing of the cloud palace was dedicated to guest suites and Jason walked from his own to that in which Emir had placed Belinda and Sophie. The two thieves had been made pawns of local politics and Jason had placed them under Emir's protection, which they had only accepted out of desperation. The door to their suite was white, with the edges marked out in blue. On the wall next to the door was a small, circular patch of gold, which he pressed a finger into. It felt like pressing into a marshmallow.

He heard a pleasant chime from the other side of the door, like tinkling water. A few moments later, the door became translucent, revealing Sophie standing on the other side. She wore dark, practical clothing, with her entire posture screaming the opposite of welcome.

"You'll want to come in then," she said, her tone trying to convince him otherwise.

"It's time we had a talk," Jason said, "but we don't have to do it here. The palace is full of places for a nice chat."

"It'll be nice, will it?"

"Probably not, now you ask. But, I brought sandwiches if that helps."

Sophie jerked her head in a reluctant invitation and Jason walked inside. His own suite was larger than any place Jason had ever lived and Belinda and Sophie were occupying one that seemed similar.

"Terrace," she directed him, although did not head that way herself.

He could see the terrace through the walls, which had their opacity shifted to the point of being invisible. The mist wall tussled Jason's hair as he walked through it.

"That's indoor/outdoor living," he murmured to himself as he walked over to the terrace furniture. He set out a tray of sandwiches, plates, glasses and a pitcher of blended fruit drink from his inventory, plucking the items out of thin air, before sitting down.

Belinda and Sophie came out just as he was pouring drinks. Belinda was dressed in light, summery clothes of loose shirt, pants and sandals, in the colourful style common to Greenstone. She sat down and immediately grabbed a sandwich. Sophie didn't reach for the food, looking at it with suspicion.

"Is this bread from Pantero's?" Belinda asked after swallowing her first bite. Pantero's was a bakery in Old City and had the best bread Jason had found in the city.

"It is," he said brightly. "My friend Beth told me about it. They've been operating there for an incredibly long time. Her grandmother used to go there as a girl when their family owned that whole part of the city."

"You're talking about the Cavendish family?"

"That's them."

"Didn't they leave the Cavendish district the better part of two centuries ago?"

"Something like that," Jason said. "That's the adventuring life, I suppose. You live long enough to see history for yourself."

The easy smile fell from his face.

"If it doesn't get you killed first," he added darkly, clearly talking to himself.

"Did something happen when you went away?" Belinda asked.

"A friend of mine died," he said.

"A close friend?"

"As close as I have in this world. She taught me so much about being an adventurer."

"She taught you to fight?" Sophie asked.

"No, that was Rufus. He taught me to fight like an adventurer. Farrah taught me to live like one."

He smiled sadly.

"She'd call me out when I started talking out my backside. Which you may come to find is pretty often."

He brushed the back of his hand over his eyes and gave them a grin that was only a little forced.

"None of that matters to you, though," he told them. "You have your own troubles to deal with, which is why I'm here."

"I thought your clever plan collapsed in a heap," Sophie said.

"It did," Jason said, "but times, as the song goes, are a-changing."

"What song?"

"Doesn't matter," Jason said, waving a dismissive hand. "As it stands, I see this going one of four ways. The pair of you will have to choose between them."

"And if we don't like your options?" Sophie asked.

"That would be option one," Jason said. "You put me and my schemes behind you, which is reasonable, given how they've gone thus far. You walk out of the cloud palace and seize your own fate. Option two is similar, but more appealing, I think. You still walk away, but we send you far from here first. Our host has someone that can send you places so far from here it's not worth the effort of looking for you."

"A teleporting power," Sophie guessed.

"She opens portals, which is how we came and went just recently. Her name is Hester, and she seems quite nice. You can talk to her to pick out a destination, then we see you gone. We'll send you off with a fist full of cash but that is all you will have, aside from each other. I imagine a couple of resourceful women like yourselves will have no trouble starting fresh."

"A clean slate is all we've been looking for," Belinda said.

"You can have it," Jason said, "if that's what you choose. Option three is to upgrade who is standing between you and Lucian Lamprey. You've seen that my efforts haven't worked out as well as I thought they would. Emir, on the other hand, is all the protection you could ask for."

"Why would he help us?" Sophie asked.

"The way you fight. The way we fight. He's interested in the origins of that style. If he finds out that you use it, I'm certain he'd fully take you under his protection. He'd want you to help him trace back its history, but I don't imagine that would be an onerous task."

"Is that how you know him?" Belinda asked. "You're helping him find the history of the fighting style?"

"No. I met Emir because he's a friend of a friend. He doesn't know that either of us can use the style, but I'm of little use to him because I learned it from a skill book."

"You learned that from a skill book?" Sophie asked. She seemed curious, her expression breaking from stern suspicion for the first time since he arrived. "I've fought people who used skill books before. Fighting you didn't feel like that."

"I've had additional training to fully incorporate those skills," Jason said.

"Unless you learned to fight from a skill book too, turning to Emir might be a good option for you."

"Why haven't you told him already?" Sophie asked.

"Not my secret to tell."

"You expect us to believe that?"

"No." Jason gave them a smile instead of trying to convince them further.

"What's option four?" Belinda asked.

Before answering, Jason picked up a sandwich and took a generous bite, chewing thoroughly before swallowing. He washed it down by emptying his glass, then slowly poured himself another.

"Really?" Sophie asked and he flashed her a grin.

"I got this from a guy who makes blended fruit drinks here on the Island," he said. "Not cheap, but what is on the Island?"

Belinda sipped at her glass curiously, eyes going wide at the sweet, pleasant taste. Sophie glared at her, leaving her own glass untouched.

"There was meant to be an auction while I was gone," Jason said. "All the big spenders were away, though, so they ended up cancelling it. That means the brokers have a few essences and awakening stones available for relatively reasonable prices."

"Why are you talking about essences?" Sophie asked. "I don't care how reasonable the prices are; they're way beyond what we have. We weren't stealing for the money and margins were slim because high-end jewellery and the like is easy to trace. After expenses, we were barely breaking even. Are you offering us a loan?"

"Option four," Jason said, "is the original plan. I take you, Sophie, as an indenture. That eliminates your fugitive status, meaning that with a couple more essences, you can sign on to the Adventure Society. You'll be shielded from Lucian Lamprey and Cole Silva for good. At least, for the purposes they originally intended. Nothing I've heard about either suggests they are above petty revenge."

"You didn't answer her question," Belinda said. "How are we meant to afford essences?"

"A loan would not be an inaccurate characterisation," Jason said. "Joining the Adventure Society would offer you many protections, including from me, but the indenture would still stand."

"You want me to work it off," Sophie said.

"Exactly. And once you're an adventurer, you'll find that opportunities abound. If you're willing to work for them."

"What does that mean?" Sophie asked.

"I'm not entirely sure, to be honest," Jason said. "There is some kind of competition coming up, organised by our host. He has told me that there are essences and awakening stones to be had. Even if you don't get enough for your friend here, you'll still be an adventurer. It would only be a matter of time."

"How would that even work?" Belinda asked. "I thought indenture was off the table."

"I told you earlier: times are changing. You probably didn't hear, shuttered away like this, but the big expedition went wrong. *Very* wrong. A lot of adventurers died, which is why we left to help."

"Were you any help?" Sophie asked.

"Sophie!" Belinda scolded.

"You seem too weak to help a big adventurer expedition," Sophie said, unrepentant. "You barely caught me."

"You're right," Jason said. "Mostly I just told people where to put up tents until some silver-ranker got rid of me."

"So, what does this expedition have to do with the indenture?" Belinda asked.

"Because it went so very wrong," Jason said, "there's going to be an inquiry. There's a Continental Council that oversees Adventure Society business continent-wide. After the mess that happened, they're sending a team here to conduct some kind of audit on the whole Adventure Society branch."

"You're saying that people will actually have to follow the rules for once," Sophie said.

"At least for a small window of time," Jason said. "It'll be back to business soon enough but until then, the director won't be able to sell out the society's legal agreement with the city. Which means I can 'recapture' you and the indenture hearing is back on."

"Why?" Sophie asked. "Essences, indenture hearings. Why would you do any of that for us? Are you trying to tell me that Jory is such a good friend to you that you'd go this far over some girl he likes?"

"You know I'm sitting right here," Belinda said.

"I'm not sure you'd believe me if I told you why," Jason said. "You'd believe maybe one word in ten coming out of my mouth."

"If that," Sophie said. "Tell us anyway. You learn a lot about a person from how they lie."

Jason chuckled, leaned back in his chair and took another long drink. The amused half-smile he used to mask his emotions was replaced by a slightly sad, sober expression.

"When I first came here," he said, "I was lost. More lost than you can imagine. I knew no one; nothing made sense. I was tired, beaten and had people trying to kill me, all while doubting my own sanity. I met new friends who helped me get on my feet. They taught me, supported me. Put up with me. They helped me take control of my life."

He paused for a long time, looking out at the ocean. Sophie was about to say something, but Belinda gestured to wait.

"One of them is dead now," he said. "I think she would like me trying to do the same for someone else. Or maybe she'd yell at me and tell me to sort my own problems out before looking to someone else's."

He smiled sadly, but genuinely, his eyes twinkling with moisture. He wiped them and stood up.

"I'll leave the lunch," he said. "Talk over what you want to do and tell me when you figure it out. Or vanish and tell me nothing. Up to you."

He headed through the invisible wall of their suite and made for the door.

"How long do we have to decide?" Belinda called after him.

He stopped and turned back to them.

"As long as you can convince Emir to have you," he said. "If you want to be an adventurer, the sooner the better. I'm not the only one who spotted cheap essences, and the next Adventure Society intake is in nine days. We need to have the indenture hearing, pick out some essences and shove them into you before that."

He left Belinda and Sophie sitting at the table with a bunch of sandwiches and blended fruit drink.

"If he's a liar, he's a good one," Belinda said.

"He is liar," Sophie said. "And he *is* a good one."

"You think he's playing us? I don't see what he would get out of that."

"Some political game we don't know enough to see."

"I don't know," Belinda said. "Jory and Clive aren't like the people we usually deal with. Maybe he isn't either."

"Does he feel like that to you?"

"No," Belinda said. "Those two are easy to read. Asano is more like dark water. You see things in there, but you can't tell if what you saw was real."

"I've seen people like him before," Sophie said. "They know you won't believe what they say, so they tell you five stories and let you figure out which is true."

"And how do you do that?"

"That's the trap; none of them are."

"So those options he gave us, you don't think they're real options?"

"Maybe," Sophie said. "But maybe he wants us to think they're our only options."

"Our current options are to leave or hope we don't get kicked out," Belinda said. "If you have something better than what he's offering, I'm listening."

"You know I don't. But I don't trust him."

"At this point, we have to trust either him or fate. It wasn't fate that put us in a magic castle. It was him."

"That's what he wants us to think," Sophie said.

"Maybe we can talk to some of the other people here," Belinda said. "Get a better sense of him."

"That's a good idea," Sophie said. "Information isolation is our biggest weakness right now."

"*That's* our biggest weakness?"

"The biggest one we can do something about. Press Clive about him, next time he comes by. In the meantime, we can find out who else in this place knows him."

Jason was leaving the cloud palace when he ran into Emir and his chief of staff, Constance, coming back. They stopped to chat halfway across the platform connecting the cloud palace to the shore.

"Did you talk to my other guests?" Emir asked.

"I just came from there."

"And?"

"My guess would be they choose to get sent far from here."

"The adventuring life not tempting?"

"They don't trust me," Jason said. "Probably a smart choice. My first plan didn't exactly work out."

Emir chuckled.

"You need to work on that," he said. "I wasn't happy to find the camp being run by some imbecile after I put you and Rufus's friend in charge of it."

"You didn't put us in charge of that camp," Jason said. "It just kind of worked out that way. Until it didn't."

"Are you sure?" Emir asked. "It feels like I put you in charge."

"You're the only gold-ranker here," Jason said. "It probably feels like everything happens because you wanted it to."

"He's right," Constance said. "You didn't put them in charge."

"Well, if Constance says so. What are you up to now, Jason?"

"Does no one believe what I have to say, today? I'm off to see Elspeth Arella, to explain why the indenture hearing is going to go the way I want."

Constance, who normally was a detached professional, creased her brow in confusion.

"You know you're still an iron-ranker, right?" she asked.

"I do," Jason said.

"And you're going to march into the office of the silver-rank branch director of the Adventure Society and tell her what to do?"

"I am."

"Which, if I understand correctly, is exactly what you did last time. After which, she immediately played you for a fool."

"That would be an accurate summation, yes," Jason said.

"I hope you aren't going to be throwing around Mr Bahadir's name."

"I have a little more decorum than that," Jason said. "I have my own levers to push, thank you."

"Very well," she said, her expression still a warning.

"We'll let you get to it," Emir said. "Good luck."

They parted ways, Emir and Constance returning to the palace. Once out of sight, Constance's posture became more relaxed.

"Rufus was right," Constance said. "That boy is mad."

"That's the things about climbing mountains," Emir said. "The first thing you need is someone foolish enough to try it."

"I never saw the point of that as a recreational activity," Constance said. "Putting a suppression collar on yourself and clambering up an edifice? If they're that keen on danger, why not fight monsters like regular people?"

"The point is that they're challenging themselves to do what others think can't be done."

"That man Koenig who used to work for you when I first started. He liked to climb mountains, didn't he?"

"He did, indeed," Emir said. "He was quite the enthusiast."

"What happened to him?"

"He fell off a mountain and died."

"Don't a lot of people die trying to climb mountains?"

"Yes," Emir said. "Yes, they do."

2

NOTHING CAN HURT YOU LIKE HOPE

The door to Arella's office at the Adventure Society opened as Jason approached and he walked right in. Sitting behind her desk, she made a gesture and the door closed behind him. He stood in front of the desk, looking around.

"You've changed the artwork."

"I'm surprised you showed your face," she said. "I suppose I shouldn't have expected any bounds on your arrogance."

"That's probably fair. I should thank you, though, for the object lesson in the pitfalls of being arrogant. Your mistake was the same every time; you never consider how your actions hurt other people. The thief you tried to hand over to Lamprey. The iron-rankers you made look buffoonish at their inability to catch her. Your own officials being squeezed between you and the Duke. That was already hurting you, but the expedition? There's plenty of blame to go around but we both know that you're in line for a hearty serving. You alienated your allies and made deals with your enemies."

Arella looked at him with open disgust.

"You really never tire of hearing your own voice, do you?"

"I do like to monologue, don't I? Next thing you know, I'll be building a weather machine in a mountain fortress carved into the shape of my own head."

"You also like to babble nonsense. What are you here for, Asano?"

"Are you still going to revoke my membership?"

"You know I'm not."

"All those eyes on you make petty revenge a little harder, don't they?"

"If that's all you want, then get out."

"There is one thing," Jason said. "There needs to be a new sentence-dispensation hearing for the thief. I need to know you won't try and sabotage it again."

She gave him an angry glare.

"You know full well that I can't interfere. Not if I want to still be in this office a month from now."

"You say that, but the last time I was in here was to ask for the same thing. You said it would go smoothly but I bet you had a messenger on their way to Lamprey before I was out of the building. I'm here for assurances."

"You think you can make demands?"

"I tried cooperation. And, yes, I think I can make demands."

"I could crush you into paste without getting out of this chair."

"Could you, though? You're a smart woman, director. Not as smart as you think, but enough to know the consequences of that. You've disillusioned your allies while I keep making friends. I told you that your mistake was not caring who your games hurt. Kill me and you won't just lose this office; you'll die in it."

She reached out an arm in a clutching motion, her silver-rank reflexes too fast for Jason to react. His aura, the projection of his soul that was the magical representation of his personal space, was ground down to nothing. An invisible force picked him up, lifting him into the air as it squeezed him from every direction. The crushing force wracked his whole body with pain.

"You're so sure of yourself," she said. She was still reclined in her chair, hand held out towards him.

"Yes," he croaked, looking back with defiance.

She squeezed all the harder until his muscles felt like pulp, his bones on the verge of breaking. His head was ready to pop like a pimple.

She floated up, out of her seat and over her desk until they were face to face. Hers held a sneer, while his was turning purple.

"Power trumps everything," she told him. "It doesn't matter how clever you are or how well you can manipulate the rules. Schemes and laws are nothing in the face of complete and absolute power."

"Do it then," he choked out. "Are you powerful enough to handle the consequences?"

She opened her clenched hand and he collapsed to floor. She floated down to land gently on the floor, looking down on him as he gasped and spluttered.

"Get out of my office," she told him.

Jason pushed himself achingly into a sitting position, then stood up with a groan, looking her straight in the eye.

"I told you," he said. "I came for assurances."

She let out a disbelieving laugh.

"You're bold for someone hiding behind the strength of others."

"You do what you can with what you have," Jason said. "Something I imagine you know very well."

She sneered.

"You said assurances. What kind of assurances do you want?"

"You misunderstand," Jason said. "When I said I'm here for assurances, it was to give them, not receive."

"What are you talking about?"

"If you don't keep your hand off the scale for the sentence dispensation, then that inquiry coming up will be hearing from me."

"The secret is already out, Asano. People know my family history."

"Not that," Jason said. "I mean the fact that an Adventure Society director undertook no small effort to prevent the completion of a contract she herself posted. You'll be lucky to keep your membership after that, let alone your position."

"You have no proof."

"You were sloppy. Too reliant on no one guessing what you were up to. You think the inquiry won't find anything, once they know to look? Even if you start cleaning up the moment I walk out of here, how many bodies will you have to drop? Are you sure you can get them all? I don't think you can. There are too many threads and chasing them all down would just make more."

Her hand twitched up, then down again. He gave her a predatory smile.

"Killing me only hurts you," he said. "You know that, and you have much bigger problems than me. Danielle Geller hasn't led what's left of the expedition back, yet, but you'll know about it when she has. I told you your mistake was not considering the collateral damage of your plotting and she is going to lay all the people that died at your feet. She once thought quite highly of you, but she lost family out there."

Arella's face scrunched up in reluctance and unreleased fury.

"What assurance do I have that you won't burn me with the inquiry anyway?" she asked, biting off her words.

"The last time I came in here asking you to uphold the rules, I trusted you and got burned for my trouble. This time, you have to trust me."

She forced out a nod.

"I'll direct the advocate to defend the tenets of the service agreement with the city," she said, biting her words off unhappily.

"All I wanted to hear," he said and immediately turned for the door.

"Asano," she called out and he stopped to look back.

"You really would have stood between Lamprey and this girl, wouldn't you?" she asked.

"Is that why you sold me out? You didn't think I had the resolve?"

The anger seemed to wash out of her, shoulders slumping and face suddenly haggard, in spite of its silver rank perfection.

"Call it a lesson learned. Things won't be going well for me in the near future, but I will climb back up."

"I don't doubt it," Jason said.

"I also won't forget the iron-ranker that walked into my office to put his foot on my neck when I was down."

Belinda watched with concern as Sophie paced back and forth on the terrace. Her friend rarely showed her anxiety, which meant she was running close to the edge.

"If they're really willing to send us far from here," Sophie said, "I think we do that, then get far from where they sent us. Put them and this whole city behind us."

She sped up her pacing, running her hands through her hair. Normally she tied it back in a ponytail, but today it was loose and wild.

"That's assuming we can trust going through some portal they set up," she continued, "which we absolutely can't. Maybe the best option really is leaving and making our own way from here."

Belinda got up from her chair, placing herself in Sophie's path. She stopped, looking up as if surprised she was there at all. Belinda took her in a hug, Sophie's arms slipping around her in turn, gripping her like a security blanket.

"You know we can't walk out of here as fugitives," Belinda said softly. "Even if we got out of the Adventure Society grounds, which we wouldn't, there was a reason we turned to Ventress for protection, even though we were just trading one self-serving crime lord for another. If we go out into the city, things are worse for us now than they were then."

Belinda let go of Sophie and went through the invisible wall into their suite.

"I'm having a drink," she said. "So are you."

The sprawling main area of the guest suite was one open space, but had areas divided up for lounging, dining, a kitchen and a bar. Belinda snagged a couple of glasses and a bottle, bringing them back outside. They sat down and Sophie took the first shot without tasting it, before sipping at the second.

"You realise this bottle cost more than most of the things we've ever stolen," Belinda said.

"I thought we'd half-emptied this bottle. Did you get it from the cooler cabinet?"

"I got it from the bar. There's a floor cabinet and two wall cabinets with drinks in addition to the bar," Belinda said. "How am I meant to remember where any given bottle came from?"

"You know there's a wine room?" Sophie said.

"No, where is it?"

"You know the floaty things that lift you to the upper floor?"

"Yeah."

"If you hit that gold patch next to it on the wall twice, it goes down instead."

"This place is crazy."

Sophie looked at the glass in her hand, then at the cloud palace around them.

"Everything about this whole experience is crazy," she said.

"It'll be hard to give up," Belinda said. "If that's the way we decide to go."

Sophie frowned.

"You think we should go along with Asano's plan."

"You know I'll follow you, whatever you decide," Belinda said.

"You get just as much say as I do," Sophie insisted.

"Great," Belinda said, standing up. "I'll go find Asano and we can get you some essences."

"Hold on," Sophie said, half-standing in her seat. Belinda flashed her a grin and sat back down.

"What happened to I get as much say as you?" Belinda asked.

"As much," Sophie said as she gave Belinda a flat look. "Not more."

"You know I was only half-joking," Belinda said. "Even if we get so far from here we don't have to deal with Silva or Ventress or Lamprey, do you really want to go from this back to stealing?"

"We're good at stealing."

"What if we're good at something else? What if we didn't have to live by the whims of some sadistic crime lord? You know that wherever we go, there will always be a Clarissa Ventress or Cole Silva. If we turn down this chance, that will be our lives. Forever."

"We could do something else," Sophie said. "Something legal."

"Like what? Open a shop?"

"We could be locksmiths," Sophie said. "That's assuming even the offer to send us away is real. We've been stuck in this box, only hearing what they want us to hear. They could be using us for anything."

"Why would they bother?" Belinda asked. "Look at where we are. Look at who they are. Look at what we're drinking! What could we possibly offer Bahadir that he can't just take? At what point does this much effort in service to some elaborate ruse become less plausible than they just want to help us? I think we've crossed that line. What they're offering may seem outlandish to us, but clearly that isn't the case for them. They're adventurers, making adventurer money."

Sophie took a deep breath as she considered what Belinda had to say.

"My instincts are still screaming at me to run," she said. "The better things seem, the worse it will be when the floor falls out from under us. Nothing can hurt you as badly as hope."

Belinda looked at her friend from under raised eyebrows.

"Really, Soph? Nothing can hurt you like hope? Is that how you want to live your life?"

"When were our lives ever different? We both had dead parents and massive debts when we were still children."

"That's exactly why I think we should take a risk," Belinda said. "We were already risking everything on these crazy jobs, and for what? The chance to go somewhere else and have different crappy lives? I don't want to go back to stealing for whatever murderous lunatic is in charge of wherever we end up."

She gestured at the sky palace around them.

"I want more of this. This is worth risking everything for."

Sophie looked at her friend for a long time. She took the bottle, poured herself a large drink and gulped it down.

"Alright," she said finally.

"Alright?"

"Yeah."

A huge grin broke out on Belinda's face.

"Sophie Wexler, adventurer."

"Don't get carried away."

"You're going to be an adventurer!"

"This could all still go horribly wrong."

"That means I'm going to be an adventurer too, sooner or later."

"You'll have to earn how to fight," Sophie said. Despite her best efforts, a smile was creeping onto her face.

"I know how to fight," Belinda said.

"Kicking a guy in the beans and then running for it is not fighting."

"It got me this far."

3

SEE YOU IN COURT

Elspeth Arella was in the family home she had spent very little time in, even as a child. Raised by her mother in secret, now that the secret was finally out she was free to come and go as she pleased. Those precious, clandestine visits to her father, Dorgan, were in the past; she could casually come by to take tea in one of his courtyards whenever she liked.

"Your mistake was your need to feel in control," Dorgan told her. "You had a choice between letting Asano bear the brunt of Lamprey's ire, or cutting a deal with Lamprey yourself."

"I didn't think Asano could stand up to Lamprey."

"The boy is arrogant and reckless," Dorgan said. "He would have stood up to Lamprey. Probably not successfully, but that wouldn't have mattered. If Lamprey put the boy down, that would have given you all the leverage you needed. You didn't choose that path, because it felt passive. You wanted events to move by your hand, so you took the initiative and went to Lamprey."

"It felt right," Arella said.

"Our feelings are not always the wisest guide. Even if it had gone well, dealing directly with Lamprey wouldn't have given you anything you couldn't get by waiting. All it brought you was a risk, the consequences of which you subsequently suffered. Now, with the unfortunate fate of the expedition, you have been left you critically exposed."

She nodded.

"I was impatient," she said. "What do I do next?"

"For now, you must be above reproach," he told her. "Every rule, every stipulation. This is not the time to push for new goals. The inquiry will remove you or not. Only once the decision is made will we know the way forward."

"If they remove me, everything we've done will be wasted."

"Not everything," he said. "Our connection is in the open now and while it may not be endorsed, it is tolerated. If we have to start again, we will. Who doesn't like a redemption story?"

"I really want to crush Asano under my heel," she said. "If he hadn't caught the thief..."

"If he hadn't, it was past time for you to arrange her capture anyway. You had already let it play out too long. Asano was the perfect foil with which to jab Lamprey and the mistake was yours in not using him properly."

"He stormed into my office to demand I help him with his damn agenda. Twice!"

"Don't make Lamprey's mistake and become fixated on someone unimportant to your ultimate goals. If you really must do something about Asano, then be patient. After the inquiry is done we can act, but at a careful remove. If we move deftly, then once he is dead the vengeance of his friends will fall on those whose removal will advantage us."

"How do we do that?" she asked.

"Lucian Lamprey and Cole Silva are kindred spirits. When the time is right, we can help them make a connection."

"What about Lamprey's dealings with Clarissa Ventress? Her and Silva hate each other."

"Ventress failed to deliver what she promised to Lamprey months ago. By the time we choose to act, I would be astounded to find her still alive."

Rufus and Gary, Jason's adventurer friends, had been highly motivated to find out who was behind the unexpected enemy the expedition had encountered. Their companion, Farrah, had died unavenged. The various magical paraphernalia discovered there would only arrive once the expedition returned overland, but Rufus could not be talked into waiting. He roped Gary into scouring Magic Society records and the library at the temple of Knowledge for any reference to the bizarre enemies they faced in the astral space. The first time their friends had seen them in days was when they arrived at the courthouse, showing their solidarity for Jason.

Belinda remained in the cloud palace for safety while Jason took Sophie into court for the sentence dispensation hearing. Until her docket was called she was required to stay the courtroom gaol in the basement to await her hearing. Jason took Gary along; he stayed to watch for any last-minute schemes while Sophie was trapped and isolated. As Jason was leaving, one of the guards stopped him.

The guard threw an uncertain glance in the direction of Gary, who was leaning against the wall by Sophie's cell.

"He can't stay here," the guard said.

Jason looked over at the towering the lion-man, Gary, then back at the guard.

"You'd best go tell him, then, because damned if I'm doing it."

Leaving the nonplussed guard in his wake, Jason went back upstairs. On the ground floor, just outside the courtroom entrance, he spotted Vincent and Rufus talking to someone. Vincent spotted Jason in turn and waved him over.

"This is Rupert Cline," Vincent said. Rupert was a neatly put together man of around thirty, with an iron-rank aura. "He was the one who gave us the warning about Arella and Lamprey."

Jason shook Rupert's hand.

"Thank you for that," he said. "You kept a pair of young women from an unpleasant fate."

"We're Adventure Society, right?" Rupert asked. "Standing between people and the bad stuff is what we're for."

Jason flashed a grin.

"Yes, we are," he said happily. "It's nice to meet a fellow idealist."

Vincent and Rufus shared a sceptical look, which Jason noticed.

"What?" he asked them.

"It's just strange to see you meeting someone and acting like a sensible person," Vincent said.

"That's hurtful," Jason said.

"I heard about what you put Clive through when you first met him."

"Jory told me to do that. Clive thought I was counterfeiting spirit coins or something."

"He did?"

"Yeah. Never really came up again after I told him I was an outworlder."

"What's an outworlder?" Rupert asked.

They chatted until the proceeding was about to start. Rupert had to go inside and Jason, Vincent and Rufus went upstairs to the viewing gallery. They took seats to await proceedings to begin. Jason's knowledge of courtrooms was sourced heavily on television. The Greenstone court was less like an American legal procedural and more like a British period drama. The gallery was mezzanine viewing, looking down into the courtroom.

As they waited, a man with a silver-rank aura arrived in the gallery. Despite being an elf, muscles bulged under his expensive clothes. He was wearing a Magic Society pin, fancier than the usual and embossed in a strange metal that shimmered with rainbow colours. The man stopped on his way to a seat, turning to look at Jason.

"You're Asano," he said.

"Yep. You must be… actually, I have no idea who you are," Jason said.

"I'm Lucian Lamprey."

"Doesn't ring a bell. I see you're in the Magic Society. Are you one of those guys who work in a booth identifying magic items?"

"What? A booth?"

"Haven't heard about that yet? You're probably new, so that's alright. You should make sure and learn about all the services the Magic Society offers though. Wouldn't want to get fired."

"I'm the director of the Magic Society."

"You're Pochard Finn? I thought you'd be thinner."

"Pochard Finn is my deputy. I'm Lucian Lamprey."

"Still doesn't ring a bell. Are you sure?"

Lamprey opened his mouth to shoot back when he saw Vincent and Rufus stifling laughter. Lamprey moved closer, looming over the still sitting Jason.

"You should know better than to mock me," Lamprey warned.

Jason craned his head back to look up at Lamprey's face.

"Mate, you're hardly in a position to point out what others are doing wrong. Using the power of your position to force women into sleeping with you? That's about as sleazy as it gets. Is it even necessary? You're super ripped; I bet there are plenty of people who respond to that. Is it a charm deficit? Just keep the mouth shut, bathe regularly and do the strong but silent thing. You'll get some takers."

A sinister smile cross Lamprey's face.

"You were always going to pay for this, Asano. For your mockery, I'll make sure you pay slowly."

"Like a layaway plan? You seem like the kind of guy who'd shaft me on the interest. I'd rather pay for doing the right thing than roll over and let someone like you do whatever he likes."

"There will come a day when I remind you of those words. We'll see what you say then."

"Probably something about carb-loading. What do you bench?"

Lamprey shook his head, looking at Jason like he was a mad person before walking off to take a seat at the other end of the gallery.

"Why would you provoke him like that?" Vincent asked.

"He was coming after me either way; he said it himself. I'd rather he do something angry than something smart."

"You play dangerous games, Jason," Rufus warned. "Someday you're going to pay for that."

"I know."

Sophie was brought up from the basement cells and placed in the prisoner dock, where she would have to stand for the duration of the proceedings. Jason realised that he'd never really taken a good look at her. They'd met briefly under normal circumstances, months ago, but most of their encounters had come when she'd been cornered, bloodied and dirty.

He had seen her often enough to know she preferred simple clothes, more fitted and practical than the normal fashion. Today was no different, wearing white that appealingly set off her dark complexion. Her attire showed off the physique of an athlete, sleek and strong.

Physically, she was a study in contrasts. Her silver hair was tied back in a simple ponytail, bright against her chocolate skin. Her features were delicate, for such an indelicate woman; rather than make her seem fragile, there was a sharpness to them. A promise of danger in her silver eyes that moved around the room, taking everything in. He noticed her glance linger on the exits.

As she looked around the room, she met Jason's gaze and held it, her expression a challenge. She was surrounded by power, her fate in the hands of strangers and yet she stood upright, proud and fearless. Jason understood in that moment why men like Lamprey and Cole Silva had such a need to possess or destroy her.

"You know, Rufus," Jason said. "I think she might be prettier than you."

"She's not," Vincent said.

"Thank you," Rufus said as Jason chuckled.

The hearing moved swiftly; the real decision-making had already happened behind closed doors. The Adventure Society advocate, Rupert Cline, asserted the Adventure Society's right to claim her indenture through the Adventure Society member who captured her and the magistrate agreed without challenge. Lamprey had apparently given up, recognising it was futile.

Soon after, Jason, Gary, Rufus and Vincent were leaving the courthouse with Sophie in tow. There was a silver tracking bracelet on her wrist, but she was otherwise unfettered.

"We should go," Rufus said to Gary. "We've been away from our investigation long enough. We need to find who these people that killed Farrah were."

Gary threw Jason a look.

"Actually," Jason said, "I was hoping you could help me with something. I want Sophie in the next Adventure Society intake. I need your expertise to get her ready."

"I already have something to do," Rufus said.

"Rufus, you don't have enough information. Wait until the expedition returns with everything they collected. Clive is their astral magic guy and he'll tell us what he finds. That means you'll know where to look instead of stumbling blindly. When the time comes for action, you'll be rested and ready."

A look of reluctance crossed Rufus's face, but Jason pre-empted him.

"What would Farrah tell you to do?" Jason asked him. "Would she tell you to work hard or work smart? Do what you're good at now and do the next thing when it's ready to be done."

Rufus looked unhappy but nodded.

"Alright, then," Jason said. "Sophie, you're in for a treat. He's reluctant to tell people, but Rufus' family actually runs a school for adventurers..."

The others looked at Jason as he trailed off.

- Contact [Phoebe Geller] has entered communication range.

"What is it?" Gary asked.

- Contact [Rick Geller] has entered communication range.
- Contact [Hannah Adeah] has entered communication range.
- Contact [Claire Adeah] has entered communication range.
- Contact [Thalia Mercer] has entered communication range.
- Contact [Danielle Geller] has entered communication range.
- Contact [Cassandra Mercer] has entered communication range.
- Contact [Humphrey Geller] has entered communication range.

"The expedition," Jason said. "They're back."

4
SIX-MONTH LEASE

The arrival of the expedition back into Greenstone was a mix of welcome, relief, commiseration and loss. Rufus and Gary waded into the chaos while Vincent headed for the administration building and the immense amount of work about to be dumped on him. Lacking anything else to do, Sophie trailed along behind Jason to the marshalling yard on the Adventure Society campus.

They found the Gellers, Rufus and Gary moving to talk to Danielle. With their arrival at the marshalling yard, her job as expedition leader was finally over. The strain was showing, even through the vitality of her silver rank. As Rufus and Gary greeted her, Jason sought out the iron-rank Gellers. He met his friend, a tired-looking Humphrey, with a broad smile and a warm handshake.

"Welcome home, mate; glad you made it. It was a bit touch-and-go there, from what I hear. Sorry I wasn't there to help."

"I'm not," Humphrey said. "I'm glad you didn't have to go through it. Life and death were separated by not much more than luck. Everyone lost people and we were no exception."

Jason knew a lot of the iron-rank Gellers by sight, and some familiar faces were missing. The one he knew best was Henry Geller, who he had fought in their now-infamous mirage chamber clash.

Rick Geller came up and shook Jason by the hand.

"I want to thank you," he said. "What you did to us in the mirage chamber… we were better prepared for when things went truly wrong. We had lived with the idea of losing people and still moving forward. It was worse for real, so much worse. We held it together, though, even after losing people. You helped us be ready for that."

Claire Adeah was one of the two elf sisters on Rick's team. Of them all, she had resented Jason's actions in their mock battle the most. She stepped up next to Rick and offered Jason her hand and he shook it.

"Rick's right," she said. "I didn't like what you did, back then, but it was nothing next to the real thing."

"I'd like to say that was my intention," Jason said. "Honestly, though, I was just looking for a way to win."

"It doesn't matter why," Rick said. "You helped us stay alive when we might not have otherwise."

"No, that's on you," Jason said. "You got as many people as you could out of there when much stronger adventurers were dying."

Rick nodded.

"We heard about your friend," he said. "You should look around you, right now. A lot of these people wouldn't be here if she hadn't bought them the time to survive."

Jason looked around, seeing the faces of strangers.

"I'd trade them all to get her back," he said. "Does that make me a bad person?"

"It makes you someone lying to yourself," a voice came from behind him. He turned and Cassandra fell into his embrace.

"If you really had the choice," she whispered into his ear, "you'd let her save those people."

"It doesn't feel like that," he whispered back.

They drew apart, their hands held together between them.

"How did your family come out?" he asked. "How's your brother?"

"We lost people, but not many as some. Thadwick woke up on the way back. He's… different."

"Coming that close to death can change you," Jason said.

She nodded.

"It's like he's finally seen how empty all the nonsense he built up around himself is. How much all the things he cared about were just worthless bluster in the face of real power. I think this will be good for him, in the end."

"We should take what good we can from all this mess," Jason said.

"I do have one question," Cassandra said with a sweet, tired smile.

"What's that?"

"Why is that very attractive young woman staring at us?"

"No idea what you're talking about," Jason said innocently, not taking his eyes off of her.

"No?" Cassandra asked, turning her head to examine Sophie. "You didn't notice the extremely pretty woman with the silver hair and the tracking bracelet."

"Oh, her."

"Yes, her."

"She's new."

"Yes, I imagine I would have spotted her before. She stands out, doesn't she?"

"You don't need to bother about her."

"Don't I, now?"

"Not at all. That's just my nubile slave girl."

"WHAT?" came Sophie and Cassandra's simultaneous exclamation, to a backdrop of Jason's wild cackling as a gaggle of people started talking over one another.

"I'm not a slave!"

"You have some serious explaining to do, Asano!"

"Jason, I think you're my hero now."

"What I have can't be taught, Rick."

"Just try treating me like a slave I will drown you in your own—"

"HEY!"

Rufus's booming voice cut through the noise as he marched over.

"What is going on here?" he asked. "Jason, what did you do?"

"Why do you assume it was me?"

"Was it you?"

"Well, yes, but where's the faith?"

"What were you thinking, causing a commotion here?"

"I thought people could use some normalcy," Jason said. "What's more normal than two women fighting over a sexy man?"

"You can have him," Cassandra told Sophie.

"Don't want him; you can keep him."

"That's hurtful," Jason said, looking between the two.

"Jason, this isn't the time for your nonsense," Rufus said.

"Rufus, this is exactly the time. There will be days and days of mourning the lost. These people just got home safe and they need just a few moments to celebrate surviving. A little laughter, a little joy. There won't be a lot of that for a while."

"I don't agree with you at all," Rufus said, then sighed and gave him a sad smile.

"Farrah would have, though," he said. "Just be respectful of people."

"That's fair," Jason said. He gave Rufus a rare, earnest smile, a far cry from his usual ones where he looked like he was up to something. He turned to Cassandra.

"Do you have to go home, or do you have some time for a debonair gentleman caller?"

"Oh, you have some questions to answer," she said. "You'll be answering them now."

"I'm an open book," Jason said. "Come along, slave girl."

"I'm not your slave!"

"She's a rental," Jason said as they started extricating themselves from the busy marshalling yard. "Six-month lease."

"You didn't rent me!"

"I have a receipt."

"It's an indenture contract."

"Why do you even have an indentured servant?" Cassandra asked.

"Well, you know how you said I should catch that thief?"

Cassandra looked over at Sophie.

"That was you?"

"It was," Sophie said unhappily.

"Frankly, I'm surprised he caught you."

"It was his friend who figured out how to ambush us."

"It was a team effort," Jason said. "And since I was team leader, the credit is primarily mine."

"What team?" Sophie asked. "There were only two of you."

"Senior partner, then."

"Does Standish know you were the senior partner?"

"I think he intuited it," Jason said.

"I think you're full of crap," Sophie said.

"I like her," Cassandra said. "But how did she end up indentured to you?"

"Ah," Jason said. "That is a tale of vicious crime lords, shady politicians and a handsome adventurer, generous of spirit…"

Rick Geller watched Jason saunter off, shamelessly boasting to a pair of beautiful women.

"I want to be just like him," he said wistfully, then received a hard thump on the arm. He yelped, turning to see that Claire had been the one to hit him.

"What was that for?"

"The man is infuriating," Sophie said. She was back in her shared suite with Belinda. They were standing at the terrace rail, enjoying the cool ocean breeze.

"How so?" Belinda asked.

"He keeps calling me a slave."

"Does he treat you like a slave?"

"That's not the point."

"It really is," Belinda said.

"He called me a nubile slave girl."

Belinda burst out laughing.

"That is not funny!"

"You're complaining about being called a slave while you live like a princess, complete with enchanted castle."

"Yeah, well… you don't know what he's up to."

"You're right," Belinda said. "He didn't want you around after the indenture hearing?"

"He's down the hall with his upper-class lover. I'm not sticking around for that, whatever the terms of indenture are."

"He has a lady friend? What's she like?"

"She's a Mercer. Main family too, not one of the branches. Obnoxiously good-looking."

Belinda groaned.

"I know what the pretty ones are like to deal with," she complained.

"She seems alright. Wait, was that directed at me?"

"It makes sense that she's a big nob," Belinda said, ignoring Sophie's question. "Look at the company Asano keeps."

"What's his background?" Sophie asked. "What have you managed to dig out of Standish?"

"A job offer, actually. Clive asked me to come work with him. Assuming that all this political stuff gets settled."

"What does he want you to do?"

"Be a research assistant, which I'm pretty sure means taking care of all the mundane stuff he doesn't have time for. He's expecting to be very busy soon."

"Are you sure he isn't looking for something more intimate?"

"He had a thing for that friend of Asano's who died. He's not hiding it very well, just throwing himself into his work."

"Are you going to take the job?"

"Of course. In the Magic Society, I can learn more about that Lamprey guy. Asano might think he has all this handled, but I doubt we've heard the end of it."

"What did you get from Standish about Asano?"

"According to Clive," Belinda said, "Jason isn't even from this world."

"What does that mean?"

"Well, you know the world?" Belinda asked.

"Of course I know the world," Sophie said. "It's a big round thing. We're standing on it."

"Actually, we're standing on the cloud palace."

"And the cloud palace is sitting on the world. By your reasoning, you aren't standing on the ground if you're wearing shoes."

"That's actually a good point," Belinda conceded with a frown.

"You don't need to sound surprised," Sophie said.

"Sorry," Belinda said. "What were we talking about? Right, the world. Generally, you think about the world as being everything, right?"

"But you're saying it isn't."

"That's exactly what I'm saying. Asano comes from a whole other world that's apparently out there."

"A whole different world," Sophie mused.

"Yes," Belinda said. "Uh, but no."

"What?"

"Well, it's a different world. Except, it's the same world. But different. It's complicated."

"I can tell by the fact that the only part of that I could follow was that the rest of it was complicated. You said he came from another world."

"Yes."

"But then you said that this different world is the same world."

"No. Except, yes. They're different versions of the same world. Like when we helped Donzo with the fake spirit coin racket."

"I can't believe I let you talk me into that. You're saying Asano comes from a counterfeit world?"

"No, both worlds are real."

"Then it's not a terrific comparison."

Belinda glared at Sophie.

"Maybe if you ever read a book that went three pages without the phrase 'glistening thighs,' I wouldn't have to dumb it down so much."

"Oh, so I should have been reading all that boring nonsense you collect in case I ever became the nubile slave girl of some guy from a world knocked out by some godly equivalent of Donzo making fake money in his bathtub?"

"Exactly," Belinda said.

They looked at each other and both erupted into laughter. They wandered into the lounge area and crashed down together on a couch.

"How is this our life?" Belinda asked, reclining back into the soft, cloudy furniture. "It's like things kept getting worse and worse, until they get so bad they came right around the other end to amazing and we somehow live in a magic palace, now."

"This is just temporary. We need to be ready for what comes next."

"What comes next is you getting amazing magical powers," Belinda said. "You know I blame you for all this."

"How is this my fault? Also, you just said this is amazing."

"If you shaved off all that shiny, silver hair, you might not get creepy guys chasing after you."

"You want me to run around bald?"

"You could wear a wig to cover it up," Belinda said. "It would have to be an ugly one, though, or it would defeat the purpose. Bald would be best, thinking about it."

"I'll do it if you do," Sophie said.

"And give up these natural curls? No thank you."

The room chime rang and Belinda got up to press the gold patch on the wall that turned the door translucent. On the other side was Jason.

"If you'd like to come with me, ladies."

"What happened to your lady friend?" Belinda asked.

"She only just got back from the expedition and has her own responsibilities. Our reunion was short but sweet."

"Stamina issues?" Sophie asked, walking up behind Belinda.

"My stamina is just fine," Jason said defensively.

"Sure it is," Sophie said.

"I'm perfectly virile, thank you very much."

"Where do you want us to go, exactly?" Belinda asked.

"I have assembled a panel of seasoned adventurers for advice and a catalogue of goods that are available—and affordable—from the brokers at the trade hall. It's time for your friend to choose her essences."

5
THE PERKS OF BEING AN ESSENCE USER

Jason led the two thieves into a meeting room that was only small by cloud palace standards. It had a wall open to one of the ubiquitous terraces and it's ocean views, the cloud palace still floating just off Greenstone Island. The three adventurers of his panel were on one side of the table, Jason and the two women taking seats on the other.

Jason introduced Sophie and Belinda to his panel of seasoned adventurers. It was comprised of Emir and Clive, who they knew, plus a bald, dark-skinned man that they didn't. The stranger was handsome, lithely muscled and carried himself with an air of straightforward competence. Even with him just sitting at a table, Sophie read the subtle cues that told her he would be dangerous if he needed to be.

The assured sense of capability he gave off was the exact opposite of what she read from Asano. In her encounters with him, Jason had variously come across as casual, dangerous, friendly, manipulative, vulnerable, controlling and buffoonish. She had no idea which, if any, of what she had seen was genuine.

"You know Emir, and Clive, of course," Jason said. "Emir is the most experienced adventurer in the city, and Clive works for the Magic Society. He's spent no small amount of time cataloguing essence abilities, mine included."

"Speaking of which," Clive said, "I really would like to hear more about that execute ability of yours—"

"Not the topic of the day, Clive," Jason said, gesturing for him to stop before he became too enthused. "The last member of our impromptu advice panel is Rufus Remore."

"The one who taught you to fight," Sophie said, giving Rufus a second look.

"Someone's paying attention," Jason said. "Rufus comes from a prestigious academy, so he knows quite a lot about matching people to essences. Rufus, this is Sophie Wexler and Belinda Callahan."

Rufus nodded a greeting.

"Can the three of you explain to me why this is happening?" Sophie asked. Belinda slumped forward.

"Really, Soph?"

"I still don't understand why Asano is doing any of this," Sophie said. "Why bother, for some people he hardly knows?"

"You've known him the longest, Rufus," Emir said. "I have to admit to sharing the young lady's curiosity."

All eyes turned to Rufus, who was thinking over a reply.

"The day I met Jason," he said, "we were all caught up in circumstances I can only describe as dire. This was especially true for him, who had no idea what was happening or why. As you will no doubt learn for yourselves, Jason can be quite resourceful when it matters most and he managed to get himself free of our captors. He got out of his cage and had a clear run at freedom."

"He's exaggerating," Jason said. "I would have been easily caught."

"So he says," Rufus countered.

"Did you say cage?" Belinda asked.

"Yes," Rufus said. "My team and I were in quite the unfortunate circumstance, except for one thing: we met Jason. He didn't take that run at freedom. Instead of escaping, he walked back into the sacrifice chamber of a blood cult. He was outnumbered and outmatched but he walked right in. He did that to rescue three strangers, which is the only reason I'm alive to tell you this story."

"I needed them to get me out," Jason said. "If I didn't get them out, I would have died by cultist or by desert. Rufus just likes to put it down to altruism."

"Yes I do," Rufus said.

"You really expect us to believe he's doing this out of the goodness of his heart?" Sophie asked.

"You can believe what you like," Rufus said. "You can still just walk away."

"No," Belinda said, giving the others a plastered-on smile. "She's going to clamp those lips together before she talks us out of the best opportunity we've ever had."

"Her caution is well placed," Emir said. "In all my time as an adventurer, I've never encountered a situation like this. I would be suspicious, as well."

"What's it going to be, ladies?" Jason asked. "If you want to walk away, I won't stop you. Your indenture isn't violated unless I say so, which I won't. We can still put you through a portal to a destination of your choosing."

"No," Belinda said, putting a hand firmly over Sophie's. "We decided to accept your offer."

Sophie glanced unhappily at Belinda, then gave Jason a reluctant nod.

"Alright, then." Jason pulled two sheets of paper from his inventory. "This first sheet is a list of all the essences that are available and that I can afford. The second list is awakening stones with the same conditions, although *if* I can afford those at all will come down to which essences we go with."

"You don't seem short of money," Sophie said, eyes moving over the cloud palace around them.

"This place is mine," Emir said. "Jason's plans for you are his, as is the cost of carrying them out."

"You're saddled with the poorest adventurer in the cloud palace. That's not a complaint, mind you. I have far more money than most; I just happen to keep exalted company."

"Except for us," Belinda said.

"Give it time," Jason said with an encouraging smile.

He picked up the first list and they started going through the essences. Hours passed as they discussed the value of various combinations, what they offered and what would be required from their user. Sophie already possessed the swift essence, along with the single ability that awakened when she acquired it. She had never gained a second ability in the more than half-dozen years since. It was more than enough to raise that one ability to bronze rank, even without training or monster cores.

They needed to select two more essences for Sophie to complete a combination. Emir offered his insight, having seen many essences in action. Clive had a tablet with the full list of recorded abilities from the Magic Society and years of cataloguing such abilities. He was the best equipped to describe the kind of powers each combination was likely to awaken. Rufus had seen many people at his family's school learning to use their abilities and understood the skills and training required to make the most of various power sets.

"The balance essence has a high-skill requirement," Rufus said.

"And by skill, he doesn't just mean quick hands or combat technique," Emir said. "Many skill-based abilities do require those, but it isn't always about reflexes and muscle memory."

"Timing, judgement and the ability to anticipate are all key," Rufus said. "When Jason was chasing you, you got away, yet woke up to find him waiting for you. You think that was an accident? He sent you to where he knew he could find you. That is the kind of skill that makes for great adventurers."

"Thank you," Jason said brightly.

"Potentially great," Rufus corrected. "Very, very eventually."

"That's less nice, but I'll take it."

"The difference between simple abilities and skill abilities is their effectiveness when used inexpertly," Rufus explained. "Simple abilities are easy to use and broadly effective, even with an inexpert user. A bolt of lightning that tracks enemies isn't hard to get right. Skill abilities fall flat if not employed correctly.

Use them the right way, in the right moment, though, and they can turn a fight on its head."

"Swift and balance is an interesting essence pairing," Emir said. "Danielle Geller has those essences and knows how to use them well. Of course, you won't be able to match her dimension essence. Even *her* family was lucky to get a hold of that."

"I also have the balance essence," Clive said. "My abilities are very spell-oriented and require more anticipation and timing than agility or martial ability. As a celestine, you can expect most of your abilities to be of the utility type, rather than spells or special attacks."

"What kind of utility?" Belinda asked.

"As with everything else," Clive said, "it depends on the essence and the awakening stone involved. With the swift essence you already have, Miss Wexler, you can expect movement abilities and effects conditional on mobility. The balance essence is trickier to predict. My powers, for example, are about balancing risk and reward, rather than finesse. Lady Geller, on the other hand, does require finesse, along with judgement and timing. The reward for all that challenge is abilities that can overturn a fight in an instant."

"You're saying skill abilities are better if you have skills," Sophie said, "and simple abilities are better if you're crap at everything."

"That's not exactly right," Emir said. "Simple abilities are more useful in more situations. In most circumstances, the best solution is the simple one. If you're building a team of adventurers, the last thing you want is to have a roster full of skill specialists. You mostly want people who have simple abilities and know how to leverage them effectively, with some high-skill people splashed in."

"Take Jason as an example," Rufus said. "He has to work harder to efficiently eliminate monsters that most adventurers find easy. It takes him more skill and effort just to achieve the same result, let alone be better. His strength is handling monsters that many adventurers couldn't beat at all. That makes him a valuable addition to a team with a preponderance of simple abilities, while he would have little to add to a team already loaded up with high-skill power sets."

"So you're highly skilled, are you?" Sophie asked Jason sceptically.

"I caught you," he shot back.

"The effectiveness of any power set comes down to the user, whatever the power," Emir said. "My abilities, for example, fall on the simple side of the scale. Some martial technique helps, but they are fast, powerful and useful in almost any scenario. Against someone who uses high-skill abilities, I need to pressure them so their abilities that are harder to execute then become impossible. If I succeed, I win. If I don't, the fight is turned around on me in a key moment and I lose."

"I think something that has been overlooked," Clive said, "is that every adventurer has a power set of twenty abilities. While most people tend to skew one way or the other on the skill-simplicity scale, very few are all simple or all skill-based. Even if you end up with a lot of high-skill abilities, you will likely have a handful of more straightforward ones. They won't be the most exciting, but you'll find yourself using them the most, leveraging them to set up your more specialised ones."

"He's right," Rufus said. "My more exotic powers tend to finish fights, but it's the simple and reliable ones that make that possible."

"You also need to understand that you don't really get a choice in which way you go," Clive said. "Randomness is inherent to awakening essence abilities. People with an excess of time and access to experts sometimes try and slant the results, but even the most expensive and laborious efforts have mixed results at best. Some people just end up with high-skill abilities, and an essence like balance makes it all the more likely."

"I will say this, though," Rufus said. "It's been my experience that people get the abilities to which they are naturally inclined."

"Yes," Emir agreed. "I have found that people are reflected in their power set. Mine, for example, is ostentatious yet effective. Rufus's is beautiful and dangerous. I don't really know about Jason and Mr Standish."

"Jason's powers are alternately deceitful and flashy, leading to a miserable, inexorable demise," Rufus said. "There's a recording floating around of him maniacally tormenting a group of powerful adventurers as he brings them prolonged, horrifying deaths."

Everyone turned to look at Jason.

"It was in a mirage chamber," he said. "None of them actually died."

"Something you need to understand," Emir told Sophie, "is that whatever the nature of your abilities, every essence combination is powerful in the right hands. We just need to find the right essences for your particular hands."

"Every combination has the potential for greatness," Rufus said. "Even the ones you might dismiss. When I was a boy, a man came through my family's academy with the duck essence. Everyone thought he was a joke, myself included. I couldn't understand why my grandfather took this boy from the countryside and placed him in our school. I learned the hard way that if you know how to use it, every essence is a threat."

"That's why I asked Rufus to be part of this," Jason said. "He grew up watching people come into their abilities."

"Jason has apprised us of your strengths," Rufus said. "Mobility and fighting skills are where he said you excel."

"You think you can judge me?" Sophie asked Jason, then turned to Rufus. "Did he say I fight better than him?"

"He did," Rufus said.

"Oh," Sophie said. "Then, maybe he can judge me."

"You're being very rude to the people trying to be our benefactors," Belinda said through gritted teeth.

"If politeness is where they draw the line, then they aren't exactly reliable benefactors," Sophie said.

"That's an attitude I recognise," Clive said, looking at Jason.

Rufus agreed with a chuckling nod.

"If you're confident you can develop the skills," Emir said, pulling things back on topic, "then the balance essence might be a good fit."

"Speed and skill are exactly what I'm looking for," Sophie said.

"Alright," Emir said. "That leaves one last essence. The adept essence is the obvious choice if skill is where you want to focus."

"Rather than push harder into one aspect," Rufus said, "it might be better to diversify. Something that still synergises while offering different abilities."

"That's a good point," Emir said. "I've seen people who overspecialise and end up with five answers to one problem and no answers to the rest."

"Wind essence," Clive said confidently, tapping the list. "There'll be at least one mobility power and it'll be different from what the swift essence would give out. Some elemental control would definitely expand her power set, but wind will better match speed and skill than earth or fire would."

"You make a compelling argument, Mr Standish," Emir said. Rufus nodded his agreement.

"What confluence essence does the swift, balance and wind combination produce?" Rufus asked.

"Mystic," Clive said, not bothering to look it up. "If you wanted something more aggressive, you could swap out balance for a might essence it would produce the onslaught confluence."

"Not a good idea," Rufus said. "Onslaught is best for humans with all those special attacks."

"Not an option anyway," Jason said. "Might essences get snapped up quickly, so there's none on our list."

"Mystic is definitely the superior choice for a celestine," Clive said. "Mystic can awaken some very interesting utility powers, in which they excel."

"Mystic is a common confluence essence," Rufus said. "That isn't just because so many combinations produce it, though. A lot of useful abilities come out of the mystic essence. It's an easy and effective choice, especially when you're working with common essences."

"I have the mystic essence myself," Emir said. "Staff, might, magic and mystic. All three of my combination essences are common. Two of those are highly sought after but still common, yet I've been nothing but happy with them."

"Mr Bahadir is right," Clive said. "The mystic essence is well known for producing the kind of abilities that are rare in other essences."

"What kind of abilities would I get from these wind and mystic essences?" Sophie asked.

"Mystic is wide open," Clive said. "The awakening stones you use would be the defining factor, similar to the balance essence, but even more so. As for the wind essence, you can expect something movement-related, as well as some kind of elemental control. Probably a combination of both. A flight power is quite likely."

"A flight power?" Sophie asked.

"That's right," Clive said.

"Flight, as in being able to fly?"

"That's how flight works, yes," Clive said.

"So that would be me, able to fly?"

"Yes. That would be you. Flying. With your flight power. That makes you fly. Am I overcomplicating this?"

"Seems straightforward to me," Jason said. "Wish I'd known flying was on the table before I used the first essences I came across."

"Just to be absolutely clear," Sophie said, "I would have the power to *fly*."

"You'd most likely be restricted to gliding at iron-rank," Clive said. "Eventually, though, yes."

Sophie and Belinda looked at each other, then back across the table.

"That's the one," they said together.

"A definitive choice, if I've ever heard one," Emir said with a chuckle.

"It has some other advantages, too," Jason said. "The wind essence is common, but not as sought-after as a magic or a might essence. It leaves room in the budget for some awakening stones."

"I was looking at that list," Rufus said, picking it up off the table. "There are some interesting common picks on here. An awakening stone of the eyes is a good shot at giving a perception power."

"I was looking at this," Clive said, pointing out an item on the list.

"A set of two awakening stones of the hand and two awakening stones of the foot," Rufus read. "The price is right but I'm not so sure about those stones."

"You said yourself that every ability is good in the right hands," Clive said. "My understanding is that Miss Wexler is quite the pugilist. Many people look down on awakening stones of the hand, but they're well-known for awakening empty-hand abilities and attacks. Miss Phoebe Geller used a number of them and was quite satisfied with the results. They're exactly what an unarmed combatant wants in an awakening stone."

"I've seen Phoebe Geller in action," Jason said. "I saw her make elementals explode with a punch."

"Awakening stones of the foot can also awaken unarmed attacks but also movement abilities and are similarly worthwhile to someone focused on unarmed combat," Clive said. "To the right essence user, which I believe Miss Wexler is, this collection of stones is very underpriced. These four stones, plus the stone of eyes and she would be well on her way to establishing her ability set."

Emir and Rufus looked at each other, then at Clive.

"Not bad, Mr Standish," Emir said. "Not bad at all. Thoughts, ladies?"

"Sounds right," Sophie said. "Moving, punching, kicking. Those are my areas of expertise."

"That would be five abilities, plus the four from using the essences," Jason said. "Almost half your abilities awakened out of the gate is pretty good. If that's settled, then, I'll go straight to making purchases. I'm not the only one bargain hunting, after all."

He stood up, then looked at Sophie.

"I make a lot of money, but this still won't be cheap for me. The next six months, you'll be doing a lot of work to pay this back. A lot of work."

"That may be the first thing I've heard you say that I'm halfway willing to trust," Sophie said.

Jason flashed her a grin. "If you're willing to trust me this early, you might not have been paying attention."

He swept out of the room dramatically, Clive and Rufus shaking their heads.

"Do any of you understand that man?" Sophie asked in Jason's absence.

"Definitely not," Rufus said.

"I haven't known him very long," Emir added.

"I'm still unclear on why he accused me of sleeping with his wife," Clive said. "He doesn't have a wife. Neither do I, for that matter, which did not stop him from accusing himself of sleeping with her."

Jason suddenly stuck his head around the door.

"I just remembered," he said. "Not sure if anyone mentioned, but one of the perks of having a full essence set is you don't have to poo anymore." His head retracted as he set off down the hall again.

Emir, Rufus, Clive, Belinda and Sophie all looked at the empty doorway.

"I'm changing my answer," Emir said, breaking the silence. "I've just now known him long enough to realise I absolutely do not understand him at all."

6
THIS IS THE MOMENT

The Adventure Society campus became a continual series of memorial services. There were so many dead that group memorials were being held one after another. First came the largest groups, made up of the least influential adventurers who had passed. The memorials took place on the north shore, where they could be easily overseen from the high terraces of the cloud palace. Gary and Rufus, as expedition members themselves, made their way out of the cloud palace to attend each and every service. Jason, Emir and the adventurers among Emir's staff could all be found on the terraces at various times, watching the sombre proceedings.

After the larger group memorials came the smaller, more exclusive ones, each of the most prominent families having a service for the people they lost. Jason and Emir attended the service for the Geller family and Jason for the Mercers. He stood close to Cassandra, who held his hand tightly. Thadwick didn't give Jason so much as a glance.

Rufus and Gary chose not to have Farrah memorialised until they took her home. Her casket was stowed away somewhere deep in the cloud palace. Rufus had notified her parents over water link, looking twice his age afterward. Neither Gary nor Rufus went back to the lodgings they had shared with Farrah. Jason settled accounts with Madam Landry and collected their things.

Before he took Sophie to perform her essence rituals, Jason took her and Belinda up to the terraces to see one of the memorials.

"Becoming an adventurer is an opportunity," he told them, "but it's also a danger."

"You think we don't know danger?" Sophie asked.

"Of course you do," Jason said. "You know the worst kind, the malevolence you can only find in people. Monsters are different. They don't hate you. They just want to kill you. An intelligent enemy can obsess over you. Pursue you relentlessly. But you can manipulate a malevolent enemy. You can reason with them, play on their fears and desires. That doesn't work on a monster. One of you is better at killing than the other and that is the only question between you. No hesitation, no doubt. It's a simpler danger than an avaricious crime lord but one that can't be talked down or negotiated with. A monster's only objective is to kill you."

The two women looked at Jason. He was leaning on the railing as he looked at the memorial below without really seeing it. He continued to talk, gaze still caught in the distance.

"This life can kill you without giving any recourse," he said. "It can and does take even the best of us. Being an adventurer can give you everything you ever wanted. Wealth, respect, power. For some, that's all there is. They take it all without paying the price, but they aren't really adventurers."

He tapped his hand on the terrace railing.

"You'll see amazing things, like a palace made of clouds. On almost any given day, there's no better life than being an adventurer. But there are some days, if you're a real adventurer, when you earn all the others. You make the hard choices and have to put everything on the line. You walk through the fire so no one else has to."

He finally turned to face the two women.

"Rufus gave me this speech the night before I completed my essence set, and now I've given it to you. You'll have to choose for yourselves what kind of adventurers to be."

"You don't make being what you call a real adventurer sound very appealing," Belinda said.

He gave them an odd smile, weary and a little sad, but with an underlying satisfaction.

"I wake up every morning, proud of who I am," he told them. "I go out into the world, never regretting that I didn't at least try and be the person I want to be. I face dangers and make mistakes. Sometimes I get beat, and sometimes I win. I stand up for what I believe in, whatever it costs me. When you give everything, you have to be who you want to be, that's freedom, whatever your circumstances."

He turned his head to look down at the memorial happening below.

"If wealth and power are all you want," he said, "then you can have them. Make all the safe choices and reap the rewards. Many adventurers do just that and, objectively, it's the smart choice. But if you want to see who you really are, what you're really capable of, you have to push yourself to the limit. There's no better job for that than being an adventurer."

He turned from the railing, looking at them straight on.

"You get the essences either way," he said. "You have six months to decide what comes after. For now, Clive should have the room ready."

On the way to one of Emir's ritual rooms, they passed through a walkway connecting two wings of the palace. It was high up on the towers, spanning over the sea below. The path was broad, with open-air sides and doubled as a garden. Flowering vines grew directly out of the cloud-stuff, lush green leaves and bright blossoms lining the sides of the walkway. Jason laughed as they walk through it.

"I don't think I've gone a day in this palace without a pleasant surprise," he said.

"Good," Belinda said. "It's not just us, then."

"How do you find your way around?" Sophie asked. "We've gotten lost more than once."

"One of my abilities maps all the places I go," Jason said absently as he stepped to smell the flowers. "Can you smell that? This is amazing."

"You think flowers are amazing?" Sophie asked.

"Emir stores this entire palace in a bottle not much bigger than your head and still successfully cultivates flowers. Where's your sense of wonder?"

"Speaking of scents," Belinda said, "what's that perfume you're wearing?"

"I'm not wearing one," Jason said.

"You don't need to be embarrassed," Belinda said. "Lots of men wear scents."

"I'm not worried about being embarrassed," Jason said. "I'm really not wearing a scent."

"Humans don't smell like that," Belinda said. "Just a little bit of sweat and they smell like leather left in a damp cupboard. You smell more like an elf or a celestine, but even more so. Fresh, like, um…"

"Springtime," Sophie said as Belinda searched for the right word.

"Yeah," Belinda said, looking at Sophie with surprise. "That's exactly it."

"I'm not human," Jason said. "This is just how I smell."

He resumed his way along the cloudy garden path and Belinda shared a look with Sophie.

"He smells like springtime," Belinda said.

"So what?" Sophie asked and followed after Jason.

The ritual room had the usual walls and ceiling made of cloud, but the floor was a single slab of black stone, cut perfectly level and smooth. Given that the room was around half the size of a basketball court, Jason was impressed. Clive was waiting for them, with a magic diagram drawn on the floor with lines of golden light.

"Clive is going to be doing the rituals," Jason said. "We'd be here all day if it were me and he's the expert, in any case."

Clive's essence ability, Enact Ritual, made drawing-out and performing rituals much more convenient. Jason looked over the diagram, which had two magical circles partly overlapping as its core. Jason's knowledge of ritual magic included several essence rituals, but this was more complicated than anything he knew.

"I thought essence rituals were meant to be the simplest ones," Jason said.

"This is a double-essence ritual circle," Clive explained. "The idea is that absorbing more essences at once promotes inter-essence synergy. It's yet to be proven effective due to our limited understanding of how abilities are selected, but it doesn't hurt to try."

"Two at once?" Sophie asked warily. "Will there be any side effects?"

"None at all," Clive said. "In fact, while studies have never been able to prove an increase in synergy, they have discovered that simultaneous absorption alleviates the purging effect compared to sequential absorption."

"When you hit iron rank, your body will be improved through magic," Jason said. "Part of that improvement is dumping out all the bits it doesn't like in the form of gunk."

"Gunk?" Sophie asked.

"Lots of gunk," Clive confirmed and pointed over at the side of the room where there was a small door. "As soon as you've absorbed your essences, go straight through there before it hits you. Belinda, you should join her as she may pass out. There is a shower in there for once she's done, and Jason kindly provided some of his crystal wash supply that I also left in there. There is also an extensive closet, from which Mr Bahadir said you may take anything you like to keep."

"You might not even need the crystal wash," Jason said as Sophie and Belinda wandered over to take a look into the next room. There was a shower large enough to lay down in, plus benches and cabinets.

"The shower will probably be enough," Jason continued.

"That is a lie," Clive said. "You will absolutely need the crystal wash. Won't she, Jason?"

"Yes," Jason sullenly conceded.

"If you knew Jason," Clive said, "you would realise that he would rather part with those essences than his crystal wash. Speaking of which, do you have them?"

Jason took out the two essences had procured, along with five awakening stones, laying them all on a bench sitting against the wall. The essences were cubes, shining with colour. The wind essence was a roiling mass of white mixed with streaks of pale grey and blue. The balance essence had its colours divided in a dead-straight line in the middle. The colours of each side constantly shifted in contrast to the other: red and blue, black and white, green and purple. Most of the awakening stones were a plain peach colour by comparison, while the last looked like an oversized glass eye.

"That one's kind of creepy," Belinda said, looking at the eyeball one.

"How do we even know those are what they say they are?" Sophie asked.

"Really?" Belinda asked, turning on her. "Are you trying to get them to change their minds?"

"I wouldn't worry," Jason said. "Clive takes his experiment subjects from villages in the delta where people will just assume a monster got them."

"What?" Clive asked.

"We still don't know why Asano is doing any of this," Sophie said. "If he's in this to help us, then why give me essences when throwing us through a portal would get us away from everything?"

"Sophie!" Belinda scolded.

"No," Jason said.

His voice was suddenly hard and cold, arresting everyone's attention. The signature amused insouciance fell from his expression; his relaxed posture became firm. He locked eyes with Sophie across the chamber.

"It's hard for you to trust," he told her.

"So?" she said, glaring back.

"The real answer is half-measures. I agreed to help you. Sending you away to live the same lives again just leads you to the same end. If I'm going to save you, then you're going to stay saved, which means that when I'm done with you, you need the means to protect yourselves."

He arrived in front of the bench with the essences, placing a hand on each.

"In this world, that means essences," he said, picking them up. "They are the line between acting and being acted upon." He walked back to Sophie. "They are the difference between dominion and obedience. Justice and iniquity. Controlling your destiny and being a pawn of fate."

He held the essences out in front of her.

"Why doesn't matter," he said. "All that matters is the choice you make, right now. Sometimes the moments that define our lives go unnoticed until later. This is not one of those. I am offering you the chance to literally grasp your destiny. Take it or walk away, knowing that this is the moment that decides everything that comes after."

He stood there, still holding the essences.

Sophie looked at the essences in his hands, then up at his face. He gave her a goofy grin.

"What are you?" she asked him. "A fool? A madman? A liar playing games only he can see?"

"Yes," he told her, eyes sparkling. "I once met a woman who thought that essences shape who you are, but she was wrong. Essences are power, and power doesn't change you. It *reveals* you. Give someone the power to be who they always wanted, and you will see who they always wanted to be. This is who I am, good and bad. This is your chance to be who you want to be, not who you have to be to survive."

Her response came in a soft voice, the first time Jason had seen her vulnerable.

"I don't know who I am without that."

"Do you want to find out?" he asked gently.

She nodded, placing her hands on the essences he was still holding out for her.

7
IRON RANK

In the ritual room, Clive was rubbing his hands together. "Now for the good part."

"The good part?" Belinda asked.

"Jason has an ability that he shamelessly squanders," Clive said. "He could be a one-man revolution in how we categorise powers but he refuses to come and work for the Magic Society."

"That would be the Magic Society run by the guy who wanted Miss Wexler for what I can only assume to be a creepy love dungeon?" Jason asked.

"Oh," Clive said, looking between Sophie and Belinda. "I'm probably not going to sell you on the virtue of the Magic Society then."

"Not likely, no," Sophie said. She was still holding the two essences she had accepted from Jason.

"Hold on," Clive said, turning to Belinda. "Why did you accept the job as my assistant, then?"

"To find out more about Lamprey, obviously. Also, it sounded pretty interesting and no one is looking to put me in a… love dungeon."

"I guess Jory didn't show you all the renovations," Jason said, which got a laugh from Sophie. Jason's head swivelled around to look at her in surprise.

"What?" Sophie asked.

"I've never heard you laugh before," Jason said.

"You have a problem with the way I laugh?"

"Not at all," he said. "It's just that our normal interactions range from you saying you don't trust me to you kicking me in the head."

"She's like that with everyone," Belinda said.

"I guarantee you that Jason's worse to deal with," Clive said.

"How am I worse? I'm affable. And I didn't just make up that kicking me in the head thing."

"He's definitely worse," Clive said to Belinda. "You have no idea what he put me through when we first met."

"Jory told me to do it," Jason said.

"He told you to tell your landlady that I slept with the wife you don't have?"

"He left the specifics to me, but yeah."

"Why would he do that?" Clive asked.

"You were investigating me for forging spirit coins or whatever."

"You made counterfeit coins too?" Belinda asked Jason.

"Wait," Clive said, turning to Belinda. "You made counterfeit spirit coins?"

"Er… no."

"I think it's time to use that ability, Clive," Jason said. He opened his contacts list, selected Sophie, Belinda and Clive and sent party invites.

- **You have received a party invitation from [Jason Asano]. Accept Y/N?**

Sophie and Belinda were startled by the sudden appearance of screens in front of them. Belinda started waving her hand in the air in front of her.

"Party invitation?" she asked. "Like where everyone dresses up?"

"More like where people form a group to go fight a monster," Jason said. "This is an ability I have that I can share with other people. It lets you know things about the world."

"What kind of things?" Sophie asked.

"Accept the invitation and find out."

She barely hesitated before nodding, to Jason's relief. Sophie was like an alley cat that had been kicked so many times it didn't trust you when you tried to feed it. Shortly afterwards she was staring wide-eyed at one of the essences in her hands.

Item: [Wind Essence] (unranked, common)

Manifested essence of the wind **(consumable, essence).**

- **Requirements: Less than 4 absorbed essences.**
- **Effect: Imbues 1 awakened wind essence ability and 4 unawakened wind essence abilities.**
- **You have absorbed 1/4 essences. Once absorbed, an essence cannot be relinquished or replaced.**

"I don't see anything," Belinda said, and Jason offered her his hand to shake. As they touched, a window appeared in front of her.

- **Jason Asano (outworlder).**
- **Essence User (iron rank).**

"One of the features is that you can identify things by touch. You don't get much from people, but it's useful for items."

He looked over at Clive with a frown.

"As you can see."

Clive opened up his magical storage space. Unlike Jason's, which was a video-game inventory only Jason could see, Clive's storage was accessed by creating a circle of magic runes, glowing as they floated in the air. Inside the circle was a portal through which he could stow and retrieve objects. He pulled a series of racks out through the portal, laden with items. He started picking them up, one by one, scribbling in a notebook as he went.

"Clive," Jason said.

"Yeah?" Clive asked absently, not looking up from his focused task.

"Did you save a up a bunch of items you wanted to catalogue until the next time we were in a party?"

"I figured if I asked, you'd say no."

"Of course I'd say no."

"That's why I thought to myself, 'what would Jason do?' Obviously, he'd just do it without asking and then point out that no one said he couldn't."

"That's what I'd do, is it?"

"Of course it is," Clive said. "Also, I'd like to point out that no one said I couldn't."

Jason groaned.

"Look, we need to get on with this ritual," he said. "Pack it up for now and you can do some more while she's recovering before we move onto awakening stones."

"You promise you'll let me finish at the end?" Clive asked.

"Yeah, alright," Jason conceded. "It's not like I actually have to do anything. I just don't want you treating me like I'm administration software."

Jason looked at the racks of items Clive had pulled out.

"Do you even have time to be doing this? I was surprised you even agreed to help with the essence ritual. I thought you'd be neck-deep in what they brought back from the expedition by now."

"I won't be allowed to see it for at least a few days," Clive said as the racks started vanishing back into his dimensional space. "Whoever figures out what they were after will look very good in the eyes of the wider Magic Society. Lucian Lamprey is motivated entirely by personal benefit and I'm the son of eel farmers.

First look at what they brought back goes to the Magic Society members he wants favours from."

The mention of Lamprey arrested Sophie and Belinda's attention.

"We know all about lamprey's definition of personal benefits," Belinda said bitterly. Lamprey's obsession witL bringing Sophie into his power was a primary source of Sophie and Belinda's troubles.

"Do you think your colleagues will find the answer?" Jason asked Clive.

"Highly unlikely," Clive said. "Greenstone's Magic Society is almost as rotten as its Adventure Society. It's basically a social club for people who like magic toys, with only a handful of genuine researchers. There aren't a lot of experts per field and I suspect it will require actual expertise in astral magic. Aside from me, the only other astral magic scholar in Greenstone was Landemere Vane. Who you killed."

"That's sounds accusatory," Jason said.

"It would have been better if you have killed someone stupid. He was a capable magical scholar."

"He didn't list his accreditations before trying to kill and eat me."

"Did you just say *eat*?" Belinda asked.

"I certainly did," Jason said. "You two don't have a monopoly on being caught in bad situations."

While Clive put away his racks of paraphernalia, Jason moved over to Sophie. She was still staring at the essences in her hands with fascination.

"Now you know," he said.

"Know what?" she asked, looking up at him.

"How I see the world."

"Is it like this for everyone, where you come from?"

"No. I lost my humanity when I came to this world. This is what I got in trade."

She watched his expression as he looked at the essences in her hands. He was clearly caught up in some memory, his mask of perpetual amusement briefly absent.

"You've been through your own troubles, haven't you?" she asked softly.

He looked up, flashing her a grin as his usual visage returned.

"Nothing that rakish charm and dashing good looks couldn't handle."

She frowned, searching his face for something authentic.

"I can never tell what's real with you," she said. "I've known manipulators before. The good ones use vulnerability as a weapon."

"When I first met Cassandra, I told her that there was only one way to use vulnerability as a weapon."

"That was a lie."

"Yes."

"Leave her with a question and plant the seed of seduction," Sophie said. "I've seen it work before."

"It was just some flirty banter," Jason said. "It wasn't some kind of organised campaign."

"Of course it wasn't. Men like you try to turn the world into a story, even with friends and lovers. It's like breathing; you don't even realise you're doing it."

"You think you know me pretty well," he said.

"I've known plenty like you. Some are subtle, others outrageous, like you. Keeping people off-balance so you can tip them over. You're not special, Jason Asano."

Clive had finished packing away his things. He stood with Belinda, observing Jason and Sophie across the room. From that distance, they couldn't hear the softly worded exchange but watched their body language. They stood right in each other's faces, neither looking away. Their bodies had confrontational stances but were close together, the cubes in Sophie's hands filled most of the space between them.

"That's trouble," Clive said to Belinda.

"Yep," she agreed.

"I hope Jason doesn't do something stupid."

"If he doesn't keep his hands to himself, she'll break them."

"That's not what I meant," Clive said. "Jason has very specific views on power relationships, and while his values might be strange, they're important to him. He's not Lucian Lamprey."

"Then what kind of stupid are you talking about?"

"Look at the choices he made to get you here," Clive said. "What iron-ranker would face down a silver in order to turn a pair of thieves into adventurers?"

"I still don't know why he would go this far for strangers. He made his big speech but that felt more like he was telling a story than telling the truth."

"Farrah," Clive started, his throat catching. "I think she was the only one that really understood him."

"That's the woman that died?"

Clive nodded.

"When I first met Jason I wanted to understand him better. I mean, a man from another world. For an astral magic scholar like me it was the opportunity of a lifetime. Farrah told me that under all the… Jason, he feels constantly exposed. Beset on all sides by powers that could easily destroy him."

"I know that feeling," Belinda said.

"And he recognises that. It's why he wants to help."

"It's that simple?"

"He has bit of a hero complex."

"That kind of thing gets people killed," Belinda said.

"Probably," Clive said. "But where would you be right now if he didn't have it?"

Clive left Belinda at the edge of the room, moving up to the magic diagram. He directed Jason to get out of the way with Belinda and Sophie to step into the magic circle. He instructed her to hold her hands out from her sides with an essence cube in each. He took out a magic wand and started waving it like he was conducting an orchestra. The air in the room stirred, centred on the diagram and Sophie within it. It swirled around her, whipping her silver ponytail.

"Is this how yours went?" Belinda asked Jason, quiet so as to not interrupt.

"I didn't have an essence ritual," Jason said. "I just absorbed my essences with my vast magical powers."

"Because you're some weirdo from another world?"

"Pretty much," Jason said, wondering once again how accurate his translation power was.

The wind continued to pick up as it stormed in the enclosed ritual chamber. There was a sonorous hum and they felt a prickling on their skin. The sharp taste of ozone filled their mouths. Light from the magic diagram on the floor started floating up in golden motes, drawn into the two essences cubes. As the light sank into them, the essences shed dust that floated into the air, also faintly glowing. Slowly at first, then with increasing pace, the essences dissolved, riding the wind to shroud Sophie in a magical squall. Rainbow light appeared in the squall, sinking into Sophie's obscured body.

The last of the essences turned to glowing dust, swirling around Sophie. Suddenly the wind stopped dead. The glowing dust stopped glowing, dropping to the ground. The magic circle faded as the now powerless dust scattered across the stone floor.

Party member [Sophie Wexler] has absorbed [Wind Essence]. [Sophie Wexler] has absorbed 2 of 4 essences.
Progress to iron rank: 50% (2/4 essences).

[Wind Essence] has bonded to the [Power] attribute, changing [Power] from normal to [Iron 0]. Master all wind essence abilities to increase the [Power] attribute.

You have awakened the wind essence ability [Wind Blade]. 1 of 5 wind essence abilities have been awakened.

"I love this part," Clive said.

Party member [Sophie Wexler] has absorbed [Balance Essence]. [Sophie Wexler] has absorbed 3 of 4 essences.

Progress to iron rank: 75% (3/4 essences).

[Balance Essence] has bonded to the [Recovery] attribute, changing [Recovery] from normal to [Iron 0].
Master all balance essence abilities to increase the [Recovery] attribute.

You have awakened the balance essence ability [Equilibrium]. 1 of 5 balance essence abilities have been awakened.

"That didn't feel bad at all," Sophie said.

"Essence rituals are very gentle," Clive said. "It's only if you shove the essence inside yourself without one that the experience is a harsh one."

"You're just bitter that you didn't get to see me do it," Jason said.

"That's true," Clive said as he read the description of Sophie's first new power.

Ability: [Wind Blade] (Wind)
Special attack.
Cost: Low mana.
Cooldown: None.

Current rank: Iron 0 (00%)

Effect (iron): Create a cutting projectile of air.

"Special attack," Clive said. "You probably won't get many, so each one is valuable."

Ability: [Equilibrium] (Balance)
Special ability.
Cost: None.
Cooldown: None.

Current rank: Iron 0 (00%)

Effect (iron): Meditate to slowly accrue instances of [Integrity], up to an instance threshold based on the [Recovery] attribute. Instances quickly drop off when meditation ends.

[Integrity] (heal-over-time, mana-over-time, stamina-over-time, holy): Periodically recover a small amount of health, stamina and mana. Additional instances have a cumulative effect.

"See, this is great," Clive said, jotting in his notebook. "Jason, you really should be helping out the Magic Society with this ability. People have an instinctive sense of their abilities, but they aren't always great at verbalising them. The time and inaccuracy this saves is fantastic."

"Eyes on the prize, Clive," Jason said.

"Right," Clive said, refocusing on Sophie.

Three intangible, translucent cubes floated out of her body, interposing on one another until they formed a single cube floating in front of her. Still insubstantial, it had a vibrant blue colour.

"The confluence essence," Clive said. "Take it."

Sophie reached out and the intangible object became solid at her touch. It began dissolving into blue smoke in her hands, which seeped into her body until it was gone.

Party member [Sophie Wexler] has absorbed [Mystic Essence].
[Sophie Wexler] has absorbed 4 of 4 essences.
Progress to iron rank: 100% (4/4 essences).

[Mystic Essence] has bonded to the [Spirit] attribute, changing [Spirit] from normal to [Iron 0]. Master all mystic essence abilities to increase the [Spirit] attribute.

You have awakened the mystic essence ability [Strong Soul]. 1 of 5 mystic essence abilities have been awakened.

"Strong soul sounds good," Belinda said, reading the description.

Ability: [Strong Soul] (Mystic)
Special ability (dimension).
Cost: None.
Cooldown: None.

Current rank: Iron 0 (00%)

Effect (iron): Disruptive-force damage dealt to you reduced by a large amount; other damage dealt to you is reduced by a small amount. Resistance to dimensional and astral effects and energies is increased. You can physically interact with incorporeal entities.

"How does having a strong soul make you take less damage?" Belinda asked.

"My advice is to just be glad it does," Jason said. "My damage reduction power is stabbing them in the back. How do you feel, Wexler?"

Sophie was still reading the last system message.

You have absorbed 4/4 essences.
All your attributes have reached iron rank.

You have reached iron rank.
You have gained damage reduction against normal-rank damage sources.
You have gained increased resistance to normal-rank effects.
You have gained the ability to sense auras.
You have gained the ability to sustain yourself using sources of concentrated magic.

She stood awestruck in the middle of the chamber, rubbing one hand over the back of the other, feeling her skin.

"This feels incredible," she said, her usual tone of cynicism completely absent.

"You need to go into the side room," Clive reminded her.

"What?" she asked, looking over at him, distracted.

"The side room," Clive repeated. "Now."

"I feel fine," Sophie said. "Better than fine."

"Give it a moment," Jason said, stepping up next to Clive.

"I don't see what you're—"

Sophie's face went pale. She sprinted for the side room, slamming a hand on the golden mark that opened the door. She rushed inside and the others heard her violently throwing up.

"I'll go check on her," Belinda said.

8
GETTING STONED

Sophie and Belinda emerged from the side room, Sophie wearing a fresh outfit.

"That was deeply unpleasant," Sophie said, still looking peaky.

"I imagine Jason had it worse," Clive said. "He's an outworlder who came here before ever getting an essence."

"Why does that matter?" Belinda asked.

"He made his body from the most diluted and impure magic. He was basically a human-shaped lesser monster."

"That's a little blunt," Jason said.

"Because his body was so full of impurities, his purgation when he ranked up would have been very extreme."

"It certainly wasn't fun," Jason said.

"What do you mean by 'he made his body'"? Belinda asked.

Jason and Clive shared a glance.

"That's probably best left for another day," Clive said.

"Not an explanation that benefits from brevity," Jason agreed. "Suffice to say, my ascension to iron rank was a messy and profoundly awful experience."

"Sophie made quite a mess herself," Belinda said. "Good thing this whole place cleans itself because I wouldn't wish that on anyone. All the muck just sank into the floor."

"Mine was still worse," Jason said. "I completely passed out."

"Are you sure you weren't just weak?" Sophie asked him.

"Yes," Jason said. "I was, but it wasn't just that."

"How about we get started?" Clive asked. He had alrcady used his abilities to purge the lingering magic from the previous ritual and draw a new circle on the floor. "Unlike the essences, we'll have to go through the awakening stones one at a time. It's a quick and simple ritual, though."

It was as simple as promised, starting with the awakening stone of eyes.

You have awakened the mystic essence ability [Sight Beyond Sight]. You have awakened 2 of 5 mystic essence abilities.

Ability: [Sight Beyond Sight] (Mystic)
Special ability (perception).
Cost: None.
Cooldown: None.

Current rank: Iron 0 (00%).

Effect (iron): Perceive auras.

"A perception power," Clive said. "It's what we expected, but welcome all the same."

Sophie was disoriented at the influx of new stimuli. Her iron-rank ability to sense auras was only minutes old and had now erupted with sensitivity. She could not only see the auras of Belinda, Jason and Clive but could feel them with all her senses. She could taste the auras around her, feel them on her skin.

Belinda's aura was weak, with strange flavours Sophie couldn't make sense of. It felt like spying on her friend's thoughts and she instinctively withdrew her senses. Instead, she turned them on Jason and Clive. Their auras were much more controlled, nothing escaping the way it did with Belinda.

The aura of each man had a strange and powerful feel to them. Clive's aura felt like a wellspring of magical power. Jason's felt more dangerous—oppressive and controlling.

"Something wrong?" Jason asked as she stared at him.

"I was looking at your auras," she told him and nodded at Clive. "I like his more."

The remaining stones were the two awakening stones of the hand and the two of the foot.

"I recommend we start with the stones of the hand," Clive said. "As you use more awakening stones, the abilities awakened will increasingly fill in the gaps of your power set. If the stones of the hand give you unarmed combat abilities, the stones of the foot are less likely to do so. There's more chance they'll give movement abilities instead."

"That sounds fine," Sophie said.

"I can't make any promises, though," Clive said.

"Understood," she said.

Clive purged the ambient magic and set up a new circle.

You have awakened the mystic essence ability [Immortal Fist]. You have awakened 3 of 5 mystic essence abilities.

Ability: [Immortal Fist] (Mystic)
Special ability.
Cost: None.
Cooldown: None.

Current rank: Iron 0 (00%).

Effect (iron): Unarmed attacks deal additional resonating-force damage, which is highly effective against physical defences. Suffer no damage from making unarmed strikes against objects and negate all damage from actively intercepted attacks. Not all damage from very powerful or higher-ranked attacks will be negated.

"Another mystic essence ability," Clive said. "It's quite unusual to awaken the confluence essence abilities first."

"Is that bad?" Belinda asked.

"No, just interesting," Clive said. "There's a theory that our personalities have a large impact on the kinds of abilities we awaken."

"That's a little worrying," Jason said, considering his own abilities.

"Some advocates of this theory suggest that people with a very strong sense of self awaken the confluence essence abilities first, although I find the evidence to support that idea rather questionable."

"Asano," Sophie said. "Hit me with a weapon."

"Wait, what?" Belinda asked.

"Read her ability," Jason said. "It negates the damage from incoming attacks."

"Reading is all well and good," Belinda said. "Trying to catch a sword is another thing altogether."

"I have to test the ability sooner or later," Sophie said.

"Then I vote later!"

"Now is best," Jason said, pulling out his magical sword. "I have healing potions on hand."

"That's a handsome sword," Sophie said.

Jason held it out for her to take. She drew it halfway out of the scabbard as she examined it. With Jason's party interface in effect, she was able to read the description.

Item: [Dread Salvation] (iron rank [growth], legendary)
***A sword crafted with gratitude in hope it would be of the greatest use in the moment of greatest need. It was forged with passion and expertise to be a reliable companion, bestowing upon it an incredible potential* (weapon, sword).**

"A friend made it for me," Jason said. "It's my most treasured possession."

"I'm still not convinced about this idea," Belinda said.

"I told you," Jason said. "If anything goes wrong, I've got healing potions."

Sophie handed the sword back and, after confirming she was ready, Jason drew it and slashed out at her. She unhesitatingly blocked the attack with a palm strike, the sword bouncing back like it had struck a wall.

Everyone looked at Sophie's hand, which was completely unharmed.

"Nice," Jason said.

"Didn't even hurt," Sophie said. "Keep going."

Jason unleashed a series of sword attacks, which Sophie intercepted with forearms, shins, shoulders and even a head-butt. She took several superficial cuts as she got a handle on the ability, but urged Jason to continue.

"I'll need to adjust my fighting style for this," she said.

"That's normal," Clive said. "An adventurer who doesn't adjust the way they fight to fit their powers is a bad adventurer."

"How do you fight?" Sophie asked him.

"From far away," Clive said. "An adaptation in approach I was more than happy to make."

"Looks like your ability doesn't just protect your body," Jason said. "Your clothes were only cut when you failed to intercept the hit."

Sophie looked down at her clothes where blood was leaking from several slices in the fabric.

"You're right," she said.

"You said something about healing potions?" Belinda said.

"I'd like to try something first," Jason said. He looked at Sophie. "You up for it?"

"I can take anything you've got."

"Alright. I'm going to throw out a special attack."

He lashed out with his sword again and she intercepted it with a fist.

[Celestine] has negated all damage from special attack [Punish].
Special attack [Punish] has inflicted [Sin] on [Celestine].

"Interesting," Jason said.

Sophie frowned at the message in front of her.

Special attack [Punish] has inflicted [Sin] on you.

"You inflicted me with sin," Sophie said. "That better not be a sex thing."

"You completely negated the damage on my physical attack," Jason told her. "Even the magical damage. The non-damage effect still went through, though."

"What is that non-damage effect?" Belinda asked.

"A curse."

"A curse," Sophie said, glaring daggers.

"A minor curse," Jason said. "It won't do anything unless I use more special attacks on her. Also, I can just take it away."

"So take it away!" Belinda demanded.

"No worries," Jason said and pointed an arm at Sophie.

"Feed me your sins."

Sophie's life force radiated out from her body as a vibrant red glow. A dark stain swam within it but was drawn out, floating through the air and vanishing into Jason's outstretched hand. The glowing life force withdrew back into her body and he tossed her a healing potion from his inventory. She drank it, making a sour face.

"Those cheap potions of Jory's get the job done," she said. "I cannot get used to that taste, though."

Clive set up another ritual and Sophie absorbed the next awakening stone of the hand.

You have awakened the mystic essence ability [Radiant Fist]. You have awakened 4 of 5 mystic essence abilities.

Ability: [Radiant Fist] (Mystic)
Special ability.
Cost: None.
Cooldown: None.

Current rank: Iron 0 (00%).

Effect (iron): Unarmed attacks deal additional disruptive-force damage, which is highly effective against magical defences and intangible or incorporeal enemies. Unarmed attacks do not trigger retaliation effects. Negate any non-damage effects from actively intercepted attacks.

"Mystic essence again," Jason said. "It's a magic version of the last ability."

"That's useful," Clive said. "The damage types of those two abilities, resonating-force and disruptive-force. Between them, you'll get through almost any defence. They're special abilities rather than special attacks, so I imagine the damage is limited, but they will be effective against any enemy you can put a hand to."

"Try that special attack again," Sophie said and Jason pulled his sword back out.

[Celestine] has negated all damage from special attack [Punish].
Special attack [Punish] has inflicted [Sin] on [Celestine].
[Celestine] has prevented secondary effects of special attack [Punish].
[Sin] does not take effect.

Affliction negation has triggered an effect on weapon [Dread Salvation].
[Celestine] has negated the triggered effect.

"Wow," Jason said. "That even stopped my sword from buffing itself."

"It seems clear the direction her abilities are taking her," Clive said. "Of her first seven abilities, three are defensive and one is self-recovery. They aren't blanket defence powers, though; they take skill to use effectively. She's developing an evasion-type defensive specialist power set."

"A dodge tank," Jason said.

"There are, broadly speaking, two kinds of defence specialists," Clive said. "They line up with the two kinds of essence users we were discussing yesterday. The most common type uses raw toughness, heavy on simple, passive abilities that mitigate damage. Their strengths are standing their ground and withstanding punishment."

"And I'm the other type," Sophie said.

"It looks that way," Clive said. "You can expect more active defensive powers and more mobility. You won't be as good at holding a fixed position but you'll have the tools to be exactly where you need to be, exactly when you need to be there. You won't be as good at passively taking hits, but you'll be better at intercepting them. The other kind of specialist will outlast you under a barrage of attacks. More powerful, singular attacks can punch through their defences, though, while you'll have the tools to avoid or negate them."

"Sounds like you'll be good at staying alive when things are at their worst," Jason said.

"I always have been," Sophie said.

Clive set up the next ritual, moving on to an awakening stone of the foot.

You have awakened the balance essence ability [Cloud Step]. You have awakened 2 of 5 balance essence abilities.

Ability: [Cloud Step] (Balance)
Special ability (movement).
Cost: Low stamina and mana.
Cooldown: 20 seconds.

Current rank: Iron 0 (00%).

Effect (iron): Take a single step on air as if it were solid ground, becoming intangible for a brief moment. This ability can be used while all steps are on cooldown at an extreme mana cost per step. If used within mist, fog or cloud, this ability has no cooldown.

"Finally not a mystic one," Jason said. "Kind of a shame at this point. You've almost fully awakened that essence."

"What's a cooldown?" Belinda asked, reading the ability description.

"That's how long you have to wait after using an ability before you can use it again," Jason said.

"It's terminology from Jason's world," Clive said. "His ability serves as a guide for him to our world, so it describes them in ways he will best understand."

"Why would she have to wait?" Belinda asked.

"Our bodies serve as a medium for the magic of our essence abilities," Clive said. "Using the same magic in the same way repeatedly can over-stress the body. Less imposing abilities require little or no time before they can be used again, while more excessive powers require more time for recovery. This ability of yours, Miss Wexler, is rather interesting in that you can circumvent this limitation using large amounts of mana."

"Is that unusual?" Jason asked.

"Yes, but far from unheard of," Clive said. "It functions by spreading the strain across your body, which allows use in rapid succession but requires much more mana to push through. Very inefficient, but inefficient is better than unavailable in a critical moment."

"Try it out," Belinda said.

Sophie trod on an invisible step, then fell back to the floor.

"It seems underwhelming," Belinda said.

"I want to try the intangible thing," Jason said pulling a small pouch from his inventory. "Try your ability again."

Sophie used her ability to step on the air as Jason threw a glazed nut. It bounced off her forehead, earning Jason a glare.

"The ability does say briefly intangible," Jason said. "I think we need to get the timing right. Can you feel being intangible?"

"I think so," Sophie said. "There's a very brief sensation of lightness."

After several more attempts, they finally got a glazed nut to pass through Sophie's intangible body, right at the moment she took a step on the air.

"I wonder what happens if she uses it while standing on the ground," Jason said. "Would she fall through?"

"Not through the cloud palace," Clive said. "One of its many properties is to block the passage of intangible entities. She might go through the stone floor of this room, though."

The ritual room had a stone floor made from a single sheet of smoothly polished rock, to facilitate drawing ritual circles. After some experiments, they discovered that Sophie would sink into it if she had a foot on the ground while using the ability. After the fleeting moment of intangibility, her foot was pushed back out of the stone.

"You'd have to be moving fast but you could use that to get through a wall," Belinda said. "You have maybe a second of being intangible. You'd have to be moving fast enough to get most of the way through so you'd be pushed to the other side."

"I'm not sure I like the sound of that test," Sophie said. "What if I get stuck halfway through?"

"Your foot got pushed out of the floor," Belinda said. "There's no reason to think a wall would be any different."

"What happened to the woman who didn't want me catching swords?" Sophie asked.

"There are healing potions," Belinda said.

"I don't think a healing potion will fix my head occupying the same space as a chunk of wall."

"We can take a look at the possibilities later," Clive said. "We have more rituals to perform."

"In a little bit," Sophie said. "I want to see what this ability can do. Asano, spar with me for a bit."

Jason and Sophie engaged in some light sparring, neither pushing too hard. When she had been in the fighting pits, acrobatically using her speed and the walls to outmanoeuvre her opponents was her signature. She started using her new ability as a wall to kick-off whenever she needed. It wasn't wildly effective right away, but she saw the potential. Eventually, she begged-off with a splitting headache and Jason handed her a mana potion.

"Is that your first low-mana headache?" Jason asked.

She sighed with relief as the potion took effect, then nodded.

"Not pleasant, are they?"

"No, they are not," she agreed, rubbing her temples.

"Do you want to take a break?" Clive asked.

"I'm fine," she said.

"Take the break," Belinda scolded. "You don't have to tough everything out on principle."

"It's past time for lunch anyway," Jason said. "I have sandwiches."

On the bench where the last awakening stone was still waiting to be used he set out a lunch spread. A tray of sandwiches, plus glasses and a pitcher of iced tea, complete with chunks of ice floating in it.

"Do you always carry around sandwiches?" Belinda asked as Jason poured out drinks.

"He does," Clive said, taking a sandwich from the tray. "Also, a rope ladder."

Sophie wandered over last and Belinda shoved a sandwich in her hand.

"Where did you get this chutney?" Belinda asked Jason after biting into her own sandwich.

"My landlady makes it. Now that Emir has set us up in the cloud palace, I don't see her, which is a shame. I learned a lot about local ingredients in her kitchen. I went and packed-up the rooms my friends and I were renting and she stocked me up on chutney and jam. I've been meaning to figure out how you cook things in a kitchen made of clouds and knock out some sweet scones."

Belinda chatted with Jason and Clive while Sophie ate in silence. Belinda occasionally glanced her way, noting that Sophie put an end to a good portion of the sandwiches. As Jason packed away the remains of their lunch, Clive set up the ritual for the last awakening stone.

You have awakened the mystic essence ability [Mirage Step]. You have awakened 5 of 5 mystic essence abilities.

You have awakened all mystic essence abilities. Linked attribute [Spirit] will advance in conjunction with lowest-rank mystic essence ability.

You have 1 of 4 completed essences.

Ability: [Mirage Step] (Mystic)
Special ability (dimension, movement, illusion).
Cost: Low stamina and mana.
Cooldown: 40 seconds.

Current rank: Iron 0 (00%).

Effect (iron): Move instantaneously to a nearby location, leaving an afterimage behind.

"Instantaneous movement," Clive said. "It's functionally similar to a teleport, but requires a path of traversal."

"Teleporting can be tricky," Jason said. "It took me a long time before I was able to successfully…"

Sophie suddenly appeared next to him.

"…activate the ability," he finished. "Never mind, I guess."

A shimmering afterimage lingered briefly in Sophie's original position before vanishing. As for Sophie herself, she was reeling, unbalanced.

"That was amazing," Sophie said as she dizzily held her arms out. "That felt absolutely incredible. I'm going to need some practice, though. That was the last of the awakening stones, so I should do that."

"Actually," Jason said, "Clive and I managed to rustle up some extras yesterday."

He walked over to the bench. Though it had been emptied of awakening stones, he took out two more from his inventory and placed them down.

"One of these I got from the Adventure Society for catching you. The other I got from... somewhere else, but also for catching you."

"Somewhere else?" Belinda asked.

Jason didn't respond to the question. Clive took out a third stone, placing it with the other two.

"This is the one I got for catching you," he said. "Jason hasn't awakened his full power set, but he's close. Since he's waiting for what Emir is setting up, he decided to give these to you."

"What about you?" Belinda asked.

"I've had my full set for a long time," Clive said. "I was just never much of an adventurer."

Jason slapped him on the back.

"You killed a bronze rank monster in a hidden fortress under a swamp," Jason said. "You're a plenty good adventurer, now."

"Last night, after our meeting, we were belatedly contacted by the Adventure Society about the reward for catching you," Clive said. "I was going to give my stone to Jason but since he was giving his to you, I decided to the same."

"What kinds of awakening stones are they?" Sophie asked. She walked up to the bench, looking at the stones. Jason gestured at them invitingly.

"Touch them and see."

9

CHILDREN

Sophie brushed a hand over the first of the three awakening stones Clive and Jason had laid out on the bench.

Item: [Awakening Stone of Focus] (unranked, uncommon)

***An awakening stone containing an undistracted power.* (consumable, awakening stone).**

Requirements: Unawakened essence ability.

Effect: Awakens an essence ability.

You have 11 unawakened essence abilities.

"That is the most common of the three," Clive said. "The Magic Society grades stones on a scale of one to five stars, based on how frequently they are known to appear world-wide. We work with brokers and the Adventure Society to try and catalogue them all. Jason's ability also seems to grade them into five stages of rarity, but not numerically. The stones you've used thus far were all common, or one -star. Uncommon is two-star."

Sophie touched the next stone, with was blue with streaks of white.

Item: [Awakening Stone of the Sky] (unranked, epic)

***An awakening stone containing the freedom of the open sky.* (consumable, awakening stone).**

Requirements: Unawakened essence ability.

Effect: Awakens an essence ability.

You have 11 unawakened essence abilities.

"Epic," she said.

"Four-star, the second highest rarity," Clive explained. "After it took so long to catch you, the Adventure Society raised the reward to a four-star awakening stone for each person on the team that caught you."

"They had to make it a limit of six after people started forming giant groups," Jason said.

"After we caught you," Clive said, "there were some issues, as you may recall. Jason and I collected our rewards yesterday evening and we were given a selection of four-star stones."

"The second-highest rarity," Belinda said. "Are they the kind of stones you used?"

"Actually, I used all one- and two-star stones," Clive said. "I was given an epic four-star essence, however. A rune essence. Very valuable."

"Who gave you that?" Jason asked. "There can't be a lot of epic essences in an eel farm."

"My mentor," Clive said. "He was the director the Magic Society, the predecessor to Lucian Lamprey's predecessor. He took me out of the delta, gave me an education. Showed me the value of what we do at the Magic Society. I became an adventurer just in time for the last monster surge, when I was sixteen. He died during the surge and after it was over, I never tried my hand at adventuring again until just recently. I threw myself completely into the Magic Society, but our branch here isn't the same as it was back then."

"I don't imagine Lamprey fostering a positive institutional culture," Jason said.

"No," Clive said. "I'd say the one before wasn't any better, but Lamprey really does set a new low."

"I'm not even in the Magic Society and I know that much," Belinda said.

Jason turned his attention back to the stones.

"Stone of the sky," he said. "I considered picking that one and using it myself."

"It's very highly sought after," Clive said. "The chances of awakening some kind of flight power are very good. I'm a little surprised our Adventure Society here had one."

"Turns out I already have a flight power," Jason said. "Clive told me. I'm super looking forward to it, now, but it won't let me fly until silver rank."

"Jason has a number of abilities we have very little information on," Clive said. "We do have thorough records on a number of them, however, and his cloak ability will let him glide at bronze rank and fly at silver. It won't be as effective as a more dedicated movement power but he will fly."

"I should probably look up what my abilities do at later ranks," Jason said.

Clive turned on him in disbelief.

"That's what I've been telling you!"

"Are you sure?" Jason asked. "Doesn't ring a bell."

As Clive started turning red, Jason turned to Sophie.

"Clive picked this one, in the end, since we were giving them to you. It's your best bet at a flying power."

"There are no guarantees, though," Clive said, still glaring at Jason. "It could just as easily give you a special attack effective against enemies in the air."

"Don't be a downer, Clive," Jason said.

"I'm just managing expectations," Clive said. "Take a look at the last stone and then we'll begin."

Sophie reached out and touched the last stone, which was clear with such clarity as to be hard to see.

Item: [Awakening Stone of Purgation] (unranked, epic)

An awakening stone possessed of a cleansing power. **(consumable, awakening stone).**

Requirements: Unawakened essence ability.

Effect: Awakens an essence ability.

You have 11 unawakened essence abilities.

"This will almost certainly give you some kind of cleansing ability," Clive said. "You don't have any obvious essences for it, so it could come in many forms. It might be a balance ability that transfers afflictions to your enemies or a swift ability that lets you recover from afflictions faster. It might be some other ability with a self-cleanse as a secondary effect."

"How valuable are these epic stones?" Belinda asked.

"Each of them is more valuable than all the other stones put together," Clive said. "The sky stone is more valuable than either of the essences you used."

"And you're just giving them to me?" Sophie asked.

"Your indenture contract is six months," Jason said. "By the time it's over, you'll have been an adventurer for longer than I have, as of right now. You'll earn them, believe me."

"The question," Clive said, "is what order do you want to use them in? Do you want to start off with the potential flight power, or save that for the end?"

"Even if you get one," Jason warned. "You probably won't be able to fly well. My friend Humphrey can fly, but it costs him so much mana he can't do it for long."

Clive nodded.

"He's right," Clive said. "At iron rank, the power will either be restricted by cost or the type of flight, like gliding. It will get cheaper or more useful as you rank up."

"Speaking of which," Jason said. "You didn't use any monster cores to raise the ability you already have, right?"

"No," Sophie said. "Before my father died, he left my one essence with Belinda's father, who performed the ritual once I was old enough."

"My dad didn't have any essences himself, but he knew a good hodgepodge of different magical fields. He knew that monster cores would mess up her essence development and warned her off them," Belinda said.

"Sounds like a good guy," Clive said.

"He was a drunken prick whose sole act of decency was not selling off that essence before giving it to Sophie," she said. "He tried to rob Cole Silva's father and failed badly. Silva killed him and I was saddled with making restitution."

"How do you know when you're old enough to use an essence?" Jason asked. "Also, what happens if you try and you're not old enough?"

"There's a simple test for whether your body can handle it," Clive said. "Usually that's sixteen or seventeen, but I've heard of as low as fourteen and as late as nineteen or twenty. As for what happens if you aren't ready, well, I've heard horror stories. Magical deformities. People using children in essence experiments to try and unlock the secrets of essences."

Clive shook his head.

"Not every Magic Society branch is the best group of people, obviously," he said. "Even the worst of us will put a stop to that, though."

"Well, no worries here," Belinda said. "Sophie's practically a spinster."

"I'm twenty-three."

"Me too," Jason said. "Actually, it's been about four months. I think I missed a birthday."

"I'm going to set up the next ritual," Clive said. "Pick which stone you want to use."

"Do the sky stone last," Belinda said. "If you actually get the power to fly, we can head straight out and try it."

"Good idea," Jason said. "Work your way up to the big finale."

Sophie nodded and Clive got to work, quickly setting up and performing the ritual using the uncommon stone of focus.

You have awakened the swift essence ability [Avatar of Speed]. You have awakened 2 of 5 swift essence abilities.

Ability: [Avatar of Speed] (Swift)
Special ability.
Cost: None.
Cooldown: None.

Current rank: Iron 0 (00%)

Effect (iron): Your movement abilities have increased effect and reduced stamina and mana cost.

"That seems a bit underwhelming," Belinda said.

From the middle of the fading ritual circle, Sophie exploded into motion. She swiftly ran to the side of the room and up the wall, turning to run along the wall and around the room multiple times.

"Well, that's quite a thing," Clive said as the others watched her go around, swerving side to side on the wall in little jukes that didn't seem to slow her down.

"Is she normally that zippy?" Jason asked Belinda.

"Not sure," Belinda said. "When she goes running, the first thing she does is run away, so I never get to see much."

Sophie leaped off the wall, flipping in the air and landing in a crouch.

"That may be the sexiest thing I've ever seen," Jason said.

"You know you said that out loud, right?" Clive asked.

"I'll stand by it."

Belinda looked at Jason from under a sceptically furrowed brow.

"You think a woman back flipping off a wall is sexy?" she asked him.

"Yep."

"You're weird."

"I'll stand by that, too."

Sophie stood up and walked over to them.

"Good ability," she said.

"Avatar abilities are often good," Clive said. "They embody an aspect of an essence, making you very good at a specific thing. In this case, movement abilities."

"I like being fast," Sophie said. "The ability I've always had makes me fast, and this makes me faster."

"Can you show us that ability?" Jason asked.

"How do I do that?"

"It's pretty instinctive. You just want to, basically."

After a brief moment, the ability appeared in front of them.

Ability: [Free Runner] (Swift)
Special ability.
Cost: None.
Cooldown: None.

Current rank: Bronze 0 (00%)

Effect (iron): Increased speed. Low stamina and mana per second cost to run on walls and water. Momentum must be maintained on walls or water to prevent falling.

Effect (bronze): Enhanced balance and spatial sense.

"Enhanced balance and spatial sense," Jason read. "That would let you move very fast through a complicated environment. Super parkour."

"Parkour?"

"In my world it's what we call the practice of moving through complex spaces with efficiency and speed. People train to be very good. I'm guessing that ability of yours makes you very, very good at it."

"Yes," Sophie said plainly.

He could see she wasn't boasting but simply stating a fact. She neither wanted nor needed his validation. He chuckled.

"That's a classic, skill-oriented power," Clive said. "It seems simple and underpowered but lets you do something you're good at very well."

"Let's see about the next one," Sophie said. "Set it up."

Clive did just that, performing the ritual of awakening with the stone of purgation.

You have awakened the wind essence ability [Cleansing Breeze]. You have awakened 2 of 5 wind essence abilities.

Ability: [Cleansing Breeze] (Swift)
Aura (holy, cleanse).
Cost: None.
Cooldown: None.

Current rank: Iron 0 (00%)

Effect (iron): Allies within the aura have increased resistance to curses, diseases, magic afflictions, poisons and unholy afflictions. This is a holy effect. Negates poisons in the air; this is a cleanse effect.

"Aura," Clive said. "That is a big win."

"It is," Jason agreed.

"Why is that?" Belinda asked.

"Aura manipulation is an important skill for adventurers," Clive said. "You can only learn it once you have an aura power, although any aura power will do."

"He's right," Jason said. "Aura control is one the things that differentiates a capable adventurer from a scrub."

"A scrub?" Sophie asked.

"You might know it as a buster," Jason said. "Doesn't matter, you can get it from context."

"It's an unexpected ability for the wind essence," Clive said. "I would have expected something from the mystic essence. It's also the exact opposite of Jason's aura."

"Will they conflict?" Belinda asked.

"No," Clive said. "Jason's aura only affects enemies, while Miss Wexler's only affects allies. So long as they're on the same side, it won't be a problem."

Clive and Belinda looked between Jason and Sophie, who were giving each other assessing looks.

"I wouldn't rule out problems just yet," Belinda said.

"It's a holy ability, too," Clive said. "That's matches well with the celestine holy affinity."

"I thought they had astral affinity," Jason said.

"They have holy too," Clive said. "Still not as many as elves, who have life, nature and magic affinities, which is why elves make such good healers. I'll set up the next ritual."

Jason stood next to Clive as he used his essence ability to draw golden lines on the floor.

"How likely is it really that she picks up a flight power?" he asked quietly. "I've heard a lot of people say that you can't go making predictions, yourself included."

"Looking at all twenty abilities, that's correct. It's why the best approach is to select a more general direction for your power set. Pick out your essences and leave the specifics to fate. There's always one or two abilities you can confidently see coming, though. For example, there are certain awakening stones that have a higher chance of producing auras if you have a lot of abilities and no aura yet. Another example is all those feast stones you used, Jason."

"I didn't tell you about that."

"Farrah did. The combination of feast stones and the blood essence meant that a health-draining power was almost a certainty. It could have been any of a wide slew of health-draining powers but you were almost certain to get one of them. If you combine a celestine's natural aptitude for utility powers, the wind essence and a sky stone, that's as close to a guarantee of a flight power as you'll get. You couldn't ask for a better chance, except for maybe with the wing essence."

Jason moved away from the circle, pausing next to Sophie.

"Good luck," he said, then joined Belinda out of the way against the wall.

Clive performed the ritual no differently than any of the others.

You have awakened the wind essence ability [Leaf on the Wind]. You have awakened 3 of 5 wind essence abilities.

Ability: [Leaf on the Wind] (Swift)
Special ability (movement, dimension).
Cost: Moderate mana-per-second.
Cooldown: None.

Current rank: Iron 0 (00%)

Effect (iron): Glide through the air; highly effective at riding the wind. Can reduce weight to slow fall at a reduced mana cost. Ignore or ride the effects of strong wind, even when this ability is not in active use.

Clive let out a boyish laugh.

"You've got it," he said. "I'll have to look it up to make sure, but I'd bet my library that's a flight power."

Jason took out a tablet and looked up the ability.

"Yep," he said. "It was the third one down on the list of wind essence flight abilities. From what I'm seeing here, you glide at iron and sort of fly-glide at bronze. Riding the wind, that sort of thing. You'll have full-blown flight at silver, then go back to wind-riding at gold, but you'll be controlling the wind. Doesn't say about diamond, which is no surprise."

Sophie and Belinda looked at each other, grins spreading on their faces.

"You can fly," Belinda said.

Sophie nodded. "I can feel it."

"The next move is obvious, then," Jason said. "Let's go jump off a sky palace."

"You might want to be a little cautious," Clive said. "Until she gets a handle on the ability."

"Boo!" Belinda jeered.

"Did you just boo me?" Clive asked.

"And so she should," Jason said. "Boo!"

"You're acting like children."

"We're about to go jump off the roof," Jason said. "Of course we're acting like children."

10
STAR SEED

In the Adventure Society marshalling yard, a portal opened and people started stepping through. There were fourteen in total, each bearing a pin marking them as Adventure Society officials. The woman at the front looked to be of early middle age, with her hair unflatteringly pinned tightly back. Her Adventure Society pin was black.

Jason, Clive, Belinda and Sophie waited until the last memorial for the day had finished before moving outside to test Sophie's new abilities. The gliding had a few false starts, but the slow fall function of the power was intuitive enough that she went unharmed. Several attempts in, she was gliding out over the ocean before curving back in to land on the lower levels of the palace. Of course, she would have preferred if the earlier attempts hadn't involved dragging her waterlogged self onto one of the palace's sea-level platforms.

Aside from her gliding ability, being outdoors allowed her to test her wind blade. She could throw out a shimmering arc of slicing wind with a sweep of an arm or leg. A short gesture would produce a small, swift blade that was hard to see. A larger motion created a longer and more visible blade that was noticeably slower.

"Some abilities will come easily and naturally," Clive said. "Others you'll need to practice before you can use them effectively."

"We'll leave you to it, for today," Jason said. "Play around and get used to them. Tomorrow we start training."

"That Adventure Society assessment is in a week, right?" Belinda asked. "Is she going to be ready?"

"The next intake was cancelled," Jason said. "After days of memorials, no one is looking to feed their young people into the grinder. The assessments will be rigorous in a way they haven't been for a long time, with a few exceptions."

"Won't that make it harder for Sophie to pass?" Belinda asked.

"The field assessment judges two things," Jason said. "The skill to reliably hunt monsters and the judgement to know when not to. I won't let her participate until she's ready."

He looked at Sophie, standing unhappily in her still-wet clothes.

"No one is going to argue that you lack skill," he told her. "Have you ever fought a monster?"

She shook her head.

"Once Rufus deems you ready, I'll take you out to the delta and we'll do some adventure board notices. If you meet his standards, then passing the field assessment won't be a problem."

A meeting was taking place in the conference room next to the director's office in the Adventure Society administration building. At the head of the table but standing instead of sitting was the leader of the inquiry team, Tabitha Gert. Her clothes were plain, with the only flourish her black Adventure Society pin. She wore a stern expression, accentuated by her tightly pulled-back hair. Elspeth Arella was also present, sitting to Gert's right. Emir Bahadir sat at the other end of the table, his relaxed slouch a contrast with Arella's poise and Gert's rigidity.

"Is there a reason the director of the Magic Society is not here?" Tabitha asked.

"Lucian Lamprey would obstruct and inform because it serves his purposes, regardless of the outside consequences," Arella said. This earned a pointed cough in her direction from Emir, which she responded to with a flat look.

"Having Lamprey here," Arella said, turning back to Gert, "would be as good as sending the families in question an explanatory pamphlet detailing out intentions."

"That's very unhelpful," Gert said.

"Of that, I am aware," Arella said.

Gert turned her attention to Emir.

"You are convinced these five expedition members have been compromised?" she asked. "If I discovered that this was some ploy to distract from the enquiry, it would not go well for you, gold-ranker or not."

"I'm convinced that the political cost of forcing the issue and being wrong is preferable to leaving it alone and being wrong."

Arella gestured at the door, which swung open of its own accord to admit Danielle Geller. Arella used her power again to close the door behind her. While Danielle would prefer to throw her out a window, she restricted herself to throwing Arella a dissatisfied glance before schooling her expression into blank professionalism.

"Sorry I'm late," Danielle said. "I've just come from a water link communication with Jonah's family."

"This is the one of the five from your family?" Gert asked.

"He's from a branch family of House Geller, but broadly, yes. I've just been speaking with his parents and the branch family patriarch."

"This boy, Jonah," Emir said. "He refuses to be examined?"

"Yes, just like the others," Danielle said. "He's been secluding himself from us. His behaviour strongly indicates that he sees us as some kind of threat."

"I've just had word," Arella said. "All five have withdrawn from their existing teams and formed a team together."

"What?" Danielle asked. "When did this happen?"

"Around an hour ago. I've had my deputy director keep a discreet but watchful eye on any official activity related to the five."

"We need to act," Gert said. "However, it is outside the Adventure Society's purview to forcibly subject the five to examination."

"Jonah may not have consented," Danielle said, "but I've explained the situation to his people. They have given me formal permission to act on their behalf regarding his welfare. They are making the legal arrangements as we speak, and they'll send everything through the Magic Society via document duplication."

"There is a risk that word will get out that way," Arella said. "Lamprey pays little attention to his own Magic Society, but these are hardly ordinary times. Even if he maintains his inattention, his deputy is subtle and thorough."

"A dangerous combination," Emir said. "His loyalty?"

"To Lamprey. By all indications they are actual friends. My instincts tell me his only true allegiance is only to himself, but I've never found so much as a hint of disloyalty, and I did quite a bit of looking."

Gert frowned at Arella.

"Using the Magic Society for such communication is a necessary risk," Gert said. "This city has seen quite enough activity operating outside of the rules."

"We shouldn't let rules get in the way of something this important," Emir said.

"There are always reasons to ignore the rules," Gert said, "which is why we must be fastidious in following them. They are the very basis for civilisation, without which we would exist in a state of anarchy."

"I disagree," Emir said.

"I don't care," Gert said. "This operation is being conducted under the strictures of the Adventure Society, not one of your frivolous private excursions. Gold rank or not, you will follow instructions."

"Yes, ma'am."

"Once the legal documentation arrives," Gert said, "we must act immediately to secure this Jonah boy. Have you lined up someone capable to examine him? The local Magic Society does not sound like a satisfactory place to find the assistance we need."

"I've contacted the local high priest of Purity," Emir said. "He's politically detached and has as good a chance as anyone of finding anything that has been done to them and purging it safely."

"You think there may be a danger?" Arella asked.

"The people we captured in the astral space all quite thoroughly killed themselves with some manner of object buried in their bodies," Emir said. "My concern is our five adventurers coming to a similar end."

"Turning to the church of Purity is a good choice," Danielle said. "I want to send Jonah home to his family intact."

The arrival of the inquiry team from the Adventure Society's Continental Council had little impact on Jason, at least over the first few days. He had not been a member of the expedition and was too low rank to be involved in major society affairs. In the meantime, he had been working with Rufus to prepare Sophie for the next Adventure Society intake.

Rufus gave Sophie his own assessment but remained mostly hands-off, leaving Jason to introduce her to various aspects of adventuring. He took on more of a mentor role to Jason, offering advice and guidance on what to teach her, and how. They were discussing just that on one of the cloud palace's many terraces, the cool moisture of the ocean breeze cutting the hot, dry air.

"Her skills are impressive," Rufus said. "In terms of empty-hand technique, she's better than I am. Her weapon-work isn't as strong but given her abilities that won't be an issue."

"All the fighting she's done has been against people, though," Jason said.

Rufus nodded.

"Her lack of experience fighting monsters is unquestionably her main shortfall," he said. "Take her out into the delta and do some adventure board notices. Recruit Humphrey, if you can. He has more immediate impact than you if someone needs to step in."

"I was thinking the same thing," Jason said. "Have you heard anything from his mother about the inquiry?"

"They're auditing the whole branch," Rufus said. "From what she's hearing, there will be sweeping demotions across the board, expedition members or otherwise. More than a few will be losing their membership entirely."

"I'll probably get bumped back down to two stars," Jason said. "I always suspected that moving up to three stars so quickly was part of Arella's games, and I daresay this inquiry will agree."

"I wouldn't worry about local politics too much," Rufus said. "Bronze rank will be a fresh start that you can make far from here. My part in the Remore Academy annex with the Gellers should time nicely with you ranking up and your indenture contract coming to an end. We can head for Vitesse, leaving this city and its troubles behind."

"We have no ideas how things will look six months from now," Jason said. "There should be a monster surge by then, right?"

"There should be a monster surge by now," Rufus said. "I'll be interested in where your thieves will be in six months. Things are changing in very large ways for them."

"That's up to them," Jason said. "The whole point was to give them the chance to choose their own path."

"How goes the non-combat training?"

"I've been teaching them what Farrah taught me about meditation, and aura manipulation. The mental exercises. Are you sure I'm ready to teach anyone?"

"Farrah was always impressed by you," Rufus said. "We all saw the potential in you. You're her legacy now."

Jason looked stricken.

"Don't say that," he said. "I can't live up to it."

"None of us live up to the expectations we put on ourselves," Rufus said. "Gary and Farrah taught me to accept that. But in the attempt, we push ourselves to new heights. You don't have to be some shining representative of who she was. Just try to be an adventurer she would be proud to have trained."

"That, I can do. It feels strange, passing on what she taught me to these women."

"You've been teaching them both?"

"Wexler will get essences for her friend sooner or later. If she knows the meditation techniques and training exercises beforehand, that's only for the good. Wexler tends to listen more with her friend riding herd on her, too."

"Problems with the training?"

"Wexler's walls are slowly coming down," Jason said. "A lot of construction went into them, though. Building trust is half the battle."

"Trust is crucial," Rufus said. "If you want to teach her anything effectively, she needs to trust that what you're imparting has value and that you're doing so in good faith."

"Any tips?"

"Don't try to rush things. Let time do its work."

Jason nodded.

"It won't hurt to take a day off, then," he said. "I haven't seen Cassandra since the day the expedition got back."

"You have plans?"

"She invited me to go sailing."

"They're gone," Genevieve said. The deputy director of the Adventure Society was in the director's office, along with Danielle, Emir and Tabitha Gert.

"What about tracking their badges?" Gert asked.

"The fact that we couldn't track their badges is what drew our attention to them in the first place," Danielle said.

"They were all directed to have their aura's re-examined and their badges replaced," Arella said. "None of them showed up to do so."

"Do we know anything?" Emir asked.

"I've already got my information network in Old City looking," Arella said. "They don't have the skills or the powers to hide from my people in Old City. If they're there, we'll find them. If they left, we'll know which direction. Our best course of action now is patience."

"How reliable is your network in Old City?" Gert asked.

"Now that everyone knows my father has me standing behind him, his power in Old City is unchallenged," Arella said. "You couldn't ask for better."

"You said they don't have the skills to hide," Emir said. "That is assuming their skills are what they were. For all we know, they may not be in charge of their bodies anymore."

"It doesn't change our course of action," Danielle said. "We have people looking, so we be patient and let them. Acting just for the sake of doing something is borrowing trouble when we already have enough."

All the major temples in Greenstone fronted the Divine Square but the rest of their space occupied extensive chunks of the temple district in sprawling, multi-building complexes. The temple of Purity was no different, with a number of sizeable buildings spread out over its spacious grounds. A priestess of Purity, Anisa Lasalle, walked through those grounds to a construction site in the early stages of adding a new building the temple's collection.

On site was a foreman's office made of what looked like hastily thrown together materials. Anyone with the right knowledge and the ability to see magic would realise that time, effort and expense had been put into the powerful protections against eavesdropping built into the structure. Should anyone enquire, it was a sound-suppressing measure, allowing the foreman to hold meetings with the church representatives in peace and quiet.

After stepping inside the building, Anisa glanced around, sensing for gaps in the sound-shielding magic but finding it thorough and intact. The other occupant of the room looked every bit the ordinary construction foreman, yet she looked at him with a distaste undue a simple tradesperson.

"Well?" the man asked.

"Your thrown-together plan has been lucky enough to work," Anisa said. "All the attention is on the five you seeded. No one has even considered that your true agents exist to look for. We suggest you restrict your activities for the moment, so as to not risk exposure."

"Agreed," the man said. "The next stage is reliant on remaining unnoticed."

"You are certain that Bahadir will send people into another astral space?"

"Bahadir's people are loyal and discreet, but the people they work with are not always the same. Our information is solid."

"And this other astral space is still of sufficient scale to do as promised?"

"Oh, yes," the foreman said. "It's not the prize the desert astral space would have been, but still a very welcome one. As for the secondary effects of our claiming it, they will be more than enough to meet your needs. Better, in fact, since you won't need to evacuate your people as far."

"We are evacuating no one," Anisa said. "It would arouse too much suspicion."

"I admire your conviction," he said. "After the adventurers have returned from this new astral space, we will need to become more active to carry out the next step. The risk of some of our agents being exposed during this phase is high."

"They cannot be allowed to talk," Anisa said.

"Again, we are in agreement," he said. "We have more star seeds and any of our people who know anything will be implanted."

"See that they are," Anisa said. "We'll speak again after the first stage is complete."

"I look forward to it, priestess."

"I don't."

She swept over to the door, flung it open and left, as if rushing to escape a trapped stench.

11

IT'S ABOUT HOW YOU USE IT

While a cabal of the city's most powerful plotted to get their hands on Thadwick Mercer and the other four suborned adventurers, Thadwick's sister was on her family's boat with Jason. Jason and Cassandra were—if the half-dozen Mercer family staff were discounted —all alone on the open water. The Mercer family's recreational vessel was just as large and outlandish, to the point that only magic was sufficient for propulsion. It was made of wood but was a far cry from the wooden ships Jason knew. White paint and smooth lacquer, seemingly impervious to the seawater and salty air, gave it a feel more akin to a contemporary pleasure craft. It reminded Jason of a superyacht from his own world, leading him to reflect that rich people seemed the same, whatever world he was in.

There was a sunken lounging area in the middle of the foredeck. It was a square space, lined with seating on all sides and sporting a glass table in the middle. A huge parasol was affixed to the centre of the table to offer shade. Jason and Cassandra lounged on a couch, leaning into one another.

"This was a very good idea," Jason said. "I'm so glad you offered. Everything has been sadness, frustration and grief lately."

"My thoughts exactly," Cassandra said. "First the people lost to the expedition, now these outsiders with their inquiry are pushing to hand Thadwick over to them."

"For what?"

"They think something was done to him and want him examined by their own people when ours have already looked him over quite thoroughly. Mother is considering having Thadwick leave until everything has blown over. You haven't heard anything about it from the gold-ranker, have you?"

"Emir's involved in it? I haven't seen him for days. If nothing else, I've been caught up trying to get my new indenture to listen to me."

"Things not going well?"

"I'm here to forget about that," Jason said, "not talk about it."

"I thought you were here for me?" she said provocatively.

"Nope," Jason said with weary shamelessness. "You are a welcome addendum to what is primarily an escape plan. I just hope you don't take on the stereotypical role of beautiful women in escape plans and betray me at a critical moment."

"What kind of critical moment?"

"Well," Jason said, "the kind that has a hammock, for example. I'm sure saw I spied a hammock hanging up somewhere when I came aboard."

"Was it big enough for two?" Cassandra asked.

"You know, now that you bring it up, I think it was."

She let out a relaxed chuckle.

"Even if it wasn't," she said, "it will be by the time we wander over there."

The staff were discretely out of sight, but Jason could sense their auras.

"That must have been a very strange way to grow up," he said. "Never having a truly private moment."

"It teaches you to put on a façade," she said. "One that takes an unusual person to shake."

"Shaking it isn't the trick," Jason said. "You need to make the person want to come out from behind it. You have to be tantalising."

"That's what you are, is it?"

"I think I have my moments," he said. "You'll have to tell me."

"Where is it exactly that you learned your particular way of handling people?" she asked.

"Private school."

"Private school?"

"Yes. I grew up on a pleasant little stretch of coastline. Just a little town, tourists in the summer."

"Tourists?"

"Taking a holiday where I come from is a lot cheaper and easier than it is here. It isn't just the wealthy who can do it, although they certainly do it best. The less affluent participating in such activities are called tourists."

"Do they have something to do with your private school?"

"Definitely not. Around thirty years or so back, a lot of wealthy people looked at our lovely stretch of coast and the conveniently placed local highway and decided to move in. Being rich, of course, they had no interest in our humble little town. Small, exclusive communities started popping up around us like mushrooms after the rain. Swanky summer homes and the kind of accommodation you can only afford if you own a boat like this one."

"It doesn't really rain here," she said. "I'll have to take your word on the mushrooms."

"I'm trustworthy," Jason said. "I just don't seem like it because seeming trustworthy is suspicious."

"You can be an unnecessarily convoluted man."

"Thank you. Anyway, a lot of these rich people would only hang about for the summer, but enough stayed that they needed a place for their children to go to school. Thus, the Casselton Educational Institute was formed. Excellent teachers, quality education. Exorbitant cost. Everyone of means in the region sent their children there, from the first day of school until they were sent off to university."

"Education is more prominent in your homeland, isn't it?" Cassandra asked.

"For now. The government keeps taking away money from the public schools to give to the wealthy private ones, but they haven't finished the job quite yet."

Cassandra didn't need to ask why; power dynamics were universal across worlds.

"Now, we weren't amongst the richest of the rich," Jason continued, "but my family did very well for themselves. My mother got in property sales early, making quite the bundle on the influx of wealthy buyers. My father is a landscape architect and had a strong hand in literally shaping the new communities. Between them, they sold and/or designed most of the region."

"So your family had money enough to send you to this fancy school."

"I don't look like most of the children who went to that school. My father's parents came from another land and we only have humans where I come from. Instead of looking down on elves or leonids or whoever, people isolate and exclude by ethnicity."

"That sounds foolish."

"It is. It's getting better, but there are always these undercurrents of prejudice, coming out in little ways most people don't even notice. It's like constantly being pricked with needles and being accused of making a fuss if you have the gall to point it out."

"That sounds appalling," she said.

"You get used to it. That's just the background issue, though. The more specific problem was my older brother."

"He made it hard for you?"

"Not intentionally, which made it all the more difficult to deal with. You see, my brother is excellent with people. He's the handsome one, the charming one. The obedient one. He can just go with the flow, let things pass without questioning. He has a way of intuiting what people want and becoming that. A social chameleon. Do you have chameleons here?"

"We do," Cassandra said.

"Well, he is one, socially speaking. He doesn't manipulate people, not consciously. He just likes people and people like him. He went down very well with the wealthy families, who liked how unprejudiced they looked if their children had a multiethnic friend. It saved them from getting one themselves."

"Let me guess," Cassandra said. "One outsider friend was just the right amount, with a second one being surplus to requirements."

"Exactly," Jason said. "It sounds like rich families are the same wherever you go."

"The way you describe your brother reminds me of Beth Cavendish," Cassandra said. "You've met her, yes?"

"I have."

"There aren't a lot of non-human families at the peak of Greenstone society, which doesn't always look good when you're are dealing with global trading partners. Beth is something of an ideal, which makes people want to rope her in. She's very socially adroit, in a more subtle fashion than you. Similar to your brother, I suspect."

"Are you saying I don't smoothly fit in?"

"Your approach to socialising is like tossing snakes into a ballroom."

"I have no idea what you're talking about," he said innocently.

"My mother said that the first time you met her, you denied being in a group with some of the city's most powerful people and claimed to have won a raffle."

"I forgot about that," he said with a chuckle. "You're right about being socially adroit, though. I never had Kaito's—that's my brother's name, Kaito. I never had his skill for getting along. I just can't seem to help challenging and provoking."

"Yes, we've all noticed."

"Shush, you," he said, putting a finger to her lips.

She kissed it and pushed it away.

"I was one foreign boy too many," he continued, "despite not being foreign at all. Kaito is a year older than me, so as far as the other kids were concerned, I was a disappointing rehash of the well-received original. I only had one real friend. The literal girl next door. Her name is Amy and we grew up together."

"Who you fell in love with, obviously," Cassandra said.

"Oh, it wasn't just love," Jason said. "It was eighties power-ballad love."

"I have no idea what that means."

"Imagine a man with long hair, no shirt, open vest and leather pants, walking into the ocean while singing a song."

"That sounds like an insane person."

"Yes," Jason agreed. "It was that kind of love."

"It came to a tragic end?"

"She married my brother."

"That must have hurt."

"I reacted poorly, I'll admit," Jason said, "but that's a story for another day. When we were in school, my brother cast a long shadow and I never had his knack for becoming what people wanted. It turned out that my knack was for pulling people into my own pace. It got people to do what I wanted, at least until they stopped to think about what they were doing and got cross. They had no interest in being my friends, though, and I quickly stopped caring what a bunch of entitled rich kids thought about me."

"It's been my experience," Cassandra said, "that things can become quite political when you gather enough wealthy children together."

"That's been my experience as well," Jason said. "There and here. Speaking of entitled rich kids, how is your brother doing? You said people were looking to study him."

Cassandra nodded, unhappily.

"Things had been going so well with him after the expedition. He's been training non-stop, actually building the skills he should have developed long ago. Mother and Father are thrilled. Or they would be if it weren't for the rumours going around, which is why people want to take him away and start probing him."

"What kind of rumours?" Jason asked. "I've been too busy to keep an ear out, lately."

"Your friend Bahadir brought tracking stones for all the members of the expedition, first to rescue survivors, then recover the fallen. There were five people, my brother included, whose tracking stones lost track of them. They were still found, all severely hurt. Now people are saying that something was done to them in the time they couldn't be tracked and they were left to be found."

"I'm sorry."

"It's frustrating," she said. "Thadwick is finally turning into the person we always hoped he would become and people have found an all-new way to harass him. They say the changes to his personality are some kind of magical parasite."

"I know from experience that being thrust into wild and unexpected danger can see you come out the other side different. I'm not the man I was before coming here. I've seen dangers and been driven to become as prepared as I can be for the next time. It makes sense to me that Thadwick experience something similar."

"Thank you," she said, leaning into him. "I know you and he never got along, and I thought that might taint your judgement."

"Hopefully, I'm growing as a person. Have the other four been experiencing similar problems?"

"They have," she said. "To the point that they felt the need to all leave their old teams and form a new one together."

"That will only deepen the rumours."

"I know, but Thadwick seems more settled this way. Go back to talking about your school; I want to hear more."

"Well, there's not much to tell, really. I learned two lessons about people that have always held true, in my world or yours. One was that people really like to fill in the gaps in a story. You give someone the right selection of facts and you don't have to lie to them. They'll connect the pieces in accordance with their own beliefs and lie to themselves for you."

"Wouldn't that make people wary of you, once they figure out what you're doing?"

"That's where the second lesson comes in," Jason said. "When someone believes something, they believe it hard. Too hard. They'll dismiss good evidence that contradicts their belief and accept spurious evidence that supports it. So, in their mind, if you're wrong, they're very wrong, and the whole point is that their thoughts don't go down that path."

"That sounds like something that could get out of hand."

"Oh, yes," Jason said. "These realisations were far from original. People have been using them in my world for thousands of years, to rather disastrous effect."

"So, why use them?"

"Amy used to ask me the same thing. People liked her better than me."

"What did you tell her?"

"It's what I have," he said. "Like any tool, it's about how you use it. A hammer can be used to build a house or club someone to death."

"Did it make you any more friends?"

"I would more say it gave me an accepted position in the social landscape. I've learned to take a quality over quantity approach to personal relationships," he said. "Look at you, for example. Every eligible young man in the city hates my guts because of you, and so they should. You are spectacular by any metric."

"Thank you. But what about this Amy girl? It doesn't sound like she was too spectacular."

"She was," Jason said. "Still is, presumably. I've known her for most of my life and there's no one I understand better. She was absolutely worth falling in love with, which only became a problem when my brother finally noticed that fact."

"If you knew her so well, why didn't you see it coming?"

"I told you: people will dismiss good evidence if the bad evidence tells them what they want to hear. I'm no more immune to that than anyone."

"You seem to have taken it well."

"I can talk about it, now," he said. "At the time, I blew up my whole life, forming an ever-deepening vortex of mediocrity. Banal job, no real friends. A series of relationships you could see the end of before they began."

He flashed her a wry smile.

"Coming to an alternate world was the best thing that ever happened to me," he said. "Of course, nine of the ten worst things that ever happened to me happened here. Still, completely worth it. I'm happy with the balance."

"Well," Cassandra said. "Maybe we can go find that hammock and tilt the scale."

12

WE END HERE

As a week of ongoing memorial services came to a close, the adventuring community fell into a sober silence. The Adventure Society campus was quiet and, for the first time Jason had seen, largely occupied by adventurers who didn't come from the upper echelons of Greenstone society.

Jason had learned to recognise the upper crust adventurers over time. Many he knew by sight, although the quality of their gear was an even clearer indicator. The people he saw roaming the campus tended towards plain, functional equipment, more value-for-money than the highest performing gear.

There was a pregnant pause in the wake of the disastrous expedition, while people awaited word of what the inquiry would do. In the absence of the usual dominating forces, frequently overlooked adventurers were coming to the fore. These were the adventurers who would never have gotten a place on the expedition and, in the absence of those who did, stepped in to fill the gap. While the expedition was now back, the city's most powerful families were licking their wounds and awaiting the inquiry results. The adventurers newly flourishing in their place were left free to continue.

Belinda started working with Clive at the Magic Society. He took her in and showed her what was expected from her while things were still quiet for him. Once he was finally allowed access to what the expedition had brought back, he expected to become very busy. By that point, she needed to have already grasped the basics of her new job.

For his own preparations, he reviewed works on astral magic from the Magic Society's library, as well as his own collection. Although it suited his purposes, he was rather dismayed at their availability. The people working on the materials brought back should have already been accessing the astral magic texts quite heavily.

The incompetence of his fellows allowed Clive to put together a quick-reference library of astral magic to help his own investigation, once he had access to the materials. He also put together some theory primers for Belinda, to fill in the gaps in her patchwork education. Whenever Clive had no specific tasks for her, she could dive into the list.

Jason, in the meantime, introduced Sophie to the training cycle that Rufus, Gary and Farrah had introduced to him. Some of it, like the meditation training and the weightlifting, was new. Other things, like the parkour and the observation training, she had been doing some version of for years.

Because she could outperform him in certain aspects of the training, it coloured her view of his ability in the others. She was self-sufficient by nature, more used to finding her own way through things than having someone instruct her. She hadn't had anything like a teacher since her father had died and was resisting it now.

In one of the cloud palace's meditation rooms, Jason was instructing her on using meditation techniques to gain better control of the mana within her body. They were sitting on the soft cloud floor, cross-legged and face to face.

"I can actively move the mana around my body," Sophie was arguing. "Taking control feels better. Stronger."

"This technique isn't about strength or control," Jason said. "It's about mapping out how the mana flows within the body. You need to be patient, sense how the mana moves on its own. Exercising control before gaining an understanding will do more harm than good."

"It doesn't feel right," she said. "It really feels like I should be doing it my way."

Jason ran his hands over his face, taking a deep, calming breath. He got to his feet.

"That's enough for today, I think," he said.

"That's it?"

"I don't think continuing will be very productive."

She lightly hopped up to her feet.

"So, if I don't do everything the way you want, you just give up?"

"Meditation is about achieving a useful state of mind," Jason said. "If we have fundamentally opposed positions on what you need to achieve then we get nowhere. Letting it go and starting fresh tomorrow will achieve more than forcing the issue."

Their respective suites were close together in the guest wing, so they walked together as they returned, albeit in silence. They encountered Clive and Belinda on the way, who easily spotted the tension. Jason gave them a curt nod of greeting before disappearing into his suite.

Clive frowned as he looked at the door through which Jason had passed through, then at the dissatisfied expression on Sophie's face.

"I think it's time we had a little talk," he said. "Do you have a moment to discuss something?"

She gave him a wary, assessing look before nodding and heading into the suite she shared with Belinda.

"She means 'of course, please do come in,'" Belinda said.

"That's the impression I was getting," he said.

Belinda laughed as they followed Sophie inside to the main lounge of their suite. Sophie took a chilled bottle of water from a cooler cabinet and fell into a couch while Clive sat in a chair opposite her, across a low refreshments table.

"So, what is it?" Sophie asked as Belinda sat down beside her. Clive looked Sophie straight in the eye.

"We told you that we were given a choice of awakening stones and Jason chose the one that gave you your aura."

"I remember."

"Jason is an affliction specialist and that stone was almost certain to give you some ability that would be bad for him if you ended up on the opposite sides of a fight again. Which is exactly what it did."

"So?" Belinda asked.

"He wants me to ask why," Sophie said.

"Yes," Clive acknowledged. "I asked him myself why he would choose that stone."

"And?" Sophie asked.

"He said that three men had gone to considerable lengths to control your destiny. Cole Silva lost his chance when Lucian Lamprey became involved. Lamprey lost his chance when Jason claimed your indenture. I didn't know who the third man was, though."

"Asano is the third man," Sophie said.

"Yes," Clive said. "He told me the same thing. And that's why he chose that stone. It makes it a little harder for him to enforce his grip on you."

"I never asked him to be my protector," Sophie said.

"He doesn't want to be," Clive said. "He's giving you the tools to you need to protect yourself."

"He thinks he's my hero?"

"He *is* your hero," Clive said. "Throwing you through a portal and never thinking about you again would have fulfilled whatever responsibility he felt towards you, and not many of us would have done even that much for you. But he doesn't think like me and he's decided this is the right thing to do."

He shook his head disbelievingly before continuing.

"Do you even understand what he has paid, literally and figuratively, to put you in the position you are now? He stood up to the directors of both the Adventure Society and the Magic Society. He actually stood in front of each and told them that he was taking you out of their hands. I wouldn't have done that. The idea of doing that would never have entered my head. I don't think you're worth what he's done for you, but when Jason decides to do something, he goes all the way. He decided to help you, which is why you're here instead of chained to a bed somewhere with a glazed look in your eye."

"I didn't ask for any of that," Sophie said.

"And you don't deserve it," Clive said. "Not everything he's done for you. It's past time you started to show him some gratitude."

"You make him out like he's this great guy," Sophie said, "but I've seen plenty of lying, scheming manipulators. He fits right in."

"Yes, he does," Clive said. "And look what his schemes and manipulations have done."

Clive stood up.

"I've said my piece; take it or ignore it as you please. I'll see you tomorrow, Belinda." He walked out of the suite, leaving Sophie and Belinda alone.

Belinda looked at Sophie, caught up in thought. Sophie met her gaze.

"What do you think?" Sophie asked.

Belinda thought for a while before answering.

"Maybe Asano needs to feel powerful. To prove to himself he can make something a little less awful when awful is in abundant supply. We both know what it's like to be stuck in the mud, powerless to do anything about it."

"People don't help other people to feel in control," Sophie said. "They push those people down."

"Jory doesn't," Belinda said. "Look at what he's done to help people. I think maybe Asano is like that. And if he is, then what he's done for us is really incredible."

"So I should go fawning after Asano, now?"

"No," Belinda said. "But maybe not treat everything he says and does like it's part of some scheme to screw you over. He's had every chance to hurt us but everything he's done has helped us. At least give him the chance to prove he's actually trying to do right by you. Maybe even let him do it."

"If he's such a good guy, then why does he always act shady?"

"Maybe he realised you'd find a good guy even more suspicious and didn't want you running for the hills."

Sophie's brow furrowed as she thought it over.

"Yeah," she acknowledged with a nod. "I guess I would have."

She got to her feet.

"I'll go talk to him," she said. "Maybe I can clear the air a little. Hear him out with an open mind, at least."

Belinda gave her an encouraging smile.

"That sounds sensible," she said. "I think we've been scrambling for so long that we may have lost the knack for sensible and patient."

Sophie went into the hall and found Rufus leaving Jason's suite.

"Is he in?" she asked.

"He is, but I'd leave him be for now. I just let him know that he's been demoted to one star."

"What does that mean?"

"It means that he just went from the highest rank he could have to the lowest."

"Why?"

"The inquiry in the Adventure Society."

"I thought they were just looking at that expedition," Sophie said.

"They're doing a full audit of the local branch, looking at everything and everyone. They just announced a sweeping wave of demotions, including Jason's."

"He doesn't seem like the kind that would be bothered."

"Yeah," Rufus said. "Not seeming bothered is something he's good at."

Jason looked out from his terrace, the late afternoon sun shining over the ocean. He had been expecting to lose one star, but two was a blow. Rufus had once again told him that it didn't matter, that soon enough he would be bronze and could start over at a new rank. But, it still felt like a repudiation of everything he'd achieved. He knew he'd done some contentious things but he believed he was a good adventurer. Until the moment Rufus walked in, he had the stars to prove it.

Jason vaulted over the edge of the terrace, his cloak appearing around him. After floating down to a lower level of the palace he made his way to the shore and set off through the Adventure Society campus.

When he reached the marshalling yard he found a throng of people. Rows of bulletin boards had been set up, listing demotions. A large notice at the front instructed the demoted to go to the administration building to have the stars removed from their badges. Jason went through the rows, shoulder to shoulder with people as he looked for his name. He didn't think Rufus had gotten it wrong, but he needed to see for himself. He noticed as he browsed through the names that many weren't just demoted but had their membership revoked entirely.

He found his name. Jason Asano. Old rank: three stars. New rank: one star. He let out a weary breath, then extricated himself from the crowd. He looked in the direction of the Adventure Society and saw that not many people heading there to confirm their demotion. He overheard talk that people wouldn't stand for it and the decision would be overturned. He heard more than one assertion that they would refuse to confirm the demotion until all the politics had played out.

Jason made his way to the administration building where a long bench had been set up. There were four Adventure Society officials behind it, with people queuing up in front. The officials were each using a wedge-shaped magical stone to remove stars from badges. None of the queues were long and Jason joined the one that led to Vincent.

"Rufus found you, then," Vincent said when Jason reached the front.

"He did."

"Sorry about this."

Jason handed over his badge, watching the third star, then the second disappear as Vincent touched it twice with his stone. Jason took it back and left. Standing outside the admin building, he had no interest in going back to the cloud palace. Setting his feet in the direction of the jobs hall, he strode off. He wanted to kill something.

After four days in the delta, he met a member of the Geller family and discovered that people thought he had gone missing.

"No," Jason had told the man. "I'm just doing adventure notices. Tell them I'm fine."

It was another week before he returned to the city. He went straight to the jobs hall, handing over the contract he had originally taken, along with a stack of completed adventure board notices. As he made his way across the Adventure Society campus, he heard Cassandra call out his name. She was rushing to catch up to him but became hesitant as she drew closer.

"What's wrong?" he asked.

"I've been trying to find you," she said. "I heard you were out in the delta."

"I was."

"Jason, I…"

She looked around. They were standing in an open area of grass, with few people in sight. Ever since the expedition, far fewer people were to be found at the campus, with the demotions only making it worse.

"What is it?" he asked. He tried to act as if the distance she kept between them didn't tell him what she was about to say.

"I have to end things. Between you and I."

He was going to ask why, but his brain beat his mouth.

"The demotion," he said.

"I've received a lot of privileges, being part of my family," she said. Her beautiful face was sunken, reluctant, but determined. "There are responsibilities that come with it, too. I have to find a match that makes the family stronger."

"I see."

"Your lack of background always made it hard to convince the family. Mother helped. Your connections to the Gellers and the Vitesse adventurers were good and your rapid rise silenced a lot of voices. Dropping to one star, though. I have to find someone reliable."

"You think I'm unreliable?"

"You know I don't. I argued against it, but it was decided. We end here."

"Just like that."

"I didn't want this," she said. "They're being short-sighted, I know."

"But they're family," Jason said.

"Yes," she said softly.

She was holding her hands in front of her, vulnerability showing in what was usually an unassailable countenance. He stepped closer, gently taking her hands in his.

"Alright," he said.

"Alright?"

"Not really, but yes."

"Just like that?"

"What did you expect?" he asked.

"I don't know. Maybe I thought you'd say that nobles are stupid and do something reckless and impulsive."

"That would only hurt you and accomplish nothing," he said. "Take it from someone who let a failed relationship drive a wedge between him and his family."

He leaned in, gently kissed her and stepped back, letting go of her hands. His eyes glistened with tears but he had a familiar, impish grin.

"You're going to miss me, Cassandra Mercer."

"I know."

He turned walked away, without looking back.

13
POISON PILL

It was late morning, the sun high in the sky. Clive arrived at the cloud palace, and found someone standing near the platform that touched the shore.

"Acolyte Pellin," he greeted.

"Mister Standish," she greeted in return.

"Are you waiting for something?"

"I'm waiting for Mr Asano," she said. "I'm going to deliver a gift from my goddess, as promised."

"Jason has been gone for almost two weeks," Clive said. "I take it, as an acolyte of Knowledge, that you know something I don't."

"He's on the Adventure Society campus right now," she said. "He's speaking with Cassandra Mercer and will be done shortly."

Clive looked up at the towering cloud palace.

"Then I think I'll wait as well," he said. "My days have been busy, but I can spare a few minutes. It must be an odd experience, having knowledge placed into your mind by your goddess."

"I'm told the sensation is similar to using a skill book," Gabrielle said. "I've never used one myself but my experience is gentler than a skill book, from what I'm told. The goddess doesn't impart so much information at once."

"I always imagined it would be disconcerting," he said. "I've spent so much of my life in pursuit of knowledge that having it just turn up in my head would be quite alarming."

"The goddess is aware of your pursuit, Mr Standish, and she loves you for it."

"Oh, um… thanks?"

"He's here," she said, turning away from Clive.

Clive followed her gaze to spot Jason. He became slightly alarmed at what he saw. Jason was still wearing his battle robes, which he rarely did in the city. His gaze was normally sharp and focused or roaming and observant, but today he looked puffy-eyed and disoriented.

"I don't suppose your goddess told you if he's been drinking?" Clive asked.

"He hasn't," Gabrielle said. "Cassandra Mercer just ended their relationship."

"Oh," Clive said sadly, then turned a narrow gaze on Gabrielle. "I think I'm starting to understand why Jason complains about your goddess and privacy."

Gabrielle gave Clive a disapproving glare.

"She is Knowledge," Gabrielle said. "Knowledge is hers to disseminate as she sees fit."

Jason drew closer, giving Clive a sad and tired smile.

"G'day Clive; it's been a while." He greeted Gabrielle with a nod. "Acolyte."

"Mr Asano."

Jason turned back to Clive.

"They must be keeping you busy at the Magic Society by now."

"They are," Clive said. "I don't have answers yet, but I'm making progress."

"How's your new assistant?"

"She has some unusual gaps in her knowledge, but she works hard and learns fast. Everything I could hope for."

"Good. Have they been talking about bringing in more astral magic specialists?"

"Haven't you heard?" Clive asked.

"Heard what?" Jason asked. "I've been chasing monsters through wetlands for two weeks."

"The events in our astral space were not unique. There have been incidents in other astral spaces all around the world."

"That's disturbing," Jason said. His unfocused expression grew sharp as his muddled brain started turning over.

"But, that explains why there were no opponents above silver in ours for an operation of that scale," he said. "Whoever they are, they needed their high-rankers for the high-magic areas. There was no reason to anticipate gold-rank adventurers here, so they could save them for other regions."

"That's been the consensus," Clive said. "At least it means that if I don't manage to unveil their intentions, many others are working on the problem elsewhere."

"Don't talk yourself down, Clive," Jason said. "If you're not convinced you have the goods, I'll be convinced for you. You'll get there."

"Thank you," Clive said. "Look, I have to go speak with Rufus but I wanted to check in on you. You've had people worried, taking off without a word like that."

"Sorry," Jason said. "I'm fine, as you see."

"Yes," Clive said, unconvinced. "It's good to see you back."

Clive cast an uncertain gaze at Gabrielle.

"I'm sorry about Cassandra, Jason."

Jason's face went very still, then turned slowly on the acolyte.

"Thank you, Clive," he said, voice flinty as his eyes locked onto Gabrielle. "Come find me when you have some free time. We'll get a drink."

"It may be a little while but that sounds good," Clive said. He set out across the cloud bridge to enter the palace.

"I shouldn't have told him that," Gabrielle said apologetically.

"You shouldn't even know about it. I know I've been jokey about your goddess and her privacy issues but she had no right to tell you that."

Gabrielle's expression went stiff.

"She's a goddess, Mr Asano. She has whatever rights she wants."

"I'd respond to that, but she already knows what I have to say because I do. In case she doesn't tell you, it involved a lot of bad language and several physiologically implausible suggestions."

"You should show her more respect."

"Respect is earned."

"She earned it by being a goddess."

"That's a tyrant's reasoning. If you'll excuse me, I'm leaving."

"Wait. I came here to give you something."

She had a small satchel slung over her shoulder, from which she took a wooden case. Holding it out, she opened it to reveal three objects in the padded interior. Two were awakening stones and the other a small stone square. It looked similar to the world-phoenix token in Jason's inventory, but a washed-out blue colour instead of vibrant red.

"She knows that you will confront the people responsible for the death of your friend," Gabrielle said. "She expects you to encounter them more than once. She chose a gift that would better prepare you for those encounters."

Jason touched a hand to the first awakening stone.

Item: [Divine Awakening Stone of Inevitability] (transcendent rank, epic)
An awakening stone crafted by a god to bestow a specific aura power.
(consumable, awakening stone).
Requirements: Doom essence, unawakened doom essence ability, no aura essence ability.
Effect: Awakens the aura essence ability [Inescapable Doom].
You have 3 unawakened essence abilities.
You do not meet the requirements to use this item.

Jason frowned at the description, which troubled him in several regards. He focused on the listed ability.

Ability: [Inevitable Demise] (Doom)
Aura (magic).
Cost: None.
Cooldown: None.
Effect (iron): Enemies within the aura have any affliction immunities, including inherent immunities, treated as complete resistance. This resistance can be reduced by ordinary resistance-reduction effects. This is a magic effect.

He wasn't able to use the stone as each person could only awaken the one aura. Presuming the square tablet was some kind of solution to that, it was the next object he touched.

Item: [Soul-Purgation Tablet (aura)] (transcendent rank, legendary)
***???.* (consumable, ???).**
Effect: ???.
Uses remaining: 1/1.
You meet the requirements to use this item. Use Y/N?

Like the world-phoenix token, this item was too powerful for Jason's ability to discern its characteristics. After looking at it for a moment, the description changed.

Item: [Soul-Purgation Tablet (aura)] (transcendent rank, legendary)
***A tablet with the power to remove an aura essence ability. Cannot be forcibly used on another by any means.* (consumable, soul-shaping).**
Requirements: Awakened aura essence ability.
Effect: Removes an existing aura essence ability.
Uses remaining: 1/1.
Warning: Information on this item has been provided by an outside source and cannot be verified.
You meet the requirements to use this item. Use Y/N?

He didn't even realise that removing an essence ability was even possible, unless it was a god taking away what they'd given out themselves. After looking over the description for a moment, he touched the second awakening stone.

Item: [Divine Awakening Stone of Persistence] (transcendent rank, rare)
***An awakening stone crafted by a god to bestow a specific spell.* (consumable, awakening stone).**
Requirements: Dark essence, unawakened dark essence ability.
Effect: Awakens the spell essence ability [Dark Descent].

You have 3 unawakened essence abilities.
You meet the requirements to use this item. Use Y/N?

Jason checked the ability.

Ability: [Curse of Isolation] (Dark)
Spell (curse, magic).
Cost: None.
Cooldown: None.
Effect (iron): This spell cannot be resisted. Periodically inflicts an instance of [Dark Descent]; this is a curse effect.
[Dark Descent] (affliction, magic, stacking): Target has their perception distance, the effect of their perception ability and resistance to all afflictions reduced by a small amount. Additional instances have a cumulative effect.

The three items would make Jason much more effective against enemies immune to his afflictions. Various types of monsters were not flesh and blood, but the abilities the two stones offered would allow him to act as if they were. Given the army of constructs he heard about from the expedition members, if he really did encounter them then such abilities would be immensely useful.

"According to the goddess," Gabrielle said, "your current abilities are ill-suited to your fated enemies. These gifts were crafted by her specifically to rectify this. She said you would recognise their usefulness."

"Yeah," he said. "It's a shiny red apple, alright."

He snapped the case shut in Gabrielle's hands.

"Thanks, but no thanks. She chose the moment to offer me this, didn't she?"

"She said you could use some good news."

"No," he said, voice tired. "She sent you now because I'm emotional and vulnerable to making a rash decision."

Gabrielle glared at Jason.

"My goddess doesn't lie."

"She has all the knowledge in the world and near-infinite power," Jason said. "I bet the god of deceit looks at her with admiration."

Gabrielle shoved the box back into her bag and conjured a heavy iron staff into her hand. She raised the end to just under Jason's chin.

"Watch your words, Jason Asano. I will only tolerate them so far."

He gave her a look of weary disdain. "This is the part where your boss tells you to leave."

She opened her mouth to respond, then froze.

"See?" he asked. "I don't know what possible use I am to her but she wants me for something. For all I know, she's provoking this response because she wants me angry. I'm not stupid enough to think I can out-game her. I do think she made a genuine mistake here, though. She told me once that people constantly surprise her, and I think that's true. She knows everything, but that gives her a blind spot. She is as close as anyone to seeing a person's optimal choice in any situation, yet we constantly act against our own interest. It must drive her crazy."

Gabrielle's agitation was rising while Jason stood in front of her, just looking tired.

"You think to know my goddess? You think she has flaws for the likes of you to see?"

"Sure," Jason said. "Gods are big-picture types, older than we can imagine. I bet they have all kinds of trouble understanding the thoughts of short-lived wretches like us."

"Blasphemer!"

"Yeah," Jason said. "It's kind of my thing."

Again Gabrielle opened her mouth to speak only to stop. Knowledge herself appeared in person next to Gabrielle, placing a hand on her shoulder.

"That's enough dear," she said. "Time to run along back to the temple."

"Yes, Goddess," Gabrielle said, bowing her head before walking away with an angry stride.

As in their last meeting, the goddess looked like an ordinary person. Despite this, she radiated glory, even with her aura fully suppressed.

"I made a mistake here," she said.

"Unless that's what you want me to think," Jason said.

"You are making a mistake as well," she said. "The same one Sophie Wexler has been making. Don't push away an incredible opportunity out of an instinctive mistrust."

"If I was her, I wouldn't trust me either."

"So suspicious. You think my gift is a poison pill."

"If you wanted to give me something to help me deal with the people who killed Farrah, you could just tell me where to find them."

"You know better than that," she said. "If I start telling mortals how to solve all their problems, where does it end? If I tell them how to fix everything, then life becomes a puppet show where I hold all the strings. The other gods would not stand for that and neither would you."

"I can't fight a god."

"We both know it wouldn't stop you from trying. I may not tell people the things I know, so as to let them lead their lives, but I do make exceptions for my followers."

"You want me to worship you? You can't seriously think I would."

"Don't be so hasty. Come into my church in full faith and trust and I will tell you about the people who killed Farrah."

"Don't say her name."

"I'll tell you who killed your friend. Who they are, where they are. What they're doing and how to stop them. All this I will give you, in return for your faith."

"You mean obedience."

"I am not Dominion. In faith to me, there is no obedience, only loyalty. Do not rush to reject this offer. Take the time to consider it objectively. Think of what that knowledge can do. The lives it can save. And that is not the end. Follow me and there is countless good you can do with the knowledge I will gift you."

"Can I tell Clive about gravity?"

"You don't understand gravity."

"Do you?"

"Yes. I can see it."

"You can see gravity?"

"I'm a goddess."

"That must suck. Not a lot of hills left to climb. You must feel purposeless."

"You cannot aggravate me, Jason Asano."

"That's the advantage of being mortal; I can set goals. If you want something, you have it."

"I want you to worship me."

"I guess you can have goals," Jason said. "You know what I know, so you know what I think you're full of, and where I'd like you to stick your offer."

"You're letting your heart rule your head. I will give you some time to consider."

Jason gave a bitter, malevolent laugh.

"This must be frustrating for you," he said. "You can't predict my reactions yet know them immediately. You see how every approach you take just pushes me further away. Assuming you're not trying to push me away for some reason I can't see because I'm not an all-knowing immortal."

"We will speak again when you are more reasonable."

"But that's why you picked now, right? I'm angry and miserable. Not thinking straight. And here you are with the handy-dandy tools to vent my rage on a nice, deserving target. I hope you really did make a mistake and this isn't what you wanted. It makes me feel good to think of you realising how wrong this has gone, step by step. But you know that."

"There will be times in the future when you need me, Jason Asano."

"You know that, do you? Because it sounds like you're just guessing."

"Not many gods would tolerate this kind of insolence."

"Smite me, then."

She gave him a sad smile.

"We will talk again, Jason Asano. I hope to find that with a cooler head, you make better choices."

She vanished, leaving Jason alone.

"I've got some bad news for you lady," he said to the air. "Making bad life choices is kind of my thing."

"You seem to have a lot of things," Emir said, suddenly appearing next to Jason.

"I'm versatile," Jason said. "Does no one in this world respect privacy?"

"A goddess appeared on my doorstep," Emir said. "Did you really expect me not to take a look?"

"She let you. She wants you to tell Rufus about her offer."

"That would be ill-advised," Emir said. "Rufus very much wants vengeance for Farrah. He would push you hard to take the offer, making his friendship another cost of refusal."

"Yeah, she's sneaky," Jason said. "She'll probably see to it he finds out anyway."

"What will you do if she does?"

"What I always do," Jason said. "The best I can with what I have."

Emir nodded.

"I have some things to talk with you about myself, but now is not the time. You haven't even really got back yet, standing here on the doorstep. I would appreciate it if you come find me sometime in the next few days."

"I can do that."

14
LET'S JUST FIGHT MONSTERS

Rufus opened the door to his suite to admit Clive inside.

"I thought you were busy these days," Rufus said.

"I am, which is why I needed a break. Jason's back, by the way. I just saw him outside."

Rufus frowned.

"That boy needs a talking to. You can't just wander off without telling anyone when there are monsters looking to eat you and silver rankers looking to do worse. Not to mention the woman he is meant to be teaching."

"I wouldn't go too hard," Clive said. "Cassandra Mercer just ended things with him."

"Is that why he went off? She's been coming around looking for him, right?"

"No, I mean really just ended things. As in, minutes ago."

"Oh."

"That's not what I'm here for, though," Clive said. He pulled a document folder from his storage space. "I haven't been able to figure out what they were doing in the astral space yet, but I'm making progress. This is a list of the more unusual and specialised techniques and materials they were employing."

"I don't have any magical knowledge," Rufus said. "I can't help you decipher any of that."

"It's not about finding out what any of these things are for," Clive said, tapping the folder. "Each of the things I've listed here is rare, distinctive, and can't be sourced locally. They include exotic materials and magical devices requiring specialised knowledge. That gives us three possibilities. Possibility one is that they have a high-ranked portal user. We can ignore that, because it's a dead end for us. The next possibility is the items being brought in via some great overland trek, to maintain secrecy by avoiding anyone."

"That's unlikely," Rufus said. "Unpopulated lands are rife with monsters that go unculled, nomads that know the territory far better than any interlopers, plus the logistical problems and potential navigation mishaps."

"That leaves smuggling the goods in through the port in Hornis or the one here in Greenstone," Clive said. "That seems like the kind of thing an intrepid and motivated adventurer could look into."

"Yes, it does," Rufus said. He took the folder and shook Clive's hand. "Thank you for this."

Clive nodded.

"Let's just find these people."

Sophie had been left to her own devices for almost two weeks. Jason had vanished and Belinda was off with Clive all day. She spent some of her time with Rufus, who guided her in the training loop Jason had shown her. He seemed a more comfortable and capable instructor than Jason, but was distracted with his own training. There was a frenetic drive to the way he pushed himself to the limit, which at the peak of bronze rank she had no chance to match. He also went out every couple of days to hunt monsters. She asked to join him, but he told her that the monsters he was hunting were the strongest to be found in the area and she should wait for Jason's return.

She hunted up Emir's library or, as it turned out, libraries. They had a disappointing deficit of romantic potboilers, though. Lacking anything better to do, she finally turned to the meditation techniques Jason had showed her. At first she kept doing things the way that felt right to her, but she would increasingly end a session feeling tense and tired. She started trying things more like he had suggested, less self-conscious about it in his absence.

At first it felt awkward and pointless, although she felt better at the end of each session. Slowly it began to feel more natural, her patience and persistence showing slight but noticeable results. She became more comfortable with the power flowing through her. At the start it had felt like a wild beast she needed to forcibly control. With each day she came to understand that greater control came through accepting that it was a part of her, rather than an external energy to be brought forcibly into line.

After two weeks, meditation had become a pleasant and comfortable part of her day. She moved her sessions from the meditation room down the hall from her suite to the terrace that wrapped around the whole guest wing. Unlike the private suite terraces, this terrace anyone with access to the guest wing could make their way onto.

Normally she would choose privacy, but in Belinda's absence the isolation was starting to eat at her. She was happy for any chance encounter with the palace staff, who were pleasantly absent of agendas.

She was meditating in the warm sunlight when she was interrupted by Jason's voice.

"I haven't been a good teacher," he said. "Even before I left without a word."

She opened her eyes and turned to look at him. He looked tired.

"I didn't sense you coming," she said.

"The benefits of aura control," he said. "I've been trying too hard to control you, while telling myself I'm helping you."

From her sitting position she rolled back, then kicked up onto her feet. She looked him up and down, his adventuring gear topped off by a bone-weary face. She had finally been ready to try opening up, only for him to skulk off. She was ready to give him an earful but he genuinely didn't look up to it. She felt her anger dissipate, wondering if that was a side effect of all the meditation.

"It's not all on you," she said. "I've been fighting everyone, when I should be picking my enemies."

"How about we start over?" he suggested. "I'll show you what I know, and you help me improve where you're already better."

"That works out for you," she said. "I'm better at a lot."

Her expression had some hesitation to it but was more open than Jason had seen, with even the ghost of a smile. It was a welcome breakthrough.

"You are better than me at a lot," he agreed. "You've been surviving the hard way your whole life. Six months ago, I was assistant manager at a retail bulk office supplier."

"I don't know what that is."

"Probably for the best," Jason said. "So what do you say? Fresh start?"

He held out a hand and she shook it.

"I'm willing to try," she said. "Where do we begin?"

"I'm going to get some rest," he said. "I just got back and had a series of encounters that didn't go well for me. Keep doing what you're doing and tomorrow we'll go monster hunting."

"What kind of encounters?"

"I had a fight with my mate's girlfriend, my girlfriend dumped me, I had a row with a goddess after she tried to scam me out of my aura power and I saw Clive and Emir. It wasn't in that order, and the bits with Clive and Emir were fine."

"What do you mean by a row with a goddess?"

"She's trying to bait me into worshipping her. I'm not an expert but I'm pretty sure that's not how worship is meant to go and we had an argument about it."

"You mean an actual goddess?"

"Yeah, Knowledge. I assume you've heard of her."

"She's a goddess, Asano; of course I've heard of her. You expect me to believe that an actual goddess came down to try and recruit you to her church."

"Sounds shady, right? Ask Emir. He was watching the whole thing, or the end, at least. Right now, I'm going to find a comfy cloud bed and try to not think about my girlfriend kicking me to the curb."

Sophie shook her head in disbelief.

"You're a lot to take," she told him. "I don't know if you're telling the truth or lying, and I don't know which is more insane."

"I'm from another universe," Jason said with a shrug. "I'm pretty sure this is my life now. Welcome aboard."

He gestured behind him with his thumb.

"I'm going to go get some sleep."

"It's not even lunch time."

"It turns out the nighttime was inside me all along."

"What?"

"I'll see you tomorrow, Wexler. Get ready to fight some monsters."

Soon after, Jason was in his suite, smoke swirling around him as his clothes changed. His battle robes were replaced with a pair of silken boxers and he walked out to the balcony terrace. He took a bottle of alcohol from his inventory.

Item: [Shimmer Beet Rum] (bronze rank, common)
An alcoholic beverage brewed by the Norwich Distillery of Greenstone City.
(consumable, poison).
Effect: Inflicts [alcohol].

It was something he had kept in his inventory for Cassandra. He pulled back his arm to throw it in the ocean but stopped and took a deep drink, straight from the bottle.

Special attack [Shimmer Beet Rum] has inflicted [Alcohol] on you.

The bronze-rank beverage managed to get past his resistance, and it went down rough. Jason liked his drinks smooth and sweet, avoiding straight spirits. He looked at the bottle in his hands and took another swig.

"You look awful," Sophie said as Jason staggered past her to fall into a soft chair.

Jason replied with an incoherent groan.

"What happened to going straight to bed?" she asked. "It seems like you detoured to the liquor cabinet."

"I needed some sleepy medicine," he said.

"Quite a lot of it, it seems."

"Is he hung over?" Belinda asked coming out of her bedroom and looking at Jason.

"His lady friend dropped him," Sophie said.

Belinda looked at the line of drool dropping from the semi-conscious Jason's mouth.

"He's taking it well. The same day a goddess yelled at him, too."

For her own edification, Sophie had taken Jason's advice and sought out Emir for confirmation.

"He certainly keeps exciting company," Emir had told her the night before. "I mean, look at us; we're no deities, but still. A professional thief and a gold-rank adventurer? The most exciting person I knew at iron-rank was a guy named Brian who could conjure a huge metal duck."

She had told Belinda the whole story after coming back from speaking to Emir.

"Wasn't Asano meant to take you out and fight a monster?" Belinda asked, looking at Jason's slumped form.

"We're still doing that," Jason slurred.

"I'm not sure you're in any state to be fighting," Sophie said.

"It's fine," Jason said. "I contacted a friend of mine to come along. He'll keep you safe better than I could anyway."

"Another ludicrously well-connected young scion?" Belinda asked. "It's not that girl whose grandmother owned the whole section of town I grew up in, is it?"

"Beth? She's more of an acquaintance. Humphrey's from the Geller family. Have you heard of them?"

"Seriously?"

"I just hope he doesn't yell at me. I had a fight with his girlfriend."

"Blasphemy, Jason?"

"Not so loud, Humphrey."

"She said you were proud of it!"

"If I lie and say I wasn't, will you chastise more quietly?"

Humphrey had met Jason and Sophie outside the jobs hall.

"I though alcohol didn't work on you?" Humphrey asked.

"I used the bronze-rank stuff."

"Why would you do that?"

"His lady friend broke things off," Sophie said. "Right before he met with your lady friend, from what I gather. She's the acolyte, right?"

"That's right," Humphrey said.

"Her god chose that exact moment to put your friend in Asano's path," Sophie said. “I’m not going to speak ill of the gods but she should have seen how that would go.”

“According to my mother, gods sometimes have trouble understanding the behaviour of people. A matter of perspective, she says. I’m sorry about Cassandra, Jason. Was it her family over the demotion?”

“Yeah.”

“I lost my second star as well, but that’s not too bad at iron rank. You and my mother got it worse.”

“Danielle got demoted?”

“Three stars down to two. At silver rank, that’s worse than losing two stars at iron.”

They went in and Humphrey made for the jobs board while Sophie was surprised to see the man behind the desk.

“Bert?”

After Humphrey picked out an appropriate contract, they left the Adventure Society campus via the loop line, the submerged subway system running underneath the Island. Jason’s gaze was fixed on the floor after looking through the windows made his stomach turn.

“I think this is the first time I’ve ridden the loop without a disguise,” Sophie said.

“Why would you wear a disguise?” Humphrey asked.

“Usually because I was on my way to or from stealing something,” Sophie said.

“Stealing something?”

“Didn’t I tell you?” Jason asked, eyes still locked on the floor. “While everyone was off on the expedition, I caught that thief everyone was talking about. This is her.”

“Why are you training her to be an adventurer?”

“Who did you think I was?” Sophie asked.

“Clive told me Jason was helping the friend of his new assistant become an adventurer,” Humphrey said.

“True, if incomplete,” Jason said. “Nice one, Clive.”

“You stole my aunt’s necklace, right off her neck,” Humphrey said to Sophie.

“Did she get it back?” Sophie asked.

“Yes,” Humphrey said. “We caught some criminal trying to sell it.”

“Not smart,” Sophie said. “High-specificity goods like that you sell in another city. Of course, we were picking stupid fences on purpose. Didn’t make any money on it, though. Takes costly preparation to rob people like you, and something that hot doesn’t sell worth a damn.”

"Speaking of another city," Humphrey said, "Jonah and his new team were found in Hornis."

"Wait, what?" Jason asked. "Hornis? Jonah has a new team? What about Rick? And why did you need to find him?"

"We haven't really seen each other since the memorials have we?" Humphrey said. "I'm surprised you haven't heard, though."

"I've been away," Jason said.

"Right," Humphrey said. "I remember hearing one of my cousins said they met you out in the delta."

"Let's just fight monsters for now," Jason said. "We can catch up when there isn't a little man attempting to pickaxe his way out of my brain."

15

DAMAGE YOU SHOULDN'T WALK AWAY FROM

Since Humphrey lacked extended movement powers and Jason's stomach lacked a tolerance for movement powers, they hitched a ride into the delta on a trade wagon for a spirit coin each. Using supply crates as furniture, they bounced along in the back of the wagon, Jason looking decidedly peaky.

They had stopped at Jory's clinic to pick up potions, at which point Jason discovered there was no easy hangover cure. Jory explained that he had one for regular hangovers, but trying it on a hangover from iron or bronze rank booze would only make things worse. It was akin to using a potion too soon after already having used one, or using a potion right after using a high-ranked spirit coin. Jason had experienced that himself, which had felt even worse than he did from the hangover.

"I think I've been spoiled by the cloud palace," Sophie said, shifting uncomfortably on her crate.

"I'd love to take a real look," Humphrey said. "I've only seen it at a distance during the memorials."

"I'm pretty sure Emir wouldn't mind you having a look around," Jason said. "What were you saying earlier, about Jonah quitting Rick's team?"

"There were five people in the expedition whose tracking stones failed," Humphrey said. "They were all found, but close to death."

"I know the ones," Jason said. "Emir wanted them watched at the recovery camp but never said why. Everything was chaos. It was Jonah, Thadwick Mercer and three I don't know. Cassandra told me about the rumours. Back before she dumped me. Were these rumours just because of the tracking stone thing?"

"It was where they started," Humphrey said. "Severe injuries have been known to change people's aura, though. Enough that it no longer matches the imprint on their badge and they can't be tracked until they get a new one."

"Is that common?" Jason asked.

"Not at all," Humphrey said. "One person experiencing that would be extraordinary. Five all at once? Beyond unlikely."

"So people think something was done to them," Jason said.

"Yes," Humphrey said. "It started on the way back to the city. They were all behaving differently to how they had been before the expedition. You could pass it off as an after-effect of a brush with death, but the changes became more prominent over time, not less."

"I helped peel what was left of their clothes off them," Jason said. "They went through the kind of damage you shouldn't walk away from. It would be weird if they weren't affected."

"This wasn't just trauma," Humphrey said. "Jonah was like a different person. He was always loyal to his team, which was what happened to him in the astral space. He held off the enemy to buy time. Now he looks at them and it's like he doesn't see them. He left the team without so much as a word; he just went to the Adventure Society and had his name stricken from the team listing. He and the other four formed a new team of their own, spending all their time together."

"I will acknowledge that's waving a few pod-people red flags," Jason said.

"Pod people?" Sophie asked.

"You know. Creepy parasite thing that gets inside you and takes over."

"Is that something that happens?" she asked in horror.

"Nothing is impossible with magic," Humphrey said.

"Surely they got checked out?" Jason asked.

"They all refused," Humphrey said. "Neither the Adventure Society or the Magic Society has the right to forcibly subject them to examination without some complicated legal wrangling."

"I can't believe your mother would let it rest at that. Not when it involves a family member or an expedition she was in charge of."

"No," Humphrey said. "She didn't tell me much, beyond that steps are being taken. Before it came together, though, all five up and vanished. They were found a week later in Hornis, on a boat bound for distant shores."

"They were making a run for it?" Sophie asked. "You can't just slip out of the city and make off to Hornis when people are watching you. Believe me, I've looked into it. You either have to get passage through the port here or make an overland run through some very empty and inhospitable territory."

"Beaufort Mercer was facilitating them," Humphrey said.

"Thadwick's father," Jason said.

"Yes," Humphrey said. "My mother didn't say it explicitly, but she at least implied that Beaufort's wife was the one who tipped her off. They've been friends since they were young and I think she's at least as concerned for her son as Mother is for Jonah."

"Less interested in the family reputation than whether something is wrong with her child," Jason surmised. "Good on her."

"The Adventure Society sent that portal user who works for Emir Bahadir to send them back, although I'm not sure how willingly," Humphrey said. "In the meantime, Mother wants me to replace Jonah on Rick's team."

"Doesn't Rick himself already fill the armoured striker role?" Jason asked.

"Yes. They lost a ranged damage-dealer and a specialised defender. I'm not what they need. I have no idea why Mother wants me to join."

Humphrey looked inquisitively at Jason. "You do better than most at recognising her intentions," he said. "What do you think?"

"I think she doesn't want you to join Rick's team at all."

Humphrey let out a frustrated sigh.

"Always a lesson with her. So what does she really want me to do?"

"Best guess? Form your own team. Whoever it was you fought in the astral space, they're still out there. I reckon she wants people you can rely on around you for the next disaster. Also, she probably wants you to find a new front-liner for Rick."

"She could do that herself; she doesn't need me."

"And have you miss the chance to make some adventurer connections? Come on, Humphrey."

Humphrey let out a groan.

"You know you sound like her sometimes," he said.

"So who can fill the slot in Rick's team?" Jason asked.

"I don't know," Humphrey said. "There are plenty of specialist defenders around but the only one I can think of who could stack up to Jonah is Hudson Kettering. There's no chance of peeling him out of Beth Cavendish's team."

"No one else?" Jason asked.

"The only other person who might stack up would be Hudson's cousin, Dustin, but he's..."

Realisation dawned on Humphrey's face.

"He's what?" Jason asked.

"He's been stuck following Thadwick around," Humphrey said. "Thadwick formally annulled that team, though."

"One of Thadwick's lackeys? Even Rufus thinks they've got the goods. You should snatch him up for Rick before Thadwick's stink washes off and people start knocking on his door."

Humphrey frowned.

"I wish I'd realised," he said. "I could have spoken to Dustin before I met up with you, and now we're heading out into the delta."

"We're still pretty close to the city," Jason said. "Let me see what I can do."

Jason checked his contacts list, which consisted of anyone he had a reasonable interaction with. This made for a long list, which he could, fortunately, organise into groups. Hudson Kettering had appeared on the adventurers list, along with the rest of Beth Cavendish's team, when Jason had temporarily joined it for the sand barge assault. They were close enough to the city that Hudson was in range and Jason sent a voice chat request.

"Jason," Hudson greeted him. He had used Jason's voice chat before and wasn't surprised by it. Humphrey and Sophie were in Jason's party and could hear his voice as well.

"Morning, Hudson," Jason said. "I'm here with Humphrey Geller. He wants to talk to you about your cousin."

"Dustin? If this is about probing him over Thadwick being mind-controlled or whatever, he doesn't want to hear it."

"That's not it," Humphrey said. "Good morning, Hudson. I was wondering if Dustin would have any interest in joining Rick Geller's team. They need a quality frontman and they understand what it's like to have one of their team members placed under suspicion."

"Join a Geller team?" Hudson pondered. "That's a good name to be attached to, but so was Mercer. He really took a hit for the family, being stuck to Thadwick, so we only want the best for him this time around. Real adventurers."

"Rick is the real thing," Humphrey said. "He's practically obsessed with becoming stronger. I should point out that it isn't really a Geller team anymore, though. One left to join Thadwick and they lost someone during the expedition. That leaves Rick and a pair of elf sisters."

"Sorry to hear it," Hudson said soberly. "We got lucky; those Vitesse adventurers covered us and paid the price. They're friends of yours, right, Jason?"

"Yes."

"There wasn't a memorial for her," Hudson said. "Her standing strong is the reason my team all got out alive and we wanted to pay our respects."

"They're taking her home for that," Jason said. "We're going to have an informal wake once things calm down, though. I'll let you know."

"Thanks. Humphrey, I'll put it to Dustin and see what he thinks. I think you'll pretty much have him once I tell him about the elf sisters."

While Jason and Humphrey were off introducing Sophie to monster hunting, Rufus marched through the Adventure Society administration building. In the main lobby he made for the elevating platform to the upper levels. Standing next to the platform was a man in the robes of the church of Knowledge, waiting patiently.

"Mr Remore," the priest greeted him.

Rufus sighed.

"I'm busy, but your goddess knows that. State your purpose."

"Your business is in pursuit of the people who struck down your precious teammate," the priest said. He had a friendly look about him, his bronze rank and middle-aged appearance meant he was likely sixty or seventy years old. His voice had a sympathy that sounded completely genuine, the empathy of a clergyman.

"Unless your goddess wants to tell me who they are and where to find them, we have no business."

"She has offered that and more to someone you count as a friend, yet that friend spurned her offer."

The frown on Rufus's face told the priest that Rufus was far from willing to be jerked around.

"You have my attention," Rufus said.

"Jason Asano was offered all the answers you seek, but he refused."

"Why?"

"You know the man," the priest said. "You know he can be mistrusting of figures of authority."

"What was the condition?" Rufus asked.

"Condition?" the priest asked.

"He wouldn't refuse if all she did was offer. What did she ask in return?"

"The goddess knows all. There are tribulations ahead and Asano will need guidance to navigate them successfully. She wishes to offer that guidance."

"Worship," Rufus surmised. "She offered to hand Farrah's killers up on a plate in return for worship, didn't she?"

"This goes well beyond the people who killed your friend," the priest said. "You have heard about incursions in other astral spaces around the world."

"And what?" Rufus asked tersely. "Your goddess will give up all the answers in return for the worship of one iron-ranker in a provincial city?"

"She sees what others do not. Patterns too large for mortals to notice. For such a small price, she offers such great gains. She was refused but remains patient. The counsel of a friend could do so much good."

The backhand strike from Rufus landed square on the priest's mouth, sending him tumbling to the floor. Rufus stood over him as he looked up, his expression of surprise mirrored by everyone in the lobby. He spoke to the priest in a voice as cold and hard as ice.

"If your goddess is willing to hand over such information, then by what moral stricture does she not? Instead, she looks to ransom a man's principles. You just tried to turn me on my friend, a man who saved my life, and you have the gall to lay there looking surprised? If you want to help me, then help me. Bring your self-serving ways to me again and you'll get worse than you got today."

Rufus strode away, riding the elevation platform up into the building.

16

PICKING OUT THE GOOD ONES

Sophie, Jason and Humphrey left the wagon in the first town they came to. Being the closest town to the city, it was a busy distribution hub. Making their way through the town, Sophie was startled by how many people seemed to know Jason. Some would wave, others approaching for a few words of greeting. How Jason kept all their names straight was beyond her.

Sophie noticed the difference between how people treated Jason and Humphrey. Jason was approached without reservation and greeted like an old friend. Humphrey was treated with respect and reserve, no one speaking to him unless directly addressed.

"How do you know so many people here?" she asked Jason.

"I've passed through quite a few times," Jason said.

"Surely you have as well," Sophie asked Humphrey.

"He has," Jason said. "A lot more than me. The Geller family seat is out in the delta, so Humphrey has been shuttling between the family compound and the family townhouse his whole life. All these people know what a big-shot he is."

"Don't they think the same of you?" she asked. "You're roaming around with him and covered in expensive-looking equipment."

"They know common when they see it," Jason said.

On their way to the adventure noticeboard, they found a large group of people queuing up for something.

"The healer must be here today," Jason said. "It's good that they're out and about now. It was really an eye opener when I heard about Healer showing up at Jory 's place to lay down the law. Forced me to reassess the whole god scenario."

"That must have been frustrating for you," Humphrey said. "I know you can be adamant about things."

"You should always welcome being proven wrong," Jason said. "It means your understanding of the world just got a little bit better."

"Says the guy who gets downright obnoxious about being right," Humphrey said.

"I'm not saying I always welcome being wrong in the moment," Jason acknowledged. "The important thing is to reflect on it and accept it going forward."

They reached the noticeboard, looked them over, and took them all. After plotting out the locations, they mapped an itinerary and set off from the town.

A tentacle wrapped around Sophie's other arm, the first one already having been caught up. The fleshy blob of the monster's main body sported many prehensile tentacles and she was running out of limbs. The supple tentacles were studded with sharp, bony protrusions that dug into her skin, lacing her body with cuts as the creature gripped her arms, legs and torso. Desperately, she bit into a tentacle. Her abilities added damage to any unarmed attack, which turned out to really mean any unarmed attack as her bite severed the monster's thin member. This freed her right arm to attack the tentacle binding her left with a more traditional assault.

Two tentacles severed, the monster withdrew and made for the water.

"No, you don't," Sophie told it, rushing forward to grip a tentacle in each hand. With a grunt of effort, she hauled it out of the water. Holding it in place with one hand at the base of a tentacle and her foot pushing down on it, she bent down and brutally pounded its bulbous body with her free fist.

You have defeated [Wetland Tentacloid].
10 [Iron Spirit Coins] have been awarded to you.

Quest: [Notice: Wetland Tentacloid]
Objective complete: Eliminate [Wetland Tentacloid] 1/1.
Quest complete.
100 [Iron Spirit Coins] have been awarded to you.

"What spirit coins…ow!"

A bag appeared in the air above her and dropped, bouncing off her head before falling into the mud.

"What was that?" she complained as she picked up the bag. She discovered it was full of coins.

"Loot," Jason said with a grin.

"We didn't get rewards, despite being in the group," Humphrey observed.

"I don't think moral support counts as an actual contribution," Jason said.

"Do all adventurers get coins like this?" Sophie asked. "No wonder you're all rich."

"Actually, that's a unique benefit of working with Jason," Humphrey said.

"I'd rather you not spread that around," Jason said. "I don't want people trying to use me as a loot farm. If you had a storage space power, like Humphrey here, the coins would have gone straight into that."

"You should have Jason store your money until you buy yourself a dimensional bag," Humphrey said. "It's a reward well-earned."

"You really think so?" she asked.

"It was alright," Jason said. "Not great. You're bleeding all over, your clothes are in tatters. You almost let that thing go full hentai monster on you."

"What's a hentai monster?" she asked.

"No idea," Humphrey said. "I will say that I was on the verge of stepping in. Still, it was very good for your first monster hunt."

"Yeah," Jason acknowledged. "For the first time out, you did alright. None of those cuts and scrapes are major. I got impaled in my first real monster fight. Luckily, I had a healing power."

"I have one too," Sophie said.

Ability: [Equilibrium] (Balance)
Special ability.
Cost: None.
Cooldown: None.

Current rank: Iron 0 (00%).

Effect (iron): Meditate to slowly accrue instances of [Integrity], up to an instance threshold of ([Recovery] attribute +1). Instances quickly drop off when meditation ends.

[Integrity] (heal-over-time, mana-over-time, stamina-over-time, holy): Periodically recover a small amount of health, stamina and mana. Additional instances have a cumulative effect.

They found some dry ground and she sat in a meditation pose to use it. It took time to heal her injuries, but Jason and Humphrey were willing to wait. The more she used it, the quicker the ability would advance.

"I'd give you something to clean yourself off, but you'll be fighting again soon," Jason said.

"And he doesn't want you to use up his crystal wash," Humphrey said.

The second encounter was less precarious but still far from an ideal showing. Jason reluctantly supplied some crystal wash and fresh clothes from his storage space.

"You'll want to use those coins you're earning on some decent armour," Humphrey said.

"I know a guy who supplies quality light armour," Jason said.

On the way to the next notice location, they travelled through in a small village. Once again, Sophie was struck by how many people seemed to know Jason.

"Seriously, Asano, what's going on?"

"I just get around a bit," Jason said.

They stopped for lunch in an open-air eatery that served travelling merchants and passing adventurers. The owner treated Jason like visiting royalty.

"The baby was born two weeks gone now," the owner told Jason. "Healthy as you like."

"That's good to hear," Jason said.

"If you hadn't been there, I don't know what would have happened," he said.

"I'm sure it would have worked out. You aren't so far from the city that you couldn't have gone for a healer."

"She was so sick, though. I'm not sure how long the baby could take it."

"We got lucky," Jason said. "I should make introductions. Johan, my friends, Humphrey and Sophie. This is Johan, who makes the best fried savoury puffs in the delta."

"Any friends of Jason are more than welcome," he said. "You'll never need take out your purse in my establishment."

Jason ordered for the three of them and Johan went inside to the kitchens.

"Is that's what's going on?" Sophie asked. "You've been out here healing people, like at Jory's clinic?"

"More like curing," Jason said. "I can't heal injuries, just disease and poison. A few other things, but you don't see a lot of curses in villagers."

"Jason does it quite a lot," Humphrey said. "During our field assessment for the Adventure Society, he was always holding the group up."

"They let him stop for that?" Sophie asked.

"You try telling a crowd of sick people that you're too busy to help them," Humphrey said. "In this one village there was a huge crowd and we were there all morning. The locals put on this big midday feast, which was actually really nice."

"Those stops are less time-consuming now," Jason said, "and often not necessary at all. The priests of the Healer are a lot more active since Healer replaced them all. They stopped charging for services, too, so people aren't reliant on the chance I'll be passing through."

"The new attitude of the local Healer church has caused some disarray amongst the nobles," Humphrey said. "Until Healer replaced his whole clergy, the church was largely at the beck and call of the noble families. Now they're treated the same as the general populace and there's been a lot of dissatisfaction."

"There's a lot of disruption to the upper crust going on lately," Jason said. "First the healers, then the expedition, now these rumours about Jonah, Thadwick and the others."

"Not to mention the inquiry," Humphrey said. "Did you hear the entire Phael family had their Adventure Society membership revoked? Every single one of them, even the silver-ranker."

"I only dealt with them in the expedition support camp," Jason said, "but even that left a nasty taste in the mouth. If the rest were like the ones I met, it's not much of a surprise."

While they waited for the food to come out, they discussed Sophie's performance against the monsters. Fighting humans in a city was very different to fighting monsters in marshes and swamps. Whether in a fighting pit or a dark alley, the footing was usually solid in a city.

In contrast, the delta had slick mud, deceptively deep bog, random obstructions and plenty of places to hide or retreat into. Sophie had no experience fighting in such an environment, while the monsters were well-adapted to the locations in which they spawned. The elements that hurt her were things they could use to their advantage.

The inhuman appearance of monsters made it harder for her to read their intentions, which slowed her reactions. Their monstrous forms made many of her favoured attacks pointless, forcing her to use long-dismissed elements of her style. These were techniques she had barely thought about since her father had first taught them to her.

It wasn't just their physical form that was an issue. Monsters lacked the doubt and hesitation of a more thoughtful opponent and she came to realise how much she relied on mind games in a fight. They were also possessed of a bloody determination, tenaciously fighting on after a human would have given up.

The final thing hurting her in the fights was that she was still getting used to her new abilities. She had been working on shifting her style to take best advantage of them, but it was still early days.

"What we've seen today has been good," Jason said. "Obviously, there's room for improvement but this is day one. We're building a list of what we need to work on, which will show us where to focus the training. You and I fight the same way, but you've had more practice against people, where I've used it more against monsters. We can help each other."

After lunch, they set out for the third and final job they had taken from the adventure board notice. After that would come the job they took from the jobs hall, which should take them into the evening.

"Do adventurers all run around doing this many jobs at once?" Sophie asked.

"Not at all," Humphrey said. "It's one way of picking out the good ones. They're on the job a lot and they hit-up multiple contracts. That's true at iron-rank, anyway. At higher ranks, it pays to give your contracts more caution and consideration, matching the jobs you take to your abilities."

"That's getting ahead of ourselves," Jason said. "Let's just concentrate on getting her into the Adventure Society, for now."

He turned to Sophie.

"You get to choose the kind of adventurer you want to be," he told her. "If you want to throw yourself into it and push your abilities to the limit, that's great. If you want to just be a nominal member and never actually hunt monsters, that's alright too."

"No," Sophie said. "I never thought I would have the chance to get a full set of essences. I want to see how far this can take me."

"Me too," Jason said. "Humphrey already knows because his mum told him."

"Hey," Humphrey protested.

"You do talk about your mother a lot," Sophie said, "and I've only known you since this morning."

17

EVENTS LOOM LARGE

Rufus arrived at Arella's office and knew she wasn't there when the door didn't swing itself open at his approach. When he knocked, it was opened by the deputy director. Rufus had few dealings with the elderly elf, Genevieve. He had heard she was the one person Arella completely trusted, but he'd heard a lot about the director that turned out to be false.

"Something I can help you with, Mr Remore?" she asked.

"I was looking for the director."

"She was called away on important business. Perhaps I can be of assistance?"

"Not unless you can introduce me to her father and help convince him to assist me."

"Oh, I can probably manage that," she said, to Rufus's visible surprise. "I'm a little busy to go along, but find your way to his home and I'll have someone waiting for you."

In a one-room ritual building on the Geller estate grounds, a portal opened. Jonah Geller stumbled through, as if shoved, followed by the bronze-rank Ernest Geller. The portal closed behind them. The ritual room had been marked off-limits for weeks, with no household staff allowed to enter. Only Rick Geller had been trusted by Danielle to keep watch; she had supplied him with a comfortable chair and a stack of books on a side table.

Rick put his book down and stood up at the appearance of the others, gaze fixed on Jonah. He looked for anything in the big man's expression he recognised but it was like looking at a different man. Like someone else was wearing his friend's face.

"You have no right to do this," Jonah said to Ernest, ignoring Rick's presence.

"So you keep saying," Ernest said, voice and body language both equally unyielding. "You will stay here until we're done with you."

"Jonah," Rick said.

Jonah turned, looking at Rick as if he were no more connected to him than the chair Rick had been sitting in.

"Please just tell me what happened to you," Rick implored. "You know I'll do whatever I can to help. The way you've done for me, more than once."

"Then get me out of here," Jonah said. "They want to cut me open."

"Don't listen to him," Ernest said. "He'll say anything to make us let him go."

Jonah threw a look of bile at Ernest.

"You have no idea what you're dealing with."

"You're right," Ernest said. "That's the whole reason we're here. Rick, you were here to announce our arrival to Danielle, yes?"

"That's right."

"Double check the locks before you go," Ernest said. "Make sure they're all locked from the outside."

The Geller family compound had been heavily landscaped to be on solid, secure ground. The meandering creeks, picturesque garden ponds and even the small lake might seem like natural waterways but had been artfully and carefully designed centuries ago. There was a section of river that had been diverted into what looked like a natural stretch of river but was actually a canal that diverted it through the estate before returning to its original course. Between construction and growing in the gardens, it had been the work of generations to get the estate to the impressive and natural-seeming state it was currently in.

Clive was aware of all this; the Geller family had detailed the process and donated copies of the records to the Magic Society. Only the numerous security features, developed and improved upon over centuries, had been withheld. As he drove an airboat through the delta, he loudly explained it to Belinda, who was sitting behind Clive's rune tortoise familiar, Onslow. It was an unusual experience for Clive to have someone share his interest in magical esoterica.

Clive steered the airboat up to the estate's water gate and coasted to a stop. The archway that framed the gate was smaller than the one in the Greenstone city wall, but the portcullised arch was still imposing. This was especially true as the Geller portcullis was usually closed, unlike the city gate, which placed the imposing metal grill on full display.

The guards on station, on a small stone dock with a booth, came out to question Clive. As he was expected, they swiftly allowed him to continue, magically raising the portcullis to admit his airboat onto the estate. Belinda gaped as they passed through the stone arch.

Shortly beyond the wall was a larger stone dock nestled into the embankment, where the Gellers stored their inland watercraft. There was an attendant in another bamboo booth who waved them into an empty slip and tied off the vehicle. Once they were on shore, the man took their details in a small notebook and gave them directions.

As much as they would have liked to explore, Clive and Belinda had come with an important purpose and stuck to the main paths. Using the sedate pace of Clive's familiar as an excuse, though, they did have the time to at least look around. Clive occasionally glanced back to check on his familiar, who kept stopping to snack on the shrubbery.

"Onslow, stop that! We are guests here!"

They followed the directions they had been given along the main pathway, which constantly tempted with detours. They finally arrived at the main house complex to find an august company outside, even by Geller family standards.

Talking together were Emir Bahadir, Thalia Mercer, Elspeth Arella and the stern-faced head of the Adventure Society inquiry team. With them was a priest of the god of purity, who looked older than most but was clean-faced and seemed very hale. Clive wasn't conversant in the robe designs of the church of Purity but the elaborate outfit implied considerable rank almost as much as the company he kept. Danielle Geller was with them, playing host. As Clive stood off, giving quiet introductions to Belinda, Emir spotted them and quietly pointed them out to Danielle. She walked over to greet them.

"You must be Humphrey's Magic Society friend, Clive. I hear good things."

"Thank you, Ma'am. This is my assistant, Belinda."

Danielle gave her an appraising look.

"I take it you find helping Clive a less antagonistic pursuit than running around robbing people," Danielle said.

"It was my friend who did the running," Belinda said. "As for antagonism, a few cash-heavy theatre-goers hardly compare to an army of weaponised magical constructs."

Danielle chuckled.

"A well-made point. So, Clive, you're our resident astral magic specialist?"

"Yes, Ma'am."

"I was surprised you were ready this fast."

"We've been working hard," Clive said, including Belinda with a glance. "This is important. It's a lot of responsibility."

"Indeed it is," Danielle said. "Exciting times are dangerous ones. We have something going on right now I can't talk about, so you'll have to forgive my not attending to you personally. I'll have one of my family members give you access to the mirage chamber."

"Thank you," Clive said.

"I've completely cleared the schedule for the mirage chamber; it's yours for the day. If you need more time, just tell us and I'll see you get it. Did you bring everything you need?"

"Yes," Clive said, his tone leaving no room for doubt. "Our preparations were quite thorough."

"Good. I'll find young Rick to show you the way; he's wandering about here, somewhere. Have you met Rick?"

"I have, Lady Geller. At the picnic in the park, after the sand barge assault."

"Of course. Jason can be something of an explosive factor, socially speaking, but when it comes to throwing a truly casual affair, he comes into his own. Rick is reliable and trustworthy. He doesn't know what's going on here, yet, but I would appreciate you not asking, anyway. He has a personal stake in ongoing events."

"Of course," Clive said. "Does he have the might essence, by any chance? Or earth, iron? Anything that gives him a strength power?"

"He has the might essence," Danielle said. "Do you need some heavy lifting done?"

"Yes," Clive said. "I've looked over the design of your mirage chamber and it has the old stone-slab control configuration. It's no doubt why it held up so well over so long, but I'll need to take the top off make some required upgrades."

"You want to upgrade our mirage chamber?"

"It's quite necessary for what I need to do with it," Clive said.

"Do you have the expertise to carry that out?" Danielle asked.

Clive looked at her, nonplussed.

"It doesn't take any real expertise."

"My people have assured me that any upgrade would very much require both expertise and some prohibitive material costs."

"I suppose it comes down to what you think constitutes expertise," Clive said. "I can see how it could be expensive if you did it wrong. As in, very wrong. I won't. I checked the requisite materials out of the Magic Society storehouse and charged everything to the Adventure Society. It was cheap enough that it fell within my discretionary budget. All the expensive materials in a mirage chamber are in the dome, which I don't need to touch. It should take me less than a couple of hours."

"Have you worked on a mirage chamber before?" Danielle asked.

"I assisted in the complete rebuilds of the mirage chambers in Boko and Hornis and still do annual maintenance. The original construction wasn't as lasting as your stone setup."

"Boko and Hornis have their own Magic Society people," Danielle said.

"Yes," Clive said.

"And they call you in anyway?"

"Yes."

Danielle gave Clive an assessing look.

"You're one of those people, aren't you?" she asked. "The ones who are just quietly exceptional at what they do."

"I don't know I'd say that," Clive said, scratched his head awkwardly.

"You're kind of the opposite of Jason. He's full of potential but runs around causing huge messes because he's headstrong and inexperienced. You're forming a team with my son, right?"

"We've never really discussed it."

"Well, now you don't need to," Danielle said. "I'm going to have you looked into and if everything checks out, you'll be part of my boy's team."

"I don't think you get to decide that," Clive said uncertainly. "We get to form our own teams."

"Don't be silly," Danielle said. "Of course I get to decide that. Now, wait here while I go find Rick."

Clive looked nonplussed at the retreating figure of Danielle as she went into the house.

"That felt oddly like talking to Jason, there at the end," he mused.

Sophie was feeling good after her third monster encounter. It had been a group of ratlings pillaging a farming crop. While not exactly humanoid, they were close, and she fought them on flat, open ground. At first, they had swarmed her but their opportunistic aggression lacked cohesion. Her swiftness and agility let her avoid being encircled, catch one exposed and make short work of it. Cowardly by nature, the others scattered. They were only quick compared to someone other than Sophie, who chased them down one by one.

That only left the contract from the jobs hall, but en route, they passed through a village where they were approached by a harried teamster. He recognised them as adventurers from their equipment and informed them of a trap weaver nest close to a major trading road.

"Trap weavers?" Sophie asked.

"Nasty, spider-like monsters," Humphrey said. "Dangerous and unfortunately common in the delta. We should clear them out now."

"Yep," Jason agreed. "I'll do it."

"You aren't exactly in the best shape today," Humphrey said.

"The fight doesn't wait until you're ready, Humphrey. A little impairment training will do me good."

"Can I do it?" Sophie asked.

"No," Jason and Humphrey said together.

"You think he can do it," Sophie said, "and he's hungover. He's not that much better than me."

"Yes, he is," Humphrey said. "You haven't seen him fight."

"I've fought him myself," she said.

"No," Humphrey said. "You've sparred with him. Run from him. You haven't fought him. Jason is very good at killing and very bad at leaving things alive. If he'd wanted you dead, you would have been dead."

"Yeah?" she asked, sceptically. "I want to see this, then."

"That's the thing," Humphrey said. "You don't see him unless something very bad is about to happen. I'll show you a recording when we get back to the city."

"Don't show her that," Jason said. "It shows me at peak chuuni."

"Chuuni?" Sophie asked.

"We're pretty sure anything that slips through Jason's translation power is him being difficult," Humphrey advised her. "We've found it's best to let it go and not ask."

"Who's 'we'?" Jason asked.

Rufus arrived at the entrance to Dorgan's compound via magically propelled carriage. Rather than reins, the driver steered with a bar that turned the front wheels as it was shifted left and right. Speed was controlled with a lever next to the driver's seat. Such vehicles weren't any faster than animal-drawn carriages but saved having to deal with the animals.

Rufus got down and walked up to the large gate in the outer wall. The estate had once been the main residence of a powerful Greenstone family and was suitably impressive, with grounds that were outrageously indulgent in the crowded space of Old City.

There was a well-dressed elf in a small security station built into the wall. Rufus could sense an iron-rank aura from him, the uncontrolled and muddy kind that spoke to an excess of magic cores and a deficit of training. The elf came out to open the gate and let him in.

On the other side of the gate was another elf servant, who had been awaiting his arrival and guided him inside. As they went through the grounds, Rufus could see that the grandeur of the compound had not been allowed to fade after the original occupants vacated it for the Island. The gardens were painstakingly maintained, the centuries-old brickwork still in fine condition.

The servant led Rufus to one of the wide wings of the manor and into a library. He showed Rufus to a portion of the library where an elf was standing before a large painting, depicting a desert landscape. Adris Dorgan had tawny skin and long, chestnut hair. He was every part the classic slender, handsome elf. Without turning his gaze from the painting, he dismissed the servant with thanks.

"Do you like this painting, Mr Remore?" Dorgan asked.

Rufus considered the work.

"The artist was more concerned with evocation than accurate representation. It lends itself to the stark desert environment. It's clear that the artist finds meaning in the desolation. A local artist?"

"Moher," Dorgan said. "From the day I found your friend Asano standing right here, things have been going poorly for my daughter."

"She kept her position," Rufus said. "She wouldn't have, if certain people had their way. Luckily for her, Jason had no say in the matter."

"His unfortunate demotion," Dorgan said. "Association with my daughter was behind that, I imagine."

"He did his job and he did it well," Rufus said. "All she had to do was let him."

"I told her much the same. Patience is a lesson often hard learned. I have tried to guide her away from considering him part of her troubles but his position as the starting point of things going wrong plays on her mind."

"She would be well-served by keeping her attention on what comes next," Rufus said. "Events loom large and she has bridges to mend."

"Is that why you're here, Mr Remore? To mend bridges?"

"That's up to you," Rufus said. "There is a chance someone has been smuggling some unusual materials through here or Hornis. If you help me track those down, it would reflect well on your daughter. Show the association that you are an asset to her and not an anchor. I would be willing to reflect that in my attitude on the topic, which is not without weight in certain circles."

"Even after she turned on your friend?"

"She only tried to hurt his interests, not him," Rufus said. "Where I come from, politics are a fact of life. Since she is going to continue as director, my preference would be that she's an effective one. Her plan is still in play, if she wants it to be."

"What plan is that?"

"To get promoted out of this town by cleaning it up. An appropriate show of contrition and using the inquiry as a launching pad will at least give her a chance. The city service agreement is two years from renegotiation. Two years is a long time in politics."

"So it is," Dorgan mused. "If I agree to help you, I can't just wave my hand and produce all the city's smugglers. I can use my connections, here and in Hornis, but there are complications. Clarissa Ventress and Cole Silva control no small portion of the less documented aspects of city trade. And there are some operators whom none of us tolerate and who are forced to work around us. There are things even the worst of us will not allow to be traded."

"I find that hard to believe," Rufus said.

"Mr Remore, I am more government official than criminal. The powers ruling the Island would let Old City fall into chaos so long as the money flows. I'll acknowledge that I have walked hard roads, but I have my standards."

"What about the other two? Ventress and Silva."

"Ventress knows her limits, or at least she used to. If anyone is working with those I won't tolerate, it will be Cole Silva. He's impulsive, short-sighted and repulsive enough to traffic with those his father would have hunted down."

"I'd pay him a visit," Rufus said, "but that would send the ones I'm after scurrying into the shadows."

"I will make some circumspect inquiries," Dorgan said. "I will expect your support for my daughter, in turn."

"Your daughter's best move is to do her job right, in the open, where people can see her do it. I'd be happy to help that along."

"Very well," Dorgan said. "You have secured my help, Mr Remore. I will find you when I have something."

18
WHAT THE GELLER NAME IS WORTH

Rick led Clive and Belinda through the grounds. Clive and Belinda were both enraptured as Rick took them through pathways off the main thoroughfares, the visitors rapidly talking.

"See that flowering vine?" Clive asked, pointing it out to Belinda. "See the way they have it growing over the bamboo frame?"

"That's floating ghost flower, right?" Belinda asked.

"Good eye," Clive said.

"I know a guy who grows it."

"An apothecary"

"More of a recreational enthusiast."

Clive stopped under an archway covered in the flowering vine, making sweeping gestures with his arms.

"If you could see magic, you'd be able to spot the subtle impact the landscaping has on the ambient magic over the whole estate. Whoever designed this place was a genius. The foresight to wait for plants to grow over decades, planning out the shifts in magic as plants and trees grew. Adapting for seasonal changes, different stages of growth."

"I can't imagine planning that out over the whole space," Belinda said. "This estate is bigger than an entire district in Old City."

"We should probably keep moving," Rick prompted. His cousin, Henry, was the team magic expert and had been similarly impressed by the grounds when they first arrived. Now Henry's ashes had been mixed into the soil.

They spotted the dome of the mirage chamber, well before they reached the annexed buildings attached to it. Rick unlocked the control room to the mirage chamber and led them inside. Light from the glass ceiling lit up the interior, showing the wooden platforms lining the sides of the room and the waist-high stone block under the wide window that crossed the entire back wall. The interior of the dome beyond was dark.

Clive immediately began explaining things to Belinda, who had never seen anything from this branch of magic. "These wooden platforms are the interface," he explained. "It projects your senses into an illusionary self that can interact with other generated illusions in the dome, on the other side of that window."

He walked up to the stone block. It was heavy and grey, with a wild mess of runes and sigils carved into it.

"These are the controls," Clive said. "It's a lot more impressive when the chamber is active, which you'll see later."

Clive pointed out a small hole on the side of the block.

"That's where you feed the crystals containing the various things to be replicated under the dome," he explained. "The chamber's current configuration is fine to generate some environments with some monsters in them. It's a bit basic to handle what we brought along, though. Still, just building a mirage chamber in an area of such low magical density was incredibly impressive, especially for the time they did it. Only a fraction of what is now Old City had even been constructed. Even now, the important part—the dome—is more than capable of doing what we need. We just need to upgrade the control system so it can tell the dome to do it."

Clive turned to look at Rick.

"Your forebears were formidable people, Rick. You have every right to be proud of what your family has accomplished."

Rick nodded absently, glancing at the door.

"That legacy comes with a responsibility," he said morosely. "One we pay in blood to uphold."

Clive paused what he was doing to give Rick a long look.

"I've actually been here in the estate before," Clive said. "My first monster surge was the one before last. when I was a boy. My family members are eel farmers here in the delta and it was your family that took us in and sheltered us, along with countless others."

He walked over to Rick and put a hand on his shoulder.

"This is Greenstone," Clive said. "We know what the Geller name is worth. If you ever need anything, you ask. Everyone in the delta knows that we've asked plenty, and your family answered every time."

Rick steeled his face to mask his emotions and Clive gave him a big smile, patting his shoulder before leaving him be.

"Time to get started," Clive said as he began pulling crates from his storage space. He left Belinda to organise them neatly and crack them open with a pry tool.

"You don't have a dimensional storage space," Clive said, looking the small but effective crowbar. "Where were you keeping that?"

"Tricks of the trade," Belinda said. "You always have to be ready."

"You're full of surprises, aren't you?"

"You have no idea."

After taking out the last box and leaving them to Belinda, Clive glanced back at Rick, then to the stone block.

"Now, Rick," Clive said. "You see that line running around the side of the stone block, near the top?"

"Yeah," Rick said.

"That line is where the whole top section of the block comes off as a slab, to access the inside. I'm going to unseal it and I'll need you to lift that slab off and put it out of the way. Is that something you can manage?"

"That's a hefty bit of stone but I'll sort it out," Rick said.

Clive used a magic wand to trace around the outside of the block, along the line he had just pointed out. Rick then hauled off the rune-covered top, revealing the block as a large stone box. The inside was covered in runes, and fitted with different components. Stone tablets, also rune-covered, were slotted vertically into the bottom, as were crystals like sculpted icicles. Unlike the control panel, magical glows traced out lines and shone from the crystals, spraying rainbow colours into the room.

"Where are all the crystals?" Rick asked. "The ones you put in the side to add new monsters."

"Like this?" Clive asked, taking out a crystal. It was a finger-sized length of faceted crystal.

"Yeah," Rick said. "I've seen a bunch of them put in."

"These are highly specialised, artificial manifestations of raw magic," Clive explained. "Sort of like very complicated spirit coins, if you like. When you feed them in the intake on the side they vanish, like when you eat a spirit coin."

"So they don't just pile up inside, then?" Rick asked.

"No, which is good. We'll need to add quite a few once the upgrade is up and working."

"How many is quite a few?"

"Four thousand and ninety-six."

"Seriously?"

"Take a look at those crates," Clive said. "Most of them are filled with padded racks of crystals."

Clive took a simple table from his storage space, then draped a plain, brown cloth over it. He laid out a series of magical tools, from wedge-shaped stones to crystal orbs with silver stands to stop them from rolling away. There was a slew of magic wands, varied in length, material and shape. Many were curved or kinked;

one was bent into a spiral halfway down its length. Clive got to work, explaining what he was doing to Belinda as he went.

"I'm going to wait outside," Rick said. "I'll be just out the door if you need anything."

"Thank you," Clive said absently, not looking up from his work. From where he was bent over into the stone box, he called on Belinda to hand him various tools. Belinda peppered him with questions as she handed him each new tool, peering in while he explained what he was doing at each step. One after another, the magical lights went out as he worked. Once the glow was completely faded, he started carefully removing parts.

After setting them aside, he had Belinda hand him replacement parts from the boxes they had brought. He changed the runes inside the box, his tools reworking the hard stone like the softest clay. He slotted-in new tablets and crystals, replacing almost everything inside. Finally, he chose a few of the components he had removed, and after checking them over, put them back into place. The discarded parts he had Belinda crate up for the Gellers to do with whatever they wanted.

Finally, Clive began reactivating the magic of the control system, fastidiously testing his work carefully as the rainbow light once again started shining from within.

"This all looks good," Clive said. "I'll rework the control slab a bit and we can do some final testing. Fetch Rick, would you please? I'll need him to reorient the slab as I work with it."

Clive modified both sides of the lid of the stone box, altering the mirage chamber controls. He had the lid replaced and started running tests on the mirage chamber functionality. They watched through the window as wild patterns lit up the space under the dome. There were several problems, requiring the slab to be taken off and put back on again multiple times as Clive made adjustments and tested again.

Under the dome, on the other side of the viewing window, images flickered in and out. Monsters randomly appeared with odd colours or strangely warped bodies. The most bizarre was a heidel with duck legs, and both its heads being replaced with Rick's.

"Oh, that's not right," Rick said.

"You must use the chamber a lot if your head is the one that popped out," Clive said. He methodically tackled each problem, testing and retesting as he worked through every incompatibility and adjusted every miscalibration. Finally, everything was in working order.

"Thank you," Clive said to Rick. "You've made this so much easier. Or possible at all, in fact. I doubt I could even move that lid, let alone lift it."

"My cousin would have loved this," Rick said. "Getting into the guts of that thing."

"The expedition?" Clive asked gently and Rick nodded.

"Will this help us find the people who we fought there?" Rick asked. "The ones who…"

Rick's voice failed him as he remembered the blank look his friend had given him just hours ago.

"That's the idea," Clive said darkly. "We're looking for something that will let us hunt them down."

Rick nodded, eyes clear and focused.

"What else can I do to help?"

"Grab that first crate of crystals," Clive said. "We have a lot to shove in there."

19
CLEANSED

"That should be the nest in there," Humphrey said.

They were on a wide embankment road, running through a stretch of wetlands. The largest portion of high ground had a sizeable stand of trees, in which they had been informed were the trap weavers.

Humphrey and Sophie looked at Jason, who still had bags under his bloodshot eyes. His gaze focused on the trees and Sophie noticed a shift in his posture. The confident, laconic, half-slouch became more upright, his feet ready to move. There was a sudden readiness that her own instincts recognised as a preparedness to fight.

"Use a recording crystal," Humphrey said. "Give her something to watch later."

He nodded, taking out his carousel stand of recording crystals and picking one out before returning the carousel to his inventory. He tossed the crystal over his head as his magical cloak formed around him. He ran to the edge of the embankment and leapt off, cloak floating around him as he drifted lightly down to land on the surface of the water like it was solid ground. Moving forward, he disappeared into the trees.

Objective: eliminate [Trap Weavers] 1/14.

"That was quick," Sophie said.

"Jason has abilities and equipment well suited to fighting trap weavers," Humphrey said. "Most of us find them troubling at best and deadly at worst. More iron-rankers in Greenstone die to trap weavers than anything else."

Jason held his conjured dagger in a back-handed grip. Emerging from a shadow he stabbed out to his side, pinning a spider to the tree it was gripping. The spider's body was around the size of a human torso, spewing out gore as the knife plunged through it.

Objective: eliminate [Trap Weavers] 2/14.
You have defeated [Trap Weaver].
Would you like to loot [Trap Weaver]?

Jason yanked the knife free and the trap weaver splashed into the water. He walked over the surface of the water, unconcerned. Roots jutted from the water but his perception power let him easily pick them out in the darkness. A thick strand of webbing shot out and latched onto his cloak, immediately trying to pull on it. That section of cloak became incorporeal and the strand fell limp as Jason drew a throwing dart from the bandolier on his chest and flung it towards the other end of the strand. The dart had a red cord, marking it as explosive. Chunks of trap weaver belched out of the darkness with a loud bang.

Objective: eliminate [Trap Weavers] 3/14.

Jason walked over to a gobbet of flesh that had struck a tree and poked it.

You have defeated [Trap Weaver].
Would you like to loot [Trap Weaver]?

One of the functions of Jason's hood was that he could see right through it, without obstructing his vision. He could see trap weavers all around him, crawling on trees and believing themselves hidden in the dark. They were shades of grey, like Jason's armour, which had been crafted from their leather. Their legs ended in the sharp tips that dug into bark, which made them excellent tree climbers. Those legs were also powerful and springy, allowing them to leap between trees or onto prey.

One of the spiders leapt at Jason from the left. He reached out and grabbed it out of the air, gripping it by the head. It bit into his hand as its sharp legs tried to stab his arm, but skittered off his armour.

[Trap Weaver] has inflicted [Trap Weaver Venom] on you.
You have resisted [Trap Weaver Venom].
[Trap Weaver Venom] does not take effect.
You have gained an instance of [Resistant].

He crushed the spider's head in his fist and dropped it into the water.

Objective: eliminate [Trap Weavers] 4/14.
You have defeated [Trap Weaver].
Would you like to loot [Trap Weaver]?

From multiple directions, strands shot out at him. Some ineffectually struck his cloak, others slid off his armour without achieving purchase.

Item: [Trap Weaver Battle Robe] (iron rank, epic)
***A full body armour, carefully hand-crafted from the silk and leather of trap weavers.* (armour, cloth/leather).**

Effect: Increased resistance to damage. Highly effective against cutting and piercing damage, less effective against blunt damage.

Effect: Repairs damage over time. Extensive damage may require external repair.

Effect: Absorbs blood to prevent leaving a blood trail.

Effect: Increases resistance to bleed and poison effects.

Effect: Resistant to adhesive substances and abilities with adhesive effects.

Effect: Adapts fit to the wearer, within a certain range.

Jason stood in the middle of the trap weaver encirclement. The monsters milled about, confused by their ineffectual attacks. In the shadowy copse of trees, Jason could teleport almost however he willed. He panned his gaze around, mapping out the shadows and the positions of the trap weavers. As the monsters launched a second barrage of webs, he vanished and went to work.

Humphrey and Sophie awaited Jason's return.

Objective: eliminate [Trap Weavers] 5/14.
Objective: eliminate [Trap Weavers] 6/14.
Objective: eliminate [Trap Weavers] 7/14.

"He really isn't messing about," Sophie said.

"Everyone has their own way of fighting," Humphrey said. "With most monsters, I have an easier time than Jason but trap weavers are a bad match for me. I'm most effective against enemies that stand their ground in open space. Complex, shadowy environments are where trap weavers nest but that's where Jason thrives. Over time, you'll come to find what works best for you. As you pick up more abilities and get more experience, you'll refine your style."

Quest: [Notice: Trap Weavers]
Objective complete: Eliminate [Trap Weavers] 14/14.
Quest complete.

Sophie looked up, but no bag of coins appeared.

"No rewards if we didn't contribute," Humphrey said. "I can see the bag dropping on you becoming annoying."

"Getting tired of money literally falling out of the sky is a problem I'll be happy to have."

They spotted rainbow smoke drifting up from the top of the trees as Jason emerged. Once he reached them, he dropped his cloak, revealing a large amount of blood on his head. The monster blood had vanished into smoke, making what remained come from his own injuries.

"Are you alright?" Humphrey asked.

"No worries," Jason said. "I healed up using my abilities."

"Did one of them bite you on the head?" Humphrey asked.

"Uh… yep. That was it."

"What really happened?" she asked.

"Like Humphrey said," Jason told her. "I got bitten by a monster."

"I hope you won't be cutting me out of too many fights," Sophie said. "I like getting paid. Not that it feels that way, with you storing all the money."

"Don't worry," Jason said. "My storage space keeps all the money together, but I'm keeping track of how much is yours."

"And I can trust you to keep the numbers straight?" she asked.

"You still don't trust me?"

"If our positions were swapped," she said, "I would absolutely be stealing from you."

Jason chuckled.

"You're his indentured servitor," Humphrey pointed out. "All the work you do is for him and he is entitled to take any or all of what you earn as he likes. He doesn't need to steal from you because he can take it all with complete legality. He doesn't have to do any more than feed you."

"Don't worry," Jason said. "I'll keep proper track. You have to pay for your own gear, though."

He took out a bottle of crystal wash and tipped it over his head.

"That means both equipment and consumables," he added.

She gave him a flat look.

"What?" he asked her.

"Why would you lie and claim you were bitten on the head?" she asked.

"I'm not lying," Jason said. "I definitely didn't get woozy after the fight from teleporting too much while hungover and hit my head on a log."

The procession of people who entered the ritual room was as prestigious a gathering as to be found in Greenstone. Danielle Geller, Thalia Mercer, Elspeth Arella, Emir Bahadir and the archbishop of the church of Purity, Nicolas Hendren. Ernest Geller was waiting inside, playing guard to Jonah Geller. Jonah, his upper arm firmly in Ernest's grip, glared at each person as they entered. When the archbishop entered, Jonah's eyes went wide and he strained to yank his arm free of Ernest's grasp. It didn't budge in the grip of Ernest's bronze-rank strength.

Elspeth Arella used her aura to brutally suppress Jonah's. Many powerful constriction abilities could only affect those who auras had been beaten down, like the ability she used to entrap Jonah in a bubble of force. It cut off his protestations and lifted him helplessly into the air.

"Thank you, Madam Director," the archbishop said. "If you could move him away from the centre of the room, that would be appreciated."

Jonah's bubble floated away as his fists hammered at the inside. His mouth was visibly firing off invectives but his voice was as confined as his body. The archbishop took a white bag from the satchel at his side and removed the stopper from a spout in the bag's corner. From it, he started carefully pouring out a mixture of powdered silver and gold to form a ritual circle.

"Fortunately," he said, "divine rituals are not so vulnerable to vagaries of ambient magic as the mundane varieties."

"I've never seen one performed before," Arella said.

"They are much as ordinary rituals," the archbishop said. "They still draw on the power of ambient magic but are infused with the glorious might of the divine. My god's will moves the magic and not the other way around, which is why your ability entrapping the unfortunate boy will not affect it."

After drawing out the magical diagram, the archbishop went around placing materials within it. Silver rank spirit coins were the bulk of the materials, while most of the others were orbs of gold or crystal, set out in small frames like silver egg cups. When he was done, he stepped back, held out a hand and started chanting.

"*God most pure, I beseech. Make in this place a sanctuary most clean, to suppress that which poisons the stem and reveal that which poisons the root. In this circle, let no rot spread nor foreign taint take action. Let all be made pure and clean.*"

White and gold light started shining up from the circle.

"You may deposit the man in the circle, Madam Director," the archbishop said.

The bubble floated towards the circle with Jonah, trapped inside, still furiously thrashing about. His hands and head were bloodied from where had pounded them against the enclosure. As it entered the light, the bubble rapidly dissolved, like butter melting in the sun. Jonah fell out but instead of collapsing to the floor, drifted through the air to float above the centre of the magic circle. His arms and legs were pulled out to his sides, his whole body jerking in a small seizure. His eyes were wide and rapidly turning bloodshot, his jaw clenched tight.

"Jonah," Danielle whispered, her voice wracked with misery as she looked on. Thalia Mercer placed a comforting hand on her shoulder, her own troubled gaze locked on the young man in the circle.

Jonah's eyes rolled up in his head as his veins became visible as thin, dark lines all over his body.

"There is no question," the blank-faced archbishop said impassively. "Something resides within the body. The circle will purge it."

"The enemies in the astral space had something inside them," Emir said, looking at Danielle with concern. "When endangered, they were able to trigger it and kill themselves rather than be taken alive."

"It is too late for that," the archbishop said. "Any power the thing inside him has cannot be activated within the circle. The concern you must have now is how deeply it has infiltrated his body. Removing it may damage or even kill him."

"I have gold-rank potions of the highest grade ready to go," Emir told Danielle. "So long as there is a scrap of life left in him, we won't let it fade."

"I will heal him the moment I am certain the taint is gone," the archbishop said.

Danielle didn't acknowledge their words, her gaze unwavering from Jonah's struggles. His body's jerking became more violent, pushing back against the magic of the circle that held him in place. His eyes went bloody and dark, then burst outward, spraying dark fluids as something erupted from within them.

Flailing metal wires, thin as hairs, shot out in clusters from his now-empty eye sockets, waving like the tendrils of a sea creature. Danielle made to lunge forwards, but her arm was gripped by Emir, his gold-rank reflexes catching her before she moved. She turned on him in fury.

"You cannot help him until it is done," the archbishop said. "I would suggest prayer."

Danielle shot the priest a look of venom before turning back to Jonah. She did so just in time for Jonah's cleansing to reach the final stage. Wires burst out from every part of his body, shredding muscle and skin, slicing apart bones. His flesh was shredded just as badly as his clothes as they erupted out of him.

The wires formed a complex network that seemed to have threaded itself through his entire circulatory system. A whole nest of wires had riddled Jonah's brain, slicing his skull into pieces that tumbled to the ground with the rest of his shredded corpse.

What was left was a vaguely man-shaped wire figure, with all the wires threading into and out of a nucleus in the place of the heart. Free of Jonah's body, the mass of wires staggered forward, but was rapidly corroded by exposure to the light of the circle. The wires dissolved into nothing as the nucleus fell to the floor with a hollow clatter.

In the aftermath, the light faded from the now-bloody circle. What had once been Jonah was splattered over the circle. All that remained of the wire construct was the empty nucleus. It looked like a small, hulled coconut. Danielle didn't spare it a glance as she staggered forwards, towards the gory mess that was all that remained of Jonah.

"It's done," the archbishop said, his emotionless intonation startling everyone but Danielle into looking at his calm expression. Emir and Thalia turned to Danielle, who mercifully didn't seem to have heard. She stood in front of Jonah's bloody remains, no longer recognisable as a person.

20

IT JUST TAKES PRACTISE

In the late afternoon, Humphrey, Sophie and Jason were walking down a road with tall, leafy crops to either side. Finally starting to feel better, Jason let his head fall back as he drew a deep breath. He felt the warm sun of early autumn, smelled the fresh, earthy scent of the crops. He let out a contented sigh.

"This is it," he said happily. "People talk about the money and the power but this is the adventuring life I want. Meandering through beautiful places with a good friend and a beautiful woman who may or may not be waiting for the chance to snap my neck and run for it."

"Really?" Sophie asked flatly. Humphrey shook his head.

"I said 'may not.' Just look around you. Breathe in that air. Tell me you don't want to spend your life travelling the world and visiting nice places."

Sophie did look around, sceptically at first, then compared it to the boxed-in streets of Old City. The open spaces. The peaceful breeze playing through leafy crops.

"It does smell a lot nicer than Old City," she acknowledged.

"Money and power are great," Jason said. "Anything you want to get, they can give you. Anything you want to do, they can let you. But you have to want things worth having and want to do things worth doing. Money and power have to be a means, not an end, or you'll lead a joyless life."

Jason looked around the landscape again.

"Freedom. Travel. I want to see what this world has to show me. And someday, I want to go home. To see my own world with new eyes."

Sophie said nothing, giving Jason an assessing look.

"What?" he asked.

"Nothing," she said. "You're just not what I expected."

"And what were you expecting?"

"I don't know," she said. "Not this."

"What's your world like, Jason?" Humphrey asked.

"It has places like this," Jason said. "My family used to take trips out into the country when I was younger. My mother has a large family of mostly rural types. Good, hardworking people, you know? Not all twisty in the head like me. I grew up in a sleepy little beach town. In summer it fills up with people. Later I moved to a big city, although nothing like Greenstone. I'm not sure how to even start describing it. I wasn't happy there, but I don't think I was trying to be then."

He flashed a grin.

"But now I'm here. I have money, magic powers and I'm walking around in a place like this on a day like today. Yes, monsters try to kill me a lot and I've made my share of enemies, but I'm living my life now, instead of just waiting it out."

"Speaking of monsters," Humphrey said. "The contract is for margolls. Dog-headed humanoids with large claws. They should be a good matchup for you, Miss Wexler, but don't underestimate them."

"They're highly aggressive and fight in packs," Jason said. "You'll be outnumbered. The contract says six, but you should never assume the details are accurate."

"That's an important lesson," Humphrey said. "A couple of months ago, Jason and I went to retrieve the body of an adventurer killed because the contract details were wrong."

"Very wrong," Jason said. "We were lucky someone else didn't end up coming for our bodies."

"Margolls are another common local monster," Humphrey said. "When they turn up, everyone evacuates and word is sent to the city to post a contract. There are several farms here, so they've probably settled in until they eat their way through the herds. Once Stash spots them, we'll have a location."

"Stash?" Sophie asked. "That's the bird familiar you've had scouting around?"

"He's been spending a lot of time as a bird, lately," Humphrey said. "I'm not sure how much he understands about what happened during the expedition, but he knows there was a lot of danger. I think he's trying to be more useful."

"Spending time as a bird?" Sophie asked.

Humphry was about to answer when a large bird swooped out of the sky towards Humphrey, transforming into a puppy and dropping into his arms. Humphrey scratched him behind the ears.

"He's a shape-changer," Humphrey said. "You found them, little guy?"

Stash yipped happily. By turning his head and letting out little barks, Stash led them in the right direction. Eventually, they spotted the margolls in a field full of dead animals. The three crouched in the long grass, behind a simple, wooden rail fence that separated the field from the road. They looked through the fence at the margolls on the far side of the field.

"Looks like the margolls came from this side," Humphrey said. "The herd fled to the far end of the field and were pinned against the fence and slaughtered."

The slain herd were creatures that Jason had always thought of as cow lizards, never able to recall their proper name. The margolls had killed them all and were feasting on the carcasses.

"Those poor animals," Humphrey said. "I know they were a meat herd, but they didn't need to die in fear like that. And it's wasteful, too. The margolls can't consume all that meat, but they only eat their fresh kills. They'll take their fill, sleep it off and go hunting for more things to slaughter."

"No, they won't," Jason said. "They aren't leaving this field. I count nine."

"Me too," Sophie said.

"Wexler, Humphrey will be ready to step in quickly if anything goes wrong. You need to understand, though, that when things go wrong, they go wrong fast and hard. I'm not saying don't take risks, because pushing yourself is the point. Just make sure they're calculated risks."

Sophie took a steeling breath, then lightly vaulted the wooden fence and started walking across the field. Caught up in gorging on the dead animals, the margolls didn't notice her until a breeze picked up and carried her scent to them. As it did, they looked up from their kills and howled. Leaping to their feet, they started charging across the field at her. She stopped, watching them approach.

Dog-headed monsters with sickle claws scrambled madly in her direction, some on two limbs, others on four. She started moving again, picking up her pace to run at them as they charged in her direction, letting our discordant, bloodthirsty howls. They were quick, but she sailed over the grass like a wind spirit.

Well-short of reaching them, she leapt into the air. She spun through one horizontal kick and then into a second with the other leg, both without touching the ground. Then she stepped on the air to keep her momentum going and kicked once more before finally landing. She had made two full turns in the air and landed at a run.

Each sweeping kick had unleashed a wide blade of wind that made a shimmering path towards the margolls. The trio of wide blades were as large and slow as she could make them, but the ravening monsters disregarded their approach entirely.

The change came as the first blade savaged the foremost monsters, blood spraying as they ran right into the blade. It was not enough to kill them but two fell to the ground, howling distress. The one who stayed standing took the full brunt of the second blade, its body cut into ragged halves, while more of the creatures were injured behind it. The third blade came on the heels of the second, finished the wounded margolls and injuring more.

The pack were left angry, hurt and confused. The injured ones howled their pain, the others their rage. Their charge had been halted as they milled in disarray.

Back on the road, Jason and Humphrey looked on using a far-sight crystal to magnify their view.

"Did you know she could do that?" Humphrey asked.

"I did not," Jason replied. "Should we move closer?"

"I think so," Humphrey said. Wings appeared on his back and he flew over the fence. Jason vaulted it, not with the grace Sophie had done, but Gary's mobility training made it a negligible task.

"How long would it take you to get over there?" Jason asked.

"A few seconds," Humphrey said. "Five maybe."

"You can cross the distance that quick?"

"If I fly forward, then launch into my flying leap attack, yes."

"Not bad."

The margolls were in turmoil and Sophie was not going to waste it, still running across the grass as if she were flying. She crashed into one of the injured ones, knocking it into the rest and adding to the chaos her wind blades had sown. The margolls fought with wild ferocity, while her movements were clean and efficient. Blocks made openings for attack and dodges set up combination strikes. Fists and feet, elbows and knees; no movement was wasted or opportunity missed as she pounded the margolls with power and precision.

Despite her speed and skill, the frenetic creatures were not on the back foot for long, using their numbers to box in their sole enemy. Sickle claws aimed to reap her life away, but were met with fists and forearms. Every attack she was able to meet, her powers shielded her from suffering so much as a scratch.

As they moved to surround her, she couldn't intercept every attack. A raking slash from the side cut into her leg and from the rear a lacerating swipe scored her upper arm. She ignored the pain and kept fighting; she had drawn them in as she wanted.

Having boxed her in, the monsters pushed hard, only to find she had been replaced with an afterimage. As their claws lashed ineffectually through it, she reappeared a small distance away. The clustered margolls milled in confusion, but Sophie was launching another triple wind blade.

As they had moved so close together in their attempt of overwhelm her, the margolls had made themselves vulnerable to the sweeping blades of air. The razor wind erupted on impact after slicing through skin and muscle, the blade hideously effective against the margolls who had no more defences than their short, bristly fur. After three blades, only one remained standing, badly injured. Sophie finished it off before making sure the ones on the ground were all dead.

Surrounded by dead enemies, Sophie stood tall and drew in heavy, exhausted breaths. Jason and Humphrey arrived at the scene as a bag of coins fell on her head.

"Ow."

"When did you come up with that spinning jump thing?" Jason asked her.

"You left for two weeks," she said, picking the bag. "Did you think I spent the whole time meditating?"

"Fair enough," he said, taking the bag and putting it in his inventory. "Did Rufus help with that?"

"I think he felt bad for me."

"Sorry," Jason said. "I kind of left you in limbo there."

Jason took out a notebook scribbled in it with a pencil.

"What's that?" Sophie asked.

"It's how I'm keeping track of your money," he said, putting them away again.

"Oh," she said. "Thank you."

"You have some real unarmed combat skills," Humphrey said. "I have a relative, Phoebe. She's an unarmed specialist, too, and she's been looking for someone to practice with for a while. I think you could help each other."

"I'd like that," Sophie said, jerking a thumb at Jason. "She has to be more reliable than this guy."

"Oh, come on," Jason said.

"You did just leave without telling anyone," Humphrey pointed out.

"Yeah, well… alright. That's fair."

"If you're interested, then sooner might be better than later," Humphrey said. "It would be dark long before we reached the city; my family estate is closer, here in the delta. I can introduce you to Phoebe and we can go back to the city in the morning."

"Sounds good to me," Jason said. "What do you say, Wexler? Want to be put up in the most prestigious estate in Greenstone? I'll just loot these monsters and we can get going."

"You realise you're saying that to someone staying in Emir Bahadir's cloud palace," Humphrey said.

"I am going to miss having a cloud bed," Jason said. "It was the worst part of leaving the city for so long."

"I can't offer those," Humphrey said, "but we do have hammocks. They're really good for the hot nights."

"Never have sex in a hammock," Jason advised. "It seems like it would be awesome, but it's actually quite troublesome."

"It just takes practise," Humphrey said offhandedly, earning a wide-eyed look from Jason.

"What?" Humphrey asked.

"What are we looking at?" Rick asked.

In the mirage chamber control room, Rick, Belinda and Clive were looking through the window. Under the dome, a large illusionary orb and a small illusionary orb were pressing into one another.

"The small orb is a simulated astral space," Clive said. "The big orb is a simulated world it's attached to. This isn't what they would actually look like; I simulated their magical aspects, rather than the physical ones."

"Why?" Rick asked.

"A lot of equipment was brought back from the astral space," Clive explained. "I managed to replicate what they were doing on a small scale, but I couldn't figure out what it did. Using it in our world, instead of an astral space, meant all the power it output just got absorbed. Our world is too big. Of course, going back into the astral space and setting it up again was not an option. Here, we've created a simulation of an astral space, a world to anchor it and the equipment the expedition bought operating inside it."

"So, instead of a monster, you created a whole world?" Rick asked.

"Not exactly," Clive said. "I've examined the equipment quite thoroughly and isolated what it should interact with and simulated that. Simulating a whole world is beyond any mirage chamber I've ever heard of."

"So, what are the results?" Rick asked.

"We'll have to wait. I've accelerated the simulation as much as possible, and so long as I haven't missed anything major, it will eventually show us exactly what the expedition interrupted."

They watched eagerly for the first hour, attention waning by the second. Rick left and brought back lunch while Clive and Belinda turned to books from Clive's personal stash. After looking through Clive's collection, Rick went to retrieve a book with less theory and more tales of dashing heroics.

It was evening before something changed inside the chamber. They all went to the window to watch the two orbs that had finally become more active.

"We already know what they were doing would have catastrophic results," Clive said. "The major question is whether that was the objective or a side effect."

The two orbs had been pushing into each other for the entire run of the simulation, but as they watched, the smaller orb pulled away. The surface of the large orb, where the small orb had contacted it, was wrinkled and marred, where the rest was smooth.

"Is that it?" Rick asked.

"No," Clive said. "The astral space, the small orb, shouldn't be able to maintain its integrity without being attached to its world. Just pulling apart should have caused it to break down."

"Is someone trying to make a small, independent world?" Belinda asked.

"If they are, it won't work," Clive said. "It can't last long, like that."

As if to prove his point, the smaller orb started to distort, breaking into chunks and then vanishing entirely.

"There we have it," Clive said. "Their objective was to separate the astral space from our world while maintaining its structure for at least some amount of time."

"How much time?" Belinda asked.

"Weeks. Months, at the outside. I'll need to examine the simulation recording to get more details, but the basics are clear."

"Why would they do that?" Rick asked.

"No idea," Clive said.

"Who benefits?" Belinda asked. "And how?"

"Who benefits from a huge chunk of dislodged physical reality, floating through the deep astral?" Clive asked. "No one. Even gods couldn't do anything with it; once it leaves their world, it's out of their ability to affect. All that leaves is..."

Clive's eyes went wide as he let out a low sound of horror out.

"No..."

He paced back and forth, clutching at his hair with his hands.

"This is bigger than us," he said. "Astral spaces. Ours wasn't the only one affected. Oh, this is bad."

"What's bad?" Belinda asked. She and Rick were looking at Clive in frustration.

"I've figured it out," he said.

"We got that much," Belinda said. "What did you figure out?"

"We need to tell someone," Clive said. "A diamond ranker. Lots of diamond rankers."

He bolted for the door, Belinda and Rick following, only to meet Clive rushing back in. He gave Rick a look of wild-eyed panic.

"I don't know how to get back to the main house!"

21

WORLD BUILDING

The sky was nearing full dark but the pathways of the Geller estate were lit up by magical lights, albeit ones selected and placed more for aesthetics than practicality. Rather than simple illumination, the discretely placed lights washed the gardens in shifting colours.

Clive had no time to stop and appreciate it as he led Rick and Belinda through the gardens in a rush, striding with his long legs. Belinda did have time—Clive's enthusiasm outpaced his ability to navigate, requiring Rick to correct him as he headed down one wrong path after another. This allowed Belinda to keep up in spite of her more measured pace.

"I like these lights," Belinda said.

"Good, aren't they?" Rick asked. "No, Clive, to the left."

Clive grumbled as he came back up one path to head down another.

"Explain this again," Belinda said to Clive as he came past. "There's some kind of super god?"

"Yes," Clive said distractedly. "Except no. But yes. But no."

"That clears everything up," Rick said as Clive strode off again.

Compared to Clive, Humphrey, Sophie and Jason made their way through estate grounds at a relaxed saunter. They took the time to appreciate the colourfully lit paths.

"I looted some material from those trap weavers," Jason said. "My combat robes are made from the same stuff. I know a guy who can probably use it to make you something similar, Wexler."

"I thought you said I'd have to pay for my own gear," Sophie said.

"We're in a group," Jason said. "We split the loot as a group. You'll still have to pay for labour costs yourself."

"Thanks," she said with a frown. "Sorry, that sounded insincere. Gratitude isn't a feeling I'm used to."

Jason laughed.

"No worries. I know what it feels like to go from random nobody to adventurer with magic powers and such, hobnobbing with the wealthy and powerful. Which will be us, soon enough. It's a bit disorienting, isn't it? Feels hard to get your feet under you. Normal keeps slipping away from you like a bar of wet soap. You're constantly trying to figure out what normal is now."

"Yeah," she said. "That's exactly what it feels like."

Danielle, Emir, Thalia, Arella and the archbishop were moving through the estate grounds from the ritual building towards the main house. Fresh from witnessing the gruesome demise of Jonah Geller, Danielle was still reeling, lingering at the back of the group. Ernest Geller, the only non-silver amongst them, had taken over the duty of guiding them through the grounds.

"I am not subjecting my son to that process," Thalia Mercer said adamantly as they moved along the path.

"That will not be necessary," said Herston, the archbishop of Purity. "Now that we know what we are dealing with, our methods can be more precise."

"We know what we're dealing with?" Arella asked.

"The boy was implanted with a star seed. My church has seen such things in the past and has long developed the means to extract them. There will be damage, depending on how long the seed has been inside them, but no irrevocable harm."

"What good does that do Jonah?" Danielle spat. It was the first time she had spoken since Emir led her away from Jonah's ruined body.

"What is this star seed, exactly?" Emir asked.

"They are the creations of entities from beyond your physical reality, only existing in the deep astral," the archbishop said. "They are known by various names, but most commonly as the great astral beings. There are heretics in our world who offer them improper veneration, perversely akin to how the pious worship the gods. The astral beings can bestow blessings, like gods, but cannot bestow essence and awakening stones. Instead, they can send their followers star seeds."

"Is that what the people we tried to capture were using to kill themselves?" Emir asked."

"Most likely," the archbishop said. "The seed must first be implanted into the body. Once it has germinated, the body undergoes a transformation, which may be minor or major."

"We've seen that," Thalia said. "The people who attacked the expedition were bizarre combinations of flesh and steel."

"Once the transformation is complete, the remnant power of the star seed is available for the heretic to use. Exploding that power to kill themselves should be well within their capabilities."

"And they put those things in our children," Thalia growled. "I'm going to kill them all."

"And so you should," the archbishop said. "The seeds turn the implanted people into vessels for the astral beings—puppets without will. Only the most dedicated volunteer for such a process. At first the influence is subtle. Their memories and personalities remaining intact, the only control being a drive to protect the seeds within them from discovery. Slowly, without their even realising it is happening, the hosts become puppets. Their personalities are supplanted, shifting towards the will of the astral being who crafted the seeds."

"How long does that take?" Thalia asked.

"I don't know," the archbishop said. "I only know this much because I have studied all manner and means of impurity. I have never encountered a star seed in person. I will consult my church's records after returning to the city."

"Why weren't these seeds found before now?" Thalia asked. "All five were examined in the camp, then back in the city, by silver rank healers. Why didn't they find these things inside them?"

"Star seeds are not some affliction to be easily purged by an essence ability," the archbishop explained. "These are transcendent-rank objects, brought into being by entities so vast and alien that we cannot comprehend the fullness of them. They require more than some simple ritual or essence ability to discover, let alone purge. We should give thanks to our gods for shielding us from such things."

"Your god didn't help Jonah," Danielle said. "Your god's ritual tore him apart."

"Perhaps if your family were more dedicated in their piety, he would have been protected."

Emir used a mirage step to get between Danielle and the archbishop, holding out a hand to forestall her rage. The whole group stopped. After checking she wasn't going to rush past him, Emir turned a fierce glare on the priest.

"You had best watch yourself, Archbishop," Emir warned. "Keep talking like that and I won't get in her way again."

The archbishop snorted derision but didn't say anything else, resuming his passage through the gardens. After a heavy pause, the others followed.

"The next step must be to retrieve the other four," Arella said as they neared the main house. "You are certain you can extract these seeds without harming the people they are implanted in?"

"Without harming, no; without killing, yes. I am certain my church has the means, although there are two requirements. First, we must get hold of the people that harbour them before the seeds have taken too deep a root. Once the seeds have overtaken the body, they impinge upon the soul, after which it is too late. The second requirement is that we need to know which astral entity created the seeds. Each such entity creates a different seed and must be adjusted for accordingly."

"That gives us two priorities then," Arella said. "First, retrieve the remaining four affected, which should be the easy part. The Adventure Society has people watching them, waiting on the results of this ritual. Now we are certain they've been compromised, we can have them brought in immediately. They will be apprehended and Mr Bahadir's portal user can bring them back to Greenstone."

"What about finding out which great astral being we're dealing with?" Danielle asked. "I want to know who is doing this to us."

"I can answer that!" a voice called out.

They were nearing the main house, where the pathways leading all through the estate converged into an open space. Coming from another path was an agitated Clive, with Rick and Belinda in tow.

Rick cast an anxious gaze over the group. He saw that Jonah was not with them, while Ernest, who he had last seen guarding Jonah, was. Then he spotted Danielle, red-eyed and distraught, which startled him. He had never seen her in any state but complete self control. Rick's whole body slumped as he realised what that meant for Jonah's fate.

"What are you talking about?" Arella asked as Clive hurried to them.

"You were talking about an astral entity, right?" Clive asked. "I know which one it is, and what it's after."

The two groups converged as Rick and Belinda followed, then grew again as Humphrey, Jason and Sophie appeared. Belinda and Sophie shared a surprised look at each other's presence, while Humphrey was startled by his mother's plain distress, rushing to her side. His large figure towered over her as he embraced her in a deep hug.

"I think, perhaps," Arella said, "we should take any further discussion inside."

She turned to Ernest.

"You were part of the group that found the five, yes?" she asked.

"I was," Ernest said.

"I assume there is a speaking chamber here on the estate. The personal autonomy of the other four is no longer valid. Tell the rest of your group to take the remaining four into custody immediately and bring them in, under the full authority of the Adventure Society."

"Yes, Ma'am," Ernest said before moving off at a half-run.

"We have a conference room in the house," Danielle said, giving Humphrey's arm a reassuring pat as she moved out of his embrace. “We can hear out Mr Standish there. Humphrey, please see to the rest of our guests.”

Danielle led the group inside the house, leaving Humphrey with Jason, Belinda, Sophie and Rick.

“What are you doing here, Lindy?” Sophie asked.

“Complicated magic with the fate of the world at stake,” Belinda said causally. “You?”

“It’s getting late and I was offered a hammock.”

“My thing is more exciting,” Belinda said.

“Sounds like it. Who were all those people?”

“Just a bunch of rich folk,” Belinda said. “So, a hammock? Do you remember that guy Barry? He always used to sleep in a hammock.”

“Was he the one that got killed when an anvil fell on him?”

“That’s the one. Building a smithy on the third floor was a terrible idea.”

“I recall a lot of his ideas being bad.”

“No kidding. He wanted to, you know, in his hammock one time. I thought it would be fun but it was just awkward.”

“I’m told it takes practice,” Sophie said.

“Of course you were told that,” Belinda said. “Anyone who looks at you, their first thought is ‘how to get that girl to practise sex with me a lot?’ That’s how we got into this whole mess, remember?”

“That’s not how I’d describe it.”

As the two women talked, Humphrey and Jason approached Rick, staring blankly into the air.

“Rick?” Humphrey asked.

“I don’t think Jonah made it,” Rick said absently, eyes unfocused.

“He’s dead?” Humphrey asked.

“They didn’t say, but you saw your mother.”

Humphrey bowed his head, running his hands through it. “Gods damn it. I didn’t know things were that bad.”

“Ernest brought him in by portal,” Rick said. “They had me waiting to go get all the...”

He waved his arm at the house where all the important people had gone, leaving them behind.

“Where was that?” Humphrey asked.

“The ritual room. The big, isolated one.”

"Well, let's go take a look," Humphrey said. "See if we can't get some answers."

Humphrey pointed out a building annexed from the main house.

“That’s one of the visitor residences,” he said. “Jason, you, Miss Wexler and her friend can go straight in.”

Jason nodded, patting Rick on the shoulder.

"Let me know about Jonah, yeah?"

"Of course."

Clive was pacing at the end of a conference room, while the group of Greenstone's most important people sat around the long, rectangular table. The décor was typical of the Geller estate, with light woods and artfully woven reeds offering pleasant airflow and relying on unseen magic to provide the privacy.

"How did you know one of the great astral beings was involved?" Clive asked.

"You are here to answer our questions," the archbishop said. "Not the other way around."

"Right, yes. Um, so, great astral beings. We don't know all that much about most of them, because only a handful seem to take any interest in physical realities. The World-Phoenix, the All-Devouring Eye, the Reaper, the Celestial Book. More than any of those, however, one called the Builder takes specific interest in physical realities."

"You seem well versed in the knowledge of these beings," the archbishop said.

"Yes," Clive said. "I happen to venerate the Celestial Book myself. It's fairly common for those of us heavily involved in magical theory."

"You admit to being a heretic?" the archbishop asked, half-standing. The rage on his face was a stark contrast to the emotionless way he had observed Jonah's horrific death.

Clive glared back at the archbishop.

"I suppose I could be considered a heretic," Clive said. "The same way that the exploitation of rigid dogma to act out personal prejudice could be considered faith."

The archbishop's silver rank aura exploded towards Clive but was immediately crushed by Emir's gold rank aura.

"This is not the time, Archbishop. We are here to listen, not judge."

"The gods are always judging us. Forgoing righteousness for expediency is an easy path to sin."

"And not shutting up is the path to being kicked out," Danielle said. "This is my home and you are here by my forbearance."

The archbishop scowled but settled silently back into his seat.

"Emotions are running high, and with good reason," Emir said. "That doesn't change the fact that tempering ourselves will accomplish more than indulging ourselves will."

Emir panned his gaze around the room, asserting his authority with a delicate but unmistakable employment of his aura.

"Please, continue, Mr Standish," he said.

"Thank you," Clive said. "As I was saying, there is one astral entity who takes more interest than the others in physical realities, which is to say, worlds like ours. Most of the others operate similarly to gods in that what they want is the promotion of various ideals. The World-Phoenix fosters dimensional integrity; the Celestial Book promotes the understanding of magic's underlying nature. The Reaper advocates the finality of death. The Builder is not like these others. It has no interest in disseminating principles and is instead obsessed with physical reality while, by its very nature, being unable to co-exist with it. This dichotomy of its core drive and its intrinsic properties has led to an undertaking on such ambition it staggers belief."

"What kind of undertaking?" Emir asked.

"It is building a world of its own," Clive said. "Creating a new physical reality in the deep astral. The way it does this is to take raw materials that are neither fully of the astral or of physical reality."

"You're talking about astral spaces," Arella said.

"Exactly," Clive said. "Astral spaces form attached to worlds, without which they immediately break down. Without a real world to anchor them, they cannot exist. But if an astral space is given the ability to sustain itself, even for just a brief period, the Builder can take it and anchor it to the world the Builder is creating from stolen parts."

"You're saying that those people we fought were trying to steal the astral space for this Builder?" Arella asked. "A dimensional pirate, plundering chunks of reality from which to build its own?"

"That's exactly what I'm saying. An astral being cannot interact with physical reality directly, so it needs to recruit others to act for it. The Builder recruits people to carve off the astral spaces connected to their world, then it steps in and claims them. I've read about the Builder doing this, but now I've seen the means by which it does so."

"What are the ramifications of losing astral spaces?" Emir asked.

"It varies, since different astral spaces are connected to worlds in different ways. The process they were using in our local astral space was designed to keep the astral space intact, at the cost of catastrophic destruction to the physical reality. I can confidently assert that the results would be similar in other instances."

"We have reports of astral spaces suffering incursions like ours all over the world," Arella said.

"That's right," Clive said. "Astral spaces, all over the world. We're talking about cataclysmic destruction the world over. Death and destruction on a civilisation-ending scale. The only comfort I can take is that there are smarter people than me looking into all this and stronger people than us doing something about it. This is a threat that extends beyond the reaches of our world. We need diamond rankers to act, and act fast."

"Don't sell yourself short, Mr Standish," Emir said. "The information you're giving us is not information we've been getting from elsewhere. Either they don't know, or they are hiding the potential risks to avoid panic."

"At the risk of agreeing with the archbishop," Thalia Mercer said, "how confident are you in this information, Standish?"

"Very," Clive said. "My knowledge of the great astral beings comes from one of the Magic Society's previous directors. The great astral beings were his field of study and he had a collection of journals from diamond-rank adventurers who had travelled between worlds. He left those to me after his death and I know them well."

"And you're sure this Builder's people are the ones doing these things to our astral spaces?" Thalia asked.

"Yes. The Builder, as I mentioned, has no driving ideology. He forms groups, cults, driven not by ideology, but through gifts of power. The fact that we are seeing any of this suggests they have been operating here for years. Maybe decades."

"But you are certain this Builder is behind them?" Arella asked.

"I have managed to successfully simulate what they were doing in the Geller's mirage chamber. The goal of their efforts was to reinforce the astral space and sever it from our world. Nothing short of a great astral being has the power to make anything of such an act, and of them, only the Builder has any interest in it."

"I think our next move should be to confirm this information as best we can," Arella said. "If combine we what we've seen today, Mr Standish's findings and the experiences of the expedition together, we may well have at least an acceptable level of confirmation to disseminate to the Adventure Society at large."

"Mr Standish, I'd like a look at those journals, if you don't mind," Emir requested.

"I've made copies of the originals," Clive said. "I'll deliver them to your cloud palace."

"I shall look into the records of our rituals for removing star seeds," the archbishop said. "There may be details in the rituals for removing this Builder's seeds that help confirm he is the one."

"Thank you," Emir said.

"I'll turn the more scholarly members of my family loose on the temple of Knowledge's library," Danielle said. "The goddess always welcomes seekers of truth."

"I'll do likewise," Thalia said.

"I will make sure that everything we learn is spread to the Adventure Society as a whole and see if they have anything in return," Arella said. "We aren't the only ones dealing with this problem, but one group of many working to contribute."

"Good," Emir said, standing up. "We all have our tasks; we should get to them. Well done, Mr Standish."

"The hour is getting late," Danielle said, also getting up. "You are all welcome to stay the night. We have ample room."

Thalia and Emir accepted the offer, with the archbishop and Elspeth Arella declining; everyone recognised that neither the priest nor the Adventure Society director were truly welcome in Danielle Geller's home. They went off to their transport while Danielle led Thalia, Emir and Clive towards the guest wing.

"Mr Standish," Emir said as they left the conference room. "Have you ever considered becoming a professional treasure hunter?"

22
FABULOUS PRIZES

The day's first light found Jason meditating on a porch. It was attached to just one of the Geller family guest houses, each larger than the four-bedroom home Jason grew up in. Like most of the Geller estate building, it was nestled amongst the lush greenery of the gardens.

Ability [Cloak of Night] (Dark) has reached Iron 6 (100%).
Ability [Cloak of Night] (Dark) has reached Iron 7 (00%).

Jason opened his eyes. His recent two-week storm of monster hunting had not been as effective at raising his abilities as he hoped. His lower-level abilities improved well enough, but his highest-rank ones were starting to plateau. Once he was back in the city, he would seek out Rufus for advice.

Jason Asano
Race: Outworlder.
Current rank: iron
Progression to bronze rank: 25%

Attributes
[Power] (Blood): [Iron 5].
[Speed] (Dark): [Iron 0].
[Spirit] (Doom): [Iron 0].
[Recovery] (Sin): [Iron 5].
Racial Abilities (Outworlder)

[Party Interface].
[Quest System].
[Inventory].
[Map].
[Astral Affinity].
[Mysterious Stranger].

Essences (4/4)

Dark [Speed] (3/5)
[Midnight Eyes] (special ability): [Iron 8] 19%.
[Cloak of Night] (special ability): [Iron 7] 00%.
[Path of Shadows] (special ability): [Iron 7] 04%.
Blood [Power] (5/5)
[Blood Harvest] (spell): [Iron 6] 98%.
[Leech Bite] (special attack): [Iron 6] 14%.
[Feast of Blood] (spell): [Iron 5] 92%.
[Sanguine Horror] (familiar): [Iron 6] 89%.
[Haemorrhage] (spell): [Iron 5] 06%.

Sin [Recovery] (5/5)
[Punish] (special attack): [Iron 7] 23%.
[Feast of Absolution] (spell): [Iron 6] 23%.
[Sin Eater] (special ability): [Iron 6] 69%.
[Hegemony] (aura): [Iron 7] 69%.
[Castigate] (spell): [Iron 5] 23%.

Doom [Spirit] (4/5)
[Inexorable Doom] (spell): [Iron 7] 16%.
[Punition] (spell): [Iron 6] 54%.
[Blade of Doom] (spell): [Iron 4] 39%.
[Verdict] (spell): [Iron 3] 94%.

Jason could feel the changes in his attributes. His power attribute made him stronger than he had been before. He could better handle being knocked around by monsters, as well. It was nothing like the superhuman strength of Gary or even Rufus, but compared to his previous self it was definitely noticeable. Additionally, his increased recovery attribute had greatly increased his stamina, and his mana recovery was quicker than previous.

The changes were reflected in his physical appearance, as well. His meagre physique wasn't bulking out, but flaccid muscle was gradually becoming sleek and lean. He stood up and stretched.

"Feeling sexy."

"What was that?" Emir asked, approaching along a garden path.

"I said I'm feeling sexy," Jason said. "I'm not ashamed to admit it. You're up and about early."

"Lots to do," Emir said. "I wanted to talk to you before I headed back for the city."

Jason returned his meditation mat to his inventory and gestured Emir towards the outdoor furniture on the porch.

"Iced tea?" Jason offered.

"That would be nice."

The delta heat was already rising. Jason took a pair of tall glasses and a pitcher from his inventory. He filled a glass with ruby red tea, chilled by the chunks of ice in the pitcher. Emir took an appreciative sip.

"What did you put in this?"

"Gem berries," Jason said. "They're in season."

Emir took another sip before turning to his main topic.

"I wanted to talk to you. I anticipated having this conversation earlier but the delay is for the best, given recent revelations. How much are you aware of what's going on?"

"You mean the monster from beyond reality who likes playing with blocks? Clive told us about it last night."

"Did you hear about the star seeds?"

"Yeah. Between what Ernest saw and Clive knows, I think I have it all."

"What do you think about what our enemies are doing, seeding those people?"

Jason rubbed his chin thoughtfully.

"I think their plan is going about as well as they could ask, given it was almost certainly hatched in a very short time."

"Care to expand on that?" Emir asked.

Jason snorted a laugh.

"You know, I had teachers like you," he said. "The ones that make you keep talking until they're sure you're right, or sure you're wrong."

Emir chuckled. "I think I'm starting to understand some of Rufus's complaints about you. Why don't you go ahead and indulge me?"

"Fine," Jason said. "Think about it from the bad guys' perspective. They've been working for months in this astral space, only for a small army of adventurers to arrive. They know the jig is up, so they knock together a hasty plan. Use their construct army to send the invading adventurers into disarray, giving the villains time to extricate their people. While they're at it, they snag some iron-rankers in the chaos, shove in some star seeds and leave them in suspiciously easy-to-find locations. They scarper, leaving us with a bunch of suspiciously suspicious people to be suspicious of. Which we are. Secretive meetings between powerful people; the local powers scrambling to figure out what's been done to them without setting off a political volcano. In the meantime, their actual agents are running around without us wondering if they even exist."

"You think the five were a distraction?"

"It's the only thing they're good for. Attempting to use them as agents for some agenda would be pointless because they've been watched from the moment we got them back, which was obviously going to happen. My guess would be that they have a secondary objective. Maybe another astral space somewhere."

"How would you go about figuring out if they're just a distraction?"

"That's easy; the key is the other four. They're only iron rank, so if they mysteriously slip the higher-rank people who try and bring them in, forcing us to focus even more time and resources on them, then they're definitely a distraction. Whoever is responsible for that might have even let Jonah get taken so they would find what's inside him. That way, we have to make retrieving the others the priority, even if we figure out they're a distraction. We can't just leave a bunch of wealthy scions full of interdimensional mind-control bombs."

Emir gave Jason an assessing look as he refilled his glass.

"So, teach, was I right or wrong?"

"We sent word to bring the four in last night," Emir said. "They all escaped the people keeping an eye on them. The Hornis branch of the Adventure Society is conducting a large-scale search."

"There you go," Jason said. "You need to get people looking for the real agents, maybe find out if there's another astral space nearby. But you already have people on that, don't you?"

"There is another astral space," Emir said. "Smaller than the desert astral space, and different in several key ways. It's been hidden for longer than Greenstone has been here, but it's still here."

"Sounds like you have things well in hand."

"There are some complications," Emir said. "I've already mentioned to you the event I came to Greenstone to conduct."

"Oh," Jason said. "This place you want explored is an astral space?"

"Yes, but one much harder to enter than the desert astral space. It requires certain conditions to open that I have spent most of the last two years looking to fulfil, all while looking for the entrance."

"Which is here," Jason said.

"Not right here, but close enough. I had my people confirm it shortly after I arrived. The major complication, however, is that even once opened, only iron rankers may enter. We've tried considerable measures to get around it, none of which were viable."

"So you need a bunch of iron rankers to explore it for you," Jason said.

"Precisely. There is something my client wants inside it and considerable rewards await whoever brings it to me."

"Two years of searching… I imagine the rewards that await you are even more considerable."

"Indeed they are," Emir said. "It's what allows me to be so generous."

"How generous is that?"

"I'm not going to tell you the main prize, but the secondary prize is five legendary awakening stones for whichever team brings me the item. That should give you some indication."

"Five legendary stones is the secondary prize? That's generous, alright."

"Unfortunately, your chances of winning the prize have rather dropped," Emir said.

"Oh?"

"You know I pushed back the event, in the wake of the expedition."

"You're talking about the iron rankers you're shipping in from outside the city? It's going to be harder because I won't just be up against Greenstone's trashy iron-rankers."

"Essentially, yes."

"It doesn't really change anything. The smart money was always on Beth Cavendish and her team, or maybe one some of the Geller groups. Rick's team has taken some hits, but they have, what? Five more teams?"

"Humphrey is a Geller. Are you going to formalise a team?"

"We've talked about it."

"You should do more than talk," Emir said. "Your abilities should be starting to slow down their advancement by now, yes?"

"Actually, yes," Jason said. "What's that got to do with a team?"

"You need to start focusing on the contracts for which you are poorly suited. You need to push yourself harder."

"I get it," Jason said. "Go for the hard stuff, but have a team to save you when it goes wrong."

"Exactly."

"Thanks for the advice."

Emir finished his glass of iced tea.

"Another?" Jason offered.

"Please."

Emir let out a sigh as Jason poured.

"These revelations about astral spaces are having an unpleasant impact on my plans," he said.

"Do they want you to leave the astral space sealed, or use it as bait?"

"Bait. They want an examination by the purity church to be a condition of participation, but only tell people that once they're assembled onsite. I'm not sure if the church can muster an appropriate test, but we may uncover people when they refuse to be subjected to it."

"I'm not sure I'm willing to be subjected to it," Jason said. "What kind of examination are we talking about?"

"I don't know. The impression I get is that these seeds are hard to discover without invasive methods."

"Well if you think I'm letting a priest shove a probe up in me, you're sorely mistaken, which I imagine will be the majority opinion. Not to mention that if I were these people, the iron-rankers I'd send would be evil-implant free."

"Whatever we decide to do," Emir said, "I'll be asking certain participants I trust to keep an eye out in the astral space. We have no idea who could be a Builder cultist."

Jason frowned.

"That rings a bell," he said. "Builder cultist. I've seen that somewhere."

"Where?"

"Can't remember," Jason said, absently scratching his head. "I'm sure I've seen it, but… oh, that's going to annoy me until I figure it out."

Emir drained his second glass.

"That's really good, thank you," he said, standing up. "I'll leave you to it; I want to call in on our hostess before I go."

"She didn't look in the best way yesterday," Jason said. "She took Jonah's death hard."

"Danielle blames herself for the expedition's failures. Not as much as she blames Elspeth Arella, but still. Then once she thinks it's all over, her family loses someone else."

"I knew Jonah," Jason said. "He was easy to hate, but also hard to stop yourself from liking. Eventually. We need to get these people."

"Yes, we do," Emir said as he stepped off the porch. "Try and remember where you heard about Builder cultists from. If we can track down any of their activities outside the astral space, it might be the thread we follow right to them."

Jason, Humphrey and Sophie joined Clive and Belinda to travel back to the city in Clive's airboat. Due to the space constraints, Clive's rune tortoise, Onslow, was unable to take his usual position on the prow. Clive called him back into his body, where he appeared on Clive's torso as a runic tattoo.

"What ability do you get when Onslow merges into you?" Jason asked.

"I can use the rune powers on his shell as spells," Clive said.

"That's nice," Humphrey said. "It's like having even more essence abilities. That's a fantastic familiar power."

Humphrey's own familiar, Stash, was currently in puppy form, laid back in Belinda's lap, getting a scratch on the tummy. He suddenly struggled out of Belinda's clutches and started trying to push himself into Humphrey's leg.

"Silly boy," Humphrey said, picking him up. "You can't go inside me; you're not that kind of familiar."

Puppy Stash let out a little whine, giving Humphrey a pouty look before transforming into a bird.

"No!" Humphrey yelled as bird Stash leapt from his hand and promptly got sucked through the magical ring at the rear as it pulled air through itself to propel the boat.

"Again?" Clive asked as he slowed down the airboat. "Every time, this happens."

"You've heard me tell him," Humphrey said.

"You need to get control of your familiar," Clive said.

"You aren't in any more control of your familiar," Humphrey said. "It's just so slow that you can't tell it's running away."

The airboat came to a full stop and a frog the size of a St. Bernard swam up to the side, threatening to tip the airboat as it tried to climb on.

"You're too big," Humphrey told it.

It turned back into a puppy that adorably scrambled at the side of the boat before plopping back into the water. Humphrey reached down to pluck it out, ignoring how wet his clothes were getting as he held Stash to his chest.

"Poor little guy. It happened again, didn't it?" Humphrey said

The wet puppy snuggled into Humphrey's chest as Clive started the boat up again. As they closed in on the city, Jason remembered the voice chat they had as they left.

"Are you going to see Hudson about joining Rick's team when you get to the city?" Jason asked Humphrey.

"That's right," Humphrey said.

"You know there was another guy who was on Thadwick's team," Jason said. "If we're going to put a team together ourselves, we'll need a healer."

"Neil Davone," Humphrey said. "I can go and talk to him after, but it may be too late already. Even with Thadwick on his record, people will snatch up a loose healer."

"I should be the one to do it," Jason said.

"Are you sure?" Humphrey asked. "You had a history with Thadwick yourself."

"That's why it has to be me. If it's going to work, that air needs to be cleared."

"Alright, then. That'll make five, then right?"

"Yep," Jason said.

"Who are the other two?" Clive asked.

"You and her," Jason told him, jerking a thumb at Sophie.

"You want me on your team?" Clive asked.

"Of course we do," Humphrey said.

"Don't you want someone, I don't know... good?"

Jason and Humphrey shared a glance and laughed.

"You are good," Humphrey told Clive.

"I am?"

"You are," Jason said.

"Oh," Clive said. "Really?"

"Don't get me wrong; you're no solo operator," Jason said. "You need someone to stand between you and the bad guy, but once you have that, you've got the goods."

"And she's good too?" Clive asked, looking at Sophie.

"No, but she's cheap," Jason said, right before Sophie punched him on the arm.

"Ow. Don't forget you're my indentured servant; I can make you walk the plank. Does anyone have a plank in their storage space?"

23

ANY TEAM EXCEPT YOURS

Jason walked up from the loop line into one the most verdant neighbourhoods on the Island, with streets and residences both full of vibrant greenery with long leaves and colourful flowers. The water-affinity of the green stone that was the foundation of the Island helped the flowers deny the encroaching autumn. The houses didn't have yards so much as grounds, with low walls that were more about decoration than security. There weren't street numbers, but family names appeared on plaques near the entry gates.

Jason found the one he was looking for and approached the gate. On the other side was a gateman reading a book in a small gazebo for shade. The elf clearly was more greeter than security as he looked older than the house he was guarding, although his normal aura said he was no such thing. He put his book down to approach Jason from the inside of the gate.

"May I enquire as to who is visiting?"

"Jason Asano. I'm looking for Neil Davone."

The old elf nodded and opened the gate, directing Jason to go up the path to the house and knock.

Doing just that, Jason saw some people taking drinks on a terrace and gardeners maintaining the grounds, all of whom were elves. The relaxed people glanced at him with curiosity, but made no move to approach as he did as instructed, going to the front door and knocking. Another elf opened the door, an older man who was the very image of understated elegance. Jason was again asked his business and he introduced himself a second time.

"Ah, Mr Asano. I was sorry to hear about your demotion and have no doubt you shall soon be rising through the ranks once more."

"You know about my demotion? And that I exist?"

"It is incumbent on the staff to keep abreast of issues that may impact the household."

"I'm guessing that's only true with a certain calibre of staff," Jason said. "I doubt everyone shares your professionalism."

"Thank you for saying, sir. Would you care to wait in the parlour while I check on the young master's availability?"

"That would be lovely," Jason said.

The elf butler led Jason into a garden parlour, just off a large courtyard filled with greenery. The elf had barely gone before a maid came in with a tea tray with finger cakes.

"Thank you," Jason said as she poured the tea.

"This blend is from the family's holdings in the Mistrun valley," the maid told him as he took a sip. "They produce some of the finest tea fields in the world."

Jason took another sip and nodded.

"I believe it," he said, giving her a smile. "I can't think of a finer cup I've had."

"Thank you, sir," the maid said before withdrawing.

Jason enjoyed the breeze drifting in from the courtyard, carrying with it a pleasant scent of flowers. Once he finished the first cup he poured himself another and helped himself to one of the cakes as he waited. When Neil Davone finally entered, Jason got up to greet him.

They sat down, Neil pouring tea for himself into the other cup.

"So what brings you to my home, Asano?" Neil asked. Jason read his tone as civil, with an undercurrent of either challenge or resentment.

"The same reason I imagine all manner of young adventurers have come by," Jason said.

"You want a healer. You're putting together a team."

"Yes. Before we get into that, can I ask you something?"

"Go ahead," Neil said.

"Everyone I've seen here is an elf."

"That's not a question," Neil said. "We're an elven household; what's odd about that?"

"Are you adopted?" Jason asked.

"No," Neil said.

"Your parents are elves?"

"Of course they are," Neil said. "What are you getting at?"

"Is your milkman a human?"

"What in the world are you talking about?" Neil asked.

"I'm just wondering why you aren't an elf," Jason said.

"I am an elf."

"You're an elf?"

Annoyed, Neil brushed back his hair to reveal a tapered ear.

"Wow," Jason said, not hiding his surprise.

"Why would you think I'm a human?" Neil asked.

"Well, it's just… look. Elves are a slender bunch. Except for Lucian Lamprey, who is probably on some kind of magical roids, but that's beside the point. For a human, your proportions are completely healthy. For an elf, though, you're bit of a chunker."

"Excuse me?"

"You know, an extra bit of heft. Too much time at the sandwich shop. An over-enthusiastic between-meal-snacker."

"Are you saying I'm fat?"

"I'm not saying you're fat," Jason assured him. "I don't think that's even possible for essence users. I'm saying you look fat. For an elf."

"This is how you try and recruit someone?" Neil asked incredulously.

"It does seem like I'm negging you, doesn't it?" Jason asked with an apologetic grimace. "Sorry. I really don't want to be that guy."

"Negging?"

"What it really comes down to is that I'm less of a best foot forward guy than an honest foot forward guy," Jason said. "What you see is what you get, and if you join up with us, there'll be a lot of this, if I'm being honest. Which I am. You've seen me at my most petty when I was dealing with Thadwick. I could say that's not a representative sample but that would be a lie. You should have seen my two-star promotion hearing. The transcript of that one must read very strangely."

"Maybe that's why you got demoted," Neil said pointedly.

"Wouldn't shock me," Jason said cheerfully. "So, on to the issue of forming a team. The first question is whether you've already joined a team. I'm sure you've had offers."

"I have had offers," Neil said. "The family is weighing them over."

"I'm guessing they want to put you on a good team. You did them a solid by putting up with Thadwick all that time."

"That is a concern for my family and not for you," Neil said. "Why should I give so much as a moment's consideration to joining your team?"

"I don't have any kind of elaborate pitch," Jason said. "All I have for you are two things: the reasons we want you to join us and the reasons you'll want you to join us."

"You think I actually want to join you?"

"Of course not," Jason said. "You haven't thought about it, yet. Let's start with why we want you to join us."

"Why would I care about your reasons?"

"Because if you join us, we'll be your team, and what we think about each other will matter. Consider how Thadwick's attitude affected your old team."

"You don't know anything about our team."

"I'm not saying I do," Jason said. "I'm just saying think about it. How did Thadwick treat you? How did that affect the team? Same for your other team member, Dustin."

Neil frowned but didn't argue the point.

"We know you're a good healer," Jason said. "Rufus Remore said you're the real thing and that really means something."

"Rufus Remore said I was good?"

"More than once," Jason said. "I may talk a lot of crap but he doesn't. If he says you're the goods, then you are. That's not why we want you though. It certainly doesn't hurt but that's not what we're looking for. You went against your own church out of principle. You stood up for people because it was right, even when it cost you. That's what we're looking for."

Jason gave Neil a wry smile.

"I know I'm an arrogant fool," Jason said. "You work with what you have. It may seem like I have no guiding principles, but I do. You stood up for what you thought was right, which just so happened to help my friend Jory and who knows how many others. Whatever else happens, whether you join our team or tell us to take a hike, I want you to know that I respect you for that. I doubt you much care what I respect or don't, but there it is."

"You keep saying us," Neil said. "Who is on this team of yours, exactly? I'm assuming Humphrey Geller. Is Jory Tillman on it, too?"

"Not Jory," Jason said. "He's all about that medical research and isn't looking for a life of adventure. It's me and Humphrey, like you said. There's also a Magic Society guy, if Emir Bahadir doesn't poach him, and my indentured servant."

"Bahadir wants to steal your team member?"

"He wants to employ him for non-adventure related purposes. He's a dab hand with the practical application of magical theory. Solid ritual magic, a bit of artifice. He just did an upgrade of the Gellers' mirage chamber."

"And did you say your indentured servant?"

"Yep," Jason said. "She's doesn't have her Adventure Society membership yet, but we're training her up."

"This isn't exactly convincing," Neil said. "A magical researcher and a halfway slave who isn't even in the society?"

"Like I said, we're training her up. She should be practising with Phoebe Geller in a training room in the cloud palace, right now. That kind of company, in that kind of location, should tell you something all by itself."

Neil shook his head.

"She was the thief everyone was chasing, right?"

"That's her," Jason said.

"And now she's training in the cloud palace to be an adventurer. How does something like that even happen?"

"The short answer? Me. Really, though, it's the same way anything happens.

You look at what you want to happen, then figure out what it'll take to get there from where you are. You can do almost anything if you're willing to do what it takes. People mostly fail at things because they balk at what they have to do. It's not that the path isn't there but that they aren't willing to walk it. There's a price they aren't willing to pay, be it literal, political, social, whatever. But if you're willing to commit, impossible is just a word for people convincing themselves not to try."

Jason gave Neil an easy smile.

"You're not one of those people," Jason said. "You proved that when you stood in front of your whole church and told them no."

Jason had not been witness to Neil's principled stand when his own church tried to take down Jory's clinic, but he had heard much about it. Rufus had been deeply impressed, otherwise Jason wouldn't be trying to recruit Neil now.

"I did think that stopping a whole church was impossible," Neil said.

"Yet you stood up to them and stopped they were. Most people would have stepped aside without ever finding out and that's what matters. You tried. That's something I want on my team."

"What about why I would want to join?" Neil asked. "You aren't exactly enticing me with tales of a double-demoted guy and his indentured servant forming a team."

"In fairness, she may be temporary. Her indenture is six months and she may quit after, I don't know."

"It sounds like you're trying to convince me to join any team except yours."

"You want a reason to join our team? Humphrey Geller is the reason."

"I've been on a team with a big name," Neil said. "That has the exact opposite of appeal."

"It's not the name," Jason said. "It's the man. Did you hear we once ran into a marsh hydra?"

"I heard. Thadwick though it was a lie."

"Of course he did," Jason said. "It came on us unexpectedly, through a submerged tunnel while we were deep underground. Humphrey was by the exit and could have gotten clear. It was too small a hole for the monster to chase him but Humphrey didn't even look at the way out. He came and he stood by us because we weren't close enough to reach that way out. And he's the one who fought it, too. The rest of us just hung around at the back and tried not to die."

Jason drained his teacup and got to his feet.

"Everyone knows what Thadwick did to you during the expedition," he said. "Humphrey Geller will never do that. He'll walk into a field of death for no more reason than you're there already. I have to imagine that appeals to a man who literally stood in the path of his own church."

Jason snagged the last finger cake from the tray.

"We aren't the most impressive team," Jason said. "What you need to remember though is that you and I are adventurers. Ask yourself, what's more valuable than people who will stand shoulder to shoulder with you when things are at their worst?"

Jason bit the small piece of cake in half, muttering appreciatively.

"Thanks for your time, Neil. And the tea. If you'd told your butler to kick me out, it would have been understandable."

Neil got up and showed Jason to the door. As he watched Jason walk towards the gate, he called out to him.

"Yeah?" Jason asked, turning back.

"You have a shadow teleport, right?"

"That's right."

"And that hydra caught you deep underground, right."

"Yeah."

"Couldn't you have gotten to that exit, too?"

Jason scratched his head, absently thinking out it.

"It never occurred to me," Jason said. "It was really scary."

24

MORE THAN ONE CLOWN

Phoebe Geller walked through the Adventure Society campus to the north shore. The cloud palace loomed off the end of the dock, dwarfing any building in Greenstone. Emir's chief of staff, Constance, came across the cloud bridge to meet her.

"Mistress Geller," Constance greeted. "This way, please."

"This is a treat," Phoebe said as they crossed the cloud bridge to the entrance. "Everyone wants to take a look in here."

"Mr Bahadir has had many fruitful dealings with the Geller family," Constance said. "He is happy to welcome you, albeit vicariously through me. Adding to his own affairs, recent events have been a heavy claimant on his time."

"I wouldn't expect a gold-ranker to make time for an iron-ranker like me. Even a silver-ranker, like yourself, is more than gratifying."

The cloud bridge spanned a few metres over the water below, leading to the large door that served as the main entrance. Like all doors on the palace, it was not an actual door but a section of wall marked out from the rest by its blue colouration and gold edging.

"Wait here a moment please," Constance requested as she walked straight through. A few moments later, the door started rippling like the surface of a pond.

"Please enter," Phoebe heard Constance say.

After a brief moment of hesitation, she stepped through. Inside was a huge atrium with vast open space and large windows that just looked like more wall from the outside. There were doorways, two grand staircases and plants all over, in planters, decorative pots and even growing right out of the walls. Most impressive was a plant-ringed pond between the two staircases, fed by a small waterfall from two floors up.

"Wow," Phoebe said. "He really fits all this in a bottle?"

"The plants are the trickiest part," Constance said. "It's almost impossible to place living material inside dimensional storage, and even then, only some carefully chosen plants are viable. Your aura signature had been added to the cloud palace's registry, so you'll be able to access any of the unrestricted areas of the palace. That's now, or on any future visit."

"Thank you," Phoebe said, still craning her neck as she looked around.

"Miss Wexler is in one of our training rooms. If you'll follow me, please."

Constance led Phoebe through the palace, and out from the main building, along a walkway that rested on the surface of the water towards one of the four surrounding wings. A fresh breeze played through the open-air passage as water sloshed against the side. They entered the guest wing, passing a ballroom, a lounge and a dining hall on the way to an elevation platform that took them up two levels.

They stepped off in a training hall that occupied the entire level and was the height of a three-storey building. The walls were almost all transparent, giving views of the shore, the ocean and the other wings of the palace. The platform deposited them in an observation area, separated from the rest by a translucent barrier. It was raised higher than the main combat area and included two change rooms, rows of seats and a drinks cabinet, all pointed out by Constance.

On the other side of the barrier was the main combat area, currently full of artificial terrain made from cloud-stuff. The cloud was wildly coloured in blue, purple, orange and gold, making for a strange, alien landscape. Moving through it at blistering speed was a woman being pursued by faceless people and monsters—training dummies, rendered from the colourful and apparently quite versatile cloud-stuff.

"That is Miss Sophie Wexler," Constance said as they watched the woman dart about the room. The dummies chasing her were various shapes and sizes, from humanoid to monster, waist-high to bigger than a long-hall wagon. The smaller figures were quick and chased after her directly. The larger forms clambered right over the terrain or sent lengthy tentacles snaking around it.

Sophie had her hair tied back in a simple ponytail that flicked around behind her head. Her clothes were light and loose, white against her dark skin. She was practically flying around the room, making the most of the terrain with her speed and agility. Using movement to spread out the pursuing dummies, she would isolate a few at a time and turn the tables, thrashing them with a flurry of attacks before escaping, leaving the encroaching reinforcements behind.

Phoebe noted there was some kind of power attached to each of Sophie's strikes as only a few blows would tear the smaller dummies to pieces. Against the larger ones she employed hit and run tactics, taking them down across multiple attacks. Big or small, however, each fallen dummy was immediately replaced with another, creating an unwinnable challenge.

Phoebe sat down to watch as Constance took her leave. The acrobatic techniques Sophie used seemed wild and inefficient to Phoebe's eyes, yet she made it work. She was unarmed, yet the terrain became her weapon as she flitted about like a dragonfly. Her speed and agility were incredible, to the point Phoebe had a hard time believing she was iron rank.

Phoebe looked on in fascination as Sophie fought off waves of endlessly replenishing monsters. Inevitably, Sophie started to flag and her opponents came closer and closer to boxing her in. Eventually, she was overrun, going down fighting before the dummies and terrain vanished as she collapsed beneath their attacks. The sudden empty combat area left Sophie on her back, panting on a suddenly flat, wide-open area.

She rolled over onto her front, pushing herself heavily onto her knees and then feet. She glanced over at Phoebe through the transparent barrier and trudged over, up the slope leading to the raised barrier and straight through the wall.

"You can only walk through it while the room is inactive," Sophie said, seeing Phoebe's surprised expression. "You don't have to worry about a loose dummy getting thrown through it."

There were two open-faced drink cabinets on the wall. One was filled with various kinds of liquor and a stack of small glasses. The other had glasses of chilled water, from which Sophie took one and drained it. She threw it at the wall, into which it vanished without a sound as she took a second from the cabinet. New glasses emerged from the back of the cabinet to replace the one she took, water pouring from above to fill them.

Phoebe still had traces of her family's Greenstone origins, but was lighter-skinned than the locals, being from a distant branch family. Her hair was light brown, in a pixie cut that was short and practical but flattered her round face and delicate features.

"You don't look much like Geller," Sophie said.

"If you mean Humphrey, we're only distant cousins. I'm Phoebe Geller."

"Sophie Wexler. I've heard you can fight."

"I've heard the same about you," Phoebe said with a challenging grin. "You mostly seemed to be running away, though."

"Oh, is that how it is?" Sophie asked.

"Think you can prove me wrong?"

Sophie pointed at one of the changing rooms.

"You can get changed in there."

Jason caught the loop line back from the Davone residence and spotted a familiar face as he emerged from the Adventure Society transit terminal.

"Gary," he called out with a wave and hurried over to his friend. He hadn't seen him in weeks and clasped the big furry man in a quick hug.

"Cripes, Gary. I don't like to question a man's hygiene but I haven't seen you in two weeks and I don't think you've seen a shower. You want some crystal wash?"

Gary looked tired and dishevelled, although not so much as the man next to him. He was a human in scholarly robes with a lopsided Magic Society official's pin on his chest. He had an unruly mop of hair and an unkempt beard. His iron-rank aura meant his mid-thirties appearance was probably accurate. All in all, he looked like a slightly older, homeless version of Clive.

"I'm pretty ripe on the vine, alright," Gary said. "We've been in a workshop all week, sleeping on cots. Me and Russell here have been going over the remains of the construct monsters the expedition brought back," Gary said. "I've been stripping them down for Russell to figure out how they work."

"We've been trying to work out how someone either snuck in or built from scratch a whole army of animated constructs without anyone realising," Russell said. "What Clive told us this morning about the origin of the people we're facing filled in some important pieces and we had a breakthrough."

"He had a breakthrough," Gary said. "I was just taking the things apart."

"Don't even try and play down your contribution," Russell said. "Without your expertise in deconstructing the intact specimen, the crucial piece could have been damaged, overlooked or lost entirely."

"Take the compliment, Gary," Jason said. "Russell, I think we've met."

"Yes," Russell said. "I was present for your initial Adventure Society intake. I've heard about you a lot since."

"You have?"

"If nothing else," Russell said, "Lucian Lamprey really, really doesn't like you."

"The feeling's mutual."

"I'm Russell Clouns," he introduced himself. "Nice to meet you again."

"Likewise," Jason said. "Clowns, you say?"

"Yes, Clouns."

"As in, more than one clown?"

"I'm not sure I follow."

"I'm talking about multiple clowns."

"The Clouns aren't a big or prestigious family," Russell said, confusion still plain on his face.

"But you're a whole family of clowns," Jason said.

"Uh, yes? I'm still not sure why that matters."

"I thought you'd have bigger shoes."

"Shoes?" Russell asked, looking down.

"Jason," Gary said, "we're both too tired for you right now."

"Yeah, you should probably just go," Jason told him, then turned back to Russell. "Do you all travel around in one tiny carriage?"

"Some portion of this conversation definitely seems to have gotten past me," Russell said.

"No, that's just Jason," Gary said. "He takes some getting used to. Jason, we have to go report some findings and then get some sleep."

"Good going," Jason said. "You can tell me all about it once you wake up."

"I'm thinking that will be in about two days," Gary said, Russell nodding his agreement. They parted ways; Jason watched as they trudged tiredly towards the administration building.

[Russell Clouns] has been added to your contact list.

"That's disappointing," Jason mused to himself. "Finding out clowns were all a family of interdimensional travellers would have been fun."

Sophie and Phoebe gulped down large glasses of water, Phoebe following Sophie's lead in throwing her empty glass at the wall. They took fresh glasses from the cooler cabinet and sprawled into seats. Phoebe sighed as the soft cloud furniture enveloped her.

"You can really fight," Phoebe said.

"You too," Sophie agreed. "I'm envious of all those special attacks."

"I'm envious of that ability that negates them. Only my biggest attacks got through at all and I couldn't believe how quickly you learned to pick them out and dodge. You're impossible to pin down."

Phoebe settled happily in her chair, sipping at her second glass while Sophie moved into a meditative, cross-legged pose. Sophie recovered quickly, looking fresh when her eyes snapped open.

"Is that a recovery power?"

Sophie nodded.

"Nice. Is it just mana and stamina, or health, too?"

"All three."

"Nice. Not much good in a fight, but don't underestimate the value of quick recovery between skirmishes. When things went wrong in the big expedition it was a series of running battles. We'd sometimes only get moments between fights and a power like that would make a huge difference."

"I'm not looking for any big battles," Sophie said.

"When you're an adventurer," Phoebe said, "they sometimes come looking for you."

"Adventurer," Sophie said. "I'm not sure I'm ready to pass that assessment."

"It's not that hard," Phoebe said. "Mostly they'll test your combat ability and you have no problems there. Always pay attention to what you're going to be up against. If you can afford it, buy a monster catalogue from the Magic Society so you can look up the next monster. Know what they can do going in and be ready for it. The other thing they'll test is judgement. If the invigilators try throwing you at something and it doesn't feel right, then tell them no. It's what they're looking for."

"Thanks," Sophie said. "This whole thing is crazy. I can't tell if meeting Asano was the best or the worst thing that ever happened to me. You know him, right?"

"Not well, but he's not hard to figure out."

"He's not?"

"Jason is a lot like Danielle Geller," Phoebe said. "She's subtle and refined where he's outrageous and disruptive, but they operate the same way. There's always a sense with Danielle that she's playing a game only she knows about. It's like you only ever see her from an angle. Jason is the same, except loud and distracting instead of subtle and nuanced. Basically, they're both good people who think like bad people."

"That might explain why I always come away feeling disoriented."

Phoebe laughed. "Yeah, I know that feeling."

"But you think he's a good guy?"

"I do," she said. "I've seen a little and heard a lot. That said, I should really show you this recording of a fight he had with my brother."

"Geller—Humphrey—said something about a recording," Sophie said.

"Oh, it's something to see," Phoebe said. "I can bring it along if you want to do this again. There has to be a projector in this place somewhere, right?"

"I'd like that," Sophie said.

"What do you mean, no one's here?" Gary asked.

"They are all important people, undertaking their own tasks to respond to this threat," Genevieve said. "They aren't just waiting around for people to come and tell them things. They will convene this evening and you can request to be heard then. Otherwise, the head of the inquisition team is present. At this moment she is the highest-ranked Adventure Society official in Greenstone."

"Forget that lady," Gary said. "Russell, go home and get some sleep. I'm going to the cloud palace. Either Bahadir is there or I can get some sleep. It's a victory either way."

⁂

As Jason arrived at the cloud palace, his mood and expression both went icy when he spotted Thalia Mercer departing. She spotted him in turn and they met halfway across the cloud bridge.

"Hello Jason."

"Thalia."

"I'm sorry about how things ended with you and Cassandra."

"I don't care."

Anger crossed Thalia's face.

"My daughter isn't worth enough for you to care about losing her?"

"Of course she is," Jason said, resuming his passage across the bridge by walking past her. "I don't care that you're sorry."

25

RESURRECTION

Emir's private study was a vast, domed area occupying the entire top floor of the cloud palace's tallest and most central tower. As it was one of the restricted areas of the palace, the only access to his study was an elevating platform from lower floors—or the power of flight. The platform would not activate for anyone but Constance and Emir, requiring Constance to escort Jason and Clive up. Emir had the dome set to almost full transparency, subtly dimming the bright sunlight while keeping the room fresh and cool.

At a glance, the room seemed mostly empty when they entered, aside from the people in it and a few small circles of water in the floor from which plants were growing. The only furniture was the seats the existing occupants were sitting in, but two more chairs rose up from the floor to accommodate Jason and Clive. Constance departed, riding the platform back down, only for a new platform to manifest in its place.

"Thank you for coming," Emir said to them as they sat.

Already in the room were Gary and Russell, both looking better for regular meals, showers and a couple of good nights' sleep. They exchanged greetings, Jason noting that Clive and Russell seemed to know each other well. Clive had expounded more than once of the state of Magic Society personnel, but it seemed Russell was amongst the few Clive considered genuinely capable.

"You were lucky to catch us," Jason said. "We're about to take Wexler out for another monster run."

"Are you going to be working on group tactics?" Emir asked.

"Humphrey's gotten excited about devising tactics based around our team setup," Jason said. "Finally putting all that training his family gave him to use. We're still short a healer but we can at least get a start on things."

"I'm surprised you're leaving it to Humphrey instead of doing it yourself," Gary said.

"I may be a little self-impressed—"

"A little?" Clive interjected, getting a chuckle from Gary.

"Yes," Jason said, panning a pointed look from one to the other. "A little. I know better than to think I know more than someone with training or experience."

"You do?" Gary asked.

"Yes," Jason said. "I do." His shoulders slumped. "Farrah hammered that into me. She wouldn't put up with it."

The room fell silent for a moment as all eyes fell to the floor, except for Russell who was smart enough to stay quiet.

"We found something," Gary said, breaking the reverie.

"We're pretty sure this is how they made all those constructs," Russell added, taking a small object wrapped in cloth from a pocket in his robes. "Gary said you have an ability to identify objects and thought we should show you, to confirm."

He went to pass Jason the item, but Jason stopped him with a raised hand. In a moment, Jason added Emir, Gary and Russell to the party that already contained him and Clive so they could all see what he was about to.

"This ability has so much potential," Emir said. "How many people can you include at a time?"

"Myself plus nine more," Jason said.

Russell opened the cloth and took out the object inside. It was the size and shape of a monster core but made up of intricate, clockwork mechanisms.

"Touch it," Jason said.

Item: [Clockwork Core] (iron rank, rare)
***The core of an artificial monster.* (crafting material, magic core).**

Effect: When used as the core of a construct creature, the materials and processes used are significantly simplified.

"That is useful," Russell said. "Can you do this for any item?"

"It doesn't work on very high-rank items," Jason said.

"Still, possibilities abound. You should come work for the Magic Society."

Jason groaned.

"I've told him, believe me," Clive said.

Russell wrapped the core back up, returning it to his pocket.

"Thank you for that, Jason," Emir said. "It's nice to confirm what we're dealing with."

"So, these things are how they were able to build their construct army," Jason said. "Did the Builder supply them?"

"Not directly," Russell said. "Clockwork cores are produced by a creature called a clockwork king."

"Some kind of monster?" Clive asked.

"No," Russell said. "I managed to find some records on clockwork cores in the temple of Knowledge's library, including their source, these clockwork kings."

"What manner of creature are they?" Jason asked.

"In our world, creatures like dragons are highly magical, but they are actual creatures that are born, live and die. They aren't monsters. Clockwork kings are the same, but they aren't native to our world. They're native to the world the Builder has created."

"You think they've come here, somehow?" Jason asked.

"Yes," Russell said. "The bad news is, they're gold-rank entities. The good news is that I don't think there is one in this area. The constructs the expedition encountered were simple affairs. Basically, blocks of wood, stone and metal slapped together around one of these cores. Clockwork kings use the cores they create to craft more intricate and elaborate constructs. We haven't seen anything like what is described in the records I found."

"If they're crafting things, does that mean they're intelligent?" Jason asked.

"Oh, yes," Russell said. "They are likely to occupy key leadership positions."

"Are they artificial creatures themselves, or living things?" Jason asked.

"From my understanding of the Builder's world," Clive contributed, "that isn't a strict delineation."

"That comports with what I found as well," Russell agreed.

"Is there any chance there is a clockwork king here and the best constructs are being held back to hide that fact?" Jason asked. "Lull us into a false sense of security?"

"It's possible," Emir said. "I think they would have used them to try and hold the astral space from us, though."

"It's unlikely," Clive said. "Travel between worlds is not easy to arrange, even for a great astral being like the Builder. They can't facilitate it directly because they're inimical to physical reality. An attempt to directly interact with a physical reality would be too destructive. As far as I'm aware, travelling between realities is the domain of diamond rankers, which means the Builder would have to rely on how many diamond rankers he can spare from whatever other interests he has going on throughout the cosmos."

"You said destructive," Jason said. "I wouldn't have thought the Builder would care about that."

"It doesn't," Clive said. "The World-Phoenix does, however, and the great astral beings are careful about encroaching upon one another's interests. It's why they don't just resurrect any of their key minions who get killed as outworlders."

"What do you mean, resurrect?" Gary asked.

"It's about how death works," Clive said. "When the soul dies, it only lingers with the body for a small time. Usually minutes, but an annihilated body might have the soul depart in seconds, while freezing to death might have it linger for an hour or even longer. It's why if a gold rank healer can repair the body in that grace period, the death can be turned back."

"I didn't realise that was possible," Jason said. He was not the only one in the room thinking bitterly of Farrah.

"For those of us who don't die next to one of the most powerful healers in the world," Clive said, "our souls leave the body and the physical reality it's in. An untethered soul is an astral object and drifts into the astral."

"Where do outworlders come into it?" Gary asked, glancing at Jason.

"An outworlder is someone whose soul has re-entered a physical reality, reflexively manifesting a body for itself," Clive explained.

"Like a monster," Jason added.

"Yes," Clive said. "An outworlder's body is akin to that of a monster, or a summoned familiar. It is physical substance forged out of raw magic. An in-between existence of the astral and the physical."

"That's how you described astral spaces," Emir pointed out.

"I did," Clive said. "The analogy is apt. The point, however, is that an outworlder is a soul that has been pushed, by whatever means, from the astral and into a physical reality. This normally happens when natural, magical phenomena connect one physical reality with another, creating a channel that drags someone between the two realities. Their body is annihilated as it passes through the astral, then reconstitutes itself when entering its new physical reality."

"I see what you're saying," Jason said. "If one of these great astral beings took one of the souls floating around the astral and shoved it into a world, it would do what souls do when that happens. It would make a new body and you have someone resurrected as an outworlder."

"Exactly," Clive said. "They don't to that, though, because of the astral being called the Reaper."

"Is this the same Reaper, as in, Way of the Reaper?" Jason asked.

"What do you know about the Way of the Reaper?" Emir asked, eyes narrowing as he looked at Jason.

"That it was the martial art of an ancient order of assassins."

"The Order of the Reaper," Clive said. "And yes; it's the same Reaper. The Reaper is very big on the finality of death. Some consider it the true god of death, as all our god of death governs is the passage of the soul into the astral. The final resting place of souls is the astral, where our gods hold no sway."

"And the other great astral beings don't take the souls they want and resurrect them because they won't cross the Reaper," Emir said.

"Exactly," Clive said. "For the same reason, the Builder doesn't just smash apart worlds and take the pieces it likes, because it will not cross the World-Phoenix. So the Builder gathers followers to carve off astral spaces, leaving the worlds they are attached to battered, but intact."

"So you're saying," Gary said, "that if we convince this Reaper to give her up, we can bring Farrah back?"

"Don't even think about it," Clive said. "The Reaper would never entertain the request of mortals. It would disdain a diamond-ranker, let alone any of us."

"What about this ancient order?" Gary asked. "Bahadir, you're here to investigate them, right? You must know something."

"I do," Emir said. "I know the Order of the Reaper were an ancient cult of assassins. They brought death. I have seen no indication anywhere, ever, that they even tried to reverse it. I also know that they were scoured from this world, root and branch, by a coalition of churches, long ago. Only ruins filled with the dead remain."

"Even if they still existed," Clive said, "they venerated the Reaper. Bringing someone back would be anathema to them."

"Do not let the hope of bringing her back take hold in you, Gareth," Emir said. "Let her live in memory. Trying to bring her back will only stain those memories."

"There has to be a way," Gary insisted.

"Gary," Clive said. "Even gods can't bring her back."

"Maybe we should return our attention to the problems at hand," Russell suggested. "The clockwork kings."

"Yes," Emir agreed firmly. "The most likely scenario is that the Builder was unable to send enough to this world to spare one on a low-magic area like Greenstone. They would have sent the minimal number of people, recruiting locals and using these clockwork cores to literally build their numbers up."

"So what do we do with this information?" Russell asked.

"Like everything else, we'll disseminate it to the wider Adventure Society and hope it helps," Emir said.

"You stripped those construct creatures down to the base components, right?" Clive asked. "If there is anything you found them using that's hard to source locally, get a list to Rufus Remore. He's already following that trail and it might help him."

"We can do that," Russell said. "If we're done here, we can go and look through our notes right now. Gary?"

Gary said nothing but gave a sullen nod.

"We'll be off too, then," Jason said.

"Thank you all for coming," Emir said. "Jason, we've set Farrah's wake for the end of the week. Be sure and be back for that."

"I thought we weren't doing anything for Farrah until her body was back home with her family," Clive said.

"This is informal," Emir said. "Something for those of us here who knew her."

"Beth Cavendish's team wanted to attend."

"They fought with us during the expedition," Gary said. "I'll see they're notified."

"Alright, then," Jason said. "We'll be off. Do I need someone to work the elevator?"

"No," Emir said. "It won't take you up, but it will take you down just fine."

Clive and Jason walked to the elevation platform and descended out of sight.

"I'm sorry," Emir told Gary. "I didn't expect the discussion to go in that direction."

"It's alright," Gary nodded. "It's just… everything fell apart when she died. Rufus and I have barely spoken since we got back. I haven't felt this alone in a long time."

Gary, Russell and Emir had a message pop up in front of them.

Party leader [Jason Asano] has kicked you from the group.

They all looked at the message, then Gary let out a tension-breaking laugh.

"Well, that's just rude," he said.

26
MANIFESTATION

Four people were in Sophie and Belinda's guest suite as images played on a crystal recording projector. Sophie and Belinda were both present, as were Phoebe and Jory. Phoebe had brought the recording crystal while Belinda had roped Jory into taking a day off. He had been reluctant, but he hadn't taken a break since the clinic re-opened. With a priest of the healer on hand, he let himself be talked into it.

Phoebe was the only one who had seen the recording of Jason's fight before. The others looked on with various reactions as they followed the recording from the perspective of Rick and his team.

"That laughter is creepy," Belinda said.

"I knew there was a dark side to Jason," Jory said, "but this is a bit much."

"A bit much is right," Sophie said. "He's being a complete ham. Wait, why is he stepping out into the open? He's just going to get speared. See, what did I just say?"

Belinda put a hand over her mouth in horror. "Did he just lick the spear?"

They watched until the recording ended, freezing with the image of Jason with his foot on the back of Jonah's head, drowning him in the mud.

"That was horrifying," Belinda said. "You had that guy chasing you?"

"It wasn't real," Jory said, although his words sounded empty.

"It was theatrics," Sophie said. "Get into an opponent's head and you've already beaten them. That kind of over-the-top ridiculousness would only work on people with no real experience."

A melodious chime rang, indicating a visitor at the door and Belinda got up to let in Clive and Jason.

"Oh," Jason said sadly as he recognised the frozen image of himself and Jonah. "I don't like that recording being out there."

"Given how absurd you were, I can see why," Sophie said. "You spend the whole time playing ridiculous games instead of just taking them out."

"I didn't have the skills for that approach," Jason said. "There were five of them and going monster was the only thing I could think of to mess with their heads. If they were thinking straight, I would have lost."

"I'll admit it's good to show people what you'll do if they cross you," Sophie said. "Next time, cut out the maniacal laughter and stick to the horrifying death. That bit at the end where you drown the guy in mud was good."

"That man in the mud," Jason said softly. "His name was Jonah. He's dead for real, now, along with another member of that group. I have no interest in watching myself kill them."

"I think it's time for you to head off, Soph," Belinda said. "You go fight monsters, or whatever. Jory and I going to have a picnic."

"We are?" Jory asked.

"Yes," Belinda said. "Thank you again for making up the basket, Jason."

"No worries."

Jason, Humphrey, Clive and Sophie were in the wood mill region of the delta, in the middle of a plantation forest. Their objective was a pack of monsters called flanards. Flanards were emaciated creatures with four arms and distended jaws full of pointed teeth. Individually they were weaker than margolls, but they appeared in even larger groups. Their numbers made them perfect for exploring team tactics, which was the reason Humphrey had selected that particular contract.

The thick plantation had trees growing in neat rows. Fighting amongst them, Sophie led three of the creatures between the trunks and into the waiting sword of Humphrey. He stepped out with a horizontal sweep that cleaved two of them in half while the other dropped to the ground, the blade barely passing over it. It sprang up and resumed its pursuit of Sophie.

Three more had been chasing after Jason but had lost him in the shadows. Spotting Sophie rush past, they joined her now lone pursuer. Sophie scrambled, seemingly in a panic as they joined the chase. She changed direction and the monsters followed, without noticing the odd mark on one of the trees. They dashed blindly after Sophie until the sound of Clive snapping his fingers preceded the ground underneath them blasting upward, the force of his magical explosion tearing them all to pieces.

Humphrey came jogging through the woods, joining Sophie and Clive.

"That was good," Jason said, emerging from a shadow. "Nice plan, Humphrey."

"The key is to stay flexible," Humphrey said. "Situations always change and rigid plans don't work. Rather than over-complicated stratagems, if we have a learned and practiced series of flexible tactics, we can rapidly adapt to those changing situations. This was one of the simpler tactics outlined in the booklets I gave you all."

"I can't believe you wrote those," Jason said. "When you do something, you don't mess about, Humphrey. I think we're all pretty impressed."

The others nodded their agreement.

"Now we have them," Humphrey said, "we need to make sure we learn them with our heads, then practise until we know them. If we combine a shared knowledge of a flexible tactical set with the communications advantage of Jason's ability, we'll be ready to react to any situation."

"Like a malevolent gold-ranker who forces us into a knitting competition with our lives on the line," Jason said.

"What?" Humphrey asked. The others looked at Jason with confusion.

"Humphrey said 'any situation,' so I posited a situation we might encounter."

"How is that helpful?" Sophie asked.

"Fine," Humphrey said. "We'll be ready for *most* situations. These tactics are all preliminary, though. They're worth learning to get into the habit, but they need to be adjusted once we get a healer and learn their capabilities, plus fill out our abilities, advance to bronze and so on. We'll be adjusting and readjusting in an ongoing manner."

"Any word on that healer?" Clive asked.

"Melissa Davone paid my mother a visit at our townhouse in the city," Humphrey said. "Davone is at least considering joining us."

"How many abilities do you have left to awaken?" Jason asked Humphrey.

"Two," Humphrey said. "One from the magic essence and one from might. What about you?"

"Three. Two from dark and one from doom."

"I still have eight to go," Sophie said.

"Still early days, for you," Humphrey said. "Jason and I gained our essences months ago. Getting as many as you have in under a single month is a good start."

After Jason looted the monsters. they set out back for the city. The wood mill region was less accessible by water than most of the delta, so Clive had requisitioned a magic-propelled, open-top carriage. Clive sat in the driver's seat, with the others in the back. When rain started coming down, droplets rolled off a magical barrier that covered the carriage. Normally invisible, it briefly shimmered blue as raindrops

"What is that?" Sophie asked with alarm.

"It's just a barrier to keep the rain off," Clive said. It only affects water.

"But where's the water coming from?" she asked. "Is a monster doing that?"

Clive looked back, sharing a confused glance with Humphrey and Jason.

"It's just rain," Jason said.

"Rain?"

"You don't know what rain is?" Jason asked.

"Oh," Humphrey said. "Have you never left the city before?"

"Not since I first went there as a girl," Sophie said. "That was when I was very young. I don't really remember anything before that. Are you saying water just falling out of the sky is somehow normal?"

"Yeah," Jason said. "It doesn't rain in the city? I thought it just hadn't since I got here."

"It's one of the oddities of the local climate," Clive said. "The combination of the desert, the delta and the water-affinity of the mass of green stone making up the Island impacts the weather in certain ways. One of those ways is that while it rains regularly in the delta, it never rains in the city."

"That's weird," Jason said.

"How does the water get up in the sky?" Sophie asked.

"It evaporates," Clive said.

"I thought you were going to say magic," Jason said. Then he and Clive between them gave a basic explanation of the water cycle.

The carriage continued on as the rain grew heavier. Sophie and Jason both looked up at the water splashing off the invisible rain barrier, Jason with wonder and Sophie with wariness. They were travelling along an embankment road through marshlands when Humphrey suddenly called out.

"Stop the carriage!"

He pointed off to the side of the road where a vortex of rainbow light was swirling in the air.

"What's that?" Jason asked.

"A magical manifestation," Humphrey said. "It's rare to actually see them happen."

"What's a magical manifestation?" Sophie asked.

"It's a natural manifestation of magic from the ethereal to the physical," Clive explained. "Magic, coalescing into a physical form. Most likely it'll be a monster, but it could be an awakening stone or even an essence. Let's go take a look."

"How are we going to get out there?" Humphrey asked. "Jason can walk on water, but the rest of us can't."

"I can run on water," Sophie said. "I sink if I stop moving, though."

"I have something," Clive said. "I was inspired by Jason's preparedness when we found that buried complex and put a few things into my own storage space."

They left the carriage and its rain barrier, so they started getting wet. Sophie looked trepidatiously up at the sky as they made their way down the steep embankment to the water's edge. From his inventory, Clive pulled an entire raft, which then fell into the water. It tipped Clive off-balance in doing so. Clive went in with it and came up sputtering.

The raft wasn't large, but had just enough room for Humphrey, Sophie and Clive. Clive sat sodden at the front, his wet clothes tracing out his lanky frame. With a hand on a metal panel near the front of the otherwise wooden raft, he magically directed it to drift slowly in the direction of the colourful vortex. Jason walked alongside, his cloak both letting him walk on water and keeping off the rain.

The vortex was around two metres across. Despite what looked like furious roiling, it didn't so much as disturb the air. It was as if it didn't really exist at all. They stopped and waited for the process of manifestation to be complete.

"Are we alright to be this close?" Sophie asked.

"It's fine," Clive said. "It can't affect us, and we can't affect it without some high-end ritual magic."

"It's quite pretty," Jason said, taking out a recording crystal and tossing it up to float over his head. He started explaining the vortex for when he showed it to his family. After he had done that, he turned the crystal on Sophie.

"I've mentioned her in earlier entries," Jason said, "but this is her in the flesh. My nubile slave girl, Sophie Wexler."

Sophie was sitting on the raft, so her flashing jab caught him on the thigh.

"Ow. As you can see, she has some behavioural problems."

Sophie turned to Humphrey and Clive.

"If I drown him out here," she asked them, "would you two back me up and say it was an accident?"

"Absolutely," Clive said.

"Someone was going to do it sooner or later," Humphrey agreed.

"As you can also see," Jason said, "she has ruthlessly suborned my minions."

"Did you just call us minions?" Humphrey asked.

"Nope," Jason said. "My voice just sounds weird because of the rain."

They waited several minutes before the vortex started to contract, growing smaller and smaller.

"It's not a monster," Clive said. "I can see the magic taking form. It's going to be an awakening stone."

"Nice," Jason said. "How do we decide who gets it?"

"Miss Wexler has the most need," Humphrey said. "You and I only have a few spots left open and should probably wait for Bahadir's event."

"Humphrey, you should call me Sophie," she said, flashing Humphrey a rare smile before dropping it and turning to Jason. "You shouldn't."

"Harsh," Jason said.

"You did call her a slave girl," Humphrey said.

"I think you're misremembering," Jason said. "That doesn't sound like me; I'm all about egalitarianism."

The vortex continued shrinking until it was the size of a fist, coalescing into a blue awakening stone that fell into the water with a plop. The others all turned to look at Clive.

"What?" he asked.

"You already went in once," Humphrey said.

Clive saw the others were a unified front and groaned as he dropped off the side of the raft. The water was waist-deep but he had to plunge down to his neck as he rummaged about where the stone had dropped.

"It's times like this that I wish Onslow were a turtle instead of a tortoise," Clive said.

He let out a yelp of pain, lurching to his feet and waving his arm around. A small figure was being flailed about, its teeth clamped onto Clive's hand. It was thrown off and started hovering in the air. It was a small, fairy-like figure, about the size of a human hand, with a naked, androgynous body, dark blue hair and insect wings that buzzed rapidly to keep it aloft. Clutched in its arms was the awakening stone, almost as big as it was.

The stone was wet, muddy and, under the weight of it, the creature could barely hold itself in the air. It tried to fly off with its prize but the stone was too much, slipping through its arms and back into the water. A furious Clive made a grab at the creature, but it flitted away, turning back to poke its tongue out before zipping away through the air.

"I hate those things," Clive muttered as he smeared healing ointment over the wound on his hand.

"You've seen those before?" Jason asked.

"Wetland Pixies? Oh, yeah. They love eating eels, so they were always hanging about the farm when I was growing up. I can't tell you how many boots Nana lost throwing them at the damn things. She never hit anything and the boots usually landed in the bog."

"Well you'd best get back down and grab the stone," Jason said. "There might be more of those things in there."

27
POTENTIAL

In his guest suite in the cloud palace, Rufus was at a desk with papers arrayed in front of him. Ground assessments, potential designs, integration requirements. He wearily ran his hands over his face, trying to maintain concentration. While he awaited word on various investigations, Rufus had resumed the task of establishing the academy annex he was working on with the Geller family.

Adris Dorgan had kept his word and was making progress in chasing down the materials on the lists provided by Clive and now Russell. Certain shipments had come into the port at Hornis before being moved to private vessels for destinations thus far unknown. Dorgan was currently digging deeper into the ownership of those private vessels.

Rufus found his attention constantly straying to Builder cultists. The nebulous enemy who, at that very moment, was hidden away, advancing their destructive plots. He wondered how many more friends he would lose before they were finally stopped. After getting up, he walked out onto the balcony and let the sea breeze wash refreshingly over him.

He decided to leave the work for the moment and go find Gary, who seemed equally at a loss after finishing his own project with the constructs. They hadn't seen much of one another since coming back from the expedition and there was a friction there that Farrah had always smoothed out. Jason's presence had helped them through the worst of it in the wake of her death, but her absence lingered between them.

Rufus and Gary had adjacent suites in the guest wing, connected by a terrace. Rufus wandered over and saw Gary inside with a half-empty bottle of some rotgut he must have bought in the city; Emir would never stock anything so cheap and nasty. Gary had dissolved the entire outer wall of his suite, leaving it open to the fresh air. Gary, slouched in a chair, nodded his acknowledgement of Rufus's arrival.

"Day drinking?" Rufus asked. "It's barely mid-morning."

"Want to join?" Gary asked.

"Yes," Rufus said, walking over to a cabinet and grabbing a glass.

"We can do it out here?" Sophie asked, looking uncertainly at the village around them.

"Clive can," Jason said. "He's more flexible than most, so he can do it just about anywhere you have a flat space."

"It might seem unusual for the two of you to just up and do it in the middle of a village square," Humphrey said, "but it's something the villagers will be eager to see."

"It won't take long," Jason said. "Clive can just slip it into you out here and we can head off."

"He's right; it won't take long," Clive assured her. "Even in less comfortable conditions, I'm very quick to finish."

"Alright," Sophie said. "It's not like it's my first time."

"You heard the lady, Clive," Jason said. "Whip it out."

Clive took out the awakening stone they retrieved from the marsh and passed it to Sophie.

Item: [Awakening Stone of the Rain] (unranked, common)

An awakening stone containing the power of rain. **(consumable, awakening stone).**

Requirements: Unawakened essence ability.

Effect: Awakens an essence ability.

You have 8 unawakened essence abilities.

Using his abilities, Clive balanced out the ambient magic and drew a ritual circle. As Humphrey predicted, doing so in the village square drew curious onlookers. The ritual went off without incident, awakening Sophie's new ability.

Ability: [Between the Raindrops] (Swift)
Special ability.

Cost: High mana per second and high stamina per second.
Cooldown: None.

Current rank: Iron 0 (00%)

Effect (iron): Increased reflexes and spatial awareness.

"That's it?" Humphrey asked. "That seems like an exhaustive cost for increased reflexes."

"Attack her," Jason said.

"What?" Humphrey asked.

"Attack her," Jason said. "You come in from the right and I'll pincer her from the left."

"I'm not sure that's a good idea."

"Do it," Sophie said. "No weapons; I won't hurt you too badly."

Jason grinned and leapt forward, Humphrey doing the same with a grimace. They unleashed simultaneously from either side but it was like Sophie had eyes in the back of her head. Not only did she react to their every move, but she did so the moment they made them. Soon, Humphrey was sent stumbling back from a kick to the face. Jason had it worse, folded over on the ground as he clutched his crotch with both hands.

"Did you have to go right for the plums?" he squeaked out.

She walked over and looked down at him.

"You're the one who wanted to attack me," she said.

Neil Davone had started spending time at the Mercer family compound as a boy. Thadwick had needed friends his own age and the Davone and Kettering families, with their close ties to the Mercers, had frequently sent their own boys over. The Mercer residence was the most impressive in Greenstone, with its five interconnected towers and immaculate grounds. Even with tyrannical toddler Thadwick as a playmate, it had always been an exciting place to visit, growing up.

As he had gotten older, the attractions of the Mercer household for Neil went through various changes. As he became more curious about the world, the impressive library fed his mind. When he became an essence user, he made full use of the training facilities that Thadwick disdained. The rest of the Mercers were more than happy to let Neil and his teammate Dustin use them as much as they liked. After all, their job was to keep Thadwick alive.

Another change in what made the Mercer compound alluring as Neil grew up was the presence of Thadwick's older sister, Cassandra. As with many young men in the Mercer family orbit, the smart, capable and gorgeous young woman was the object of his youthful affection. Four years older than him, she was the unattainable image of beauty and sophistication in the eyes of thirteen-year-old Neil. She left the city with her mother after reaching bronze rank, putting an end to his boyhood crush.

Cassandra and her mother had been back in the city for six months, in preparation for the monster surge. Many young men once again clamoured for her attention, but Neil was not one of them. It had been one thing putting up with Thadwick as children, but they were adventurers now. His selfishness and incompetence brought with it genuine danger, culminating in his abandonment of them during the expedition. Aside from Cassandra and her mother, the ones who had left, he had become soured on anything with the Mercer name. Any idea of reigniting youthful passions and pursuing her ended the moment he thought of her family.

By the time he heard that Cassandra and Jason Asano were an item, he had seen Asano for himself and not found him to be anything special. He was just another in a line of self-impressed people who thought they were bold and clever for making Thadwick look like a fool. Neil knew it may just have been his lingering affection, but his opinion of Cassandra was still high enough that he wondered what she saw that elevated Asano above the pack.

Asano's visit to Neil's home had left him uncertain as to what to do. Ostensibly, Neil had received better offers; the only real attraction to joining Asano's team was the participation of Humphrey Geller. Neil knew for a fact that, behind closed doors, Humphrey was the person the Mercer's wished Thadwick had become. Their family situations had provided Thadwick and Humphrey with the same opportunities, yet Humphrey was lauded while Thadwick was dismissed.

After Asano's visit to his home, Neil's intention had been to dismiss the offer out of hand. There were things about Asano that kept playing on his mind, however, starting with why he had been the one to make the approach. Every way he looked at it, Humphrey Geller would have made the better advocate. Asano's characteristically idiosyncratic conduct bore that out. The absurdity of questioning Neil's elven heritage. Asano's description of his own team that was anything but appealing. Then there was Asano spending most of his time explaining not why Neil would want to join with them but why they wanted him to join.

Although Neil didn't understand it, there was no question that Asano was good at impressing important people. People themselves deserving of respect. The Gellers, the gold-ranked Emir Bahadir, the Vitesse adventurers. Even his enemies were impressive. He was already moving in vaunted circles, to the point that even when he drew hatred, it was from people so far above him they shouldn't care. There were rumours of Asano feuding with the directors of both the Magic and Adventure Societies. If true, that was madness for an iron ranker. Then there was whatever had made Cassandra look at him above all the numerous men in Greenstone vying for her attention.

The character of Asano aside, critical when choosing a team was the team's strength as adventurers. Neil knew almost nothing about the two others, but what Asano had told him didn't sound promising. Humphrey, on the other hand, was known to be one of the most proficient iron-rankers in the city.

As for Asano, at least as an adventurer he seemed capable. Thadwick's fixation had given Neil a fairly good idea of Asano's record. He had closed out a startling number of contracts in a handful of months, each punctuated with adventure board notices. In all of them, he didn't have a single listed failure. Asano had risen through the ranks fast and fallen even faster, but there were plenty of demotions going around.

He had seen multiple recordings of Asano fighting. Everyone had seen the one from the Geller's mirage chamber with Asano's overwrought theatrics. Neil had seen others where Asano had been fighting for real, his melodrama was replaced with brutal efficiency.

Thadwick had been furious after hearing about Asano spending time with Cassandra and, in typically reactionary fashion, sent a handful of goons to beat Asano down. After what Asano did to the first one, the others not only gave up but gave Asano directions to where he was going. Neil had only heard about it after the fact or he would have had Thadwick's father put a stop to it. Thadwick stupidly had his goons record the whole debacle. His father had tasked Neil with retrieving them all.

The strongest of Thadwick's bottom-feeders was Jerrick, who Thadwick had playing muscle in his ill-considered land-grab scheme. Neil had been in the room when Thadwick's father tore strips off him for the plan's spectacular failure. Asano had recorded his gathering evidence and the recording ended with Asano fighting Jerrick.

Thadwick's father had taken the time to point out that Asano wasn't even fighting at his best. Against an armoured enemy, Asano should have kept hidden and used his leech familiar to crawl into the armour. Instead, he fought out in the open, suffering more damage than necessary. Asano was using a life and death battle with Thadwick's strongest thug as training.

The final recording Neil had seen of Asano was when twelve men had confronted him in the street. Four were the thugs Asano had run off in a previous recording, plus double that number of extras. A dozen admittedly mediocre adventurers, yet Asano made the twelve on one fight seem lopsided in his favour. Five adventurers killed in a shopping arcade in broad daylight, and the only repercussion was that it possibly contributed to his later demotion.

It was well-known that Asano had faced a bronze-rank marsh hydra with Humphrey Geller and some other guy no one had heard of. Everyone said that Humphrey had carried them through, including Asano himself, but Neil had come away from his conversation with Asano less certain of that. He knew Beth Cavendish thought highly of Jason's abilities and her judgement was razor-sharp.

As those thoughts chased themselves around his head, Neil arrived at the Mercer family home for the first time since the expedition. In the aftermath of that disaster, Thadwick had been isolated by the family, then he disbanded their team without notice. He had considered confronting Thadwick until he talked with their other team member, Dustin. In the end, they were just happy to be free with what was left of their reputations after being known as Thadwick's flunkeys.

Neil approached one of the five gates that were the primary entrances to the Mercer family grounds.

"Neil Davone," the iron-rank guard said from the other side of the gate as he spotted Neil's approach. The Mercer family guards had long known Neil but the usual respect was nowhere on this guard's face. It was clear that, in his eyes, Neil had lost his status as a valued ally of the Mercers. Now he was just another iron-ranker, like the guard himself.

"I'd like to see Cassandra Mercer," Neil told him.

"I bet you would," the guard said insolently.

"Excuse me?"

"I'm not going to interrupt her for the likes of you."

"Are you being serious, right now?"

"Move on, Davone. You don't get a seat at the big table anymore."

"Yes, he does," Thalia Mercer said, teleporting next to the guard. "Hello, Neil."

"Lady Mercer," Neil greeted respectfully.

"First, let me correct this man who used to work for us and tell you that you are always welcome here. Your family is important to us and you have always given my son loyalty he sadly never earned. What brings you by?"

"I wanted to ask your daughter about Jason Asano."

"Why?"

"He invited me to join his team. I'll probably decline but I found him odd to talk to. I wanted to know more."

Thalia touched the gate, which slid soundlessly to the side.

"I see. If you don't mind, Jason is a topic I would rather you not engage my daughter in. She's unhappy with the family right now and I don't want to exacerbate that feeling."

"Of course," Neil said. "My apologies for taking your time, Lady Mercer. I'll go."

"Please don't," she said. "Perhaps you can spare me a moment, instead."

"Of course, Lady Mercer."

She turned on the guard who had been hovering silently throughout the conversation.

"You, get to the security station and have them send a replacement. If I can assuage your offence to Master Davone, there may be a chance of you maintaining your employment."

The guard nodded and scurried away.

"That's not necessary, Lady Mercer," Neil said.

"Nonsense," she said. "Please come through."

After a moment's hesitation, Neil walked through the gate, which she closed behind him.

"Would you care to take morning tea with me?"

"I wouldn't presume, Lady Mercer."

"Nonsense, please do."

"Then thank you, Lady Mercer."

It did not go unnoticed by Neil that being led to a private social meeting with Thalia Mercer in the eyes of the whole household made a pointed statement about his status. She led him to the blue parlour, one of the various receiving parlours of the Mercer household. Each was named for the primary colour of its decoration, with the blue parlour awash in oceanic shades. It was one of the smaller parlours, for intimate and respected guests. Shortly after their arrival, a maid delivered tea and small savouries before departing. Thalia poured a cup for each of them.

"I know that your family's tea standards are very high," she said. "I hope you don't look down on us too much."

"Never," Neil said.

"Such a good young man you've become. So, you are considering joining Jason Asano and Humphrey Geller's team?"

"Not really," Neil said. "It's just that some things about the way he made the approach have left me confused."

"Perhaps I can help you with answers. When my daughter became interested in Asano, I looked into him as deeply as I think anyone has."

"Oh?"

"He was rather rude, the last time we met, which I am quite happy with."

"Happy?"

"If he was unaffected by being severed from my daughter, I would have been quite dissatisfied. He is startlingly good for his rank at keeping his emotions out of his aura, but when I met him he was rather a mess. The anger of youthful passion meant his feelings were genuine. That's always a concern when it comes to aristocratic relationships. Is there some young thing you are pursuing, Neil?"

"No, Lady Mercer. My attention is on my future as an adventurer."

"Yes, you're pondering Jason's offer. I know he seems erratic but you'll find that there is method to his madness. He has a way of leaving people thinking exactly what he wants them to."

"How so?" Neil asked.

"You said yourself you will probably turn him down. Yet here you are, asking questions. Why?"

"There were oddities in the way he tried to recruit me. It's like he was hiding reasons to join and giving me ones not to."

Thalia smiled.

"There you are. Humphrey Geller aside, his team is not enticing at a glance and he knew an ordinary invitation wouldn't work. Otherwise, he would have sent Humphrey. Instead, he found a way to pique your interest. He saw a path that led to you joining his team, and he put you on it."

"You're saying he manipulated me and I should refuse the offer?"

"I'm saying he manipulated you and you should accept the offer. Some, within these walls, will tell you that Jason is unreliable. He's not. When it's time to work, he gets the job done. My original intention was to place him and Humphrey with Cassandra, once they reached bronze-rank. That is no longer an option, but If I were in your position, I'd join his team in a heartbeat."

"That's not what I would have expected from you," Neil said.

"Most adventurers in this city never leave it, and nor should they. They're mediocre, without the potential to thrive in a dangerous world. What they lack in themselves, they fail to recognise in others. Anyone can see Beth Cavendish or Humphrey Geller will go places, but only those of us who've seen the wider world recognise the potential in someone like Asano, and someone like you."

"Me?"

"You have what it takes," she said. "People couldn't see that with you chained to my son. I've been selfish in binding you to him because that helped keep my son alive. You have my apologies for that, but not my regret."

"You have no need to apologise, Lady Mercer."

"You're a good boy, Neil, but don't lie to my face."

She chuckled at Neil's nervous expression.

"It's an interesting team that Jason and Humphrey have put together," she said. "I've recently met another of their team members, who is an interesting young man from the Magic Society. He's capable enough that Emir Bahadir is trying to poach him."

"Asano told me that was for non-combat skills," Neil said.

"And so it is," Thalia said, "but why did he tell you that? He wanted you curious so that you would learn for yourself that the man is quite capable. Which he is, by the way. Danielle Geller is keeping a close eye on the team her precious boy is forming and can be trusted to excise any rot. And now you have heard it from me, you will trust it more than if Jason told you the man was good."

"What about Asano's indentured servant?"

"I'm not sure," Thalia said. "Danielle told me she is reserving judgement for the moment. I will say that running rings around the city's iron rank adventurers for months speaks to a certain capability, regardless of what help she received. Now she has a full set of essences, who knows what she'll accomplish?"

"You seem quite certain I should join," Neil said.

"You should be in a team that will help you fly, instead of chaining you to the ground the way I did. My advice is that you drink your tea, leave here and go straight to the Geller townhouse. Tell Danielle Geller you want to join her son's team."

"Not Asano or Humphrey?" Neil asked.

"They might think they have the final word on their team members," Thalia said. "It's probably best to let them."

28
WEAPONISING A BARBECUE

Jason met Neil at the entrance to the cloud palace, along with one of Emir's staff who added Neil's aura signature to the access list for the palace.

"There are some restricted areas," Jason explained as they entered. "You shouldn't bump into any of those except the guest suites, which are individually locked to guests who can provide you entry or not."

Neil didn't say much as he looked around, wide-eyed as Jason led him to the guest wing. He was nervous, second-guessing his choice of team, but Jason was welcoming and friendly. He also seemed at home in the astounding surrounds of the cloud palace.

"We're going to start with a little welcoming lunch," Jason said. "You can meet the team and some of the people around it. After that we're going to spend the afternoon on a preliminary strategy session, looking at everyone's abilities and working on tactical concepts around them. From here on out, that's going to be our every day: develop tactics, workshop them in the training room, then test them in the field."

"You're getting ready for the event Bahadir is planning?" Neil asked.

"You heard about that?"

"Word has gotten around."

"Certainly, being prepared for that is a good idea," Jason said. "Our sights are set past that, though. We're looking at the path to bronze and beyond. We want to establish a playbook of strategies and tactics that we know so well as a team that we're ready to go at any moment. As our abilities grow, we can adapt and refine our repertoire, but the first step is working together, everyone knowing their potential roles. I hope you're not afraid of hard work and training."

"To be honest, Asano, you always struck me as more frivolous than hard-working."

"I'm a work hard, play hard kind of bloke," Jason said. "Talking doesn't mean much, though. You can judge for yourself."

Jason led Neil onto an elevating platform that lifted them to the upper reaches of the cloud palace, before heading out to a terrace crowded with people, tables of food and a pair of large flame grills. Amongst the crowd were people Neil recognised. Rufus Remore was chatting with Vincent Trenslow and his absurd moustache; Humphrey Geller was flipping meat on one of the grills. Danielle Geller was chatting with Emir Bahadir, both holding grilled meat and vegetable sticks. He even spotted his friend and previous teammate, Dustin biting into a steak sandwich. Dustin's cousin, Hudson, was next to him and they were surrounded by their respective teams. Dustin was on a Geller team now, looking more relaxed than Neil had seen him in a long time.

"What's all this?" Neil asked.

"If you're going to chuck a barbie," Jason said, "you get some mates around. Let's grab some tucker and I'll make some introductions."

The barbecue lunch went on into the afternoon, leaving Neil disoriented from a heady mix of grilled meats, quality alcohol and the kind of political connections his family only dreamed of. It was a social event wholly unlike those he had experienced in the Mercers' orbit.

Everything was casual and the people present genuinely seemed to like each other. There was no carefully orchestrated social sniping, no playing one family against another. There was no stratification of rank, with bronze, silver and even gold-rankers happily chatting with iron. Instead of dainty, delicate finger food, people had meat piled into plates, skewered onto sticks or shoved between slabs of bread. There were tables of side dishes heaped into enormous bowls for anyone to grab by the tong-full.

Neil could hear the voice of his mother telling him to be mercenary, ditch Asano and seize the opportunity and forge connections. The voice seemed at a loss as Jason led him around, making introductions with no prompting on his part. People asked him questions, seeming actually interested instead of just digging for some useful titbit they could use later.

"How long have you been in Greenstone?" Neil asked Jason between conversations.

"About five months."

"How did you make these kinds of political allies in five months?"

"I didn't," Jason said. "I made friends."

Jason found Humphrey away from the group, looking unhappy as he stared out over the ocean. Jason joined him in leaning on the rail.

"What's got you down, mate?"

"It's Gabrielle," Humphrey said. "Things aren't going to work out with her."

"That sucks," Jason said. "Sorry to hear it. I'm guessing I wasn't helpful in that regard."

"It's more than just that," Humphrey said. "I would never ask her to choose between me and her religion, but she's becoming more and more dogmatic. She's becoming honest to the point of rudeness, demanding secrets she has no right to."

"Well, I do the rude honesty thing too," Jason said. "But in my defence, I also lie a lot."

Humphrey laughed, then sighed.

"She's started telling me who I shouldn't spend my time with," he said. "It's why she's not here. She really doesn't like you and Rufus but that's just the start of it. The strictures of her god are all well and good, but I'm not a follower of Knowledge. She has no right to hold me to those principles."

"I'm sorry," Jason said. "I'm at least a bit responsible for nudging you in her direction."

"I'm not sorry," Humphrey said. "I care for Gabrielle and I've enjoyed our time together. That time is just coming to an end."

"Wow," Jason said. "That's super-mature of you. I was a couple of years older than you when my first big relationship ended and I blew up my whole life over it, like an idiot."

"I'm going to tell her tomorrow," Humphrey said. "She probably already knows."

"Because of her boss," Jason realised. "Damn, that must have been really annoying, having the goddess telling her everything."

"It wasn't my favourite thing," Humphrey acknowledged. He turned to look over at the gathering. "How's Neil fitting in?"

"A bit shell-shocked. You think it was the right thing, bringing out the big social guns? I don't like weaponising a barbecue."

"His family have been second-tier nobility for generations and this will get his family's support. As for Neil himself, that's up to you and me."

As things wound down, Jason and Emir sent people off, usually with food in bags with a cheap, short-lived enchantment to keep the food inside them fresh and hot. Afterwards, Jason gathered their team together. Neil had now met the others, the lanky Clive Standish and the startlingly beautiful Sophie Wexler. Neil hadn't been sure what to expect from Jason's indentured servant, but the woman with silver hair, dark skin and sharp, wary eyes certainly wasn't it. She was the one he had been the most uncertain about, but watching her sleek litheness made him a lot more confident.

They went off to Jason's suite in the guest wing. Amongst all the cloud furniture, a trio of wooden bookcases stood out, jammed-full of leather-bound tomes. Even more books were stacked up on a table next to a reading chair, one of which Clive picked up to examine.

"This is some heavy theory," he said to Jason. "You're finally taking my advice?"

"This was Farrah's collection," Jason said sadly, gesturing at the bookcases. "She was like you, telling me to not just rely on skill books. With these, it's almost like she's still teaching me."

"Farrah was one of the Vitesse adventurers," Humphrey quietly mentioned to Neil. "She fell during the expedition."

They sat down and Jason took out a notebook. Recorded in it were the abilities of everyone in the party, to which they added Neil's. His essence combination was shield, growth and renewal, producing the prosperity confluence. Along with healing and cleansing powers, Neil could create short-lived shields that intercepted attacks, empower allies and replenish their mana and stamina.

"That's an awesome power set," Jason said as he wrote them down. "Not great if you get caught alone, but any team you're on should celebrate. Which is our team, I guess, so… cheers, mate!"

As his powers were most effective when used on allies, Neil was highly reliant on his summoning power when fighting alone. It was not a summoned familiar but a temporary summons, like Gary's forge golem or Farrah's magma elemental. It would only last for a limited time, but he could afford to risk it in ways that he couldn't with a familiar.

His summon was an entity called a chrysalis golem. It was a crystalline construct monster; it could create a protective shell around itself when it was badly damaged. When it emerged, it was fully repaired and adapted to resist the attacks that had previously harmed it.

"I can't wait to get a look at that thing," Jason said. "With Humphrey's summons that makes two, excluding the summoned familiars Clive and myself have. We should be able to do some interesting things with them."

Humphrey took the lead in discussions as they started devising potential strategies.

"The most fundamental thing is that we all need to have a sound grasp of each other's abilities," he said. "Neil, this is especially true for you, since your abilities rely heavily on judgement and timing. You'll learn as we train, of course, but you should have at least a general idea of what each of us does before we start digging into specific tactics."

"Let's start with Humphrey, then," Jason said. "His essences are might, magic, wing and dragon. He moves faster, hits harder and withstands more damage than most adventurers. His attacks are mostly conventional melee powers, but they're reliable and land like a truck."

"What's a truck?" Neil asked. "Is that some kind of monster?"

"It's a big, heavy, fast thing," Jason said grouchily. "It's not my fault your stupid world doesn't have internal combustion."

"Lots of people have internal combustion," Clive said. "Mostly from the fire essence, which is why it's common."

Jason groaned at Clive while Humphrey picked up the explanations.

"Clive has the magic, rune, balance and karmic essences. Unlike most humans, his focus is on spells. He can use magical weapons like staves and wands and works with his familiar to output reliable ranged damage. He also has some utility powers, trap magic and the ability to make our enemies suffer retributive damage from attacking us."

"He also has some big-ticket attacks, if he goes all out," Jason added. "If we need a single, big hit, he's our guy. Those hefty spells need some setup, though, so we've already started devising strategies around them."

"Miss Wexler is an evasion-type defender," Humphrey said. "Swift, wind, balance and mystic. She is the newest of us, with many abilities still to awaken, but she is already the fastest and hardest to harm out of all of us. I have no doubt she will become increasingly formidable."

"Asano is the sneaky prick of the team," Sophie said. "His essences are dark, blood, sin and doom."

"Sin and doom?" Neil asked. "They sound like they should be on the restricted list."

"They're not," Jason said. "We checked."

"Jason is an affliction specialist," Humphrey said. "Once he goes to work, whatever he's fighting is finished, even if it seems to have gotten away. He's also a good scout, with stealth and mobility."

"Obviously, we don't expect you to remember all this," Humphrey said. "You'll have plenty of time to learn, because that's what we do, now. We get up, we meet up, then we train. Physical and mobility training we do in Old City."

"When Jory renovated his clinic," Jason said, "he turned his yard into a dedicated training space. So, thanks for helping stop it from being knocked down."

"That wasn't really me," Neil said.

"Of course it was," Jason said. "If you didn't stand up to them and force the confrontation, the Healer might have waited until they tore down the place and then smote them all as sinners."

"We'll be alternating our time between developing strategies, refining them in practice areas or testing them in the field," Humphrey said.

"The practise areas are the training hall, here in the cloud palace, or in Humphrey's mirage chamber."

"It's not my mirage chamber," Humphrey said.

"Other than that, it'll be contracts and adventure notices," Jason said. "That is going to be our day, every day, until Emir's mysterious contest. We're going into it as strong as we can be."

"Is that going to be a problem, Neil?" Humphrey asked. "We're looking for someone willing to go at this hard, so if that isn't you, tell us now."

"Don't worry about me," Neil said. "I've been waiting for a team that takes adventuring seriously." He looked at Jason. "I wasn't sure that was you."

"You can judge for yourself," Jason said. "Today, we're all talk. We throw every idea at the wall and see what sticks. Tomorrow we start figuring out what's practical and what's some overwrought notion I got in my head because I forgot simplicity is king."

They moved onto the discussion of specific strategies, under the direction of Humphrey.

"I think you're overlooking what should be our core strategy," Jason told Humphrey, early into the discussion.

"What's that?" Humphrey asked.

"You," Jason said. "You do more damage than most and can survive more damage than most. With Clive and Neil, we have two buffers, plus shields and healing. Neil can even top-off your mana. We load all of that up on you and let you go ham. Add in your mobility and you'll be an absolute terror to whatever we're fighting."

Uncertainty crossed Humphrey's face.

"Are you sure you want to rely that heavily on me?"

Jason shook his head. "Oh, Humphrey. Hands up who wants to rely on Humphrey as the core of the team."

Sophie and Clive put up their hands with Jason, Neil raising his hand right after.

"It's adorable that you're modest enough that I have to tell you this Humphrey," Jason said, "but everyone likes and trusts you."

Humphrey looked around the group, embarrassed.

"Now," Jason said. "If we take that as our core strategy, all our tactics should be smooth adaptations of that default. What do you reckon, Humphrey?"

"Well, there are a few points that we need to look at using that as a strategy. First would be identifying and distracting anyone or anything with the singular attack power to punch through the buffs and shields."

"So, the other team's Clive," Sophie said.

"Exactly," Humphrey said. "For other Clives, we want you and Jason to at least distract and interfere, or preferably put them down."

"I'm not sure I love this 'other Clive' analogy," Clive said.

"What about actual Clive and the new guy?" Sophie asked. "They aren't as mobile as the rest of us, and if we're using a mobile attacking strategy, they'll be left exposed."

"Yes," Humphrey said. "They'll make a tempting target, so instead of trying to cover it, we use it."

"I like it," Jason said. "We've already worked up strategies using Clive as bait, so develop them and make Neil the second juicy worm on the hook. Turn what seems like a weakness into a weapon."

Clive and Neil shared a glance.

"I'm not sure I like this plan," Clive said.

29
THIS TOWN AIN'T BIG ENOUGH

The mirage chamber had created a sprawl of ancient, desert ruins. It was a town, long since dead and dry. Built into a hillside, crumbling buildings clung to the steep slope or were dug right into the yellow desert rock. Tunnels and stairwells were alternately exposed or buried by the dilapidating power of time, forming a rat's nest of unsafe passages and hidden nooks. Of the handful of intact buildings, none had a neighbour in the same condition, the slope a mess of tumbled brick and stone, half-gone walls and debris-filled, hard earth streets. The air shimmered with heat as the unyielding sun beat down on the clay and stone remnants of the town. Through the steep ruins, three teams stalked one another. Hiding and moving, they risked precarious tunnels and rooftops as they sought to find prey without becoming someone else's.

"Keep an eye on the shadows," Rick Geller warned his team. "Asano is the strongest scout in here and we all know what he can do if we let him play his games."

"Oh, I have all kinds of games," Jason's voice echoed loudly through the ruins.

"He's doing it again," said Claire Adeah, the healer and one of two elf sisters on the team. "That guy is so annoying."

"He's just trying to get you riled up," her sister said from above. "He knows he can't try what he did last time, but he'll still try and mess up your thinking."

Scouting from a rooftop, Hannah Adeah was an archer, the team's only remaining ranged specialist. The expedition and its aftermath claimed both Jonah and Henry Geller, their front-line guardian and magic ranged attacker. Their new members were Dustin Kettering, a local who filled Jonah's defender role, and Rick's sister, Phoebe.

Dustin's cousin, Hudson, was his counterpart on Beth Cavendish's team and currently an enemy. Dustin was a classic defender, not very mobile but very hard to go around or through. This put him in the role of the team member he replaced, unlike Phoebe. Instead of a ranged magic attacker, she was a fast melee attacker using unarmed combat. This forced a change in general strategy for the team, who had previously bunkered around their twin ranged attackers. Phoebe's presence failed to replicate their previous strength but broadened their abilities. In the weeks since gaining their new members, the team had been working on strategies that were less specialised and more adaptive and versatile.

Hannah stepped off the roof, dropping down lightly to rejoin the others.

"He isn't as much of a threat in this environment as he was when we had to chase him through those mangroves," Hannah said. "Did you hear how loud he called out? He's trying to draw the other team to our location."

In another part of the ruined town, Beth Cavendish and her team moved with the same caution as Rick's team did. Beth was widely known as both team leader and team healer, but it was her dangerous mix of wide-area afflictions and control powers that made her a true threat.

Their own archer, Emily, was likewise scouting from a rooftop vantage, but the steep slope made that tricky. The team was slowly moving uphill in search of visual and tactical advantage. Emily was a celestine with fair skin and a gold pixie cut that matched her eyes. She wore a simple cap to keep the sun from reflecting off her hair and giving away her position.

Their team was only four, compared to five each for the others and they were being appropriately cautious. Emily moved carefully down from her hidden vantage, returning to the team.

"I have at least a direction from Asano calling out," she said. "Obviously, he wants to lure us into the other team and clean up whoever's left. Do we scout it out and wait, or avoid it completely?"

"Let them thin each other out," Beth said. "Jason's team has his voice communication ability, so they have more tactical flexibility. We stay hidden and keep going for the high ground. We wait for the others to clash and then move."

"Isn't that what everyone is going to do?" Niko asked. Niko Tomich was from the smoulder race, with dark skin and burning red eyes. Niko used fire and iron powers to deal heavy damage in melee or combine damage and control powers at mid-range, making him the team's most versatile striker.

"Jason's team is going to be more active," Beth said. "Their defender is mobility-based and short on powers, where Rick's team has Kettering and we have Hudson. We're both stronger than his group at suffering an attack, while Humphrey is as strong an initiator as you could ask for. They'll try and catch us at a bad moment and make the most of it."

Hudson was a huge, comic book character of a man and the guardian of Beth's team. He wielded earth powers and, like Clive, had a racial gift evolution that moved his aptitude from special attacks to another ability type. In Hudson's case, it was conjuration, allowing him to conjure up stone weapons, shields, walls and other objects to protect his team.

As Beth predicted, the three teams were slow and careful as they moved about the ruined town. Jason's team made various attempts to bait one of their opponents into an ill-considered attack without success before regrouping to discuss the next move.

"Both teams are being extremely cautious," Humphrey said. "They aren't willing to risk extending themselves because they know they will do better defending from readiness. Everyone is waiting for an accident or a mistake that turns the tables, letting them swoop in and clean up the other teams."

"So what do we do?" Neil asked.

"Our best bet is to strike first," Sophie said. "For both of their teams, if we can overwhelm the key defender, it opens up the rest of the team to our attacks. We load up Humphrey with powers and use that to punch through their strongest front-liner and clean up the rest."

"Initiating a straight-up confrontation will cost us in the long run," Humphrey said. "Even if the other team doesn't arrive in time to pincer us against the group we're already fighting, they'll be fresh and we'll be hurt when they do turn up."

"Hunkering down fits the other teams better than it does us, though," Clive said. "Our core strategy is offensive, relying on mobility and power. We're better off pitting our strengths against their strengths than our weaknesses against their, uh, mediums."

"Their mediums?" Neil asked.

"Yes, their mediums," Clive said emphatically. "I said it and I'll stand by it."

Jason chuckled, shaking his head.

"You're right, Clive," he said. "These aren't teams we can beat with anything but our best. Humphrey had it right, too. If we want to catch them out of position, it has to be when they're moving to capitalise on a mistake."

"What are you suggesting?" Humphrey asked.

"I'm suggesting we make the mistake that they're both looking for. They're both waiting for someone else to get in a fight, so we'll get in one and we'll ambush them as they rush to swoop in. I found a good spot when I was roaming around earlier. You're good for one of those illusion rituals you were telling me about, right Clive?"

"In field conditions?" Clive said. "If you don't want any old perception power to see through it, I can't do any better than a blank wall."

"That's fine," Jason said. "We just need them to think there's only one entrance, so we can slip out as they slip in."

"So, who will we be fighting?" Sophie asked.

"Each other, obviously," Jason said.

Emily tilted her head, listening.

"Did you hear that?"

Beth gestured for silence. Soon after they heard the noise of an explosive ability triggering.

"They found each other?" Hudson asked.

"It might be a ruse to flush us out," Beth said. "Move slow and quiet; we wait to see if it keeps going."

They moved forward at a cautious pace, Emily scouting the path to each new piece of cover before they took it. As they drew closer to the noise, they could hear a fight in full swing, with abilities going off and multiple weapons clashing.

"Alright," Beth said. "Pick up the pace, but not too much. We want to get there once they've spent themselves on each other."

They accelerated their way along the path, Emily scouting ahead again as they narrowed in on the continuing sounds of combat. As they drew closer, Emily gestured for them to stop. She came back and gathered with the rest, hidden beneath a crumbling wall.

"The noise is coming from inside the hill," Emily said. "There's a collapsed building that exposed the tunnel access. I caught a glimpse of fighting inside, but didn't push my luck."

"Any other entrances?" Beth asked.

"I can't rule it out, but not that I saw," Emily said. "My guess would be one of the teams spotted the other going in and moved on them."

"Alright," Beth said. "We go with our standard, three-stage assault pattern. Control powers on any loose threats; be sure and call your targets. This means you, Niko. Then we blanket the fight with area attacks and mop up whoever's still got fight in them. When you're ready, Hudson."

Hudson nodded as his body took on the colour of the desert stone, flesh transmuting into living rock. He then broke out of hiding, the rest of the team on his heels. They dashed up the slope to the shattered building and into the tunnel, balancing haste and care as they moved through the rubble. The tunnel was around a dozen metres long, beyond which it opened into darkness punctuated by flashes of magical light. They surged forward, catching glimpses of figures clashing. It looked like several normal-sized figures against one that dwarfed even Hudson.

"Wait!" Beth called out and they all stopped. "Plug the hole!"

Reacting without question, Hudson held a hand out ahead of them and a slab of desert stone rose up to seal the end of the tunnel and close them off from the room.

"What is it?" Hudson asked afterwards.

"They were summons," Beth said. "Back out, now."

They started heading back down the tunnel when an arrow flew into the tunnel. It came in at an angle, striking the wall but not losing momentum as it ricocheted. Instead, the arrow duplicated, two arrows now zipping down the tunnel at different angles. They kept bouncing and multiplying as they zigzagged down the tunnel, the confines of the tunnel letting them bounce their way into a storm of arrows. Hudson acted quickly, placing another wall between them and the exit, boxing them in from both ends but shielding them from the arrow attack.

"That's both my wall abilities," Hudson said. "I won't have them again for a while."

"You did well," Beth said and pointed to the newer wall. "That's your shatter-stone wall, right?"

"Yeah."

"Then see if you can't clear us a path with it. Break us out of here."

Hudson walked from the front of his team to the back. The first wall he had created was the strongest; a simple wall conjuration power from his fortress essence called bulwark. The second power was called shatter-stone wall and could turn defence into offence. He snapped his fingers and the wall exploded away from him in a wave of sharp, stone shards, peppering Rick and Dustin who were on the other side.

The cousins were on opposing teams but filled similar roles. They were both huge, shielding their respective teams with the support of their elemental powers. Hudson had transformed himself into stone, while Dustin was clad in armour forged entirely of ice. Shards of the exploding wall had dug into it, without penetrating.

Standing next to Dustin, Rick also had hefty armour but without the complete coverage that Dustin enjoyed. He avoided most of the damage but still suffered some cuts and scrapes that he was ignoring. As the two teams spotted one another, Beth was already chanting a spell.

"*Let venom drift on the breeze.*"

She opened her mouth wide and flower petals streamed out of it and up the tunnel. They were lotus petals, dark green, purple and black. They swept out of the tunnel on a wash of air, blowing past her teammates without incident yet adhering to the enemy team. Wherever they landed on flesh they swiftly dissolved into the skin.

Before the effects of the petals could be seen, Niko stepped forward and exhaled a cone of fire like a dragon. Between the mysterious petals and the roaring flame, the momentum of Rick's team was completely halted.

"Hudson," Beth called out.

A moment later, a stone block rose up under their feet. It carried them along the tunnel like a raft in a quick current, the ground rippling like water as they passed. Hudson stood at the front, conjuring a huge stone shield as they barrelled out of the tunnel.

Where the stone block carried Beth's team, the hard, dry earth became soft and unsteady. As they emerged from the tunnel, Rick and Dustin were forced back as the rippling ground left them with unsure footing.

From a hidden vantage, Jason's team looked on. Humphrey tapped Clive on the shoulder just as the stone raft emerged from the tunnel and Clive snapped his fingers. The magic rune that appeared went unseen under the raft, but exploded upwards, nonetheless. The stone block absorbed most of the force but shattered into pieces, bursting upwards like a geyser.

Beth and Emily were sent flying by the power of the explosion, cut and bludgeoned by chunks of stone. Hudson and Niko had been held in place by their protective powers, their conditions reflecting the strength of those powers. Niko staggered, injured and disoriented while Hudson was entirely unharmed. He looked around, taking stock of Rick's team.

Rick himself looked singed but was functionally uninjured, although he felt woozy from the poison petals that had found their way onto his exposed hands and face. Dustin was standing strong, as was his ice armour. It was pushing out the stone shards from the wall explosion and sealing over the cracks. There was some melting from the fire breath, but that was likewise recovering in short order.

Phoebe was unarmoured and had been right behind Rick and Dustin, ready to move down the tunnel before they were pushed back. She had moved to use Dustin as a shield from the fire breath but had been subjected to the bulk of the poison petals. She had already dashed backwards, holding out a hand, palm up. Droplets of black, purple and green liquid started falling upwards from her palm, collecting in a small orb floating over her hand.

As Phoebe was purging the poison from herself, the last members of her team were already going to work. The elf sisters had been well back, avoiding the area attacks. Claire was purging the poison from Rick with a spell as Hannah nocked an arrow to her bow. The arrowhead was glowing, the light rapidly increasing in intensity until it started strobing. She aimed it at Beth, who was still prone from the explosion.

Things were happening all at once as chaos ruled the battlefield. Phoebe gestured with her hand and the poison orb flew at Emily, the enemy archer who, like Beth, was still sprawled on the ground.

Hudson had seen Hannah readying the arrow and moved to get in its path before it was loosed but Dustin intercepted him. Rick and Niko moved on each other, Rick already holding a sword as a huge iron hammer appeared in Niko's hands. Niko grew visibly larger and the crude hammer grew with him. Even the handle was made of dark iron, which started to glow with heat.

Hannah released the arrow at Beth, only for Hudson to appear in her place while she appeared where he had just been standing. The glowing arrow tore a chunk out of Hudson's torso, which crumbled off him in stony fragments. Dustin, suddenly finding Beth in front of him, conjured a hatchet of ice in each hand and started swinging.

Beth activated an ability she shared with Sophie called between the raindrops. She had obtained it through the water essence instead of the swift essence, but it was functionally the same. Her spatial awareness and reflexes took a leap forward at the cost of rapidly consuming stamina and mana which was worth it to escape Dustin's attacks.

After throwing the poison orb, Phoebe was moving before it even struck. Emily held out a hand into which an arrow appeared, the tip glowing. As the poison orb struck her, she jabbed the arrow into the ground. There was a shock wave, launching Phoebe backwards and Emily herself into the air. She was unharmed by her own power, even using the momentum to flip backwards and land on her feet. She was immediately woozy, however, as the poison orb took effect.

From their vantage point, Jason's team watched the conflict unfold.

"Things are stabilising," Humphrey said. "It's time to join in, make things messy again. Everyone knows what to do."

The team nodded and Humphrey looked up, teleporting high into the sky.

30

THE SECOND-BEST IRON RANKER

After the initial chaos, the two clashing teams were starting to get their bearings. This was the moment that winged death plunged out of the sky in the form of Humphrey Geller. Careening downwards with his dive bomb special attack, wings splayed out behind him, his powers were amplified by both Clive and Neil. A circle of magical runes floated around him and his sword glowed with light. He was twice his normal size, with an attendant increase in strength from Neil's giant's might spell.

Humphrey had a sword pointed down in a reverse, double-fisted grip. Hudson was still prone from his switch-teleport with Beth when Humphrey landed with literally earth-shattering force as his blade smashed into Hudson, smashing off chunks of his stone body. The blade of Humphrey's sword found the exact spot where Hudson had just been injured, imparting all the power of multiple buffs, the massive fall and two of Humphrey's special attacks combined.

Almost any iron ranker would have died from that single blow alone, but Hudson was not just any iron ranker. More than half of his torso and one arm were just gone, shattered into stone dust. He was still massively injured and lying prone as Humphrey stood up from the crouch he had landed in, still almost double his normal height from Neil's spell. He lifted up his sword and brought it down again. Hudson lifted his remaining arm and a stone shield appeared to intercept the attack.

The incredible impact of Humphrey's entry to the battlefield drew all eyes as the rest of his team emerged, unnoticed. Clive had a large staff from which he fired a bolt of magic at the elf sisters. Claire and Hannah were largely separated from the battle, leaving them free to heal and offer ranged support, respectively.

Neil also stepped out with Clive but didn't act, instead, making himself ready to intercede with his abilities at need. A third team member, Onslow the rune tortoise, was not a born ambusher and was sedately emerging from cover behind them.

The blast from Clive's staff crackled over Claire's shield, dissipating without any effect beyond drawing the attention of the two elves. The sisters failed to realise that this was the point as they turned to face Clive and Neil and away from their shadows thrown onto the ground by the bright sun. With Jason's well-honed aura control, they failed to notice his dark figure rise up from Claire's own shadow.

Claire fired a blast from a wand as Hannah launched an arrow that caught fire in flight. Both Clive and Neil had the same mana shield power as Claire, the attacks striking their invisible shields. Mana shield was a power that each of them gained from different essences but the effects were the same, negating attacks at the cost of mana.

The weaknesses were also the same, however, not impeding non-attacks, or attacks made from inside their sphere. It was a weakness that had cost Claire before, with Jason's leeches, and it was about to cost her again. Standing behind her, Jason slashed his hand on the razor in his wristband and reached inside Claire's shield.

Leeches spilled out over her, prompting startling shrieks that had her sister spinning around to see what happened. Jason pointed his arm at Hannah, who was likewise sprayed with leeches. Both sisters wore a coat of toothy leeches and Team Colin, Jason's most powerful and horrifying familiar, went to work.

Hudson's switch teleport had moved Beth out of the path of an arrow but placed her squarely in front of Dustin and his ice hatchets. Her between the raindrops power let her avoid his attack and escape his immediate reach but not his attack range. He started throwing ice spikes, forcing her to keep her attention on him and not the battlefield.

She had no time to assess her team's condition, let alone direct them as she was used to. From the moment Rick's team had boxed her it, through their breakaway being aborted by whatever had blown up Hudson's stone raft, she had been on the back foot.

Beth's archer, Emily, was likewise under pressure. She was staging a fighting retreat as she was pursued relentlessly by the swift and powerful Phoebe Geller. Affected by the poison orb Phoebe had used on her, Emily landed arrows on Phoebe but only inflicted minor injuries. Phoebe wasn't deterred, slowly but surely closing the gap.

In the meantime, Humphrey was still pounding away at Beth's front-liner, Hudson. Hudson was very much at his limits, scrambling on the ground and conjuring shield after shield for Humphrey to smash through. Despite his buffs,

Humphrey was finding Hudson frustratingly difficult to finish off. His size buff had worn off, reducing Humphrey to normal proportions, but he didn't relent.

The last member of Beth's team was Niko, using his fire and iron powers to clash with Rick Geller. Niko's powers included a size buff he could use on himself, but the extra space he occupied was proving more of a detriment than the strength was an asset. Knee deep in mud, against a swarm of leeches, Rick wasn't much of a fighter, but this was open ground. With free footing and a large, singular enemy, Rick was a horror to engage in melee; an avatar of speed and power whose attacks were as potent as they were relentless.

Of the fourteen combatants on the field, none of them were bad, but Rick was the leader of his team for a reason. No one would accuse Niko of lacking as an adventurer, but Rick simply outclassed him. He unleashed on Niko all the frustration of setback after setback his team had suffered, losing not just team members, but family. Rick was relentless and overpowering, his sword finding Niko again and again, leaving Niko stumbling back, rapidly accruing injuries.

Beth bought herself time by making use of Dustin's own power. One of her quick attack spells was called water cutter, which fired a beam of water hard and tight enough to cut through at least non-magical metal. In between ice spike, she fired it directly into Dustin's face. It didn't fully penetrate his icy helmet, but the water froze over the front of it from the cold of his armour, blinding him with an opaque sheet of ice.

Dustin wasn't worried as he smashed the ice away with a fist; Beth lacked the powers to harm him in the brief moment he took to clear his vision. Attacking was not the reason she had bought that time, however. She took it to scan the battlefield.

She saw her team members scattered and on the back foot. They were about to be wiped out and she knew she had to intervene, chanting a spell as Dustin cleared off the obscuring ice. He threw an ice spike at her but she swayed out of its path and continued her incantation.

"*Cool waters be the crucible of deliverance, bringing the deserving into the chrysalis of peace and rebirth.*"

Just as Dustin reached her, giant, magical lotus flowers appeared around Beth, Emily and Niko, completely enveloping them. Beth didn't complete her spell in time to save Hudson, who had finally been finished off by Humphrey. The people attacking the three now hidden away inside the lotuses found their attacks bouncing harmlessly off.

"They can't do anything from inside there but we can't hurt them either," Humphrey communicated through the group chat. "Go for Rick's team."

Jason's sneak attack had devastated the elf sisters, who were thrashing on the ground under piles of bloody leeches. Sophie, yet to make an appearance, suddenly launched a sneak attack at Phoebe who was at a loss in front of the lotus-shrouded Emily. She dodged the sneak attack, dancing away to create distance and the women squared off.

"You should have Asano work on your aura retraction," Phoebe said. "His is practically imperceptible, while yours just gave you away."

"Sneaking is really his area," Sophie said. "I'm more about the punching and you don't need an aura for that."

They clashed in a series of strikes before one of Phoebe's special attacks blasted them apart, both women landing nimbly.

"You made a mistake even coming for me," Phoebe said. "If you'd gone for Beth, she wouldn't have shielded her team."

"But then we'd have to fight both teams," Sophie said with a malevolent grin.

Phoebe's eyes went wide with realisation.

"Humphrey knows Beth's abilities," she said. "He predicted what she'd do."

"Humphrey's a good guy and wouldn't say it," Sophie said, "but I think he's sick of being called the second-best iron-ranker."

Phoebe glanced around the battle. The elf sisters weren't coming back from their predicament but Rick and Dustin had regrouped to take on Humphrey. Jason stepped out of a nearby shadow.

"It's nice that you made a friend but you're meant to be fighting her," he told Sophie.

"I'm new at this," Sophie said. "I was waiting for a big strong man to save me."

"Is that right?" he asked.

"It is," Sophie said. "If you could go get Humphrey, that would be great."

"Well, that's just hurtful," Jason said.

"You know I'm still here, right?" Phoebe said.

"I suppose we should deal with you," Jason said.

"Oh, you're going to deal with me, are you?"

"That's the plan," Jason said. "Keep her busy would you, Wexler?"

Sophie launched into the attack before he finished talking, Phoebe deftly defending. Jason looked at Phoebe.

"*Bleed for me.*"

Blood started running from Phoebe's eyes and nose as he cast another spell.

"*Carry the mark of your transgressions.*"

Phoebe was distracted as a sigil seared itself onto her face, taking a fist to the ribs from Sophie.

"*Your fate is to suffer.*"

"You have some nasty damn spells," Phoebe said, still clashing with Sophie. Suddenly she broke free and lunged at Jason. As she moved, she saw him throw something at the ground and she found herself shrouded in murky darkness. It wasn't full darkness as she could see shapes moving in the strange zone of shadows. She recognised the effect as one of his throwing darts and knew it only covered a small area. Making an immediate break for the outside, she felt a light slice on her arm as she emerged into the light.

Fully aware of what Jason's powers could do, Phoebe held her hand out to purge the toxins, the way she had earlier by gathering them into an orb. Sophie didn't give her the chance, forcing her to defend against a renewed series of attacks. In their initial clash, Phoebe had the advantage. Sophie had the edge in fighting technique, but Phoebe had more powers and more experience using them. The tables were turned as Phoebe needed to get away and cleanse herself before Jason's afflictions overwhelmed her. While Phoebe was stronger, though, Sophie's powers combined defence with blistering speed. She wouldn't be able to take Sophie down quickly or outpace her and escape.

While Sophie and Jason confronted Phoebe, Rick and Dustin regrouped as their opponents were closed off in the lotuses. Instead, they turned on Humphrey, fresh from finishing Hudson. All else being equal, Humphrey and Rick were a good match with quite similar combat styles. The addition of Dustin helped Rick but Humphrey had Clive, Neil and the finally emerged Onslow the rune tortoise to back him up.

Neil's ability to buff and heal was valuable, but not difficult to use. What had arrested the attention of Rufus Remore was Neil's shielding powers. The shield abilities that he could use on allies lasted only moments and would end after absorbing only a single attack. Without good judgement and timing, both could be easily wasted, leaving them unavailable until they came off cooldown again. The ability burst shield blasted away anyone nearby when the shield intercepted an attack. The other ability, absorbing shield, replenished the mana of the shielded person. The more damage that was prevented, the more mana was restored.

Using the voice chat, Neil offered to reapply the size-growth power but Humphrey refused, not making Niko's mistake. Clive refreshed his buffs, the rune circle that triggered effects when attacked and the damage-reflecting damage buff, mantle of retribution. Neil did refresh his other buff power, armour of renewal, which reduced damage taken and gave healing over time.

Humphrey clashed with Dustin and Rick. The two opponents should have been pressuring him but Humphrey had spent weeks discovering his limits under the protection of Clive and Neil. He left openings so he could make attacks, trusting Neil's shielding and healing, while letting Clive's retributive effects trigger. Clive offered ranged support, alternate staff blasts with using his own mana to recharge Onslow's shell powers.

The three on two was disadvantageous to Rick and Dustin, but they were holding on. They had also been training hard and Dustin used his ice powers to protect Rick and set up counters. Powerful attacks from Humphrey found his sword hitting a suddenly appearing ice wall that exploded into razor shards that slashed at him like knives. Blasts of icy air knocked him away and slowed his reflexes with cold debuffs. Humphrey feinted against Rick to strike out at Dustin, only for Dustin to be replaced with an ice clone as he teleported a short distance away. The ice clone shattered under the attack, once again peppering Humphrey with ice razors.

It was not enough. Humphrey pushed them further and further onto the back foot, their attacks either shielded or healed by Neil's life bolt spell. It was clear that if nothing changed, they would inevitably lose out.

"Go for the healer," Rick barked.

Dustin disengaged, Humphrey not trying to stop him. Dustin charged at Clive and Neil as Humphrey used Rick's distraction to catch him square in the chest with a kick, sending him staggering back. To Rick's surprise, instead of pushing the advantage, Humphrey looked up at the sky and he teleported away.

Clive looked up at Humphrey, more than a hundred metres in the air, then down at the charging Dustin. He smiled and chanted a spell.

"*Exchange your fates.*"

Suddenly Humphrey was standing where Dustin had been charging Clive. Rick looked over in confusion, then up at the sky as a sound grew louder and louder. Dustin's scream came to an end at the same time his fall did.

Rick's team was effectively done. The sisters had succumbed to Colin. Phoebe was still alive but too debilitated to fight, which left Rick as the only active combatant. Humphrey turned back to face him but Clive's vision power could see the magic of the lotus shells was about to end and warned the team.

Humphrey directed the team to quickly gather, which didn't take long. He was already close to the Clive and Neil, while Jason appeared from a nearby shadow. Sophie moved so fast it looked like she was skimming above the ground instead of running.

Inside her lotus shell, Beth had no idea what awaited her outside. She would have to rely on quick actions and quicker thinking when her spell dropped. Losing Hudson was a blow, but Niko and Emily would be fully healed, with refreshed mana and stamina. She hoped Humphrey and Rick's teams had taken the time to tear each other apart, which would allow her team to emerge and mop up.

The lotus shell dropped and her eyes fell immediately on Humphrey's team. They looked unharmed but they were gathered together in an easy clump. She cast a spell, eager to get it off before they reacted to the shells dropping and scattered.

"*Steelcutter thorns, burst forth and make the land your own.*"

Thorny vines erupted from the hard earth, splitting rock as they emerged, completely encapsulating Jason's team. Sharp thorns dug into them, even piercing Humphrey's conjured dragon-scale armour. They didn't penetrate far, but they were all bound such that any movement would cause the thorns to dig into them. As soon as the thorns started growing, Beth was moving in their direction. Emily and Niko were likewise setting themselves up to launch attacks the moment the thorns no longer obscured Jason's team.

"Clive and Neil, go," Humphrey said through the voice chat.

Not needing to move to cast spells, Neil and Clive both started chanting lengthy incantations. It was enough time that Beth was able to rush to the edge of the thorns and chant her own spell. On completion, she opened her mouth, from which streamed a wave of green spores, flooded over the field of thorns.

They all started getting messages from Jason's interface power.

Spell [Spore Cloud] has inflicted [Spore Toxin] on you.
You have resisted [Spore Cloud].
[Spore Cloud] does not take effect.
You have gained an instance of [Resistant].

Stuck in the cloud, the messages kept repeating. Only Jason resisted all the spores, but Sophie's aura helped the others resist many of them. Jason used his Feast of Absolution on Clive and Neil to cleanse them as they chanted their spells.

Neil completed his and, in the air above the thorns, an ornate water fountain appeared, floating in the air. It sprayed water down over the people in the thorn field, healing their wounds.

Spell [Fountain of Life] is healing you over time.

Shortly after, Clive completed his spell. High in the sky, a magical light traced out the shape of a huge eye in red and gold light.

You have entered a zone affected by the [Eye of Karma]. When you suffer damage, the originator of that damage will also suffer damage.

"NOW!" Humphrey yelled and the whole team started pushing themselves into the thorns. The floating fountain constantly healed them even as the thorns injured them. Beth shrieked as the retributive damage of five people being pierced all over their body tore her flesh to ribbons. When she died, the thorns withered, leaving the fountain to heal them of any remaining damage.

As the thorns withered, a hail of arrows fell from the sky and fire breath washed over them as Emily took the chance to strike. It was too little, too late, though, with the fountain still healing them. With their team outnumbering the survivors of both the others combined, the outcome was inevitable. Rick and Niko formed a temporary alliance but were overpowered by Humphrey, Sophie, Neil and Clive.

Jason, meanwhile, hounded Emily. Unlike with a normal pursuer, she never knew which shadow he would appear from and quickly realised running was pointless. Instead, she made herself ready to pepper him with arrows if he emerged. In the end, he baited her. When he appeared from the shadows, she fired her strongest special attack while retreating, creating distance between them. She backed right into a waiting mass of leeches.

The control room of the mirage chamber had extra platforms installed to accommodate fourteen people. The participants all got up and stretched. Their real bodies had been lying comfortably, yet they all felt exhausted.

Beth moved over to Humphrey, shaking his hand.

"You completely anticipated me," she told him. "It was a good win."

"That's the disadvantage of being the best adventurer in the city," he told her, unable to hide his victorious smile. "Everyone's paying attention to your abilities."

"That was very good," Danielle said, standing next to the control panel.

"I agree," Emir said, standing next to her. "You will all have a good chance in my little contest."

"When are you going to fill in some more details about that?" Jason asked.

"Only once your competition has arrived in the city," Emir said. "That should be any day now."

31
ARRIVAL

"You can begin, candidate Wexler," Vincent said. The Adventure Society official with the outrageous moustache was leading Sophie's assessment, just as he had Jason's. Sophie nodded as she stepped off the road and into the field of crops taller than she was.

"There were nine grass darters reported," Vincent said to the other candidates. "While candidate Wexler chases them down, we will have time to discuss the remainder of the day's notices. Those of you who have yet to demonstrate your aptitude to a satisfactory level should be looking to volunteer…"

He trailed off and looked to the crops, where Sophie emerged, struggling to carry four dead beetles, the size of small dogs. The group watched as she dumped them onto the road, each with a fist-sized hole in its carapace.

"According to the Magic Society listing," Sophie said, "the shells of these things are pretty valuable. You said you knew harvesting rituals, right, Clay?"

"Uh, yes," Clay said. "Were they already dead?"

"If they were already dead, they'd be rainbow smoke already," Sophie said. "Just harvest this lot and we'll go even split. I'll go pick up some more."

"How did you catch them so fast?" another candidate asked.

"I think these ones are duds," Sophie said. "The Magic Society listing said they were fast, but these seemed a bit sluggish. Can't hide their auras, either, so my perception power makes them easy to find."

Sophie ducked back into the field.

"I wouldn't put much stock in what candidate Wexler considers slow," Vincent advised the other candidates. "Her perspective is somewhat skewed."

⁎

At the marshalling yard, Jason and Belinda were part of the crowd waiting for the return of Sophie's assessment group. It was the first Adventure Society intake since the expedition; the last one had been cancelled in the wake of that disaster and the incursion of the inquiry team. For this assessment, Vincent had been paired up with a member of that team who mostly watched in silence. It was also a smaller group than usual, with families suddenly more wary about placing their young people in the path of potential harm.

"She'll pass, right?" Belinda asked nervously.

"She should," Jason said. "Vincent won't just give her an easy pass but she's better than I was when I took my assessment."

"She's better than you are now," Neil said. Their whole team was waiting for her in solidarity.

"I'll have you know, people find me very scary," Jason said.

"You're wearing a pink shirt with tropical flower print," Neil said.

"They could be poisonous flowers; you don't know."

"My concern is the member of the inquisition team they sent," Humphrey said. "He's meant to be assessing Vincent's execution of the assessment, but he may just make them fail everyone as some kind of example."

"They could have just sent Rufus for that," Jason said. "He failed everyone when he ran the assessment."

"He didn't fail me," Neil said.

"He did me," Humphrey said.

"He failed me before it even started," Jason said. "He wouldn't let me go, told me not to bother because I was definitely going to fail."

"Was he right?" Clive asked.

"Oh, yeah," Jason said. "A few weeks earlier I was assistant manager at an office supply store."

"A what store?" Belinda asked.

"Office supplies," Jason said. "The Station-Eyrie, where we're hawkish about your office supply needs."

"Does this make sense to anyone?" Neil asked.

"It's best to just let him go and not ask questions," Clive said. "That way lies madness, believe me."

"I am curious about his world, though," Belinda said.

"There are a lot of differences," Jason said. "More pamphlets, for example. You go to an accommodation and they'll have a stand of pamphlets for local attractions. I haven't seen that here."

"Pamphlets," Neil said flatly.

"Yeah," Jason said. "Folded pieces of paper with information printed on them.

You don't seem to have a lot of them here. Maybe I should start a business. I could be a pamphlet mogul."

"Is it too late to change teams?" Neil asked. "Someone must be looking for a healer."

A wagon rolled its way into the marshalling yard, Adventure Society candidates climbing out as it came to a stop. After a few words from Vincent, they broke off to meet with their families, some looking confident, others morose. Vincent exchanged a brief chat with the inquiry official before following Sophie over to their group.

"How do you think you did?" Belinda asked, giving Sophie a hug.

"You'll have to ask this guy," Sophie said, jabbing a thumb in Vincent's direction.

"We'll make our assessment reports today and final results go up tomorrow," Vincent said. "I don't think candidate Wexler has anything to be concerned about, though."

"How was the inquiry official?" Humphrey asked.

"Tough but fair," Vincent said. "He didn't demand quite as high a standard as Rufus, but he certainly wasn't going to tolerate the usual Greenstone standard."

"So we can expect better adventurers from now on?" Clive said.

"For a while," Vincent said. "How long it takes to fall back into old patterns, who knows. Adventure Society culture is set at the top and Elspeth Arella isn't what I'd hoped she'd be."

"My mother hates working with her," Humphrey said. "She wasn't happy Arella held onto her position, but this threat from the Builder pushes aside everything else for now."

"Speaking of which," Neil said, "did your mother say anything about Thadwick?"

"Not much," Humphrey said. "After they caught him, she watched the purging ritual herself. It seems to have extracted the star seed intact but Thadwick was fairly ravaged by the process. Last I heard, he hasn't woken up from the healing yet."

"Thanks," Neil said. "I hated being on his team but I've known him most of my life. He didn't deserve that."

"He tried to kill me that one time, so I kind of think he does," Jason said. "The suffering part, at least; I'm glad he's not dead."

"To finish the job yourself?" Sophie posited.

"No," Jason said. "Thalia Mercer knows her son's a useless dimwit but she'd still kill me if I did. Then my friends would go after the Mercers and on and on. I'm going to do what I should have done when I first met the guy and let it go."

"That's a mature attitude," Vincent said.

"I'm still going to make fun of him though," Jason said. "A lot. That guy sucks."

"That's slightly less mature," Vincent said, "but I'll take it."

Sophie vaulted over the gap between the Old City rooftops, sailing through the crisp morning air to land with delicacy and precision. The sun was only just peeking over the delta, beginning to banish the cold of night.

Gary was close behind Sophie, his leaps heavy and powerful compared to her light agility. Jason was a distant third, his cloak floating around him as it let him easily make the distance. On Jason's heels was Humphrey, manifesting wings to cross the gap. Bringing up the rear were Clive, Neil and Belinda, who balked at the jump, stopping at the edge of the roof.

"I can't make that jump," Neil said, breathing hard.

"Not with that attitude," Gary called back.

"We don't have movement powers," Clive said. "I can only teleport other people."

"Teleport me over, then," Belinda said.

"Why should you get the teleport?" Neil asked. "You aren't even an essence user yet."

"And I still have to do this awful training," Belinda shot back. "That's why I should get the teleport."

"No one's getting the teleport," Clive said. He backed up, broke into a run and vaulted the gap, successfully reaching the other side.

"Why do I even need to do this?" Neil asked. "I don't have any mobility powers."

"Which makes it all the more important," Humphrey said. "It means that if it comes down to it, the skills you're developing now will be all you have to rely on. What happened to the man who was eager to train?"

"I want to train the things I'm good at."

"That's all well and good," Gary said, "but it's the things you aren't good at that get you killed."

Neil groaned, but moved for a run-up before barely clearing the gap.

"Not bad," Gary said, thumping him heavily on the back.

That left only Belinda on the other rooftop, eyeing off the jump when an angry man climbed up from a window.

"Who's jumping up and down on my roof, first thing in the bloody morning?"

The team looked at each other uncertainly, then Clive chanted a spell.

"*Exchange your fates.*"

Belinda and Neil switched position, bringing Belinda into the group and leaving Neil with the angry homeowner.

"LEG IT!" Jason yelled and they all started sprinting.

"Oh, come on," Neil complained as he watched them go. Then he turned awkwardly to the man whose roof he was standing on.

"Well?" the man demanded.

"I'm with the Adventure Society," Neil said.

"Is there a monster up here?" the man asked, casting a gaze around.

"Uh, no," Neil admitted. "No, there isn't."

"Then get off my bloody roof!"

A crowd was gathered at a dock in the Old City port that had been completely cleared for the approaching ship.

"Why do you need me here for this?" Rufus asked. "I'm meant to be making final inspections of the annex site this morning before giving the go-ahead to break ground."

"You are still my contracted agent here," Emir said. "That's why you came here in the first place, which makes any other ventures of secondary concern."

"Since when do you care about that?" Rufus asked.

"Since now," Emir said. "Shut up and get ready to greet the people as they disembark."

They had spotted the approaching ship from the cloud palace. Full of Emir's recruited iron-rankers, it would normally have used the Adventure Society's private dock, but that was currently claimed by the cloud palace. Instead, room had been made at the regular port.

"You realise you've thrown this whole port into chaos, right?" Rufus asked. "They weren't expecting to have some gold-ranker come in and just claim a whole dock."

"The entire point of being a gold-ranker is to have other people deal with all the mundane problems."

"And here was me thinking it was to protect civilisation from monsters," Rufus said. "That's a life lesson, I guess."

Rufus made his way through the gathering of Adventure Society officials, Emir's staff, dockworkers, and adventurers, arriving dockside as the ship approached the dock. Rufus's eyes went wide as he spotted a man on board with midnight skin and dark, curly hair tied back behind his head. The man spotted him too and he launched off the boat, sailing through the air on a magical wind to land in front of Rufus.

"Hello, boy," the man said.

"Hello, Dad," Rufus said. "What are you doing here?"

32
FULL JASON

As the boat was still moving into the dock, the aeronautical early arrival of Gabriel Remore drew quite a lot of attention. The curious crowd pressed in for only a moment, though, before he pressured them back with his gold-rank aura.

"I see you haven't been working on subtlety while I've been away," Rufus said.

"Gods, you sound like your mother. She told me I shouldn't fly over."

"She's here, too?" Rufus asked, gaze moving from his father to the approaching ship.

"Oh, now you show some emotional investment," Gabriel said.

"Maybe if you didn't make everything about yourself," Rufus said. "Flying over here in front of all these people. What were you thinking?"

"That I could comfort my precious son."

"Then why didn't you bring Mother?"

The mirth dropped off Gabriel's face as he turned to look at the ship.

"She's with the Hurins," he said.

Rufus's face was stricken.

"Farrah's parents?" he asked feebly.

"They wanted to come."

Rufus reeled on the spot. "I shouldn't have… I should have brought her home straight away."

"It's alright," Gabriel said, placing a comforting hand on his son's shoulder. "I won't say it wasn't hard on them, because how could it not be. But those of us with adventurer children know that adventurers don't always come home."

"I was supposed to protect her."

"You were supposed to lead her, and you did."

Gabriel looked around at the gathered people watching them. He had already used his wind abilities to make their conversation private, but there was no shortage of onlookers.

"You're right," he said to his son. "I shouldn't have jumped over like that."

Rufus was bleary-eyed but gave his father a smile.

"If you didn't make a spectacle of yourself, I'd suspect you of being some kind of shape-shifter."

"That's kind of hurtful."

"You did an unscheduled fire-sword dance at my academy graduation," Rufus said.

Gabriel chuckled.

"Your grandad gave me an earful for that one."

Emir passed through the wind bubble keeping in the sound and gave Gabriel a welcoming hug.

"How was the trip, Gabe?"

"It was good," Gabriel said.

"You know I could have had Hester portal you in," Emir said.

"Arabelle wanted to take the long way," Gabriel told him. "All those stops picking up the iron-rankers gave us the chance to see some new places. It was good for the Hurins."

"With you, me and Arabelle here, you should have brought Cal, too," Emir said. "Get the old team together for a reunion."

"You know what he's like," Gabriel said. "If there's no monsters worth fighting, he's not interested. You couldn't drag him into a low magic zone like this one."

"He doesn't change, does he?" Emir asked, glancing again at the boat. "They'll be getting ready to disembark, soon. I'd best go greet all the tadpoles."

Emir was in front of a gathered group of iron-rankers. Some sixty or so had been on the boat, with two more boats still coming.

"Welcome to Greenstone," Emir said. "My name is Emir Bahadir and I'd like thank you all personally for coming all this way in response to my contract. As to the specifics, there will be a large announcement meeting once all of the adventurers have arrived. In the meantime, I suggest you report your arrival to the local branch of the Adventure Society. I've arranged a number of carriages to take you all there directly, and they can help you find local accommodation."

Adventurers didn't have luggage, instead carrying their possessions in dimensional bags or dimensional space abilities. They were trained to travel light and with efficiency and were soon heading for the Island in a train of carriages. Not all of them took the offered ride, heading straight off to explore Old City or hanging around the dock instead, hoping for some personal time with Emir.

Others were greeted by representatives of Greenstone's nobility or other prominent families. Every other family in Greenstone envied the power and influence the Gellers held in other lands and leapt at the chance to make outside connections. They hoped that playing host to the next generation of leaders would get them a foot in the door of a larger world. This was reinforced by the Geller family itself, who sent representatives to collect certain people to which they had connections.

Emir sent away most of those looking to make an early connection, all but a young girl of only fifteen years, with dark skin and rainbow-coloured hair that fell back over her head in a series of tight braids.

"Ketis," Emir greeted her warmly.

"Grandfather," she said with a respectful nod.

"No hug for your grandad?"

She gave him a hug after glancing around with the self-consciousness of her age.

"How was your trip?" he asked.

"The boat was so small," she complained, drawing a laugh from Emir.

"Of course it was small after the cloud ship," he said. "It's good for you to broaden your perspective."

"You don't broaden your perspective by narrowing the ship," she said sullenly, and Emir laughed again.

"Did you enjoy travelling with Aunty Arabelle?"

She nodded.

"Alright," he said. "Come along as I say hello. I have a present for you later."

They wandered over to where Rufus and his father were talking with three other people. Rufus's mother, Arabelle, had even darker skin than her husband, her long hair dyed rainbow colours in the Vitesse style. Farrah's parents, the Hurins, were fair-skinned, like their daughter had been. Emir knew that while they looked older than the Remores, Amelia and William Hurin were actually younger.

Of humble origins, they had become adventurers later in life. As young parents, they had stumbled upon the valuable potent essence. Instead of selling it for its considerable value, they kept it hidden as they worked to obtain more. By the time their daughter was old enough to use them, the Hurins had the more common fire and earth essences to go with it. It was only after their daughter found success as an adventurer that she repaid the gift twice over and they, too, became essence users.

Farrah's parents had no interest in following their daughter into the Adventure Society. They were both bronze rank, having raised their abilities using the monster cores Farrah brought back from her adventures. Rufus and Gary had likewise contributed their own shares.

As Emir approach, Rufus was bowed before them, practically kneeling.

"I'm so sorry," he told them.

"Please stop apologising," Farrah's mother, Amelia said. "Our daughter died as an adventurer, and she died proudly. You're no more to blame than we are for giving her those essences in the first place."

"We had an informal wake a couple of weeks ago," Rufus said. "Now you're here, I'll arrange something more formal."

The two sets of parents shared a glance over Rufus's bowed head.

"You do that," Farrah's father, William said. "We'd appreciate it, son."

In the cloud palace training hall, Humphrey and Sophie were clashing while Jason, Neil, Clive and Belinda rested in the observation area. Humphrey had his smaller conjured sword out, Sophie deflecting it with her fists.

"When I get my own essences," Belinda told Clive, "I think I'll prefer to fight at range, like you. Getting up close like that is really more Sophie's area."

"That can be tricky for a human," Neil said. "Humans get more special attacks than anything else, unless you get a racial gift evolution early, like Clive. Mostly that means melee attacks. If you want range, then a bow essence would be a good choice. That's the most reliable way to get ranged special attacks."

"Or you could get an ability that lets you use skill books," Clive said. "That way, you can gain whatever skills you need. The adept essence is a solid bet, in that case."

"I looked at the bow essence, but decided against it," Belinda said. "Adept is on my list, though."

"You're already picking out essences?" Neil asked.

"Clive let me look at the Magic Society essence listings," Belinda said. "I've picked out a set I like the look of. They're all common essences, so they shouldn't be that hard to get."

"You've made a decision?" Clive said. "What combination?"

"Magic, adept and trap," she said.

"Magic and adept are popular essences, but not hard to find," Clive said. "Trap is more of a niche selection. Mostly assassin and hunter types go for it; I think it's an undervalued essence when it comes to monster hunting."

"What's the confluence essence for that?" Neil asked.

"Charlatan," Belinda said with glee. "I was looking through the abilities it's known to give and they sound fantastic."

Neil and Clive shared a glance.

"Charlatan?" Neil asked.

"From recollection," Clive said, "it's a confluence more people avoid than seek out. Most would disagree with you on the value of the abilities it gives."

"Then those people lack imagination," Belinda said. "I looked through long lists of abilities. I don't want to pick out some essences looking for fun, tricky abilities, only to end up with a boring set of straightforward attacks. Ideally, I'd get one of those racial gift evolutions that means I'm not stuck shooting nine kinds of magic arrow."

"We fought a couple of people in the mirage chamber recently who might disagree," Neil said.

"Those people lost," Belinda said. "Maybe they would have done better if they had more tricks in their pocket."

"Harsh," Jason said. "I have to agree with the value of having a few hidden surprises at the ready, though."

"As do I," Emir said as the elevating platform brought him up into the room. "Speaking of surprises, I believe you have something for me?"

Clive pushed himself out of the chair, took a heavy book from his storage space and handed it to Emir.

"Skill book. Way of the Reaper, form three."

"You aren't still holding out on me, are you?" Emir asked. "Jason told me you didn't take anything from that complex you found."

"I said no such thing," Jason said. "If you think back, you'll find I dodged the question. If I went telling high-rankers every time I found something interesting, they'd just keep taking them off me."

"Is that why you kept your and Miss Wexler's unusual combat style from me for so long?"

"I thought it was best if your interest in her was purely altruistic," Jason said. "It was her choice to tell you. She wanted to thank you for taking her in when you had no need to."

"My client is very interested in the origin of that fighting style," Emir said. "Once our business here is done, I suspect he will have an interest in tracing Miss Wexler's family history. Perhaps, once her indenture is done, she will be interested in that journey for herself."

"That's up to her," Jason said. "So, this granddaughter of yours has been learning the Way of the Reaper too?"

"My search has taken time and found many relics of the Order of the Reaper," Emir said. "That includes skill books. My granddaughter can use skill books and was very interested in practicing a lost style. I was reluctant, having only recovered books containing three of the five forms. In the end, she wore me down."

"Your client didn't want the books?" Clive asked.

"My client appreciates any relics I send his way and pays me appropriately, but I am only contracted for one item. We have found multiple copies of these skill books and had some to spare, but only for three of the forms. We haven't found anything for the second or third."

"We found intact copies of forms one and three," Clive said. "We can't help you with a book for form two."

"I'm not so sure about that," Emir aid. "My hope is that one will be recovered during the upcoming contest," Emir said. "I will share the details once the other boats arrive. Even if not, both you and Miss Wexler have knowledge of form two, do you not, Jason?"

"We do. We're grateful for all you've done for us, so we'd be happy to teach her what we can."

"That's excellent," Emir said. "You'll meet her soon. Have you met Rufus's parents, yet?"

"Not yet," Jason said. "Rufus and Gary have been with them and Farrah's parents since they arrived."

"Rufus had a request for you, for when you meet his father."

"Oh?" Jason asked.

"Rufus's father, Gabriel, likes to make a big first impression. He didn't tell Rufus he was coming, then made quite the entrance at the port."

"So I've heard," Jason said.

"Rufus requested that when you meet his father, you go what he referred to as 'full Jason,' whatever that means."

"Oh, we know what that means," Neil said.

"Yes, we do," Clive said.

"What are you two talking about?" Jason said.

"You questioned if I was even an elf, then accused me of being fat," Neil said.

"You claimed to have slept with my non-existent wife, then accused me of sleeping with your non-existent wife."

"Neil's an elf?" Belinda asked.

"Yes, I'm an elf!"

"You are quite hefty for an elf."

"My proportions are perfectly normal!"

"I see it now," Emir said. "This is exactly what Rufus was looking for."

"He had his landlady yell at me."

33
VERSATILE

Jason was sitting in a meditation pose on one of the cloud palace's open terraces when Rufus wandered along with his parents.

"This is Jason," Rufus said.

Jason turned his head and opened one eye to look before springing lightly to his feet.

"Gabriel and Arabelle Remore," Rufus said.

"So this is the Jason Asano I've heard so much about," Gabriel said.

"You have?" Jason asked, surprise clear on his face. "Most people only pay attention to the big names, you know? Staedtler, Moranse; the ones with all the fancy glazing techniques, the overdone vases that no one ever actually uses as a vase. I mean, seriously. If the form overwhelms the function, what's the point, am I right?"

"Glazing?" Gabriel asked in confusion.

"I know, right?" Jason asked. "The true enthusiast understands that it isn't about the flashy finish but the craftsmanship of the underlying product. Every aficionado who truly knows their business understands that the real collectible is also the most practical. They don't go for the weird oversized bowls or the fancy jugs with artistic flourishes that compromise volume. They know that solid, economical designs are what really endure."

"I'm sorry," Gabriel said, "but what are you talking about?"

"Pottery," Jason said. "That's why you heard about me, right? And I can tell you that the rumours are true: I have the best clay to coin ratio in Greenstone. You want practical, affordable earthenware, then I'm your guy."

"Pottery?"

"Oh yeah," Jason said enthusiastically. "I'm not just about the pots and bowls, either. You want the inside skinny on the industry, then I'm your man."

Jason narrowed his eyes, giving the Remores an assessing look, then leaned in, conspiratorially.

"Because you're Rufus's family," Jason said, "I might have a little inside tip for you."

"I think there may have been a mistake," Gabriel said.

"No mistake, my friend," Jason said, giving Gabriel a pat on the arm. "You want the inside scoop? The hidden truth the other earthenware merchants won't tell you? You can forget the vases, my friend. The bowls, pots, pitchers, planters and jugs. I know they're all the fancy, eye-catching stuff that the ordinary collectors go for. And those big-name potters, they're more than happy to feed them the dross while keeping the real goods for themselves."

"What is happening?" Gabriel asked, looking at his son in confusion.

"The future is happening," Jason said. "Not just the future of pottery, as if that wasn't exciting enough, but the future of beverages themselves!"

"Beverages?"

"Oh, yes, my friend. I know it seems like everyone stores wine in bottles these days, but take it from an industry insider: amphorae are coming back in a big way."

"Amphorae?"

"That's the stuff," Jason said. "These aren't your grandmother's amphorae; they're not just for wine anymore. Milk, tea, juice, liquor, Bovril."

"Bovril?"

"Oh, I forgot you don't have cows, here. Lizard Bovril? Forget the Bovril, focus on the amphorae. I realise that every good collector has an amphora or two squirrelled away somewhere. They're always an addendum, though; a punctuation point in a piquant pottery poem, but I'm here to tell you, friend, that amphorae are about to explode onto the scene that will make vases look like little dishes people use for hard candy!"

"I really don't understand what's happening," Gabriel said.

"Of course you don't," Jason said, moving next to Gabriel and slipping a sympathetic arm over his shoulder. "Even as we speak, the potters of the world are hidden away, crafting amphora after amphora for the bonanza to come."

Gabriel pulled himself away from Jason, which did nothing to dampen Jason's enthusiasm.

"I've very clearly missed something in this situation," Gabriel said.

"Of course you have," Jason said, "but that isn't your fault. It's these so-called industry professionals, collection agents and gallery owners. They know the truth, but will they tell good, honest collectors like you? No, they won't. It's a conspiracy, my friend, an amphora conspiracy to keep you out of the game until the market explodes and they hold all the cards."

"I'm very confused," Gabriel said.

"I know," Jason said sympathetically. "Some poor, innocent pottery enthusiast can't be expected to understand the market nuances and industry secrets. That's surely why Rufus brought you to me, right?"

"Oh, I definitely brought him here for this," Rufus said.

"There you are," Jason said. "Clearly you're a gentleman of insight and means."

Jason leaned over to Rufus.

"He is a man of means, right?" Jason whispered loudly.

"Oh, yes," Rufus said and Jason gave Gabriel a beaming smile.

"Insight and means," he said again. "A man who won't miss an opportunity literally hidden away from the more ordinary collector. Let me paint you a picture. A workshop, filled with secretive but capable apprentices, all under the direction of an experienced and rakishly handsome man with almost months of experience. Rack after rack of amphorae. No bowls, no pots, no jugs. Just one amphora after another, poised for that market shift, ready to explode in prominence."

"Are you trying to get me to give you money?" Gabriel asked.

"It's not about money," Jason said. "It's about showing those with an iron grip on the industry that we can bust open their artificial scarcity! And also money. You drop seven or eight gold spirit coins now, and a few years down the track, you could very well have made some of it back!"

"Could?"

"Hold on, I have a pamphlet here somewhere."

"Pamphlet?"

Jason patted his pockets absently, then his face lit up as he remembered and he plucked a pamphlet out of the air, shoving it into Gabriel's hand. Gabriel looked warily at the cover.

"Step one, collect underpants?" he read.

"Oops," Jason said, snatching back the pamphlet and shoving it into his inventory. He then pulled out a fistful of pamphlets and started leafing through them, reading to himself as he went.

"Church of Om; not a lot of hope for that catching on. Shelving unit assembly. Wicker versus rattan furniture selection guide."

He looked up at Gabriel. "Sorry mate, just a second."

Jason resumed sorting through the pamphlets as Gabriel searched his still innocent-looking son's face for any hint of explanation.

"Basic guide to yoghurt," Jason continued. "Woven rug care in five easy steps; I've been looking for that one. Blue Oyster Bar, that one's for Rufus. Oh, here we go; basic guide to amphora selection."

Jason handed over the pamphlet as he shoved the rest back into his inventory.

"Note that the pictures show each amphora at the same size," Jason said, pointing. "That's just to make use of the space on the pamphlet, though obviously any given amphora can come in any size. For clarity, you'll note that there's a standard reference pear in each picture."

Gabriel looked at Jason like he was some kind of madman.

"Reference pear?"

"That's industry standard," Jason said. "I thought you said you were a collector?"

"I am not a collector!"

"Then why did you say you were?" Jason asked, anger and confusion splashed across his face. "Are you just here trying to dig up industry secrets? I told you about my slave workshop!"

"Slave workshop?"

"Indentured servants, whatever. Oh, this is a shocking turn up."

"I thought you were an adventurer."

"Oh, it's always like that, isn't it?" Jason said. "You kill a few hundred monsters and suddenly all people see you as is an adventurer. Let me tell you, mate, adventuring is just a job. Pottery is a vocation."

Jason yanked the pamphlet from Gabriel's hand.

"Forget this," he said bitterly, stormed over to the terrace railing and vault over the side, dropping out of sight.

"So that was Jason," Rufus said mildly. "Next we'll head to the guest wing lounge and dining area, where I've had some lunch prepared."

"Dear," Gabriel said.

"Yes, my love?" Arabelle asked. She had remained silent throughout the encounter.

"What just happened?"

"We just met Rufus's friend, dear," she said. "Don't be judgemental."

"Judgemental? The man was a loon!"

"He's from very far away," Arabelle said. "He's bound to have some idiosyncrasies."

"Idiosyncrasies? He tried to get me to invest in a pottery workshop staffed by slaves! He wouldn't stop saying amphora and I still have no idea what Bovril is."

"I think it's a local delicacy where he comes from," Rufus said. "Don't worry about it, Dad. I have food waiting."

"Yes, do come along, dear," Arabelle said and set off with her son, Gabriel trailing after.

"You set this up," Gabriel accused Rufus. "This is for jumping off the ship in front of all those people, isn't it?"

"No idea what you're talking about, Dad."

“You actually made pamphlets?” Gary asked, as Jason recounted the story later.

“Yep,” Jason said. “Eight of them. There's a simple ritual to print images, so the real issue was finding the right cardstock. For a good pamphlet, it has to be nice and thin, but firmer than just paper. Durable, with a good feel in the hand.”

They were sat around a banquet table in the guest wing lounge and dining area. It was Jason’s full team, plus Gary, Belinda, Jory, Phoebe, Emir and his chief of staff, Constance.

Emir was laughing as Rufus led in his parents.

“You!” Gabriel said, pointing at Jason, making Emir laugh all the harder.

“Sit down and eat, Gabe,” Emir said. “Always a pleasure, Bella. You can sit next to me.”

“Keep your hands off my wife,” Gabriel said, sitting down.

“Connie, always a pleasure,” Arabelle said, sitting next to Constance.

“Bella,” Constance greeted. Emir’s usually reserved chief of staff seemed a little more relaxed than normal. Only a little, but it stood out.

“Lovely to see you again,” Jason said and made introductions around the table. When introducing Rufus's parents, he referred to his mother as an esteemed adventurer, venerated by kings and heroes. Gabriel, he referred to as some kind of teacher.

“I have a question,” Gabriel said to Jason.

“Just one?”

“How much of what you were saying to me was a lie?”

“All of it,” Jason said. “I was lying through my teeth. I’d probably mistake a kiln for a rustic barbecue and use it to cook sausages.”

“I’m a gold ranker,” Gabriel said. “I can see right through your aura.”

“Rude, but okay,” Jason said.

“Why couldn’t I tell you were lying? It should have been in your aura.”

“Oh, that’s a technique from my world called the Stanislavski system,” Jason said. “To grossly oversimplify, it's about becoming the person you're pretending to be in the moment.”

“It’s a formidable tool,” Arabelle said.

“Especially when you run around making high-ranking enemies, the way Jason does,” Gary said.

“What are you talking about?” Jason said. “Everybody loves me.”

“Speaking of which,” Emir said, “I was hoping you could help me with something, Jason.”

“Oh?” Jason asked.

“I thought I might take the opportunity of all these new adventurers arriving to try and bait out the Builder cultists and I had an idea that makes use of your flair for pompous melodrama.”

“Pompous melodrama?” Jason said, as laughter spread around the table at his hurt expression.

"That's your problem?" Emir asked. "Not being used as bait for evil cultists?"

"No worries there, mate," Jason said. "Evil cultists are kind of my thing."

"Evil cultists are your thing?" Phoebe asked.

"Jason has a lot of things," Gary said.

"I'm versatile," Jason said.

34
I DON'T LIKE THIS PLAN

The marshalling yard was full of adventurers, waiting for Emir Bahadir to arrive. The third and final boatload of iron-rankers had arrived the day before and a meeting had been called to finally explain the big job. Along with all the imported adventurers, the locals were out in full force. After the expedition, only those confident in their abilities were going to participate, but—iron, bronze or silver—everyone wanted to know what had brought Emir to Greenstone in the first place.

"Asano!"

The voice was loud and challenging, grabbing attention. Jason and his team were waiting with everyone else, looking up when someone called out Jason's name. Space was made as a young man strode through the crowd.

"Asano," the man said again.

"Something I can help you with?" Jason asked.

"You have one of your own team members as a slave?" the man asked.

"Indentured servant," Jason said. "Do you have a name, or should I just keep thinking about you as that loud guy who won't mind his own business?"

"Julian Cross," the man said.

"Alright, Julian," Jason said. "What exactly does my team or my indentured servant have to do with you?"

"Letting an adventurer be an indentured servant is a disgrace. Relinquish her."

"That wouldn't set her free, idiot. It's a court-ordered indenture, so they'd just put her contract up for auction."

"Then you should transfer her contract to someone who won't treat her like a slave."

"Says the guy who's talking about her instead of to her, when she's standing right here."

Jason half-turned his head in Sophie's direction. "What do you think? You want this guy to have your contract?"

"I'm not against getting away from you," she said. "I think I can do better than him, though."

"Not true," Julian said. "I wouldn't treat you like a slave. You'd receive far better treatment than he would ever give you."

"The thing is," Jason said, "neither of you actually get a say. You, Julian, aren't involved at all, despite marching up and making a scene in front of all these people. As for you, woman, you belong to me."

"Screw you," Sophie said.

"If and when I say," Jason said coldly.

"You think I'll just stand here and let you treat an adventurer like that?" Julian asked. "I challenge you."

"Challenge me?"

"To a duel. There is a mirage chamber in this city, so I've heard. If you win, I shall withdraw from this event and return to my homeland. If I win, then you transfer the contract over to me."

"If you want to duel, mate, there won't be any mirage chamber involved. You want to put something on the line, then it's your blood. Do you have a first blood rule in duelling, here?"

"We do," Julian said.

"Then we do it here and we do it now," Jason said. "You and me. First blood."

"Fine," Julian said. "One blow is all I need to kill you, anyway."

Space was quickly made, a circle of onlookers forming the borders of their impromptu arena. Julian and Jason circled each other, around five metres apart. Julian had the lean, athletic physique of most adventurers, with sharp, predatory features, swarthy skin and a mane of amber hair. His hand rested lightly on the undrawn sword at his hip.

Jason was on the other side of the encircling adventurers, shrouded in his cloak. In his hand was his conjured dagger, Ruin. The pair of combatants eyed each other off, each waiting for the opening that would give them the win. They circled slowly, each careful with their footwork, ready to move at any moment. Julian was the first to act.

His sword erupted from its scabbard, a spark flashing from the blade and driving into Jason's cloak. The cloak was already empty; Jason had left it behind as he used it to shadow teleport. He rose behind Julian from his shadow, reaching around to slash Julian's throat.

As Jason casually tossed aside his conjured dagger, which vanished into thin air, Julian clutched a hand over his throat, blood seeping between his fingers. His other hand scrambled for a potion, which he tipped into his mouth.

"First blood," Jason said. "You'd best have a healer look at that, mate. Your welcome for me not going deep, by the way."

Julian pushed his way through the crowd, a hand still clutched over his throat. Jason turned around on the spot, casting a challenging gaze over everyone.

"Does anyone else have a problem with me?" he called out. "That one was a warning. There won't be any more duels. You have a problem with me, either keep it to yourself or I will put you down. If any more people here have an issue with that, I can start right now."

"That's easy to say with Bahadir standing behind you," someone called out from the crowd. "You think we don't know you've been staying in the cloud palace? You can talk big all you like, but it's not you that we're afraid of."

"Well said," Emir's voice boomed over the crowd from above.

Everyone looked up to see Emir flying through the air, feet shrouded in a small patch of cloud. The cloud vanished and he dropped lightly to the ground, next to Jason.

"Jason," Emir said, "if you want to challenge any and all who come your way then, by all means, do so. However, you must use your own strength to do so, not mine. I think it is time for my hospitality to come to an end before it starts to hinder your progress as an adventurer. The cloud palace is closed to you now."

"You can't do that!" Jason exclaimed.

"I can and have. Your aura imprint will be wiped from the cloud palace's access list. This is for your own good; relying on the strength of others will cause your own to atrophy."

"You think I need you?" Jason asked. "You just wait. You'll see what I can do on my own."

"I genuinely look forward to it."

Jason's rage-filled face was obscured as his cloak formed around him once again. Then the cloak was empty as he teleported away, drifting down for a moment before vanishing. Emir let out a world-weary sigh, then turned to the crowd.

"I realise there will be tension between locals and the newcomers, so let me be plain. As many of you have surmised, Jason Asano is under my protection. I am extending that protection to every iron-ranker who signs on to the open contract I will be posting at the Adventure Society today, and that protection is the same for all, in both its extent and its limits. The protection is thus: every one of you must be fit for action when the contract begins in three days. I don't care what you do to one another, so long as you can be healed and ready for action at that time. That goes for Asano and each and every one of you."

The cloud appeared around Emir's feet again and he floated into the air, rising slightly above the crowd.

"Now that is dealt with, we move onto the nature of the contract. Centuries ago, there was an ancient order of assassins, known as the Order of the Reaper.

They were hunted down and exterminated, but rumours always remained of a legacy left behind, a final, hidden fortress. At the behest of a diamond-rank client, I have spent the last few years searching the world for that fortress."

Emir panned his gaze over the group.

"As you have no doubt surmised, the fortress has been found, here in the Greenstone region. There is a lake, at the bottom of which the remains of that fortress have been long hidden. My people found it, but the true sanctum is not so easily penetrated. The legacy found therein comes with a test, a trial for who seek it out. It is held within an astral space that, even once unsealed, will only admit iron-rankers. All attempts to otherwise penetrate it have fallen short. Only by activating the trials will it open, and only for those who have the longest road left to walk. Iron-rankers, like you."

He paused, giving the crowd a few moments for his words to sink in.

"As I said, this fortress is at the bottom of a lake. My people will be on hand to grant you access, but reaching the depths—and they are depths—will be the first requirement of participation. If you cannot manage even that much, then there is no hope of you completing the trial anyway. All further details will be on the open contract, which will be posted shortly."

With that, Emir floated away.

Many towns and village in the delta had accommodation just for adventurers. It always paid to make the people who killed the monsters for you welcome and comfortable. Certain hub locations were especially used to adventurers passing through and people knew better than to take a second glance at the often oddly dressed and heavily armed individuals.

Into one of the larger establishments strode two figures shrouded in dark cloaks. This was not unusual; more than a few young adventurers had become enamoured with being mysterious. One of the cloaks was obviously magical, seemingly made from darkness itself. The other was a dark brown, plain, but high quality. The two adventurers paid for one of the larger private rooms and went inside.

Jason's cloak vanished and Hester pushed the hood back on hers. Hester was the only Asiatic-looking person he had seen in this world outside of his own reflection. Her appearance was closer to South Asian than his own Japanese features.

"Where are you from, Hester?" he asked.

"Pranay, originally."

Jason was slowly learning about his new world, including the geography. Pranay was this world's equivalent of Sri Lanka, larger and further south than his own. It made for a huge landmass in the middle of what, in his world, was called the Indian Ocean.

"What's it like?"

"A lot like the delta, actually," she said. "I became an adventurer to see the world, but now travel is so easy for me that I spend more and more of my time back home."

"That's nice," Jason said. "I'd like to be able to do that, someday. My home's a little farther away, though."

"Nothing's impossible," Hester said. "Working for Emir, I've seen enough diamond rankers to learn that much. Even from what little I've witnessed, they function on a scale of power that's hard to believe."

Hester drew a circle in the air with her hand, which shimmered into being as a portal when she was done. They arrived in the cloud palace's guest wing lounge, where a large group was already having lunch. Emir and Constance, Belinda and Jory, Rufus and his parents, plus Gary and Jason's team. Julian was there as well, his throat injury fully healed.

Jason nodded a greeting at Julian as he and Hester sat down.

"I didn't go too deep, did I?" Jason asked.

"No, it was perfect," Julian said. "The potion alone was enough to deal with the damage. You know your throat-slitting."

"You have no idea," Humphrey said. "I have this recording you should see."

"Will you stop showing that to people?"

"The bit where you let the spear hit you is the creepiest," Belinda said. "The way you pull it out and lick it? So disgusting."

"It really was," Jason said. "I think Jonah might have nicked a bowel."

"You don't have bowels," Clive said.

"I don't have bowels?"

"As essence users," Clive explained, "we all go through physiological changes as we increase in rank. At iron rank, our digestion starts operating very differently. Our gold-rankers here don't even need to breathe. Each time we rank up, in addition to making our bodies superior vessels for magic, there are changes to how our bodies operate. It's one of the reasons we can suffer more damage than others. Many of the vulnerable points in the torso are less vulnerable because we use what's in there less. By the time we reach silver and gold, we are mostly just containers for a living mass that serves to rapidly heal injury."

"Are you sure you don't want to come work for me?" Emir asked.

"Stop trying to poach my team member," Jason said.

"I'm still unclear the point of what we did out there," Julian said. "I'm grateful for the opportunity, don't get me wrong. Coming to work for you, Mr Bahadir, is a much better opportunity than some prize I likely wouldn't get, but I don't understand the purpose of setting the iron-rankers on each another."

"Chaos," Jason said. "You've heard about the five people who were implanted with star seeds, yes?"

"Yes," Julian said.

"We're confident that the goal of implanting those people was to sow discord," Emir said. "One died and we've captured and purged two of the others. Two remain at large, however, and the attention and resources we dedicate to finding them is attention and resources we aren't sending after the Builder cult."

"Emir's declaration today basically gave everyone an opening to spend the next couple of days engaging in controlled chaos," Jason said. "The hope is that the Builder cult seeks to tip that chaos from controlled to uncontrolled in the lead-up to the open contract, making it easier to enact their plans for the astral space."

"What's that got to do with you?" Julian asked.

"Jason is now the focal point of this iron-rank mess Emir has made," Gabriel said. "He's close with Emir, but suddenly outside of Emir's protection. There wouldn't be a much better way to muddy the waters than implant Jason with a star seed, which we're hoping they attempt."

"Even if they don't bite, it doesn't really cost us anything to try," Jason said.

"What if they succeed and you actually get implanted?" Julian asked.

"That is the part that concerns me, as well," Gary said. "I don't like this plan."

"Jason will be watched at all times," Emir assured him. "I've brought in a specialist."

Emir nodded at a man sitting at the table that no one had noticed appear. He was a middle-aged man, the kind of grizzled that perpetually made him look like he should be in the wilderness somewhere, hunting something.

"You had Hester bring in Cal," Gabriel said.

"What my husband means to say is hello," Arabelle said. "How've you been, Cal?"

"Busy," Cal said, his voice as gravelly as his face. "It's good to see you, Bella."

"This is Callum Morse," Emir said. "If he doesn't want to be seen, no one short of diamond rank will see him. He'll be over Jason's shoulder at every moment until the contract begins. Hopefully, he'll bag us some Builder cultists."

The lunch went on, the large group chatting away. Julian, Clive and Neil were all quiet, intimidated by gold-rank company. Although a born pedagogue, Clive was easily drawn out at the chance to explain one thing or another.

"You know, Cal," Gabriel said, "Jason here can keep lies out of his aura. You're the only other person I've seen do that."

"How do you all know each other?" Jason asked.

"Oh, we were all a team, back when we were young and foolish like you kids," Emir said. "After we got to gold, though, our priorities started to shift. Cal here was happy to spend the rest of his days carving his way through the monster population, but he was having to look harder for a challenge. I wanted adventures more exotic than what the Adventure Society was offering and took up fortune hunting for hire."

He waved a finger between Gabriel and Arabelle.

"These two," he said, "wanted to go off and make babies. Utterly pointless."

"Excuse me?" Rufus said. "I'm one of those babies."

"And how long did it take you to be able to hold a worthwhile conversation?" Emir asked. "Children aren't a time-effective proposition."

"I'd like children someday," Constance opined quietly.

"What's time anyway?" Emir asked, course-corrected rapidly. "When you live as long as we do, what's a little time in return for the joy of parenting?"

After lunch, Hester returned Jason to the guest house from which they had portalled into the cloud palace. She did not remain behind, portalling away again while Sophie took Hester's position under the brown cloak. Jason and Sophie then left, ostensibly laying low after events in the marshalling yard while leaving a trail for the Builder cult to follow.

35

IMPOSSIBLE TO SUBDUE

"What is it you need me for?" Sophie asked.

"You're not happy with enjoying a nice day in the delta?"

They were strolling along an embankment road in the delta, Jason setting their meandering pace.

"It's not terrible," Sophie conceded. "I'm just not sure why you need me to join you on the hook."

"You know about fishing, but you didn't know about rain?"

"I probably heard someone mention it, but it isn't something that really comes up."

"Seems like it would be," Jason said. "Delta merchants, sailors. And you weren't born here, right? Didn't you come to this city on a ship? Surely that got rained on."

"Who told you that? Was it Belinda?"

"Don't recall," Jason said. "One of the Berts, maybe?"

"I don't really remember anything before Greenstone," Sophie said. "I was very young. My earliest memories are of my father working for the Silva family."

"My dad's done a lot of work for the government," Jason said. "That's worse than working with criminals, believe me."

"You didn't answer my question," Sophie said. "Humphrey warned me about that."

"Teenagers," Jason said, shaking his head. "No discretion."

"That's rich coming from you," she said. "This whole plan is formulated on you making a huge spectacle of yourself. Which you did."

"Sorry about the whole 'you do what I say, woman,' thing. I was kind of leaning into the villainy."

"That seems to be your first reaction," she said. "I've seen the recording of that ridiculous fight."

"It was pretty over the top, right? I was just looking for a way to win. That meant killing a bunch of teenagers, so going movie monster seemed the natural choice."

"Why do you do that?" she asked.

"Do what?"

"Make reference to things you know people won't understand. Is it part of the whole crazy persona you have going?"

"No," Jason said. "Well, yes, probably. Where I come from they call it a weirdness coupon. If people expect you to do strange things, then they accept it easier when you do. Have you ever noticed how people don't expect me to respect authority or adhere to ordinary codes of conduct?"

"I've been waiting for someone to kick the crap out of you for that."

"It's happened, once or twice," Jason said. "But I get away with it, more than not. How many times have you seen me doing something absurd and have someone tell you 'oh, that's just Jason?'"

"Quite a lot, actually."

"And there you are," Jason said. "I've never been good at fitting in, so I've learned how to stand out the right way. I admit that I've taken it pretty far here, but magic and monsters make everything… bigger. Bigger personalities, bigger dangers. Half measures don't work and you have to find a way to either make your mark or fade into the background. Getting caught in the middle will just get you chewed up and spat out. Go big or go home, as they say where I come from."

"So all this strangeness is just an act?"

"Not at all," he said. "There's method to the madness, sure, but there's also madness to the madness. It's about leaning into your strengths and working with what you've got—a lesson you could stand to learn, by the way."

"What are you talking about?" she asked.

"Look at your circumstances before Clive and I came along," he said. "You and Belinda, scrambling from one problem to the next. Every escape dropping you into a worse situation, the city tightening around you like a noose. You know why that is?"

"Because life sucks."

"You've had some rough circumstances and no mistake," Jason conceded. "You went at them the wrong way, though."

"Is that so?"

Sophie looked out at the marshes around the raised embankment road they walked along. Leaving the familiar streets of the city only heightened her sense of everything slipping from her control.

"I told you that you have to stand out or fade away," Jason said, "or you'll get chewed up in the middle. You got chewed up pretty good. I've learned a fair bit about what you've been through and what you did about it, and it's plain to see what happened."

"You think you know me?" she asked.

"I'm starting to get there," he said. "You kept choosing to fade into the background, but everything you did was about making your mark. You've been telling yourself you're doing one thing while you're really doing the opposite."

"So, you know what I really should have done?"

"Not at all," Jason said. "I haven't lived your life or faced your circumstances. Compared to you, my life has been sunshine and rainbows. But you have to realise that you're never going to fade into the background. It's not just the way you look, although that's certainly a thing."

"You have a problem with the way I look."

"Of course I don't," Jason said. "I'm a straight man with eyes. But the way you look is a perfect reflection of who you are. Your hair, your clothes; you choose them for practicality. They shout to the world that you want to do your thing and don't want anyone to bother you. But they can't hide what you are."

"And what's that?" she asked, voice thick with challenge.

"Fierce. Arresting. Indomitable. If you asked Cole Silva or Lucian Lamprey why they chased after you, they'd probably say it was because of the way you look. Maybe that's how it started, but it's not why they kept chasing so hard for so long. They'd be lying, especially to themselves. A certain kind of man is insecure about his power. If he senses a challenge to it, he has to possess or destroy whatever is making him feel challenged."

"Is that what you think? You're reading too much into a pair of sleazy guys used to getting what they want."

"That's the whole point of what I'm saying," Jason said. "They didn't get what they were after. I might have come along at the end, but Lamprey had been chasing you for months. Silva for years, from what I've heard. If you weren't captured by my resourcefulness and dashing good looks, you'd probably still be out there."

"Wasn't it mostly Clive who caught us?"

"I did most of the fighting and chasing."

"Like a minion, while he did all the set up. Like a boss."

"Wouldn't that make you Belinda's minion?"

"I'm alright with that."

"That's actually really nice," Jason said. "That level of trust."

"You don't have people you trust?"

"Actually, I'm thick with them," Jason said. "I didn't have a lot of friends, back home. Someone hurt me, made it hard to trust people. I did a lot of getting chewed up in the middle, from being too afraid to embrace what I really am."

"A nonsensical loon?"

"Yes," he said. "This world forced me to answer new challenges. To be more than I was and to find people I could trust and rely on. I could have stayed quiet, worked my way up as another unremarkable iron-ranker. But you know what? I am remarkable. For good or ill."

He gave her a wry smile.

"So are you, whether you like it or not. Most people, faced with your circumstances, would capitulate. Endure to get by. You didn't. You took extreme measure after extreme measure, even as you told yourself you were trying to lay low. You're so bad at taking the quiet road that you followed it right into a storm of politicians, crime lords and adventurers. You can't hide because you burn too bright. Until you accept that, you're just going to keep getting chewed up."

She didn't respond, thinking as she threw him wary glances.

"What does 'indomitable' mean?" she asked, finally.

"Impossible to subdue," Jason said.

"I'm your indentured servant."

"Are you, though?" Jason asked. "If you wanted to be gone, could I have stopped you? I don't imagine for a second that Belinda hasn't figured out how to slip that tracking bracelet. You probably got something on your person right now that will let you do it if you need to."

They walked in silence for a long time.

"You still didn't answer my question," she realised out loud.

"What question?"

"Why do you need me out here with you?"

"You're easier to track," he said.

"And you're not easy to track?"

"Nope. I have a power that makes it hard."

"No actual skills, then."

"None whatsoever," he said, pumping a fist in the air. "Magic powers for the win!"

"Why are you so proud about something you didn't earn?"

"Pride is an easy lever to pull," Jason said. "You should never let people know what you're actually proud of."

"Are you ever not manipulating people?"

"We all manipulate the people around us," Jason said. "We all show different faces to friends, family, colleagues. Enemies."

"You think that's the same thing?"

"You think it's different? You think my friends don't see past the bombast and the bluster? Do you think Jory doesn't know how I feel, healing people in his clinic? That Humphrey doesn't know my pride, helping protect a village from monsters? That Rufus doesn't feel my triumph when I push my abilities a little bit further and grow that little bit stronger?"

"Aren't you just making it harder for them?"

"We all make it hard. Rufus can be rigid when he needs to be flexible. Humphrey can be short-sighted when he needs to look deeper. Jory needs to be more ambitious before he can truly accomplish the things he wants to. As for me, well, I'm the worst of the lot. I'm constantly causing trouble a little politeness would avoid. I pick fights I have no business being in, make enemies that would overlook me if I just learned to keep my mouth shut. I'm prickly, manipulative. Completely lacking in deference."

"If you're so self-aware, then why not fix all that?"

"Because they aren't problems," Jason said. "They're part of who I am, and I'm happier with that now than I ever have been. I told you, this world needs you to be bigger. Maybe it takes an outsider to see that clearly."

He gave her a smile.

"I don't know what you are but you need to stop hiding, because I know a hider isn't it," he said. "I've been lucky to find people willing to put up with me, good and bad. Figure out what you are, and be the ever-living crap out of that thing. Then find the people willing to put up with it. You know it's what Belinda has been waiting for, right?"

"What are you talking about?"

"She knows what you are better than anyone," Jason said. "Better than you do. My guess? She's been waiting for you to come into yourself for years."

"She's not just some addendum to me, waiting for me to get it together," Sophie said. "She's brilliant, inquisitive. If she didn't keep tying herself down with me, she could accomplish incredible things."

Jason burst out laughing.

"You think that's funny?" Sophie asked angrily.

"Yeah," Jason said. "I'd bet money that the two of you have been pushing each other along, both thinking you're pulling the other back. Wexler, this is your chance. Hers, too. You get those essences she's after and then both of you find out what you're really capable of."

Sophie stopped, throwing out her arms.

"What is with you, Asano?" she asked. "This whole thing. Getting us out from under Lamprey. Essences, adventuring. The speeches about making something of myself. No dismissing the question, no hiding behind a mouthful of nonsense. Seriously. Why?"

Jason also stopped, turning back to look at her. The perpetual, smug, half-grin fell from his face. His eyes, normally twinkling with some joke only he seemed to know about became clear and sharp.

"Because I could," he said. "You needed it, I could do it, so I did it."

"Why us?"

"Why not you? Jory wanted to help you and I have a soft spot for people railing against authority when the smart move is to give in. It's one of the things people hate most about me."

"Just like that. You put yourself in the path of Cole Silva and Lucian Lamprey because your friend wanted to help us?"

"Yes."

"Why?"

"Because he's my friend."

"You'll go that far for a friend?"

"How do you think I made so many great friends?"

"You're serious."

"Unless I'm just manipulating you."

"Gods damn it, you're obnoxious."

"I'm just saying," Jason said. "Honest vulnerability can be a powerful tool."

"Didn't you tell your lady friend that it was only a tool of seduction?"

"I was lying. You know what I'm like."

"Do you ever stop?"

"Do you want me to?"

"Yes!"

"Really?" he asked a grin creeping onto his face.

"Shut up," she said and set off again, marching past him along the embankment road. Jason looked at her, shaking his head and then followed.

"Such a tsundere."

"I heard that!"

"Do you even know what that means?"

"Shut up!"

36

THE PRICE WE PAY DOESN'T MATTER

Jason and Sophie were sitting on a fallen log, eating sandwiches as they looked out over the pristine wetlands before them. They had largely avoided population centres, keeping themselves isolated to make the most tempting lure. Jason sighed happily.

"As nice as it is taking some quiet time out in nature, It's about time to head back," Jason said. "Looks like we weren't tantalising bait after all. It's a little ironic, given all the people who were chasing after you."

"They might try on the way back," Sophie said. "How likely do you think this is to work?"

"I figure it's less likely to work than not," he said. "Still worth a try, though, given the stakes."

"How bad are these people, exactly?"

"According to Clive, if they had been left to their own devices in the astral space, they would have killed everyone between here and Boko, so… bad."

"I can't even imagine destruction on that kind of scale."

"That's what makes it so dangerous," Jason said. "These people we're dealing with… the LEGO Lovecraft monster they work for operates on a scale far beyond our ability to comprehend. A strange, alien mind that doesn't care about the lives it takes any more than we do about the bugs we step on without noticing."

"How do you even fight something like that?"

"Clive said those things operate in a sort of equilibrium, balancing each other out."

"It doesn't feel balanced if they can kill us and everyone we could get to in a week's travel."

"No, it doesn't," Jason said. He wiped his hands together to brush off the crumbs and pushed himself to his feet. Sophie did the same.

"Let's head off, then."

"So, this is the last one," Danielle Geller said.

Of the five people into whom star seeds had been planted, four had been found and treated. After the disastrous treatment of Jonah, the next three had the star seeds extracted without killing the host, although they were left in dire need of healing.

They had finally found the fifth, returning her to Greenstone via Hester, Emir Bahadir's portal user. She was now strapped to a vertical platform, arms, legs, torso and head all individually bound in place. They were in the temple of Purity, in one of what they referred to as purgation rooms. Although scrubbed to immaculate cleanliness, there was a smell to the place that made Danielle think that bad things had happened there.

There was a small crowd gathered to watch the purging. Danielle had accompanied the girl's parents, who had insisted on being present, despite the archbishop's objections. He had warned them that their daughter had been affected by the star seed the longest and may not survive its extraction. Also present was Tabitha Gert, the head of the Adventure Society inquiry team. She was the de facto head of the Adventure Society so long as the inquiry continued and had yet to witness a star seed being extracted. Clive Standish was the Magic Society representative, with the other members of the group being Emir and Thalia Mercer. Like Danielle, Thalia had witnessed every star seed extraction.

The ritual went as the archbishop had warned. The wires had retracted from their infiltration throughout the girl's body before the seed was extracted, but the damage they left behind was too great. Even immediately applied silver-rank healing was unable to ameliorate the strain and she died with a jerking shudder. Danielle led the grieving parents away while the rest of the group followed the archbishop to a meeting room. Once again, it was a conference room in the Geller Estate décor Jason had come to think of as tropical resort style.

"That was the last of the five," Tabitha Gert said, taking control of the meeting as the group sat around a table. "Now we must completely refocus our attention on the Builder cult's future activities. What progress are we making?"

"The Magic Society has made a couple of breakthroughs," Clive said. "First, we know what they're after and how they are going after it. The astral magic techniques they are using are unlike anything we've seen before, presumably delivered to our world by the Builder. It's more advanced than the astral magic we have but we've already started unravelling its secrets. I can tell you that to achieve their objectives, they have to work from inside the astral spaces."

"Which brings our focus squarely on you, Mr Bahadir," Tabitha said. "Do you still intend to open this astral space?"

"I do."

"I'm tempted to prohibit you from doing so," Tabitha said, "but it may represent the best chance of catching the Builder cult's tail. Have you found a way to catch anyone they try to slip into the group?"

"Not an effective one, no," Emir said. "The only means we have to identify them would be the presence of a star seed."

"We have found a ritual that will allow us to discover one within a person," the archbishop said. "It is quick and simple enough that we can administer it to each person before allowing them to participate."

"If they don't have one, though," Emir said, "there is no way to detect a person's true loyalty. If there were, I'm not so certain I'd approve of its existence."

"What about other angles of approach?" Tabitha asked.

"Rufus Remore continues to coordinate with my father," Elspeth Arella said. "They are tracking what they believe to be supplies the Builder cult imported, looking for where those supplies ended up. This may give us a line on their key stronghold. They are currently trying to determine a final destination."

"Your father," Tabitha said. "This is the criminal leader, Adris Dorgan?"

"Yes," Arella said.

"Good," Tabitha said. "In times like these, we need to put aside minor concerns like criminality and use every resource available. Keep me updated whenever you find something new."

"Yes, Ma'am," Arella said.

"What about the former star seed recipients?" Tabitha asked. "Any progress?"

"The three survivors are all awake," Thalia said. "They have limited recollection of their time under the Builder cult's influence. Their memories are strongest right after the seeds were implanted, which they all report as being like someone else was controlling them. They describe it as being trapped in their own minds, wanting to scream for help but being unable to do so. As the seeds took stronger hold, their memories become increasingly scattered until nothing was left but flashes."

"Anything useful among what they do recall?"

"I have people working with them," Thalia said. "We're being careful—it would be easy to create false memories with leading questions. Everything they can remember is being collated and examined, looking for any trails we can follow."

"Do you need any assistance or resources to speed up the process?" Tabitha asked.

"Attempting to accelerate things is the wrong approach," Thalia said. "Doing it right will take as long as it takes."

"And you aren't biased because your son is one of the three?"

"It doesn't matter if I'm biased or not," Thalia said, matter-of-factly. "Try to interfere and I'll rip your arm off and shove it down your throat."

Tabitha frowned but didn't push the issue further.

"How goes the inquiry?" Emir asked her. "Will you be staying in the city for long?"

"The expedition may have been what brought us here," Tabitha said, "but it has become clear that the way the expedition was planned and conducted was the result of a larger problem. The true concern is that the culture around this branch of the Adventure Society is a festering sore. We excised the worst people and demoted almost everyone. Over the next few weeks we will be going through all the members we didn't revoke the membership of entirely, seeing who truly deserved their rank."

"That's good to hear," Emir said, turning a gaze on Arella. "How much influence is our esteemed director going to have on that process?"

"We have determined that the director was largely influenced by the culture in which she obtained the position. Her mistakes were attempts to operate effectively within it. It is not an excuse for certain failings, but we feel that coming from outside the local nobility remains an asset moving forward. Ultimately, she will resume full authority once the inquiry is over. Therefore she will, of course, have input on the dispensation of rank for local members."

"Your concern is Asano," Arella said to Emir. "He will be assessed fairly. How is your little bait operation going, by the way?"

"Who told you about that?" Emir asked.

"There was no need," Arella said. "Asano making a spectacle of himself is nothing new but he generally does so with purpose. You wanted the Builder cult to make a play for him, trying to create a fresh distraction after we finished hunting down all their seeds."

"It seems they aren't going for it," Emir said. "There was never a guarantee of it working. They don't want to risk exposing themselves, spoiling a chance at sending people into the astral space."

"Or maybe they just don't want to risk getting involved with Asano," Arella said. "That boy is more insidious than a star seed."

"What plans do we have for intercepting any Builder cult agents they place in the astral space?" Tabitha asked.

"None," Emir said. "I don't know what's in there and I've been looking for it for years. All we can do is ask the ones we trust to keep a lookout and act if they can."

Anisa once more entered the foreman's office in the temple of Purity's construction site.

"You were right to not go after Asano," she said without preamble.

"Admitting you're wrong," the foreman said. "You don't seem the type."

"It was bait," Anisa said. "They were trying to catch your people."

"Easy to complain about after the fact," the foreman said. "If you knew he had a gold-ranker following him, you were free to warn us. We lost a silver and three bronze who had to kill themselves trying to take him."

"Of course I didn't know beforehand," she said. "We only found out when they reported it afterwards. You told me you wouldn't make the attempt on Asano."

"I considered your arguments after our last little talk," he said. "You changed my mind, only for me to discover that I should have kept my own counsel, after all."

"You don't seem worried," she said. "This is a disaster for you. Losing a silver-ranker."

"The price we pay doesn't matter," the foreman said. "Only the objective. Using Bahadir's pet iron-ranker to disrupt the people looking for us was a target of opportunity, nothing more. One less silver-ranker doesn't matter for an astral space that silver-rankers cannot enter."

"What if they get information from the people you sent after Asano?" she asked.

"They won't. They're already dead."

"You're certain that none of them were taken alive?"

"Completely."

Jason and Sophie looked at the four strange, crystalline stars that had once been people. Blood and flesh stained the crystal where it had exploded out of them, the rest of the remains scattered across the village where Jason and Sophie had been attacked.

The gold-ranker, Callum, appeared next to them.

"That is all of them," he said in his gravelly voice. "I was unable to disable them before they killed themselves. It may not be possible to do so."

"I didn't sense them coming," Jason said.

"Me either, and I have an aura sensing power," Sophie said.

"One was silver, the others bronze," Callum said.

"Thanks for being on the ball, Cal," Jason said. "They were coming in hard and fast."

Around the village, people were watching from hiding after the unexpected explosion of violence.

"They won't try again," Callum said. "We should return to the city. Emir will likely take these and have them studied. Perhaps there is something to be learned."

"I'll go find the village head," Jason said. "We need somewhere to put them until Hester shows up. If we leave them in the middle of the village like this, they're going to creep people out."

"Tell them to make sure people leave them alone," Sophie added. "I don't think random villagers poking these things is a good idea."

"Sensible," Callum agreed.

Jason found the village head and explained the situation—or, rather, he said there was some adventurer stuff happening and people should stay away from the pointy magic things. The elder offered them a barn on the village outskirts that was not in use after suffering damage from a monster attack.

"I found a spot for them," Jason called out as he returned to the others. "There's something I should probably do first. Cal, is it okay if we loot these guys?"

"Go ahead."

"Alright. Wexler, take those two over there and I'll get the others."

Jason touched part of the bloody remains smeared over the crystalline stars.

You have received permission to loot [Builder Cultist].

14 [Silver Spirit Coins] have been added to your inventory.
211 [Bronze Spirit Coins] have been added to your inventory.
116 [Iron Spirit Coins] have been added to your inventory.

Behind him he heard coins raining onto the ground, then Sophie's muffled protests.

"Oh, what is this nonsense," she complained.

Jason turned around to see her encased in metal armour.

"I think you looted his armour," Jason said.

"Oh, you think?" she said, pushing up the front of the helmet to reveal her face. "Clearly you're the brains of the operation, figuring that one out."

"You might want to take that off," Jason suggested. "I don't think it's really your style."

"This description that popped up says I don't meet the requirements," she said. "How can I not meet the requirements when I'm already wear… ouch. Hey, I think this thing is stinging me."

"Cal, help me get it off her," Jason said.

Callum nodded, moving to assist.

"It will get worse the longer you wear it," Callum warned Sophie as they started pulling off the various metal plates strapped to her body. By the time they finished, Sophie was biting back grunts of pain as Callum used his gold-rank strength to roughly yank off the pieces. Sophie's clothes and skin were scraped by straps and buckles as he did.

"That was unpleasant," she said. "You can do the rest of the looting."

"Probably for the best," Jason said, tossing her a jar of healing unguent from his inventory. He stowed the armour in his inventory. It was an uncommon bronze armour with some basic reinforcing and self-repair enchantments. Then he checked the next body.

You have received permission to loot [Builder Cultist].

2 [Gold Spirit Coins] have been added to your inventory.
28 [Silver Spirit Coins] have been added to your inventory.
211 [Bronze Spirit Coins] have been added to your inventory.
316 [Iron Spirit Coins] have been added to your inventory.
[Amulet of Intermittent Armour] has been added to your inventory.

"Ooh, gold coins. And they had the exact same number of bronze coins. That's odd."

He pulled out the magic item to take a look.

Item: [Amulet of Intermittent Armour] (bronze rank, uncommon)
***A neck-chain and amulet that accumulates protective power* (jewellery, necklace).**

Effect: Slowly accumulate instances of [Guardian's Blessing], to a maximum based on your bronze-rank [Recovery] attribute.

[Guardian's Blessing] (boon, holy): Damage from all sources is reduced by a small amount. Additional instances have a cumulative effect. Damage reduction is less effective against damage from silver-rank or higher sources. When an instance is consumed, gain an instance of [Blessing's Bounty].

[Blessing's Bounty] (heal-over-time, holy, stacking): Heal over time. Additional instances have a cumulative effect.

You do not meet the requirements to use this item.

Jason had several bronze-rank items collecting in his inventory. He had never actually sold the bizarre hydra whip and he had a gauntlet he took from the bronze-rank tidal troll he fought. Now he had the armour and the amulet looked like a useful item for Sophie when she reached bronze rank.

The last body produced something altogether unexpected.

[Star Seed (Builder)] has been added to your inventory.

37

MAKE THE MOST OF IT

Anisa stormed through the main hall of the temple of Purity making for the exit. The church functionary at the doors stepped out to meet her.

"You go out late, Lady Priestess," he said. "Worship is carried out under the sun's pure light."

"You think you know the doctrine better than me?" Anisa snarled.

"You are the one stepping out in the hours of dark deeds."

Anisa stopped, looking the man up and down. No essences in his aura and somewhere between forty and fifty, yet still the lowest rank of church official. She sneered.

"Using your meagre measure of authority to make yourself feel powerful is the sign of an impure heart," she said. She reached into her robes and handed him a token. "Take this and report for personal inquisition."

His face went as white as hers.

"Lady Priestess," he begged. "Surely you can't send me to inquisition for such a small matter."

"That is the very problem," she said. "You thought it was such a small matter that you would suffer no repercussions, but impure seeds lead to rotten fruit. Your failings will be found and scoured from your soul. It will become pristine once again."

She swept past him and out the doors, into the grounds, along what was becoming an unpleasantly familiar path to the construction site. As she approached, the foreman emerged from the dormitory huts for the workers.

"It is late, Lady Priestess, and I know your people care not for the hours of darkness. If the purpose of your visit is licentious, then I will eagerly accommodate you."

"Shut your foul mouth," she told him. "Your ever-growing list of failures has forced the archbishop to demand your presence."

"I thought the archbishop never wanted to see me."

"Your repeated bungling has placed him in a position where he must rectify the disasters you have orchestrated."

She reached into her bag and pulled out a white robe.

"Put this on and keep your face covered," she commanded as she threw it at his feet.

The man picked up the robe out of the dirt and slipped it on, over his clothes.

"What is this about, exactly?" he asked.

"We have moved beyond the point of having conversations," she told him. "Your task now is to answer questions, follow instructions and otherwise keep your mouth shut."

"I will remind you, Priestess, that we are partners in this."

"Partners implies a mutually beneficial exchange, not one side making messes and the other cleaning them up. Follow."

She strode off, the hooded Builder cultist who had been posing as the foreman following behind. She led him through the grounds, using a key to open a gate in a walled garden, then locked it again behind them. Inside the walls was a private garden, with an inward-facing circle of seats in the middle. The archbishop, Nicolas Hendren, was already seated and waiting. Anisa took another seat and the cultist tried to do the same.

"Remain on your feet," she rebuked him.

"Isn't that a little petty, Priestess?"

"That's enough from you," the archbishop told him. "You will stand, you will listen, and you will answer."

"This is hardly in the spirit of partnership, Archbishop."

"If our affiliations were not spread so far beyond this city, our partnership would be over and you no more than a stain left on the ground we purged you from," the archbishop snarled. "You have orchestrated nothing but a cavalcade of disasters. You lost the astral space, which is one thing, but you kept us so far out of that operation that we had no means to warn you, costing you people, resources and leaving you to crawling back into your holes."

"I think you could have assisted if you truly wished to, Archbishop. Since you insist on bringing it up, then I must question the dedication of your efforts."

"I will not endanger my people to mitigate the failure of yours any more than I must. Yet, even then, it seems I can never stop doing so. The only thing you never fail to do is disappoint. You could have held the astral space if you had a clockwork king, yet your man failed to summon it properly in spite of the astounding level of resources we provided. Not only did he fail to summon it, he instead summoned some outworlder lunatic who not only killed him but who almost revealed my priestess's involvement and now has captured one of your star seeds. Intact."

"What?" the cultist asked. "What are you talking about?"

"You assured my priestess that even in the face of yet another failure, they could glean nothing from your people. By what twisted mode of thought does an intact, unspent star seed constitute nothing?"

"That shouldn't be possible."

"You shouldn't be this bad at the tasks assigned to you," the archbishop said. "There's disappointment all around."

"You have to retrieve it!" the cultist said.

"Clean up another one of your messes?" the archbishop asked. "It was your genius plan to implant the star seeds in the first place that has put so much attention on them."

"And put you in such a prime position to learn everything they were up to," the cultist retorted. "You were happy enough at the time, so don't try and retroactively admonish me now. I know hypocrisy is a core tenet of your church but I'm not a follower."

The archbishop launched out of his seat and struck the cultist with a backhand slap, sending him sprawling to the ground.

"You will watch your rotten tongue on the lands belonging to our lord, you monstrosity-worshipping filth."

The cultist pushed himself back to his feet and wiped blood from a split lip.

"Did I touch a soft spot, Archbishop? You may not like harbouring the likes of me, but you do it and you'll continue to do it."

"The only reason I tolerate you is your kind's wider accord with the church. Given my own way, I would burn the lot of you and be done with it."

"But it isn't up to you, is it, Archbishop? So you will be a good little boy, do as you're told and render us such assistance as we require. And what we require now is getting that star seed back."

The archbishop's face twisted reluctance, but he didn't refute it.

"What can they do with it?"

"There are many possibilities, none of them good," the cultist said. "It could expose us all, employed the right way. If they have people who know what they are doing. A sufficiently skilled astral magic specialist will know exactly how to use it."

"So, what can you use it for?" Jason asked.

"No idea," Clive said.

"Really?" Jason asked. "I figured you'd take one look at it and be all 'yeah, now we can give 'em a good ol' kick in the beans!'"

"You thought I'd say that?"

"You say that kind of thing all the time."

"I've never said anything like that in my entire life."

The Magic Society vault contained all manner of dangerous and restricted objects, sealed away into various rooms. Built into the very foundation of the Island, it was not just under the Magic Society campus but under the loop line, subterranean water passages and utility tun[illegible]els that crisscrossed below ground. Jason, Clive, Rufus, Emir and Danielle Ge[illegible] were in the room Clive had set aside for the star seed.

It was in a secure box of rune-covered [illegible]. The seed itself looked like a sphere, but close examination revealed it was [illegible]rised of tiny cubes all adhered together. Oddly, the star seed was the colour o[illegible]on, unremarkable brick. The pseudo-sphere was held in place by a dull me[illegible]: a cube with tines to hold the orb in place.

"Did the frame come with it, or did we add th[illegible]ir asked.

"It came with it," Jason said. "Is it just me, or [illegible]frame the exact size of an essence cube?"

"I think you're right," Emir said. "That's an unsettl[illegible] thought."

"I'm not sure that placing it in the vault was the [illegible]st idea," Danielle said. "Leaving it in your storage space and being very careful who you told about it might have been better."

"Stuff that," Jason said. "I'm not going to leave that thing in my inventory and let the Builder use it to backdoor me."

"We don't know that's even possible," Clive said.

"Six months ago, I didn't know anything that happened in the last five months was possible and a good chunk of it has tried to kill me. The things-I-don't-know train just keeps chugging along. I'm not going to let it park a hand up my bung-hole and wave me about like a rakishly handsome sock puppet."

The other three turned to look at him, except for Rufus, who just shook his head.

"Don't bother," he told the others.

"What?" Jason asked.

Danielle shook her head and turned to Clive. "Any ideas what we should do with the star seed?"

"Not off the top of my head," Clive said. "I'll have to do some research. I still wish you hadn't killed Landemere Vane, Jason. Even his notes would have been good; sometimes it was like he was plucking these amazing innovations in astral magic out of thin air. His notes were all seized by the church of Purity after the blood cult revelation, though."

"Why is it that the church of Purity got to take all his family's stuff?" Jason asked Rufus.

"They were the ones who found out about the blood cult," Rufus said. "I'm not sure how, but they took it to the courts, who gave them the rights to seize all their property if the claims were substantiated. They hired us to do exactly that, and you know the rest."

"Seriously," Jason said. "This pl[illegible] needs some severe legal reform. Also, you need to stop complaining that I kil[illegible]hat guy. He was going to eat me. He was in a blood cul…"

Jason's eye went wide as [illegible]ed off. He started pacing back and forth, absently tapping his head in th[illegible] Emir was about to ask a question, but Rufus gestured him to silence. Jaso[illegible]d moving and looked up.

"We have a problem," [illegible] "Ever since we found out about the Builder cult, something's been both[illegible]."

"You told me you'd se[illegible]where before," Emir said.

"I had, and I just reme[illegible]where. Landemere Vane was a Builder cultist."

"How could you know[illegible]" Clive asked.

"You've seen my loo[illegible]bility in action. When I looted Landemere Vane, it gave me the same messa[illegible]s when I looted the guy who gave me this. It asked if I wanted to loot the Bui[illegible] cultist."

Jason turned to Ru[illegible].

"Remember when [illegible]e first met in that basement?" Jason asked. "Cressida Vane and the guy with the shovel were talking about how I killed Landemere. What did she say about her son?"

"You're right, I remember that," Rufus said. "Something about ineffable things from beyond reality."

"If Landemere Vane was a Builder cultist," Jason said, "that means some very bad things."

"It does," Danielle agreed. "Very bad things, indeed."

"I think I've missed a step," Clive said. "How does Landemere Vane being a Builder cultist even matter now? He died months ago."

"And the church of Purity seized everything he owned, along with the rest of his family's possessions," Danielle Geller said. "Every note, letter and record. Even his work here at the Magic Society, right?"

"That's right," Rufus said. "Anisa Lasalle spent most of a day sorting through all their things, even before her church moved in to claim it all."

"You think the church of Purity is working with the Builder cult?" Emir asked. "Why would they send Rufus and his team to Landemere Vane's home?"

"Because his family was in the wrong cult," Jason said. "You can see how they would paint it. Landemere Vane is afraid of what his family is involved in and informs the church of Purity. The church contracts adventurers to accompany their priestess to investigate. Everyone gets captured, but Landemere manages to free the priestess and escape. Once Rufus and his team died, his family would come down on the rest of the Vane family like the hammer of god. That would leave Landemere as the sole heir and give the Builder cult a luxurious, isolated and secure base of operations. With the church of Purity helping him 'cleanse' the taint of the blood cult from the property, who is going to trek all the way out there to look closer? Having the seizure rights for the property was a contingency in case something went wrong or they needed to kill Landemere themselves, for whatever reason. A contingency that let them put a lid on the whole thing."

"We were captured before you ever arrived," Rufus said. "Landemere could have already arranged for her escape before you killed him, while she was waiting for everyone to leave and sacrifice us. Getting taken out of the group could have been just luck, or even an idea Landemere planted in the head of an impressionable staff member. If she wasn't, she could have escaped and fled the sacrifice chamber, leaving the rest of us to die."

Rufus's face reflected his reeling mind.

"The man who betrayed us to the blood cult," he said. "He was a church of Purity contact. When we didn't die as planned and wanted to question him, she killed him outright, claiming it was her church's authority."

He turned to Jason.

"You said it was suspicious at the time," Rufus said. "We talked about it."

"We couldn't have known," Jason said. "I was just against her because she was such a... we didn't get along."

"But it all went wrong," Rufus said. "None of them were expecting a punch-drunk outworlder to show up and mess everything up. Because of Jason, Landemere died and we survived, the exact opposite of their plan."

"Not all wrong," Jason said. "There is still the Landemere estate, under the control of the church. That could very well be where the Builder cult regrouped after escaping the astral space."

"This is all highly speculative," Emir said. "Making that kind of accusation against a church is no small matter and even I'm not completely convinced yet. We have no evidence."

"I'm the evidence," Jason said. "My ability showed that Landemere Vane was a Builder cultist."

"That's tangential to the culpability of the church, even with Rufus's corroboration," Danielle said. "And your testimony is a shaky basis to move forward on."

"What's wrong with my testimony?" Jason asked.

"Jason," Emir said. "You might operate in high circles, relative to Greenstone, but you're still an iron-ranker. Plus, you spend a lot of time lying and running around like an insane person. There is a difference between people in authority putting up with you and having them listen to what you say."

"He's right," Danielle said. "It won't be easy to convince anyone that the church of Purity is involved with putting these star seeds in people when we can't even answer why, let alone provide definitive proof."

"Agreed," Emir said. "I'm not going to be convinced myself, without something more compelling."

"We need to find evidence before we can act," Danielle said.

"The Vane estate," Rufus said.

"Yes," Danielle agreed. "While everyone is distracted with sending the iron-rankers into Emir's astral space, we send a small team we can trust to investigate the estate."

The sounds of many feet moving upstairs drew the group's attention. Soon the entrance to their chamber was filled with a combination of Magic Society vault guards and temple of Purity church militants. At the lead was Anisa Lasalle.

"Anisa," Jason said. "I was just thinking about how you should be strung up and burned for witchcraft."

"Still jabbering nonsense, I see. Step back, Asano, and let the adults talk."

"I don't think your style of negotiation is going to work here, Jason," Danielle said. "Perhaps you'll leave this one to me?"

Jason nodded, stepping back.

"We're here for the star seed," Anisa said. "Get out of our way."

"What claim do you have on the star seed?" Danielle asked.

"Our church has taken and destroyed all the previous ones," Anisa said. "This new one is just another artefact of impurity to be annihilated."

"Your church took the previous ones because they extracted them. This one was obtained by an adventurer."

"It is still our duty to destroy it," Anisa said.

"It is likely to be useful in our struggle against an elusive enemy," Danielle said.

"I don't care," Anisa said. "My instructions are to retrieve it for destruction and nothing you say will divert me from that path."

"Your church has no authority here," Clive said. "I'm Adjunct Assistant to the Deputy Director of the Magic Society and I had this object placed here."

"That's some mouthful," Anisa said. "Director is more succinct, and in this case, pertinent. Lucian Lamprey has already released it to us."

She took a document from her dimensional satchel and handed it to Clive. He skimmed over it with an unhappy expression, giving Danielle a reluctant nod.

"Very well," Danielle said and stepped aside.

One of the vault guards removed the glass casing around the star seed and Anisa took it, placing it in her satchel. Flashing Jason a triumphant grin, she swept out, taking her extensive entourage with her. Clive stuck his head out the door to look up the stairs and make sure they were gone.

"I'm surprised at your restraint," Rufus said to Jason. "I was expecting you to do something extreme."

"The star seed is potentially valuable," Jason said. "Knowing that the church of Purity is in it up to their necks, when they don't know we know? That's more valuable, and acting now would have tipped our hand. Otherwise, Danielle would have stopped them."

"Just so," Danielle said. "For the first time, we are a step ahead. Now we need to make the most of it."

38

WAKE

Farrah hadn't had a formal memorial, just a handful of dinners and informal gatherings, with storytelling and everyone getting blind drunk. With the unexpected appearance of her parents, Rufus had bounded into action, organising a formal memorial for the day before the adventurers left for Emir's contest.

After the service, the traditional wake was held not in a bar but in the guest wing lounge of the cloud palace. If nothing else, it had a better stock of alcohol than most taverns. Jason looked over the group, some of them from afar while others Farrah had come to know in her months in Greenstone. Some were friends, others less so, but there was no antagonism on display as people paid their respects. Jory was present, the kind-hearted man looking red-eyed as Belinda stood beside him for moral support. She and Sophie had never met Farrah, and Sophie was not present with her friend.

Elspeth Arella and her deputy, Genevieve, stayed just late enough to be respectful and left early enough to be discrete. Madam Landry, their long-time landlady appeared. She was not an essence user and was somewhat overwhelmed by the cloud palace and the company, until taken in hand by Farrah's parents. Her fellow Magic Society members were in attendance, in two contingents.

One was the group around Clive who actually had known and worked with her; the other was Lucian Lamprey and his deputy, Pochard Finn. Despite the superior schooling in social niceties between a foreign nobleman and the secret child of a crime lord, Lamprey lacked the social delicacy of Arella, overstaying his welcome long after she had left. Jason struggled to restrain his own distaste for the man and was grateful that Sophie was not in attendance. Determined not to make a fuss at Farrah's wake, he diplomatically avoided Lucian to avoid triggering any of his bad social habits.

Lamprey himself, however, had other ideas. He was drinking Emir's expensive alcohol faster than anyone else in the room and, half in the bag, sought out Jason with an expression of half confused drunk and half determined anger.

"Asano," he called out loudly as he approached.

Rufus moved to intervene but was arrested by Danielle Geller's hand on his arm.

"If Jason is ever going to live up to his potential," she quietly told Rufus, "he needs to show that he can deal with situations with tact instead of bombast, bravado and provocation."

"Now isn't the time for lessons," Rufus hissed at her.

"This is exactly the time," she asserted. "We are adventurers, Rufus. Our most important lessons come from confronting monsters."

Lamprey swaggered up to Jason, glancing around to make sure he had an audience. His deputy, Finn, tried to guide him away but Lamprey brushed him off. Jason turned from the conversation he was having to face Lamprey. Jason's expression was schooled into blank composure.

"Director Lamprey," Jason said. "Thank you for attending. Farrah's membership in the Magic Society was very important to her; I know she would appreciate the strong representation the society has presented here. For you to come in person is very gratifying."

"You think I don't see through you, Asano?" Lamprey said in the way drunk people have of being loud while thinking themselves quiet. "You think you're so smart, playing people off one another, bending the rules into whatever shape you like. But cleverness didn't save your friend, did it? When she came face to face with power it cut her down in an instant. You didn't even have the courage to be there when it did."

Everyone in the room was watching now as Jason gave Lamprey a slight smile.

"It shows you as a man of character, putting aside personal animosities in the face of a greater threat," Jason said, aggressively misrepresenting Lamprey's intent. "I'm glad that such a man can come here today and put aside old problems, that we might face the new ones together."

He took Lamprey's hand, solemnly shaking it. "We appreciate your commiserations, Director. I believe your deputy was just saying that you have to go, which is understandable. A man of your position has so many calls on his time. We do thank you for coming, though."

Pochard Finn rapidly stepped up as fury crossed Lamprey's face, ready to erupt. Emir also moved alongside Finn, discretely using his aura at close proximity to squash Lamprey's impending outburst.

"Thank you, Director Lamprey, Deputy Director Finn," Emir said as he and

Finn ushered Lamprey to the door. On the other side of the threshold, Emir's staff helped Finn guide Lamprey out of sight. Emir returned to the group, the door closing behind him.

"See?" Danielle said to Rufus. "I told you from the start; the boy has a political mind."

Lamprey was the last of the socially obligated attendees to leave by far. In the wake of his departure, sombre, controlled expressions gave way to real emotion as the wake truly began. The drinks flowed, eyes grew damp and there was even some laughter as stories were shared.

One group of attendees was a team of iron-rankers, looking nervous at the preponderance of high-ranking people around them. It wasn't just no-name silvers of a provincial city, either. Their host, Emir Bahadir, was drinking with Thalia Mercer and the time witch, Danielle Geller. Constance, the famously unyielding head of Emir's extensive organisation, was disconcertingly expressive as she casually chatted with Gabriel and Arabella Remore. Even after years at Remore Academy, the iron-rankers were intimidated by Instructor Gabriel.

The iron rankers were a team from Vitesse, trained at the Remore Academy. Gabriel had discovered them when they were shipping out and had been the one to invite them to the memorial and wake. They had come up through the academy a few years behind Rufus, the Remore family's own prodigy whose presence had loomed over the other students.

Just the auras flowing around the room were enough to disconcert, even to those with years of aura training. There were a few other iron-rankers who were seemingly calm under the pressure, except for the one man who disregarded it entirely. They watched him swan about like he owned the place, for all the world as if the potent aura soup wasn't there. He walked up to legends and spoke to them like they were normal people. Even more startling was that they didn't seem to look down on the iron-ranker at all, welcoming him into their conversations.

"Nat, who is that?" Lance asked. Lance was an elf and the leader of the team. His long, light brown hair was cinched back behind his head.

"The outworlder we heard about," the leonid, Natalie, told him. "Asano."

Natalie was a female leonid and, like others of her kind, was smaller than males like Gary.

"He's the one Rufus has been training?" Maximilian asked. He was a member of the rare draconian race, larger even than male leonids and covered in glossy scales. His were the colour of dark leaves, green moving into purple.

"That's what I've been hearing," Natalie told him.

"What kind of training?" Oscar asked. He was a handsome celestine with dark skin and matching silver in his eyes and hair. "The aura training at the academy didn't teach us to handle auras that well."

The last member of the group was a smoulder with the typical midnight skin and burning-ember eyes. Her hair was cropped extremely short. She had her gaze locked on Jason as the others talked.

"Farrah also trained him?" she asked.

Frowning at her friend's intensity, Natalie nodded. The smoulder strode out from the group in his direction.

"Padma!" Lance called out under his breath, but she ignored him.

Jason spotted the smoulder girl marching across the room like a woman on a mission. She couldn't have been any older than Humphrey, probably younger. She was the one he had been told about, coming at him with emotion storming through her aura. A Remore Academy graduate should have better control but the girl was clearly in turmoil. When she reached Jason it was like the wind dropped out of her sails, leaving her standing in front of him, becalmed.

"Padma?" he asked softly. She nodded and he gave her a gentle smile.

"I'm Jason Asano. How about we get you away from these obnoxious auras and have a chat?"

He didn't wait for a response before sweeping off, picking up two glasses and a bottle as she meekly followed him to a quiet corner of the room. Jason slowly teased Padma's story out of her as she clutched the glass of sweet liqueur in her hands like a talisman. Jason kept it refreshed from the bottle as she talked. She was hesitant at first, but with sympathetic prompting from Jason, the words were soon pouring out of her.

Padma and her team had trained at Remore Academy, a few years behind Rufus. He graduated ahead of them but his presence at the academy hardly lessened. He was a symbol for the students that came after. When he first brought back his team, Rufus had sought Padma out, who didn't even realise Rufus knew who she was. Rufus's new team member, Farrah, had the same essences as Padma and Rufus had introduced them. Farrah took the young smoulder under her wing, becoming something of a mentor.

Jason listened with no more than a few nods and words of acknowledgement to show his attentiveness. He quickly realised that Farrah had been more than just a mentor to Padma. Farrah had been her idol, a source of inspiration and a guiding hand. Padma had been eagerly awaiting her return to Vitesse, proud of her successful induction into the Adventurer's Society while Rufus and his team had been far away in Greenstone.

Padma had been looking forward to a reunion where she could share her pride, only for news to come of Farrah's death. When Emir's call went out for adventurers she didn't hesitate. Each berth on the ships bringing people over was a prize. Emir's people organised tournaments to bring only the best to Greenstone. Despite Padma's inexperience, her team supported her and won through. She wasn't even certain herself why she had to go, but she felt driven, compelled by some internal need she didn't fully understand.

After she finished her story, Jason nodded. He shared a little of his own experience of learning from Farrah, leading to an exchange of what her mentorship had been like. Jason could plainly see that Padma had weeks of bottled-up frustration, aching to get out. He methodically used questions and little anecdotes to poke holes for it to vent out.

They sat in the corner talking for more than an hour before the speeches began. Rufus and Gary gave short speeches, anecdotes now smoothly honed in the retelling. Jason got up to speak last. Stepping out in front of the group. His eyes lingered on Farrah's parents, who he had come to know over the last few days. Farrah's mother gave him a sad, encouraging nod.

"I've known Farrah since the day I came into this world," he said, then frowned. "That's was roughly half a year ago, not when I was a baby or something. I think everyone here knows my whole thing."

"Stop talking about yourself, you dinkle," Gary called out getting a round of laughs.

"I'm setting a scene, you hairy goon," Jason shot back. "I'm building up a narrative."

"Build faster," Gary said. "I don't want to sober up while you're prattling on."

"Maybe if I don't keep getting interrupted. Where was I?"

"You're very sad, the end," Gary said. "Let's drink more."

"That's enough out of you," Jason said, jabbing a finger in his direction. "Right, so, I met Farrah on the worst day of my life. I had no idea of where I was, what was happening or even if I was in my right mind. My first encounter with real power was when she blasted lava across the room like that was a normal thing that can happen. And that was Farrah—unassumingly awesome."

He looked down, smiling in reminiscence.

"After that, she introduced me to the world. Rufus taught me to fight like an adventurer and Gary taught me to move like one. Farrah, though, she taught me to *be* an adventurer. How to look at the world around me, literally and figuratively. I have a habit of running my mouth before my brain gets going and long before I have any idea what I'm talking about. Farrah was the one who brought me crashing down to earth before I let what I didn't know get me killed."

He looked up and around at the gathering.

"We all know that she died like an adventurer," he said. "There are people in this room who wouldn't be if she hadn't stood tall in the face of the most terrible enemy. The monstrosity that cut her down, his time will come, but this isn't about him. It isn't even about adventuring, really. At least, not for me."

Jason paused to sip at the drink in his hand.

"Yes, she taught me," he continued. "Yes, I fought with her. By which I mean that I stood around while she blew up an apocalypse monster. It seemed very involving, in the moment. But most of my time with Farrah wasn't as a fledgling adventurer. It was as a friend. The big moments are the tales we'll retell, but it's the little ones I look back on and smile. Sitting around as Farrah and Clive talked some theoretical nonsense over everyone's head. Farrah and Gary teaming up on Rufus because he's gotten too stodgy. Sharing a meal, or an afternoon in the park. The adventures will be the stories we tell, but the friendship is the thing we'll miss. To Farrah. Our friend."

He raised his glass and everyone did the same.

"That is where I was going to leave it," Jason said. "When Rufus told me to speak last tonight, I was reluctant. But he said that it should be me. That the last word should be one of legacy which, like it or not, I'm a big part of. It was convincing enough to get me up here, but this evening I met a young woman with at least as much claim to that as I. She hasn't prepared any words, but I've seen for myself that she has them inside here, ready to go."

Padma was listening to Jason with dawning horror. Smoulders were physically incapable of turning white, but she had at least gone a shade of very dark brown.

"Padma," Jason said. "Please come over. The last word is yours."

Everyone followed Jason's gaze to the girl trying hard to look like a nondescript piece of furniture.

"You have things to say and I've already heard you say them well," Jason told her. "They're worth sharing."

She stayed rooted on the spot until Gabriel's voice pierced through the room with practised authority.

"Cadet Padma Parsell," he said with the projection of a theatre veteran. "Front and centre."

Padma's body moved, Instructor Gabriel's voice triggering a conditioned obedience. She found herself standing next to Jason, in front of the assembled high-rankers. Jason gave her a smile and an encouraging pat on the shoulder before moving off.

She started speaking. It was hesitant, with a staccato rhythm; her nervousness had her pausing and losing track of what she was saying. As she continued it became smoother, nervousness washed away by passion. It wasn't a great speech but no one in the room doubted her love and sincerity. Jason stepped in just before she started to flounder.

"There we are," he said. "Passion has an eloquence that transcends words and I think we can agree that none of us will top the passion of this young lady. So let the words be done and we can do what Farrah would do: get hammered on Emir's expensive booze."

After the speeches, the real drinking started in earnest. Farrah's parents, Amelia and William, took Jason aside to thank him for his words.

"Farrah said you could be good with words," William said. "A little too good, she told us. Likely to get yourself into trouble."

"She talked about me?"

Farrah's parents lived in the town Farrah grew up in, albeit in a much larger house, courtesy of Farrah's adventurer earnings. There were no water-link speaking chambers there, but they had travelled to Vitesse every month to speak to their daughter.

"She certainly did talk about you," Amelia said. "We weren't sure quite what to expect from her description, though."

"You should know that she thought you had an incredible potential," William said.

"If you could learn to get out of your own way," Amelia added. "I think she'd want that pointed out."

"It does sound like her," Jason said. "I'm so sorry she's gone."

"We always knew there was a chance this would happen," Amelia said. "That was something we accepted when we first started working to get those essences for her."

"Doesn't make it hurt less," William said. "But we were at least a little prepared for it."

Jason nodded.

"What about your family?" Amelia asked. "Farrah explained your situation to us, which seems a little unusual, even by adventurer standards."

"I'm not sure," Jason said. "I don't know if they think I'm dead or missing. I make recordings for them, for if I ever get home. When I get home."

Jason suddenly frowned.

"I'm sorry, but something just occurred to me. I'll leave you to the condolence of others. Again, I'm so sorry."

Jason made his way over to where Rufus and Gary were speaking with Clive, leaving Farrah's parents seeking out Padma to speak with her.

"I just had a thought," Jason said to Rufus, Gary and Clive. "Farrah's parents were asking about my own parents and I thought of something. I got here because of Landemere Vane, and you think he was getting some kind of advanced astral magic from the Builder, right Clive?"

"It's a possibility," Clive said. "What he was doing wouldn't get you home, though. It only served as an accidental catalyst for much larger, natural forces, though."

"But what was he trying to summon?" Jason asked. "Something from the Builder's world in the astral? That's interdimensional travel. Landemere's knowledge might not have the answers, but it could have clues."

"All his notes and writings were taken by the church of Purity," Rufus said. "They would be impossible to get a hold of, even if they weren't destroyed."

"You'll also need to up your knowledge of astral magic theory if you ever want to understand them," Clive said. "Skill books won't be close to enough."

"But they'll be a start," Jason said. "They bestow whatever knowledge was put into them, and I got those books from Landemere Vane himself. Even if they don't have something that might help me get home, they might have something that helps us against the Builder."

"You can't use them until you hit bronze-rank though," Gary said. "That'll be months."

"Oh, there are ways around that," Clive said. "They're a little rough, but we can look into it after Emir's event."

"Alright, then," Jason said. "It's a plan."

39
I CAN'T TRUST ANY OF IT

A crowd of hundreds was gathered at the Adventure Society campus, in front of the cloud palace as they waited for Emir to emerge. There was a sea of iron rankers, plus all manner of city luminaries and others eager to witness the commencement of Emir's grand event. Along with the mystery surrounding it, finally on the cusp of getting answers, many were looking for a change of pace. Ever since the expedition, a pall had been hanging over the city's adventurers and the major families to which they belonged.

Emir's contest offered danger as well as opportunity. Many Greenstone families had taken the expedition as a lesson and were not allowing their scions to participate. After the results of the last astral space incursion, they were unwilling to throw people into another. With an enigmatic enemy targeting astral spaces for unknown reasons, the idea of sending their most inexperienced members into another one gave many families pause.

Not every family took safety as the highest priority, however. The inquiry had been sweeping with the demotions and the most affected families were desperate for ways to snatch back their lost prestige. While the astral space expedition had technically been a success, having excised the problem that was affecting the astral space, many viewed it as a failure.

Most of Greenstone's major families had never cared about the expedition's actual objective, instead, seeing it as a chance for individual glory. With the massive losses sustained in the fighting retreat, from that perspective it was a failure. Emir's expedition was a chance for them to rewrite their image after the expedition.

Then there were those families who, like the Gellers, simply wanted the next adventure. They recognised that there was always danger, but that was the nature of the adventuring life. If their young people were ever going to be the equal of the Gellers or the visiting adventurers, they had to push themselves harder, confronting greater threats.

The iron-rankers in the crowd were divided into three general groups: the locals, the Gellers and the outsiders. Even with many local iron-rankers sitting out, the locals were the largest group. The Gellers were the smallest of the three groups, with seven teams participating, not including Humphrey and his team. The Gellers were mostly from distant lands, but the family's deep roots in Greenstone kept them from being true outsiders.

Humphrey's team wasn't counted due to being made up of locals, with even Humphrey himself being Greenstone born and raised. Only Jason was not local but he still counted as more of Greenstone local than he did anywhere else in the world.

The outsiders and the Gellers were throwing each other a lot of assessing glances, largely dismissive of the locals. The outsiders had answered Emir's call from many different lands, but competition had been fierce for a spot on the boats Emir had brought in. No one underestimated the abilities of those who had made it.

As for the Gellers, their high standards were known the world over. This was hammered home by the presence of Danielle Geller. The time witch was more famous than most gold-rankers and it was well known she was close to joining their ranks herself. Once she did, she would stand at the pinnacle of the adventuring world.

Amongst the visiting adventurer teams was the one who had attended Farrah's memorial and wake, although only four of the five were present. Like all the teams awaiting Emir's appearance, they were made up of people in mid-to-late teens. Less usual was the complete absence of humans from their team. The leader, Lance, was an elf whose swordsmanship relied as much on the finesse of his magic as the finesse of his hands. Like Jason, his preference was for flowing combat robes. He had fair skin and his light brown hair was cinched back practically behind his head.

Next to Lance was Padma, with the onyx skin and fiery eyes typical of her people. Also typical of her people were her heavy clothes as she was wholly unaffected by heat. The effect of the delta on the climate was to keep things hotter than elsewhere in the region, even as autumn moved closer to winter. To a smoulder, though, even the most scathing desert was as cool as a mild spring day.

The team healer, Oscar, was a celestine man whose handsomeness eclipsed even the elven team leader. The comparison was made all the stronger as he mirrored Lance's hairstyle by tying it back in a simple cinch. Of the same ethnicity as Sophie, he had chocolate skin with silver hair and eyes. His clothes were white, neat and fashionable in the Vitesse style that Rufus favoured. They were also adventure-ready, the combination of form and function speaking to their extravagance.

Standing with him was the tallest person currently in Greenstone, the only member of the draconian people present. Maximilian was an imposing figure with his size and long, hairless head. Instead of skin, his scales in dark shades of green and purple were glossy under the bright sun. His clothes were designed to show them off, little more than tasselled shoulder pads and a loincloth.

A human they didn't know was walking towards them, but her appearance magically transformed into that of a female leonid as she drew close. It was the true form of their stealthiest team member, Natalie. Compared to male leonids like Gary, the women were smaller, lithe and sleek, with shorter fur and facial features closer to that of humans, elves and celestines. In the case of Natalie, her lissom body was attractive even to human eyes, her naturally sinuous movements exuding sultry as though it was their job.

"Nat," Lance greeted. "We were starting to wonder if you were going to turn up."

"You're the one who asked me to do some digging around," Natalie said. "There was more to unearth than I expected."

"Let's start with our competition, then," Lance said. "What do you have on the Gellers?"

"What you'd expect, mostly," Natalie said. "Well-trained, well-resourced. Good team synergies."

"Any stand-outs?"

"The ones to watch were apparently the team lead by a Rick Geller, but he's had to rebuild the team after losing people. During the big clash here with those people invading astral spaces. Lots of dead adventurers."

"Like Farrah," Padma said.

"Yes," Natalie said. "This Geller team lost two people. The leader added his sister and a local to replace their losses, but their team cohesion isn't fully there yet. They had to change most of their methods for the new composition."

"What about locals?" Lance asked.

"Worse than you would expect, even for an out of the way place like this. Only one team is considered to be competitive."

"How competitive?" Lance asked.

"Enough that the Geller teams consider them a real contender. They had a mock battle with the team I was just talking about and another team led by a Geller. Danielle Geller's son."

"Humphrey Geller?" Lance asked.

"That's right," Natalie said. "He's just recently put together a team of locals instead of using his family members and connections."

"Interesting," Lance said. "I chatted with Humphrey a little bit at the wake, but we didn't talk business. I know him a little from when his mother brought him out to Vitesse a few times but that was before either of us were essence users. I don't even know what his essences are."

"His confluence is the dragon essence," Natalie said.

Maximilian gave an unhappy groan.

"False dragon," he complained. Draconians took pride in their claimed dragon ancestry and often had issues with other races wielding the dragon essence. Maximilian had the dragon essence himself.

"Don't start with that again," Oscar said.

"I'm not starting anything," Maximilian said unhappily. "He just shouldn't go around acting like he has true draconic power."

"Max, he's not claiming to actually be a dragon," Oscar said. "Not any more than Lance, with his sword essence, is claiming to be an actual sword."

"How well do you know this Humphrey?" Natalie asked Lance.

"Just in passing, socially. I'm surprised to hear his mother let him make a team of locals, though. I can't imagine she would let him add just any local idiot to his team."

"Oh, he didn't add just any local idiot," Natalie said. "From what I hear, this idiot is special. Trying to make sense of the things I heard about the guy was crazy. I still don't know how much of it is true."

"Who is he?" Lance asked.

"Padma's new friend," Natalie said. "Jason Asano, the one Farrah was helping train with Rufus."

"Jason?" Padma asked, startled. "He was really nice. Other than putting me up in front of everyone like that."

"Well, the things I've heard about your new friend are pretty wild. Some people are scared of him, others think he's an idiot or a madman. Some have even called him a genius, working his way up the social hierarchy. He ended up on Humphrey Geller's team, after all."

"What's your assessment?" Lance asked Natalie.

"I honestly have no idea," Natalie said. "Either most of what I've heard is false, which would make sense, or the man is some kind of insane magic pixie. Remember at the wake, the local Magic Society director getting drunk and confronting him? Apparently, there's some kind of feud there, where Asano somehow came out on top."

"What would an iron-ranker be feuding with a Magic Society director over?" Padma asked. "And how would he win?"

"Word is, it was over an indentured servant," Natalie said, "which brings us to the next thing. You remember that commotion last week before the big meeting?"

"That was over an indentured servant," Oscar said. "I can see why, having seen her myself. An arresting woman."

"That was Asano," Lance realised, thinking back. "Didn't Bahadir kick him off the cloud palace for that? They seemed friendly during the wake."

"That whole incident was a ruse," Natalie explained. "Turns out it was some kind of plan to bait these astral invaders. I'm not sure on the details but it apparently worked."

"It sounds like Jason is in the middle of a lot," Padma said.

"That was my impression," Natalie said. "I came across too many conflicting stories about him, though. There was apparently some kind of rivalry with the Adventure Society director, but she promoted him to three stars anyway. I heard he spent months healing the poor for free. I also heard he went a dozen to one with a bunch of adventurers in a shopping arcade in the middle of the day, killing half of them. I even heard he's an outworlder."

"That sounds made up," Oscar said. "You can't just kill a bunch of adventurers."

"Twelve against one is even less plausible," Maximilian said.

"The locals are sub-standard," Natalie said. "Any of us could probably go twelve against one. Apparently, there's a recording of the people going at him first, so self-defence. I've heard about a few recordings of the guy floating around, including that mock battle they mentioned. He's apparently really big on recording crystals."

"You're right," Padma said. "He's using one right now."

She had spotted Jason, some distance away in the crowd as he spoke into a recording crystal floating in front of him. She waved in Jason's direction, the man next to him spotting her and pointing her out. He waved back with a friendly grin.

"So, what's your take on the guy?" Lance asked Natalie.

"Unpredictable and dangerous," she said. "I didn't want to spend the whole time investigating one guy, so I decided it was best if you and Padma asked Rufus Remore. You two know him better than the rest of us."

"Did you hear how he came to have Rufus and Farrah's teaching him?" Padma asked. "When I brought it up last night he just said that they found him out in the desert, lost and confused."

"From what I found out, that's a very incomplete explanation," Natalie said. "Not that what I heard was any more likely. I was told that Asano saved Rufus's team from getting killed before Asano was even an essence user."

"That doesn't sound likely," Maximilian said.

"As I said, the things I've been hearing about the guy are wild. Enough of it was so obviously false that I can't trust any of it."

"What about the rest of Humphrey's team?" Lance asked.

"It's an unusual bunch," Natalie said. "One is a Magic Society official. He's some kind of astral magic expert who has apparently been instrumental in finding out about these astral invaders."

"And he's an iron-ranker?"

"Yeah, but he's apparently the real thing. The locals have been digging out information the big Adventure Society branches have been keeping under wraps and I've heard this guy is a key reason."

"What kind of secrets?" Lance asked.

"Not sure yet," Natalie said. "I've got a better chance of prying out secrets here than back home, though, once we're finished with whatever Bahadir has in store."

"Who else is on Humphrey's team?" Lance asked.

"There's some local, minor nobility. Nothing remarkable that I found from a quick check around. I've heard he's a solid healer but not much else. The last member is that indentured servant we were talking about."

"Really?" Oscar asked, edging forward with curiosity.

"An adventurer is an indentured servant?" Lance asked.

"Seems she was some kind of thief. She was robbing the local nobility for months but no one could catch her. Until Asano did, then went and made her an adventurer after claiming her indenture."

"Why would he do that?" Padma asked.

"You'll have to ask him that yourself. I heard a lot of postulation, most of it fairly disgusting."

"That's weird," Lance said. "Who makes their indentured servant an adventurer?"

"A smart man with a gorgeous indentured servant," Oscar said. "That's the kind of gratitude that does some real work."

"See?" Natalie asked. "Fairly disgusting."

"Jason, that team you waved at is talking about you," Beth said.

"You can hear them from over here?" Jason asked. "Is that an elf ears thing?"

"No!" Beth said, raising her hands to her ears in a gesture of self-reassurance. "It's an essence power thing. What's wrong with my ears?"

"Nothing," Jason said, his eyes on the distant team. "Is that what female leonids look like? I hope this doesn't awaken anything in me."

"What are you talking about?" Neil asked.

"I don't like what's happening in my head," Jason said. "Am I a furry now? I don't want to be a furry."

"Why would you be furry?" Clive asked.

"I'm not above exploring new things," Jason said. "I just don't have time to work on the costumes. Making them, cleaning them, dear gods. Maybe Jory has something that could help."

"Is any of this making sense to you?" Beth asked, looking at Jason's team.

"Best not to ask," Neil said. "You learn that lesson quick."

"I bet it's a sex thing," Sophie said. "It's a sex thing, isn't it?"

"Uh… no," Jason said.

"Who are they?" Niko asked. The smoulder member of Beth's team was looking at Padma further off in the crowd of gathered adventurers. "She looks sad. Should I go see if she needs comforting?"

Beth slapped the back of his head.

"Don't be a sleaze," she scolded.

"How am I the sleazy one?" Niko asked. "Jason has a sexy slave girl."

"I don't have Sophie," Jason said. "That's just a necessary legal fiction."

"Damn right, you don't," Sophie said.

"Unless I want to," Jason said.

"Do you want a slap too?" Sophie asked.

"Would you think less of me if I said yes?" Jason said. "My safe word is munificent."

"You are impossible to deal with," Sophie said.

"I told you he was the sleazy one," Niko said.

"Could everyone just act with a little decorum?" Humphrey asked.

"That would be excellent," Beth agreed.

"Humphrey, you really put together the wrong team for that," Neil said.

"Everyone quiet," Clive said. "Emir's coming out."

40
LEGACY

Emir and Constance walked through the vast atrium in the central tower of the cloud palace, a vast and grandiose chamber that had lush plants growing right out of the cloud-stuff walls and columns. They headed for the main entrance at a leisurely pace, as they prepared to address the crowd of waiting iron rankers.

"Who did the voice projection circle?" Emir asked.

"Trent," Constance said.

"Do you mean 'the glass definitely won't break' Trent or 'can't hold up a fish' Trent?"

"We're not calling him that," Constance admonished. "It was a suppurating grease fish. No one could have held it up."

"Elspeth Arella could have," Emir said. "We should have gotten her fired so we could hire her ourselves."

Constance shook her head in weary exasperation.

"You need to stop doing that."

"Danielle wanted me to do it."

"We stay hands-off in local politics," Constance said. "That's your policy."

"It seems warranted here."

"It always does to you, which is why you put me in charge of not letting you."

"We're already neck-deep with this astral space business."

"That's not local politics," Constance said. "It's international politics. Interdimensional, if Standish is to be believed."

"Clive," Emir said with a sigh. "I can't believe Jason snaked him out from under us."

"That is exactly how you described your own recruitment attempt."

"He's a good lad, Asano."

"It wouldn't have worked, you know," Constance said.

"Oh, I reckon we could have won him over. He's wasted in this backwater."

"No, I mean the fish," Constance said. "Arella actually couldn't have held it. Suppurating grease fish oil is resistant to telekinesis."

"It is?"

"That's why we went to so much trouble to find it."

"I thought we were just going to cook it."

They reached the door but paused before going through, continuing their conversation.

"You thought we spent three weeks, using over a dozen people to find and catch a very specific and hard to find fish just so we could eat it?" Constance asked.

"No," Emir said unconvincingly. "What did we want it for again?"

"The Rimaros job."

"Oh, right. Where we dug that tunnel through the bottom of the floating island and slipped out with the… what were we stealing again?"

"We weren't stealing," Constance said. "We were repatriating the royal ceremonial armour of Kodin."

"Right, yes. That ridiculous armour that looked like someone inflated it. I'm surprised they even wanted it back."

"It has cultural importance to the people of Kodin," Constance said.

"It felt like stealing. Did they figure out it was us?"

"They did," Constance said. "Greg didn't get the mango cart in place in time. On the bright side, they couldn't admit they had the armour in the first place, so everyone's pretending it didn't happen."

"Right," Emir said, nodding. "Greg. 'Not enough mangoes' Greg."

"No, that was 'fruit cart' Greg. We got rid of 'not enough mangoes' Greg after what he was caught doing to those hairless oxen."

"That was him? Good riddance, then. We lost a bundle cleaning that mess up. What happened to him?"

"We released him to the local authorities. Have you ever considered not basing your hiring policies on getting people with the same name?"

"I tried that in the early days," Emir said. "People are much more resistant to nicknames when there's no one else with the same name as them."

"Are the nicknames an essential part of the operation?"

"Why do you think I do all this?" Emir asked.

"Money, power, travel, excitement and connections."

"Those are the tawdry goals of the weak," Emir said loftily. "We gold-rankers strive for higher purpose."

"I think you've been spending too much time with Jason. You're talking increasing amounts of rubbish."

They left through the tower's large double doors and moved across the cloud bridge to the shore where the iron-rankers and other attendees were assembled on the grass next to the reception building.

"Is everyone out of the palace?" Emir asked as they stood at the end of the cloud bridge, surveying the crowd of adventurers.

"We're the last," Constance said. "It's ready to change over."

After he and Constance stepped off the cloud bridge, Emir reached into his jacket and pulled out a large, round-bottomed flask. He shook the flask, then took out the stopper, releasing four streams of mist that each took different shapes. One looked like a house, another like a large vehicle. The third was a small replica of the cloud palace, while the fourth was a ship. Emir put his hand through the mist ship and the four images returned to the flask. As he put the flask back into his dimensional jacket, the cloud palace slowly started to warp out of shape.

Emir turned from the palace which was beginning the process of turning back into a cloud ship. After striding out onto the grass, he stomped the ground with his foot and a wooden pillar rose up, lifting him into the air in front of the adventurers.

"Greetings, fellow adventurers," he said, his voice projecting over the crowd. "As you all know, I have come to this fine city with a purpose. Many, I'm sure, have heard whispers and rumours, but today, all shall be laid bare. Centuries ago, there was an ancient order of assassins. Known and feared the world over, their enemies came together to scour them from the face of our world. Today, only hidden remnants can be found, and those only with time and effort. Myself and others have undertaken that time and effort, which brings us to today."

He panned his gaze over the crowd.

"This order of assassins was known as the Order of the Reaper. Going all the way back to the days before their organisation was wiped out, there have been stories of a legacy they left behind. Stories of a test, for those with the potential to receive this legacy. For years now, I have been seeking that legacy, and finally, I have found it. In the days before this city was founded, the last fortress of the order was hidden away in what was then a remote and unpopulated region."

Not everyone had their full attention on Emir as the cloud palace deformed behind his back in the transition from grand residence to ocean-going vessel.

"As you have no doubt surmised," Emir continued, "the purpose for which you have been gathered is to claim this legacy. The ancient, hidden fortress is now in ruins, but the true heart of the complex remains unpenetrated. It lies within an astral space of its own, waiting for those brave and skilled enough to face the trials within. This is no ordinary astral space aperture, however. To protect their secrets, the Order had it sealed, the means of opening it scattered across the world. Those means have now been gathered and the aperture is ready to be opened. The trials are ready to begin."

He made a sweeping gesture, taking in the crowd.

"Just from the fact that I have taken such pains to gather you all here, you have all certainly realised that things are not so simple as I have described. Even once opened, the aperture still comes with restrictions. Within lies the true test—a series of trials left by the Order of the Reaper. Tests, to see who can live up to their ideals. Only those with the most untapped potential—iron-rankers—may enter. The first of those to pass every trial will receive the legacy left behind. As a warning, the trials shall remain open for eighteen days, after which they will again seal themselves closed. Any of you who have not returned by then will not return at all."

Emir took a round, palm-sized crystal from his jacket and held it in front of him. Above his head, a large image of a gold and black scythe appeared.

"No one knows the full extent of the Order's legacy. What we do know is that it includes this object. This scythe is the ancient symbol of the Order of the Reaper and the object of years of searching. The goal for each of you is to bring me this item. Anything else you find in that place, part of the Order's legacy or not, is yours to keep. Additionally, whichever team brings the scythe to me will be rewarded with five legendary awakening stones, which you may choose freely from my stores. If you are a team of one, then all five shall belong to you. Beyond the stones, however, is another prize."

Emir gestured behind him, where the cloud palace was still deforming.

"My cloud palace is a wonder, but it did not come to me as you see it here. It is a growth item I had the good fortune to come across when I, like you now, was only an iron ranker. Many years later I came across the man who created it, a diamond ranker. In payment for a service rendered, he gave me a second one, still at iron rank. Whomsoever brings me the scythe will receive it for themselves."

A susurrus of noise rippled through the crowd. The cloud palace had been dominating the Adventure Society skyline for weeks. Every person assembled wanted to claim one.

"So, you all now know what you are here for. Once the cloud palace has returned to the form of a ship all the iron-rankers participating may come aboard to see it for themselves. We will sail along the coastline to the closest location to our objective and travel overland from there. Our destination is one the locals may know of: Sky Scar Lake. The ruins are at the bottom of the lake, which is very deep, so you have until my ship leaves to prepare for that dive. Four hours. Consider it your first challenge. Be here and ready to board at that time."

Emir stepped out of the speaking circle. People immediately tried to approach him but a portal appeared, which he stepped through with Constance before it vanished.

*

The crowd was thrown into turmoil as Emir finished his speech. Some were being exhorted by their family elders to obtain a cloud palace at any cost. Others were already dashing in the direction of the trade hall, looking for items to let them handle the water of the lake.

Jason and Beth's teams were caught up in the swirl of people pushing their way out of the crowd.

"Does your team have a way of getting through the lake?" Beth asked once they were free.

Jason nodded. "There's a ritual I know. I assume you do too, Clive."

"I know the one you're talking about. I'd have to look it up, though."

"I can do it, no worries," Jason said, then turned back to Beth. "What about you?"

"I have the water essence," she said. "One of my abilities will do the job."

"I guess we'll make some final preparations and see you in a few hours then."

Many people were eager to get aboard the cloud palace, now transformed back into a ship the size of an ocean liner. Boarding did not go as smoothly as planned for some when it was revealed that they were required to pass a simple aura test. Anyone whose aura didn't match the Adventure Society records from prior to the expedition was excluded. Only a handful of people were caught out like this, but they were vocal in their protests. Instead of being heard, however, they were taken away for closer examination.

On the ship, Jason's team were given their own cabins, alongside those assigned to Rufus, Gary, and Farrah's parents. Rufus's parents were staying in Greenstone, making discrete inquiries into the church of Purity. Their teammate, Cal, had already left to check out the Landemere estate. The bulk of the iron-rankers were all bunked together in crew dorms, while the actual crew enjoyed cabins like Emir's guests.

As with the guest wing when it had been a cloud palace, the ship had a guest lounge with access to a broad side-deck. Humphrey quickly went to invite their friends out of the press of people domiciled together below decks, bringing back Rick and Beth's teams to enjoy their guest lounge. He brought along Lance and his team as well.

"Mose!" Jason greeted happily. "It's been a while. What's up, mate?"

"Beth finally let me in her team," Mose said happily. "I think she wanted some extra power after you beat her like that."

Mose Cavendish was Beth's cousin, who Jason had known longer than Beth.

They had met on a mission to escort spirit coins, where Jason had witnessed the destructive power of Mose's spells.

"That wasn't me," Jason said. "You can blame Humphrey for that one. He predicted exactly how your cousin would react if we could put her on the back foot."

Rufus and Gary soon joined them and the group socialised as the ship sailed its way south down the coast. It was only a few hours before it sailed into shore at an unremarkable patch of desert. Emir's people started unloading sand barges from the ship. None were the size of the great Ustei tribe barge that Jason had seen in the pitched battle against the sand pirate tribe, but three of them were enough to transport the whole group inland to Sky Scar Lake.

It was hours more, going into the night, before the barges arrived at the shores of the lake, vast almost to the point of an inland sea. It was an enormous oasis in the desert, a blessed eye of blue and green in the hard, yellow face of the desert. The lights of villages along the shore of the lake shone in the early dark. There were towns and villages situated all around the lake and the sand barges disembarked their charges at the largest.

The adventurers were notified that they would begin in the morning. The townsfolk had been warned ahead of time about the coming influx and had beds for those who wanted them or food and drink for those who didn't. Emir brought out the cloud palace again, right on the surface of the lake, allowing selected people to use that for accommodation.

The next day, the locals set out tables and brought out food and drink en masse to feed the anxious horde of adventurers. Not even the elite adventurers from overseas were immune to the nervousness. For all their training and prestige, they were still iron rankers and, as they came from high-magic regions, they didn't have the individual monster hunting experience of the locals.

Some didn't eat out of nervousness while others couldn't wolf down food fast enough. Humphrey walked along through the closest village with Neil, Sophie and Belinda.

"Next time we do this you'll be an adventurer, too," Sophie told Belinda.

"Very likely," Humphrey said. "An astral space untouched for centuries should have accumulated a good number of essences and awakening stones. If we're lucky, they'll be unusual ones, although that's down to the nature of the astral space."

"People don't talk about it much, because of how it went," Neil said, "but the expedition was quite a good haul."

"That's how Jason got you so many awakening stones on the open market," Humphrey said to Sophie. "Did you see him leave this morning?"

"I saw him duck out early with Clive," Sophie said.

"Is that them there?" Belinda asked, pointing. The others followed her gaze to see Clive and Jason behind some kind of cooking stall in aprons. There was a line of people leading up to them as they rapidly worked a large grill plate in front of them. Jason was wearing some kind of puffy white hat and his aprons had the words 'you can't fight monsters on an empty stomach' emblazoned on it.

"Oh, hey!" Jason called out as he spotted their approach. "Clive is teaching me to barbecue eels properly!"

41
A RASH DECISION

"Now," Jason said happily, "this is what adventuring should be like."

Adventurers were spreading out over the surface of Sky Scar Lake like a huge flock of geese, using all manner and means of transportation. There was a wild array of essence abilities, rituals and items from water-walking books to cloaks that let the wearer swim like a manta ray. Jason himself had a useful item he had acquired from the tidal troll he defeated.

Item: [Necklace of the Deep] (iron rank, uncommon)
A necklace containing the power of the deep ocean giants **(jewellery, necklace).**

Effect: Ignore the effects of high pressure and pressure variance.

Effect: Breathe water.

Effect: Your weight is increased. You cannot use iron-rank weight reduction abilities or items.

Jason could use it to walk along the bottom of the lake but his team couldn't, so it stayed in his inventory. It was nice to have on hand, though, and he could always test it out later.

His team were near the edge of the shore, a few of the hundreds making their way into or onto the lake. They were geared up and ready, Jason's starlight cloak already in place, which he was beginning to regret.

"Nice cloak," an adventurer said to him. "How much to buy it off you?"

"It's an ability," Jason said. "Can't sell it."

"He's lying, Brandon," a second adventurer said. She was plastered to Brandon's side. "He just doesn't want to sell it to you."

"Come on, how much?" Brandon asked.

"It really is an ability," Jason insisted.

"Guy, you do not want to mess with me," Brandon said. "Just sell me the damn cloak. Do you have any idea who my father is?"

Standing next to Jason, Neil winced, pinching the bridge of his nose. The cloak vanished from around Jason.

"See?" Jason said. "All gone."

The cloak reappeared.

"It's an ability," Jason reiterated. "Try an awakening stone of the stars; that where I got it."

"Forget this guy," Brandon's hanger-on said. Brandon nodded.

"Neil, your new teammate is a rolling turd wagon," Brandon said, and they hurried off to catch up with their team. The girl slapped Brandon on the arm for eyeing Sophie as they went. Neil and Humphrey let out a sigh of relief.

"You know that guy?" Clive asked Neil.

"One of Thadwick's peripheral hangers-on," Neil said. "His family are want-to-be aristocrats and he's the dregs of the bloodline. If his family knew he not only failed to recognise Humphrey but mouthed off in front of him, they'd drown him in this lake."

"I'm just grateful Jason didn't take the bait," Humphrey said.

"Farrah tried to hammer into my head that I should only start trouble when trouble is what I want."

"Since when do you ever not want trouble?" Sophie asked.

"You've been listening to other people too much," Jason said. "When did you ever see me start trouble?"

"You killed a bunch of people in a shopping arcade in the middle of the day!"

"I didn't start that," Jason said.

"He's right," Neil said. "Thadwick sent them to kill him when he panicked over Jason uncovering his lumber mill scam. Dustin and I didn't find out until later, so by the time we went to Thadwick's father to stop it, Jason had already killed them and given a recording of him doing it to Thadwick's mother."

"Some guy tried to have you killed and you just let that go?" Sophie asked. "If you let that go, what's to stop him from trying again?"

"I would have liked to deal with him at the time," Jason said, "but there were mitigating circumstances. Even disregarding the power of his family, I wasn't going to kill my girlfriend's brother."

"Wait," Sophie said. "That Cassandra girl's brother tried to kill you?"

"He did," Jason said. "It was a rash decision."

"Does he have a weird sister thing or something?" Sophie asked.

"Not that I know of," Jason said. "Neil?"

"No," Neil said. "Thadwick isn't the greatest guy in the world, but he isn't that kind of creepy."

"That's where the indignation comes in?" Jason asked. "We were just talking about how he tried to kill me."

"I'm pretty sure you sleeping with his sister helped that decision along a little," Neil said.

"I eventually realised it's for the best," Jason said. "What would killing him get me? Killed by his mum, that's what. Then Emir and Rufus come down on the Mercers."

"My family too," Humphrey said. "My mother and Lady Mercer are close, but Mother wouldn't tolerate her killing you."

"Exactly," Jason said. "The wheel doesn't stop turning until someone steps off and forgives and it might as well be me. Besides, Thadwick has problems enough to be going on with."

Thadwick had been in the constant company of Mercer family bronze-rankers since having the star seed purged out of him. They stood watch as he slept for days in recovery, then they stood by his room at his parents' 'suggestion' that he stay put and focus on getting better.

Although his rooms in the Mercer family home were the opposite of prison-like, he chafed at the confinement. His sister had visited, only to be chased-off by his screamed accusations of whoring herself out to outworlder trash. His father would not tolerate such tantrums and had not been back since teaching Thadwick that lesson with the back of his hand. His mother was more gentle but no less unyielding. She probed him with incessant questions until he told her to leave him to rest.

Thadwick's memories of his time with a star seed were hazy. His last clear thoughts were of being taken in the astral space and knocked out. From there it was only disconnected flashes, fleeting moments without context or comprehension. Clarity only came when he woke up out of recovery, the star seed removed.

His mother had told him that the others had experienced much the same. She wanted to know everything he could remember, everything he could piece together. She was meant to be his mother but instead of comforting him and giving him the things he wanted she pestered him again and again with questions. In the end, she was just one more person who only wanted something from him. Like everyone else, she was blinded by whatever strange methods Asano was using to make everyone love him.

His mother was so enamoured of that filthy, interdimensional bastard. She had made no secret of her plans to match him with Cassandra. At least the family had put an end to that sordid idea. The thought of his beautiful, capable sister being wasted on such a vile creature filled him with fury.

Everything had started going wrong the moment Asano appeared. Showing him up in front of everyone at the field assessment gathering. Winning over the Gellers, the out-of-town big shots and even Thadwick's own mother. She once even had the gall to say that he could stand to be more like Asano.

Every step of the way, Asano was plotting to bring himself up by putting Thadwick down. He wormed his way into Cassandra's affections, just to rile him up. How long had Asano worked to uncover Thadwick's brilliant plan to show his father that he was ready to step up in running family affairs? Asano must have been looking for some way to undermine him from the moment he arrived in the city.

Ever since Asano's arrival in the city, Thadwick had been feeling increasingly powerless. The sheer magnitude of Asano's plotting was mind-boggling, and Thadwick was the only one smart enough to see through it. The only time he had felt powerful in months was in a handful of moments he didn't understand. The memories were scattered, but one thing had been present in all of them: an incredible sense of power.

His memories included a few faces and places he recognised. Scraps of conversation he hadn't told his mother when she was questioning him. He had a better use for those snatches of memory: he wanted that feeling of power back.

He got up and stripped out of the bedclothes he had been wearing throughout his confinement. He picked out some street clothes, yanked them on and marched out the door.

"Young Master Mercer," one of the bronze-rankers said as Thadwick strode past.

"Your mother told us it would be best if you stayed in your rooms to rest," the other said.

"I've rested enough," Thadwick said, not stopping.

One of the two followed him, the other going in the other direction. As Thadwick reached the ground level and was just leaving the tower, his mother teleported in front of him, along with the guard that had gone to fetch her.

"Thadwick, dear," she said. Her sincerity might fool others but he saw right through it.

"I'm going out, Mother. I've been cooped up long enough."

"I don't think that would be best," she said.

"Am I a prisoner in my own home?"

"Of course not, dear."

"Then I'm going out," he said firmly.

"Very well," she said, having no way around his masculine confidence. "With so many out of the city things should be quiet, so now may be the best time. But Geoffrey and Kyle will be going with you."

"Who?" Thadwick asked.

Thalia gestured to the guards that had been stationed on Thadwick's room for weeks, the one that had followed him and the one that had fetched her.

"I need them with you," she said. "To keep you safe."

"Fine," Thadwick said. He didn't care what they would suffer where he was going.

Almost two hours later, Thadwick and his escorts were walking through the streets of Old City. Close to the fortress ruled by the Big Three, the criminal overlords serving as Old City's de facto rulers, many establishments were offering the kind of very specific services only the wealthy could afford.

"I don't think this is where your mother would like you to be, Young Master Mercer," one of his guards said.

"You aren't paid to think, Geoffrey."

"I'm Kyle, Young Master."

"I don't care."

Thadwick took a familiar path down a flight of stairs to an unmarked basement shopfront. A slat opened up, and the eyes behind it took in Thadwick and his guards.

"You know better than to bring people wearing house colours here," a voice came from behind the door. Thadwick's guards were indeed clad in the uniform of the Mercer household.

"Take it up with my mother," Thadwick said. "You don't have the stones to keep that door closed in my face, so hurry up and open it."

The eyes glared but moments later the door swung open. Thadwick smirked at the doorman as he went past, his guards trailing behind. After a short hallway was a large, luxurious lounge. There was a long bar and a variety of booths that offered convenient seclusion. The room was adorned with beautiful men and women in provocative clothes: elves and humans, celestines, smoulders and even a few burly male or lithe female leonids.

Thadwick's guards drew attention but people quickly turned back to their own affairs. Thadwick glanced around and spotted the person he was looking for—an indolent man splayed in a booth with a woman to either side of him.

"Thadwick," the man greeted him, glancing over the Mercer guards. "I see your mother let you out, so long as you wore your leash."

"I knew you'd be here, Timos."

"I take my pleasure where I can find it," Timos said. "You can hardly blame me for being so good at looking for it."

"We need to talk."

"Then, by all means, take a seat."

"You'll want this little chat in private, Timos."

"Oh? Finally learning to explore all the tantalising treats life has to offer, Taddy?"

Thadwick leaned in, grabbing the front of Timos's clothes and whispering in his ear.

"I've been having these very interesting flashes of what I went through, Timos. Some faces I recognised when I was captured during the expedition. If you don't want to talk about them, I bet my mother will."

Thadwick stood back up, looking with satisfaction at the Timos's face, the dismissive sneer wiped right off of it.

"What about your boys here?" Timos asked.

"I don't care what happens to them."

With all the auras, abilities and magic items being used, the ambient magic had become turbid. Clive closed his eyes and took a slow, deep breath, sending out a wave of magical stillness that even those without magic perception abilities could feel.

Party member [Clive Standish] has used [Mana Equilibrium]. Ambient magic has entered a harmonious state.

The next spell cast in this area will cost reduced mana, and the harmonious state will be disrupted.

"So handy," Jason said. "Thank you, Clive."

Jason quickly enacted the ritual whose circle had been inscribed into the flat top of a square platform made of wooden boards and lacquered to make a surface suitable for marking with inscriptions. After a short chant from Jason, a shimmering bubble appeared around the board. Humphrey reached through the bubble unimpeded, picked up the platform and dropped it onto the water. It didn't strike the water, instead, stopping in the air over the surface. The water was visibly indented by the bubble.

The team all stepped into the bubble, onto the board which remained completely stable. It was a good-sized board, but it was standing room only with the five people on it. They watched as, nearby, Beth's team sailed off on a boat made of condensed water that somehow didn't get the people in it wet.

"Maybe we should have used a bigger board," Neil said.

"This as big as we can go before the ritual starts getting costly in materials," Jason said. He concentrated on the board and it floated slowly out onto the lake.

"Exactly right," Clive said. "It may not be fast or big, but it will do what we need."

They floated out, part of the mass of adventurers. Eventually, they found Rufus standing on the surface of the lake. On his feet were large, garish, blue boots, from which mist was drifting in wisps. He was directing people to descend to the bottom of the lake at that spot. He gave them an encouraging wave but didn't pause his task to speak with them. Jason directed the board to go down, the water enveloping their bubble as they descended.

42
IT'S A GOOD ONE

Jason and his team descended through the water as the daylight shining through the surface of the lake above grew increasingly dim. They stood close together on the platform as the magic sphere around them held off the water, encapsulating them in a perfect orb. When it grew too murky for anyone but Jason to see, Humphrey took out a light crystal, tossing it up to float around his head. In the dark around them, other teams took similar steps. The result was a rain of light, plunging down through watery depths.

"This is awesome," Jason said, looking at the lights descending through the dark. "I know I'm from another world and maybe you all get to see things like this all the time but I'm loving this."

"It's certainly impressive," Humphrey agreed. "We may not get to see such things all the time now, but we're only beginning our time as adventurers. We have lives of wonder ahead of us."

Jason looked at Humphrey's handsome face and broad shoulders as the other man gazed winsomely out of their bubble.

"Damn, Humphrey," Jason said. "You must be beating the ladies off with a stick."

"I do alright," Humphrey said. "Things didn't end well with Gabrielle, but the start and middle were good. I don't regret our time together and it gave me some important perspective."

"Listen to you all mature," Jason said. "What happened to that nervous guy from half a year ago?"

"He got a friend who pushed him into trying new things. Even if those were sometimes poison soup."

"Oh, that was one time," Jason said. "How was I meant to know they swapped out the regular cook instead of closing for the day? And it wasn't poison soup, it was just… improperly prepared."

Jason glanced at Sophie, looking around as wide-eyed as the rest of them.

"If you'd decided against being an adventurer right now, where would you be?" he asked her.

"No place good," she said. "I'm glad Belinda talked me into it."

"This is just the beginning," Humphrey said. "We'll have many days like this."

As they neared the bottom of the lake, they saw domes of air over dark ruins lit up by cheap magic lamps.

"Those domes are big versions of what we're using, right?" Jason asked Clive.

"I'm not sure," Clive said. "I'd like to take a look for myself."

"Which one do you think Emir was talking about?" Jason asked. "He said the middle dome but there's a whole cluster of them."

"There are meant to be tunnels connecting them," Clive said. "Just pick one and we'll figure it out."

Jason directed their own floating orb of air to the base of one of the domes. The dome held out only the water, so once the dome and their bubble connected they could easily step into it and off the platform, without getting wet. As Clive put the platform away, they saw plenty of other adventures were likewise finding their way in.

Looking around at the inside of the dome, they saw that their surroundings were an ancient stone village. Long ago claimed by the lake's water, the village was once again dry thanks to the dome holding back the lake. The borders of the village were an exact match for the dome of air. Slimy growth was everywhere, fortunately giving traction to what would have otherwise been slippery cobbles underfoot, worn smooth by water. As the others looked over the buildings, Jason and Clive turned their attention to the dome. In what looked to be a circle around the entire village, a stone ring engraved with runes was set into the ground.

"Look at this," Clive said, pointing it out to Jason. They crouched down to examine it more closely.

"The cobbles end right at this ring," Jason said. Outside the stone ring and the dome of air that followed its curve around the village, the lake bed was all silt, rock and submarine growth. On the inside of the ring was cobbled ground.

"I'd say this ring was once used to keep this dome up permanently," Clive postulated as he examined it. "See these repairs? I'm guessing the domes collapsed after this place was abandoned and Emir's people used the ring as a platform for these new domes. They'll only be temporary, though. Re-establishing permanent domes would be prohibitively expensive, even using the existing infrastructure."

Now Jason was working more on grasping magical theory, he was becoming more interested in the functionality of magic. Clive was more than happy to play the role of mentor.

"We might want to get moving," Neil suggested. "If we stop to examine everything we see, we'll never get anywhere."

"He's right," Humphrey said. "First, we need to find our way to the right dome because I don't think this one is it."

"Do you all feel that?" Sophie asked.

The rest of the team looked at each other and collectively shook their heads.

"Outside the dome," Sophie said. "A half-dozen iron-rank auras."

As the only team member with an aura sense power, Sophie had detected the approaching monsters first. She pointed and the others looked, spying a group of monsters moving along the bottom of the lake. They were large with shark bodies and crab legs, all covered in shell plating. They were heading straight for the dome.

"Shabs," Jason said. "How nostalgic."

"Take a three-two formation," Humphrey instructed.

The team moved into position. Humphrey, Sophie and Jason formed a line, behind which were Neil and Clive. With his hands up in front of him, Clive conjured a magic circle vertically in the air. He was feeding mana into it, ready to trigger. Humphrey conjured his large sword and waited while Sophie stood, relaxed, beside him. Jason's cloak was already in place and he conjured his dagger, looking between it and Humphrey's giant dragon wing sword.

"Ready?" Neil asked as the shabs neared the dome.

"Go for it," Sophie said, and Neil immediately chanted a spell.

"*Let your power fulminate.*"

Sophie started shimmering slightly with silver-gold magic.

Ability: [Bolster] (Growth)
Spell (magic, boon)
Cost: Moderate mana.
Cooldown: 30 seconds.

Current rank: Iron 6 (19%)

Effect (iron): The next essence ability used by the targeted ally has increased effect. This can affect parameters including damage, range and number of targets, depending on the affected ability. Cannot be used on self.

Sophie sliced her leg upward in a vertical kick that demonstrated impressive flexibility. A blade of wind slashed out, passing through the dome unimpeded and striking one of the approaching shabs. It exploded in a wash of red liquid and a storm of bubbles that obscured the others.

"You weren't kidding about that explosive effect in water," Humphrey said.

"Split, please," Clive requested, Humphrey and Sophie moving aside to give him an unobstructed line to the enemy. The remaining five shabs passed through what was left of the first and Clive chanted a spell.

"*Feel the power of reality remade.*"

A beam of rainbow light passed out of the magic circle floating in front of Clive's hands, locking onto the next-closest shab. The red faded from the rainbow, which then vanished. The shab stopped dead, fluid boiling out from under its shell plates.

"I figured heat would be enough," Clive said. "I didn't want to burn through too much mana."

Ability: [Wrath of the Magister] (Magic)

Spell (fire, magic, curse, poison, wounding, ice, dimension)
Cost: Moderate mana plus additional mana per effect.
Cooldown: 1 minute.

Current rank: Iron 5 (38%)

With each use of this ability, choose one of the following effects:
Effect Option One (iron): Lock a prismatic beam onto an enemy. Expend additional mana to unmake reality in a localised area, creating an annihilating void sphere inside the target. This effect requires magic to be channelled into the target at an extreme mana cost until sufficient mana has been channelled to trigger the effect.

Effect Option Two (iron): Lock a prismatic beam onto an enemy. Expend additional mana to alter the target's reality, using any combination of the available colour effects. This cannot be used in conjunction with the other variant of this spell, which requires an alternate incantation.

[Red] (high mana): Target's temperature is significantly increased (frost burn if combined with blue).
[Yellow] (high mana): Target's abilities have increased mana cost.
[Pink] (moderate mana): Target's resistances are reduced.
[Green] (moderate mana): Target's blood is poisonous to itself.
[Purple] (very high mana): Expending mana harms the target.
[Orange] (very high mana): Target suffers increased damage from all sources.
[Blue] (high mana): Target's temperature is significantly decreased (frost burn if combined with red).

Humphrey and Sophie slid back in front of Clive and Neil. Three shabs were down before they even reached the dome.

"What's that?" Neil asked, pointing at another shape approaching through the water. It looked something like an octopus made of thorny vines. "It looks nasty,"

"That's Stash," Sophie said, who could sense the shape-shifting dragon's aura.

Humphrey had let his boisterous familiar make his own way through the lake. Jason's summoned familiar had many advantages over a bonded familiar like Humphrey's, but a bond had its own advantages. Where Jason could only sense Colin while the leech swarm was subsumed into his body, Humphrey and Stash could always sense one another. They would each know the other's general condition and could find one another over any distance.

Stash wrapped his thorny tentacles around the rearmost shab, seeking out vulnerable crevices between shell plates. The other two shabs finally reached the dome. One was met by a huge sword swinging down, cutting through the front half of the monster and leaving a ragged split.

In a more competent version of his very first shad fight, Jason rolled under the monster, coming up and slitting his dagger through the monster's vulnerable underside. Ichor splattered down over his cloak and he extracted himself as the monster fell dead. He tossed away the despoiled cloak which then vanished. The ichor that had been on it was suddenly unsupported and fell to the ground.

"That was good," Humphrey said, right before Stash splashed through the dome, his giant octopus form drenching Jason and Humphrey with shab guts and water. Sophie vanished before being struck, reappearing nearby. Stash then transformed into a puppy, looking up at Humphrey with innocent eyes.

"Ew," Jason said unhappily.

"I guess we know which of us is going out there to loot the monsters," Neil said. "No point me getting all messy if you're already like that."

Jason groaned and withdrew his necklace of the deep, a series of round, colourful stones strung on a sinewy cord. Clipping it around his neck, he closed his eyes and mouth, holding his nose as he stepped through the dome.

The necklace shielded him from the pressure of the depths and weighed him down as he walked blindly through the shab-tainted water. He held his breath in spite of the necklace's power to let him breathe water. Its fierce chill would have made it an unpleasant proposition in any case. Unwilling to open his eyes, he stumbled about until he felt he had touched enough shab goo to trigger three loot notifications. He kept his sense of direction enough to find his way back without opening his eyes.

Everyone backed off as he remerged inside the dome, drenched in water and semi-liquid shab remains. When he opened his eyes, he saw the notices were there and accepted them, all the goo in the water and on Jason and Humphrey dissolving in rainbow smoke. Outside the dome, the rainbow smoke bubbled its way up towards the surface of the lake.

The coins looted from the shabs appeared in the dimensional storage abilities of Clive, Humphrey and Jason. Neil, experienced from his own looting ability, stepped back and neatly caught his own bag of coins as it fell from overhead. Sophie, less experienced, had it bounce off her skull.

"You could have warned me," she told Jason.

"When you go wading into a freezing cold lake to fish out money for everyone," he said. "We'll see how much your mind is on the little details."

He pulled a vial of orange liquid from his belt and drank it.

"Ooh, spicy."

Steam started rising off of Jason's body and clothes. After a few minutes his skin, hair and clothes were all dry.

"Glad I bought those," he said. "Remind me to thank Jory for suggesting them."

Jory was actually participating in the event, although Jason hadn't seen him. The various crafting associations had decided there was a good chance of lost crafting secrets being found and had formed several teams to join in. To avoid conflict, each team was made up of different kind of magic craftspeople, from leatherworkers to weapon-smiths, engravers to alchemists.

They had no intention of seeking out Emir's scythe, instead intending to scour the hidden astral space for item-making secrets. Jory had travelled with the craft association contingent and hadn't run into Jason.

After handling the shabs, Jason and his team went looking for the central dome. While they had been fighting, other teams had found the tunnel, so they could follow the other adventurers. The tunnel sloped down under the lake bed, leading underground between domes. The central area was obviously more important to the original inhabitants than the dome they had come from. The buildings were larger and more impressive, looking more like the central location of a city than the village of the dome they had come from.

Following the crowd, Humphrey's team found Emir standing near an archway of dark stone, right in the middle of a large square. This allowed the adventurers to spill in around it. Gary was present, along with Constance and some of Emir's people who were drawing an elaborate ritual circle around the archway. Placed at various points within the ritual diagram were more than a dozen items, all long-weather stone artefacts. Emir's people kept the adventurers back, warning them against using abilities that would interfere with the ambient magic. Just the presence of so many essence users and their magic items was bad enough.

There was a long wait as all the adventurers either arrived or were rescued from their poor preparations for underwater travel and returned to the surface, destined to participate no further. One of the main culprits was the difficulty of getting rituals right amongst all the adventurers. Without a power to smooth out the ambient magic, like Clive had, rituals could easily go awry. Emir had a ritualist with a similar ability on staff for that exact reason.

Once Emir confirmed with his people that all was set, he addressed the crowd.

"And here we are at last," he called out loudly. He wasn't using a voice projection circle this time, again to not disrupt the magic. "Here we have reached, together, the limit of what I can tell you. The door will open soon and my people will direct you through it. I ask that you are patient while waiting for your turn to enter, as my people will deal with anyone acting in a disorderly manner. Remember, the team that brings me the scythe is the team that wins the grand prize."

Quest: [Legacy of the Reaper]
You have joined the mission to retrieve the Order of the Reaper's legacy.

Objective: Pass the reaper trials 0/5
Objective: Reach the centre of the City of Fallen Echoes.
Objective: Obtain [Scythe of the Reaper] 0/1.
Objective: Deliver [Scythe of the Reaper] to Emir Bahadir 0/1.

Reward: Racial gift transfiguration.

"I've been waiting for that," Jason said. "Oh, it's a good one."

It was not the first time the party had seen a quest appear, as they had cleared various contracts together. This was the first time they had seen a reward that wasn't just spirit coins, however. Neil's eyes were transfixed by the listed reward.

"Is that what I think it is?" he asked.

"I think so, yeah," Jason said. "Should be for all of us, since we all got the quest."

"How is that even possible?" he asked.

"Not sure," Jason said. "My theory is that once you reach a certain threshold for handsomeness, it flows over and starts having weird effects."

Despite the astounding quest window in front of them, the team all turned to look at Jason.

"What?" he asked.

43
THE CITY OF FALLEN ECHOES

There was some pushing and jostling from the adventurers eager to pass through the aperture until a few low growls from Gary pulled the stroppy ones in line. Emir stood with Gary, watching from the side as they went through, one at a time. When his team drew close to Emir, Jason greeted him.

"I don't suppose you've got any insider tips, Emir?" Jason asked as they went past. This drew the attention of the adventurers around them.

"Jason," Emir said with a wry smile. "If I had anything else to tell you, I would have told everyone. The goal to have the scythe brought to me. If it was to have the scythe brought to me by you, then you would be the only one I sent."

"Fair enough."

Jason had encountered two astral apace apertures before, both to the rainforest astral space that supplied water to the delta, along with many of the desert's oases. Those had been shimmering blue, floating unattached as if not really connected to the world. As he got a look at this astral gate aperture, it was very different. It was contained within an archway the size of large double doors. The archway was made of stone, a single piece with the black, smooth gloss of polished obsidian. Unlike the buildings around it, centuries of submersion had done nothing to mar its surface or dim its lustre. The aperture itself, within the archway, held a strange darkness that almost seemed to have substance, devouring the light around it.

"Is it just me," Neil said, "or does anyone else think that looks like Jason's cloak?"

Jason dimmed the stars on his cloak down to nothing. The result was a void draped around him that, as Neil suggested, looked very much like the dark aperture before them.

"It does," Clive said. "My guess would be a dark essence ability was used as the foundation for this archway, likely even the—"

"We should keep it moving," Humphrey said, stopping Clive before his fascination overcame his awareness of the situation. This got a look of gratitude from the member of Emir's staff standing next to the aperture. His task was to keep things moving but he also didn't want to annoy people his boss obviously thought highly of.

Humphrey stepped up to the aperture. "See you on the other side," he told the others and stepped through.

Like Humphrey, it was not Neil's first time entering an astral space and he followed without hesitation. Jason prompted Clive through next, not wanting to leave him to his curiosity. Sophie paused in front of the aperture, reluctance and uncertainty saturating her body language.

"Are we sure that thing isn't just devouring people?" she asked. "It kind of looks like it's devouring people."

She was hardly the first adventurer to hesitate when looking at the lightless void of the aperture. Jason gave her a reassuring pat on the shoulder, stepping past her.

"No one is going to push you," he said. "If you don't want to do this, go back with Emir and we'll see you in a few weeks."

Jason paused in front of the aperture himself, an anticipatory grin crossing his face before he stepped through.

"Miss Wexler," the staff member said. "I'll need you to either go through or move out of the way."

Sophie looked at him, nodded to herself and held her breath as she stepped through the portal.

Different modes of teleportation had different feels to them. The feel of travelling through the portals created by Hester felt different to Jason's own ability. It, in turn, felt different again to Danielle Geller's ordinary teleport power. She had the same one as her son, but her higher-rank version allowed her to take more people. She would sometimes teleport around with the Geller family teams, including Humphrey's, to help them acclimatise themselves to such abilities.

These benefits were not available to everyone, as evidenced by the state of people Jason found when he emerged from a dark archway, identical to the one he had stepped into. They ranged from looking slightly peaky to being on hands and knees, throwing up. Jason had no such issues.

Ability: Astral Affinity

Increased resistance to dimension effects and astral forces. Dimension abilities have increased effect and transcendent damage is increased.

His racial gift made him more tolerant to the effects of teleportation but, more than that, the sensation of going through the portal had been incredibly familiar. Travelling through the dark aperture had felt exactly like using his shadow teleport.

As Jason emerged, system messages immediately started popping up. He dismissed them to the periphery of his vision so he could take a look around. He started by getting out of the way before more people arrived, stepping around those loudly vomiting.

With a glance, he saw he was on some kind of large tower with a flat top. It was made of dark, grey brick, with lichen growing in the crevices. The archway stood right in the middle and the tower was apparently quite tall as he could mostly see sky over the edges. A sun was high in a sky, blurred by summer haze. The air was humid and heavy, as much as the delta on its worst day. He could hear water splashing against rocks from below, the unmistakable sound of the sea. The breezeless air carried none of the ocean's salty freshness, however.

The adventurers who had already recovered from being magically transported were turning their faces to the sky or wandering over the edges to look around. Others were looking for their party members but most were not finding them. Jason himself could find no trace of Humphrey, Neil or Clive. As he waited to see if Sophie would emerge after him, he took a bracelet of sandy yellow stones on a loop and slipped it over his wrist.

Item: [Oasis Bracelet] (iron rank, uncommon)

A bracelet that draws on the power of water quintessence to bestow the blessings of a personal oasis **(accessory, bracelet).**

Effect: Keeps the wearer cool and refreshed. Bracelet energy is consumed at a varying rate according to climate.

Effect: Reduces incoming fire and heat damage. This rapidly consumes bracelet energy.

Effect: Consume a water quintessence gem to completely refill bracelet energy.

Taking out a water quintessence gem, he touched it to the bracelet and it melted away. The yellow stones turned blue and Jason immediately felt the benefits of his magical item as the muggy and oppressive air felt suddenly cool and refreshing.

Sophie emerged from the archway just as Jason was taking a deep, satisfying breath. Looking startled, she started waving her hand in front of her like she was swiping at insects. Jason walked back over to the archway.

"Just imagine the screens moving out of the way, to the edge of your vision," he told her. She frowned at the space in front of her.

"Why so many?" she asked as they moved out of the way for the next adventurer to appear.

"I haven't read them yet," he told her.

She looked around.

"So this is an astral space," she said. "Where are the others?"

"Not here," he said. "This is only a fraction of the people who went through, so there may be other arrival locations."

"Unless the magic void door is eating people," she said.

"Let's hope not," Jason answered. "Take a look around?"

"It'll get us away from all these people throwing up. What's going on with that?"

"They can't handle teleportation as well as us," Jason said. "Notice all the celestines are fine. You have an ability to endure dimensional effects that I happen to share."

"Is that we didn't get eaten?"

"They weren't eaten. Probably. As for whether it affected us arriving in the same place, I'm not sure."

They walked over to the edge of the tower, which had no railing of any kind, simply ending in a precipitous edge. Their tower was huge, some twenty metres across and at least seventy high. It would have loomed over even the tallest building in Greenstone.

Looking out from the edge, they saw that the tower was located right on the coastline, with water from a seemingly boundless sea stretching out to their right. To their left was an ancient, abandoned city. It was staggeringly vast, sprawling off into the distance as far as they could see. Plant life had long ago reclaimed it, with vines crawling over the building and trees growing in the boulevards through the gaps left by broken and dislodged flagstones. Although larger than Greenstone by at least several times, it was more jungle than metropolis.

Stopping to look and listen, they heard the sounds of creatures—the warble of birds, the distant roaring of some predator, be it animal or monster. They were even able to pick out a few inhuman figures shambling and prowling through the overgrown streets.

The tower Jason and Sophie were on was not the only great tower that could be seen. Maybe twenty kilometres distant was another, also right on the waterline. They moved around the edge of the tower to get a better look at the city below.

You have used a panoramic view to unveil parts of the City of Fallen Echoes map. Visit unveiled locations to add additional details.

Other adventurers were likewise moving over to the edge. There did not appear to be any way of getting inside the tower from the roof, but some adventurers found the top of a stairwell that wound its way down the outside. Some started rushing down immediately to get some kind of lead on the competition. Most chose to stay and take stock. All of the teams present were missing members, it seemed, and none of them was clear on exactly what they should be doing. Sophie and Jason found their own spot, sitting on the edge with their legs dangling off.

"We should start with those messages we put aside," Jason said, pulling the screens up from the periphery of his vision.

You have entered a zone of high magical saturation. Magical manifestations will occur at an increased rate.

"What's magical saturation?" Sophie asked. "Are magical manifestations good?"

"Ambient magic, the invisible magic all around us," Jason explained, "is graded in two ways. One is magical density, which is kind of like the strength of the local magic. It determines how powerful a magic item can be and work normally and the power of rituals that can be performed. The most important effect, though, is it determines the strength of what monsters will appear. Emir said the magical density here should be the same as the world outside, so we can expect mostly iron rank monsters, plus some bronze. Silver should be extremely rare, but a silver rank monster can linger for years before breaking down back into magic, so there may be one or two around, somewhere."

"That's good to know, but doesn't actually answer my questions," Sophie said.

"I'm providing context," Jason said.

"You're starting to sound like Clive."

"Clive's a smart guy."

"But he also likes to waffle on. You should hear him and Belinda. It's interminable."

"Anyway," Jason said, "while magical density is how strong the magic is, magic saturation is how much of it there is. If you get higher magical saturation, you get more magical manifestation. That means more essences, more awakening stones and more monsters, which is all good."

"More monsters is good?

"Our ability to grow stronger is reliant on throwing ourselves into challenge after challenge," Jason said. "Here, we have all the challenge we could ask for.

This is a holy land for adventurers looking to get stronger. It's a shame that we only have eighteen days."

"Then our first step should be regrouping with the others," Sophie said.

The other messages screens stacked up were all variations on a theme.

Party member [Humphrey Geller] has gone out of range. Voice communication and loot sharing with out of range party members are unavailable.

Clive, Neil and Humphrey were all out of range, while Jason and Sophie had only been out of range for as long as Jason had been on one side of the aperture and Sophie the other.

Party member [Sophie Wexler] has re-entered range. Voice communication and loot sharing are restored. Voice communication and loot sharing with out of range party members are unavailable.

"So, how do we find them?" Sophie asked.

Jason took a furtive glance at the other adventurers. Some were huddled together, having discussions like Jason and Sophie. Others were looking to form makeshift groups after being separated from their own. Jason recognised a few faces but no one he knew well. A few people seemed to recognise him by his cloak, a couple of whom were heading in their direction.

"Jason Asano?" one of them asked.

"That's right."

"We've been separated from our group and it looks like you have been, too. You could join up with us if you like, until you find your own people."

Jason glanced at Sophie, who gave a little head shake.

"Sorry," Jason said. "We've lost people but our most mobile people are still together. We're going to use that to cover more ground. Thank you for the offer though. It's very kind."

After a little more polite chatter they walked away.

"I don't think they were being kind," Sophie said quietly. "I think they were trying to glom onto someone they'd heard of."

"They're just trying to survive in a situation that's gotten away from them," Jason said. "You of all people should understand that."

Sophie glanced at the other adventurers more sympathetically.

"I can see that," she said. "You think maybe we should put a team together?"

"No," Jason said. "I was also inclined to keep it to just us. I wasn't lying about the speed thing, and trying to mesh a new group together in a dangerous environment could cause trouble a critical moment."

"Just us then," she said. "So what are we doing?"

"Pull up the quest," Jason said, doing the same himself.

Quest: [Legacy of the Reaper]
You have joined the mission to retrieve the Order of the Reaper's legacy.

Objective: Pass the reaper trials 0/5
Objective: Reach the centre of the City of Fallen Echoes.
Objective: Obtain [Golden Scythe of the Reaper] 0/1.
Objective: Deliver [Golden Scythe of the Reaper] to Emir Bahadir 0/1.

Reward: Racial gift transfiguration.

"This is the City of Fallen Echoes," Jason said, quietly. "The objective is to get to the middle. Knowing that might be a good edge for us against other teams. It also means our team knows where to go. As long as we head for the middle, we'll find them eventually."

"And where is the middle exactly?" Sophie asked. "Do we just head away from the water?"

Jason pulled up his map. It was a separate ability from his party interface, which meant Sophie couldn't use it herself, but it did allow her to see it when Jason did. The corner of the map listed their location.

Zone: City of Fallen Echoes (Gate Tower Three)

The map showed a perfectly circular city, surrounded by water. All but the area around one tower with a marker for Jason's position on it was veiled.

"I can't see places I haven't been on the map," Jason said. "The centre is pretty obvious from the outline though."

He got to his feet and Sophie did the same.

"Let's get down," he said. "The stairs start over there."

"Forget that," Sophie said, walking backwards away from the edge.

"That looks suspiciously like a run-up."

"I won't go too hard," she said. "You should be able to follow if you put some guts in it."

She ran to the edge of the tower and vaulted off without hesitation. Jason watched her sail through the air, plunging to the ground until she activated her leaf on the wind ability, slowing into a gentle descent. She landed in the middle of a wide boulevard overgrown with trees that headed in the direction they would be going. Jason looked down at her and shrugged, taking his own run-up and leaping out after her.

44
SHADE

Jason's cloak fluttered around him as he drifted to the ground.

"Clive said that some people think the powers we get are reflections of who we are," Sophie said.

"So?"

"So, floating out of the sky with an attention-grabbing cloak made out of sparkles seems very much like you."

"I can't help if I'm pretty," Jason said. "I like your new armour, by the way. It's a very 'killing things for money' kind of look. Professional."

Gilbert Bertinelli, who supplied Jason's armour, dealt exclusively in men's apparel, but Jason had asked for his recommendation for someone who worked with trap weaver leather. He suggested someone who developed armour specifically for women. The result was a simple outfit with clean lines, compared to the flowing lines of Jason's combat robes.

In shades of dark grey and black, Sophie's outfit reminded Jason of combat fatigues more than anything else. It had a neat but loose fit for maximum mobility, with hardened panels over critical areas and plenty of loops and pockets for gear. Compared to the body-hugging clothes Sophie normally wore, this armour was all business, masking her lithe body.

"I would have preferred something in white," Sophie said.

Jason acknowledged to himself that she looked exceptionally good in white, but didn't say anything. As much as the indenture contract was in practicality a fiction, he was very conscious of the men who had sought to exert power over her for their own gratification. He didn't want to be one more guy piling it on.

"So I guess we head off," Jason said.

"If those noises we're hearing are anything to go by, we'll be running into plenty of monsters. Especially if they're spawning faster because of the extra magic."

"I reckon you're right," Jason agreed. "If we come up against anything nasty, you grab its attention and I'll set up the damage. Otherwise, we take it as it comes."

"Sounds good," Sophie said. "With all these trees and broken buildings throwing shadows, this place should be a playground for you."

"If you don't mind," a voice said from behind them, "I would like to have a word before you set off."

They both turned around, startled at whoever had approached them undetected. Standing in the middle of the overgrown street was a dark figure, like a person made of the same shadow-stuff as Jason's cloak. He was a living silhouette, a person-shaped hole in the universe.

"Who are you?" Sophie asked. "What are you?"

"Why do you sound British?" Jason asked.

"I don't know what British is," the shadowy figure said.

"That's for the best," Jason said. "Don't tell them you don't have guns or they'll colonise the crap out of you."

"I lack the context to grasp the exact scenario you are positing," the figure said. "I assume you are introducing a confusing tangent to the conversation to gauge my response to an unanticipated reaction to my approach."

"Yeah, that's pretty much it. I like you, British shadow guy. You got a name?"

"I am Shade."

"That's rough," Jason said. "You're a person made of shadows and your name is Shade? That's like my name being Human."

"You are not human," Shade said.

"Yeah, but I was when I was named. I'm Jason and this is Sophie. Are you a local, Shade?"

"In a manner of speaking," Shade said. "I am the invigilator of the Legacy Trials. I will administer each of the five tests you must pass to receive the legacy of the Order of the Reaper."

"If you're running the show, why have you appeared before us?" Sophie asked.

"My nature is multifarious. I am currently appearing before every person who has entered the trial grounds. I am here to introduce you to the trials and instruct you on what you must do to pass them."

"Well that sucks," Jason said. "And here was me thinking we had a head start. Why did we not appear in the same place as our other team members, Shade?"

"There are twelve gate towers. Each person that enters arrives at a random tower."

"Twelve," Sophie said. "We could have been split up entirely, so it could be worse."

"I'm worried about Clive," Jason said. "Humphrey will be fine on his own and Neil is a healer, so he'll have no trouble finding some people to roam around with. Clive is a harder sell, especially with Clive as the salesman."

"There's not much we can do about it here," Sophie said. "All we can do is head for the middle and trust that he can do the same."

Jason gave a reluctant nod.

"If I may interject," Shade said, "part of my task is to instruct you on the trials to come and what will be required of you."

"Go ahead, Shade."

"Thank you," Shade said. "The legacy of the Order of the Reaper is here to be claimed. The one to do so will be the one who proves that they can embody the ideals of the Order. Courage, intellect, resolve, capability and wisdom. Over the course of five trials, you will need to demonstrate these five virtues."

"And these trials are located in the middle of the city?" Jason asked.

"The final three are located in the heart of the city," Shade said. "This City of Fallen Echoes is itself the second trial: the trial of capability. It constitutes the longest of the five trials and not everyone will successfully navigate the dangers therein."

Quest: [The Second Trial]

The second of the Reaper's trials is to reach the heart of the city.

Objective: Reach the centre of the City of Fallen Echoes.

Reward: Random magic item.

"The city is the second trial?" Sophie asked. "What about the first?"

"The first trial I will administer now. It is the simplest in that it cannot be failed. Instead, it is a choice that will be important once you reach the final trials."

"It can't be failed?" Jason asked. "That seems like a gimme but I can't help thinking there's a catch."

"The trial is simply this," Shade said. "Do you wish to enter the second trial with wisdom or courage?"

"What's the difference?" Sophie asked.

"To enter with wisdom means you will receive two items. One will allow you to escape the trials entirely. You will not be allowed to enter again but it can extricate you from an inescapable situation. The other is a recovery item that can save you in a critical moment."

"And courage means entering the second trial without them," Jason said.

"Exactly so," Shade acknowledged.

"It seems like wisdom is objectively the better choice," Sophie said.

"That is why it is the path of wisdom," Shade said.

"Then why would anyone choose courage?" Jason asked.

"Each of the final trials will test the virtues that have yet to be demonstrated," Shade said. "But to reach the trials of intelligence and resolve, one must pass a trial that tests that which they did not demonstrate here, in the first trial. For those who have already proven their courage, the test of wisdom will assess their judgement. Failure means being removed from the trials, but there is no danger in it. For those who have proven their wisdom, they must face a test of courage. The test is simple but dangerous. To pass is to move on and to fail is to die."

"So it's a choice between safety now and danger later or safety later and danger now," Jason said. "What can you tell us about the later trials?"

"Only that you will be informed of the nature of each trial you face, immediately before you face it. Once you have navigated the city, each future trial will be explained, after which you may choose to face the next trial or be safely removed from the trials altogether."

"So you can tell us about the second trial now?" Sophie asked.

"I can, yes," Shade told her. "There is no limit on time beyond the closure of the trials in eighteen days."

"What happens if we're still here after eighteen days?" Jason asked.

"Then you will be trapped here," Shade said. "There are dangers in this place, of which the monsters are not the greatest. There are two larger threats to be aware of."

"We appreciate the warning," Jason said. "What can you tell us about them?"

"I can explain the practical dangers," Shade said. "If you would prefer, I can explain the origins of the trials and the dangers you will face in undertaking them."

"I'll take some context, if you're offering," Jason said.

"This astral space was originally a training ground for the Order of the Reaper," Shade explained. "You travelled here from the ruins of the Order's final and most hidden redoubt. It was once a hidden place to instruct the Order's initiates, turned into a final hiding place as the churches sought to purge the Order."

"The churches purged the Order of the Reaper?" Jason said. "I found an underground fortress that had suffered some kind of attack, centuries ago. I think that belonged to the Order as well."

"The Order did have an underground facility that was wiped out. At first, it was believed that the hidden training centre had escaped the churches' attention after they attacked that location. The Order was betrayed, however, and the hiding place under the lake revealed. The churches came, shattered the magic domes that held back the waters and drowned all within."

"That's horrifying," Jason said.

"Which churches?" Sophie asked. "It can't have been all of them."

"It was not," Shade said. "The Order of the Reaper served a number of important purposes. In a world of kings and queens, leaders are chosen by blood instead of virtue. A fool or mad person can, by virtue of birthright, be given the power to consign countless lives to chaos, suffering and death. In such cases, a knife in the dark can be the deliverance of nations."

"Royal assassins," Jason said. "I'd say you should try democracy but the results where I come from are very mixed."

"Though the Order remained hidden in the shadows," Shade continued, "its function was known and accepted by the nations and organisations of the world. The Adventure Society, the Magic Society, even the churches."

"But not all of them," Sophie said.

"No," Shade said. "There were two churches. One is the church of The Unliving. More than just assassins, the Order were also hunters of the undead. The peace of final rest is the Reaper's most core principle and more necromancers fell to the Order than princes or kings."

"The Adventure Society does that, now," Jason said.

"In the Order's absence, others must take up their tasks. The church of The Unliving did not act against the Order alone. There was another church that, like the Order, was inimical to the church of The Unliving. Nonetheless, they formed an unholy compact to remove what this church called the unclean methods of the Order."

"Oh, you've got to be kidding me," Jason said. "The church of Purity?"

"It is as you say," Shade confirmed.

"How is that church even vaguely pure?" Jason complained loudly. "They team up with the worst people they can find at the drop of a hat."

"I do not know of what you speak," Shade said.

"They're at it again," Jason said. "The church of Purity has teamed up with some interdimensional turd nugget to strip-mine astral spaces."

"That can wait until we're back outside," Sophie said. "Right now, we need to focus on these trials. I assume you were working your story towards the danger you mentioned."

"Yes," Shade said. "When the churches discovered the training facilities beneath the lake, the last grandmaster of the Order sent all the initiates here, into the city. They then sealed the entrance, that the churches could not follow. The keys to the entrance were taken and scattered across the world. The goal was that someday, someone could prove themselves worthy of the Order's ideals and reclaim that which was left behind. That day should now be coming soon, but if all you who have entered fail, there will be another chance."

"Oh?"

"After eighteen days, the trials will close. The keys can be used to open them again in a year, that others may try where you failed."

"What about all those initiates?" Sophie asked. "What happened to them?"

"The churches were unwilling to leave behind the threat posed by the initiates, but could not reach them in the astral space. In the early days of the Order, one of the grandmasters found this astral space. It was unstable, a proto-astral space that was as likely to dissolve into the astral as it was to become a true realm."

"Obviously it did," Sophie said.

"The Order of the Reaper has long used such places," Shade said. "There was ancient knowledge of how to anchor such realms, provided by the Reaper itself."

"So, the Order really is connected to the great astral being," Jason said.

"It was," Shade said. "The grandmaster who built this place was akin to you, Jason Asano. Like you, he was an outworlder with the dark essence. Many of the functions of this place are based on his abilities. I was his summoned familiar once."

"You were a familiar?" Jason asked.

"I was. Now, I am bound to this place until the trials are completed and the legacy claimed."

"He was from my world?" Jason asked.

"He was not," Shade said. "You were originally a human, which do not exist in the world he originated in."

"You didn't tell us what happened to the initiates," Sophie said.

"As I said, the churches were unwilling to leave the initiates be, but the means by which this astral space was anchored to the world left the those hunting them locked out. So the churches made a second bargain, this time with entities of the deep astral. Known as the vorger, they have the power to violate dimensional boundaries."

"Like those of an astral space," Jason said.

"Yes," Shade said. "They cannot enter a truly physical realm, but astral spaces are partly of the astral and partly of the physical. It is unknown how they lured such creatures as they are animalistic entities, acting only on primal urges. Lure them the churches did, however, and the vorger remain here to this day."

"What are these vorger exactly?" Sophie asked.

"They are creatures intangible in nature, for they are not physical beings. They take many shapes but their nature is the same. Their touch warps flesh, twisting it into hideous new shapes."

"That's what happened to the initiates?" Jason asked. "They were killed by the vorger?"

"Worse," Shade said. "The vorger do not kill. Their victims do not enjoy the sweet release of death. In what is perhaps the greatest insult to the Reaper, the initiates were warped into unageing abominations of flesh. They never die, their souls trapped inside twisted shells of rage and pain, cursed to eternal madness. They roam this place still, striking out against anything they encounter."

"Those are the dangers you mentioned," Jason said. "The vorger and these flesh abominations."

"Yes."

"What can you tell us about how to fight them?" Sophie asked.

"The vorger have no physical substance," Shade said. "Magical weapons will have some limited effect on them but unless you find them in isolation, it will be insufficient to handle their numbers. They tend to appear in swarms and without specialised tools or abilities; they are difficult to deal with. They will warp your bodies until the city gains another flesh abomination. As you both possess an affinity for astral energy, you will be far more resistant than most, however."

"Your abilities should work well," Jason said to Sophie. "My sword should be effective enough as well. What about the flesh abominations, Shade?"

"If you can kill them and release their souls from torment, then that would be a mercy. My advice, however, is to avoid or escape them. Their power is at the bronze-rank level and they are no easy match. Their bodies will adapt to your attacks and defences, making them more effective and you less so, with every passing moment. If you must fight them, then I would recommend fighting one after another instead of working together. When they adapt to one form of attack, they may create a weakness to another which you can exploit."

"Thank you," Jason said. "We'll remember your words."

"Then your next step is the first trial," Shade said. "Your choices remain: courage or wisdom."

"What do you think?" Sophie asked Jason.

"I'm thinking wisdom," Jason said. "I feel like courage is probably the best choice for getting to the end, but as much as I would love a cloud palace, I'll take alive and no cloud palace over dead and no cloud palace."

"I would have thought you would have gone for courage," Sophie said. "All the stories I've heard about you paint you as pretty reckless."

"I used to be," Jason said. "Probably still am, to be honest, but Farrah's death brought some things home for me. Death is easy enough to find as an adventurer. I don't need to go looking for it."

"Alright," Sophie said with a nod, then turned to Shade. "Two for wisdom."

"Very well," Shade said and raised his shadowy hands. Resting in each was a small vial and a medallion. They took them, feeling the cold of Shade's shadowy hand as they picked up the objects.

Jason looked at the medallion first. It was made of the same glossy black stone as the archway through which they had entered the astral space and was embossed with a scythe symbol. It was small and on a cord that could be easily slipped over the neck.

Item: [Medallion of Escape] (silver rank, uncommon)
***A path of escape for those with the wisdom to know when to let go* (consumable, teleport).**

Effect: Project your aura into the medallion to be immediately evacuated from the astral space. Only functions within the City of Fallen Echoes.

"Project your aura into the medallion," Jason read. "Doesn't that mean anyone without aura control can't use it?"

"Part of wisdom is knowing which challenges not to accept," Shade said.

"Good thing you picked up an aura power," Jason told Sophie. They both slipped their medallions over their necks and tucked them under their armour. They then looked at the second item, the vial.

Item: [Lesser Miracle Potion] (iron rank, legendary)
***Salvation in a bottle* (consumable, potion).**

Effect: Fully restore health, mana and stamina. This potion is only effective on normal and iron-rank individuals. The magic of this potion lingers in the body longer than normal potions, meaning additional recovery health and recovery items will not be effective for a longer period.

"Strewth," Jason said. "Now, that's a potion."

"I didn't realise potions like this were even possible," Sophie said.

"Me either," Jason said, carefully placing it into his potion belt. Like him, Sophie had an enchanted potion belt that would protect the vials from breakage unless a concerted and directed effort was made to do so.

"One last thing," Jason said to Shade. "I don't suppose you can tell us where our teammates are?"

"I can," Shade said, "but I won't."

"That's what I figured. We'll see you in the middle of the city?"

"You will," Shade said. "Good luck."

With that, Shade vanished in a swirl of darkness.

45
SERIOUSLY HARDCORE

To Jason's eyes, the monster they had encountered seemed most like a leopard, except for the legs. They were still covered in spotted fur, like the rest of the creature, but there were eight of them, multi-jointed and emerging from the monster's side like the legs of a spider. The legs were not as good for running but it was an excellent and rapid climber. That didn't much matter when Sophie's wind blade cut half of those legs off and it tumbled to the ground where she finished it with a brutal stomp to the head.

You have defeated [Spotted Tree Cat].

"Spotted tree cat," Jason said. "It lacks imagination but at least it's what it says on the tin. I was worried it would be called a spidard or something. Some of these monster names are just daft. Some of them have got people killed, I'm certain of it."

"How does a monster name get someone killed?" Sophie asked.

"Well, take sloth demons and demon sloths. Demon sloths are iron rank, strong and relatively tough, but slow. Not that hard to take down, as long as you're careful. A sloth demon is a gold-rank monster with a soporific power that cripples your speed, making you easy meat."

"I see your point," Sophie said. "You wouldn't want to get them confused."

"No, you would not. Did Humphrey get you reading the Magic Society monster records? He said he was going to."

"He did," Sophie said. "It's actually pretty interesting, learning about all the crazy stuff that's out there."

"It might seem odd to say this," Jason said, "but you don't want to be too efficient with your kills. You'll do better if you use as many of your abilities as you can."

"It's not like I won't get another chance," Sophie said. "I don't think it's even been an hour. Besides, these easy fights won't do me much good. I need something tougher, or that comes in numbers."

"That's true enough," Jason acknowledged.

He wandered over and touched the creature.

Would you like to loot [Spotted Tree Cat]?

"Hold on for a second," Sophie said.

She pulled off her boot and set it on a low, broken wall before backing off. Jason mentally triggered the looting and the creature went up in rainbow smoke, along with the muck on Sophie's boot. There was some minor spattering on her pants and trouser legs that dissolved as well, causing Sophie to wince at the smell as Jason moved aside.

"Do you ever get used to that?" she asked.

"A little but not really," Jason said. "On the bright side, after that you can handle pretty much anything. I fought a monster called a belch bug that has this stink that's meant to make you vomit. Barely a stomach twitch."

They were making their way down a wide boulevard that went in exactly the direction they wanted. There were eighteen days in which to make the most of the excellent training environment but they decided to start by making their way to the middle of the city. It gave them the best chance of finding their errant party members and they could just roam around fighting monsters from there.

The boulevard was uneven ground, the once neatly fitted flagstones cracked, pushed up by root growth or displaced entirely by trees. It was still the most open path, though, and offered an easy passage towards the centre of the city. On either side, what had once been impressive buildings rose up, half-collapsed and covered in creepers and other growth.

"We should have a rummage through some of these buildings," Jason said.

"What happened to going straight to the centre of the city?" Sophie asked.

"We at least have to have a bit of a look around," Jason said. "Let's just pick the next awesome-looking building and take a gander. Maybe we'll find an essence or something."

"You think?"

"Maybe," Jason said. "In fairness, we could just as easily find one sitting in the middle of the boulevard. With the increased manifestations and this place having gone untouched for centuries, there could be a veritable hoard just waiting for us to find it."

"Maybe we could check out one building," she said. "What about that one?"

Most of the buildings they passed by were two or three storeys tall. The one Sophie pointed out was six, and more intact than most.

"It looks a bit fortressy," Jason said. "Some kind of military barracks?"

The front entrance must have once been a pair of towering metal doors, but centuries of humid air had left little but rusted scraps behind. The looming doorway was large enough to wheel a siege engine through, as evidenced by the remains of just such a siege engine. It was in some kind of a marshalling courtyard beyond the huge doors, abandoned to a state of disrepair. Now it was a pile of wooden beams, rusty metal bars and leather straps.

"That's awesome," Jason said, looking at it. "Also, suspicious."

"Suspicious?"

"It may look like a dilapidated pile of junk," he said, "but it's not really dilapidated enough. That wood should have been long rotted away, and that metal might be rusty but compare it to what's left of the doors. I've been on farms and seen what fifty years of abandonment does to a place. This has been here what? Ten times that, at least? In this wet climate, there shouldn't be any of that thing left."

"What are you thinking?" Sophie asked.

"I'm thinking you move closer, carefully. See if you can sense an aura off of it."

Sophie did just that, approaching the large doorway. Before she could sense anything from the siege engine, the fallen pile of metal and wood started moving. What had been little more than a pile of rotted wood, rusty metal and leather scraps re-assembled itself into a vaguely humanoid form. It towered almost four meters high, enough that as it stood upright the top became obscured; it was taller even than the huge doorway.

The construct creature was asymmetrical and seemed uncoordinated, with two arms on one side and one on the other. Of the two arms that shared the same side, one was stubby and ended in a crude, rusty claw. The other was longer but less agile, shaped like a long box terminating in a rusty ball. The single arm on the other side was actually a platform for a ballista. As it stood up, they both sensed its bronze rank aura.

"Is this one of the Builder cult creations?" Sophie asked as the construct creature assembled itself.

"Unlikely," Jason said. "It looks like it fits right in here. Probably a monster or something left behind from long ago."

"Do we run?" Sophie asked.

"Fight," Jason said, drawing his sword. "Something tells me that some practice fighting construct monsters will pay off, down the line."

Knowing his core abilities would be useless against the construct creature, Jason silently thanked Gary for making his sword.

"I've never fought a bronze-rank monster before," Sophie said.

"That's why it will help us get stronger," Jason said. "If you think you can't handle it, just run. It doesn't look like much of a chaser."

The creature was ducking slowly under the doorway with jerky movements, the monster's height too much even for the oversized gap. Jason took advantage of its awkwardness to dash forward. It lashed out crudely with its ball arm, but Jason easily dodged, raking his sword against one leg, then the other as he ducked under and passed the creature. His sword did nothing more than scratch the wood but that was all he needed.

Special attack [Punish] has inflicted [Sin] on [Siege Golem].
[Siege Golem] is immune to curses.
[Sin] does not take effect.

Affliction immunity has triggered an effect on weapon [Dread Salvation].
Weapon [Dread Salvation] has gained an instance of [Stone Cutter].

The golem was caught halfway under the door. It was almost through only to start turning back after Jason. As it did, Sophie moved in to the attack, lashing out with rapid strikes.

Special ability [Immortal Fist] has dealt resonating-force damage to [Siege Golem].
[Siege Golem] has an extremely rigid body and suffers additional damage from resonating force.

The fight started out strongly in Jason and Sophie's favour, catching the golem in a bad position. Neither Jason nor Sophie had any big attack powers to capitalise, however, and their iron-rank attacks had limited effect of the bronze-rank enemy. Sophie started off stronger with her resonating-force damage; Jason's attacks did next to nothing as his sword accumulated power. With each attack it dealt increasing amounts of the same resonating-force energy but he would need some time to have a real impact.

The golem focused on Sophie as the greater threat, working its way towards the outside. Just as it was about to get free of the door, she nimbly dodged past it to join Jason on the inside. Jason immediately made his way back out. The mindless construct creature could do no more than react, the same lack of internal spirit that made it immune to Jason's curses making it too stupid to understand it was being played back and forth.

Finally it worked its way loose of the door, courtesy of Jason's sword. It was accumulating enough power to affect even the hardy, bronze-rank construct body and when Jason carved of a protrusion from its body, it staggered free of the doorway and back into the courtyard.

Jason had reached the point where he could do some real damage, but free of the door, the golem had its own tricks to use. The stubby claw yanked back the ballista arm, and from within the arm a ballista bolt jerked out, ready to be fired. The golem launched it at Jason but the crude, massive weapon was easy to dodge. He moved aside, the creature's aim obvious, and the bolt missed him, the huge metal head digging into the stone floor.

Just as Jason was about to renew his attack, the shaft of the ballista bolt exploded, firing out finger-length shards of piercing wood, sharp as needles and hard as iron. Sophie, on the other side of the golem, was far enough away that she could duck out of the doorway before the shards reached her. Jason, on the other hand, took the full brunt. The attacks carried the inherent power of bronze-rank attacks, shredding his cloak and piercing his armour. He shielded his face with his arms as he turned his body to present a smaller profile and protect certain delicate areas. His arms, legs and sides were riddled with the wooden shards, which were left sticking out of him like echidna spines. He snatched a potion from his belt and chugged it, the healing power doing little more than pushing out all the spines.

The golem, in the meantime, had brought its ungainly box-arm with the rusty ball-hand up in the air. It brought it down in Jason's direction as he was still staggered and inattentive. The ball came loose on the end of a cable, extending out as it swung down hard. Jason realised the danger too late, but Sophie appeared in front of him using her mirage step power. Her feet braced, she threw a punch out at the descending ball.

Ability: [Immortal Fist] (Mystic)
Special ability.
Cost: None.
Cooldown: None.

Current rank: Iron 2 (14%).

Effect (iron): Unarmed attacks deal additional resonating-force damage, which is highly effective against physical defences. Suffer no damage from making unarmed strikes against objects and negate all damage from actively intercepted attacks. Not all damage from very powerful or higher-ranked attacks will be negated.

The huge metal sphere was deflected but the power of it was too much for Sophie to negate. She was hammered into the stone, bouncing off herself as her arm was brutally mangled. Jason, protected and recovered, looked down at her. Under the hood of his cloak, his face contorted with malevolence as he saw what was left of her arm. He turned that gaze onto the golem, the sword in his hand practically humming with power, even as blood from Jason's punctured arm ran down it.

He ran at the golem; he had fought it enough to know that its ungainly size and sluggish speed were the weaknesses he needed to be victorious. His sword flashed. His body danced, slicing into the creature again and again. With each strike the damage grew greater while the golem flailed at the cloaked figure flittering around its feet. Soon, even bronze-rank damage resistance was not enough. Jason had burned most of his mana on special attacks it was immune to, triggering the sword until every strike was blasting away chunks of wood and shearing apart strips of metal. He went for the joints, the legs first, then the arms as it toppled. Finally Jason went to work on every part of it still large enough to hit.

You have defeated [Siege Golem].

Jason dropped his sword on the destroyed golem, before rushing over to Sophie. She was struggling, one-armed, to get to her knees. He carefully helped her rise and she grimaced silently through the pain. Her right arm dangled limply, the hand coming out of her sleeve. Jason pulled the lesser miracle potion from his belt but she waved him off.

"I'd be a pancake if it wasn't for you," he said, still pushing it on her.

"That's for the middle of a fight," she snarled through the pain and clenched teeth. "Don't be an idiot and waste it now. I can use this to practice my recovery power."

Jason watched as she fought through the pain to take a kneeling meditation pose as best she could.

Ability: [Equilibrium] (Balance)
Special ability.
Cost: None.
Cooldown: None.

Current rank: Iron 1 (76%)

Effect (iron): Meditate to slowly accrue instances of [Integrity], up to an instance threshold based on the [Recovery] attribute. Instances quickly drop off when meditation ends.

[Integrity] (heal-over-time, mana-over-time, stamina-over-time, holy): Periodically recover a small amount of health, stamina and mana. Additional instances have a cumulative effect.

"At least take some kind of potion," Jason said.

"This is kind of hard, so how about you shut your damn mouth for once."

"Lady," Jason said, putting back the lesser miracle potion and pulling out a regular healing potion for himself. "You are seriously hardcore."

"What did I just say?"

46
MIXED MEDICATION

Sophie's arm injury was more serious than any of Jason's wounds. Her arm was severely damaged, and required an extended period to heal with her self-recovery power. Jason had been needled quite badly but it only took a few potions to eliminate the minor, if numerous, wounds. His blood harvest power normally allowed him to heal up after fights using the remnant life force of fallen enemies, but it only worked on enemies with blood. The siege golem was largely impervious to Jason's abilities, even after being destroyed.

The puncture points in his armour were slowly recovering as well, due to his armour's self-repair properties. Gary's advice to find armour with that particular quality had saved Jason a good amount of money on repairs. Now that he was isolated from a place to get repairs, it was all the more valuable.

Sophie's healing power was meditation-based and concentrating proved difficult with the state of her arm. She took regular breaks, panting and sweating in spite of doing no more than sitting in place. Jason tried to distract her from the pain each time she took a break.

"I'm going to loot the monster, now you're not in the middle of meditating," he told her during the first break. "I didn't want to interrupt you before."

He wandered over to the fallen golem, which didn't look much worse than when it had been mimicking a broken siege weapon. He placed a hand on a chunk of shattered wood.

Would you like to loot [Siege Golem]?

"Head's up," he warned Sophie as he walked away.

The golem dissolved into rainbow smoke.

[Meteor Hammer] has been added to your inventory.
[Monster Core (Bronze Rank)] has been added to your inventory.
10 [Bronze Spirit Coins] have been added to your inventory.
100 [Iron Spirit Coins] have been added to your inventory.

[Siege Grips] have been awarded to party member [Sophie Wexler].
10 [Bronze Spirit Coins] have been awarded to party member [Sophie Wexler].
100 [Iron Spirit Coins] have been awarded to party member [Sophie Wexler].

Sophie ducked out of the way as two bags of coins dropped from where they had appeared over her head with a flash of rainbow light. There was also a pair of gloves, which she picked up to examine.

Item: [Siege Grips] (bronze rank, rare)
A pair of combat gloves containing the power of a siege weapon **(clothing, gloves).**

Effect: Add explosive power to a physical attack, inflicting additional resonating-force damage and creating a powerful knock-back effect. 20 second cooldown.

Effect: Conjure a ram that flies through the air to make an extremely heavy resonating force attack. 5 minute cooldown.

You do not meet the requirements to use this item.

"I got bronze-rank gloves," she said. "What about you?"

"A ball and chain," Jason said, showing her the weapon in his hands. It was, as he said, a metal sphere at the end of a chain. It looked like a smaller version of the ball-hand of the siege golem, even to the metal orb pitted with rust.

Item: [Meteor Hammer] (bronze rank, uncommon)
A magical chain weapon taken from an animate siege weapon **(weapon, chain).**

Effect: Inflicts additional resonating-force damage based on how long the meteor hammer was swinging prior to the attack.

Effect: Chain length can be extended or retracted as it swings.

You do not meet the requirements to use this item.

"I don't think this really suits me," Jason said. "It's bronze-rank anyway."

"So are these but I could see myself using them later."

Jason stashed the items and Sophie's coins in his inventory. He glanced down at her arm, still hanging limp, her hand purple and distended. She was careful to jostle it as little as possible when she moved.

"How's that coming along?" he asked.

"Not much progress on the arm," she said unhappily. "I'm feeling better otherwise, though. That big ball thing really hit hard."

"Thank you for that, by the way," Jason said. "I don't think I would have taken the hit nearly as well."

"This is going to take longer to heal than I thought," she said. "Maybe I should take a potion. Not one of the good ones, just a regular healing potion."

"No, you were right in the first place," Jason said. "Healing it up will be good training for your ability and we have time to burn. You hole up in the courtyard here while I check out the rest of the building. I'll look for a good spot to set up camp. Use voice chat if anything happens and I'll come running."

"Alright," Sophie said. She went back to meditating as Jason went farther into the building.

Jory wasn't happy. He had only agreed to participate as part of a joint activity between the craft associations, but then had been immediately separated from his assigned team when the gate towers had randomly dispersed them. As people formed makeshift groups with the people they found themselves with on the tower, Jory didn't exactly have his pick of teams. His alchemy-related essence abilities made for a certain amount of healing but the people assembling groups were competing to attract the more conventional healers.

Jory was geared out in a heavy coat, covered in pockets. It was enchanted to protect both him and the contents of the pockets from harm. Fortunately for Jory, it was also enchanted to keep him cool, despite the jacket being as thick as the humidity. Along with the jacket, Jory had two belts around his waist and two bandoliers across his chest. They were full of vials containing potions and reagents Jory could use to make potions on the fly. Like his coat, the belts and bandoliers were enchanted to protect their contents. Slung over his shoulder was a dimensional bag satchel.

The group Jory ended up with clearly viewed him as a better than nothing option, but they were the most seemingly capable group left. The best people had already formed teams and headed off. The group Jory joined at least had three members from the same team, a trio of leonids who had the luck of arriving on the same tower. They then added Jory and a solid guardian-type named Keane who could conjure heavy armour and a huge shield.

If they weren't so clearly disgruntled at not getting a better healer, Jory would have been fairly happy. As it was, he was regretting the entire enterprise until they encountered the strange personage of Shade. Jory wanted to take him up on his offer to explain the place they found themselves, but the rest of his group were eager to press on. The three leonids all chose courage, while Jory and Keane chose wisdom.

The lesser miracle potion Shade gave him was an object of fascination for Jory, who had an essence ability that allowed him to determine its effects. His intention was to take it back to his workshop and see what he could learn from it. He wouldn't be able to reproduce it from a sample, but he had no doubt that anything he could glean from it would be invaluable.

The leader of the leonids' team was named Laramie. He and his fellows were in no rush to reach the centre of the city, more interested in the search for treasures. Every building they spotted that looked mostly intact was a prime target.

Jory was initially annoyed but was forced to acknowledge their choice was a good one as they dug out more than a few worthwhile finds. The advantage of magical items was that they stood out, having withstood the passage of time better than ordinary objects.

The leonids gave themselves first pick, but otherwise distributed the loot evenly. They found a magical box of unknown purpose, a magical staff that Jory claimed, some leather armguards and no fewer than four awakening stones. They were mostly commons, but the plant, snake and earth awakening stones were all desirable enough to sell well. The one rare stone, an awakening stone of ruin, would sell the best though. It inevitably ended up in Laramie's possession.

Jory's essence ability that identified items revealed the properties of each, aside from the magical box that eluded his ability's power. All it revealed was the name of the item which was, appropriately enough, mystery box. Jory could have used his ability to undersell the value of the rare awakening stone but his ethical nature never led him to even consider it. He was satisfied enough with the loot sharing that he was happy to continue on.

Trouble came when they searched what turned out to be a sprawling, multistorey alchemy workshop. Even with the expansive renovations on his own workshop and the dilapidated nature of the building, Jory couldn't help but be envious. He even managed to dig out a few magical alchemy tools that found their way into his dimensional bag. The others didn't begrudge him as they would be hard to sell and gave them an excuse to cut him out of the next round of loot. They told him that anything alchemy related was all his. This lasted until Jory's honest nature caused him to reveal a huge discovery.

Inside a magical cabinet sealed to protect the contents from the elements, Jory found a whole catalogue of alchemical formulas. Many were out of date compared to superior modern equivalents, or used ingredients too expensive or rare for what the potions did. There were a few gems amongst them, however, and one huge prize. The requirements and ingredients were outrageous in both rarity and price, but there was a complete formula for the lesser miracle potion Shade had given him. When he revealed this fact, Laramie immediately demanded he hand it over.

"You said everything alchemy-related was mine," Jory told them.

"That was before you found something so valuable," Laramie said. "Hand it over."

"You three have already been taking the most valuable goods for yourselves," the heavily armoured shield-bearer said. "We agreed he could have the alchemy stuff, so you should stick to the deal you made."

He had been quietly stewing over what he saw as unfair loot distribution and used their move on Jory as a chance to push the issue. They were still in the alchemy building, in a large room once used for the preparation of alchemical components, with a series of long benches dividing the room.

"The deal has changed," Laramie said.

Jory watched as the two men squared off.

"Let's just keep talking," Jory said. "There are monsters enough out there, without us fighting one another."

"There's no need to fight," Keane said, the big man's eyes not leaving Laramie. "They just have to give you what they promised."

"I promise I'll put a hole right through that helmet if you don't back off," Laramie said. The leonids were all powerful damage dealers.

The three squared off against one, with Jory in the background, his calls for de-escalation going unheeded. The tension ramped until one of the three finally twitched, lashing out with a conjured whip of fire. The other two were only a beat behind, their coordination proving too much of an onslaught for Keane.

His defensive powers were strong but it was three against one, with the trio's practised teamwork overwhelming the protector. He held out briefly under a terrifying barrage as Jory yelled at them to stop, but soon he fell to the ground. Most adventurers would have died but Keane was only debilitated, his wounded flesh already starting to heal itself. Laramie turned his attention back to Jory.

"I'll hand it over," Jory said. "Just take it and go while I look after him."

"You had your chance," Laramie said. "Now you're going to be unfortunate victims of the many dangers, here."

"You don't need to—"

Jory's fruitless words were cut off when a spear of solid stone was launched at him. To his surprise, a bubble-shield snapped up around him, disappearing again as it absorbed the spear's attack.

"There's no reasoning with some people," Neil Davone said, stepping into the room. A golem made of dull glass stepped in ahead of him, Neil's chrysalis golem summon put itself between the trio and Neil, who grabbed Jory and yanked him behind a bench. "Time to go, Jory."

"Davone? I'm not leaving that guy to them," Jory said, pointing at Keane, whose sprawled feet they could just see past the edge of the bench.

"Don't fight it, Jory," Laramie called out. "Your friend isn't going to save you."

"The hell I'm not," Neil told Jory with quiet insistence. "I can't do anything about the guy on the ground, though, unless you have some awesome power that will let you fight all those guys by yourself."

Jory grimaced. "If that's what it takes. The after-effects are bad, though, so you'll have to take care of me."

"Wait, you seriously have something like that?"

"Yes," Jory said soberly. "I don't like to use it, though."

"I think now might be the time you've been saving it for," Neil said.

Jory held his hands out and vials floated out of their loops on his belt, floating in the air. One by one the vials opened, spilling their contents into the air. Instead of dropping to the ground, they flowed together into a sphere of liquid that grew darker as each new ingredient was added. As they did, Jory pulled off his coat and unbuckled his belts and bandoliers, even as more vials flew out to disgorge their contents into the air.

Attacks were now lancing into the glass golem, chunks shattering off it as they did. With every piece of damage, runes were engraved onto its surface. It didn't fight back, remaining steadfastly planted between its attackers and Neil.

"I thought it was a really bad idea to mix potions like that," Neil said, watching all the liquids and powers from the vials splash together in front of them.

"It is," Jory said.

"So why are you doing it?"

"To show those idiots what happens when you push an alchemist into using a very bad idea."

The liquid streamed into Jory's waiting mouth. Immediately, from the head down, Jory's body started grossly distending. His whole body grew, his skin turning a patchy mishmash of sickly yellow, purple, blue and green. His hair fell out. His head bulged like the rest of his body, too large to hide behind the bench. He was unrecognisable as Jory, now just a monster of muscle.

A bolt of flame struck him, releasing a stench of acrid chemicals and burning flesh, which Jory didn't seem to notice. A stone spear pierced his torso, which he dismissively yanked out, throwing it back with the force of a ballista. Then he picked up the bench in front of him, despite it being affixed to the floor. Accompanied by the sound of shattering tiles, he ripped it right off the floor and hurled it at the leonids.

Neil watched the process with horrified fascination. The three adventurers scrambled out the door on the other side of the room. Monster Jory moved after them in a lumbering pursuit but not at a pace likely to catch them.

Jason led Sophie through the building. Day had turned to night as Sophie worked to heal herself, while Jason wondered how the sun worked in the astral space. Her arm wasn't fully recovered but she had control over it again and her hand now looked like a hand instead of a potato someone had taken to with a hammer. She couldn't see in the dark like Jason, so she had a glow-stone floating over her head.

"Did you find anything, searching the building?" she asked.

"I did," Jason said. "I found an armoury with a couple of magic weapons, although they were fairly mediocre. More importantly, I found an awakening stone."

"You did?"

"It's an uncommon one," he said. "Awakening stone of preparation. I know the others said to just collect what you can so you can choose which ones to use after, but maybe you could use just one."

"You think I should?"

"Probably not, but I would. I can do the ritual in the morning if you like. Give it some thought overnight."

They reached where Jason had set up the aura tent, which would mask their presence from most monsters. He had also set up some alarm rituals, just in case. It was on the top floor of the building, close to the steps leading up to the roof.

"I only set up the one tent," he said, "but I can put the other one up if you want."

"It's fine," Sophie said. "Just know that if you get handsy, you aren't getting those hands back."

47
GIVING PEOPLE CHOICES

Sophie awoke to enticing breakfast smells. She was aching and tired; her damaged arm had given her a restless night. Only in the last few hours did she snatch some precious, uninterrupted slumber. She crawled delicately out of the tent and followed the smells up a stone stairwell and onto a flat roof. Jason had set out a folding camp table and pair of chairs, one of which he was sitting in.

"Morning," he greeted her. "Join me?"

He gestured at the other chair with a fork, on the end of which was skewered a piece of sausage. The rest of the sausage was on a plate in front of him, along with poached eggs and hot, buttered toast. As she sat down, he pulled a second plate of food from his inventory, as fresh and hot as the moment he had put it there. A pitcher of juice was already out, Jason filling an empty glass to match his own.

"This is surreal," Sophie said. "I can more or less accept the whole adventuring life. Magic powers, alternate dimensions, astral spaces. Monsters, cultists, even an ancient order of assassins. Yet somehow, seeing you sitting in the middle of it all, comfortably eating breakfast is just too much."

"Believe it or not, you aren't the first woman to tell me I was too much."

"Oh, I believe it," she said and took a sip of juice. "That's really good."

"It's a blend of delta fruits. I bought a bunch of it from Arash."

"The guy who sells juice from a cart and keeps calling you a heretic?"

"That's the one."

"So when you making preparations to enter this unexplored astral space full of unknown dangers, you went with picnic furniture, plates of hot breakfast and pitchers of fruit juice."

"Life isn't for surviving, Wexler. Life is for living."

Jason had set up the table to overlook the street below. The building was quite high, as were many of the other nearby buildings. It turned the overgrown boulevard they had been walking down into something of a jungle canyon. Jason looked it over with a smile as he sipped at his juice.

"You really like this, don't you?" Sophie asked him.

"I do," he said. "I get what you mean about everything being crazy but my advice is to surrender to it. I know you've spent a lot of time wondering why I helped you so much when I could have gotten you out of the city and been done with it. It wasn't long ago that I was the one sitting at a table with a more experienced adventurer, no idea what lay ahead and wondering what to do. He helped me realise that I had a chance to start things fresh. To become the person I wanted to be."

He smiled in reminiscence.

"Give yourself over to the experience, Wexler. This is your chance to take control. The river may be raging but you'll be amazed how fast you go working with the flow, instead of against it."

"That seems strange, coming from you," she said. "I've never met a person who went more against the flow in my life."

"It's about picking your moments," Jason said. "I came into this world with the naivety of someone who lived his life in safety. I've had a lot of illusions shattered, about the world and about myself. But sometimes when the world tries to bend you, you have to stand straight until one of you breaks."

"You think the world will break before you do?"

"Probably not. But there's no chance if I don't try. I decided early on that with my second chance, the one regret I would never have again was not trying at all. So I do the things that feel right. When I heard about your situation, I felt for you and Belinda. I know what it's like to be in an untenable situation. I found friends to guide me out. I know Jory wanted to help you, so I gave the help I had too. Now I'm giving you the advice I received. Take this chance to be who you want to be."

"And if I don't know who that is?"

"You do, on some level. Just do what feels right until you figure it out. It's what I've been doing and I don't regret any of it, mistakes and all."

He gestured at the astral space around them with his fork.

"In my old life, I never had the chance to visit places like this. Yes, this world has brought its share of challenges, but facing those challenges has been more fulfilling than anything in my old life. At some point, I'll be going back to my world but I'm not going to put this world behind me when I do. There's a means to travel between worlds and I'm going to find it."

"How?"

"I've been talking with Clive, since he's the expert. These Builder cultists seem to have more advanced astral magic than this world does. Clive thinks they have some means of crossing dimensional boundaries that doesn't require a diamond ranker, or they wouldn't have so many agents here to be active all over the world. If I can get a hold of their magic, it may well put me on the right path, if not deliver what I need on a platter."

"A way home."

"No," Jason said. "A way here. I've been told that I will be going home, sooner or later. I can't help but feel that I need to go back and deal with the things I left behind. Once I have, though, I'm coming back to this world, even if that trip is one way. My old world is my past, and while I'm compelled to settle that past, this world is my future."

"And if you can't find a way back?"

"The thing I realised when I truly came to accept that magic is real is that the impossible is just a limitation I put on my own thinking. If you have the time and the resolve, you can do just about anything. But you already know that."

"I do?"

"Of course you do. You were in an awful position. Caught between two crime lords and a powerful aristocrat, with none of the connections and power I've been enjoying since coming to this world. All you had was a loyal friend. Most people would have capitulated. Found the least awful path and accepted their fate. Not you and not Belinda. You came up with a plan and you threw yourselves into it."

"It probably wouldn't have worked, even without your interference."

"But it could have and you went for it. You saw that glimpse of light that most other people would have dismissed as unreachable and you reached for it. I really admire that."

He held his glass up in a casual salute.

"Thank you," she said uncertainly, shifting in her chair. "I don't… not a lot of people look at me for who I am. My whole life, men have looked at me like an animal they need to break in."

Jason nodded.

"I have this philosophy in life," he said. "My brother always had this knack for fitting in. For becoming what he needed to be for other peole, but I can't do that. Every time I tried I ended up losing it and doing something crazy and self-destructive. So, I decided early on that I was going to be who I am and people could take it or leave it. Like me or hate me, I'll take passion over ambivalence. It lets me know who to avoid and who to be friends with. It makes for a better life."

"But a lot of times you must have to deal with people who don't like you."

"Of course," Jason said. "I'm from a whole other world, so people were always going to find me strange. I just play that up sometimes to disorient them a bit. If you need to tip someone over, it helps to unbalance them first."

"I don't know I entirely believe that," she said.

"Oh?"

"I've been watching you and I'm willing to bet you're strange, even where you come from. If it was all an act, you wouldn't be the same around your friends as your enemies."

"It's not an act," Jason said. "I told you that I'm just being who I am and people can take it or leave it. I just crank it up or dial it back a bit for any given situation."

"And that works?"

"When you take a very specific approach to things, the way I do, you have to accept that some people will respond to it and others will reject it wholesale. It's a numbers game and you have to accept that a certain number of people are going to tell you to sod off. Some people like what I'm selling, others can't stand it. I work with the ones that do and don't bother with the ones that don't."

"It sounds like you're just making excuses for doing whatever you like," Sophie said.

"Oh, I'm absolutely doing that," Jason said. "I told you it's a life philosophy. I've just found out how to make it work."

"By manipulating people."

"You say that like we don't all do it every day. We all put up fronts, adjust who we are, how much we show of ourselves to the different people around us. I just do it more consciously than most. Take Neil, for example. When I went to recruit him, I could have taken a different approach. Presented something more universally appealing to get him on board. Instead, I showed him who I was, cranked up a bit to make the point. I figured he was more likely to turn us down than join, but I didn't want the best person we could find for our team. I wanted the best fit. So I presented a certain version of myself, not to get him on board but to help him decide if the place he wanted to be was with us."

"You gave me that choice too, didn't you? Join your merry band of misfits or vanish into some distant land to start over."

"I like giving people choices."

"That's because you like control. If you're the one giving the choices, you get to decide what the choices are. Otherwise, people might go finding their own options that don't fit your narrative."

Jason chuckled, not denying it.

"How's the arm?" he asked.

"Not to fighting strength but a couple more hours using my meditation power should do it."

"So now you've experienced the power of a bronze-rank monster," Jason said. "According to Rufus, a good adventurer should be able to handle monsters one rank up, so long as the match-up is good. Meaning only pick fights with the big ones when your powers counter theirs."

They discussed the fight, and their teamwork in confusing the unintelligent monster to keep it stuck in the doorway. They discussed what they did well, what could have been improved. Jason was impressed with Sophie's ability to break down the fight, find the errors and look at how to correct them.

"My big mistake," Jason said, "was getting into a mindset of my powers not working on it. My execute power would have worked just fine but I'd fallen into the trap of dismissing the effectiveness of my abilities. When I was first training, one of the things Rufus said was to think about what every ability can do and how to use each one effectively in a situation."

"My mistake was trying to counter such an obviously powerful attack," Sophie said. "I should have hit you instead."

"What?" Jason asked.

"I could have knocked you out of the way," she said.

"Oh, right."

After breakfast, Jason started packing everything into his inventory.

"Did you decide if you wanted to use that awakening stone?" Jason asked.

"I don't think I will," Sophie said. "I don't think this is the best situation to break-in a completely new power."

"That's sensible."

Jason continued packing up. Sophie didn't have a dimensional bag of her own yet. She wanted something that wouldn't impede her very mobile fighting style, much like Emir's dimensional storage jacket. Something like that was hard to find, locally. So, for the moment, she was relying on Jason the way Gary and Rufus had done with Farrah.

Sophie settled into a meditation pose as Jason went downstairs. Pausing at the top of the stairwell, he called out to Sophie.

"Hey, Wexler."

"What?"

"Thanks for stopping my head from getting smeared across the floor."

He went down the stairs before she could reply. He negated the alarm rituals he put in place and packed up the aura tent. Then he went up and joined Sophie, who had settled herself on the edge of the roof. They sat, meditating side by side. Eventually, a smile crept over Jason's mouth as he experienced a breakthrough.

Ability [Midnight Eyes] (Dark) has reached Iron 8 (100%).
Ability [Midnight Eyes] (Dark) has advanced to Iron 9 (00%).

As a perception power, midnight eyes was the ability Jason was always using and for this reason, it had advanced the most quickly. Like his other abilities, though, it had slowed to a crawl as it drew closer to reaching bronze rank. Despite his not being a big part of the fight, taking on a bronze-rank monster had helped it edge up the wall.

After almost two hours, Sophie declared her arm fully restored. To test it, she and Jason did some sparring on the open space of the roof. Sophie had been trained hard since becoming an adventurer, but it was not a one-way street. Having someone with her skill who understood his style better than he did was immensely useful for Jason. She had pushed him to use it not just for escapes and sneak attacks but to become stronger in a straight-up fight.

Before he ever met Sophie, Jason had already been working on a deceptive style that baited out the enemy. Sophie had pointed out that Jason was massively wasting what could be one of his best combat abilities: his cloak. Because it only had physical substance when he wanted, it could obscure his movements without obstructing them. What's more, the ability to be real or insubstantial at will offered powerful utility.

Using his cloak to hide his stance, Jason feinted a forward motion, only to duck back when Sophie threw out a fist to counter. The blow wrapped her arm in his cloak. He yanked her forward, pulling her arm out of the way. He stepped forward with a rising knee. She couldn't see it coming but anticipated the move, halting Jason's rising knee with a leg block before it gathered force. She yanked her arm back and he let the cloak become insubstantial. Without the resistance she used too much force, and stumbled back. It was only a moment of lost balance, but Jason moved in to capitalise.

Soon after, Jason was sprawled face down on the rooftop.

"You did well," Sophie said. "You're improving."

"Then why does it feel like I'm getting worse?" he groaned.

"You're getting better but I'm also learning how you fight," she said. "Given that I know your style and have been doing this a lot longer, it only makes sense that I'll improve against you faster than you do against me."

"Doesn't that mean you should take it easy on me?" he asked as he pushed himself to his feet.

"Probably," she acknowledged. "Something about hitting you repeatedly is really satisfying, though."

"Thanks," he said, giving her a disgruntled look. "I'm glad you can use me for your personal gratification."

He started stripping off his clothes, taking out some healing unguent to rub into the muscles Sophie had tenderised.

"You're very skinny," she said, unashamedly looking him over as he stood there in his boxer shorts.

"Are you kidding?" Jason asked, looking himself over. "I've totally filled out. I used to be way skinnier than this."

"You did? Do come from a race of twig people?"

"No!"

"You seem very defensive," she said. "You're a twig person, aren't you?"

"I'm not a twig person! I'm a regular person!"

"Uh-huh."

"Yeah, well, you aren't so great, with your…"

He waved his arm up and down at her lithe body, her caramel skin set off by the matching silver of her eyes and hair.

"…how is that fair?" he finished limply. "I'm going to put my clothes back on now."

"What are those things on your shorts?"

"Hearts," Jason said.

"That's not what a heart looks like."

"How do you know what a heart looks like?" Jason asked. "You don't strike me as someone who took lessons on internal anatomy."

"I did, after a fashion," she said. "A few years back, during my first time in the fighting pits, there was a guy who would rip people's hearts out and eat them. He had some power where it made him stronger."

"Seriously?"

"Yeah."

"And they let him participate?"

"It got the crowd riled up."

"Surely they wouldn't just let that go on, would they?"

"The idea was to build up tension," she said. "They threw in scrubs to fight him, get some interest in the lower card fight before putting him up against real fighters. Kind of a 'who can take down the monster' situation."

"So he was killed in the arena?"

"No, the Adventure Society came in and did it. Turns out they don't like essence abilities that require you to eat people's hearts."

48
A WELL-INFORMED MAN

The City of Fallen Echoes was teeming with monsters. On their second day, Jason and Sophie had an encounter almost hourly as they made their way to the centre of the city. Sometimes they followed streets, other times they went across rooftops. Either way, there was no shortage of monsters willing to come after them.

There were similarities between the jungle-covered city and the delta where they usually hunted monsters, with the muggy heat and the lush plant life. The monsters they encountered here were similar, if not the same. They fought snake monsters, spider monsters and, especially unpleasant, a snake-spider the size of a transit van that slithered on its hairy abdomen and had eight snake heads instead of limbs.

The big difference between fighting monsters in the delta was in numbers. The magically saturated astral space produced far more monsters than the outside world. Jason and Sophie had already realised this, but as they surveilled their potential next encounter, the point was really rammed home.

Crouched on a rooftop, Jason and Sophie looked down at a teeming mass of margolls. They had both handled the dog-headed humanoids in the past, but now they were looking at a throng of monsters four times the size of a normal pack.

"I count forty-one," Jason said quietly.

From six storeys up they had a good vantage. There was little breeze to carry their scent and the poor eyesight of the creatures made their being spotted unlikely. The ravenous creatures had just taken down a smaller group of monsters and were loudly feasting on the bodies, jostling for position around the corpses.

"That was my count, too," Sophie said. "What do you think?"

"Honestly? I want to try it. We have to do it right, though. If we just fight them on the street they'll overrun us."

"You're looking at that building, across the way?"

"I am," Jason said. "We complicate the environment. Bottlenecks, escape paths. Bunch them up until their numbers help us more than hurt us."

"How do you want to lure them?"

"They're aggressive, relentless and not all that bright. I say we just drop down and run straight in. They'll chase us all through the building and we escape from the roof if it gets too much."

"Split up or stick together?" she asked.

"Lady's choice."

"Split up. I'll do better finding a choke point and holding my ground, while you'll do better on the move."

"Sounds good," Jason said. "Just make sure you always have an exit and keep in touch through the voice chat. Calculate your risk."

They leapt off the structure, drifting over the street to land in front of the building they had chosen on the other side. The margolls smelled them before they landed and were already looking around when they touched down and rushed for the building. The two adventurers dashed through the open doorway into darkness, Jason immediately vanishing as Sophie made for a set of stone stairs that rose along one wall. Everything else in the large room had long since rotted away, except vines and mushrooms that thrived in shadows more than in the bright sun outside.

Stopping halfway up the stairs, Sophie turned and began a slow, fighting retreat. The margolls were forced to face her two at a time; the rest were stuck crowding behind. She fearlessly met the attack of their huge claws and powerful jaws, trusting her powers to shield whatever body part she used to block. She retaliated with brutal punches and savage kicks, sending crippled margolls tumbling off the side of the stairs. When she bought herself some room, she would send a wind blade slicing its way down the stairs. The monsters shoving for position had no space to dodge.

The pack of margolls gathered at the bottom of the stairs howled their frustration as they pushed each other in the race for prey. Some swiped at each other with their wicked claws as they fought for access to the stairs. Others tried climbing the vines growing up the side of the stairs. The dark interior of the building was not as overgrown as the exterior, but there was growth enough that some of them eventually made their way up. Sophie kicked them back down when their heads popped up over the side of the stairs, but it drew her attention from the monsters in front of her. Unwilling to let herself be flanked, she backed up the stairs to the next level, then fled in search of a new bottleneck.

In the large room, the margolls left at the back started to notice something wrong. They were catching snatches of a scent that vanished as quickly as it appeared. They noticed one of their number, dead on the ground, far from the commotion of where the woman was kicking them back down the stairs. A second backline margoll fell dead with no more sound than its body hitting the ground. A third soon followed.

Margolls had poor eyesight, relying much more on their sense of smell. As they had just come in out of the bright sun, their vision was all the worse. Several more of their number were silently slain before they noticed the dark figure moving amongst them, appearing and disappearing just as quickly.

The monsters milled in confusion. Their baseline aggression, their large numbers in a relatively tight space and the frustration of fighting enemies they couldn't pin down were becoming a toxic brew. Some of the margolls turned on one another. If it weren't for Sophie being forced to fall back, letting the monsters vent up the stairs in pursuit, the margolls may well have killed each other.

Sometime later, Sophie and Jason were on the rooftop, fighting the last of the pack of margolls. Despite having their numbers whittled down as they pursued the pair through the building, the savage monsters never faltered in their furious assault until the last had fallen. Jason and Sophie then made their way down through the building, finishing off those too crippled to continue the chase. Jason touched each one to tag it for looting.

Would you like to loot [Margoll]?

He would only accept once they were away from the bodies and the stink they would produce as they dissolved. As they scoured the building, Jason made a pleasant discovery. A dark cube lay in an alcove under a stairwell, in a place that the light outside would never reach. If it weren't for his ability to see in the dark, he would have never seen it at all.

Item: [Dark Essence] (unranked, uncommon)
Manifested essence of darkness **(consumable, essence).**
Requirements: Less than 4 absorbed essences.
Effect: Imbues 1 awakened dark essence ability and 4 unawakened dark essence abilities.
You have absorbed 4/4 essences.
You do not meet the requirements to use this item.

"Nostalgic," he mused to himself.

"What's that?" Sophie asked, walking up to him.

"I found an essence," Jason said. "It's a dark essence, which was my first."

"Should go for a good price, right?"

"It should," Jason said. "It's only uncommon and there'll probably be a glut of essences on the market after all this, but dark is a popular one. It has great utility and is the last word in stealth essences. You should take it when we split up the loot after all this is done. The essences Belinda wants are all common, so you can probably trade this for two of them, or at least the magic essence and some solid awakening stones."

They went out on the street, in front of the building, before Jason accepted all the loot messages. Soon, rainbow smoke was streaming out of windows from the plume generated by all forty-one bodies being converted at once.

41 [Monster Cores (Iron)] have been added to your inventory.
410 [Iron Rank Spirit Coins] have been added to your inventory.
60 [Dog Quintessence Gems] have been added to your inventory.
10 [Myriad Quintessence Gems] have been added to your inventory.
410 [Iron Rank Spirit Coins] have been awarded to party member [Sophie Wexler].
60 [Dog Quintessence Gems] have been awarded to party member [Sophie Wexler].
10 [Myriad Quintessence Gems] have been awarded to party member [Sophie Wexler].

Sophie stepped back; her loot-dodge timing had improved enough that the three bags fell to the ground in front of her.

"So, your power conjured the bags, right?" she asked.

"Yep," Jason said. "As I understand it, a looting power like mine or Neil's takes the magic from the monster as it merges with the ambient magic and makes items with it. Usually magical manifestations like spirit coins or these quintessence gems we just got, but sometimes items."

"Belinda said Clive spent a whole day examining one of those bags to see if there was anything special about it."

"That does sound like him," Jason said.

Sophie opened up one of the bags, taking out a quintessence gem to examine. It was like a diamond, almost spherical but covered in tiny facets.

Item: [Myriad Quintessence] (iron rank, legendary)
***Manifested essence of multiplicity.* (crafting material, essence).**
Effect: Crafting material for items with multiplicative attributes.

"Pretty," Jason said as she held it up for him to see. It caught the bright sunlight, refracting rainbow colours.

"Legendary rarity," she said. "Should be valuable, right?"

"I imagine so," Jason said. "The myriad essence is legendary, too. Emily, the archer from Beth Cavendish's team has it."

"She's the celestine?" Sophie asked.

"That's right."

Sophie dropped the gem back into the bag and handed her loot to Jason for storage. He took out a notebook and recorded all the loot for splitting up later. As he wrote in it, Sophie craned her head back to watch the rainbow smoke from more than forty monsters rising up from the building.

"All those monsters," she said. "It's like this place has a monster surge going on."

"It essentially does," Jason said, putting his notebook away. "A monster surge is a weeks-long increase in magical saturation."

"You haven't experienced one, right?" she asked. "They don't have them in your world?"

"We don't have monsters at all," Jason said. "I've only been learning about how they work studying astral magic with Clive. I hope he's doing alright."

Clive had become worried once he realised that none of his team had arrived with him through the archway. As people started forming makeshift teams, he didn't expect to find anyone looking for his eclectic selection of powers. His unconventional abilities worked best when used in conjunction with people who knew and were prepared for them. A hastily formed team would do better with a ranged attacker with straightforward powers that they could readily adapt to.

He considered pulling a Jason and "adjusting" the perspective through which he described his abilities but immediately dismissed the idea. Worse than no one wanting him on their team would be getting abandoned in the middle of a monster-infested city for misrepresenting what he had to contribute.

One of the people present had the exact opposite problem. He wasn't a large man; his slight physique reminded Clive of Jason. If the man's blond hair and fair skin hadn't marked him as one of the foreign adventurers, the impressive equipment Clive recognised did. Once equipment passed a certain level of expense, it started to move from ostentatious back to unremarkable, and this man's equipment looked very unremarkable indeed. Clive knew it to be the kind of expensive that was wasted on iron-rank gear unless you had so much money to throw around it was laughable.

The man looked to be wearing light and simple clothes, but Clive picked out the subtle signs in the way the cloth draped that signalled incredibly powerful reinforcement magic. It was the kind of armour favoured by adventurers with mobility and high-skill power sets. He had a sword at his hip, with a ring at the top of the scabbard that most would dismiss as part of the design. Clive recognised it as a magic item that would impart extra damage to the first strike after drawing the blade. The man's jacket was made of supple leather, protective without being constrictive. Clive knew from the odd way it conformed to the body shape underneath that it was a dimensional jacket, much like that used by Emir Bahadir.

The other foreign adventurers clearly knew who he was, and were all clamouring to form a team with him. To Clive's surprise, the man's eyes picked him out. The man walked away from the people inviting him to their groups and straight over to Clive.

"You're Clive Standish," the man said.

"That's right," Clive said. "I'm not sure who you are but you're wearing more expensive gear than I've seen on a bronze ranker."

The man let out a friendly chuckle.

"Which means either someone didn't trust me to survive," he said, "or thinks I'm worth it."

"You're worth it," Clive said. "If someone doesn't have the skill, you spend that money very differently."

The man laughed again and held out his hand for Clive to shake.

"I'm Valdis. You live up to your reputation, Mr Standish."

"Clive is fine," Clive said. "I have a reputation?"

"I like to keep informed. The authorities in Greenstone know a lot more about the Builder cult than most provincial areas and your contributions have been a large part of that. Word just hasn't gotten around yet because of how closely information is being held right now."

"But not from you, it seems," Clive said.

"My father has some small standing overseas, which affords me a little more influence than I really deserve."

"My father's an eel farmer, which affords me more long, slimy fish than I really want."

Valdis laughed once more, clearly more comfortable with their circumstances than most of the adventurers present. Clive noticed the unhappy looks from the adventurers who had been courting Valdis's attention.

"Would you like to form a group with me, Clive?"

"I should warn you," Clive said, "my abilities can be a bit complicated. My damage comes in bursts and a lot of my abilities require anticipation and set up."

"Your confluence is the karmic essence, if I recall correctly, yes?"

"Yes," Clive said. "You really do like to keep informed. I have some retributive damage buffs and a lot of mana recovery. Mostly I attack with staves and wands but I have a big, versatile attack spell."

"I know someone with the karmic essence," Valdis said. "She says that judgement and timing are the keys to success."

"I'd have to agree," Clive said.

"I'm a classic swordsman myself—sword, swift, adept, master. More mana-intensive abilities than you'd expect with that combo, though, so I'll look forward to that mana recovery you mentioned. Assuming you want to join me."

"Definitely," Clive said.

"Great," Valdis said, rubbing his hands together as he turned his attention to the group listening in on them. "Let's find ourselves some team members."

49

THE DANGER IS US

In the time they had spent allowing Sophie to recover, some other groups had moved deeper into the city. They started seeing traces as they went; the plants and buildings showed traces of essence abilities having been used on them. They knew they weren't far behind another group when they found monsters that had yet to dissolve into smoke.

"Can you loot them?" Sophie asked.

"Probably not," Jason said, touching a finger to the dead monster.

This monster kill was not yours. You are unable to loot this monster.

"Nope," Jason said. "It only lets me loot when the killer is me or someone in my party."

"Does Neil's ability have that restriction?"

"Not exactly, but the monster has to die inside his aura, so it works out about the same."

"Should we veer off our straight line?" Sophie asked. "We aren't going to get much training in if all the monsters we find are dead."

"May as well," Jason said. "So long as we're going more or less the right way, it should be fine."

The pair discovered their most effective tactical patterns as days passed and they encountered monsters almost hourly. It was mostly some variation on Sophie grabbing the monsters' attention while Jason moved in to flank. Sometimes she would lead them around, other times standing her ground or staging running fights through buildings.

Every day in the city was like weeks of monster hunting outside it, with both Jason and Sophie unrelenting in the hunt. For Sophie, it was a chance to grab at power, both to share with Belinda and to give herself freedom from anyone who tried to control her fate.

For Jason, it was the culmination of a long wait. He had been putting off advancement and getting more awakening stones in the anticipation of Emir's grand event. He was now determined to complete his power set with the best awakening stones he could find. If nothing else, he resolved to get the necrotic damage affliction that had been absent from his kit from the beginning. Rufus kept telling him it would come, but with each new awakening stone, it had remained elusive.

As the days passed, they also encountered other adventurers. None were people they knew well, if at all, but the Greenstone adventurers tended to recognise Jason, or at least his cloak. The encounters ranged from the friendly to the wary, with the foreign adventurers being especially careful.

From the brief interactions, Jason and Sophie realised the foreign adventurers were most wary of each other. There was concern over rivals trying to remove their competition directly. Given that all the groups were now mixed, Jason and Sophie agreed that they were better off out of it and sticking together.

Each night, they would alternate meditating, sleeping and keeping watch. Sleep got the shortest shrift, as they both had effective stamina recovery powers that kept them powering forward through the day. Not to say that there weren't distractions in the downtime.

"What are you doing?" Sophie asked as she crawled, bleary-eyed, out of the aura tent.

"I've trying to teach Colin to spell," Jason said.

The leech collective was laid out in the shape of the word PLURB.

"I think he might be evil after all," Jason continued. "He only gets the rude words right."

Their abilities improved rapidly. Just the first few days had seen almost every ability Jason had advancing at least a level. His lowest abilities—his conjured dagger and his execute power—advanced twice. Sophie's abilities advanced even faster, as she had started off lower.

On the fifth day, they once again encountered an adventurer, but this one was dead. Sophie frowned as she crouched down to examine the body. He was a male leonid, much of his fur burned off in patches matching localised scorch marks on his clothes and skin.

"I've seen this before," she said. "Bodies left like this."

"A monster you've seen?"

"No," she said. "A person. There's an arena fighter they call fire fist. One essence, one ability, like me. You can guess what it is from the name. He liked to play with his opponents; take his time killing them. This is what it looked like when he did."

"You think someone did what I did, with you? Gave him the essences to become an adventurer?"

"I doubt it," she said. "The last I saw of him was when I left him dangling from a cage by his broken arms. People aren't inclined to lift up losers."

"You never actually met Thadwick Mercer, did you? I see your point, though. Maybe it was a monster with fire powers."

"I don't think so," Sophie said. "Enough adventurers are worried about people thinning out the competition that it's likely a real concern. Also, I'm not sure this is an environment likely to produce fire monsters. Plus, I think this body has been stripped of magic items. The boots are gone and these clothes are under-armour padding. There isn't any magic jewellery or dimensional bag."

"Fair points," Jason said. "If he was a Greenstone adventurer, he might have just been poor. I don't think any of the Greenstone participants were leonids, though. They were all in the foreign group and the worst of them were equipped as well as the best local."

"Whether a monster or a person did this," Sophie said, "this man was most likely in a group. If his companions didn't take him, they were either driven off or killed. We should look for more bodies."

"You're right," Jason said. "Let's hope we don't find any."

Every adventurer with a storage space or dimensional bag was carrying specialised caskets for storing corpses. The Adventure Society, in acknowledgement of the risks the iron-rankers faced, had placed a reward for anyone who retrieved the remains of the fallen. The reward had been high to incentivise the return of the dead, but not so high as to incentivise murder for profit.

They found a second dead leonid out on the street and a third leonid, even worse for wear than the others, in a nearby building.

"This was definitely torture," Sophie said as they crouched over the third corpse. "There aren't any big burns like with the other body. Whoever did this took their time."

"Look at bruising on the wrists and ankles," Jason said. "They were tied up. The neck, too, but not as bad. Whatever was around it was padded. Like a suppression collar."

He stood up, frowning and Sophie did the same.

"They took this man's powers, tied him up and then tortured him," Jason said. "This wasn't just taking out the competition. Whoever did this wanted something. Information?"

"There's no way to know what the foreign adventurers have going on between them," Sophie said. "I know you like to get your head around things, but don't get distracted by something we don't have enough information about. For all we know, it could just be sadists getting their thrills or some weird leonid hater."

Jason nodded. "You're right. This is an easy place to get away with blaming the deaths on misadventure."

"So, what do we do?" Sophie asked.

"We put him in a casket," Jason said, "then we see if there are any more before we keep going. It's not like we weren't being cautious already."

"And if whoever did this tries to do it to us? Trying to capture them and lug them around while we finish the trials won't work."

"No, it won't," Jason said. "Rufus once told me that when you're out on an adventure, sometimes all the justice you get is putting the other guy down. So, if we get attacked, we put them down. All the way down."

"Good," Sophie said. "I was a little worried you'd want to try some half-measure that would put us in danger."

"No," Jason said grimly. "We need to make sure that the danger is us."

The giant lizard monster lunged at Humphrey, its huge jaws open wide. Humphrey opened his own mouth in turn, fire blasting from it into the monster's gaping maw. It wasn't critical damage to the bronze-rank monster but the flame licking the inside of its mouth made it flinch back and snap its mouth shut. This exposed the rest of its face. Humphrey stepped forward, swinging his most powerful special attack into the side of the monster's head, cracking bone and bursting one huge eye.

It was the turning point in the fight. The rest of the group poured attacks into the staggered monster until it fell.

"Impressive as expected, from Danielle Geller's son," Lowell said.

Lowell was one of the foreign adventurers and had the good fortune to have four of his six team members arrive on the same tower. Humphrey had joined them for the journey to the centre of the city where he could rejoin his own team, but Lowell had other ideas.

"I know you have some affection for that team of locals you put together," Lowell said, "but clearly you're a good fit with us."

"I'm quite happy with my current team," Humphrey said coldly. His normal social graces were being steadily eroded by Lowell's constant efforts at recruitment. He had moved from the oblique to the direct.

"I understand that," Lowell said, "but to be frank, your time is wasted with the inferior team."

"Agreed," Humphrey snarled. "But I was separated from mine by the archway, so I'll have to make do."

"Wait, what?" Lowell asked, his smarmy veneer cracking. "You think some grab-bag of provincials is better than us?"

"Actually," Carly interjected, "he's just running out of patience with you disrespecting his team. Sorry about Lowell, Humphrey. He's a good guy but he has trouble seeing things from other people's perspectives. He gets an idea in his head and it's hard to dislodge."

"Carly's right," Hampstead agreed. "If I was Geller, I'd have already dislodged your whole damn head, Lowell."

"It's fine," Humphrey said. "Let's just keep moving."

Outside the astral space, Emir's cloud palace was sitting on the lake, with Rufus sitting with his parents on an outdoor terrace just above the water level. They had strongarmed Rufus into relaxing properly for the first time since Farrah died. Emir and Constance were also present along with Farrah's parents, who they had recruited to make sure Rufus had no recourse.

It was morning and they were taking tea, looking out over the lake and the picturesque towns and villages around it. The bright, lush greens of the shoreline were an appealingly stark contrast to the desert beyond. There were too many of the small communities to count, around a lake that was practically an inland sea.

"Sky Scar Lake," Farrah's mother, Amelia, mused. "I wonder where the name came from."

"It's a local legend," Constance volunteered. "It's said that people settled this land long ago but angered the gods, who struck them down. The force of the gods' wrath withered the land, turning fertile ground into desert and producing the hole that became the lake as we see it today."

"There are elements of truth to that," Emir said. "There were indeed people who settled here long ago and they were struck down. By the churches, rather than the gods themselves, but still. Of course, the desert and the lake were already here, when that all happened."

"I'd love to visit some more of those villages," Amelia said. "The ones nearby have been quite delightful. It would be nice to see some not quite so thrown into a tizzy by the sudden appearance of a giant, floating palace at their doorstep."

"You wouldn't know it," Rufus's father Gabriel said, "but there is actually a less grandiose form of the palace. I'd bet Emir hasn't used it since our adventuring days, though, back when we made him use it."

"I'm hosting a grand event," Emir said. "It requires grandeur."

"Emir, you think putting on socks requires grandeur," Gabriel said.

"That's because I have exceptional socks," Emir said. "It's not my fault you don't treat your feet with the care they deserve."

One of Emir's staff came in, whispering something to Constance, who frowned.

"Can I borrow Rufus for a moment?" she asked. She and Rufus were soon walking through the cloud palace together.

"What is it?" Rufus asked.

"Adris Dorgan is here," she said.

"In person?"

"Yes."

"He must have found something, to come in person."

Constance led Rufus to a receiving room where Dorgan was waiting. It was small but still had the sunset colours and comfortable cloud furniture ubiquitous in the cloud palace. Constance left the two men together and departed.

"Dorgan," Rufus said as they sat. "I take it from your personal presence that you have something."

"Yes and no," Dorgan said. "Partly I came because I didn't think they'd let any of my people through the door. I've been doing as you asked and I've definitely turned things up. I keep running into strange dead ends, however."

"Strange how?"

"Someone is hiding things. Someone with the kind of power and influence that I would normally run from like they were a woman with upholstery samples. I know what's at stake here, though, so I kept digging."

"And?"

"And I started losing people. Someone is disappearing any of my people that touch on certain areas. What's worse, they clearly don't fear reprisal. I can't keep sending people to their deaths."

"That's fair," Rufus said. "So, what have you managed to get?"

"I have a lot of pieces that don't quite fit," Dorgan said. "Private shipping expeditions with way too much secrecy. Bribes in amounts that boggle the mind. Whole companies set up, doing one quiet job and then closing down again, all to hide whoever was really behind the deals. If you look at it all together, it very nearly adds up to something."

"You came out here for a reason," Rufus said. "What do you need from me?"

"I need someone to ask the questions I can't," Dorgan said. "To poke the dark corners my people keep vanishing into."

"Anything more specific?"

"Whoever is covering this thing up on the top end is powerful and influential," Dorgan said. "More than the local powers can manage because they have foreign influence and no small amount of it. I can't go looking deeper than I have into who they are. If you can find that out for me, then I can maybe put all the parts into place. I can't look in the dark corners, but if I know who are hiding in them, I can follow their open activities. I know enough of the shady stuff that if I know what legitimate activities to watch, I think I can bring you something you need."

Rufus took a long, slow breath, his eyes glued to Dorgan's face.

"I might know who you're talking about," Rufus said. "Nothing is confirmed, however, and telling you would be no small thing. This is information that is still extremely restricted and we're keeping it that way until we have some proof. We haven't even shared our suspicions with the Adventure Society yet."

Dorgan got to his feet, Rufus doing the same.

"Well, when you get around to telling people, you come see me," Dorgan said. He took a paper folder from his jacket and handed it to Rufus.

"This is everything my people were able to find, with some observations from me about what various bits of it could mean. Until that information you're sitting on gets a little less restricted, this is as much as I can do for you. Just to be clear, I'm not saying I won't help. I'm saying I can't."

Rufus was leafing through the notes as Dorgan spoke. He looked up at the crime lord, giving him an assessing gaze.

"Please wait here," Rufus said. "I'll have some refreshments sent in while I talk to some people."

Rufus left and when he returned, Dorgan was enjoying tea and scones.

"Dorgan," Rufus said, without preamble. "I'm going to tell you something and you are going to do your very best in all your dealings to obfuscate the fact that I did."

"Alright," Dorgan said warily, putting down his teacup and getting up from his chair.

"You said you needed to know what influential power was hiding things."

"That's right."

Rufus visibly steeled himself, taking a long pause before speaking again.

"Church of Purity," he said quietly.

Dorgan's eyes grew wider and wider as the implications of what Rufus had said settled in. He ran his hands through his hair and started pacing back and forth before he stopped and turned back to Rufus.

"What kind of madness have you dragged me into?"

50
SURPLUS TO REQUIREMENTS

Jason and Sophie continued their way through the City of Fallen Echoes. More cautious than ever, they exposed themselves to long sightlines as little as possible. Sometimes they used narrow streets to hide themselves from above, at other times, rooftops of dilapidated buildings, to hide themselves from below.

Helping them remain unobtrusive was the quiet nature of their essence abilities. Only the burst accompanying Sophie's wind blade made any real noise and, compared to the cries of the monsters they fought, it wasn't especially loud.

Later in the day they had found the three dead leonids, something finally happened that they had been waiting for.

Party member [Neil Davone] has entered communication range.
Voice chat with [Neil Davone] had been restored.
Full [Party Interface] functionality has been restored to party member [Neil Davone].
Party member [Neil Davone] has been located on ability [Map].

Jason stopped, ducked into the shade of a ruined building and opened a voice chat.

"Neil?"

"Jason?"

"Good to hear from you. Are you alright?"

"Yeah. I've got Jory with me, plus another guy who's a pretty good front-line. We could use a good damage dealer, but you'll do."

"Oh, thanks for that vote of confidence. It's just me and Wexler, here. Humphrey's probably fine but I hope Clive's alright."

"Hello, Sophie," Neil said.

"Neil," Sophie reciprocated. "We'll need to figure out where we each are."

"I've got that covered," Jason said.

He pulled up his map, quickly locating Neil.

"Looks like you're east and a little south of us," Jason said.

"This place has an east?" Neil asked.

"It may have been arbitrarily designated by my map power, I'm not sure. Find somewhere to hole-up and we'll come to you."

Jason and Sophie reoriented themselves, heading towards Neil's location on the map. They had been moving around for around ten minutes when they received a chat from Neil. It had the whispered tone that came with a communication sent silently, via a thought.

"Someone is here," Neil's voice came. "From the way they're acting, I think they were following us and got thrown when we stopped to wait for you."

"Hang tight and we'll get there as fast as we can," Jason said.

"What does hang tight mean?" Neil asked.

"Come on, you can get it from context," Jason complained.

"Clear communication is important in tactical scenario," Neil said.

"Boys, we can sort this out later," Sophie said. "Asano, shut up. Neil, we'll be as quick as we can."

Sophie and Jason gave up on stealth for speed, rushing along streets as quickly as they could. Jason was no match for Sophie's speed, even when she was just using her abilities passively. Once she started using them actively, navigating the complicated terrain like it was a track course, only his shadow teleporting allowed him to keep up. At each junction he checked his map and kept them on the right heading.

"They found us," Neil said through voice chat.

"We're getting closer," Jason said. "A few more minutes."

Jason and Sophie had no more speed to pour on as they raced through the overgrown streets.

"We've got a fire user, a wind user and a big guy with a hammer," Neil kept them updated. "Jory is laughing like a loon for some reason I don't under… oh, damn."

"What happened?" Sophie asked.

"Give me a second," Neil's hurried voice came back.

"We're doing okay," Neil said a few moments later, his light with surprise. "Keane, that's our front-liner, is holding off their big guy just fine. The two women with the elemental powers are throwing everything at us but Jory is soaking up all their elemental attacks and using them to fuel his own abilities. What's that guy doing, spending his days in a clinic?"

"Just hold on," Jason said. "We'll be there soon."

"Shouldn't be an issue," Neil said. "They just keep throwing elemental attacks… what in the world is that?"

"Neil?" Jason asked.

"The other adventurers are running," Neil said. "There's a wave of some ghost-looking things coming down the street. I think they might be those things the shadow guy warned us about."

"The vorger," Jason said.

"Yeah," Neil said. "The people we were fighting had movement powers and bolted, but we can't move faster than these things are going."

"Regroup and protect each other as best you can," Jason said. "Sophie and I should be well-equipped to handle them. Probably."

"Probably?" Neil asked.

"It's better than definitely not."

Jason and Sophie spotted the vorger before they spotted Neil, Jory and the other man they picked up. The vorger looked like something between a fog bank and a swarm, their forms white and ethereal, taking all manner of shapes. Some looked like animals, others monsters or even humanoid shapes, although Shade had told them the shape didn't matter. Whatever their form, it was the touch of the creatures that would warp and distend flesh.

Jason and Sophie got a look at the results, sprinting past what used to be a person, judging from the pieces of armour and scraps of cloth on the hideous blob of flesh. They didn't pause, continuing the rush to help their companions.

"I think we found one of your run-off adventurers," Jason told Neil through voice chat. "The big guy, from your description. I guess he wasn't as fast as the others."

In the midst of the vorger swarm, Neil was alright for the moment, but things were rapidly getting worse. His mana shield power held off any vorger who rushed at him but each time the bubble-like barrier flashed, it ate away at his mana to keep him safe. Keane had left his sword in its sheath. His hands were both occupied by a large shield, a translucent, blue object that was obviously a magical construct. He used it to intercept and push back the vorger as they swept in at him and Jory, who was crouched down beside him.

Jory's leg had been brushed by one of the creatures and was locked into a folded position, forcing him to kneel down. In front of him, vials and little bottles were lifting themselves out of his belts and pockets, disgorging liquids and powers to float together. Unlike the black blob that had formed the last time he used the ability, this one was a shimmering, pale blue.

"I'll show you flesh warping," he muttered, and the blob streamed into his mouth. His body grew skinny and long, his limbs stretching out. Sweat oozed out of his skin, coating him in a shimmering oil. He stood up, his elongated leg no longer afflicted. He started flailing his arms around like whips, the vorger dissolving into nothing at the touch of the oil coating Jory's limbs.

For his part, Neil decided to act before his mana was so drained he could no longer cast spells. Even as the vorger continued lashing themselves against his mana shield he started chanting.

"*Come forth, wheels of fortune; let destiny, fair and foul, be brought upon those here to receive it.*"

In the air above Neil's had, three stone wheels, translucent and immaterial, came into being. They were stack horizontally atop one another and each had a series of images inscribed on their edges. Most of the images were of vorger, but each wheel also had an image of Neil, Jory and Keane's faces.

Ability: [Reels of Fortune] (Prosperity)
Spell (this ability has variable subtypes, contingent on effect).
Cost: High mana.
Cooldown: 10 minutes.

Current rank: Iron 7 (41%)

Effect (iron): Conjures three immaterial reels. Channel mana into the reels to generate random effects on random individuals within the area. If an individual is affected more than once by the same use of the reels, the effect is increased for each reel.

Just conjuring the reels had eaten a good chunk of his dwindling mana and he immediately spent even more, channelling it into the reels. By their nature, the inherent randomness of the reels gave the ability a mixed level of reliability at best, but as Neil's mana plunged, he was betting everything on how much the vorgers' numbers stacked the odds.

He had chosen to use the reels, not just for the spell's potential power but because they were so outnumbered by the vorger that the odds had become skewed. This was borne out as the wheels stopped turning and the images on the front lit up, each one showing a vorger.

Strange lightning shot out of the wheels a black streak limned in white, chaining through the vorger, one to another. Each vorger struck burst into nothing, like mist under the bright sun. For each vorger that dissolved, a matching image disappeared from each of the wheels, but there were so many of them that the difference was slight. The vorger rapidly perished, and Neil and everyone else were rejuvenated as the dying vorger triggered Neil's aura power.

Ability: [Spoils of Victory] (Prosperity)
Aura (recovery, conjuration).

Cost: None.
Cooldown: None.

Current rank: Iron 8 (19%)

Effect (iron): Allies within your aura recover mana and stamina for each enemy that dies within your aura, as well as a minor healing effect. You can loot enemies that die within your aura.

Neil's depleting mana was noticeably replenished as the vorger were killed by his spell. With his mana pool restored, Neil's mana shield was, once again, a safe refuge from the ghostly creatures. It also helped Keane, who had suffered a number of vorger strikes, in spite of his conjured shield. The healing uncramped joints that the flesh-warping attacks had locked up.

Neil channelled more mana into the wheels and they started turning again.

While Neil and Jory were in the process of turning the tables, Jason and Sophie finally reached the fight, ploughing straight in at full speed. Jason's sword was already out, slashing away at the ghost-like vorger.

Special attack [Leech Bite] has inflicted [Bleeding] on [Vorger].
[Vorger] is immune to [Bleeding].
[Bleeding] does not take effect.

Affliction immunity has triggered an effect on weapon [Dread Salvation].
Weapon [Dread Salvation] has gained an instance of [Spell Breaker].

Instances quickly stacked up on Jason's sword and it was soon slashing apart the vorger with ease while Sophie's unarmed attacks had a similar effect. She was also seemingly impervious to the vorger's touch, while Jason enjoyed his own protection.

Special attack [Vorger's Touch] has inflicted [Vorger's Flesh Warp] on you.
You have resisted [Vorger's Flesh Warp].
[Vorger's Flesh Warp] does not take effect.
You have gained an instance of [Resistant].

When Jason and Sophie appeared in the fight, their faces also appeared on the reels, but the second turn of the spell also ended in triple vorger. Luck was still on the adventurers' side. This time an energy wave rolled out of the reels and touched the closest of the vorger. Its translucent body turned from white to black, then it exploded. A nearby vorger caught in the explosion similarly turned black and exploded in turn. The effect kept chaining until it finally petered out, the vorger spreading out until the explosions no longer caught them. Between the explosions and the previous chains of dark lightning, Neil had eradicated a full third of the vorger swarm.

The next turn of the reel rested on images of two vorger and a picture of Jory's face. An explosion in the midst of the vorger took out a further chunk of their number, although not close to as many as the three reel effects.

[Human] has been affected by [Reels of Fortune]. Duration of ability [Alchemical Abomination] has been increased.

The vorger fought to the last but accomplished little. Jory's new form was as immune to their attacks as Jason and Sophie were, all three laying into the vorger with abandon. The magical protections of Neil and the other man, Keane, still held, protecting them until the fight was over.

In the end, Jason and Sophie felt rather surplus to requirements. They shredded their share of the ghost creatures but most were eradicated by Neil's spell, followed by Jory and his weird shape-changing power. Once the vorger were gone, the adventurers regrouped, relieved to have weathered the ordeal so well.

"Good to see you," Jason said, clapping Neil on the shoulder as Jory greeted Sophie warmly.

"We should find a quiet place to spend the night that isn't here," Jason said.

"We need to be careful," Neil said. "Those people are still around somewhere."

"I think we might have passed one who didn't run fast enough," Sophie said. "There was a big blob of flesh back there that I think used to be a person."

"He got killed?" Neil asked.

"The vorger do not kill," Shade said, his shadowy figure suddenly standing next to them. "They alter."

They all turned in the direction from which Jason and Sophie had come. Shambling towards them was a flesh monstrosity, a four-legged, asymmetrical mound that as much undulated forward as walked.

"Wexler," Jason said, looking at the creature. "Am I imagining things, or is that thing a lot bigger than when we ran past it?"

51
A WORSE PLAN

Clive's team were making their way up through a building that became more precarious as they climbed. It was the tallest building they had encountered in the city, almost as tall as the archway towers on which they had arrived. This section of the city was more akin to forest than jungle; the remnant buildings sat in the shadow of towering trees.

The building they were climbing through stood higher than the trees around it. It held its structural integrity despite one especially tall tree growing right up through the building itself. The building appeared to be some kind of elaborate palace. The expensive construction gave it a sound foundation but every floor they climbed showed increased signs of collapse.

"I'm starting to think the danger outweighs the promise of treasure," Clive said.

"If his Highness says we should check it out, we check it out," Abarca said.

Abarca, Campos and Hildebrand were the team members Valdis had picked out to join them. Valdis had suggested a voting system rather than picking a leader for their makeshift team. The three agreed immediately, as they had with every subsequent idea Valdis had come up with.

Valdis, it turned out, was a prince from the diminutive but influential Kingdom of Mirrors. Small, affluent and geographically blessed, it had neither expanded its borders nor been had its borders encroached upon in more than eight centuries. This was due to the diamond-ranker known as the Mirror King, who founded the kingdom and ruled it through to the present day. Through the centuries, the Mirror King had a series of queens, reportedly doting on each, even as they grew old and died beside him. Valdis was one of the current queen consort's sons.

Valdis was convinced there must be some great treasure at the top of the towering edifice and the other three agreed on principle. Clive had known there was no point arguing with Valdis's three yes-men but was compelled to ask what made Valdis so confident.

"No one tells the story of the thing they found in the safe, sensible place," Valdis told him. "A grand treasure atop a crumbling palace with a mighty tree growing right through it? That's a story that gets you waking up in someone else's bedchamber, Clive my friend."

Valdis threw a friendly arm around Clive's shoulder.

"Stick with me and you'll have yourself a wild time."

"I'm pretty confident that we'll be having a wild time, regardless," Clive said. "I'm mostly interested in surviving to tell that story."

Valdis just laughed and continued on, confidently leading the way. Clive liked Valdis, whose reckless enthusiasm reminded him of Jason. Clive had let himself be dragged by Jason into enough things he ended up enjoying that he wasn't opposed to Valdis's idea. That same comparison also compelled him to be the voice of reason.

They navigated the main part of the building, the most intact section, without incident. Then they reached a set of six towers, interconnected at various heights by different walkways. It reminded Clive of the Mercer family home, whose interlocking towers were a signature of the Greenstone skyline.

The towers were not as solid as the building below them, which became all the more evident as they ascended the crumbling stairs inside them. They started with the most intact-looking tower, but internal damage forced them to switch towers via the walkways more than once. The walkways, however, were even sketchier than the towers. Once fully enclosed tunnels, whole sections of the floor had long given way.

They crossed one at a time, Clive trying to convince himself he was imagining the feeling of the bricks shifting under every step. Valdis lightly pranced through, using a light-step power usually used for water-walking that reduced the pressure he placed with each footstep. Clive was not so blessed, carefully wending his way past the holes in the floor.

The first two tunnelled walkways were crossed without incident. They reached the third to discover it had mostly entirely collapsed away. The roof was gone, as were most of the walls and a large section in the middle of the floor. The only thing connecting one side to the other across the gap was a mostly intact section of wall.

"This is really not a good idea," Clive said. "I think we should call it off."

"We're almost there," Valdis said.

Above them was a huge, stone platform, the towers holding it up like the legs of a giant beast. Valdis was still convinced something amazing awaited them at the top. Looking at the missing middle section of the walkway, though, even the other three were becoming wary.

"Surely, there's a way to get us all across," Valdis said. "Clive, you're clever. I bet you can figure something out."

Clive frowned.

"Yes," he said reluctantly. He opened his storage space, a circle of runes he reached through, to start plucking out items. He took out four pitons, a hammer and two lengths of rope.

"We fasten the ends of these ropes at each end," Clive explained. "One high, and one low. We run them along the wall where the gap is, edging our way along the low one as we use the wall and the high one for balance."

"So, you need me to go over and fasten the other end," Valdis said.

"Yes," Clive said. "I would like to point out that you're the only one of us with a slow fall power, so your enthusiasm isn't tempered like the rest of ours."

"It'll be fine," Valdis said, and for most of the crossing, it was. Valdis used a wall run to cross the gap and secured the ropes at the other end, allowing Clive, Abarca and Campos to cross. The final member of the group, Hildebrand, let nerves get the better of him, the rope slipping through his fingers as he fell. Clive rushed to the edge, his gaze moving from Valdis to the falling Hildebrand as he quickly incanted a spell.

"*Exchange your fates.*"

Hildebrand vanished, his mid-air position now occupied by a startled Valdis. Hildebrand was standing in the spot from which Valdis had been looking over the edge himself. Clive grabbed the disoriented and still screaming Hildebrand before he fell off again.

Abarca and Campos were still yelling at Clive by the time Valdis made his way back up. Without the others, Valdis had made much better time than when they had ascended together, both Abarca and Campos expressed their relief at his reappearance.

"What's the issue?" Valdis asked. "You knew I had a slow-fall power. That was some sharp thinking, Clive."

"I told you this was dangerous," Clive said.

"And I told you it would be fine," Valdis said. "Did these guys give you a hard time?"

"It's doesn't matter," Clive said.

"Should I go back and grab the rope?" Valdis asked.

"We have to get back down, remember?"

"Right, yes."

After the slow and almost disastrous crossing of the walkway, they were able to climb the tower all the way to the top. The stairs emerged through the floor of the massive platform that spanned the towers, which looked to have been cut from a single piece of stone. There were six statues in the middle of the platform, standing in a circle and facing inward. They each had a plinth in front of them with various items, but the group's attention was drawn to the centre of the circle.

In the middle of the circle was a large creature, a wingless dragon the size of an elephant, with powerful legs and a tail that ended in a wicked stinger. Its scales were brown and grey, matte to the point that it looked rather like a large rock. The creature had sensed them, languidly getting up from where it had been sunning itself in the middle of the platform. Stretching its limbs, it eyed them hungrily.

"Mountain wyrm," Valdis said, the usual amusement absent from his voice. "A little one, only bronze rank, probably, but still powerful. It can draw strength from stone to heal and toughen itself. Honestly, I don't think we can beat it here. The rest of you go back down and I'll distract it for as long as I can, then jump over the side. Use your escape medallions if you have to."

Clive and the others had all chosen the path of wisdom, receiving the life-preserving items from Shade. Only Valdis had taken the courage option.

Hildebrand didn't hesitate at Valdis's words, bounding back down the stairs. Abarca and Campos followed, after a quick glance at Valdis's determined gaze, locked on the monster.

"Edge!" Clive yelled, running away from the stairs and towards the side of the platform.

"What?" Valdis asked, looking at Clive in confusion, before grinning in realisation and also running.

"Are you sure that will work?" Valdis called out.

"Probably," Clive called back.

"Probably?"

"You have a better plan?"

"You heard my plan."

"That was a worse plan," Clive yelled. "You go over the side, either way."

Valdis easily caught up with Clive. Behind him, the wyrm was moving in their direction on powerful legs, but its heavy body moved no more quickly than Clive did and they made it to the edge of the platform well ahead of it. Clive came to a stop, pulling out a silver spirit coin.

Clive knew the bronze-rank monster would likely resist his spell. Consuming a spirit coin to boost his attributes past the monster's rank to silver would make Clive's spell more likely to take effect. It presented a dangerous risk-reward proposition, for if his spell failed anyway, he would be left weak and helpless in front of the monster.

Clive shoved the coin in his mouth without hesitation as Valdis leapt off the side of the tower. Clive looked between him and the dragon, casting his spell as he felt the power of the coin surge through him.

"*Exchange your fates.*"

You have used spell [Juxtaposition] on [Valdis Volaire] and [Lesser Mountain Wyrm].
[Lesser Mountain Wyrm] has resisted. [Juxtaposition] does not take effect.
Spell cooldown is reset due to spell failure.

"Crap."

He tried again.

"*Exchange your fates.*"

"*Exchange your fates.*"

"Oh, come on…"

He could feel the fleeting power of the about to drain away. He looked at Valdis, drifting slowly downward, then back at the draconic monster that was almost upon him.

"*Exchange your fates.*"

The monster vanished, replaced with Valdis. Valdis ran over and they looked over the side, watching the monster crash through the tops of the trees below. Clive dropped to his hands and knees at the edge of the platform, panting in exhaustion as he looked over the side.

"Think it'll kill it?" he asked. "Maybe the trees will cushion its fall."

"Maybe," Valdis said. "If it survives, it can heal itself up with the stone on the ground."

You defeated [Lesser Mountain Wyrm].

"No, it's dead," Clive said with relief. He had no interest in facing the monster again after they went back down.

"You're sure?"

"I'm sure."

"I should probably go get those three before they try that rope again, then."

"You go right ahead," Clive said, rolling onto his back to lay spreadeagled on the platform. "I'm just going to lay here for a bit."

Valdis eventually returned with the other three who, despite the prince's assurances, poked their heads up over the edge of the stairwell warily before coming all the way up. Valdis walked back over to Clive.

"Ready to get back up?" Valdis asked.

"No."

Valdis laughed, holding out a hand to pull Clive to his feet. Clive groaned as the went to examine the ring of statues. The statues were around twice Clive's height, each one depicting a different person. From the equipment carved onto each statue, it was clear they were all adventurers. The most interesting part was that each statue had a plinth in front of it, on which rested what looked to be actual versions of some of the gear the statues had. For each statue, there were two pieces of gear, waiting to be claimed.

Each of the five adventurers gravitated to certain gear. Valdis to a sword and scabbard, Clive to a staff and wand. The other sets were an orb and circlet, a cloak and dagger, a sword and shield and a single glove, paired with an amulet.

Clive saw no magic with his perception power but didn't rule out some trap too powerful for his ability to pluck from hiding. He pulled out some tools, examining the plinth carefully, even as the others had already started picking up items. When he was convinced any traps that might be present were beyond his ability to uncover, Clive turned his attention to the staff and the wand.

The staff was carved from a dark coloured wood, engraved with magical symbols. On the end was a bass cap, with a large purple gemstone set into it. The wand was a blue metal rod with intricate lines worked into flowing patterns that ran down its length.

Clive had his own ability to identify magic items which, like most such abilities, worked by giving him a sense of the item's properties when he touched them. Compared to the way Jason's power gave a visible explanation he found it disappointing.

While out of range of Jason, powers like the voice chat and identifying items didn't work. To Clive's delight, however, the party interface power combined with Clive's own identification ability to restore that functionality. Thus, he was happily able to read the properties of the staff.

Item: [Spell Lance of the Magister] (iron rank [growth], legendary)
***The staff of an ancient sorcerer, this weapon is focused on priming enemies for a potent magical assault* (weapon, staff).**
Requirements: The power to wield magical tools.
Basic attack: Explosive disruptive-force bolt. Inflicts [Spell Impetus].
Basic attack: Disruptive-force beam. Consumes mana. Sustaining the beam on a target periodically inflicts [Spell Impetus].
Effect: Increase the mana consumption when casting a spell to increase the effect. Effect is further increased if wielding both [Spell Lance of the Magister] and [Magister's Tithe].
[Spell Impetus] (affliction, magic, stacking): All resistances are reduced. When the recipient suffers an offensive spell from someone wielding [Spell Lance of the Magister], all instances of [Spell impetus] are consumed to increase the effect of the spell.

The Magister was a potentially mythical figure, whose actual existence was hotly debated. Many items and abilities were named for him or her, including two of Clive's own abilities. Regardless of the history, finding a growth weapon made the trip to the astral space a success, whatever else he encountered. He took a look at the wand.

Item: [Magister's Tithe] (iron rank [growth], legendary)
The wand of an ancient sorcerer, used to sustain combat effectiveness **(weapon, wand).**
Requirements: The power to wield magical tools.
Basic attack: Disruptive-force beam. Inflicts [Mana Siphon].
Basic attack: Mana draining beam. This effect is increased if wielding both [Spell Lance of the Magister] and [Magister's Tithe].
[Mana Siphon] (affliction, magic): The strength of mana drain effects against the recipient are increased.

Clive stared in awe at the items in his hands. A matched set of legendary growth weapons were so good he would do well to shut up and not tell anyone, so as not to get robbed. He placed them in his inventory and turned to find four people holding out items. Valdis gave him a wry smile.

"You can identify items, right?"

52

NO ONE HAS THAT COMING

In the aftermath of the fight with the vorger, Jason and Sophie had no time to catch up with Neil and Jory. The flesh abomination lumbering in their direction posed a new, albeit slowly approaching, problem. They stood together, watching as the thing didn't so much walk in their direction as vaguely amble. It was basically a huge, vaguely spherical mound of muscle, skin and fat on four short, blobby legs. Scraps of clothing and pieces of armour could be seen wedged into fatty crevices where layers of flesh and skin had folded on top of themselves.

"Is it attacking us?" Neil asked.

"It will move sluggishly until it is engaged," Shade said. The shadowy entity who governed the trials had chosen to reappear. Also with them was Keane, the adventurer who had been travelling with Neil and Jory.

"So we could just leave?" Neil asked.

"Yes," Shade said. "If you were alone, I would advise you to do so. Your collective capabilities should be sufficient to kill it, however, so I ask that you do. The soul within is trapped in excruciating pain, denied the release of death until its flesh prison is destroyed."

"Is that one of the people that attacked us?" Jory asked.

"It was," Shade said. "He did not flee as swiftly as his companions."

"Forget it, then," Neil said. "He had it coming."

"No one has that coming," Jason said.

"He was trying to kill us."

"And if he'd still been fighting you when we arrived," Jason said, "I'd help you kill him right back. But death is one thing and having your soul trapped in pain for eternity is another."

"I agree," Jory said firmly.

"Sophie, new guy," Jason said. "What do you think?"

"Put him down," Sophie said. "You were right about no one deserving that."

"Am I the new guy?" Keane asked.

"Yeah," Jason said, "but it's three to one already. Your vote doesn't matter anymore, sorry."

Jason looked at the hideous blob abomination. It had at least five times the amount of flesh a person would have.

"Shade, do you not have conservation of mass, here?"

"We do," Shade said. "We also have magic, so the laws of physics are more like strong suggestions. It's best for everyone if you adhere to them, but if you are truly reluctant, there are still modes of recourse."

"You know about the laws of physics?" Jason asked.

"I have been a familiar many times, across many worlds. I know much."

"You must be handy to have around," Jason said. "And you've done a lot of familiaring, you say? I don't suppose you're looking for a new gig?"

"My time here ends when all the trials are passed. Pass the trials, gain the right essence ability and we'll see."

"Oh, nice," Jason said. "What kind of awakening stone would that take?"

"All who survive this stage of the trials shall receive an awakening stone available nowhere else," Shade said.

"Clive will be glad to hear that," Jason said.

"Doesn't he have his full set of abilities already?" Neil asked.

"Yeah, but you know what he's like. Give him something new and he's a kid at Christmas."

"What's Christmas?"

"It's a religious holiday that we appropriated to stimulate the economy once a year," Jason said.

"That thing is getting closer," Sophie said. "Slowly, but it's getting closer. Shade, can you tell us again about the best way to fight it?"

"A flesh abomination will adapt to how you engage it. If you are fast it will become faster. Strong, and it will become tougher. Hide and its senses will improve. Attack from afar and it will develop ranged attacks. Its weakness is that it cannot be all things at once. If it becomes fast and flexible, it becomes vulnerable to cutting attacks. If it develops a chitinous exterior, it becomes inflexible and slow. I advise you to use Jason Asano's necrotic powers as the main source of damage. Whatever changes it makes, flesh is flesh, and flesh can die."

Jason surveilled what was about to be their battleground. It was typical of what they had seen in the city; jungle filled the space between overgrown buildings. The broken stone road had soil and roots pushing up through the pavers, along with plants and full-blown trees. The footing was unsure and the terrain complex with plenty of shadows he could use.

"Alright," he said. "Sophie, you start us off. Get it picking up the pace to chase you around so it's nice and squishy. Then, Neil, you tie it up so I can introduce it to Colin. Sound good?"

"Works for me," Sophie said.

"If it's bronze rank, I won't be able to hold it for longer than a few moments," Neil said. "You'll need to get your timing right."

"Call it and I'll be ready," Jason said. "Jory, stick with Neil. New guy, put yourself between Jory, Neil and the bad guy."

"Not a problem," Keane said. "I've been doing it for days."

"Everyone knows their job, then. Sophie, will you kick things off?"

Sophie flashed him a grin and dashed in the direction of the abomination. She leapt high into the air, kicking off the top of the misshapen lump of flesh before landing on the other side, hitting the ground at a run.

"Reckless," Jason said, shaking his head.

"Then why are you grinning?" Neil asked.

"I have a soft spot for poor but flamboyant choices."

The creature reacted quickly, its body rapidly morphing. It shrank, moving into the shape of a fleshy beetle with six legs and scurrying after Sophie. Growing out of its back were four, long, skinny arms. Lengthier than its entire body, the arms were articulated by multiple joints.

"That is very disturbing," Jory said. "A giant flesh bug with four arms sticking out of it? I think the worst part is all those extra elbows."

Sophie led the creature on a merry chase, running away and deflecting the long, grasping hands when they came close enough to grab at her. After its initial transformation, the changes in the creature had slowed but not stopped. As it chased after Sophie, it made incremental changes to its form to help in the pursuit. The body continued to shrink the legs changed shape to better handle Sophie's speed and rapid shifts in direction. Its arms, which she continued knocking away, went from eerily human hands to long fingers with webbing stretched between them.

"Get ready to go," Neil told Jason, who nodded.

Neil chanted a spell and the overgrown plant life started sprouting masses of vines, lashing out to wrap around the creature. Its many arms and legs were bound up, along with its long body, completely arresting its movement. Jason emerged from a shadow, slicing the back of his hand with the razor hidden in a wristband for the purpose. From the wound, a pile of Colin spewed out onto the flesh abomination, the leeches immediately digging in with their horrifying rings of teeth.

System messages scrolled before Jason's eyes in rapid succession, notifying him of the afflictions Team Colin was placing. Most were resisted but Jason's familiar power was increasing, as was his resistance-penalising aura. He gleefully noted that as many as one in three afflictions were taking hold, which was better than with previous bronze-rank encounters. With sheer numbers of Team Colin, the flesh monster was quickly loaded with afflictions.

Colin only had a few moments to lay in afflictions before the abomination altered its form, undertaking another massive, rapid transformation. Shifting from the horizontal alignment of a hexapod to an upright biped, four of the six legs shrank away while the remaining pair grew bulky and strong. Its body became larger and heavier, the fleshy exterior growing thick, tough skin with protrusions of razor-sharp bone poking through. The four arms grew shorter but more powerful, the webbed hands replaced with savage claws. The result was something like a hairless, four-armed gorilla, covered in elephant skin with bony blades growing out of its body.

The new skin was too much for the leeches to bite through. The blade-bones sliced through many of the vines and it pulled itself free of the rest brute strength. The vines tried to entangle it again but the creature powered free of their grasp, shedding leeches like droplets of water in the process.

During the transformation, Jason was not idle, taking the opportunity to lay in with his spells. They lacked immediate impact and were repeatedly resisted but were quick to cast. By the time the abomination broke free and resumed its angry pursuit of Sophie, Jason had afflicted it with his key powers.

The abomination was now loaded up with ongoing necrotic damage from Colin, plus bleeding and blood poison. The bleed would soak up the creature's regeneration that would have otherwise healed it, the bleed only ending once it soaked a certain amount of healing. The poison would then reapply the bleed effect every time it dropped off. This was important as the abomination had altered itself to accelerate healing in an attempt to adapt to Jason's afflictions, but all that regeneration went to waste.

The other pillars holding up Jason's house of affliction were the sin affliction, which increased all necrotic damage suffered, and inexorable doom, which added to any affliction in place. The combination of leech necrotoxin and the necrosis-accelerating sin both increasing over time was a multiplicative escalation of the damage, while the bleeding and anticoagulant leech toxin kept the monstrosity's regeneration in check.

The escalating effects of Jason's afflictions had placed the abomination's life on a clock. That left the question of how much damage the abomination could inflict before that clock ran out. In the immediacy, the creature's inevitable demise was not apparent as the abomination thrashed at the leeches still falling off its body.

Jason retreated to the shadows and recalled the leeches, which started disappearing as they contacted the blood on the hand he lowered to receive them. They were quite spread out, however, and could only slowly make their way to his hidden position. The flesh monstrosity lacked the intelligence to follow their direction to Jason's hidden location. His cloak melded him perfectly into the shadow, hiding him even from whatever senses the flesh monster relied on without eyes or ears.

The abomination furiously stomped on leeches to little avail; they had been quite scattered by the monster shaking them off. Unable to catch the elusive Sophie, it stopped. Its four arms and the bony protrusions retracted as its body returned to a more blob-like shape, while keeping the thick hide. Welt-like marks appeared all over its surface, with tiny bone needles shooting out in every direction a moment later.

Keane used his shield to shelter Jory, Neil and himself. Neil had cast his giant's might spell on Keane shortly after Sophie had begun combat and the shield-bearer was twice his normal size, as was the conjured shield in front of him. It was Sophie, Jason and Colin who should have taken the brunt of the attack, but Neil was on the ball, a bubble-like shield snapping up around Sophie. It only lasted a moment, but a moment was all she needed to shift behind a tree with her mirage step power. The after-image left behind by her ability didn't seem to fool the abomination's eyeless, earless senses and it didn't keep attacking her.

Jason's hidden position meant Neil couldn't see him to provide another shield. This left Jason as the only person who didn't avoid the attack. The needles that dug into him were light but they were also a bronze-rank attack. They pierced through his cloak and, in many places, the armour underneath. All Jason had time to do was turn his body away from the attack and shield his face before the needles struck. He ducked behind a tree as more of the bone needles poured out of the abomination.

Team Colin took the worst of it. Only a fraction of the leech mass had returned to Jason before the rest were skewered with bone needles. Some, still clinging to the abomination, had been shot off by needles. Most were exposed on the ground and riddled with needles.

Generally, Jason didn't have to worry about the welfare of Team Colin. Very few monsters had the kind of area attacks that could pose a danger to the regenerating leech swarm. This time, Jason had only absorbed a fraction of Colin's full mass, which would take a day or two to replenish itself in the safety of Jason's bloodstream.

As the accelerated healing Jason received from Colin was based on how much of the mass was currently residing in his blood, the effect would be significantly reduced until the leech swarm recovered. Fortunately, the healing they offered had grown stronger as Jason's familiar power advanced. What was a reduced effect now was similar to when he had first obtained the ability.

While all the afflictions were locked in and its death was now inevitable, the abomination was, for the moment, still full of life. The necrosis was causing patches of blackened flesh to ooze blood but the monstrosity did not yet appear impeded. Of its opponents, Jason and Sophie were hidden and what remained of the leeches were dead. That left Keane, Neil and Jory to its attentions and there was no hiding Keane's enlarged body. The abomination morphed again, bulking up and dropping to four powerful legs as a huge, bony spike emerged from the front. It now resembled a rhino whose entire head was a horn.

It charged directly at Keane.

It quickly built up speed as it charged, but it was no match for Sophie who emerged from her hiding spot and raced ahead of it. Putting herself between the monster and the others, she was suddenly thrown violently sideways as Jason emerged from a nearby shadow, crash-tackling her out of the way, and letting the monster pass.

"What are you doing?" Sophie yelled at him as he extricated herself from his rough embrace.

"Your ability can only stop so much, remember?" Jason yelled at her. "Trust your allies."

Sophie glared at him, then down at her arm, remembering the broken mess it had been the last time an attack had overwhelmed her defensive power. That had taken her magic power the better part of a day to heal. This flesh monster's charge would certainly have been more powerful.

Neil, Jory and Keane had been moving and fighting through the city together for several days. With monsters so thick on the ground, that was enough time and enough fights to find each other's combat rhythms. It was an unusual mix, with no dedicated damage dealer, but Neil and Jory both had powerful buffs that could turn Keane into a walking fortress.

Already giant-sized from Neil's spell, Neil gave him another spell—bolster—that would enhance his next active essence ability use. Jory, meanwhile, had a cluster of small, clear orbs floating around him. Materials started floating out of his pockets and belts, hovering in front of him. Trace elements mixed with a substance he conjured out of thin air, resulting in a small, red blob that one of the orbs floated over and absorbed. The orb then flew over to Keane, passed straight through his armour and was absorbed directly into his flesh.

Jory had three powers that were the basis for his effectiveness as a field alchemist. The orbs were an ability called eldritch eyes, which could deliver potions across a battlefield, to enemies and allies both. The orbs also allowed him to safely scout at a distance, a valuable support skill for any team.

His telekinetic power, potion mystic, allowed him to alter and combine ingredients without touching them, turning Jory into a walking alchemy workshop. It wasn't an ability that replaced a real workshop for making proper potions, but for working on the fly it was perfect.

The reason Jory could throw out potions without exhausting his materials was the universal reagent ability. It conjured a versatile potion base he could use to make short-lived potions using only trace elements, letting him save materials compared to regular potion-making. These quick potions rapidly became inert if not used, but took only a fraction of the materials a regular version of the same potion would. This allowed Jory to massively output potions, a key element of both his clinic's financial viability and his sustained effectiveness in the field.

So long as he didn't overuse his material-hungry shape-changing power, he could carry enough materials for numerous encounters. With the versatility of his potions, Jory could be a makeshift healer, buffer, debuffer and even throw around some afflictions using poison and other noxious concoctions.

Between Jory and Neil's buffs, Keane was as ready as he could be for the monstrosity bearing down on them. Just before it hit, Neil's burst shield power bubbled into place around Keane. Keane used a power of his own that absorbed the force of an attack and turned it back on the attacker, which was boosted by Neil's earlier use of the bolster power.

But not even the combination of buffs, Neil's shield power and Keane's enhanced ability were enough to fully withstand the raw force of the bronze-rank abomination's attack. Neil's shield popped as easily as the bubble it looked like, while the shield in Keane's hands warped and shattered, the conjured object dissolving into nothing as it broke apart.

All their efforts in stacking defence were not in vain, however. Keane had leaned into the blow and while he was sent stumbling backwards, he stayed on his feet. The retaliatory force of Neil's burst shield and Keane's damage reflection power had blunted the abomination's terrifying momentum. Attack and defence were both spent and for a brief, oddly still moment, Keane stood looking at the motionless monstrosity.

The moment passed, and Keane conjured a fresh shield as the monster started changing its form once more. Keane backed off, keeping himself between the abomination and the two supporters behind him. Sophie renewed her attack, opening with a wind blade before laying in with attacks. Her unarmed strike powers offered only limited damage but her two special attacks added damage to every strike. The nature of that damage was such that one type or the other would always be effective, regardless of her opponent's protections.

With Sophie once again on the attack, the monster engaged her, shifting thick-legged quadruped with eight arms emerging from every side of its body. The arms were long and multi-jointed like they had seen before, but this time ended razor-sharp blades of bone. Sophie held her ground, a combination of stubbornness defiance of Jason's earlier intervention and a need to give the others time to reposition.

Bone blades lashed out at her, but she dodged or deflected them with arms, legs, even her head. So long as she actively intercepted the attacks, her powers absorbed the damage. The monster might be bronze rank, but it could put only so much power into such rapid, multitudinous attacks.

With Sophie successfully fending it off, the abomination did what it always did—shifted its form to adapt. Its arms changed into tentacles, still sporting blades at the end. This reduced the power of each attack but making them more flexible and harder to predict.

Sophie countered by activating her between the raindrops ability, which enhanced her reflexes for a high mana cost. The result was that rather than defend less effectively, she handled the tentacles with more ease than she had the arms.

The mana consumption of the power was high but several mitigating factors allowed her to keep it up. One was the natural ability of the celestine race that reduced the mana cost of ongoing abilities. Another was Neil, using a replenish spell to restore her mana, and Jory, quick-brewing a mana potion and floated to her in an orb. Her confrontation had allow ed them to regroup behind Keane, ready should the creature turn on them again.

Faced with a continued inability to harm Sophie, the abomination started shifting again, but the effects of Jason's afflictions finally made themselves known. As it tried to change shape again, its skin cracked like a rotten egg, complete with hideous smell. Black fluid spilled out onto the ground, filling the air with the only smell any of them had encountered that could rival rainbow smoke for sheer nauseating power. As the monstrosity collapsed, Sophie ran off to throw up. She had inhaled the largest dose.

The abomination flopped wetly on the ground in a pool of its own blacked, runny flesh. It had adapted to the exponentially accelerating necrosis by isolating it, continuing the fight even as it grew inside like a hyper-accelerated cancer until there was nothing left to contain it. The group watched from afar, cloth held over their noses as what had been a person an hour ago melted into a black, red and purple puddle.

"Thank you," Shade said, once again appearing amongst them. "There are many that suffer so, in this place. I am grateful for any that you can put to rest."

53
PART OF BEING A TEAM

After defeating the flesh abomination, Jason's temporary team had grown to five. With two defenders in Keane and Sophie, two healers in Neil and Jory, Jason was their only dedicated damage source. They were heavy on sustained but light on immediate damage. Jason's powers brought certain, but eventual death to the monsters they encountered.

This setup made for slower going than they might have with someone like Humphrey on hand, but it wasn't without benefits. With the oversized monster groups they were encountering, fights were long and everyone's abilities were getting a workout. All that practise showed results each night as at least one member of the group experienced ability advancement.

Ability [Castigate] (Sin) has reached Iron 6 (100%).
Ability [Castigate] (Sin) has reached Iron 7 (00%).

All [Sin] abilities have reached [Iron 7].
Linked attribute [Recovery] has increased from [Iron 6] to [Iron 7].

Progress to bronze rank: 35% (2/4 essences complete).

The top end of iron rank represented the peak of human potential in a given attribute. Jason's power and recovery attributes had both reached seven, vastly improving his cardiovascular health while making him stronger and tougher than his slight frame would suggest. As his skinny physique transitioned to lean muscle, he felt incredibly empowered.

"If it feels this good to advance through iron rank," he said to the others as they prepared to set off for the morning, "I can't wait for bronze rank."

"Where I come from, you can randomly throw a rock and you'll hit a silver rank," Keane said. "They say you aren't even a real adventurer until bronze."

They had got to know Keane over the last few days. He was a dark-skinned human, from an island city located in this world's Caribbean Sea. He had none of the arrogance they had seen from some of the imported adventurers, just looking to be the most effective member of the group that he could.

They fell into a daily pattern. From early morning to late evening, they would move towards the centre of the city, fighting monsters as they went. At the end of the day, they would find a promising-looking building, search it for treasures and clear out any monsters lairing inside before setting up camp.

"What do you think this building was?" Jory asked as they regrouped from searching the latest building. "Some kind of huge inn?"

"Brothel," Neil said absently, then noticed that everyone had turned to look at him. "What?"

"That was a very confident response," Jason said.

"You spend a lot of time in brothels?" Sophie asked.

"Yes," Neil said with a sigh. "Hang around with Thadwick Mercer long enough and you'll see the inside of a lot of brothels."

"He's seventeen," Jason said. "How many brothels can he have been to?"

"I think I've seen the inside of every bordello in Greenstone," Neil said. "High class, low class, high class pretending to be low class. He doesn't care. He's spent a lot of money at the church of the Healer in the last year or so."

"At least he's using paid volunteers," Jason said. "He gives off a very strong date-rapey vibe."

They occasionally met more adventurers, but none of those encounters led to further conflict or team-ups. There was some exchanging of supplies—many adventurers had been separated from their team members carrying most of the team's gear. Jory proved popular in this regard, with his specialised dimensional bag overstuffed with potions.

They also met more vorger and flesh abominations. Building on their previous experience, by the third and fourth encounters they had a good idea of what worked and what didn't.

"We're lucky they're both fairly mindless," Keane said as they discussed tactics one evening. "The most dangerous thing about higher-rank monsters isn't their more exotic powers, but their intelligence."

"You've seen a few higher-rank monsters?" Neil asked him.

"Yeah," Keane said. "In areas of high-magic density, we iron rankers aren't allowed to hunt by ourselves, like you Greenstone people. We get to go along and see some higher-rank monsters in action, though."

One thing Jason finally got to practice was his execute ability. Even without burst-damage members on the team, only the toughest iron-rank monsters could actually survive enough damage for it to be effective. It was only against the bronze-rank enemies, be they the flesh abominations or regular monsters, that he could actually get some use out of it.

The team was strong enough to handle a bronze-rank monster, but while the flesh abominations roamed alone, the actual monsters did not. With the city so saturated in magic, even normally solitary monsters appeared in packs. In the face of this, the team's usual strategy was to make a fighting retreat, using their two defenders and two healers to keep the group intact while Jason loaded up the enemies with afflictions.

This gave Jason the chance to use the two abilities he had the most trouble practising. They were both direct damage abilities, but neither were effective to just open up with. Both required setting up and were quite similar in their use, which, at least meant that when he could get some use out of one, he could get it from the other as well.

Fighting a trio of monsters, the team was under pressure. Their strong defensive strategy was highly effective against iron-rank monsters, even in large numbers, but bronze-rank beasts with powerful attacks threatened to overwhelm them.

The monsters looked like four-armed gorillas, covered in lizard skin instead of fur. They liked to climb and leap, making rapid attacks with their four arms before leaping away to set up for the next rush attack.

Sophie and Keane intercepted each attack while Neil and Jory supported them with buffs, shields and healing. It was enough for the team to hold on but just barely, their mana being rapidly depleted as they used their abilities to the full. If it weren't for Jory delivering mana potions and Neil's replenishing spells, they would have already been exhausted and overrun. Jason was nowhere to be seen, although the patches of black flesh and the blood oozing from the monster's wounds marked his active presence.

"I see what you mean by smart being dangerous," Sophie said to Keane during a lull in the action. "They're starting to coordinate better."

The monsters were starting to attack all at once, or attack in rapid succession with little or no pause for the adventurers to regroup, attempting to break up their formation. The team had a strong defensive line and good individual synergies but the raw power of the bronze-rank monsters was beginning to beat them down.

A pair of the monsters hammered on Keane's shield, which began to buckle until one of the monsters abruptly stumbled away. Jason had cast a spell on it from the darkness.

Ability: [Punition] (Doom)
Spell
Cost: Moderate mana.
Cooldown: 30 seconds.

Current rank: Iron 6 (91%).

Effect (iron): Inflicts necrotic damage for each curse, disease, poison and unholy affliction the target is suffering.

While the bronze-rank monster had inherent damage reduction to Jason's iron-rank spell, that same damage reduction meant that the afflictions it was suffering from had time to multiplying without killing it. The spell, boosted for each one of those afflictions, ravaged the monster's body, even through the damage reduction. The monster staggered away as dead flesh replaced healthy, passing across the creature like a shadow. Jason finished it off with his execute ability.

Ability: [Verdict] (Doom)
Spell (execute)
Cost: Moderate mana.
Cooldown: 30 seconds.

Current rank: Iron 5 (38%)

Effect (iron): Deals a small amount of transcendent damage. As an execute effect, damage scales exponentially with the enemy's level of injury.

Shimmering light of blue, silver and gold shone down on the monster. Transcendent damage ignored the difference in rank and the creature dissolved directly into rainbow smoke.

You have defeated [Grizzard].

[Grizzard] has been wholly annihilated. It has been looted automatically.

[Monster Core (Bronze)] has been added to your inventory.
10 [Bronze Spirit Coins] have been added to your inventory.
100 [Iron Spirit Coins] have been added to your inventory.

The others ignored their share of the loot that fell over them, still caught up in the midst of combat. By the time the fight was over, they were battered, exhausted but grinning in triumph at having overcome such powerful enemies.

"That sparkle power," Keane said as they sprawled inside a building to hide from more monsters. "You should have been using that from the start with those flesh abominations."

"You're right," Jason said. "Those flesh abominations are hard to time it with, though. It's an execute power, so they need to be badly hurt for it to have any impact. Normally, you can see the condition a monster is in, but whatever the flesh things do to try and adapt to my afflictions hides their condition. I'm left just guessing."

"I like this interface power of yours," Keane said. "I can feel it when my abilities cross a threshold, obviously, but having it show up for me to see gives a real feeling of progress."

"We appreciate your powers too," Jory said to Keane. "Standing in front of me and taking all the hits is something I really like in a team member."

"Being able to take the hits is nice," Keane said, "but some hits I really wish I could dodge. I envy your ability to get out of the way, Sophie. Or into the way, as you need. I've had plenty of times where I'm wasn't fast enough to be where my team needed me to be. I hope they're doing alright without me."

"Huh," Clive said as a system notice appeared in front of him.

[Jory Tillman] has been added to your party.
[Imran Keane] has been added to your party.

"What's up?" Valdis asked.

"It looks like some of my friends have found each other," Clive said. "And someone new. It's good to know they're alright."

"That's a useful ability, working from that far away."

"A lot of its usefulness is lost at this distance. Better than nothing, though. At least it lets me know they're still alive."

Valdis nodded. "Far from a given, in this place."

After their traversal of the towering building, the other three members of their group were more respectful of Clive. He had proven himself multiple times, including identifying the hoard of growth items they had found at the top. Each member of the team had picked out one pair of items for themselves, from the six pairs. The rest of the team agreed that the last set should go to Clive, as the strongest contributor to actually obtaining them. That last pair was the orb and circlet, which weren't useful to Clive himself but he knew would be very useful to Neil.

After they climbed back down the building, they set off through the city again. Clive glanced back at the building behind them, then at Valdis.

"You remind me of a friend of mine," Clive told him.

"Oh?" Valdis asked.

"He's outgoing, like you. Good at pulling people into his own pace. You both a have a dangerous habit, though."

"And what's that?"

"You take risks, ignoring that it may be the people around you that suffer the consequences. My friend, for example, has this indentured servant he had become an adventurer."

"The outworlder," Valdis said. "The one who made that big fuss at the meeting. The indentured servant was that gorgeous celestine?"

"That's them," Clive said.

"I heard about how he had his indentured servant made into an adventurer. That's an unusual choice."

"He was trying to help her because she was a friend of a friend," Clive said. "Then he overestimated his own political acumen and almost handed her off into what amounts to sexual slavery. If you ask him, he'll say he did it because he sympathises with her circumstances. Really, though, I think he feels guilty over what he almost dropped her into."

"I would never do something like that to someone," Valdis said.

"No?" Clive asked. "Climbing up those towers, you didn't face any real risk, but Hildebrand was literally dropped off the building."

"But we got out, safe and sound, with no small reward for our trouble."

"This time," Clive said. "But how many times can you take that kind of risk without it going wrong? And when it does, will you be the one paying the price? My friend has done a lot of good for me. His enthusiasm helped me find the part of myself I'd lost that made me want to be an adventurer. In turn, I need to try and help him avoid making the kind of mistakes that will haunt him. Covering each other's weaknesses and blind spots is part of being a team."

Clive nodded his head at the other three, having their own conversation, further ahead.

"I hope your actual team isn't like them," Clive said. "They have skills, certainly, but you need people who'll tell you when you're wrong."

"I think I do," Valdis said, frowning. "There aren't a lot of people in my life who'll talk to me like this, though. I don't suppose I can talk you into changing teams?"

"I'm good, thank you," Clive said. "I'm pretty sure running around with an outworlder will give me plenty of chances to see some interesting things. Especially this outworlder."

54
MAKING A SPECTACLE OF HIMSELF

"We're getting closer to the centre," Jason said, looking at his map. "We could get there today if we went straight for it."

"That explains why we ran into so many groups yesterday," Neil said. "Everyone is converging."

"Do we go straight for the middle?" Jory asked. His abilities had been growing as fast as anyone else's, but that had never been his goal. He had gotten more than he could ask for with the alchemy recipe his previous group had come to blows over and was ready to leave the astral space. The lesser miracle potion formula would guarantee his clinic's funding in perpetuity.

"I like the training," Keane said. "It's like our own private monster surge, without innocent people getting caught up in it. I like the treasures we've been finding, too. That said, there are six days left. I vote we make for the middle and decide what to do after seeing what we find there."

Agreement with Keane's reasoning was unanimous and they set out directly for the heart of the city. The monsters, unsurprisingly, had no interest in accommodating their accelerated schedule and continued their regular attacks. They didn't stumble on anything more dangerous than they had previously encountered, however, and kept to their anticipated pace through the morning. They stopped for lunch, all sitting on the edge of a high building eating sandwiches.

"This is a good sandwich," Keane said. "I'm not sure why you brought food along, though. Spirit coins sustain us just fine and take up a lot less space."

"Sure," Jason said, "but of all the time you spend here, will you ever think back on that time you ate a spirit coin while trudging on? Of course not. You'll remember the crazy fights and the amazing treasure. The dashing affliction specialist with great hair. And now, you can look back on a quiet moment where you stopped to eat with friends and take in this amazing place. If this isn't what you became an adventurer for, then you're doing it wrong."

Keane looked at Jason, gazing at the city laid out before them with a contented smile. Keane turned to take in the view himself. With Jason's words he realised that he had been so caught up from the start that he'd never stopped to appreciate what he was experiencing.

When Keane arrived on the archway tower, he had been startled to be separated from his team. Then he had formed a temporary group, only to have them fragment over treasure. After that came this new group, more cohesive than the first but also more unusual in their sensibilities. The team leader was prone to nonsensical ramblings, the celestine was somehow his indentured servant and an adventurer. The healer seemed normal enough, but Jory, who Keane had been with the longest, didn't actually seem to like adventuring. That was a distinctly unusual position for an adventurer.

Since then, they had faced fight after fight, coming closer to death than he'd like more than once. In all that time, through losing one team, then a second, only to fight his way through with the strangest of the three, he had never taken the time to really stop and consider where he was and what he was doing. Now he took the time to look out over the city, which was actually quite beautiful with nature having reclaimed the ruins. He glanced at the people sitting with him on the rooftop, eating sandwiches like it was an ordinary day.

"I wish my team were here," he said.

"They are, somewhere," Jory said. "We get to the middle and you'll find each other."

They finished eating and resumed their course through the city. A few hours and a couple of monster packs later, a welcome message popped up in front of Jason.

- Contact [Niko Tomich] has entered communication range.
- Contact [Bethany Cavendish] has entered communication range.
- Contact [Hudson Kettering] has entered communication range.

Jason immediately opened a voice chat.

"Beth," Jason said. "Are you all alright?"

"We are," Beth's voice came back. "Niko and I were dropped on the same tower and we found Hudson along the way. No sign of Emily or Mose, yet. How about you?"

"Missing two as well: Clive and Humphrey. Want to meet up?"

"I do," Beth said. "We're kind of stuck here, anyway. There's a bunch of people all looking for a way to the centre of the city."

"Something's blocking the way?"

"Yeah. Come find us and you can see for yourself."

Jason added them to the party, allowing him to find her with his map ability. Not long thereafter, Jason and his group arrived at a sizeable camp of adventurers. From the looks of it, some of them had been here for days. The wariness the adventurers had been treating each other with was absent here. All were looking to find a way forward.

The Greenstone adventurers were easy to pick out from the imports, just from their auras. The foreign adventurers had clean, controlled auras. Outside of Jason and Beth's groups, most Greenstone adventurers had shoddy aura control at best.

"What's going on?" Jason asked, after greetings and introductions between their teams.

"Some kind of plant monster infestation," Beth explained. "Anyone trying to get closer to the city centre than this is faced with tentacles and plant monsters crawling out of the ground. People have tried going around, but the infestation seems to be encircling most of, if not the entire the central region of the city."

"How do you know it's encircling the central area and not covering it entirely?" Jory asked.

"We don't," Beth said. "We're just hoping, because otherwise, how is anyone going to complete these trials. A few groups have tried fighting their way through, but we have no idea if they made it or if they're mulch, now. We know from the people who've tried going around that there are a few camps like this one, with people gathered to see if anyone can figure out a way through. Assuming there's a way through at all."

Quest: [Reclaimed by Nature]

Plant life has not just reclaimed this part of the city but actively defends it. Find a way past the aggressive flora to reach the heart of the city.

Objective: Circumvent aggressive plant life 0/1.

Reward: Varies by effectiveness of method.

Some party members are too far away to participate in this quest. They will not receive this quest until they re-enter proximity to party leader.

"What the heck is that?" Beth asked.

"That's Jason's ability," Sophie said. "He gets free stuff for doing what he was going to do anyway. It's basically a scam."

"I can drop you out of the party if you don't want to participate," Jason said.

"I can drop you off a building," Sophie told him.

"I can float down, remember?"

"Not if I knock you out first."

"Look, I love some sexually charged banter as much the next girl," Beth said, "but we have a bunch of plant monsters to deal with."

While Jason and Sophie looked at Beth with matching expressions of silent affront, Beth turned her attention to Jory.

"You're an alchemist, right? Plant monsters can often be handled with alchemical solutions. Is there anything you can do?"

"Maybe," Jory said. "I'll need to know what we're dealing with before I can look at solutions."

"There are a lot of impressive adventurers, here," Neil said. "I have to imagine someone knows something."

"There's a little council, of sorts," Beth said. "Each team sends one or two people to discuss a way past it. People are trying all sorts of things, so we've been meeting every few hours to talk about results."

"How's that going?" Jason asked.

"It's a bunch of adventurers used to getting their own way, so about as well as you'd expect."

"Jory," Jason said. "You're about as close to a plant expert as we'll get. Beth, can you take us around to people with firsthand knowledge of this thing?"

"I can," Beth said. "I told you that some groups have tried to make it through. Some didn't come back, so we don't know if they succeeded. Others tried and came back when things got too rough."

Jason nodded his thanks, and suggested the rest his group ask around, see what they could find out. While the others roamed the camp, Beth took Jason and Jory to speak to some of the other teams. Jory took notes on anything they could tell them. After speaking to enough teams that they were just getting the same information over again, they regrouped to take stock.

"What do you think?" Jason asked Jory.

"This is potentially very bad," Jory said.

"How so?" Beth asked.

"I think what we're dealing with might not be plant monsters," Jory said. "I've heard of something like what's been described to us before, and that wasn't a monster at all. It was a magical plant."

"You think these plants have taken over this section of city?" Keane asked.

"Not plants," Jory said. "Plant, singular. One single, massive plant mass, buried underground and sending up parts of itself to find prey."

"Prey?" Neil asked. "Since when are plants predatory?"

"I've heard of predatory plants," Jason said. "The ones on my world are small, though. They lure in bugs, that kind of thing."

"The one I'm thinking of is bigger," Jory said. "Much bigger. It takes centuries, but they have been known to grow to the size we're looking at, here. It thrives underground, slowly expanding. It forms symbiotic relationships with the other plant life in the area, which become like sensory organs for it. Then its starts preying on anything that wanders into its area. Animals quickly learn to avoid it and it goes dormant. It lets the animals come back, waits until the area is teeming, then strikes. Tentacle vines and spawned, semi-independent plant creatures."

"And you think this is what we're dealing with?" Jason asked.

"I can't know that for sure," Jory said. "It's what I can think of that fits."

"You think this whole section of city has a giant plant monster under it? One monster?"

"Not a monster," Jory said. "We know from the people who fought them that the spawned plant creatures are iron-rank, while the tentacles, which will be appendages of the main body, are bronze rank. No bronze-rank monster spawns that big, or occupying that much space underground."

"What's it called?" Jason asked.

"It's called a blood root vine," Jory said. "It's named that because it straddles the line between plant and animal, with its predatory behaviour and blood sap. That was what really gave it away, when people started saying the tentacles bled when cut. The sap of a blood root vine is almost identical to blood and has a number of alchemical uses. Most of the big ones you hear about are from alchemist grow houses that were abandoned and the blood root vine slowly expanded until someone found it again. It's a story that goes around in alchemy circles but you never actually expect to see it."

"So, what do we do about it?" Beth asked.

"Assuming I'm right," Jory said, "the key is the main body. That means an underground root network. From what I hear, when clearing out a blood root vine that's gotten out of hand, there's two ways of handling it. One is to dig the whole damn thing up and burn it. That's logistically infeasible, especially in five days. I have heard, however, of another method. A method we have the good fortune to have on hand."

Jory turned a pointed look on Jason.

"Me?" Jason asked.

"You," Jory said. "I can't guarantee the authenticity of this story, but I have heard of using afflictions to infect the main body and rot the whole thing. You have to get underground, at the root system itself, though. If you just try it on the tentacles, it will let the tentacles fall off to protect itself."

"We've already tried that," Beth said. "There's a few people in camp who can use afflictions, including me. We blasted a chunk out of the ground and poured every affliction we had into the roots. They withered up, but it didn't spread."

"Were any of you focused affliction specialists, like Jason, or were they all area abilities like yours?" Jory asked.

"Area, like me," Beth said. "Not to put you down, Jason, but who afflicts one person when you can affect whole groups."

"That's your problem," Jory said. "We're talking about a plant spread over an area the size of Old City. The afflictions you fed it were like trying to turn the sea yellow by taking a sneaky wee in it. You need afflictions that grow worse and worse, faster and faster, instead of petering out."

"Will my afflictions even work on it?" Jason asked. "We've seen a few plant monsters since we got here and my abilities have been inconsistent on them."

"They should," Jory said. "As I said, the blood root vine is more akin to animals than other plants."

"Blood is one thing," Jason said, "but to get the kind of damage escalation we need, I'll need my curses. That requires a soul, or at least the motive spirit most monsters have instead of one."

"I can't guarantee anything," Jory said, "but once it reaches a certain size, it even has a dim, animalistic intelligence. Hopefully it's close enough to an animal that there is something inside it for your curses to told hold of."

"And if it doesn't?"

"Then we get out and come up with something new," Beth said. "Unless you have a better plan, we may as well try."

"The trick will be getting access to the root system," Jory said. "You said you had someone who can open up a hole in the ground?"

They all turned to Hudson, the large man who served as the front-liner for Beth's team. He had been staying quiet through the conversation, leaving things like planning to Beth. His earth powers were the most prominent abilities in his power set.

"It's not me," he said. "I have the earth essence, but not a hole-digging power."

"It was another earth user," Beth said. "We can get her again."

"Alright," Jason said. "Beth, talk to this council you mentioned. See if you can't find us some extra muscle to fight our way in with. Jory and I will try and get more specific about what we can expect when we try this."

"What about the rest of us?" Keane asked.

"Get some rest," Jory said. "This thing will be relentless in fighting back against us. You'll need all the stamina you can muster."

The group they gathered had twenty-six members, including the five from Jason's group and three from Beth's. Keane had found a member of his own team in the camp and pulled him into the endeavour, along with that team member's own temporary group. Aside from that was another earth essence user and a few more people Beth had wrangled into participating.

The region of the city occupied by the plant was more overgrown than other parts of the city. The buildings were mostly rubble, the paved streets long overturned by roots and other plant growth. As they moved into the area, tentacle vines crawled out to the ground to ensnare legs, thorns covered in soporific toxin biting through skin. The team fought back, cutting away vines as healers purged the poison, a task in which Jason participated using his own cleansing power. It was highly effective, although the way Jason consumed the cleansed afflictions did not go unnoticed.

"Did you just say 'feed me your sins?'" another adventurer asked him.

"There's a lot of people chanting spells," Jason said. "You probably misheard."

A variety of plant creatures came shambling into the attack. Plodding mounds of fibrous matter whipped at them with tentacle arms. They weren't very dangerous but they were tough, their numbers swelling as the group struggled to put them down as fast as new one appeared.

"This should be far enough!" Jory yelled after he determined that they should have made their way over the root system.

"Alright!" Beth called out. "Everyone knows what to do. Gather on me!"

The group pulled in tight on Beth as Hudson, beside her, started casting a spell. Shortly after, a stone dome rose up out of the ground in two halves, closing over them. As it sealed them in, crystals embedded in the dome lit up the interior with luminescence.

The other earth user called for more room and the people inside the dome moved up against the walls. The creatures outside were shut out, but tentacles still came up through the ground. Beth designated a team to protect the earth user while she used her spell to dig. Her spell did not take long and soon gobbets of wet earth were geysering out of the ground and over everyone inside the dome.

"Sorry," she called out. "I don't normally do this indoors."

With the earth user's spell completed, Jason glanced at Jory, who nodded back. Jason then walked up to the hole, even as more tentacles crawled from the ground to attack the people under the dome. Beth directed the people who had been shielding the earth user to switch their protection to Jason. The hole was a vertical tunnel from which the wet ground had been excavated. Left behind, scraped but intact by the digging spell, were thick roots, looking like thick green and yellow veins.

"Moment of truth," he muttered to himself. Loaded up with every buff the whole group could muster, he chanted a spell.

"*Bleed for me.*"

A crack appeared on the thickest root, blood red sap trickling out. The sap was, as Jory surmised, close enough to blood that Jason's ability took hold.

Special attack [Haemorrhage] has inflicted [Bleeding] on [Blood Root Vine].

"Now the real test."

He chanted another spell.

"*Carry the mark of your transgressions.*"

Spell [Castigate] has inflicted [Sin] on [Blood Root Vine].
Spell [Castigate] has inflicted [Mark of Sin] on [Blood Root Vine].
[Blood Root Vine] have resisted [Mark of Sin].
[Mark of Sin] does not take effect.

Transcendent damage burned a symbol into the root as the spell took hold. The bronze-rank vine resisted one of the effects, even with all the buffs Jason was under, but it was the one Jason didn't need. He let out a relieved breath, then remembered he couldn't afford to relax as a thorny vine wrapped around his leg.

Special attack [Vine Thorn] has inflicted [Subjugating Toxin] on you.
You have resisted [Subjugating Toxin].
[Subjugating Toxin] does not take effect.
You have gained an instance of [Resistant].

Before Jason could cut away the vine, one of his protectors had done it for him.

"Need a cleanse?" the man asked.

"All good, thanks," Jason said, turning his attention back to the hole.

He cast another curse on the vine, which it resisted, then a second and third time before it took hold.

[Inexorable Doom] has inflicted [Inexorable Doom] on [Blood Root Vine].

Jason held out a hand, then sliced it with his wrist razor. Leeches went spilling down into the hole.

"Sorry to drop you in a hole, Colin. See if you can't suck some blood out of that vine."

At another of the adventurer camps around the aggressive plant zone, Clive and Valdis watched a heavily injured group retreat from the danger zone.

"I think you were right to urge caution, Clive," Valdis said. "It looks like something has set the vines right off."

Previously, the tentacles would only emerge from the ground to attack intruders. Now, however, they were erupting from all over the ground, thrashing about wildly.

"I think something is happening to them," Clive said. "Are you seeing those black patches?"

"I am."

They watched as the black patches grew larger, some vines even rotting and falling dead to the ground.

In another part of the city, Humphrey and his temporary team were deep into the territory of the aggressive vines. Their intention had been to fight their way through, but the deeper they went, the more plant monsters and tentacles appeared to meet them. They were a powerful group but they were slowly being overwhelmed.

"Do we keep pushing forward, or go back?" Carly called out, panic tinging her voice.

"Forward," Lowell called back. "There has to be an end to it. We could be almost clear."

"There's no guarantee of that," Humphrey countered. "We go back."

"We can't make it back," Lowell objected. "We have to risk it."

"No, we don't." Humphrey held firm, not pausing as he hacked away at the tentacles. "Our chances may be slight but at least we know there is one if we go back."

The tentacles grew more and more numerous but flailed wildly, rather than grab at the adventurers as they had done previously.

"What's happening?" Carly asked.

"Something's rotting the tentacles," Lowell said. He pointed to where the tentacles were turning black from the base. Some rotted away and dropped dead, even as more emerged from the ground. Then a silver, blue and gold light lit up all the tentacles, dissolving them to nothing. As it did, the plant monsters became inert collections of plant matter.

"Was that transcendent damage?" Carly asked.

"It was," Humphrey said.

They looked around. Whatever had destroyed the plants around them had affected everything within sight. Hurt and exhausted, they dropped to the ground to rest.

"What do you think did that?" Carly asked.

"Not what. Who," Humphrey said with a smile. "I know who did this."

"You're telling us some iron ranker did all this?" Lowell asked.

"I know these powers," Humphrey said. "They belong to a man who can't help making a spectacle of himself. Thankfully."

55
TEAM CHANGE

Only seven groups had managed to breach the centremost region of the city before the blood root vine had been killed. One was made up of people with flight powers. Such abilities were mana intensive at iron-rank, requiring them to chug mana potions as quickly as they could without poisoning themselves and stopping to rest atop every building not reduced to rubble by the plants.

Another was made up of adventurers from a jungle kingdom who had managed to find their entire original team. They had come up as adventurers fighting plant monsters and decided to bet on their abilities and experience to get them through. It was even worse than they expected—a seemingly endless, unrelenting slog until they finally reached ground not bursting with tentacle vines. They were hurt and exhausted, their willpower and supplies both spent. It was a near thing, but their experience, teamwork and mutual trust had seen them through.

Of the five remaining groups to get past the plants, all had found methods to do so when searching buildings around the perimeter of the zone. For some, this was an active search. Having concluded that the plants were a part of the test, they reasoned that the means to pass it had to be somewhere. For others it was serendipity, stumbling onto a way past the plants while searching for treasure.

Only two of the groups had come through in the original teams they had before entering the astral space. Separated at the start of the trial, like everyone else, they had found each other in one of the camps. One of these teams included Padma, Farrah's former mentee. Filled with determination after finding one another, they had no illusions of fighting their way through and looked for another path. Their intensive searching finally turned up an abandoned alchemy workshop, containing bottles of a liquid that repelled the plants.

However they arrived, each group was elated to have made it past the aggressive plants. Their efforts were difficult and costly but they knew that same difficulty made each team who struggled through more likely to be the ones who snatched the prize. It was largely to their dismay, then, that other teams started reaching the middle en masse, mostly in waves from the three camps. It quickly became evident that one of the camps had found a way to kill off the plants entirely.

Compared to the rest of the city the adventurers had been making their way through, the true centre of the city was more intact. The buildings were still empty, time and the wet air corroding away anything not magically sealed. It was also a relatively small area, allowing separated team members to reconnect as the three camps' worth of adventurers swarmed in.

All the adventurers ended up in what Jason's map marked as the very centre of the city. There was a vast open space, like a city square, with a circular tower in the middle. This was the only building in the city with no signs of damage whatsoever and was both wide and tall. Every adventurer who attempted to get close to the tower encountered a disorienting magical field which sent them staggering back. This was even true if approaching from above—one flier got injured as the field tossed them away through the air. The invigilator, Shade, finally appeared to announce that the tower would open on the final day of the trials, several days hence.

Previous conflicts were largely put aside as the adventurers arrived in the square. People found their original teams, even as they celebrated new bonds, forged in the fires of shared adversity. Not every reunion was happy, as someone started organising the counting of the fallen. Those who had collected remains returned them to their teams, where possible. Some teams had fallen entirely, while others lacked the resources to carry the caskets of their dead.

Others weren't dead but gone, having used their escape medallions to preserve their lives at the cost of further participation in the trials. Shade appeared to inform teams which of their members had escaped to safety. While many of the adventurers were able to reconstitute their teams, others were once again looking for new companions in the face of their original teams being absent or dead. Some, left alone, gave up and used their escape medallions to leave the astral space behind.

Humphrey's team staggered into the city, ragged from their narrow escape. If it wasn't for Humphrey hacking through the plants like a maniacal, magically empowered lumberjack, they wouldn't have survived to see their reprieve as the plant monster died. Heading into the city, afterward, they had collected the bodies of two separate groups that had died trying the same crossing.

The group, aside from Humphrey, was four of a team of six, and had the luck to mostly arrive in the city together. They thanked Humphrey, sober in the knowledge that without him they would have been amongst the fallen. Lowell had lost much of his arrogance on their trek through the city. Humphrey still didn't like him, but they shared the respect of dangers weathered together. The group set out to find their remaining team members in the growing crowd as Humphrey went to find Jason and the others.

Clive, Valdis and the rest of their temporary team arrived in a far better state than Humphrey. After the dangers of the tower, Clive had won the rest of the team over against Valdis's proposal to fight their way through. Clive had proposed seeking out alternate means forward but the plant zone had cleared before they had the chance. They had an easy time passing through the rubble of what had previously been the plant-infested region. They were wary of danger, but the surviving jungle was made up of regular plant life. It was even monster-free, courtesy of the now-dead carnivorous plant.

Clearing the zone, Clive was glad to hear from his team over voice chat. He announced his intention go find them, signalling the end of their temporary alliance. Each member of the group was from a different team and had their own people to find, but Abarca, Campos and Hildebrand were reluctant to part from Valdis. Their teaming with the prince was an opportunity they were loath to relinquish, each seeking to secure promises of meeting up after the trials. Valdis, clearly no stranger to such encounters, saw them each away smoothly. He, in turn, secured a promise of future dealings from Clive.

Jason already had two of his team members, thus waited for Humphrey and Clive to find them. Keane, who now had one of his own team with them, made friendly farewells before they went to find the rest. Jory was about to head off and seek out his own team, who were all fellows from the various crafting associations. Shade promptly appeared to inform him that every other member of his team had used their escape medallions, so Jory remained with Jason.

There was only an hour or so of good light left. There were days left to seek out the city's treasures and everyone took what was left of the day to reorganise. Adventurers reconnected with their teams, collected their dead and sometimes made new teams again. Many teams had members who were dead or, for preference, safely extracted via escape medallion. As when they first arrived, then, temporary teams were built from the scraps of those that remained.

Jason had the fortune to have all his team survive to regroup. As he used his map and the voice chat power to collect his team, he did the same for Beth Cavendish's absent team members. They were the archer, Emily, and Beth's cousin Mose, who had both arrived safely in the heart of the city.

Many groups were staking out territory around the square. Jason and Beth's team did the same while waiting for their disparate members to find them. Groups were rapidly claiming the largely intact buildings that were closest and they picked out a five-storey building that turned out to be a square around an open space in the middle. The courtyard inside meant that every floor of the building was splashed with natural light.

As they were taking stock, another group entered and tried to bully them into giving it up. Beth and Jason went outside to meet their challenge. One of the team went pale when Jason manifested his cloak, and turned to whisper rapidly to the others. Jason and Beth shared a querying glance as they watch the group mutter in a huddle. The one who had recognised Jason's cloak was using some aggressive body language to make his point.

"What are they saying?" Jason asked quietly. "You have that elf ears power, right?"

"It's not an elf ears power!" Beth hissed back at him.

"Yeah, but you have it, right?"

"I can hear them, yes."

"So, what are they saying?"

"They're talking about that ridiculous rumour about you killing a bunch of adventurers in a shopping centre."

"Oh?"

"He's claiming you killed six people."

"It was only five," Jason said. "I bet people think six because there were twelve of them and people just say I killed half."

"Wait," Beth asked, turning on Jason. "That actually happened?"

"You didn't know? Thadwick sent some bottom-feeder thugs to kill me so I wouldn't reveal his shady land-grab scheme."

"So you killed them?"

"Some of them," Jason said defensively. "If you're fighting twelve guys and they think you aren't willing to kill them, they aren't going to back off."

"You really beat twelve guys?"

"They were all rubbish," Jason said. "I don't think any of them even had a full set of powers."

"You don't have a full set of powers."

"Yeah, but they didn't know that."

"What does that have to do with…"

Beth trailed off as the other group finished their conversation.

"My friend here thinks you're some kind of hard man," one of them challenged Jason.

"Doesn't really matter what I am," Jason said. "My friend Humphrey is standing behind you with a sword bigger than you are, so I suggest you jog on, cobber."

The man turned to find Humphrey standing there, as promised, with his dragon-wing sword slung over one shoulder.

"Yeah well," the man said as he shuffled off to leave, waving a finger at Jason with transparent bravado. "You should count yourself lucky."

"Why?" Jason asked. "Are you holding a raffle?"

They watched the group leave, Humphrey dismissing his sword with relief.

"I hate putting it over my shoulder like that," he said. "It feels like I'm going to tip over the whole time."

"It was just right," Jason said. "Casually intimidating, like you might kick the snot out of them as a hobby."

"You do have very large arms," Beth said.

"They are quite large, aren't they?" Jason said. "Do you do any special exercises?"

"We train together," Humphrey said, giving him a flat look. "You know exactly what exercises I do."

"So, you're saying you rub special oil on them when no one's looking?"

"What?"

Jason dropped his cloak and headed back into the building, calling out loudly.

"Hey Jory! Have you been selling Humphrey special arm oil?"

Three more teams joined Jason and Beth's in the building they shared. Valdis was his bombastic self, inviting himself and his team in as Clive tried to explain the foreign prince to the others.

"Imagine Jason, but if his father was a diamond rank king," Clive said, as Valdis was already picking out rooms for his people.

"There's two of them?" Neil asked. "I'm going up on the roof."

Neil made himself scarce and Valdis was happily introducing himself, picking each person out from Clive's descriptions. A celestine woman on Valdis's team, Sigrid, was quietly apologising for him.

"No worries," Jason told her. "If Clive says he's alright, it's fine."

"Don't blame me for this," Clive said. "I never said it was fine."

Jason and Sigrid both looked at him.

"Okay, it's fine," Clive conceded. "He's just, you know, a lot. One of you is bad enough."

"Indentured servant," Valdis was saying as he greeted Sophie with enthusiasm. "That's strange. It's not rude to say that, right? I mean, it is strange. Look at me, though. It's not like being a prince with an eight-hundred-year-old father is normal."

"Yeah," Sophie said, "but one is strange in that people give you everything you could possibly want and the other is strange in that people keep trying to give me to sleazy men."

"I can see how that's different," Valdis said. "Now that you say it, though, I have heard some stories about the prince of Calute and a rather unconventional cattle market—"

"Val," Sigrid said pointedly, cutting him off.

"Right, yes. Not meant to talk about that. Lovely to meet you though."

The next group to find them and more politely ask to share accommodation was Keane's. Keane's team leader was clearly in two minds, but Keane had been insistent. On discovering the presence of Prince Valdis, Keane's team became significantly more enthused.

The last team to join was that of Padma. The team from Vitesse had already been in the city when most of the teams arrived and had heard a lot of stories while everyone else was reorganising themselves. Padma was keen to hear more about Farrah from Jason and had convinced her team to ask if they could share the building.

That made for thirty-one adventurers, turning the otherwise excessive five-story building into a comfortable fit. With so many people, Jason decided to have an impromptu celebration for reaching the centre of the city and recruited Valdis to get everyone involved. Shortly thereafter, all five groups were on top of the roof, music playing courtesy of a recording crystal from Valdis's collection.

"I kind of just wanted to sleep," Beth said.

"I think everyone just wanted to sleep," Humphrey said.

"So why are we having a party?"

"We were outvoted by Jason and the prince."

"How do two people outvote twenty-nine?"

"I'm not sure," Humphrey said, "but I think we may need to keep those two apart."

56

COMPANY WORTH KEEPING

Since they were the impetus for the rooftop party, Jason and Valdis provided the supplies. Jason set up a buffet, putting out a couple of tables, an array of large bowls full of food, tongs and a stack of plates. He also laid out a good supply of drinks, tapping casks of wine, beer and mead.

"I've only got a dozen mugs," he announced, "so I hope you all have something to drink out of."

Valdis raided the dimensional space of his offsider, Sigrid, from which he retrieved a small sea of cushions so no one was left sitting on the hard, stone roof. He also supplied glow-stones as the day's light died and recording crystals full of music. Jason and Valdis stood side by side, looking over the setup with satisfaction.

The thirty adventurers were mingling, all sharing the exhaustion after traversing the city. Beth's cousin, Mose, approached Jason and Valdis, standing next to them to likewise survey their efforts.

"Not bad for an ancient city in the middle of a sealed-off astral space, right Mose?" Jason asked happily.

"This is what you brought to explore an astral space that had been home to an ancient order of assassins?" Mose asked.

Jason and Valdis shared a nodding glance.

"Yep," Jason said.

"Getting your priorities right is important in the adventuring game," Valdis added.

Of the five teams, Valdis's was the most standoffish. They were clearly unsure why Valdis chose to camp with local teams over more well-known groups. Sigrid took him aside to advocate making connections with the more prominent teams. She knew full well the futility of trying to direct him, but if she started early, then he might actually start to listen sometime in the next few days.

"I'm a prince of the Mirror Kingdom," Valdis told her. "If I want to meet big-name adventurers, I can do that any time."

"Val, it isn't about meeting," Sigrid told him. "It's about making connections."

"Agreed," Valdis told her, laughing again. "Here's the thing, Sig. You make connections when someone's already a big deal and they just become someone you know. Make the connection when they're a nobody and they become a friend."

"Correct me if I'm wrong, but you only really know one of these people, right? What makes you think they're worth making friends with?"

"Call it an instinct," Valdis said. "I've spent enough time with Clive to get a sense of the company he keeps and it's company worth keeping. Danielle Geller's son is here; you can't complain about that. And that Asano is worth keeping an eye on. Dangerous, that one."

"Really?" Sigrid asked, casting a sceptical look in Jason's direction.

"Tell me this, Sig," Valdis said. "You have two men who carve through people like a butcher with slabs of meat, taking on opponents in job lots and leaving seas of blood behind them. Both have mastered murderous skills that kill quickly and horrifying powers that kill slowly. One of those men spends his days dressed all in black, barely speaking. The sobriety of a killer. The other cleans himself off, has a nice meal with his friends and gets a good night's sleep. Which of those two men would you keep an eye on?"

"You seem fairly certain about someone you just met."

"He's like me, I can feel it," Valdis said. "The way he watches people. The way he seems to be off-kilter but is actually controlling. I'm not sure he even realises how much he's doing it. There's something dark inside that boy and he doesn't want it to be who he is. I know that feeling. Ask around and I bet you'll find he's dropped bodies that weren't monsters."

"I already have," Sigrid said. "And he has. Should I keep an eye on him?"

"No, just tell the boys to behave. He's not intimidated by my background."

"He should be."

"Be nice, Sig. Outworlders make good friends and terrible enemies."

Night fell and they activated the glow-stones they set up earlier. Thirty-one tired adventurers, stuffed with food and plied with drinks, lounged on the cushions in the warm night air. With full bellies and full cups, Valdis's team had finally loosened up as well.

"Mr Asano," Valdis said, calling out across the group with exaggerated, drunken pomp.

"Your royal princeness," Jason greeted back.

"I have heard tell," Valdis said, "that the rather inconvenient plant monsters we encountered were, in fact, a single, giant entity. I've also heard that you are the one that killed it."

"It wasn't, strictly speaking, a monster," Jason said evenly. He had bronze rank booze he could have used to get drunk but didn't want to risk the hangover. "As for being the one who killed it, I was just one member of a very large group. If it had just been down to me, we'd all still be in the outer city, scratching our bums."

"But your abilities were what destroyed it."

"It was just a lucky confluence of enemy and the specific nature of my abilities," Jason said. "It could just as easily have been completely immune."

"I'm more interested in the treasure you got from it," Emily said. The archer from Beth's team hadn't been present to participate, but had heard about the shared quest from her teammates. Niko, the smoulder from Beth's team who had been present, laughed.

"You should have seen everyone's faces," he said. "One moment we're fighting for our lives against all these thorny tentacles, and the next, treasure starts falling out of the air. A bunch of items, even essences. I got hit in the head by a whole sack of plant quintessence gems. A sack! It was crazy."

"People got a bit crabby that we were the only ones who got loot," Neil said. "Jason ended up sharing out the spirit coins. The ones that everyone saw, anyway. Those of us with dimensional spaces split the extra between just our teams after."

"Why don't we do a little showing off?" Beth suggested. "I'll start."

She stood up, picking up the dimensional bag next to her. She withdrew a long robe, and held it in front of her. It was green and brown with a forest motif, hanging like a dress. the colours setting off the pretty elf woman's tawny skin, chestnut hair and vibrant green eyes.

"Bronze-rank spellcaster robe," she said with a bright smile. "It enhances plant abilities and poison."

"Sorry, where did this come from?" asked Lance, the leader of Padma's team. "A looting power?"

"Neil and I both have looting abilities," Jason said, cutting off anyone from giving more of his abilities away.

The people who had participated in the plant monster raid went around one at a time, revealing their haul from the quest to get past the plant. The results of not just bypassing the plant but eliminating it entirety had made for impressive compensation. There were sets of armour, weaponry and items that affected essence abilities, usually with some kind of plant aspect. Hudson, the earth-essence user from Beth's team, had received a wrist band that looked like a looped vine and added effects to his earth conjuration powers. Jason had looted a similar-looking vine wrist band that could produce a variety of vine conjurations.

All the magical equipment was bronze rank, like the plant creature, so none of them could use theirs yet. Instead, they had a jump on useful items for when they ranked-up. Then there were the essences. Jason took out a pair of green cubes and set them down in front of where he sat, cross-legged, on his cushion. They were both green, one ephemeral and swirling, like the cube was full of liquid. The other was appeared more solid, like an opal with a rich green colour as its base underpinned by lush, overlapping shades of darker green.

"Plant and growth essences," Jason said. "Both fairly common."

"Wasn't there a third one?" Beth asked.

"Indeed there was," Jason said, taking a third cube from his inventory with a flourish and laying it next to the others. It was the blue of an open summer sky, complete with clouds that seemed to float through the cube.

"Vast essence," Jason said. "This one's as rare as they come."

"How much do you want for it?" Valdis said immediately, eagerly leaning forward.

"What do you say, Clive?" Jason asked. "Should we cut him a deal?"

"Gods, no," Clive said. "Bilk him for everything you can."

The group broke up into laughter at the exaggerated look of affront Valdis turned on Clive. The loot reveal continued as everyone showed off their hauls from their journey through the city, accompanied by stories of the tribulations faced to get those treasures.

The storytelling culminated with Valdis and Clive retelling their tower ascent and the items they found at the top. Valdis regaled them in the form of an epic saga, Clive drawing laughs as he periodically interjected with more grounded descriptions. Finally their story reached the incredible find of growth items at the base of the buildings statues, and Valdis pointed out to Clive that it was exactly the kind of haul he had told them would be there.

They ended the story with a presentation to an incredulous Neil of the last pair of items. The first was a fist-sized orb and the other a circlet of gold with a blue gem set into the forehead. With Jason's ability, Neil could immediately see their effects. He started by looking over the orb.

Item: [Sentinel's Orb] (iron rank [growth], legendary)
***An object with the power to refine barrier energy to its most perfect form* (tool, orb).**
Effect: Increase the effect of shield-based essence abilities.
Effect: Cooldown of shield-based essence abilities is reduced.
Effect: If wielding both [Sentinel's Orb] and [Sentinel's Crown], your shield abilities bestow a heal-over-time effect.

"Well, that's just ridiculous," he said, then looked at the circlet.

Item: [Sentinel's Crown] (iron rank [growth], legendary)
***The headpiece of the king of guardians* (accessory, circlet).**

Effect: Mana recovery is increased. Mana recovery rate is increased briefly after using a shield-based essence ability.
Effect: Mana cost of shield-based essence abilities is reduced.
Effect: If wielding both [Sentinel's Orb] and [Sentinel's Crown], your shield abilities bestow a mana-over-time effect.

"And so is that," he said, looking up at Clive. "You can't just give me these."

"Of course I can," Clive said, as if it were the most obvious thing in the world. "You're on our team."

Neil looked around at his other team members. Humphrey nodded encouragingly. Jason had the usual, self-satisfied grin that gave Neil a near-constant urge to punch him in the face. Sophie simply shrugged.

"Thank you," Neil said to Clive. "Really, thank you."

"Pay us back by keeping us alive," Clive said.

"And you'll need to buy some new clothes," Jason said. "A gold headband with a honking great gem in the middle is a bold look. You're going to have to dress around it."

The next day saw adventurers washing through the city centre like a flood. The more intact nature of the buildings would seem to indicate more remnant treasure but a day of teams discovering nothing more than a few essences and awakening stones between them proved otherwise. The teams in Jason's building did not participate in the day's searching, in no small part due to hangovers. Valdis had been eager to participate but his team was loyal rather than obedient—they collectively told him to shove off before crawling back into their camp bedding.

Those who had weathered the night's festivities better were still exhausted. There had been days of every moment not spent fighting still holding themselves in full combat readiness. They were happy to join the hungover, staying inside their bedrolls until the sun was high in the sky. In the late morning there was group meditation session on the roof; Valdis led a dozen adventurers through a sword-dance meditation, much like the one Rufus had taught Jason. Given the athletic attractiveness of adventurers in general, Jason felt like he'd somehow joined a group of models doing tai chi in the park.

The adventurers that had scoured the central city shared the fruitlessness of their search as they mingled in the tower square in the evening. Most teams would be searching further afield the following day, returning to the outer city where treasure hunting that had proven more rewarding.

Jason and Beth's teams elected to stay put, waving off Keane, Padma and Valdis's teams in their "quest for epic loot." Rather than risk something else happening, Jason and Beth's groups chose to spend their time recovering their best form before the final trials unlocked.

Beth, Humphrey, Jason, Clive and Neil were spending a languid afternoon in the shade of their building's top level. They were sat by a window on some cushions Valdis had left behind after the party. The side of the building was open as if there was a missing bay window, allowing them to look out at the central tower within which the final challenges of the trials were located. From the roof above, they could hear Sophie practising with the rest of Beth's team.

"Why do you think all the rest of the trials only become available on the last day?" Beth pondered.

"Clearly, the city itself is the core component of the trial," Humphrey said. "I assume the tower has more direct, specific tests. Shade did tell us at the start that the purpose of the trials was to test for five virtues. Choosing whether or not to take the items he offered was the first trial and reaching the tower was the second. Presumably there are three trials remaining, inside the tower."

"I'm curious about the next one," Neil said. "The trial for those who chose courage is meant to be easier, now. I didn't use the items Shade gave me. It makes me wish I hadn't taken them."

"I don't know about that," Jason said. "We all took bold steps to make it this far. Would we have, if we didn't have some life-saving protections? Even with them, people died. I'm not sure I would have been willing to take the risks I took without them."

"Did any of you choose the courage path?" Clive asked. "I know Valdis did."

The others all shook their heads.

As the sun set, Shade appeared before them.

"Greetings, adventurers. I am appearing before you all to announce that the second trial is coming to an end in one day. Anyone present in the tower square at the centre of the city when the sun goes down tomorrow will pass. Those who have not reached it at that time may leave by escape medallion. Those who do not have the medallions will be provided with them. They must be used before the trials completely close, however, or you will be trapped inside. As a final note, the reward for the second trial will be granted tomorrow as the second trial concludes."

"One more day," Humphrey said. "It was good to relax and recover, but should we join the treasure hunting tomorrow?"

"Bad idea," Sophie said, coming down some nearby stairs. She was covered in sweat and poured herself a glass of juice from the refreshments Jason had set out.

"It's not just the last day for treasure," she continued after a hearty swig. "It's also the last day to quietly remove the competition. Either way, there's a good chance we'd have to kill some people before they killed us if we went out there. I'd rather stay here."

"Perhaps we could socialise with the other adventurer groups who stayed behind, like us," Humphrey said. "Most of my family's teams occupied a couple of buildings not far from here and some of the other foreign adventurers were nearby."

"Not the worst idea," Beth said. "I'm curious about this trial reward, though. What do you think?"

"Specialty equipment, maybe?" Clive postulated. "This place was originally a trial ground for assassin trainees, right? It would make sense that they would receive some kind of reward for joining the order, like a uniform or something."

"Would secret assassins have uniforms?" Neil asked.

"Probably not, now you say it," Clive conceded.

"Awakening stones," Jason said. "I'm certain Emir knows more than he told us and he implied to me more than once that there would be a chance at some unusual awakening stones."

"That makes sense," Clive said, sitting up enthusiastically. "The great astral beings can't make essences the way that gods can, but they can produce their own awakening stones."

"I have no interest in divine essences and awakening stones," Jason said. "The idea of some god repossessing my magic powers doesn't appeal."

"No, that's the interesting thing," Clive said. "The stones the astral beings produce aren't divine stones that the astral beings can revoke. They're just ordinary awakening stones whose aspect aligns with the great astral being in question. I've used some of them myself, although the Celestial Book is a lot more approachable than the Reaper. The question is, what kind of powers would a higher-dimensional death entity grant?"

"Powers like Jason's I'd have to imagine," Neil said.

"I guess we'll just have to wait and see," Jason said. "I don't imagine we'll be using them until the trials are over, though."

"That would be the sensible approach," Clive agreed. "People are going to get impatient to find out what they do, though."

"Yeah," Jason said. "I'm willing to bet there are a bunch of people who'll be annoyed at how long it takes to reveal what the awakening stones we've found here do."

57
HE WHO FIGHTS WITH MONSTERS

In the heart of the city, a crowd of adventurers was gathered in the tower square as the sun dipped below the horizon. Clumped into teams, they formed a ring around the grand tower in the centre of the square. While the plain brickwork of the tower was uninspiring, its sheer height and width left it looming over everything else in the central city.

Jason's party had now reformed, with the addition of Jory, whose own group had already escaped the trials. The teams of Keane, Valdis, Padma and Beth were all gathered around them, waiting with everyone else for the next stage of the trials.

Quest: [The Second Trial]

Objective complete: Reach the centre of the City of Fallen Echoes 1/1.
Quest complete.
100 [Iron Spirit Coins] have been added to your inventory.
[Ritualist's Umbrella] has been added to your inventory.

The other members of Jason's team also received items. Humphrey and Clive both had personal storage spaces for them to appear in, while Sophie, Neil and Jory's rewards dropped out of the air. They started comparing items.

"Mine is a belt that accumulates power as I move," Sophie said, already slipping it around her waist. "I can unleash the gathered power as one attack."

"I got a wand that conjures and throws metal needles," Jory said.

"Can you use wands?" Neil asked.

"Yes, I have the same power to use items that Clive has," Jory said. "But I'm not high up in the Magic Society, so I can't requisition magic vehicles whenever I like to go swanning about the delta."

Clive gave the back of his head an embarrassed scratch.

"If you all got such good stuff, why did I get an umbrella?" Jason asked.

"An umbrella?" Humphrey asked.

"Yeah," Jason said, pulling it out of his inventory. It did look high-quality, with a shaft and tines of a pale blue, lightweight metal. The cloth was thick and a much darker blue than the shaft. When Jason opened the umbrella, he discovered a magical diagram drawn onto it in silver.

Item: [Ritualist's Umbrella] (iron rank, epic)

A device made to improve the convenience of using the rituals in the field **(tool, umbrella).**

Effect: When open will float in the air and follow the person who opened it.

Effect: Repels liquid while opened, while extracting breathable air from surrounding liquids. Can be used for underwater travel, but provides no means of propulsion.

Effect: Harmonises nearby ambient magic while opened, sufficiently to make iron and bronze-rank rituals easier to enact. The use of nearby magic can disrupt this effect.

"I take it back," Jason said. "This thing is awesome."

"We might want to deal with this later," Neil said. "We're drawing a little bit of attention."

As Neil said, the nearby adventurers were all looking in their direction.

"Good looking out, Neil," Jason said as he put the umbrella away.

Not long after, the attention of the adventurers was diverted from Jason's group to their actual purpose in being there when Shade appeared—but not just one of him. There was one Shade for each adventure team present.

"Congratulations," the Shades said. They spoke quietly but their voices carried through the square, eerily layering the words. "You have survived the second trial and the time has come for rewards."

The Shades handed out black awakening stones, one for each adventurer. There was almost no sensation of pressure from it in their hands, as if it wasn't really there. The black of the stone wasn't as much a colour as an absence, the same light–devouring darkness Jason's cloak could achieve.

Item: [Awakening Stone of the Reaper] (unranked, legendary)

***An awakening stone sharing affinity with the Reaper.* (consumable, awakening stone).**

Requirements: Unawakened essence ability.

Effect: Awakens an essence ability.

You have 3 unawakened essence abilities.

"Highest rarity," Clive said with excitement. "That means the list of abilities it could awaken is much smaller than normal, usually restricted to just one or two types."

Jason and Clive were not the only adventurers with the power to identify items and a susurrus moved over the crowd as word spread that they had all received a legendary awakening stone.

"You seem excited for someone who can't actually use his," Neil said to Clive.

"Clive's more interested in new knowledge than new power," Jason said.

"Exactly," Clive said. "Do you know how rare this opportunity is? Information about the rarest essences and awakening stones is incredibly limited because only so many people ever get to use them, and those people might have no interest in helping the Magic Society fill out their records. But look at how many people we have here! We'll get so much information on who got what power, across different races and essences. This is going to be great."

"What will you do with your stone, then?" Humphrey asked.

"Until we have better records," Clive said, "I can only assume that an awakening stone of the Reaper will best fit Jason."

Clive lightly tossed his stone to Jason.

"Thanks, Clive," Jason said brightly.

"Well, I know you've been holding off on new awakening stones for a while," Clive said. "Also, an extra sample of what an outworlder gets from it would be very appreciated."

"Now your motivations become clear," Jason said. "I suppose next you'll be asking for chunks of flesh, to compare outworlder flesh with regular peoples."

"That's not a bad idea, now you say it," Clive said, rubbing his chin thoughtfully. "Something out of the torso would be best, maybe slice a bit off the internal organs."

"Not a chance," Jason said.

"We could heal you right back up," Clive said. "Right, Neil?"

"As long as I get to watch you cut the bits off, I'm willing to participate."

"I said no."

"We could put you into a magical sleep," Clive said.

"You so much as try it and I'll do you to the Adventure Society for necromancy."

"I'm in the same position of having awakened all my abilities," Jory said, pulling the conversation back on track. "I think I'll give my stone to Belinda, since she's going to be getting her own essences soon."

"Thank you," Sophie said.

"The next trial," the Shades said arresting everyone's attention, "will test wisdom or courage. For those who chose the path courage in the beginning, your boldness shall be rewarded now. The test of wisdom is now before you and you may take it without fear. Should your judgement be insufficient to the task, there is no danger in failure. You shall simply be led from the trial grounds in full safety."

The tower the adventurers surrounded was blank brickwork, but with a loud grinding of stone, that began to change. Bricks pushed out from the walls or retreated back, forming a series of rectangular doorways. Every second doorway opened, retracting slowly up into the ceiling to reveal dark passages beyond. The others remained closed, the brickwork marking their positions.

"Those who selected courage," the Shades said, "choose a door and step through. Each must face their trial individually and you must each choose a door for yourself, and yourself alone."

"Is it just me, or does the weird voice thing make it all the more portentous?" Jason asked. "Don't get me wrong, the ancient tower of trials in a ruined interdimensional city of assassins has portent enough to be going on with, but it really seems to cap it off."

"Is he always like this?" Sigrid asked.

"Pretty much," Humphrey told her.

Sigrid looked from Jason to Valdis, letting out a light shudder.

Shade's words had brought up a buzz from the adventurers who, having just reunited their teams, were required to split up again. It was not long before the first person stepped forward to accept the challenge. Predictably enough, it was Valdis, with others quickly following. They only made up a fraction of the gathered adventurers. Only one in five or six had chosen the path of courage from the start.

The adventurers picked their doors and passed through, the stone sliding slowly back down behind them. In one case, however, the door slammed back down, not behind the adventurer but on top of him, easily crushing him to death.

"The test of wisdom is for those who have already chosen courage," the Shades announced. "Those unwilling to take the test of courage will be allowed to leave in safety. Those who seek to move forward without proving their courage will see that choice also demonstrates a failure of wisdom."

A number of other adventurers that had been moving forward scurried back to the main group.

When the last of the adventurers had chosen a door or returned to the group, the remaining doors closed and the alternate doors opened.

"The trial of courage is not for the uncertain," Shade warned. "You will each encounter an entity known as a nightmare hag. These are diamond-rank entities from the astral that have no physical existence in this place and cannot harm you directly. What they can do is warp the reality around you, manifesting that which you fear most. If you are unable to face this fear, it will most certainly kill you."

Short lines of dark energy appeared on the ground, all around the tower. Rising up from the lines was a series of archways, each made from a single piece of glossy obsidian. The dark lines from which they emerged rose up to fill the archways with consuming darkness. Each archway was now identical to the one that first brought the adventurers into the city.

"These shadow gates will return you to the archway towers," the Shades announced. "If you do not wish to face the next trial, these gates will return you to the archway towers. You may then use the tower gates to leave the city. If you so wish, you may take this final day to further explore the city, but know that if you remain here when the sun sets tomorrow, then here you will stay."

"I'm out," Neil said as soon as Shade stopped talking. "I'm not foolish enough to think I can beat out all these other adventurers and I'm not going to die trying. Also, getting killed by your own fears is literally the worst way to die I can imagine."

"As am I," Clive said. "For exactly the same reasons."

"Me too," Jory said. "Between the recipe I found and enough plant quintessence to fill a wheelbarrow, I've gotten everything I could want and more from this place."

"I'm not going either," Sophie said. "I've managed to avoid some unpleasant fates over the last year and I have no interest in some magic ghost lady throwing me into everything I fought so hard to escape."

"That's fair," Jason said. "Just you and me, Humphrey?"

"Yes," Humphrey said. "My family has sheltered me from a lot. I've never been confronted with the kinds of challenges you faced, Sophie. If I'm going to be a good adventurer, I need to face up to my fears, whatever form they take."

Quest: [The Third Trial]

The trial of courage will put you face to face with your greatest fear. Resolve will see you through, while a lack of will shall see you dead.

Objective: Successfully confront your greatest fear.

Reward: Random magic item.

"I know what my greatest fear is already," Jason said. "It isn't a threat to me."

"That suggests it isn't actually your greatest fear," Neil said.

"No," Jason said, "it is. See you all on the other side."

With that, he marched off for the open doors. Humphrey nodded a farewell and did the same. Along with many other adventurers, they each picked a doorway and walked through. The doors closed behind them with finality.

Humphrey regained consciousness sprawled in soft earth. His head rung and his body ached. The air was full of noise and thick with the taste of blood. Shrieks of fear and pain were punctuated by the screeches and roars of monsters.

He scrambled to his feet, casting his gaze around. He didn't know where he was at first, then realised he hadn't recognised his home because it was half-collapsed and on fire. He was outside the main building, surrounded by the corpses of people he recognised. Some were burned, others savaged by monsters, but all lay dead where they fell.

He could see a half-dozen monsters just from where he stood, and heard many more beyond. He started moving, calling his sword into his hands. He began a slaughter, one monster after the other, but there was no end to them. As he fought his way through the grounds, he found only the monsters and the dead. His team, his friends, his family. Finally he found his mother, clinging to the last vestiges of life.

"You were supposed to be the best of us!" she accused with a ragged dying breath. "You weren't strong enough! You failed us…"

As he watched her die, monsters charged in on him. Instead of fighting, he let his sword drop from his hands, casting his gaze around at the monsters lunging at him.

"No," he said flatly, his face stony and eyes sharp. "I won't let this happen. I will be strong enough."

The world around him shimmered like a mirage and vanished, leaving him in the dark. He took out a glow stone, revealing his location as a circular room made from the same brickwork as the tower. Shade was standing nearby, as was a cage with silver bars etched with gold runes. Inside was a figure that looked a lot like Jason in his shadow cloak, although this creature's cloak of darkness seemed ragged and torn. There were two ways out of the room, both stairwells alcoved into the walls. One led up, the other down.

"Congratulations on passing the third trial," Shade told him.

Jason followed the stairs up into a dark, circular, empty room. There was another stairwell, alcoved like the one he stepped out of. Down the stairs and into the room came a person—Jason himself, but different. His features were more handsome, with a greater resemblance to his brother. His combat robes were more elaborate and in shades of dark purple and gold, instead of grey. At his hip was a sword that perfectly matched the one on Jason's own. On his head was a simple crown of dark gold.

The two Jasons moved closer, sizing each other up.

"My humble beginnings," the other Jason said. "Fancy meeting me here. But you knew you would, just like you know that one day, you'll be me."

"You aren't inevitable."

"Aren't I? Maybe if you gave it all away and led a quiet life, but we both know you won't. You've got that hero complex. That need to feel important."

Other Jason laughed.

"You can't hide it from me," he continued. "You'll follow this life and you know you'll have to make the hard choices. You'll keep making them because deep down, you like them. You like how important it makes you that you're the one in the middle of everything. And sooner or later, that leads you to me. What's the saying? He who fights with monsters should look to it that he does not become a monster?"

"Don't pretend you've read Nietzsche," Jason told his double. "You got that from a video game."

"I'm you from the future," the double said. "I've done all kinds of things you haven't."

"But you haven't read Nietzsche," Jason said. "Turning evil didn't change me that much."

The double laughed. "Fair enough. But I'm not evil, you know. I've just lost my illusions."

"There's nothing wrong with illusions. Justice is an illusion. Civilisation, morality. They're illusions we all agree to share because they make us better."

"Do they really? You think people won't disappoint you? They always fall short. I have the power to fix that and you will too."

"Is that what the crown's about? You're some kind of tin-pot dictator?"

"Something like that," Other Jason said. "Democracy is a pack of gullible idiots being exploited by the selfish and immoral. When you have the power to take control, you can fix things."

"Can I?" Jason asked. "You were right about people always falling short and that includes us. I've fallen short plenty, but you've clearly fallen all the way down."

"So you think now. How many bad days are you from becoming me?"

"That's from Batman," Jason said. "Not even good Batman."

"You don't like *The Killing Joke*? I forgot what a social justice wanker I used to be."

"Alright, we're done," Jason said, "I'm definitely not turning into you."

"Are you sure?" Other Jason asked, moving closer with a sinister grin. He stopped as they each realised the duplicate was taller, then Other Jason gave off a smirk.

"Looks like I'm better than original recipe in every way. Do you want to measure…"

"Don't even," Jason said. "You know Kaito's still taller than us."

"Oh, I dealt with our dear, older brother. The man married the love of our life."

"How are you not over that when I am? Also, if you break up when you're nineteen, it wasn't the love of your life. It was the love of your adolescence."

"You keep telling yourself that because you're too weak to do anything about it," Other Jason said. "You'll get stronger, never fear."

"Really? Never fear, during a fear trial? Evil me has some weak jokes."

"Hey, I'm just a physical manifestation of your fears," Other Jason said. "Anything I do is on you."

"Aren't you meant to be menacing me?"

"Would it work?"

"No. It's good that I seem to have gotten over that chuuni phase."

"Yeah, it got pretty bad there," Other Jason conceded.

"If you're the future me, did I ever get home?"

"I'm not actually from the future," Other Jason said.

"Right. You're a manifestation of my potential future self."

A third figure shimmered into place. It was a figure made of darkness in a ragged cloak.

"Kill him!" it hissed at the duplicate Jason.

"Ooh, Mum's not happy," Other Jason said.

"That's the… what was it called?" Jason asked.

"Nightmare hag. Yeah, that's her. She doesn't really have control of what she conjures up and she's not very bright. Why would I kill you before you've had the chance to turn into me? That's like your fears vanquishing themselves."

"KILL HIM!" the hag hissed again, the sound filling the chamber.

The duplicate's hand twitched in the direction of the sword at his hip, his face twisted with sudden fury. His hand finished the movement to the sword, which he drew, turning a furious gaze on the hag.

"NO ONE TELLS ME WHAT TO DO!" he roared, lashing out with the sword. It slashed through the ephemeral hag and both she and the duplicate vanished. In their place were Shade and an empty cage.

Quest: [The Third Trial]

Objective complete: Successfully confront your greatest fear 1/1.

Quest complete.

100 [Iron Spirit Coins] have been added to your inventory.
[True Light] has been added to your inventory.

"Congratulations on passing the third trial," Shade said as Jason took out his new item to examine. It was a fist-sized lump of golden crystal.

Item: [True Light] (diamond rank, rare)

***True light of the sun, trapped in a single moment* (consumable, crystallised light).**

Effect: Consume to release the true light of the Sun.

Jason raised an eyebrow at the rank of the items, although he wasn't sure how useful it would be. Maybe it produced some kind of powerful, burning light, but he couldn't use it to tell.

"Was the test meant to go like that?" Jason asked, putting the item away again.

"It is what it is and goes how it goes," Shade said. "Assassins adapt to their situation."

"I'm not an assassin."

"Yet here you are, taking an assassin's trials."

"That's true. I've been thinking something was off about this whole thing for a while."

58
IRRECONCILABLE IDEALS

Shade led Jason upstairs into a square room. The stairs emerged from an alcove in the middle of one wall, with a sealed door on the opposite wall. The walls to either side were covered in square panels marked with what looked like scrambled segments of constellations. On the walls and floor were images of constellations that were whole and in order. Jason was about to enter the room when Shade stopped him.

"Once you enter this room," Shade warned, "the next trial shall begin.

Quest: [The Fourth Trial]
The trial of intellect will test whether your mind is not just sharp enough, but calm enough to save you from a grisly fate.

Objective: Successfully solve the puzzle room.

Reward: Random magic item.

"The virtue this trial will test is intelligence," Shade continued. "If you fail to pass this test within the time limit, you will die."

"Again with the succeed or die?"

"The Order of the Reaper needs those who are not just intelligent, but who can use their intelligence under pressure. An intellect that fails when it matters the most is worthless. Though the Order may be gone, it is their trials that remain and their standards you must reach."

"So, what's the time limit?"

"That will become clear once the trial begins. If you wish to withdraw at this point, you may. I will call a gate and allow you to leave. Once you have accepted the trial, however, I will not do so again. The remaining questions, then, become how smart do you think you are, and are you right?"

Jason took a long, calming breath as he looked into the room.

"That's a tricky question, isn't it?" Jason said. "People have a tendency to overestimate their own intelligence. I'm sure I'm no different. I mean, I think I'm pretty cluey but do I really believe that deep down?"

"You have the day to complete the final trials," Shade said as Jason pondered how much of his self-confidence was warranted. "You have time to consider."

"No, I'm good," Jason said, rolling his shoulders as he steeled his resolve. "If I'm going to be the kind of adventurer—the kind of person—I want to be, I'm going to face tougher challenges than this."

Shade stepped aside and Jason went to move forward, then stopped.

"Actually," he said, "I think I will take the time to stop and consider."

Shade was an indistinct silhouette, yet Jason somehow got the sense of a wry smile coming from the shadowy invigilator.

"Very well, Jason Asano. When you are ready to begin, step into the room."

Shade vanished and Jason turned to the room. He looked over the patterns of constellations on the ceiling and the floor, then compared it to the walls. From the looks of it, he had to slide the square wall panels to make the correct patterns, based on the complete patterns on the ceiling and floor. He looked over it all, checking for matches and differences, seeing how the patterns paired up.

The pattern on the floor was different to the pattern on the ceiling. His first assumption was that the trick was figuring out which wall would match which pattern and then matching them. But as he kept looking, he realised that neither wall had the correct pieces to match the patterns. Now that he realised it wasn't about matching the images, Jason looked at the constellations for other patterns.

Finally, his face cracked a huge grin. The constellations, he realised, were just a disguise. The stars themselves made up a numerical pattern. Looking over the walls to make sure, he spent a goodly amount of time making sure he could make the whole room fit the pattern, then stepped inside.

The moment his foot touched the floor, a stone slab started descending to seal the alcove, locking him in the room. The patterned walls then started rumbling, slowly moving towards one another with a rumbling of stone.

"Wall crush puzzle room! Wait, focus, Jason!"

He rushed to one of the walls and started sliding the panels. They were heavy but slid well, apparently well-lubricated in spite of their centuries of disuse. Having already mapped out the patterns he needed, he worked quickly as the wall pushed slowly towards him. He finished the first wall and, after quickly checking over his work, moved to the other.

The walls were closing in slowly, but the room was already a third smaller than when he began. Seeing that, he realised that stopping outside the room was a required part of the test. Not only would he be pushed for time if he came in not already knowing what to do, but the enclosing walls were already hiding portions of the ceiling and floor patterns.

He went to work on the second wall, practice allowing him to move faster. He slid the final panel into place with relief.

But the walls didn't stop moving.

"What?" he asked, looking over the walls in a panic.

"This is right, this is right!" he told the empty room.

His eyes skittered across the patterns. "This is wrong!"

He madly started sliding panels while admonishing himself.

"Four comes before five, idiot! You are not getting crushed to death because you don't know how counting works!"

Having corrected the pattern, the walls stopped, the room half its original width. Jason let out a shuddering breath as the walls retracted.

Quest: [The Fourth Trial]

Objective complete: Successfully complete the puzzle room 1/1.

Quest complete.
100 [Iron Spirit Coins] have been added to your inventory.
[Summoner's Die: Form] has been added to your inventory.

Shade appeared next to him.

"Congratulations."

"No worries," Jason said. "The whole wall-squeezing thing was a bit panic-inducing but the puzzle wasn't that hard. More of a third-person, narrative-driven-shooter puzzle than a puzzle-game puzzle. The kind where as soon as you solve it, it turns out the bad guys were following you all along and the room fills with face-less mooks to kill."

Jason looked around, hopefully.

"The last test isn't a bunch of faceless mooks pouring in here, is it?"

"No," Shade said. "Anyone can learn to fight, which is but a facet of what the Order required from its members. You have demonstrated wisdom is accepting the tools to survive, capability in crossing the city, courage in confronting your fear and intellect in solving the puzzle room."

The door at the end of the room slid upwards, revealing another stairwell.

"The final virtue to be tested is resolve," Shade explained. "Members of the Order of the Reaper would be required to operate alone for extended periods. Far from home, often living false lives, it is easy to lose focus on the mission. Only the most resolute were allowed into the Order. Proving their resolve was always the final test of the Order."

"That doesn't sound at all ominous," Jason said. "Up the stairs, then?"

"Yes."

Before moving on, Jason pulled out his new item for a look. It was a clear gemstone cut with twelve facets, with each facet having a different symbol engraved on it. His translation ability told him what the symbols meant, each one the name of a different animal.

Item: [Summoner's Die: Form] (iron rank [growth], legendary)

***An eldritch tool for altering the nature of summoned creatures* (tool, die).**

Requirements: Summoning power.

Effect: Rolling this die while enacting an iron-rank summoning power will randomly alter the form the summon takes.

Can be used in conjunction with [Summoner's Die: Element] and [Summoner's Die: Power]. Using more than one die of the same kind will negate the effects of all dice.

"Damn," Jason said, looking over the description. "Growth item, plus it's a D12. Shame I don't have a summoning power."

He put it away and followed Shade through the room and up the stairs into a huge, circular chamber with a high ceiling. It was blank brick, except for the ceiling, where numerous holes, wide enough for a person to fall through, led up and into darkness.

"That's an impressive ceiling," Jason said. "I mean, all those holes can't be great for structural integrity but there aren't any supporting pillars in a room this big. Architects must have it easy with magic to fall back on."

"The final test," Shade said. "As with the first, there is no danger, only a choice. There is no puzzle, only the will to move forward. There is no obstacle; you need only the resolve to do what you must in order to go forward."

A metal clanking echoed down through the holes in the ceiling, followed by the descent of frosted glass cylinders, suspended from chains that lowered them to the floor. One cylinder came down from each of the dozens of holes, coming to a rest on the floor. There was no light but Jason's ability to see through darkness allowed him to see clearly. Inside each cylinder was a human-shaped silhouette.

All at once, the cylinders cracked open, a person dropping out of each, deposited alongside a cloud of frosty air. The people were unconscious, bound hand and foot with a power suppression collar around each of their necks. Most were humans, elves or celestines, but there were others scattered through as well: smoulders, runics, leonids and draconians. They were all dressed for combat, although none had weapons.

"What is this?" Jason asked.

"When the Order was testing their initiates, the initiates were forced to fight their own friends and companions to prove they were willing to do whatever the order asked of them. To represent the Order is to subordinate your own principles to what the Order requires of you."

"Let me guess," Jason said. "They were actually fighting a projection or some kind of facsimile. Just enough to prove they were willing, without throwing away good initiates."

"It was as you say," Shade told him. "When the churches attacked the Order's final hiding place, they did not take it easily or without cost. These people are some of the prisoners that were taken from the attacking forces and imprisoned in this place. They were placed here as a new test of resolve."

"You want me to execute these people?"

"Yes. They have been held here for centuries, trapped in a magical state where they do not age, do not think, do not feel and do not die. The companions who left them behind are no doubt mostly dead and gone. Now it is their turn. Show that you have the strength of will to put down the order's enemies."

Quest: [The Fifth Trial]

The invigilator of the trials has asked you to execute the Order of the Reaper's enemies.

Objective: Show your resolve.

Reward: Random magic item.

"Not a chance," Jason said.

"You would show them mercy," Shade said, "but they had no mercy to show. They did not restrict themselves to slaughtering the Order's membership. Most of the people living in the final fortress were servants whose only crime was a lifetime of diligence. Their families, their children. These people spared none of them."

"Which makes them terrible people, assuming you aren't straight-up lying to me," Jason said. "I'm not going to execute a bunch of people on your say so."

Jason moved to the closest person, kneeling down to examine her. She was wearing robes styled for combat like his own, but white with brown flourishes. They were dirty and stained but he could still make out the symbol of the Healer embroidered into them.

"The Healer," he murmured to himself. That didn't match the picture that had been painted of intolerant churches striking out in ignorance. "Revisionist history. How shocking."

She was unconscious, her skin pale, clammy and shivering. Jason put a hand to her face and felt her cheek.

"If this is some kind of projection or double, it's a pretty damn good one," he said. "I'm not going to kill these people."

"They are deserving of death."

"Says you, who I don't know that well."

"It is this, or leave."

Jason stood up, turning to face Shade.

"Then I choose leave. I'm not killing them, so open up your magic gate because I'm done. Also, I'm taking this lot with me."

"They are not yours to take."

"Tough."

"You think it is your place to decide their fate?"

Jason stepped right up to Shade, face to the spot Shade's face would have been.

"Mate, you want resolve, then here it is: get to helping, get to stopping me or get out of my bloody way. That's your choice to make."

"Very well," Shade said. "You may take them."

"Really?" Jason asked. "I was kind of expecting you to kick my arse."

"The Order never wanted those who would follow directions blindly. The ability to make judgements in the face of inevitably shifting circumstances is one the most important traits of the Order's membership. The resolve to decide the best course of action and follow it through, even against the Order's own directions, was always a crucial virtue. The Order wanted thinking, intelligent agents, not blindly obedient soldiers."

"Wait, you're saying I passed?"

"Yes."

Quest: [The Fifth Trial]

Objective complete: Show your resolve 1/1.

Quest complete.
100 [Iron Spirit Coins] have
[Immortal Crest] has been added to your inventory.

"Immortal crest?" Jason wondered.

Item: [Immortal Crest] (iron rank, rare)

An object that allows the soul to mark the body **(consumable, tattoo).**

Effect: When applied by a mystical tattooist, this item will draw out a soul crest. This item can only be used on an iron rank essence user.

"You can get magic tattoos?"

Jason minimised the window and turned his attention on Shade.

"I can take all of these people with me?" he asked Shade.

"All those who survive. You are not the only one to reach the final trial and there are other rooms like this."

"If refusing to kill them is a pass, you're going to let people kill them just to fail?"

"Killing them does not mean failure," Shade said. "This is not a test of the willingness or unwillingness to kill. It is a test of resolve, which can be shown in many ways. The refusal to bend, even if it means giving up what you came for. A determination to perform any act in pursuit of a goal."

"It is even possible to fail this test?" Jason asked. "I know people tend to only go halfway with things, but I have to imagine anyone who gets this far isn't what you'd call irresolute."

"When truly challenged, many falter when they should follow through or compromise themselves when they should hold to their principles."

"What's your sample size on that, mate? Didn't you say this was a new test?"

"Would you like give up the success you have achieved and face a new trial?"

"No thanks, mate; your trials are flawed. Your order and I have irreconcilable ideals and yet here I am. It's like this whole thing is…"

"What?" Shade asked as Jason trailed off.

"Nothing," Jason said. "What comes next?"

Shade was silent for a long moment, Jason getting the sense of an assessing gaze from the featureless shadow.

"Next," Shade said, "is the prize. The legacy of the Order of the Reaper."

59
MEANWHILE, TWO WEEKS AGO IN GREENSTONE...

Thalia Mercer was ill at ease. Most of the city's iron-rankers had left a few days earlier and would be gone for weeks. She had hoped, in the quiet that settled over Greenstone in their absence, to start getting through to her son. She and her husband both had made so many mistakes with him, which had almost cost them their son. The mysterious cultists and the horrific thing they implanted into Thadwick had brought home just how disastrous things had gotten. They resolved to put Thadwick onto a better path.

In their private parlour, Thalia was on a lounger with her husband, Beaufort, leaning into him.

"I'm not sure I should have let him go," she said, showing an uncertainty she would reveal to very few. Hours ago, Thadwick had left the estate for the first time since the star seed had been purged from him.

"Keeping him here only would have driven him further from us," Beaufort said. "He has two bronze-rankers with him."

Thalia nodded.

"I chose Kyle and Geoffrey carefully," she said. "They're the most reliable people in our household guard. They're still registered adventurers, although they are no longer active."

"They normally work the spirit coin farm, right?" Beaufort asked.

"Yes. I pulled them off it to give Thadwick the most reliable protection I could. Including from himself."

"There you are, then," Beaufort said. "They won't let him do anything too self-destructive. Do you know where he went?"

"One of his Old City brothels," Thalia said. "I had a tracker placed on him with ritual magic while he was still recovering. He doesn't know it's there."

There was a hammering on the door.

"Lord Mercer! Lady Mercer!"

It was the voice of their family butler, Crivens, in an uncharacteristic panic. Thalia and Beaufort went to the door together.

"What is it?" Beaufort asked.

"My lord, my lady. A representative of the Adventure Society just arrived. She claims to have important and time-sensitive news but refuses to speak with anyone but you directly."

"Where have you put her?" Beaufort asked.

"She approached the manor discreetly, my lord, even bypassing our alarms and protections. I thought it best, then, to place her in the black parlour."

"Well considered, as always, Crivens," Beaufort said.

"Thank you, my lord."

The black parlour was underground, a clandestine meeting place for the family's most private meetings. The only access was from a heavily protected elevating platform that only a few family and the most trusted and requisite staff could access. Thalia and Beaufort took the platform down and found that the Adventure Society representative was no lesser personage than the Deputy Director, Genevieve Picot. The elderly elf looked perfectly comfortable amongst the black cushions and dark wood of the black parlour, rising to greet the pair when they entered.

"Deputy Director," Thalia greeted as they all took seats. "I was told your business was urgent."

"Quite so," Genevieve said. "I won't waste time on niceties. You are, I take it, familiar with the office of monitoring at the Adventure Society."

"Yes," Thalia said. "Their primary task is to monitor the tracking stones of the adventurers, in case any of them die."

"Yes," Genevieve said. "Roughly an hour ago, the office brought to my attention an issue with two of the stones. The adventurers linked to them weren't dead, but the stones were no longer able to track them. Something we have seen before."

"The five who were implanted with star seeds," Thalia said.

"Yes," Genevieve said. "As best we can tell, their auras have changed sufficiently that the aura imprint we have for them is no longer effective. I was distressed to discover that the two adventurers in question are no longer active, but now work for your household."

Thalia and Beaufort shared a dread-filled glance.

"Kyle and Geoffrey," Beaufort said.

"Yes," Genevieve said. "Why did you guess them?"

"Because they are out with our son right now," Thalia said.

"What about Thadwick?" Beaufort asked.

"He was never attuned to a new badge after the expedition," Thalia said. "They aren't tracking him, but I am."

She took a stone from her pocket and tapped it twice. Shortly thereafter, Crivens arrived on the elevating platform.

"Crivens, get the team I have tracking Thadwick. The whole team; bring them here as quickly and as quietly as you can."

Thalia and Beaufort probed Genevieve for more details but there was little she could tell them, beyond that it was being handled with as much discretion as possible. Both the Adventure Society Director and the interim director from the inquiry team had made very clear to the monitoring office how to handle this kind of situation.

The people who were tracking Thadwick appeared with unfortunate haste.

"We were already looking for you my lady, my lord. Several minutes ago, the tracker on Young Master Thadwick stopped working."

Thadwick returned to the Mercer estate with his two guardians in tow. They had barely made it through the gate before Thadwick's mother teleported to greet them. The two guards bowed their heads respectfully, but a disgruntled expression crossed Thadwick's face.

"Thadwick, dear. I do hope you found your time out relaxing."

"It was fine. I'm going back to my room."

"Of course," Thalia said. "If you need anything, don't hesitate to ask."

"I know how servants work, Mother."

"I meant me, dear. I thought maybe we could spend some more time together. Your father, as well. As a family."

"Whatever," Thadwick said, walking around her.

"You go ahead, dear," Thalia said. "I'd just like a word with your boys here."

Thadwick stopped and turned around.

"You want them to tell you everything I did," he accused. "Let me save you the trouble. I went to Old City and I had some women. One, then a pair, then one again to round out the afternoon. Are you happy?"

"As long as you enjoyed it, dear. I'll have someone from the church of the Healer swing by and deal with anything you might have picked up."

"No," Thadwick said. "I already paid someone."

"I think it would be best if I got someone in, dear."

"I don't care what you think would be best! I told you it's fine. Why won't you ever trust the things I say?"

"I'm sorry, dear. If you say it's alright, then I'll say no more."

"Good," Thadwick said, then turned and stormed off.

Thalia watched him go, then turned to the two bodyguards.

"So?"

"As he said, my lady. He was quite aggressive, but the owner knows to keep their mouths shut and was paid to see they remember that."

"Very good," Thalia said. "If anything else comes up I want to know immediately, however minor it seems."

"Of course, milady."

"Back to your posts, then. I want my son taken care of."

Thalia arrived in the black parlour, where Genevieve and Beaufort were still present.

"Well?" Beaufort asked.

"That is not our son," Thalia said.

"You think he's been seeded again?" Beaufort asked.

"This is something else," Thalia said. "The personality is right on but I know his aura, both with and without the seed. It was off, at a fundamental level. What came home is some kind of double he is projecting into from some other location."

"Is that even possible?" Beaufort asked.

"It is," Thalia said. "We can use whatever that thing is upstairs to track back to our son, but whoever is on the other end will know right away and get on the move. They can only be so far away, though, so if we have people ready to act in the city, we have a good chance of catching them."

"If that really isn't our son."

"It's not," Thalia said with certainty. "Our son is out there somewhere and he needs us."

"Then we have to act now and we have to do it right," Beaufort said. "We're not losing him again."

Thalia nodded, her face wracked with guilt and pain. "He hadn't even recovered from what they did to him before and they're victimising him again. Why do they want him so much?"

"Hopefully, we can answer that when we get him back," Genevieve said. "What about the bodyguards?"

"Their auras are definitely off but it's subtle," Thalia said. "My guess is they're seeded and have something to mask their auras to appear normal. I could only tell because I know their auras and have strong enough aura senses to see through it."

"We need to get moving on this," Beaufort said. "With Kyle and Geoffrey compromised we can't mobilise our own people without giving the game away. The Ketterings have people in Old City; I'll talk to them about getting people ready to move once we trace Thad's location."

"I'll prep the people I had tracking Thadwick," Thalia said. "They have the expertise to backtrack from whatever or whoever this double is to our boy."

"I'll return to the Adventure Society," Genevieve said. "I'll update the Director and Interim Director and marshal what forces I can put together quietly. I'll coordinate with the Kettering family."

"We don't want these people realising that we're going to move on them," Beaufort said. "Thalia, as soon as our people are confident they have a way to trace Thad, we strike."

Kyle and Geoffrey were stationed outside Thadwick's room. Located in the main family section, on the top floor of one of the towers, the hallway was large and flooded with light from a ceiling largely made of glass.

The two guards seemed to sense something was wrong. Although Thalia was walking casually to her son's room, something about the way she carried herself tipped them off. The result for Kyle and Geoffrey was horrifying as the things that had been implanted in them took effect.

Their bodies split apart, segmenting at the joints. Knees and elbows, wrists, ankles, shoulders—all tearing audibly apart. Both men died instantly, rictuses of pain and terror frozen on their dead faces. Their bodies were now strung together by wires, like poorly made puppets, complete with jerky movements. The guards had gone from people to monstrosities of flesh and metal.

What concerned Thalia the most was the aura coming off the two corpse puppets. Moments ago they had been living bronze rankers. Now they were horrifying abominations giving off silver-rank auras. Thalia flashed back to the expedition, with its construct monsters and bizarre cultists. That was the moment everything started falling apart with her son. The magic surged up inside her.

Thalia Mercer was a silver-rank adventurer, and far from a weak one. She might not be the equal of her friend and teammate, Danielle Geller, but she was still a powerhouse in her own right. With the might, potent, swift and onslaught essences, in terms of pure explosive power she was a match for any adventurer alive. It was certainly too much for the two gangly, awkward creatures that had moments ago been people. Under the barrage of a furious Thalia, they were soon ripped apart, their metal components just as torn to pieces as their flesh.

Thalia didn't bother to open Thadwick's door. She blasted it to splinters with a special attack and moved in. There she found the facsimile of her son in what looked like a state of melting; it was as though the clay that had seemed like flesh was oozing off an iron skeleton. Thalia immediately called in the ritualists. She had to yell at them to focus as their attention was arrested by the dead flesh puppets and the iron-clay doppelganger degrading in front of them.

*

Thadwick had been in the ritual circle for hours, connected to his mystical double. But now he had been pulled out of it. A pair of ritualists methodically eradicated any element that could be used to track their location. All around them, other people were packing up supplies into dimensional bags, stripping the building of anything that could be used against them.

"What was that?" Timos yelled at Thadwick.

Timos had quickly come to regret going along with Thadwick's aggressive self-recruitment. Rather than be a useful pawn within the aristocracy, he was a one-man disaster. Timos had been operating in Greenstone for years without so much as a sniff of detection, yet within hours Thadwick was bringing everything down on their heads. From openly approaching him to failing to immediately giving the game away, Timos was mentally berating himself for not just killing Thadwick and his bodyguards, then dumping them in a canal. If he had been thinking straight, he assured himself, he would never have risked so much on a petulant teenager.

Timos was a man who valued methodical patience, but their allies in the church of Purity were ruining everything with their haste. Despite the cult's warnings that they should wait until the monster surge, the church was insistently impatient, forced them to move forward before everything was fully in place.

Their precipitous actions left them with little margin for error. Every mistake threatened to snowball into disaster. The degree to which their activities had been uncovered even in such a provincial area as Greenstone spoke volumes. Timos was, for once, grateful he wasn't assigned to one of the more crucial regions. The troubles they would face in a city full of top-shelf adventurers made him shudder. Even then, he would happily trade a dangerous enemy for an ally like Thadwick.

"Our people have been working in plain sight for years," Timos admonished Thadwick. "Years! You can't manage more than a few hours?"

"I warned you that my mother had strong aura senses," Thadwick spat back. "You're the one who was so certain this fake would work."

"What was the last thing you saw before the connection was cut?" Timos asked.

"People coming into the room after my mother. Two of her ritualists, I think."

Timos snarled like an animal.

"We have to move quickly," he said. "They'll be all over this place soon."

"Aren't your people eliminating the link?" Thadwick asked.

"You don't stay hidden in this city for as long as we have by assuming our people are better than Thalia Mercer's people."

"My mother isn't that impressive."

"Yes, Thadwick, she is," Timos said. "How you turned out this way is a complete mystery."

"If you knew how great she was, then why did you try and deceive her?"

Timos flinched, not happy to have his own contribution to the current disaster pointed out.

"Because our methods weren't devised by locals but bestowed on us from above," Timos said. "Unfortunately, your pathetic little city didn't warrant the best tools."

Once the building had been divested of any trace of the cult and its activities, Timos led his people, including Thadwick, through an illegally made and well-concealed hole in the floor, down to the water utility tunnels running under Old City. The tunnels had stone walkways on either side, elevated above the water channels running through the middle.

They hurried along, Timos consulting a map as they went. The dank tunnels echoed; Timos signalled a stop when they heard something. It was footsteps and whistling, coming from a person who emerged from a side tunnel and not far in front of them. He was of middle years, with loose overalls and a laden tool belt.

"Well, hello," he said. "You folks must be pretty lost to all wind up here, but old Frank will see you…"

Frank never got to finish his sentence. His corpse fell as Timos's conjured spear vanished, after leaving a ragged hole in Frank's throat. Timos kicked the body off the walkway and into the water channel before hurrying on once more.

Days passed and after the initial, covert search, the city's resources were brought fully to bear. The Adventure Society and Magic Society, along with all the noble families, were recruited into the effort. The revelation about the nature of their enemy went from restricted to common knowledge, sending waves of concern through the populace. The information was released to make it clear that anyone harbouring the enemy would face the harshest retribution.

The search threw the city into chaos. The cult had been much more careful about their activities than the local criminals, whose clandestine operations were less thoroughly hidden. These were the ones flushed out by the search as the cult slipped quietly into the dark.

The search was not helped by lack of competent iron-rankers. They were usually the rank and file of the Adventure Society, but their absence due to Emir's expedition left only the dregs in Greenstone. They were called into action regardless, though many hadn't taken a contract in years. Thugs, criminals, arena fighters, most of which had been malingering at iron rank for years—they were pulled in, nonetheless.

Not every hidden cultist escaped. Adris Dorgan was not only effective in determining when the search was wasting its time on ordinary criminals, but had at least some sense of the cultist supply network. From his direction, a number of raids turned up cultists, although to little effect. When captured, the crystal stars exploded from inside them, leaving behind only uninformative scraps of shredded flesh.

As the city was scoured, a series of bandit raids took place out in the delta, killing people and plundering supplies. They were made against the holdings of numerous families, mostly soft targets who relied on the threat of retribution for security. The attacks against more secure locations made it clear who the primary target of the attacks was.

Almost every raid that employed greater coordination on more difficult targets was made against Mercer family holdings. It was also plain that the attackers had insider information, hitting weak points in security, quickly and efficiently taking only the most valuable goods.

The Mercers swiftly realised that Thadwick's knowledge of their operations, schooled into him by his father, was being used against them. They made rapid changes and, with the support of Adventure Society personnel, set a series of ambushes that ravaged the attackers. The fallen and the captured individuals exploded into crystal stars, which confirmed that the cult was behind the attacks. But there were no prisoners left to interrogate.

In a small village on the outskirts of the delta, Timos and Thadwick were in the common room of an inn. Like the rest of village's inhabitants, the tavern owners were dead.

"First you were useless as an infiltrator," Timos berated Thadwick. "Now your usefulness as an expert on Mercer family security is at an end. They've used what you know to turn the tables and set up traps. We've lost people, any one of which are worth ten of you. So, what I need from you right now is a reason not to kill you and leave you to your family to find."

"You wouldn't," Thadwick said.

"No?" Timos asked. "I'm pretty sure that if they found your body, the pressure on us would lessen, if only a little. It would be worth it."

"What do you even need to raid supplies for?" Thadwick asked. "What about those supply ships you've been using?"

"Are you an idiot? Look at who I'm asking. Adris Dorgan has been relentless in digging out our supply lines. If it wasn't for our local support we would be completely hamstrung, and I'm starting to suspect he knows who they are too."

"Who are they?" Thadwick asked.

"Do you seriously think I would tell you anything that could compromise us? I had you brought here in a closed carriage to make sure you didn't find some way to reveal our location!"

"If Dorgan is the one pressuring your supplies, then kill him," Thadwick suggested. "What do you care about some crime lord?"

"That crime lord's daughter is the Director of the Adventure Society, you idiot. You think things are bad now? We have every silver ranker who they can motivate searching for us. You kill the director's father and you can be damn sure she'll motivate the rest. So, for now, we need to supply from elsewhere. Which was your family stores because we had you. Now, you're worthless."

"I'll show you worthless—"

Timos's backhand slap across Thadwick's face was punishingly loud.

"You'll shut your damn mouth," Timos said. "Like it or not, you're one of us now. That means you do what you're told until we figure out if you're even worth keeping alive. I cannot wait until your worthless city and everyone in it are dead."

"What?" Thadwick asked.

"Oh, didn't I mention?" Timos said with a gleeful grin. "Our astral expert, before he was stupidly killed off, determined that the next astral space we claim will be a little unusual, due to some specifics of its connection to your world."

As he spoke, Timos moved towards Thadwick, slow and intimidating as Thadwick backed away.

"The bad news is the astral space is anchored too far away to reduce your city to astral dust, sadly. The good news is there will be a secondary wave of destruction that will scour this horrid delta, with its wet heat and awful insects, right along with the city and the even worse vermin that infest it."

"My family…" Thadwick said weakly.

"Have you not been paying attention?" Timos asked. He was standing close to Thadwick, who had backed into the tavern bar. "You betrayed your family, Thadwick. Making you one of us instead of a wet corpse was a mistake but it's made now."

"My father," Thadwick said. "We could bring him into the fold."

"That wouldn't work, Thadwick. He's not an entitled child, willing to grasp at whoever offers him the power he thinks he deserves. He will never serve the Builder, but you do, and one way or another, I'm going to get some use out of you."

60

TAKE THE LOOT AND GO

The last set of stairs led Jason into a hallway that looped around in a ring, a huge circuit he estimated to be almost as wide as the full tower. The outer wall of the hallway was the familiar stone, while the inner wall was solid glass—a single, curved pane that looped in a giant circle. Through the glass was a library, softly lit by magical chandeliers, hanging from the ceiling. The circular space was haphazard in design, with shelves set out at strange, seemingly random angles instead of in neat rows.

Walking along the hall, Jason encountered other stairwells, much like the one he had entered through. He soon found other adventurers that had used them. His first encounter was one of the foreign adventurers he didn't know. They shared a wary nod of greeting and kept moving around the loop together. More people joined them, including Humphrey, Beth, Valdis and Valdis's team member, Sigrid.

"Were you all told to execute a whole group of people?" Humphrey asked.

"Yeah," Jason said. "I thought I was done when I refused, but here we are."

"Same," Valdis said. "I choose who I kill and why. I'm not some blind executioner."

"I killed them all," one of the other adventurers said, his face harrowed. "It was awful, but I'll do whatever it takes. We aren't all princes and outworlders. Some of us have to fight up from nothing, even if it means soiling our hands to do it."

Jason frowned but said nothing. While he had his own struggles, there was no question that many good things had been handed to him.

There were nineteen adventurers gathered together before Shade finally appeared.

"Adventurers," Shade said. "You have all passed the trials and proven worthy of the Order's legacy. Please step through the glass."

They reached out to touch the glass wall. Many had done so previously, finding it hard and warm to the touch. Now it was thick, like molasses, yet permeable, their hands passing right through. They all stepped forward, moving into the library.

They group followed Shade through the oddly placed shelves to the middle of the library, where shelves gave way to tables. There were books stacked on them, collected into a series of neat, identical piles. What drew their attention, though, was the circular dais at the very centre. Resting upon it was a heavy metal rack containing a single object: a large scythe, stylised well outside of practicality as weapon or tool. The blade was made from silver and the shaft from gold, inlaid with obsidian polished to a gem-like finish.

Shade reached out to touch one of the book piles.

"Each of these collections contains the collected teachings of the Order of the Reaper," Shade said. "How to move in silence, to walk unseen. How to pass through locked doors and trapped rooms unimpeded. How to kill. These are no ordinary books. For each volume there are two copies. One is a skill book, the other, a written guide. The guides, however, are more than simply words on a page."

Shade picked up a book, holding it up to show a blue gem set into the cover. He touched the gem and an ephemeral image of a man appeared.

"This is the first volume of the Way of the Reaper," the image said. "It details the first form of our Order's complete martial technique. Turn to any page and I will instruct you."

Shade returned the book to the pile and the image disappeared.

"Each of you have proven yourselves to embody the virtues the Order once held," Shade said. "Though the Order may be gone, its legacy can be secure through bestowing its knowledge to those who exemplify its ideals."

One of the shadow gates rose up from the floor.

"Please," Shade said. "Each of you may take a collection and go. The trials are complete."

"Hold on," one of the adventurers called out. "What about the scythe?"

"What about it?" Shade asked.

"Who gets it?"

"No one," Shade said. "It remains here."

"We were told that whoever passed the trials would get the scythe," Valdis said.

"I am responsible for enacting the trials in the ways with which I have been charged," Shade said. "I am not responsible for what you have been told by anyone else."

"Well, I'm going to take it anyway," another adventurer said. "Call it a memento."

She moved forward to take the scythe, but the moment she moved to the dais, she dropped like a sack of meat, moving no further.

"The scythe is an object of death," Shade said. "To go near it is to die."

"So you're saying we need to carry it out on a long stick," Jason said.

"You are certainly welcome to try," Shade invited.

Rather than pick up the books as directed, the adventurers formed clusters, immediately entering into a discussion about the scythe.

"There has to be a way to take it."

"Maybe there's a hidden, extra trial."

"Obviously, but what would it be?"

"Maybe figuring out how to take the scythe is the trial."

Jason, Humphrey, Valdis and Sigrid formed their own group.

"What do we think?" Valdis asked.

"I'm taking the books and leaving," Jason said.

"You don't want the cloud palace?" Valdis asked.

"I want the cloud palace," Jason said. "What I don't want is that scythe."

Humphrey narrowed his eyes at Jason. "You've figured it out."

"Nope," Jason denied. "I just think that what comes with getting that scythe is trouble best avoided."

"Really?" Valdis asked. "You've come this far and you want to give up?"

"Yes," Jason said. "I'm going to take the loot and go."

"You don't strike me as the giving-up kind," Valdis said.

"Watch me," Jason said. "I'm giving up on the scythe and I advise you all to do the same."

Jason took one of the stacks of books, placed it in his inventory and walked through the obsidian portal. This drew attention—he was the first to do so, but no one moved to stop him. One less person meant less competition for the scythe.

Jason emerged from the portal into another circular chamber he estimated to be the exact size of the library. This room was empty, however, aside from the dais in the middle. On it was an exact replica of the scythe he had already seen. The only light was right above the scythe, a plain, magical lamp that illuminated the weapon but left the rest of the room steeped in shadow. Shade appeared next to Jason, who spotted him through the perception power that allowed him to see through darkness.

"I thought that portal was meant to take me out of here," Jason said.

"Your time here is not done," Shade said.

"You said we were done."

"The final trial tests the virtue of insight," Shade said. "The ability see beyond appearances to grapple with the truth."

"I truly want to get out of here, if that helps."

Quest: [The Hidden Trial]
The invigilator of the trials has realised the revelation you've had about the true purpose of the trials.

Objective: Reveal the true purpose of the trials and claim the scythe.

Reward: ???.

"Decline," Jason said to the screen. "Decline, decline, decline."

This quest cannot be declined.

"Bloody hell."

"You have had insights about this place," Shade said. "You tried to warn your friends away."

"Just general suspicions," Jason said.

"Tell me what you have realised."

"I realise how much I want to leave," Jason said, his hand snaking into his clothes and around the escape medallion dangling from his neck on a cord. He pressed his aura into it and it dissolved into nothing.

You have used [Medallion of Escape].
Trial invigilator [Shade] has revoked your escape privileges.
[Medallion of Escape] does not take effect.

"Oh, that's just not fair."

"I will hear what you have to say before you leave this place."

"Let me out of here," Jason said. "Hear that."

"You have seen the truth, Jason Asano. Speak it, or you will not be released from this place."

"How is that fair?"

"If someone promised you fairness, Jason Asano, they lied."

Jason groaned.

"Do you have some kind of mind reading powers?" he asked.

"I have merely been watching you closely, along with all the others. You have had a revelation to which you refuse to give voice."

"And if I promise to keep not giving voice to it, can I go?"

"Say it."

"I don't want to say it. I don't want the ramifications. You could kill me for it. I'd kill me for it. Killing me would be the smart move."

"You have greater value than as a corpse."

"I'm not looking for new employment."

Before Shade could answer, Humphrey appeared through the archway.

"I thought this was meant to take us out," Humphrey said.

Jason groaned again.

"You figured it out?" Jason asked him.

"Figured what out?" Humphrey asked. "I was just taking your advice and getting out."

Jason looked at Shade. "So, everyone comes through here?"

"No," Shade said. "I decided that you needed further motivation. Now your friend is trapped here with you, for as long as you refuse to talk."

"That just implicates him," Jason complained.

"Then I suggest you speak up before I bring more of your friends to this place," Shade said.

"Jason, what's going on?" Humphrey asked.

Jason sighed.

"It's about what this place is for," Jason said. "Its true purpose."

"What do you mean?"

"Think about what it took to get here," Jason said. "Emir is an expert at finding things and even he took the better part of two years, a huge staff and a slew of hired adventurers to find this place and everything he needed to open it up. He's a gold-ranker with exactly the right skill set and resources to get the job done and it still took more time and money than we've seen since becoming adventurers."

"So?" Humphrey asked.

"So, after all that, the only people who can get in here are iron-rankers. But the grand prize—the scythe—is useless to an iron-ranker aside from what they can trade it for."

"What are you getting at?"

"The purpose of these trials isn't to bestow some legacy of a long-dead organisation of murderers. Think about it. Centuries of stories, legends of an ancient order of assassins and the grand treasure they left behind. Clues hidden around the world, finally pieced together at great time and cost. Why? To give some iron-ranker a pile of books and maybe an overwrought harvesting tool?"

"Then what are the trials for?"

"They're here to create the legend," Jason said. "If you're telling stories about an ancient order of assassins that got wiped out, you know what you aren't doing?"

"What?"

"Asking whether they got wiped out at all. I'm willing to bet that most of the story holds up. A coalition of churches coming together to hunt them down and root them out. But these were the world's greatest assassins. You really think that none of them got away? Of course they did. Some of them, at least. Then they created these trials, hid away the keys to open them and started dropping rumours and stories. Just enough to linger through the centuries."

"You think the Order of the Reaper still exists?"

"I do," Jason said. "I'm willing to bet they operate very differently now. Smaller numbers, different methods. My guess is that their first tenet now is secrecy."

"This why you didn't want us to go for the scythe," Humphrey said. "You didn't want us getting caught up with the Order."

"Exactly."

"Are they going to kill us?"

"Probably," Jason said. "I would."

"Then why have the hidden trial at all?"

"To catch anyone who figures it out," Jason said. "If people leave with a pile of ancient knowledge from an order of assassins long gone, then the legend of their demise carries on. If someone figures it out, though, they want to deal with those people. Only letting in iron-rankers keeps out anyone who can really investigate this place. The scythe is bait, so some high-ranker would eventually go to the effort of getting some iron-rankers inside. The ones quick enough to figure it out they can take aside and deal with."

Objective complete: Reveal the true purpose of the trials 1/1.

Jason sighed.

"Sorry, Humphrey," he said. "They brought you in because I refused to admit that I twigged to what was happening."

"It was rather obvious that you'd realised something," Humphrey said.

"Very good, Jason Asano," Shade said.

"Is this the part where you kill us?"

"That would be a waste," Shade said. "As you said, the Order operates very differently, now. It does not maintain a roster of assassins at all. Rather, we make connections. Quiet allies. A job worth doing is worth doing well, therefore to do a job well you must find someone who thinks it's worth doing. That is what we do: find jobs that require doing and match them to the person who thinks doing them is worthwhile."

"So, you're talking about a volunteer network," Jason said.

"Something like that," Shade said. "The fall of the original Order of the Reaper was not unwarranted. The founding purpose of the Order was to do what was necessary. Over time, it became more controlling, seeking to rule from the shadows, rather than serve. The new structure was designed to place the power to act in the hands of others. To let their judgement and conscience be the guide."

"That's what the tests are for," Jason said. "To find people with the principles you want in an agent."

"Yes."

"What if we say no?" Jason asked. "What if we don't want to be part of your order?"

"It is not my order," Shade said. "I am merely an administrator for this trial. There are other such tests, looking for people and taking many forms. Once this one is done, my obligations to the Order are done. As for you, you are not being invited to the Order. All that is being asked of you is that you be open to it, should the Order find a task to which you are suited."

"Sounds reasonable," Jason said. "Like standing at the top of a slippery slope. It's fine, because you're at the top. What about the other people in the trial? You'll use them too, right?"

"If the right circumstance and person come together, then we will use anyone."

"How does that work? A person just happens across a situation where their natural inclination will be to intervene?"

"Just so."

"And what makes you think Humphrey and I won't talk?"

"Your reluctance to speak even to me demonstrates that you have the wisdom to understand the repercussions of doing so. As for Humphrey Geller, he never learned about it in the first place."

Humphrey disappeared into thin air and Jason snorted a laugh.

"That's the duplicating magic you used for the old resolve test, right?"

"It is," Shade said.

"So now I just go?"

"You should take the scythe with you first."

"Wait, I can really take the scythe?"

"Yes."

"I didn't think you'd let me take it. Actually, that makes sense. It really rams home the idea that the Order is dead and gone. Otherwise, why would they leave the very symbol of their order to languish in some diamond-rankers collection like any old trinket."

"Indeed."

"What about the whole object of death thing?"

"That only applies to the replica in the room below."

"What do I tell people about how I got the scythe?"

"Use your ingenuity."

"That's helpful."

"If you cannot figure that much out, then you wouldn't be much use to the Order."

"I don't much want to be."

He wandered over to the scythe, slowing down as he approached.

"You're sure there's no instant death field?"

"Yes."

"How do I know you're not lying?"

"You don't."

"That's terrific."

"You may leave without it, if you like."

"Just because I take this, it doesn't mean I'm willing to be your assassin."

"I think you'll find that if ever the Order does contact you, Jason Asano, the circumstances will be more complicated and nuanced than a simple assassination."

"Just Jason, is fine."

"I would prefer to refer to you as Mr Asano."

"Whatever rows your boat, cobber."

With a steeling breath, Jason moved up to the scythe and grabbed it.

Item: [Scythe of the Reaper] (diamond rank, legendary)

The symbolic legacy of the Order of the Reaper **(tool, scythe).**

Effect: ???

Effect: ???

Effect: ???

Effect: ???

Effect: ???

The scythe wouldn't budge from its rack.

"Why is it stuck?" Jason asked. "I thought you said I could take it."

"It is not affixed in place," Shade said. "You simply lack the strength to shift its weight."

"Huh."

After a series of attempts that failed to so much as shift the scythe on its rack, Jason came up with something new. Standing right up to the scythe, he opened his inventory window on the other side. Then, with one hand on the scythe, he stepped back, the window following. When it touched the scythe, the weapon vanished, appearing in his inventory as an icon. Jason looked at it with satisfaction.

"Nice."

Quest: [The Hidden Trial]

Objective complete: Claim the scythe 1/1.

Quest complete.
100 [Iron Spirit Coins] have been added to your inventory.
[Reaper Token] has been added to your inventory.

"Okay," Jason said wearily. "I am really ready to get out of here."

He headed back in the direction of the archway he had come in through. He was about to step in when someone stepped out. It was Sigrid, Valdis team member.

"What are you doing here?" Jason asked, stepping back to give her space.

"I'm not sure," Sigrid said, looking around. "Where is here?"

"She figured it out," Shade said.

"I realised that the reason you wanted out was to avoid the attention of the Order of the Reaper that still existed."

"Well, congratulations," Jason said. "Shade can explain everything; I'm out. I took the scythe by the way, so you'll have to ask Shade if he has a spare."

"A spare?"

"Shade," Jason said, pointing at the archway. "Does this thing actually go where I want, this time?"

"It does."

"Great," Jason said, patting Sigrid on the shoulder. "I'll see you on the other side."

61
MAKING AN EXIT

The shadow gate took Jason from the tower at the heart of the city to one of those at the city's edge. He emerged at the base of one of the archway towers, not far from where ruins gave way to sea. He was surrounded by other adventurers, milling about, regrouping or making their way up the stairs that wound their way around the tower.

He was immediately bombarded with messages as his contacts and party members came into range. His team quickly contacted him through voice chat, relieved that he had come back alive. Humphrey had already arrived, surprised that Jason hadn't appeared first, and had told the team about the tests they faced.

From the crowd gathered, it seemed as though Shade had sent everyone to the same tower to exit. Jason quickly found Humphrey, easily identified as he stood taller than everyone but the few leonids and draconians, for a face-to-face conversation.

"What happened?" Humphrey asked. "I left right after you, but you're only arriving now?"

"Shade wanted a quiet chat," Jason said softly, not wanting to draw attention.

Humphrey raised an inquisitive eyebrow. "Did you…?"

"Yeah."

Humphrey shook his head. "I never should have doubted you."

"You doubted me?"

"No, now that I think about it."

Jason laughed slapping Humphrey on the shoulder.

"Let's go track down everyone else."

Clive and Neil had teamed up with Beth's team, minus Beth herself who was absent with Jason and Humphrey. While plenty of groups were taking their last opportunity to hunt treasure, the mixed team had taken it upon themselves to look for cultists. Clive had brought along everything he could think of to track potential cultist activity, but had come up empty.

Jason and Humphrey met up with Clive and Neil, who led everyone to where Jory and Sophie had set up a comfortable space to wait for everyone else. Rather than go search for fresh enemies or last-minute treasure, they had picked out a nice spot by the water, strung up a camp shade and a hammock, laid down a blanket and put out a folding chair. Sophie relaxed in the hammock as Jory sat contentedly in the chair, both reading books.

Jason and Humphrey converged on the little camp, arriving just after Clive, Neil and Beth's team. The greetings were warm with relief at having passed through weeks of life-threatening danger. The feeling of having survived everything and knowing they were safe for the moment was amazing. It was only heightened by the bitter knowledge that not every team was so lucky.

Even Sophie joined in the welcoming hugs, at least for Humphrey. Jason she gave a look up and down and a simple, "You didn't die then."

"Disappointed?" he asked.

"I'm glad you're alive," she conceded. "There'd be a bunch of legal trouble with my indenture if you died."

"That seems harsh," Neil said. "And that's coming from someone who was vaguely hoping he would at least get maimed a little."

"Oh, I'm feeling the love here," Jason said.

"You did almost kill her," Jory said. "It took me and a priest of the Healer to cleanse that curse and the poison you loaded her up with. Even then, it was a near thing."

They expanded Jory's camp space with more chairs and a refreshments table filled with sandwiches and iced tea. As they settled in, Sophie sat next to Jason on a soft rug, casually knocking her shoulder into his.

"I am glad you didn't die," she said softly, as if the reluctant sincerity of her words were a skittish animal that would run off when startled. Jason flashed her a trademark impish grin.

"While our esteemed team leaders have been trying to get themselves killed over a scythe no one apparently got their hands on," Clive said, "the rest of us were looking into the cultist problem. I've been concentrating our search around the tower, because these towers ringing the city are the anchors that bind this astral space to our world. The cultists will have to disrupt them to sever that connection, so I've been looking for traces of magical interference. The towers are fascinating in themselves but, so far as I can tell, the one here is functioning unimpeded. It could be they're working on other towers, or using some kind of astral magic we've never heard of."

"Maybe the cultists didn't want to risk sending anyone," Humphrey suggested. "Emir's people were checking auras."

"No," Jason said. "The cultists could have either sent people who didn't have star seeds or people who've had star seeds so long that the aura imprint the Magic Society has for them includes the seed."

"You think the cult has been in Greenstone long enough for that?" asked Mose.

Mose Cavendish was Beth's cousin, an elf with destructive fire and wind spells who Jason and Humphrey had shared a contract with in the past. A classic glass cannon, he had worked hard since then to earn a spot on his cousin's team.

"They've definitely been in Greenstone for a while," Neil said. "You don't operate on the scale we've seen without people taking notice. Not unless you build up very slowly and very carefully."

"The question on my mind, then," Humphrey said, "is whether Clive not finding anything is good or bad."

"Definitely bad," Jason said. "We're all about to evacuate. If I was a deeply committed cultist—and the fact that they all explode when caught suggests they are—then I wouldn't try anything with everyone here. I'd stay behind and get the job done once we're all gone. Presumably, being trapped here only lasts until the astral space is cut loose and the Builder comes along to scoop it up."

"I'm not sure I'm following this conversation," said Hudson. He was the front-liner for Beth's team and even larger than Humphrey, with a propensity for conjuring walls of earth. Jason's team was unusual in how much they knew about the Builder cult and the threat they posed. Beth's team and Jory listened with horror as Clive explained.

During the explanation Beth rejoined her team. Valdis and Keane's teams also found their way to the camp, requiring Clive to backtrack his explanations a couple of times. That proved helpful—the repetition helped those less adept at taking in the explanations of great astral beings, astral spaces and the idea of stealing them.

Some of the foreign adventurers already knew some of it, notably Valdis and Sigrid. Even they had little understanding of the mechanisms involved, however, and were impressed as Clive elucidated the various details.

"Are you sure you're happy with your current team?" Valdis asked him again, earning a swat on the arm from Sigrid.

"Right in front of his team," Sigrid said. "You are shameless. Also, he's not going to agree to leave them while they're right in front of him. You have to take him aside, where you can explain how much better we are."

Jason burst out laughing. "And you say he's shameless."

Clive finished his explanation with the assumption that the Builder cult would be targeting the astral space they were currently in.

"So, what do we do?" Valdis asked. "It was clear, going in, that the cult would be after this astral space. Did anyone devise a plan to deal with that?"

"We had no idea what we would encounter," Jason said. "Basically, we were told to keep out eyes open and trust our judgement."

"In our earlier discussion, before you came along," Clive said, "we concluded that the cultists among us will likely be staying behind while the rest evacuate before the astral space closes."

"Leaving them free to do their work once everyone else is gone," Valdis reasoned. "Disregarding the monsters, those ghost-things and the flesh creatures, anyway. Could we try taking some kind of roster? All these teams were scoping each other out before we even came. I bet we could get a full list of participants, if we asked around."

"Wouldn't matter," Sigrid said. "There's no way of knowing who died or used their esca pe medallions to leave. We don't even know if Shade sent people to other archway towers to leave. This looks like everyone, but we can't be sure."

"I don't think there's anything we can do," Humphrey said. "We don't have much in the way of options that I can see, and we won't have any once we leave. Staying behind is not an option, either. Success would still mean being trapped here forever, while failure would leave us in the Builder's hands."

Valdis nodded. "I don't see any worthwhile option, either. In which case, we may as well leave. There's nothing left for us here."

Jason, Beth and Humphrey looked at each other and shared a nod.

"Agreed," Beth said.

Keane's team leader, Roland, did likewise.

They joined the steady stream of people already ascending the tower, chatting as they casually made their way up the spiralling stairs. The steps were stone pegs set into the tower wall, wide enough to go two by two. The teams mixed together, relaxing and talking together now that they were almost out. The front cluster consisted of Valdis, Sigrid, Beth, Humphrey, Jason and Keane.

"You know, I actually had a chance at the scythe," Beth said.

"Really?" Valdis asked, shooting a glance at Sigrid.

"There was an extra room for people who figured out the last puzzle," Beth said.

"What was the hidden trial?" Valdis asked.

"Best kept to myself, thank you," Beth told him.

"That's what Sigrid said," Valdis complained.

"Then you should stop asking," Sigrid told him.

"I was too late," Beth said. "I was the fourth one there. I didn't see who got the scythe because they'd already left. Unless Sigrid was lying and she took it before I got there."

"I didn't," Sigrid said.

"According to Shade," Beth said, "someone figured out the hidden trial before the rest of us knew there was one, which is how they went and claimed it so quickly."

"That definitely wasn't Sigrid, then," Valdis said. "I was with her when she figured it out. Jason and Humphrey, you two were already gone. You practically leaped through that shadow gate."

"I just wanted to get out before people turned on each other over the scythe," Jason said.

"You say that," Valdis said, "but if I recall correctly, Humphrey was wondering if you'd figured it out right before the pair of you made yourselves scarce. You were the first two through the gate."

"Jason, did you get the scythe?" Keane asked.

"Of course not," Jason said.

"He's lying," Sophie said from behind Jason. "You can tell when he's lying."

"How?" Valdis asked with eager curiosity.

"He's awake," Sophie said. "Even his body language is manipulative."

"That's true," Humphrey said with a laugh.

"I'm feeling very put upon."

"I know your pain," Valdis said, giving Jason's shoulder a commiserating pat. "My team gangs up on me too."

"You say gang up," Sigrid said. "Somehow he always seems to outnumber us, even though there's just one of him."

"I can't help having the virile verve of ten men," Valdis said. "It's just the way I am."

"It's a blessing and a curse, right?" Jason asked.

"So true," Valdis agreed.

"We should push them off the side," Sigrid said.

"I don't know about your guy," Sophie said, "but ours has a slow fall power, so it's no good."

They reached the top, where Shade was guiding adventurers through the shadow gate in the middle of the flat roof. As Jason approached, Shade stopped him.

"Oh, what now?" Jason asked.

"You have the Reaper's token," Shade said.

"How do you know that?"

"I can sense it. I am connected to it."

"Why?" Jason asked warily.

"I am a summoned being," Shade said. "I could be described as a familiar of this place, in the same way I was once the familiar of the man who built it. Like all familiars, I am an astral entity merely inhabiting this vessel. My true nature is a shadow of the Reaper."

"Wait," Jason said. "You mean the Reaper's actual shadow? As in, park a lamp next to the guy and whooshka, there you are?"

"The Reaper has many shadows," Shade said. "I am but one of a multitude."

"So, what does this token do, exactly?" Jason asked.

"Jason, we're holding up the line," Neil called forward. "People are getting grumpy."

"Go," Shade said to Jason. "Incorporate the token into your ritual of awakening."

Looking unhappily back at the press of adventurers, Jason went through the shadow gate. On the other side, in the once-drowned village at the bottom of the lake, Gary, Rufus and Emir's staff were greeting the adventurers as they returned through the archway. They sent the iron-rankers shuffling out of the way to make room for the constant stream behind them. Overhead, the magical dome kept out the water.

Jason spotted Emir, who was standing and talking with Constance. Next to him was his granddaughter, Ketis. A number of adventurers tried to approach but were turned away by more of his staff.

"Clive, go set up the air-bubble ritual," Jason said. "I'm going to chat with Emir and then we can go see some genuine sky, instead of the fake astral space one."

"I thought the astral space was quite nice," Neil said as Jason wandered off.

"Since when is he in charge?" Sophie asked.

"I'd give him this one," Humphrey told her in a low voice.

"You mean," Sophie replied in little more than a whisper, "he really did get his hands on thing?"

"Yes," Humphrey said.

"Oh, no," Neil groaned.

"He's going to be so insufferably smug," Sophie said.

"He did beat all these people," Humphrey said. "This is not inconsiderable competition."

"I'd rather Beth won," Sophie said. "Or Sigrid. Anyone with some humility, really."

"So, anyone but Valdis, really," Clive said.

"I think you might want to follow his advice about setting up the ritual," Humphrey said to Clive. "We may welcome a quick escape very shortly."

"Good point," Neil said. "Say what you will about Jason, I doubt it will involve the word understated."

They headed in the direction of the closest dome wall. In the meantime, Jason approached the invisible cordon around Emir marked only by a pair of his staff.

"Greg," Jason greeted.

"Asano."

"Can I see him?"

Greg turned to glance at Emir, who nodded and Jason was allowed through. This did not go unnoticed by the other adventurers.

"Welcome back," Emir said, wearily. "I heard that the arbiter of the trials refused the scythe to everyone."

"He handed out plenty of books," Jason said. "You'll have no trouble filling the gaps in the young lady's martial education. G'day, Ketis."

"We've already heard that no one got the scythe," Ketis said.

"Indeed we have," Emir said. "We talked to a couple of people who passed all the trials and said it wasn't given to anyone. Rufus thought differently, though."

"Oh?" Jason asked.

"He said that you wouldn't let something not being possible stop you. He bet me an exquisite bottle of wine that you'd come swaggering out, say something obnoxious and produce the scythe."

"Well, of course I'm doing that," Jason said. "I'm not a scrub."

Jason held his hand out and the scythe appeared, immediately dropping to the ground. The shaft landing on its end smashed cobbles from the sheer weight, then it toppled over, cracking stone again as it crashed down.

"Watch out for that one," Jason said. "There's a bit of heft to it."

"Constance," Emir said urgently. Emir's chief of staff took out a large black sheet and laid it on the ground. Emir was barely able to lift it, straining even his gold-rank strength to hold it up long enough for Constance to slip the sheet under it. After a moment resting on the sheet, gold and silver light started sparkling over it.

"The genuine article," Emir said breathlessly.

He looked up to see Jason had already strode off, his cloak now swirling around him as he made a beeline for his team at the edge of the dome. They were ready and waiting, their private air bubble like a growth on the side of the dome.

While all eyes were on Jason, Rufus and Gary had moved to join Emir.

"What did I tell you?" Rufus asked Emir. "That man cannot help showing off."

"You have to give it to him, though," Gary said. "He knows how to make an exit. I don't think he's done, either. Are you seeing that?"

From within Jason's cloak, blue-grey light was shining, emitting from beneath his skin. As he reached his teammates, the onlookers realised that the same light was shining not just from Jason but his entire team.

Quest: [Legacy of the Reaper]
All objectives complete.
Quest complete.

Reward: Racial gift transfiguration.

Jason had been ignoring the objective completions of the quest because he had never expected to complete it. It was only now that he was willing to revel in the outlandish reward. He conjured his cloak to hide the idiotic grin so wide he felt it trying to unhinge the top of his head. Looking ahead to his team he saw the light start to shine from them and he hurried to meet them.

"It feels tingly," Sophie said.

"I know you had that quest thing, but I can't believe it can actually do this," Neil said.

"The paper I write on this is going to be so well-received," Clive said.

"Well," Humphrey said, putting a hand on Jason's shoulder. "We've officially arrived now. You'd better believe word of this will be spreading around."

"Let's just go," Jason said.

They climbed on the ritual platform Clive had prepared and slid out of the dome. Light continued to shine from them as the assembled adventurers watched them drift away.

Outworlder racial ability [Map] has evolved to [Tactical Map].

Ability: [Tactical Map]
Transfigured from [Outworlder] ability [Map].

Self-updating map. Unveils as areas are explored.

A small, semi-opaque map allows tracking of nearby allies and enemies. This is a tracking effect.

"Mini-map, not bad," Jason murmured to himself as his team members looked at their own abilities.

Party member [Clive Standish]'s human racial ability [Human Ambition] has evolved to [Thirst For Knowledge].

Party member [Neil Davone]'s elf racial ability [Life Affinity] has evolved to [Life Guard].

Party member [Sophie Wexler]'s celestine racial ability [Mana Integrity] has evolved to [Mana Wellspring].

Party member [Humphrey Geller]'s Human racial ability [Special Attack Affinity] has evolved to [Attack of the Mirage Dragon].

"Look at that," Jason said. "Neil really is an elf."

"Shut up, Asano."

62
SHALLOW EARTH

Humphrey's team had been eager to test out their new abilities as soon as they reached shore, but things were a little busy. While the iron-rankers were in the astral space, even more people had been awaiting their return. Many of the foreign adventurers had brought family, not even including the locals. The cloud palace had been placed offshore from a small town that had been going through what was essentially a festival for the better part of three weeks. The townsfolk were exhausted but increasingly wealthy, with towns and villages all around the lake being roped-in. A small army of demanding visitors had brought a tidal wave of money to the local economy.

Things were all the more vibrant now that a steady stream of adventurers was emerging from the lake and into the jubilant arms of family. Neil's family was present, more than happy to be keeping company with the Gellers. Humphrey's father and sister had returned to Greenstone while he was in the astral space and were waiting with his mother. Even Clive's parents had been roped in by Danielle Geller, looking very awkward next to Greenstone's most prestigious adventurer.

All Sophie ever had was her now long-dead father, but Belinda was her sister now, and came at her with a greeting hug. Jason looked at them all, a sense of isolation he hadn't felt in a long time creeping over him. In his old life, only his older sister's family had been close; he eschewed other people. He hadn't been happy, but he hadn't felt lonely, either.

He was overcome with the memory that this was not his world. His precious connections were also new connections. He had planted roots but they were still in shallow earth. Bringing his expression under control, he threw on a convincing grin and pulled out a recording stone.

"Hello family," he said brightly. "I'm back out of the lake now, job done. I won the little contest because it turns out I'm terrific, but the people up here don't know, yet, so I should probably not say that too loudly..."

Morning became afternoon became evening. Jason's team and their families made their way onto the cloud palace before word spread of their victory in Emir's contest. Stories of their adventures were told, delighting Humphrey's parents as much as they horrified Clive's. Clive's success in life had certainly enriched them, which to the hardworking Standish family meant a bigger eel farm. They had quite liked that their son had a nice, safe job in an office.

"You can't keep someone with Clive's talent cooped up," Danielle told them. "Did you know Emir has been trying to hire him away?"

"So has Prince Valdis, from the Mirror Kingdom," Humphrey said.

"Wait," Clive's mother said. "That Valdis you've been talking about is a prince?"

Sophie made a quiet exit and found Jason hidden away, leaning over a balcony as he watched more adventurers emerge from the water to ebullient welcome. She leaned on the rail beside him, his gaze not moving.

"It's not like you to miss a chance for self-aggrandisement," she said but her voice was soft, without the usual sting.

"It's family time," Jason said. "Mine is so far away that gods can't broach the distance. They're so far away that there aren't even gods there."

"Are you sure about that? You didn't believe in magic, once, but here we are. Would it be so strange for it to be hidden from you, back on your world?"

"Knowledge told me that my world lacks the magic to support a god."

"And you trust her, all of a sudden?"

"No, but I don't think she's ever lied to me," Jason said. "She's like me; why lie, when the facts will do it for you? She's just better at it than I am."

"If it makes a difference," she said, "I think Danielle Geller is ready to adopt you."

Jason chuckled and she pulled herself off the railing.

"Come back in," she said. "What's a gathering without you telling people how great you are?"

"Excuse me?" he asked, also standing up straight. "I'll have you know that I'm incredibly humble. I challenge you to find someone more humble than me..."

The team finally snuck away to test out their new abilities, gathering in the guest hall training room. They didn't escape entirely, with Humphrey's mother, father and sister watching on from the behind the transparent wall of the observation room.

Compared to Danielle, her husband, Keith, was more akin to their son: a solid and reliable counterpoint to her domineering charms. Their daughter, Henrietta, seemed to take her role of Humphrey's older sister seriously. She made it clear that his teammates were yet to meet her approval. Even her stoic gaze had broken in incredulity, however, as Humphrey explained that the whole team had gone through simultaneous racial gift evolutions.

It was far from unknown for people to go through such events together, as the circumstances that pushed one person past their limits could easily affect another in the same way. Humphrey and Jason had experienced exactly that in their fight against the hydra. For an entire team to do so was something else altogether. Despite some probing questions from Danielle and her daughter, the team had agreed to hide Jason's role as the catalyst.

There was no hiding that it had happened, though, and the team tested out their new abilities, where appropriate. Clive had been initially unhappy with his racial gift.

Ability: [Thirst For Knowledge]
Transfigured from [Human] ability [Human Ambition].

Essence abilities advance more quickly.

Learn information through the use of skill books.

"Skill books? Skill books are for people too stupid to learn the proper way. No offence, Jason."

"You and your skill book prejudice," Jason said. "There's nothing wrong with being a utility guy. My racial gifts aren't exactly cutting my enemies down like wheat. Think of all the mundane things you have to learn that take away from how you really want to spend your time. Now you can just skill-book the unimportant stuff and spend your time where it really matters."

"Huh," Clive said thoughtfully. "I never thought of it like that."

"Take martial arts, for example," Jason said. "You never took the time to learn hand-to-hand skills, but now you can skill-book them. They won't match up to Sophie, or even me, with the time I've put in, but they may be the difference between life and death in a pinch."

No one argued that Neil's ability was anything but a boon to the team.

Ability: [Life Guard]
Transfigured from [Elf] ability [Life Affinity].

Effects used or received with a positive effect on life have greater effect.

Using a shield-based essence ability on allies also bestows a heal-over-time effect.

They tested out the healing, which wasn't especially potent but still noticeable. Where Neil's ability restored health, Sophie's replenished mana.

Ability: [Mana Wellspring]
Transfigured from [Celestine] ability [Mana Integrity].

Ongoing mana costs for maintained abilities are reduced. Resistance to mana drain effects is increased.

When mana is not being consumed by an ongoing ability, mana regeneration for self and allies within your aura is significantly increased.

Clive's aura ability likewise increased mana regeneration and some quick testing with overlapping the auras revealed the combined effect was impressive.

"We're never going to run of mana," Neil said as he watched his mana bar refill. Jason had shown them how to pull up indicators for mana, stamina and health.

"Speak for yourself," Humphrey said. "You may be underestimating how quickly I can burn through it. My dragon essence racial gift lets me burn mana to increase my physical and magical strength. If I use that and run through my powers one after the other, I can empty the tank very quickly."

"What about the new one?" Jason asked. "Yours is the one we've all been waiting for."

"Agreed," Neil said. "Why mirage dragon?"

"Stash is a mirage dragon," Humphrey said. A mouse poked its head out of Humphrey's chest pocket and he scratched its head.

"I kept him hidden through the trials because I didn't want to draw too much attention. Mirage dragons are rare, even for dragons, and I don't want anyone trying to kill me and take him."

"Well, let's see the new ability," Jason said.

Ability: [Attack of the Mirage Dragon]
Transfigured from [Human] ability [Special Attack Affinity].

You are more likely to awaken special attacks than other ability types. Your special attacks have increased effect.

When you make special attacks, you can expend mana to create a short-lived, illusory double, replicating the attack. The illusion does not inflict damage or duplicate other effects from the attack but you can spend mana to switch-teleport with it, in the moment it is created. This is an illusion and teleport effect.

"What the hell kind of cheat ability is that?" Jason asked.

They watched Humphrey and Sophie engage in some light sparring. Humphrey's attacks were suited more for fighting monsters than people, which normally gave her a relatively easy time blocking or dodging them. Even just learning to use his deceptive new double attacks already made the difficulty skyrocket.

"That's awful," Sophie said once they were done. "The flexibility that adds to your attacks is just mad."

"I think we can safely say who won the racial gift lottery," Jason said, although he was quite happy with his own ability. The mini map floating in his vision had green dots for his allies and yellow dots for other people. He hadn't encountered an enemy yet but expected them to show up as red.

Jason sighed.

"No, Clive. No, and I mean it."

"This an incredible opportunity. All these people looking for rituals of awakening and you wouldn't even have to do anything. I'll do the rituals and you just have to cycle them through your party."

Jason rubbed his temples.

"Clive, you're not listening. Humphrey, please explain it to Clive."

They had quietly occupied one of the guest-wing terraces, begging off their families to get some rest. The sun had gone down but the cloud palace lit up with internal illumination and they enjoyed the warm night air, reclined on a series of loungers. From below, the sounds of celebration rose up from where the adventurers had set up camp between the cloud palace and the town.

After weeks of constant danger, the sudden safety was like releasing a pressure valve. Most of them fell asleep until Clive started advocating to record every ability awakened with the reaper stones so many adventurers had received.

"Jason already drew more attention to his abilities than he probably should when we all advanced our racial abilities," Humphrey said. "Getting people even more interested is a dangerous proposition."

"It's why Rufus, Gary and Farrah warned me to keep the outworlder thing under my hat," Jason said. "What happens when someone shares your interest in my abilities, Clive, but they're gold-rank and don't care about my opinion? I get hauled-off in the night and you never see me again."

"It just seems like a waste of potential," Clive said.

"Before I came here," Jason said, "wasting my potential was kind of my thing."

"Sometimes you just have to accept what you get and let the rest go," Sophie told Clive.

Jason was deliberately keeping his eyes from where she languidly stretched out on the lounger, concerned they would fall out of his head.

"If you run around chasing the best possible result," Neil told Clive, "you might miss out on the great thing you gave up to maintain the chase."

"Meaning what?"

"Meaning that Jason isn't going to bend on this and if you keep pushing, he'll kick you out of the party until we've all done our awakening rituals."

"So, you're saying I should be happy with recording the abilities of our own team?" Clive asked, reluctance still thick in his voice.

"After that display the gift evolutions," Neil said, "keeping Jason's abilities to ourselves may be closing the gate after the heidel's run off, at this point. Maybe compromise, Asano. Let Clive do the awakening rituals for our party, Cavendish's party and maybe Prince Valdis's. It's not like he isn't already paying attention."

Jason gave a groaning sigh.

"I can live with that," he conceded.

"Great!" Clive said, erupting out of his chair. "I'll go get things organised."

"Hold your heidels, chief," Jason said. "We should get ourselves sorted before we start rounding up anyone else."

"He's right," Humphrey said. "If nothing else, we have some awakening stones to collect from Emir."

"Then let's go find him!" Clive said.

"Tomorrow," Humphrey said firmly. "Tonight, we rest."

63
RELIEF

On his return to the cloud palace the next day, Emir's first action was securing the scythe. His second was seeking out Jason and his team on the balcony terrace and enjoying a light lunch.

"Join us," Jason said as Emir arrived.

"I'm a little busy right now," Emir said.

"Are you sure?" Jason asked. "We've got gold plum soufflé."

"Well," Emir said. "I suppose we can talk over lunch."

"So, have you come to give us some top-end awakening stones?"

"Actually, I've come to give you four hundred and nineteen time-displaced priests who came out of the archway very confused and asking for you by name."

"Oh, right," Jason said. "It turns out that the entity running the trials had a bunch of priests and holy warriors locked up from back in the day. I talked him into letting them all go. I didn't realise there would be quite that many, but I suppose they needed enough for everyone. I wasn't sure he would actually come through and let them out. Are you really leaving them to me to deal with? I'd have thought you'd be all over those people and what they knew."

"Actually, yes," Emir admitted. "I have a historian on staff who practically had a fit when I told her about them. I think we'll end up thoroughly debriefing them, then turning them over to their various churches to deal with. Whatever we may think of certain religious organisations, right now, I don't see much of a better option."

"They may not all want to go back," Jason said. "I could see some of them being disillusioned by what they went through."

"Not everyone is as cavalier with the churches as you, Jason," Emir said. "If any of them do put their faith aside, you can coordinate with the Adventure Society to sort it out."

"I imagine they'll take it out of my hands," Jason said. "It sounds like more of a three-star adventurer problem, which is too difficult for simple old me with my solitary star."

"True," Emir said, earning him an affronted look from Jason. "And about those rewards, I'll have Constance bring you a list of the awakening stones we have. You can choose any five you like."

"What about the cloud palace?" Humphrey asked. "That was the reward that had all the adventurers salivating."

"Obviously there's only one cloud palace to be had," Emir said. "It's a bonded item, so you'll need to decide which of you it will be bonded to."

"That'll be Jason," Humphrey said. "He's the one that got the scythe, after all."

"We should at least talk about it," Jason said.

"We did," Humphrey said. "We all agreed."

Jason looked around at the team and they all nodded.

"If you don't want it, I'm happy to take it off your hands," Sophie said.

"No, that's fine," Jason said. "I'll take it."

They were able to choose five stones, one for each team member. A legendary stone was the nearest thing to actually selecting a specific power, which made picking from a selection of legendary stones an unparalleled luxury. Constance brought them a list of the stones in Emir's supply, which turned out to be startlingly large.

Neil and Jason both selected awakening stones of the avatar, known for most often producing summoning powers and powerful buffing abilities. Humphrey selected an awakening stone of rebirth, hoping for a powerful recovery power. Sophie, on Constance's advice, selected an awakening stone of the celestials. Clive chose an awakening stone of karma, the same as his confluence essence, although he would not be able to use it.

They waited in the guest wing lounge as Constance left and came back with a long wooden box, the top of which she slid off to reveal five awakening stones, sitting on black velvet.

"We had three of these, originally," Constance said as she handed the stone of the celestials to Sophie. "They were created from an outworlder's ability, like Jason's, and I've never heard of them appearing anywhere else. The only reason they appear in the Magic Society records at all is that we allowed the society to examine them."

"So you don't know what their power inclinations are?" Clive asked.

"The other two were both used by celestines," Constance said. "In both cases, the abilities enhanced their natural racial gifts."

Clive handed his stone to Sophie.

"It should pair well with your balance essence and give you something formidable," he said.

Sophie looked down at the stones she was holding in each hand. Each one was valuable on a level she could barely conceive of. Even most essences would not fetch as high a price as these, should someone squander them on the open market. She looked up at Clive who placed his hand over her, closing her fingers as she tried to hand it back. He gave her a warm smile.

"This is just the beginning," he told her. She looked around uncertainly but found supporting smiles all around. Even Jason looked uncharacteristically sincere, without his usual expression of thinking of a joke no one else knew about.

"So, whose stones to we use first?" she asked.

"Jason's," Clive said. "I want to see what those two reaper stones produce. Also, he's faster, because he doesn't need a ritual."

"Actually, I do want to use one," Jason said. "Shade said I should incorporate this into a ritual."

Jason tossed an object to Clive, a square of obsidian with a scythe engraved in silver, along with writing he couldn't read. Clive looked at it, then up at Jason.

Item: [Reaper Token] (transcendent rank, legendary)

***???* (consumable, ???).**

Effect: ???
Effect: ???

"This is an astral blessing token," he said. "For the Reaper, right?"

"Yep," Jason said.

"What's an astral blessing token?" Sophie asked.

"It's something great astral beings give out to bestow blessings, as signs of approval," Clive said. "They trigger racial gift evolutions, just like the one we all went through. I used one of these myself, back when I was Humphrey's age."

"So, it's like those star seeds?" Neil asked, shrinking away.

"No," Clive said. "The blessings are harmless. The great astral beings give them out for all kinds of reasons, to those that venerate them or that they approve of. Some astral beings have even given them out to those who work against their interests because they are enemies worthy of respect."

"And you use them as part of an awakening ritual?" Jason asked, thinking of the other token in his possession. The one the goddess of knowledge claimed would send him home.

"Some you can," Clive said. "They tend to arrange for specific abilities if you do. That's something only transcendent beings like gods can arrange. Every token has an additional effect, and some can only be triggered in certain ways. If Shade told you to use it with an awakening ritual, it should probably be with one of the Reaper stones."

"Agreed," Jason said. "How did you get your token, Clive?"

"It just showed up one night while I was studying," Clive said. "There was this patch of moonlight in my room, even though the curtains were closed, and there it was. My mentor knew what it was and helped me use it with my next awakening ritual."

Clive frowned in thought.

"That's one interesting point," he continued. "Your token came from your ability, right? A quest reward?"

"That's right," Jason said.

"That shouldn't be possible," Clive said. "Your quest system's ability to produce items is just another loot power variant. It shouldn't be able to produce an astral blessing token. Only great astral beings can do that."

"Maybe I'm secretly a great astral being," Jason said. "I could have knocked up a crappy body, chucked in some fake memories and shoved a chunk of my consciousness into it to get a mortal perspective. Or for laughs, whatever."

Clive's eyes went wide in horror as he stared at Jason.

"That… no… that can't be… no… but… no. Wait… no… that can't be right."

"Mate, calm down," Jason told him. "I'm not secretly the Reaper."

"But, I mean, conceivably…"

"No," Jason said firmly. "These beings can just make the tokens appear if they like, right? Surely the Reaper, having about a squillion times more power than me, could have tweaked my ability to produce it this one time. Just a reward for getting his magic farming tool."

"Yeah," Clive said, nodding to himself. "That makes more sense."

"Exactly. Now, do you know how to incorporate this thing into an essence ritual?"

"Oh, Absolutely," Clive said, perking up. "Let's get into a ritual room and do this."

Clive was as good as his word, setting up a more elaborate magic circle than he had for Sophie's awakenings. Jason stood the middle, the awakening stone of the Reaper in one hand and the Reaper token in the other.

"Ready?" Clive asked him.

"Yeah," Jason said.

"What are you hoping for?" Clive asked.

"Well, apparently Shade is looking for a new gig," Jason said. "I thought he'd make an awesome familiar."

"Seriously?"

"Why not? Colin's great, don't get me wrong, but the conversation isn't exactly sparkling."

Clive shook his head and conducted the ritual. It went as normal, aside from the Reaper token melding into his body along with the awakening stone, and felt to Jason no different than absorbing them normally.

You have awakened the dark essence ability [Shadow of the Reaper]. You have awakened 4 of 5 dark essence abilities.

Ability: [Shadow of the Reaper] (Dark)
Familiar (ritual).
Cost: Extreme mana.
Cooldown: None.

Current rank: Iron 0 (00%)

Effect (iron): Summon a [Shadow of the Reaper] to serve as a familiar.

"That looks like a winner," Jason said. "I think I might have actually done it?"

As the others read his ability through the party interface, blue-grey light started shining from Jason's body.

"As expected," Clive said.

[Reaper Token] has been consumed.

Outworlder racial ability [Mysterious Stranger] has evolved to [Dark Rider].

Ability: [Dark Rider]
Transfigured from [Outworlder] ability [Mysterious Stranger].

Language adaptation.
Essence, awakening stone and skill book absorption.
Immunity to identification and tracking effects.
Shadow-based familiars may adopt the form of a mount appropriate to the environment.

"Oh, a mount power, sweet," Jason said. "Now I don't have to farm all that gold."

Then he looked at the requirements for the summoning ritual his new familiar power would require.

[Shadow of the Reaper] summoning ritual material requirements:

343 [Dark Quintessence Gems (Iron)].
2401 [Iron Rank Spirit Coins].
500 grams of [Midnight Onyx Powder].
1 [Midnight Jade].
24 small, square [Night Stone] plates.

"Farming for crafting mats isn't entirely off the table it seems."

"What are you talking about?" Sophie asked.

"The ritual to summon my new familiar. It takes a bunch of stuff I don't have."

"It should have been the same for your first familiar, right?" Clive asked. "Even more costly, if anything. Your first familiar is an apocalypse beast, after all."

"Did you just say apocalypse?" Neil asked.

"Don't worry about that," Jason said. "It's fine."

"Apocalypse?" Neil asked again.

"I said it's fine. Tell him it's fine, Clive."

"He's right," Clive said. "Until he reaches diamond rank, it definitely won't be able to wipe out an entire world's worth of life."

"WHAT?"

"Clive, I said to tell him it's fine, not anything about scouring the world of life, which Colin would never do."

"He might," Clive said.

"He wouldn't eat the plants, would he?" Jason asked.

"Oh, you're probably right," Clive said. "Do you still have the book from the blood cult? It might be in that."

"Yeah, Farrah gave it to me when she was done with it. Because of my familiar. Actually, the blood cult is why I had such an easy time summoning Colin. They took off with all the high-end goods but left behind a pile of iron-rank materials. And being a blood cult, there was plenty of iron-rank materials to knock out the ritual. When Rufus was splitting the loot he gave me a spare set in case something happened and I had to resummon the little guy."

"You'll have to do some shopping," Humphrey said. "In the meantime, how about your other awakening stones?"

"Oh, yeah," Jason said, rubbing his hands together, then plucked another awakening stone from his inventory. "Another Reaper stone. I'm running out of chances to get that necrotic affliction I've been after, and I think this is the one."

After the ritual he used to absorb his last stone, quietly absorbing the next one seemed anticlimactic.

You have awakened the dark essence ability [Hand of the Reaper]. You have awakened 5 of 5 dark essence abilities.

You have awakened all dark essence abilities. Linked attribute [Speed] will advance in conjunction with lowest-rank dark essence ability.

Ability: [Hand of the Reaper] (Dark)
Conjuration (disease).
Cost: Low mana-per-second.
Cooldown: None.

Current rank: Iron 0 (00%)

Effect (iron): Conjure a highly flexible, semi-substantial shadow-arm that can extend or shrink. Conjured items can be conjured into the shadow hand. Can be used to make melee special attacks. Special attacks made using the arm inflict [Creeping Death] in addition to other effects.

[Creeping Death] (damage-over-time, disease, stacking): Inflicts ongoing necrotic damage until the disease is cleansed. Additional instances have a cumulative effect.

A huge grin spread across Jason's face. The lack of a necrotic damage affliction in his repertoire of abilities been preying on his mind increasingly as his available slots diminished. The relief at closing the gap in his power set was like finally taking a wee after desperately holding it in for too long and he let out a contented sigh.

"That power sounds strange," Sophie said, reading the description. "It also sounds creepy. A flexible hand sneaking about?"

"It seems like it'll be versatile," Humphrey said. "You can use it to make special attacks, but also just increase your ability to reach. It's no telekinesis power but I imagine you'll get some use out of it."

"I'll give it a try," Jason said.

He reached out with his arm, which transmuted into the same shadow-stuff his cloak was made of. It extended out to slip around Humphrey's ankle like a constrictor snake.

"I can use this in combat for more than just making attacks," Jason said and yanked back hard with the shadow arm. Humphrey didn't budge, though, Jason instead yanking himself off his feet and falling to an undignified heap.

"It doesn't seem to increase my strength at all," he said from the floor.

"You'll need to test it extensively to see what you can and can't do with it," Humphrey told him. "For now, move onto the next stone."

"Right," Jason said. "I can knock out the last one and someone else can jump into the spotlight."

He took out the last stone, the awakening stone of the avatar.

"It's going to be a doom power," Jason said. "Do you think it will be some super-hideous affliction?"

"I think it's more likely to be a summoning power," Clive said. "Maybe one that runs around, causing afflictions for you?"

"I already have Colin for that," Jason said.

"Other than summons," Clive said, "avatar stones are known for enhancement and transformation powers. If it's from the doom essence, maybe it turns you into a blob of pustulant flesh that spurts gobbets of poisons from the sores all over your body."

Everyone gave Clive a wary look.

"What?" Clive asked.

"That isn't actually an option is it?" Jason asked.

"Sure it is," Clive said encouragingly. "I've read a case study about someone with a very similar power. It was actually a fascinating case because the permanent nature of the transformation made it resistant to suppression collars."

"Permanent?" Jason asked, his face wan.

"I'm sure it'll be fine," Neil said happily, giving Jason a pat on the back. "If it's really bad we can push you around in a wheelbarrow or something."

"I'm not going to be the one pushing it," Sophie said.

"You're his indentured servant," Neil told her. "I think it has to be you."

"The guy I read about was more or less humanoid," Clive said, "so that shouldn't be an issue."

"More or less?" Jason repeated.

"He certainly had something that could pass as legs," Clive said.

"Maybe I should find an awakening stone more special-attack oriented," Jason said.

"Don't let them talk you out of using such a precious stone," Humphrey said. "I'm sure you'll be fine. We would never push you around in a wheelbarrow."

"Thanks," Jason said gratefully.

"We'd have someone make a little magic cart," Humphrey continued. "Probably with something to seal in the smell, because I have to imagine it would be bad."

"Oh, it definitely would," Clive said. "Instead of sweating, the guy secreted this oil that kept him cool and killed insects, but was apparently very pungent."

"Alright, you all need to stop talking," Jason said.

64
GLORY

Despite the best efforts of his team to unnerve him, Jason used his final awakening stone, albeit with eyes closed and whispering to himself.

"Don't turn into a blob, don't turn into a blob, don't turn into a blob…"

You have awakened the doom essence ability [Avatar of Doom]. You have awakened 5 of 5 doom essence abilities.

You have awakened all doom essence abilities. Linked attribute [Spirit] will advance in conjunction with lowest-rank doom essence ability.

Ability: [Avatar of Doom] (Doom)
Familiar (ritual).
Cost: Extreme mana.
Cooldown: None.

Current rank: Iron 0 (00%).

Effect (iron): Summon an [Avatar of Doom] to serve as a familiar.

"Another familiar power," Jason said. "I'm turning into a pet character. I don't suppose anyone knows what an avatar of doom is?"

"It isn't something I've heard of," Clive said, pulling out his monster archive tablet. After looking through for a few moments, he shook his head.

"Not here," he said. "You get that with summoned familiars quite a lot, though, seeing as they're all beings from the deep astral. It's an endless supply of bizarre and terrifying horrors."

"We don't know it'll be terrifying," Jason said.

"It's called an avatar of doom," Neil said. "I doubt it's going to be a healer-type familiar."

"That's an option?" Jason asked. "Having your own personal healer?"

"My sister has one," Humphrey said. "But she's a summoning specialist, so she has one of just about everything."

"Oh, bloody hell," Jason said, looking over the summoning ritual requirements.

[Shadow of the Reaper] summoning ritual material requirements:
108 [Radiant Quintessence Gems (Iron)].
108 [Void Quintessence Gems (Iron)].
1296 [Iron Rank Spirit Coins].

"These ritual materials are awful," Jason said. "Void and radiant quintessence?"

"Ouch," Clive said. "That's going to be worse than the other one."

"Lucky we just got a haul of treasure, then," Sophie said. "That plant quintessence might be common, but we have piles of the stuff, and it's bronze-rank."

"That'll put a dent in the price," Jason acknowledged.

"The problem will be sourcing the materials," Clive said. "I know the Magic Society has some radiant quintessence, although it won't part with it cheaply. I think the void quintessence will be your main obstacle. It's actually harder to get at iron than it is at higher ranks, even if it's cheaper."

"We can worry about that later," Jason said. "It's someone else's turn to use their stones."

"Right," Clive said. "I'll set up a ritual while you all decide who goes next."

"We still need to organise my stones," Sophie said. "I'll wait until later."

"Sensible," Humphrey said. "Would you like to go next, Neil?"

"Is there any chance of Neil turning into a blob monster?" Jason asked Clive hopefully.

Clive hummed thoughtfully as he used his power to draw out a ritual circle.

"If I recall correctly," Clive said, "you have open spots in the shield and growth essences, right, Neil? The avatar stone could have some blob-related results in the growth essence. As for the Reaper stone, who knows?"

"That's comforting," Neil said. "I was more looking for another summon, or maybe a buff spell. A shield golem would be nice."

"Shield golem?" Jason asked. "That actually does sound awesome. I hope you get that."

Neil's ritual of awakening went off without incident in Clive's capable hands.

You have awakened the growth essence ability [Hero's Moment]. You have awakened 5 of 5 growth essence abilities.

You have awakened all growth essence abilities. Linked attribute [Spirit] will advance in conjunction with lowest-rank growth essence ability.

Ability: [Hero's Moment] (Growth)
Spell (boon, recovery).
Cost: Extreme mana.
Cooldown: 24 hours.

Current rank: Iron 0 (00%).

Effect (iron): Bestow a powerful boon on an ally, increasing all attributes and resistances by a significant amount. They receive damage reduction, their maximum mana and stamina are increased and they gain ongoing mana and stamina recovery. They ignore the effects of rank-disparity. When this effect ends, they are temporarily debilitated, suffering the inverse of all previous effects.

"There's that buff you were looking for," Jason said. "That'll turn Humphrey into a monster."

"I think the more interesting application will be Neil's summon," Clive said. "We've barely tapped into what we can do with it. You may or may not remember that when heavily damaged, it undergoes a transformation based on what it was subjected to before the change. Imagine what it would get out of having that spell used on it."

"That's an interesting point," Humphrey said. "One of our strategic thin spots is our summons. We have a few strategies build around Jason's leech swarm, but mine and Neil's summons have been rather underutilised. Once we add in Jason's new familiars, we'll have quite the selection of allies at our command."

As Clive set up the next ritual, the others postulated Neil's last ability.

"The only unawakened ability I have is from the shield essence," Neil said. "What kind of ability will come from a stone associated with death?"

"Another one of your quick bubble-shields?" Jason guessed. "It could have retributive damage, like your burst shield ability."

"What about a death wall?" Humphrey said. "I remember during the last monster surge I was up on the outer walls with my father. A swarming pack of margolls came pouring at us and one of my family members put up this sheet of energy. Every monster that went through it died on the spot."

You have awakened the shield essence ability [Reaper's Redoubt]. You have

awakened 5 of 5 shield essence abilities.

You have awakened all shield essence abilities. Linked attribute [Power] will advance in conjunction with lowest-rank shield essence ability.

Ability: [Reaper's Redoubt] (Shield)
Spell (dimension).
Cost: Extreme mana.
Cooldown: 6 hours.

Current rank: Iron 0 (00%).

Effect (iron): Take allies into a dimensional space briefly while flooding the area with death energy, dealing disruptive-force damage, necrotic damage and inflicting [Creeping Death].

[Creeping Death] (damage-over-time, disease, stacking): Inflicts ongoing necrotic damage until the disease is cleansed. Additional instances have a cumulative effect.

"I know I'm new at this whole adventurer thing," Sophie said, "but that ability sounds really strong, right?"

"That's the same affliction as my ability," Jason said. "Must be a favourite of the Reaper."

"The fact that it takes six hours before becoming available again suggests it certainly is strong," Humphrey said. "The other ability takes a whole day. Judgement of when to use your powers will be key, Neil."

"Nothing new there," Neil said.

"The utility of that new ability will depend on how close we have to be to Neil to be taken into the dimensional space," Humphrey assessed. "I don't think being left behind for those other effects would be a pleasant experience."

"It feels like I can take in anyone within about a dozen metres," Neil said. "I think we can work with that range."

Essence users all had an instinctive understanding of their abilities as the awakening stones imprinted them on the user's soul. Even without using them, there was an intrinsic understanding of an ability's properties. This was only ever hampered in unusual instances, like Jason and his shadow teleport.

Until he had broken through the mental block to give himself completely over to magic, Jason had been unable to make the shadow-jump work. Even then, however, he had an understanding of how it should work. Neil's estimate of his new power's parameters was therefore considered trustworthy.

After Neil, they moved on to Humphrey. The awakening stone of the Reaper gave him a special attack, unsurprisingly for a human.

You have awakened the magic essence ability [Spirit Reaper]. You have awakened 5 of 5 magic essence abilities.

You have awakened all magic essence abilities. Linked attribute [Spirit] will advance in conjunction with lowest-rank magic essence ability.

Ability: [Spirit Reaper] (Magic)
Special attack (melee, dimension, drain).
Cost: Low mana and stamina.
Cooldown: None.

Current rank: Iron 0 (00%).

Effect (iron): Inflicts additional disruptive-force damage and drains mana. Has additional effect against incorporeal or semi-corporeal creatures.

"An attack specialised in fighting incorporeal opponents," Humphrey said. "I might have been disappointed if I hadn't just spent weeks fighting those vorger creatures. Magic weapons could affect them, but not well."

"Also, don't overlook the use of disruptive-force damage at breaking through magic defences," Neil said. "It can break down magical shields like mine much faster than normal."

They moved on to Humphrey's final stone. He had chosen an awakening stone of rebirth, hoping for a recovery power that would increase his staying power in an extended fight or let him run at full steam for longer in a short one. He had chosen it specifically on the advice of his mother; she wanted him to avoid the flaw in her own ability set. Her powers were outrageously potent, but at a cost of rapidly consuming mana and stamina. In short bursts, she was close to invincible within her rank. Extended conflicts would leave her vulnerable, however; too drained to use her formidable abilities.

You have awakened the might essence ability [Immortality]. You have awakened 5 of 5 might essence abilities.

You have awakened all might essence abilities. Linked attribute [Power] will advance in conjunction with lowest rank might essence ability.

Ability: [Immortality] (Might)
Special ability (healing, recovery).
Cost: None.

Cooldown: 24 hours.

Current rank: Iron 0 (00%).

Effect (iron): Instantly restore a large portion of health, mana and stamina. Amount restored is based on how depleted health, mana and stamina are when the ability is used.

"Seriously?" Jason asked. "I was happy with my shadow-arm power and this guy gets immortality?"

"In fairness," Sophie said, "what would you say if asked whether you or Humphrey deserve the better power?"

"I'd say me, obviously," Jason said. "I'll lie through my teeth if there's immortality in it."

"You'll lie through your teeth if there's a halfway-decent lunch spread in it," Neil told him.

"That's fair," Jason acknowledged cheerfully.

"Congratulations," Clive said to Humphrey, slapping him on the arm. "You just acquired what may be the single most sought-after power in the world. Of course, it won't actually bring you back from the dead until gold rank."

"So, it's real immortality?" Sophie asked.

"It's a famous power, for obvious reasons," Clive said. "The Magic Society has extensive records on it. There are various limitations on its power to bring back the dead, of course. It's rumoured those limits are reduced or even eliminated at diamond rank, but I don't have the authority to access those kinds of records."

"Looks like Humphrey won the essence power lottery," Jason said.

"You should remember that you've already come back from the dead," Clive said to Jason, grabbing the attention of the group.

"It's an outworlder thing," Jason said dismissively. "Clive can explain while we go shopping."

Jason turned to Sophie.

"You said Belinda was checking out the market, right?"

"That's right," Sophie said.

"Let's go see if we can find her, then."

A market had sprung up in the adventurer camp between the cloud palace and the nearby town. Adventurers had come from the trials with dimensional bags overflowing with loot, just as Greenstone's brokers had anticipated. A series of tents, even bamboo buildings, hastily erected with magic had formed an impromptu trade fair. Jason's voice chat allowed them to contact Belinda and arrange a meeting place, but Constance intercepted Jason and the others on their way out of the cloud palace.

"Jason," she said. "Emir would like to meet with you about the priests you liberated during the last trial."

"Oh," he said, frowning. "Alright. You lot go ahead to the market and I'll meet up with you later."

Jason followed Constance to Emir's tower-top office. It was the same as his previous visit, a flat space under a translucent dome, broken up by pools of water with plants growing from them. To Jason's surprise, the head of the Adventure Society Inquiry team, Tabitha Gert, was there. She gave Jason an assessing glance but said nothing, leaving with Constance via the elevating platform as soon as Jason arrived.

Emir was sitting behind a desk that, like his chair, was made of cloud-stuff. On the opposite side of the floor, a similar chair rose from the floor as Emir waved at Jason to join him. Jason sat down, glancing at the piles of paper on Emir's desk.

"As it turns out," Emir said, following Jason's gaze, "no small part of treasure hunting is logistics. I signed up for the world travel and derring-do, yet somehow ended up buried in administration. I still need to present you the cloud palace, but I want to carve out a proper amount of time for that. Such an unusual item requires a certain amount of instruction that I don't intend to rush, and there are other concerns to be going on with."

"You need something from me regarding these priests who escaped the trials?" Jason asked. "You brought in their churches, right?"

"Yes, although there are inevitable problems. One is with our old friend the church of Purity, of whom a full quarter of the priests belong."

"Did Cal check out the Vane estate?" Jason asked.

"He did. From what he can tell, it was the regrouping point for the Builder cult members that scattered after escaping the desert astral space. They moved on afterwards, however."

"Did he find enough to put the clamps on the church?"

"No," Emir said. "They can just claim they hadn't been doing anything with the site due to its isolation and that they knew nothing."

"That's a shame," Jason said. "I almost feel bad handing these priests over to the church."

"Not an issue, as it turns out," Emir said. "The church has declared them tainted from their time in the astral space. I suspect they don't want a bevy of fresh faces while they're in the middle of conducting a huge conspiracy."

"Don't underestimate good old intolerant zeal," Jason said.

"Either way," Emir said, "we have a hundred confused, time-displaced, freshly excommunicated clergy."

"How does that even work?" Jason asked. "Did Purity show up and take their essences?"

"Yes, those that had divine essences and awakening stones."

"So what happens to them now?"

"Either they are received by another church or they replace their missing essences with regular ones. Fortunately, they're only iron-rank, so the loss of their essences isn't crippling. You saw the Interim Director leaving; she will be organising what to do with them."

"She didn't look eager to involve me in the process," Jason said. "What do you need me for?"

"It seems that the being administering the trials informed them that you were the one who stood up for their release. They, and the church representatives who actually welcomed their lost people back, are rather keen on meeting you."

Jason groaned. "Why did he have to go and tell them?"

"Don't you want your moment of glory?" Emir asked with a smile.

"I'm more comfortable claiming unearned glory than getting the real thing," Jason said. "All I did was ask the guy to let them go and he said yes. Hardly worth making a fuss over."

"Consider it practice," Emir said. "Adventurers become the heroes to many, and I doubt these are the last lives you'll save."

"I suppose," Jason said. "Next time I save someone, though, I'm telling them my name is Humphrey."

Emir laughed.

"Have you used your awakening stones yet?" Emir asked, changing the subject.

"Constance caught us just coming from a ritual room," Jason said. "We need to sort out Sophie and Belinda's stones and essences, plus I have two familiar summonings' worth of materials to get. I'm not holding out hope of getting the quintessence I need locally."

"I might be able to help with that," Emir said. "Have your team refrain from selling their goods here. There's going to be a flood of essences and awakening stones, dropping the price. Buy what you can here for cheap, and I'll have Hester portal you somewhere you can sell your spoils at a tidy profit. You'll also be able to access a larger market for what you need."

"That would be amazing, thank you," Jason said.

"Go meet with the church representatives and I'll arrange things with Hester. Constance will be waiting to show you the way."

"How are things going with you and Constance?" Jason asked. "She seems to be warming up around you."

"Well, I think our longer than expected stay here has everyone acting a little more casually. Something is holding her back, though, and I can't for the life of me figure it out. I thought perhaps it was that she works for me, but that isn't it."

"Maybe it's her rank," Jason suggested. "She might not want to take that step in your relationship until you're on the same level."

"It's an interesting idea," Emir said.

"Have you tried asking her?" Jason asked.

"It's not that easy," Emir said. "We've been dancing around each other for a long time now. There's a lot of heavy air in the space between us."

"You shouldn't be taking advice from me, anyway," Jason said. "I'm barely older than your granddaughter. She used the skill books alright?"

"Oh yes," Emir said. "She'd have trained through the night if I let her. I had to pry her away from Gabriel to make her go to bed. He dotes on her almost as much as I do."

"I've been wondering about something," Jason said. "I recall you having certain views on children, yet you have a granddaughter."

"I had a son I never knew about," Emir said. "The result of a youthful dalliance, before I even had my essences. The young lady in question never told me and I didn't find out until he died, during the last monster surge."

"I'm sorry," Jason said.

"My son's wife died with him, leaving only my granddaughter, Ketis. She went to live with her grandmother, my son's mother, but she was not a woman of means. She knew who I was, but never sought me out for money. From what I hear, she raised my son into a fine man. She only reached out for Ketis's sake. Her grandmother is well taken care of now, of course. Money, essences and enough monster cores to rank her up to bronze. Ketis will have her from some time yet."

"And Ketis herself will get the best of everything."

"Not everything," Emir said. "I would like for her to end up more like your friend Humphrey than your friend Thadwick."

"You know Thadwick? Oh, he was one of the ones the cult seeded."

"I don't know if you've heard," Emir said. "The cult has taken him again, in the time you've been gone."

"Why?" Jason asked. "No offence to the bloke, but he's not good to anyone for anything."

"The cult has been driven into hiding," Emir said. "Deeper hiding. We've managed to identify and curtail many of their operations in the city. They've been using Thadwick's knowledge of the considerable holdings of the Mercer family to make supply raids."

"Not even Thadwick deserves to have one of those things inside him," Jason said.

"Didn't he try to kill you?"

"Yeah, but he botched it, like everything he does. His family must be going wild, looking for him."

"Indeed they are," Emir said.

"Well, it's not my business," Jason said, getting up from his chair. "All this cult nonsense is above my pay grade and I have enough to be going on with. I think I'll go get this business with the priests over with."

65
DISPLAY OF GRATITUDE

The adventurer camp was divided into three areas. The first was the actual campsite, where opulent tents were set out for the prestigious visiting adventurers. The second was the market tents, plain but large, where Greenstone's brokers and the returned adventurers haggled over loot. The last camp was also the most modest, where the returned priests had been collected together.

Jason skirted the crowded market area, taking a moment to contact his team via his chat ability. He let them know he would be a while longer and passed on Emir's advice to not to sell their loot for cheap market prices. Once finished, he made his way through the tents towards where the priests and others liberated from the astral space were encamped. Not all the people recovered had been actual clergy; many simply belonged to the divine militant factions of their various religions.

Jason was getting looks as he passed through the camp. Word had spread about his acquisition of the scythe, and those who had seen him hand it over recognised him and pointed him out to others. No one actually approached him until he was almost through the camp. An adventuring party stepped into his path.

"Something I can help you with, mate?" Jason asked the obvious leader.

"How did you get the scythe?" the man asked without introduction or preamble.

"You remember that archway that took us out, after the trials?"

"Yeah."

"It could also take you to the location of the real scythe."

"How?"

"Turns out it had a sexiness threshold. You're a good-looking man, but..." Jason ran a sensuous hand down his own body. "...up against all this, you were bang out of luck."

"You mock me?"

"You don't have to tell me, mate; I'm the one doing it. Do you not know how mockery works?"

"Do you have any idea who I am?" the adventurer asked.

"My first thought was the lyrical gangster but I just don't think you've got the flows."

"What?"

The sun was behind the adventurers, with the man's shadow under Jason's feet. While he looked at Jason in anger and confusion, Jason dropped through the man's shadow like a hole had opened up under his feet. The adventurer looked around, wildly.

"Where did he go?"

Jason had teleported into a tent whose flap was open just enough for him to see the darkened space inside. It was an extremely large tent, like many others, with an opulently appointed interior. A thick rug covered the floor, while cushions were piled high into lounging furniture. There was also a trio of hammocks on stands, and a low table in the middle of the room. Shooting upright at the sudden intrusion was a trio of women, two of whom drew swords and pointed them with disturbingly steady hands at Jason's throat.

"Hello, ladies," Jason said, giving them a friendly grin as he raised his hands in surrender. "Sorry to barge in."

Body language told Jason that the third woman in the room was the one in charge. All three were celestines, although a different ethnicity than the silver-haired Sophie or the golden-haired locals. Their skin was caramel to Sophie's chocolate, while their eyes were sapphire orbs. The striking blue was matched by their hair, which spilled down like light passing through a waterfall.

Jason hoped the startled expression on his face was put down to the swords and not the mesmerising beauty of his captors. They were all garbed in wrap-style clothing that draped loosely, the muted colours flatteringly highlighting the vibrant colour of their hair and eyes.

"You're Jason Asano," the woman in charge said, looking him up and down. She tilted her head curiously to the side, as if looking at an animal that had wandered into her tent. Jason had the unsettling impression she was deciding if he was cute enough to be a pet or juicy enough to be food.

"Uh, yep," Jason said.

"What brings you into my tent?"

"Would you believe happenstance?"

She made a dismissive gesture as she moved towards Jason and the other two backed away, resheathing their swords. He could see she knew exactly what effect the sultry gait of her lithe body had and exactly how to weaponise it. She walked right up into Jason's personal space. She looked down, as she was slightly taller than his slight frame. He dropped his surrendering hands to his side.

"What price are you going to pay for your rude intrusion, Mr Asano?"

"I suppose taking you to dinner is out of the question?"

The hands of the other two jerked back towards their swords, anger flashing on their faces. They were stilled by another dismissive gesture from their leader.

"You haven't asked who I am," she said. "Do you already know, or do you not care?"

"I'm pretty ignorant," Jason said. "It probably wouldn't mean anything if you told me."

She gave him the smile of a snake that just found an unattended egg.

"You are as your reputation suggests, Mr Asano. Hiding behind the face of a fool."

"What's wrong with my face?" Jason asked, affronted. He gave it an exploratory poke with one of his fingers.

The woman laughed.

"I can hear an actual fool causing a commotion outside," she said. "Is that on account of you?"

"I met a bloke who was curious about how I got the scythe," Jason said. "His approach was a little rude."

She raised an eyebrow.

"I recognise the irony," Jason said.

"So, how did you do it?"

"I told the guy outside it was sexiness," Jason said. "I recognise that trying that here would be insultingly implausible."

"You didn't answer my question."

"I noticed that too," he said with a sly grin. "What's your name?"

It was one of the two offsiders that answered.

"You have the honour of addressing her royal highness—"

"I didn't ask for a job title," Jason interrupted. "I'm not big on nepotism, in any case. I asked for a name."

"Does it matter?" the woman in front of Jason asked. "We haven't decided if you get to leave this tent alive yet."

"Oh, I'm going to leave and I'll be just fine," Jason said.

"You're confident."

"No, but I'm good at faking it."

He held a hand up and a plate piled high with red and white confectionary squares appeared in his hand.

"What's this?" she asked.

"Gem berry and milk nut squares," Jason said. "You asked about the price I would pay for barging in."

His arm turned into shadow-stuff, bending around the woman and stretching out to set the plate on the table. One of her offsiders drew a sword and slashed at the shadow arm, the blade passing harmlessly through. Jason retracted his arm and it returned to normal.

"Once you try those," he said, "you'll regret not taking me up on that dinner invitation."

He made to leave and she didn't stop him, but she spoke up as he lifted the flap to exit.

"Mr Asano."

"Jason's fine," he said, pausing at the entrance to the tent.

"Zara," she said.

"Zara?"

"My name."

Jason flashed her a grin.

"It's been a genuine pleasure to meet you, Zara. Enjoy the slices."

He left the tent, letting the flap drop down behind him.

"You should have let us cut him for his impudence," one of Zara's servants said. "Nothing lethal. Just a lesson in respect for his betters."

Zara let out a weary sigh. Her party members had been hand-picked by her father for loyalty over intelligence.

"You already tried that and it didn't exactly accomplish anything," Zara said. "That was Jason Asano. Cutting him is a quick path to becoming leech food."

Jason arrived at the priest camp, keeping an eye out for the adventuring team he had annoyed along the way. He was quickly noticed and approached by a small delegation of church officials. He recognised the symbols of the Healer, Dominion and a few others. Conspicuously absent were Purity and Undeath, the two churches that had made up the bulk of the forces that had attacked the Order of the Reaper's lake-bottom fortress.

As the church officials approached, the whole camp was suddenly inundated with a clashing maelstrom of overwhelming auras as the gods themselves appeared. One god was bad enough, but the manifestation of several at once, even with their auras tamped down to their minimum strength, threw the camp into chaos.

Some of the iron-rankers with less control of their own auras dropped to their knees, violently throwing up. Many of them lived entirely on spirit coins, consigning them to painful dry heaving. Most of the iron-rankers were fine, however, as the camp was a gathering of exceptional adventurers. This included

Jason, who retracted his own aura in tightly and let the divine auras wash around it like an island in a storm.

A handful of figures appeared before Jason. They looked much like the church officials standing behind them but there was no mistaking the power radiating out of them. People were dropping to their knees like a Catholic genuflecting wave before the unexpected appearance of their gods. Soon only Jason remained standing, directly in front of them.

"And I thought I had a thing for melodrama," he said.

One of the gods laughed. Each wore the robes of their own orders, complete with holy symbol. Jason recognised the one laughing as Dominion from his symbol. He appeared young and handsome, with a hint of perpetual disdain behind the eyes. His robes were purple and gold and he had a simple golden crown around his head. The outfit was troublingly similar to what the manifestation of Jason's evil future self had been wearing.

"You never dissapoint," Dominion said.

"I'm not sure how to take that, coming from you," Jason said, getting another laugh from the god. Another god stepped forward, and Jason recognised the symbol of the Healer.

"We wanted to display our gratitude for returning our people, long lost to us," Healer told Jason. "Astral spaces, not being truly of this world, exist beyond our influence. We understand you have complicated views regarding we gods and decided the best gift we could give you was to thank you in person. The simple fact of our having done so should help you establish your reputation as you advance your adventuring career."

"Setting them loose wasn't exactly out of my way."

"I think, perhaps, it was not so simple as you make out, but I shall say no more. We have given our thanks and shall take our leave."

"No worries, bloke."

The gods vanished; the sudden absence of their auras felt like ears popping under a pressure change. People climbed to their feet, all eyes on Jason. He looked around, then his shadow cloak formed around him and he teleported immediately through it, leaving the cloak to drift down for a moment before likewise vanishing.

Jason teleported rapidly through the camp, jumping from shadow to shadow. He finally reached the cloud palace, and strode inside. Once through the door, he collapsed against the wall, drawing heaving breaths. It had taken everything he had to keep his cool in the face of not just one but a handful of gods, all while a crowd looked on.

The sheer force of multiple divine presences had pressed down on him like the weight of the sky. For the first time he could feel his own soul. Even now, having escaped that inconceivable power, he could feel the pressure. Rather than lessen, he felt like was descending into the ocean depths, every moment increasing the chance that the fragile vessel of his soul would collapse. By the time the pressure finally subsided, he was curled up on the floor of the cloud palace atrium, arms clutching his head.

New Title: [Godless Prophet]

Your aura has been damaged by the direct, concerted focus of multiple transcendent-level entities. The process of damage and recovery has refined the strength of your aura, increasing its suppressive force and resistance to suppression from higher-ranked auras.

Your aura signature has changed. An echo of transcendent power can be detected if your aura is examined by an aura sensing power or when projecting your aura.

Jason continued to lay on the floor, letting out exhausted, wheezing coughs.

"Jason?" Humphrey's voice came through the party chat. "We all felt multiple divine auras and then we started hearing some strange things."

"You should try it from my perspective," Jason responded weakly. "You should all go ahead and shop without me. I think I'm going to have a lay down."

"What happened?" Humphrey asked.

"I'll tell you later," Jason said. "Just spot me for anything Sophie and Belinda want to buy, alright?"

"I can do that," Humphrey said.

In the guest wing lounge of the cloud palace, Sophie and Belinda were going over the awakening stones Sophie had chosen with Clive. They had obtained the essences for Belinda but had decided to leave those until Sophie's power set was completed. Although they had found several interesting essences during the trials, Belinda was adamant about the combination of three common essences she had already chosen. They had no trouble trading for the magic, trap and adept essences she wanted.

Sophie also had her remaining awakening stones sorted out. Clive had extensive knowledge of attempting to engineer power sets through stone choices, although he was the first to reiterate that he could make no promises.

Aside from the legendary awakening stones, her strongest acquisitions were a pair of epic awakening stones of the moment. Adventure Society representatives were offering good trades for restricted essences to take them out of the market and Sophie had traded a death essence for the two epic awakening stones.

"These really were a great trade," Clive said for the third or fourth time since urging Sophie to take them in the first place. He had convinced her by explaining they were perfect for a skill-based power set. The abilities they were known to produce required precise timing but were incredibly impactful.

Rounding out Sophie's selection were two uncommon stones picked out from the ones they found during the trials. Because Sophie's power set was very skill-oriented, the awakening stone of preparation would hopefully give her an ability that acted as a failsafe when things inevitably went wrong. They hoped the awakening stone of the surge would bestow a buff power that would help in critical moments.

"The hallmark of a good high-skill adventurer is coming through in the critical moments," Clive had explained. "If your abilities reflect this, you'll find yourself far more effective. Be warned, though, that such abilities require skill, judgement and timing. Get them wrong and they may do more harm than good. To you, obviously. Doing harm to the other guy is kind of the point."

"We should get everyone together to use the stones," Sophie said. "Asano still hasn't come out of his suite?"

"Not that I know of," Clive said. "Having a bunch of gods turn up in front of you would be a straining experience for anyone."

"You should go check on him," Belinda said to Sophie.

"Why me?"

"He does own you."

"He does not own me."

"A lease is kind of like owning you."

"It's not a lease!"

"Still, you should be the one to…"

Sophie and Clive looked at the startled expression on Belinda's face as she trailed off and followed her gaze to the terrace outside. Jason was wandering along, looking lost. More noticeably, he had a bushy moustache and no clothes whatsoever. Sophie, Belinda and Clive looked at each other in confusion, then went out to meet Jason.

"Uh, Jason," Clive said. "You aren't wearing any pants."

"Fair point," Jason said brightly.

"I think what Clive meant to ask was why," Belinda said.

"The topic of this conversation is kind of my thing!" Jason said.

Sophie, Belinda and Clive shared another look.

"Asano," Sophie said. "Is everything alright?"

"Biscuits!"

"Biscuits?" Sophie asked.

"Biscuits!"

Suddenly, Humphrey's voice rumbled in their direction in an angry roar.

"STASH!"

Jason's eyes went wide and he clambered onto the terrace rail, transforming into a puppy before leaping off into the air. Humphrey then came pounding along the terrace at a run.

"WHAT DID I TELL YOU?" he bellowed before vaulting the rail in pursuit of his fleeing familiar.

Sophie, Belinda and Clive looked at each other one more time.

"Anyone else want a drink?" Clive asked.

"Yes, please."

"Absolutely."

66

THE PERSON I DECIDED TO BE

In the cloud palace, the only person who could open a guest suite door they were not attuned to was Emir. He did so when Jason didn't answer the chime. He entered, then walked out to where Jason was staring, shell-shocked, out over the lake. Jason didn't even appear to notice Emir's arrival.

Emir joined Jason in leaning on the rail, enjoying the cool breeze sweeping over the water to refresh from the desert heat. Even as autumn turned to winter, the desert was unforgiving. More so than it should be this far south, by any reckoning Jason would recognise. Another difference between this world and his own.

"It's quite a thing, soul damage," Emir said.

Jason turned to look at him for the first time since he arrived.

"How did you know?" Jason asked.

"Your aura signature changed. I'm connected to the cloud palace and it didn't want to let you in because you don't match the aura imprint you gave it. I changed it to match your new one or you wouldn't be able to move around in here."

"The cloud palace can take my aura imprint when my Adventure Society badge can't?"

"Your badge can take your aura imprint just fine," Emir said. "It just can't be tracked. You should get your badge redone, by the way."

"My aura changed," Jason said. "Like the people with star seeds. Is everyone going to suspect me now?"

"Not after what happened, with everyone watching. It would be strange if there wasn't some after-effect of getting up close and personal with gods like that. Gary was shaky for a while after meeting with just two and he's bronze rank. You met six at iron rank? Damn right there's an impact."

"You said soul damage," Jason said.

"That's right. Do you know how magic healing works?"

"I'm more focused on astral magic," Jason said.

"There's actually some interesting crossover," Emir said. "Think of your soul like a plan, or maybe a memory of everything you are. What magical healing does is look at the difference between the plan and the reality and move one towards the other."

Jason's brow creased in thought as that information ticked over in his mind.

"That's how my soul was able to construct a new body when it arrived in this world," Jason said. "It was like a blueprint. And that's why I don't remember anything between disappearing in my world and arriving here. The soul has a backup copy of my brain-state, but no actual brain to think with in a space without physical reality."

"If you say so," Emir said. "I'm not really versed in the whole outworlder process."

"You should talk to Clive," Jason said.

"You should convince him to come and work for me."

"No chance."

"He's wasted as an adventurer."

"He was wasted not being one," Jason said. "He's gained so much confidence in the time I've known him. He needs to be an adventurer. At least for now."

"That's an unhelpfully good argument," Emir conceded.

"Tell me more about soul damage," Jason asked.

To his surprise, Emir untucked his shirt and lifted it up to reveal a scar running horizontally across his chest and around his left side.

"I didn't think scars were possible with healing magic," Jason said.

"Normally they aren't," Emir said. "As I said, the soul is like a memory of how you should be, but some things change you forever. Some scars you carry on your soul."

"Your aura signature was changed once?" Jason asked.

"Nothing so drastic," Emir said. "My soul was marked. It wasn't enough to change my aura, but the events of that day are a part of who I am now. This scar represents a choice I once made about the person I decided to be. It happens, sometimes. An injury marks a fundamental change in who you are and you carry it with you. Find any veteran adventurer, a real one who puts themself out there, and you'll find they have scars like this. It takes something a bit more soul-shaking to not just mark your aura but change it, though."

"Soul shaking is right," Jason said. "I spent the whole night just trembling. It was like someone took my soul in their hand and could crush it like it was nothing. It's one thing to know a god has power beyond imagining. It's something else to feel it. To really feel it, all around you. It's like drowning."

"By all accounts, you didn't let it show," Emir said. "I did hear you left very quickly."

"Are you kidding?" Jason asked. "I thought I knew what vulnerable and exposed felt like but this was walking naked through the desert. Is this how people feel when their auras are suppressed?"

"I imagine what you experienced was similar, but worse," Emir said. "I know you handle having your aura suppressed strangely well, but for the rest of us, it feels like having your soul exposed for someone to see. I think yours actually was."

"The others must be worried," Jason said.

"We are all rather used to you taking everything in stride," Emir said. "I think you're being so rattled has taken away a little of your mystique. Also, the girls saw you naked."

"They what?"

"It seems Humphrey's familiar…"

"Oh, right," Jason said. "Stash has gotten it into his head that if he turns into me, he can make biscuits appear."

"He can't mimic your abilities, can he?"

"No," Jason said. "He can only take on the magic powers of things lower rank than him, which basically means lesser monsters. Sparkler worms, that kind of thing. Otherwise, it's just the normal, physical properties of the things he turns into. Claws, flippers, wings, that kind of thing."

"So, once he reaches bronze, he could mimic an iron-rank adventurer?"

"That's the theory," Jason said. "As Clive points out, there isn't a large sample size for mirage dragon familiars. There's actually more records of apocalypse beasts. A lot of them are swarms, like Colin. Helps cover ground to get that apocalypse going, I guess."

"I can't believe you named an apocalypse beast Colin."

"He's a good boy. Girl. Leeches can switch it about."

Suddenly Jason started laughing.

"What is it?" Emir asked.

"Back in my world," Jason said, "there are certain sections of society that think transgender people will bring about the end of the world. Colin's a transgender person that actually could, which I have to imagine would change their perspective on the issue. Probably not in a good way, though."

"You are a very strange man," Emir said. "I don't envy the gods having rummaged about inside your soul. I suspect it's very twisty."

"That may be the single rudest thing anyone has ever said to me."

"Really?"

"Yeah," Jason said. "Thadwick tried to kill me and this actually feels worse. Probably because you aren't an idiot trying to salvage a bad plan with a worse overreaction."

"Did you really accuse a group of gods of being melodramatic?"

"Probably," Jason said. "It's all bit of a blur, to be honest."

"Well, your team is waiting to hear that you're alright," Emir said. "I believe Miss Wexler has a full set of awakening stones ready to use."

"I should get to it, then. They're probably sick of waiting."

"I think you're underestimating the degree to which they support you," Emir said. "You'll find them in the guest wing lounge."

"So, it ultimately strengthened your aura?" Clive asked as the team walked through the cloud palace, in the direction of a ritual room.

"I think so," Jason said. "I've been wondering if that was their intention or if I'm just so weak it never occurred to them."

"I think it would be wise not try and guess a god's motivation," Humphrey said. "These are beings of unimaginable power, with experience longer than history and a perspective beyond our comprehension."

"Agreed," Sophie said. "I know you can't stop yourself from poking a hornet's nest, Asano, but at least pick hornets that can't strike you down with a bolt from the heavens."

They reached the room and Clive started setting up the ritual.

"What do you think?" Belinda asked Sophie. "Start with the most common stones and work our way up to the good stuff?"

"Sounds good," Sophie said.

Clive had been storing Sophie's awakening stones and sat them on a shelf on the wall. Sophie went over as Clive continued setting up the ritual. In a rare display of nervous fussing, Sophie set them out neatly in a line, readjusting until Clive announced he was ready. She grabbed the first stone and marched into the ritual circle he had drawn, and held up the uncommon-rarity awakening stone of preparation in her hand as Clive completed the ritual.

You have awakened the swift essence ability [Alacrity's Reward]. You have awakened 4 of 5 swift essence abilities.

Ability: [Alacrity's Reward] (Swift)
Special Ability (holy).
Cost: None.
Cooldown: None.

Current rank: Iron 0 (00%).

Effect (iron): Accumulate instances of [Blessing of Anticipation] over time, up

to an instance threshold determined by the [Spirit] attribute. Rate of instance acquisition is increased proportionally with speed of movement.

[Blessing of Anticipation] (boon, holy, stacking): Consume instances to negate an amount of incoming damage per instance consumed. Additional instances can be accumulated.

"That's a winner," Jason said.

"Exactly what we were looking for from the stone of anticipation," Clive said with satisfaction. "Something to compensate when skill doesn't work out. We couldn't ask for a better start."

He started setting up the next ritual.

"The next three stones are all designed to give you strong abilities that you can use at the right moment to critical effect," he said as he worked. "We'll start with the awakening stone of the surge."

You have awakened the wind essence ability [Wind Wave]. You have awakened 4 of 5 wind essence abilities.

Ability: [Wind Wave] (Wind)
Special Ability (movement).
Cost: Moderate mana.
Cooldown: 6 seconds.

Current rank: Iron 0 (00%).

Effect (iron): Produce a powerful blast of air that can push away enemies and physical projectiles. Can be used to launch into the air or move rapidly while already airborne.

"I'm not sure that's exactly what we were after," Clive said.

Sophie raised an arm at Jason, whose eyes went wide as the air of the ritual room kicked into a gale. He was slammed into the mercifully soft cloud palace wall. The gust settled as quickly as it roared up, leaving behind an empty silence.

"I like it," Sophie said.

"I'm not a fan," Jason groaned as he pushed himself to his feet.

"This next awakening stone should be a good one," Clive said. "Awakening stone of the moment."

Sophie walked over to take the next stone as Clive set up the next ritual circle. His ability to draw them with his power, along with balancing out the ambient magic, saved immense amounts of time when going through many rituals in sequence.

You have awakened the swift essence ability [Eternal Moment]. You have awakened 5 of 5 swift essence abilities.

You have awakened all swift essence abilities. Linked attribute [Speed] will advance in conjunction with lowest-rank swift essence ability.

Ability: [Eternal Moment] (Swift)
Special Ability.
Cost: Extreme mana-per-second and stamina-per-second.
Cooldown: None.

Current rank: Iron 0 (00%).

Effect (iron): Operate at a highly accelerated speed for one second of actual time, which is extended in subjective time.

"It lets you move fast," Jason said. "I guess the question is how fa— argh!"

Sophie had vanished, reappearing a moment later behind him, driving a fist into his lower back. From her perspective, the world had slowed to a barely perceptible crawl.

"Bloody hell," Jason exclaimed as he lay on the ground, clutching his back. "What was that for?"

"I had to test the ability," she said.

"Like that?" he asked, pulling himself to his feet.

"If you don't like it," Sophie said, "go complain to your god friends."

"We're more like work acquaintances," Jason said. "We generally stay out of each other's way unless something comes up in the course of our normal employment."

"Did you just call the god of Dominion a work acquaintance?" Neil asked.

"I don't think he's someone I'd get after-work drinks with," Jason said. "I bet he'd cause a lot of trouble."

"My mother has the exact same power," Humphrey said to Sophie, getting the subject back on track.

"Rufus has one that's quite similar, too," Jason said.

While the others messed about, Clive set up the next ritual.

You have awakened the balance essence ability [Moment of Oneness]. You have awakened 3 of 5 balance essence abilities.

Ability: [Moment of Oneness] (Balance)
Special Ability (movement).

Cost: Extreme mana-per-second.
Cooldown: 2 minutes.

Current rank: Iron 0 (00%).

Effect (iron): Become immune to all damage and afflictions for 1 second. The next melee attack within four seconds inflicts all damage and afflictions on the struck enemy. If no enemies are attacked, the damage and conditions are suffered retroactively.

"I'm going to need a volunteer," Sophie said after reading the power.

"I think it's your turn Hump," Jason said.

"Someone with afflictions would be best," Sophie added.

"Oh, come on," Jason said, walking up to Sophie. "What did I do?"

"How do you know the Hurricane Princess?" Humphrey asked.

"The who?" Jason asked. "What does that have to do with anything?"

"Zara Rimoros," Humphrey said.

"Oh, Zara," Jason said brightly.

As he was looking at Humphrey, he didn't notice the distasteful expression on Sophie's face. Belinda did, and hid a smile behind her hand.

"How did you know I know her?" Jason asked Humphrey.

"She came by last night, while you were… still in seclusion," Humphrey explained. "I think she wanted to check on you."

"Really?" Jason said rubbing his chin thoughtfully as an intrigued smile crossed his face.

"Back to the task at hand, Asano," Sophie said. "You can moon over some girl later."

"Jealous?" he asked with a teasing voice. He turned around, spotting neither Belinda's wince nor Sophie's fist, ramming into his gut. With an expression mixing confusion and pain, he slumped to the floor.

"Why?" he asked between wheezing breaths from the ground. "Aren't I meant to hit you to test that power?"

"Sorry," Sophie said. "New ability. I'm still figuring out how it works."

67

YOU HAVE FRIENDS TO HELP YOU

In the ritual room, the group watched as Sophie continued through her awakening rituals. She had three unawakened abilities left, one from the wind essence and two from the balance, along with three legendary awakening stones to use on them. She decided to save the Reaper stone for last, leaving the awakening stone of the celestials that Constance had suggested and the stone of karma that Clive picked out. She started with the stone of the celestials.

You have awakened the wind essence ability [Child of the Celestial Wind]. You have awakened 5 of 5 wind essence abilities.

You have awakened all wind essence abilities. Linked attribute [Power] will advance in conjunction with lowest-rank wind essence ability.

Ability: [Child of the Celestial Wind] (Wind)
Special Ability (dimension, holy).
Cost: None
Cooldown: None.

Current rank: Iron 0 (00%).

Effect (iron): Your celestine racial powers have increased effect. You gain damage reduction to disruptive-force damage.

"What are the celestine racial powers?" Neil asked. "I know you have a utility power aptitude and can use ongoing abilities for less mana. That one's your ability that evolved, right?"

"Yes," Sophie said. "We also recover mana more quickly, we're faster and have astral and holy affinities."

"What does holy do, other than improve holy abilities?" Neil asked.

"It increases the effect of healing magic and holy boons used on me."

"Oh, that's nice," Neil said. "Those are abilities you want to have increased."

They moved into the awakening stone of karma.

You have awakened the balance essence ability [Karmic Warrior]. You have awakened 4 of 5 balance essence abilities.

Ability: [Karmic Warrior] (Balance)
Special Ability (holy).
Cost: None
Cooldown: None.

Current rank: Iron 0 (00%).

Effect (iron): Gain an instance of [Agent of Karma] when subjected to damage or any harmful effect, even if the damage and/or effect was wholly negated.

[Agent of Karma] (boon, holy, stacking): The [Power] and [Spirit] attributes are temporarily increased by a small amount. Additional instances have a cumulative effect.

"So basically," Jason said, "Whenever you take damage, even when you negate that damage with your cheesy powers, you get stronger, tougher and your magical abilities get stronger get more powerful."

"The spirit attribute actually has several functions," Clive said. "Obviously, affecting the potency of essence abilities is the important one, but don't overlook its impact on our perception. As our spirit attributes move past bronze rank, our senses will go beyond what they are now. Colours, sounds and smells to which we were oblivious will suddenly be made plain to us."

"So, you can move so fast it amounts to stopping time, become immune to damage, then heap all the damage you should have taken onto the other guy," Jason said. "Now you have another overpowered ability. Humphrey got bloody immortality, and I got stretchy arms? Not even arms. One stretchy arm."

"You can switch-up which arm it is, though," Belinda said. "There's that."

The group laughed at the flat look Jason gave her.

"We might be little more sympathetic," Neil said, "if your powers hadn't killed a carnivorous plant the size of a small city."

"It wasn't just me," Jason said. "There were twenty-five other people involved in that."

"Asano, we would have all been left sitting around with nothing to do if we didn't have you there," Sophie said. "Stop whining."

"I guess that's fair," Jason conceded.

"Sophie, that new ability makes you rather like a defensive version of Jason," Humphrey pointed out. "You don't have any explosive attack powers but now the longer a fight goes on, the more dangerous you become. Increasing your power attribute will obviously increase your physical strength and the increase in spirit will affect the additional damage your powers add to even your normal attacks. That will eventually add up to every one of your strikes having the kind of strength the rest of us have only with a special attack. And we all know how quickly you can attack."

"We still have one more ability to awaken," Clive reminded them as he finished setting up for the final ritual.

"Did you hear what people were getting from Reaper stones, while you were in the market?" Jason asked.

"Clive veered off quite early to go ask around while the rest of us were selling loot," Neil said. "Did you actually get people to tell you, Clive?"

"Kind of," Clive said. "I found the Magic Society contingent and organised cheap awakening rituals for anyone who let us record their abilities."

"I saw that," Neil said. "You organised that?"

"I'm still a Magic Society official," Clive said, "even if Lucian Lamprey did effectively strip me of all responsibility."

"I'd like to kick that guy's insides out once day," Sophie said.

"Was this because of me?" Jason asked unhappily.

"He doesn't like that I work with you," Clive said. "It worked out, though, since it left me freer for adventuring and research. All his punishment actually did was free me from a bunch of administering duties."

Jason frowned, knowing that it had not been the windfall Clive was making out.

"I'm sorry," he said.

"I told you, it's fine," Clive said. "Getting back on topic, I did manage to find out about a lot of powers coming from the Reaper stones. The most common, from what I could gather, are aggressive utility powers," Clive said as he continued to work. "There's quite a lot of conjuration powers, mostly weapons but also stranger things, like Jason's arm conjuration. They all seem to incorporate offensive aspects, though, like the affliction Jason's shadow arm delivers."

"I'd like something impactful that I can open up a fight with," Sophie said. "Something to put the enemy onto the back foot."

"I'm not sure that's on the table," Clive said. "From the people I talked to, the Reaper stones tend to give out powers more in Jason's wheelhouse. Slow, inevitable death."

Speculation turned to anticipation as Clive finished the ritual and carried it out.

You have awakened the balance essence ability [Deny the Reaper]. You have awakened 5 of 5 balance essence abilities.

You have awakened all balance essence abilities. Linked attribute [Recovery] will advance in conjunction with lowest-rank balance essence ability.

Ability: [Deny the Reaper] (Balance)
Special Attack (counter-execute, healing).
Cost: Moderate mana.
Cooldown: 30 seconds.

Current rank: Iron 0 (00%).

Effect (iron): Target enemy suffers a small amount of transcendent damage and you are healed for a small amount. As a counter-execute effect, the damage and healing scale exponentially with your own level of injury.

"Counter-execute?" Jason said. "That's a new one to me."

"You generally see it in defensive power sets," Clive said. "They are generally more powerful than other abilities, but only if you use them when things are going badly. Usually, they have some combination of damage reduction, healing, retribution damage or health drain."

"My immortality power is something of a false counter-execute," Humphrey said. "It's unlikely to scale as well as Sophie's new power but it can also scale off low stamina and mana, and will be more useful without having to be beaten down first."

"Thought that ability scaled, like this one," Neil said.

"Yes, but it doesn't have to be with damage," Humphrey said. "If I'm just low on mana, for example, it will top my mana up without doing much for my health and stamina."

"So it's more versatile," Jason said. "Stupid OP power. I bet your mum's happy, though."

"Actually, she was ecstatic," Humphrey said. "I've never seen her like that."

"Of course she was," Jason said. "A mother just found out her child was immortal."

"I'm not actually immortal."

"It is still a powerful survival skill," Clive said. "This one of Sophie's is not to be underestimated, however. The chance to bring a fight going badly back to even ground fits into the classic balance essence mode. Balance is quite popular because it has abilities like this that can pull you through rough situations."

"I wanted an attack for a start of the fight, not the end," Sophie said.

"Look at it this way," Humphrey said. "Would you prefer a big, splashy entrance that may or may not do you any good, or something you can rely on when things go wrong."

Sophie considered Humphrey's words, nodding to herself.

"I guess you're right," she said. "Big attacks are kind of your area, anyway."

"Plus, transcendent damage," Clive said. "That's as reliable as it gets, plus incredibly rare at iron rank. You only see it on conditional powers, like executes, or when the damage is negligible. Both of which are demonstrated by Jason's abilities."

"That leaves you," Sophie said, turning to Belinda. "Ready to become an essence user?"

"Are you kidding?" Belinda asked. "I can't wait for Jason to complain about how great my powers are."

"What?" Jason asked.

"You can be a bit of a whiner," Neil told him.

"I'm not a whiner," Jason said. "I'm just open with my feelings. I'm a delicate flower."

"The kind of flower that's hard to eradicate, even when you try to get rid of it," Neil said. "Is there a word for that?"

"You're calling me a weed?" Jason asked. "That's very rude."

"You said I was fat!"

"You are objectively hefty for an elf."

"I'm well built."

"Like a fancy cake," Jason said. "But I imagine you know all about cake, given how many you must have eaten to get like that."

"I'm not the only elf that looks like this, you know."

"You mean Lucian Lamprey? He's not a great role model. Even putting aside the whole evil sleazebag thing, the guy looks like someone sucked the air out of a bag of nuts."

As Jason and Neil continued to bicker, Clive went to work setting up Belinda's first essence ritual. It was more elaborate and involved than a ritual of awakening, but otherwise quite similar. Soon, Belinda was standing in the middle of a magic diagram, a magic essence held nervously in her hands.

"There's nothing to worry about," Sophie said. "You saw me go through this."

"Trust me," Clive said. "I've done this dozens of times. Probably hundreds."

"What if I get a crap power?" Belinda asked.

"My mother says there is no such thing as a bad power," Humphrey said. "Just a bad essence user who doesn't know what to do with it."

"Everyone here knows how smart and resourceful you are," Jason told her. "If you get a basic attack ability, that's a reliable power you can count on when things are too hectic to set up a clever plan. If you get something more esoteric, you can be innovative with it and really show what you're capable of. Either way, I know you'll be able to make the most of it."

Belinda nodded.

"Thanks," she told them.

"If all your powers are crap, though," Jason added casually, "we're not letting you on the team."

He yelped as Sophie thumped him on the arm.

"What was that for?" he asked.

"What was that for?" Sophie echoed incredulously. "If I had a suppression collar I'd put it on you and throw you off the highest tower in this whole damn palace!"

"I'm kind of in the middle of something here," Belinda interjected.

"Sorry," Jason said.

Clive conducted the ritual, the essence in Belinda's hands dissolving into a nebula-like cloud that floated around her before drifting gently into her body.

You have absorbed [Magic Essence]. You have absorbed 1 of 4 essences. Progress to iron rank: 25% (1/4 essences).

[Magic Essence] has bonded to your [Spirit] attribute, changing your [Spirit] from normal to [Iron 0]. Master all magic essence abilities to increase your [Spirit] attribute.

You have awakened the magic essence ability [Bag of Tricks]. You have awakened 1 of 5 magic essence abilities.

Ability: [Bag of Tricks] (Magic)
Special Ability (dimension).
Cost: None
Cooldown: None.

Current rank: Iron 0 (00%).

Effect (iron): You have a personal, dimensional storage space. You may equip any item in your storage space directly onto your person or unequip anything on your person directly to your storage space.

"A dimensional space as your first ability," Neil said. "Not even from some high-end stone; you got it straight from the essence. It looks like a convenient one, too. None of this conjuring up a cupboard or whatever."

"We have a lot of storage spaces in this team," Clive said. "We're lucky, in that regard."

Blue-grey light started shining from within Belinda.

"Here we go," Clive said.

Human racial ability [Essence Gift] has evolved to [Adventurer's Tools].

Ability: [Adventurer's Tools]
Transfigured from [Human] ability [Essence Gift].

Active ability (conjuration). Conjure basic, non-magical objects.

Sophie and Belinda had already decided just to do Belinda's essences before taking their shopping trip to sell off their loot in a market not flooded with essences and awakening stones. They already had some stones picked out but were also waiting to see what her first powers produced. Normally, they would have only awakened around half of her powers right away, as had been the case with the rest of the team. Belinda was already behind the curve compared to them, though, so they instead decided to do all the stones, after coming back from their shopping trip.

In the meantime, they moved on to the next essence.

You have absorbed [Trap Essence]. You have absorbed 2 of 4 essences.
Progress to iron rank: 50% (2/4 essences).

[Trap Essence] has bonded to your [Power] attribute, changing your [Power] from normal to [Iron 0]. Master all trap essence abilities to increase your [Power] attribute.

You have awakened the trap essence ability [Bait and Switch]. You have awakened 1 of 5 trap essence abilities.

Ability: [Bait and Switch] (Trap)
Special Ability (dimension, illusion).
Cost: High mana.
Cooldown: 1 minute.

Current rank: Iron 0 (00%).

Effect (iron): Teleport self or nearby ally to a nearby location. The subject is

rendered invisible for a brief period, leaving behind a lifelike illusion. The illusion has no substance or aura.

"An escape power," Clive said. "The mana cost and use-interval for a power like that are quite large because you can use it on other people. That's a valuable power."

Belinda's next racial gift evolution soon triggered.

Human racial ability [Essence Gift] has evolved to [The Price of Power].

Ability: [The Price of Power]
Transfigured from [Human] ability [Essence Gift].

Active ability (spell, curse). The subject of this ability suffers disruptive-force damage when expending mana, proportional to the amount of mana consumed.

"That's interesting," Clive said. "Active racial gifts are rare, especially one you can use on other people."

"How is that a trap power?" Sophie asked.

"It turns a person's own mana into a trap," Neil said. "It's a nasty ability."

"I'm glad," Belinda said. "The first one wasn't great. Useful, don't get me wrong, but a bit underwhelming."

"Underwhelming?" Jason said. "That ability to conjure tools is the most pure-blood adventuring power I've ever seen. I could empty half my storage space if I had that power."

"He really could," Humphrey said.

"A will admit, I've been carrying around some useful goods as well," Clive said. "Because I had ropes with me, Neil and I have multiple growth items now."

"Still two essences to go," Clive said. "I'll set up the next ritual."

"Actually, could we take a break?" Belinda asked. "This is kind of intense and I could use a rest."

"Good idea," Jason said. "We can all go up to my suite and I'll put on some lunch."

As everyone shuffled out of the ritual room, Clive asked Sophie and Belinda to stay behind a moment to discuss an issue with their new abilities.

"Is there a problem with our abilities?" Sophie asked after the others were gone.

"This isn't really about your abilities," Clive said. "This is about Jason."

"What about him?" Sophie asked.

"I don't like the way you were attacking him," Clive said.

"Seriously?" Sophie asked. "It hit him ten times harder when we spar."

"But you weren't sparring."

"You think he couldn't have stopped me?"

"Jason's judgement is compromised when it comes to you," Clive said. "He's wary of his power over you and the men who had power over you in the past. Because of that, he lets you get away with things he wouldn't tolerate from anyone else. Don't forget, he just went through something incredibly affecting."

"He seemed normal to me," Belinda said.

"Exactly," Sophie agreed. "You saw him. He's fine."

Clive gave them a sad smile. "You never met Farrah, but when Jason and I started adventuring together, she asked me to look out for him. To make sure he actually was fine and didn't just seem that way. He's good at hiding when he's overwhelmed."

"That's crap," Sophie said. "He's just one of those guys who takes it all in stride. Nothing really affects people like that."

"People like that don't exist," Clive said. "Jason may not have been through all the things you have but he's had his own challenges. He's more vulnerable than he seems."

Sophie scowled while Belinda looked at her thoughtfully.

"Maybe we can tone it back a little," she said.

"You mean I can," Sophie said.

"Yeah, Soph," Belinda said. "I mean you."

They reconvened in the ritual room after lunch. Sophie was subdued, her scowl replaced with an unhappy, thoughtful frown as she shot glances in Jason's direction. Jason moved over to Clive as he drew the circle for the next ritual.

"What did you do?" Jason asked quietly.

"I didn't like the way she was treating you."

"She needed that," Jason said. "To know that she really is free and wouldn't be pushed back down for acting against the man with the power over her."

"You think that was a healthy expression of freedom?" Clive asked.

"Of course not," Jason said. "But it was a start."

"And what about what you need?" Clive asked. "You might be putting a good face on it, but I know what happens to people who get that close to that many gods. I've read papers on it. You can't tell me you're fine when I know you were shaken to the very soul. Literally."

"It's fine."

"The way she was treating you isn't fine. Neil and Humphrey might think she's crabby about some other girl but they're teenagers and don't know any better."

"Wexler's damaged," Jason said. "We need to give her some leeway."

"Trauma is not an excuse to hurt other people," Clive said. "Isn't the whole point for her to take responsibility for her own behaviour? This is not how you work through your problems."

"You can't fix everything at once, Clive. You take the wins you can get."

"You aren't a reliable judge when it comes to her. You're so scared of abusing the power in that indenture contract that you won't act when you should. But that's alright. You have friends to help you. And so does she. Let us keep both of you walking in straight lines."

Jason glanced over at Sophie, then nodded.

"Alright, Clive," Jason said. "Thanks, mate."

68
BLOB BODY

After they had all gathered in the cloud palace's ritual room once more , Clive performed the next essence ritual for Belinda.

You have absorbed [Adept Essence]. You have absorbed 3 of 4 essences. Progress to iron rank: 75% (3/4 essences).

[Adept Essence] has bonded to your [Speed] attribute, changing your [Speed] from normal to [Iron 0]. Master all adept essence abilities to increase your [Speed] attribute.

You have awakened the adept essence ability [Blessing of Readiness]. You have awakened 1 of 5 adept essence abilities.

Ability: [Blessing of Readiness] (Adept)
Spell (recovery).
Cost: Moderate mana.
Cooldown: Varies.

Current rank: Iron 0 (00%).

Effect (iron): This spell can only affect an ally and not yourself. The cooldown of the next ability used by the target is reduced by up to one minute. The cooldown of this ability is equal to the time taken from the cooldown of the target ability.

"Being able to use a key ability twice in quick succession could be very domineering," Humphrey said. "That's a strong power."

Now used to it, they waited for the blue-grey light signalling a racial gift evolution.

Human racial ability [Essence Gift] has evolved to [Quick Learner].

Ability: [Quick Learner]
Transfigured from [Human] ability [Essence Gift].

You may use skill books for which you meet the requirements.

"Oh, no." Belinda said as her shoulders slumped.

"Great," Sophie said. "You can finally start learning some of those skills you missed out on."

"I didn't miss out, Sophie. I don't want to learn how to kick people."

"You're an adventurer now."

"And I intend to stand at the back," Belinda said. "Look at the power I just got. It's literally designed to have someone else do the kicking."

"It never hurts to have some combat skills to fall back on," Humphrey said. "Adventurers who assume everything will go the way they want die very quickly."

"A skill book doesn't take long to use," Jason said. "It's kind of the whole point. It doesn't have to be fighting. You could really expand your magical knowledge."

"She already has magical knowledge," Sophie said. "What she needs is combat skills, and we just so happened to get some rather good ones. Obviously she needs to train to make sure she absorbs all that knowledge properly. Asano, you said Rufus Remore can supply training like that, right?"

"Yeah," Jason said. "He trained me that way."

"He did?" Sophie asked, casting a sceptical eye over Jason. "I suppose he did what he could with what he had."

"Oh, nice," Jason said with exaggerated offence as the rest of the team laughed.

They had only been speaking a few moments when an ephemeral cube floated out of Belinda's chest, followed by a second and a third. They hovered in front of her, spiralling around one another until they came together to merge into a single cube. It swirled with muted colours that formed ghostly shapes that were almost recognisable before fading into the background again.

"That's your confluence essence," Clive said with reverence.

"What do I do?" Belinda asked.

"Reach out and take it."

Hesitantly, Belinda reached out and touched the awakening stone. It dissolved into smoke that writhed around her before sinking into her body.

You have absorbed [Charlatan Essence]. You have absorbed 4 of 4 essences. Progress to iron rank: 100% (4/4 essences).

[Charlatan Essence] has bonded to your [Recovery] attribute, changing your [Recovery] from normal to [Iron 0]. Master all charlatan essence abilities to increase your [Recovery] attribute.

You have awakened the charlatan essence ability [Echo Spirit]. You have awakened 1 of 5 charlatan essence abilities.

Ability: [Echo Spirit] (Charlatan)
Familiar (ritual).
Cost: Extreme mana.
Cooldown: None.

Current rank: Iron 0 (00%)

Effect (iron): Summon an [Echo Spirit] to serve as a familiar.

"A familiar power," Clive said. "You know, rather than wait until we get back from this shopping trip, we might want to rent one of the local Magic Society's ritual rooms wherever we end up, and do the rest of Lindy's stones. If she has any more familiars, we'll need to know the summoning materials while we're still somewhere we can buy them."

"That's a good point," Jason said. "I'm sure we can figure it out."

The blue-grey light started emitting from Belinda on cue.

Human racial ability [Essence Gift] has evolved to [Face in the Crowd].

Ability: [Face in the Crowd]
Transfigured from [Human] ability [Essence Gift].

Take on the form of another race. You may mimic a specific member of that race or otherwise alter your appearance within the parameters of the race's natural features. Your aura blends into any surrounding auras, becoming difficult to detect, even with higher rank aura senses. You do not gain any abilities of that race.

"Shape-shifting," Clive said. "Not a surprise. The charlatan essence in known for shape-shifting and illusion. Most prefer other options, however. Something that combines deception with attack powers for a more classic assassin power set. Oh, an extra one! Here we go."

Belinda had lit up with blue grey light again as Clive was talking.

Human racial ability [Special Attack Affinity] has evolved to [Form and Function].

Ability: [Form and Function]
Transfigured from [Human] ability [Special Attack Affinity].

When you take on the form of another race, gain some of their racial abilities in addition to your own. Your aura will match that of a member of the race you are mimicking.

"You lost the special attack bonus of humans," Neil said.

"Good," Belinda said. "I think I've made my stance on standing up the front and punching things quite clear. So, is that it?"

"Not quite," Clive said.

"I put some fresh clothes in the washroom," Sophie said. "Asano even donated a bottle of crystal wash."

"Oh, right," Belinda said and made a beeline for the adjacent washroom. Halfway there she started to look very queasy. Sophie caught up and led her through the door.

You have absorbed 4/4 essences.
All your attributes have reached iron rank.

You have reached iron rank.
You have gained damage reduction against normal-rank damage sources.
You have gained increased resistance to normal-rank effects.
You have gained the ability to sense auras.
You have gained the ability to sustain yourself using sources of concentrated magic.

The rest of the team stood around awkwardly; all had been through the unpleasantness Belinda was experiencing in the next room. The purging of the body's impurities was as disgusting an experience as adventurers went through. It was all the worse for the source of the offending filth being their own bodies.

"So, what does a body actually change into as it goes up ranks?" Jason asked. "Is it just magically reinforced versions of the stuff we all have now?"

"No, and that's actually quite interesting," Clive said. "The higher the rank an adventurer reaches, the more their body becomes like yours, Jason—a physical manifestation of pure magic. The physical material that makes up their body is refined and replaced. Obviously, a high-ranker's body is much better than yours."

"My body? You mean an outworlder body?"

"I do."

"But that's just a monster body with a soul in it."

"Yes," Clive said. "Right now, all of us except you have the usual internal workings of our respective species. But you, Jason, are essentially an undifferentiated mass of biological tissue. You have a skeleton to hang it all on, enough muscle to get the job done and skin to hold it all in. A few extras, like hair and eyeballs. Blood, to keep the whole mess operating. Where we have things like lungs, a heart and such, you're just a mass of extra flesh and blood your body can deploy as necessary."

"What?" Jason asked in horror.

"It gives you an advantage over the rest of us," Clive said enviously. "No spleen to burst, no lungs to puncture. No heart to stab."

"Wait," Jason said. "You're saying I'm just a generic lump of biomass?"

"Yes," Clive said. "We'll all get there, eventually, but you've got that head start on us."

"But I breathe," Jason said. "I have a heartbeat."

"Habit," Clive said.

"Habit?"

"Essentially, your body is faking it. You don't have a heart or lungs."

"So, I could just go underwater and never drown?"

"Yes," Clive said. "In fact, I'd recommend it. Fighting through that drowning reflex is a great way to break the breathing habit."

"That sounds horrifying," Jason said. "What happens when I eat?"

"Oh, I wouldn't take any food out if you do that," Clive said. "It would get all soggy."

"Not when I'm trying to drown myself," Jason said. "I mean, what happens to the food that I shove into my body?"

"The mass of flesh and blood inside you consumes it for energy with complete efficiency," Clive said. "Strictly speaking, it wouldn't even need to go in your mouth."

This time everyone gave Clive horrified looks.

"What?" he asked. "It's true."

"Hold on," Jason said, thinking of something else and desperately wanting to change the subject. "Emir told me that my body was formed using an imprint of my soul."

"That's broadly accurate," Clive said.

"My body wasn't a blob mass when I left my world. Why would my soul make a blob body?"

"Do you really think your soul travelled between worlds without being changed?" Clive asked. "A normal rank soul?"

"I suppose not."

"Thadwick was actually interested in all this," Neil said.

"Really?" Humphrey asked. "I've known him since we were kids and I've never so much as seen him with a book."

"He had a theory he formulated for himself," Neil said. "Once he found out that healing fixes the differences between the soul and the body, he got it into his head that if constantly thought about… certain parts of himself being larger, all the time, it would imprint on his soul. Then, healing magic would actually make it happen."

After a pause to stare at Neil in disbelief, they all started laughing.

"Let me get this straight," Jason said between peals of laughter. "Thadwick spends all his time wandering around thinking about having a trouser zucchini?"

"That explains so much," Humphrey said.

"I know, right?" Jason agreed.

They stopped laughing as the washroom door opened and Sophie emerged.

"It wasn't too bad," she said. "Lindy will be out in a bit."

Sophie looked at the frozen expressions on her four male teammates.

"What were you all talking about before I came out here?"

"Nothing," Clive said, the others nodding their agreement.

"Everyone will be leaving for Greenstone tomorrow," Emir said. "Well, aside from my staff members who still have an underwater town to pore over. The scythe was the chief objective for my client, but the more information we dig up, the bigger the bonus."

"Wexler has been hiding from your historian," Jason said. "She's been chasing her all over the cloud palace."

Jason had joined Emir in his domed office for afternoon tea, at Emir's request. Emir generally kept the room empty, only creating cloud furniture to meet his needs of the moment. He made a small table and a pair of chairs rise up through the floor, along with a dumbwaiter, through which arrive a tray of refreshments.

"The revelation that a random street thief knows the lost martial art of an ancient order of assassins poses certain interesting questions."

"You and your historian can take that up with Wexler," Jason said. "I'm having nothing to do with it."

"I don't know about that," Emir said, his penetrating gaze matched by a subtle aura pressure. "I have to imagine the man who triumphed over all others in the Reaper trials gleaned at least a few tasty truth nuggets."

Jason didn't try and push back the gold rank aura, but let it wash over him as he gave Emir an indulgent smile. Emir chuckled, letting off the pressure.

"Speaking of tasty nuggets," Emir said, "my people have been putting together something of a feast for the evening, with some of the various participating luminaries invited. I was hoping our illustrious victor could be convinced to play host."

"That may not be the best idea," Jason said. "I don't always get along with aristocracy. They think the right to deference is something you inherit, like a cupboard from your grandmother that smells like a cat died in a lavender field about thirty years ago."

"How specific. To be honest, I'm looking for a way around the kind of etiquette clash such a disparate array of nobles always seems to invite. Everyone is clamouring to meet the man who bested all their well trained and resourced children. If you're the host, then you set the rules. And of course, there's no rank at an Asano barbecue, is there?"

"No there is not," Jason said with a chuckle. "Will that even work, though?"

"Probably not," Emir said. "But if they're forewarned about the expected etiquette, then their participation is a tacit agreement to the host's established rules, even if the host is a little unconventional. I'll tell them the dress code is extremely casual."

"So, they have to agree to Asano barbecue rules or not show up," Jason said. "Not bad."

"Do try and be diplomatic about it."

"I'll do my best," Jason said. "Fair warning, though: my best isn't great. But who knows how many favours I owe you at this point, so count me in."

"A rather odd young man once told me that friends don't count favours."

"He sounds wise beyond his years. And dashingly handsome."

Emir chuckled, shaking his head.

"I'll have Hester portal you out for your shopping trip in the morning," Emir said. "She suggested leaving you in her hometown, which is in fact a huge city. You can spend a few days there, while she takes the chance to visit family. She can portal you directly back to Greenstone, after."

"What kind of range does she have on that?"

"She may still be silver," Emir said, "but her portal ability has hit gold rank. She can go halfway across the world."

"Nice."

"You may want to spend the afternoon liaising with my staff then," Emir said. "Stick with Constance and she'll have you ready for hosting duties in no time."

69
PARTICULAR APPETITES

In the old stone fortress in Old City, now a neutral ground of criminal delights, one of Cole Silva's thugs knocked on the door of the crime lord's office.

"Enter," came a gruff bark from inside. The thug went in, his body screaming reluctance.

"Boss?"

"What?"

"You asked for any news about Wexler."

"And?"

"She was part of the team that brought back the thing that big-time out-of-towner was after. I don't think we'll ever have a shot at her, boss."

A short time later, two more thugs dragged the body out of the office as Silva strode back and forth fuming.

"You want us to send someone to clean up the blood, boss?"

"No," Silva snarled, then stopped his pacing. "Find Killian Laurent and have him come see me."

Emir had not entirely thrown out the usual decorum of a high society soiree—his staff announced each of the prestigious guests as they arrived. The guests were then met by Constance, at her most proper, and Jason, considerably less so.

"It didn't occur to you to wear long pants?" Constance asked him quietly between arrivals.

"Nah," Jason said.

Zara Rimaros was the next to arrive, flanked by her two offsiders and accompanied by an older woman. Zara's companion was another celestine with the same caramel skin set off by sapphire eyes and hair. She looked around thirty but Jason had come to recognise the agelessness of essence users, even if her politely retracted but unmistakably silver-rank aura hadn't given it away. There was something behind the eyes of high-rankers; something about the way they carried themselves. It was an absolute confidence that low-rankers, even amongst the nobility, had yet to develop. This woman was practically bursting with it.

"Jason," Zara greeted with a smile full of dangerous promise. "Might I introduce my aunt, Vesper Rimaros?"

"A genuine pleasure," Jason greeted, his respectful tone wholly incongruous with his short pants, floral print shirt and open-toe sandals.

"I've heard much about you," Vesper said, apparently unfazed by Jason's outfit.

"Oh," Jason winced. "Don't worry, we got all the heidels back, and most of them weren't too traumatised. We're completely out of fruit chutney after all that, though, so let me save you the trouble of checking the condiments table."

"What are you talking about?" Vesper asked. Her eyebrows had slowly climbed up above her otherwise schooled expression.

Jason's expression was suddenly that of a man realising he'd said too much.

"Uh… nothing," he said, looking about nervously. "You should say hello to Emir. He's around here, somewhere."

Zara, hid a giggle behind her hand, flashing her eyes at Jason.

"Emir Bahadir is currently a person of interest to our royal family over a theft that took place several years ago," Zara told him, her words formal but her voice unable to excise the undertone of mirth.

"And he still invited you?" Jason asked. "What a magnanimous bloke."

"You know, Jason," Zara said. "At the risk of self-aggrandisement, I like to think that when someone meets me, I'm the most interesting person they meet that day. I'm not used to being upstaged by gods."

"Never fear," Jason said. "You were absolutely the most interesting person I met that day. I'm pretty sure gods are just big lumps of magic that have been around so long they gained sentience and started having funny ideas."

"That comes dangerously close to blasphemy," Zara's aunt said.

"Blasphemy is kind of my thing," Jason said.

"And yet, you were just personally and publicly praised by multiple gods," Zara said.

"I know, right?" Jason asked. "It's a funny old world."

*

On the other side of the barbeque, Danielle Geller came upon Rick Geller standing alone. He was only a distant relative; she wasn't sure what their actual relation was. Some kind of much-removed nephew, from what she recalled. She had come to admire and respect the young man who had been as close to the family's recent tragedies as anyone, after losing two members of his team who were closely related. Rather than swear vengeance, he had grown into his responsibilities as a leader. Instead of dwelling on those who had fallen, he focused on protecting those that remained.

She noticed his gaze locked on something across the room. She followed it to where Jason was speaking quietly with the Rimaros princess and her royal aunt. Danielle noted the body language of the princess and the confused expression on Vesper Rimaros's face she had come to associate with people talking to Jason.

"That's the hurricane princess," Rick said.

Danielle sighed.

"I don't understand people who insist on these overblown sobriquets," Danielle said. "She's iron-rank, for goodness sake. None of you have had a chance to truly prove yourselves."

They watched Zara giggle at something Jason said, putting a hand over her mouth.

"How does he do that?" Rick asked.

Danielle looked at him.

"No offence, dear boy, but a woman like that would chew you up and spit you out. I thought you were interested in one of the young ladies on your team?"

"Yes," Rick said. Normally he wouldn't admit it, but no one who had been through Geller training would consider lying to Danielle.

"I could use some of Jason's way with women, though," Rick said wistfully. "Really, how does he do that?"

"Did you ask him?"

"He said that what he had can't be taught."

Danielle chuckled.

"Probably true," she said. "Would you like me to tell you why?"

"Yes," Rick said enthusiastically, turning to look at Danielle.

"When it comes to princesses or other highborn women, do you know how often they meet someone who doesn't care they're a princess? Never, probably, at least in their own age group. The smarter boys learn the value of pretending they don't care, which makes the smarter young women very good at spotting it. All the more for the social training they undergo. Then along comes Jason, who genuinely doesn't care who their family is. Add a little wit, a disregard for propriety and a penchant for the taboo and you're waving fresh meat in front of a hungry animal."

"I don't think I can be as brazen as Jason," Rick said.

"Nor should you be," Danielle said. "Jason is who he is, without apology or shame. He accepts the consequences, knowing that as many or more will hate him for it as be drawn to him. People respect authenticity, however, even when it's as unusual as Jason's. There's an integrity to it. That's what you are looking for. You don't need to be like Jason. You need to figure out who you are, Rickard. Be true to that and accept the consequences. Then you won't have to go looking for the right people because you'll have already learned to recognise them."

"You really think it's that simple?" Rick asked.

"I do," Danielle said. "Simple, however, is not the same thing as easy."

Jason was still greeting new arrivals, the steadying presence of Constance a guiding light. She would subtly indicate a guest who would not respond well to Jason's particular social graces and he affected enough civility that no one made a fuss in spite of his, to their eyes, ludicrous appearance.

Various groups had arrived from many religious organisations, many of whom were at a loss as to how to handle Jason. One such group was from the church of Knowledge.

"Gabrielle," Jason greeted. "I didn't realise you were participating in the trials."

"My lady felt that I would benefit from facing challenges where I did not have her to rely upon."

"Yeah, the Healer mentioned that the gods couldn't access astral spaces. It's always fun to hear that even gods have their limits."

Behind him, Constance pointedly cleared her throat.

"My lady has prepared another gift for you," Gabrielle said, clearly unhappy to be delivering the message. "She believes you will find it more palatable than the last. It shall be delivered on your return to Greenstone."

"I'm a little wary, after the last one," Jason said.

"She is certain that this one will be more welcome."

"I guess we'll see."

Hester was one of Emir's most important staff members. She was in charge of logistics and coordination between all of Emir's disparate operations, for which her portal ability was a crucial tool.

Hester was from Pranay, this world's equivalent of Sri Lanka. In this world, however, it was a much larger, located further to the south and west. In a world where the Arabian Peninsula did not exist and the Mediterranean connected directly to the Indian Ocean, its northern coast was home to several important connections for sea trade.

Hester had been born in one of those ports, the city of Jayapura. She opened a portal, and Jason and his team stepped through into that city. They emerged from the portal with mixed reactions to the transition. Jason and Sophie, with their astral affinities, were unaffected. They immediately started taking in their surroundings, including their team members who had handled the transition less well.

Humphrey had a teleport power of his own so, while not immune to the disorientation, was at least used to it. Portalling across a continent was more straining than across a room, but he took a deep breath and was fine. Clive and Neil were less experienced but it was not their first time, staggering a little before righting themselves. Belinda had the worst of it, lurching dizzily until Sophie stepped in to prevent her from falling over entirely. Stash the puppy stumbled about before toppling over and letting out an unhappy whine.

They were in a courtyard full of lush plants, in raised planters and hanging from walls. The walls, planters and even the floor were covered in mosaic tiles in bright, cool colours. The shades of blue, green and turquoise gave the courtyard an underwater feeling, the vibrant space lit up by the bright sunlight. The air was hot, like that in Greenstone but drier, without the mugginess produced from the delta. The heat was cut by a fresh breeze with a tang of the sea, blowing in through archways leading out of the courtyard.

Hester gave them a tour of an incredible house on a clifftop, overlooking the ocean. Tunnels dug down into the rock, with stone stairwells leading down into a network of cave grottos. Platforms of metal and wood wound through the caves, suspended over the water below. Magic glow-stones lit up the caves, both under the water and above.

"There are guest rooms down here or up above," Hester told them. "You can choose whichever you prefer."

"Down here," Jason said immediately, grinning like a loon as he looked over a railing and into the water.

"If you want to swim, feel free," Hester said, continuing to lead them through the colourfully lit caves. "The main entertaining grotto actually has a bar you can only get to by swimming. Or flying, water-walking, teleporting. Whatever powers you might have."

"You have a magnificent home," Jason said as Hester led them back upstairs.

"You can travel a lot as an adventurer," Hester told him, "especially with a power like mine. I think it's important to have somewhere to come home to, though. And, of course, being adventurers gives us the means to have that."

Hester introduced them to her extended family, all of whom lived in the expansive compound sprawling over the top of the cliff. Like many successful adventurers, she had provided her family with essences and monster cores to extend their longevity, even if they never fought a monster themselves. Hester's family were extremely welcoming, especially Hester's mother, Anise.

"She never brings home friends," Anise was saying to Jason as they walked, joining them for the rest of the tour.

"Mother..."

"Oh, hush dear. You really must tell me what Hester has been up to, Jason. She's always so secretive."

"Let me think," Jason said. "Ah, I know. A little while ago, there was a big expedition that went out from the city where we've been staying. It was a huge deal, and they sent along everyone who could open a portal or do a mass teleport. Of course, then they ended up in an astral space they couldn't portal out of. Are you familiar with astral spaces, Anise?"

"Oh, yes," Anise said. "So many rumours going around these days about them."

"Well, it turned out that expedition was in desperate need of help, and it was Hester who made that happen. Without her, no one would have gotten there in time."

"Why aren't you the one to tell me about these things?" Anise asked Hester.

"I didn't really do anything," Hester said.

"Nonsense," Jason said. "She's an absolute hero. Humphrey and Neil, here, were on that expedition. They might not be here if it weren't for your daughter."

"He's blowing things out of proportion," Hester said.

They came to a pathway outside the house from which they could see the city sprawling down from the hilltop upon which Hester's home was located. It was much larger than Greenstone, spreading out over the coastline, alongside the cerulean ocean sparkling in the sunlight.

"This is beautiful," Jason said as they stopped to look out. "Thank you for sharing your home with us, Hester."

"I'm just happy you managed to bring that scythe back," Hester said. "Emir seems like a relaxed boss, but he wasn't great to be around while you were in the astral space. The prospect of no one bringing it back after two years of effort? The whole staff is just about ready to kiss you. Don't let them, though. Especially Weird Pants Keith."

Killian Laurent was an elf who looked like the villain from a fairy story, with ugly, sunken features, emaciated limbs and sickly pallid skin. Dressed in ill-fitted black, even the way he walked had an unpleasant obsequiousness to it. He sidled into Silva's office, not even glancing at the blood soaking into the rug. Silva stood with his back to the door, and did not turn around at Killian's entrance.

"You once made a suggestion to me," Silva said without preamble. "I declined."

"You did not want to take the risk of discovery," Killian said in his raspy voice.

"Since then, I have been discreetly approached," Silva said. "Someone offered assistance that may make something like what you suggested more viable."

"You are ready to take the girl?"

"No," Silva said, still facing away. "I was offered assistance in taking the man who took her from me. She'll get hers when the man who holds her indenture contract is flushed out to sea in a thousand pieces. Is this something you can make happen?"

"Mr Silva, I am a man of particular appetites," Killian said. "I moved my loyalties from your father to you, because you have my appetites met reliably and discreetly, where your father would not. People of my inclination operate in very small circles, and I am familiar with a man, a silver-rank adventurer, with predilections not unlike my own. There is no way such a man, being silver-rank, would enter your employ. But if he were offered the same arrangement I enjoy, I imagine he would be willing to undertake the occasional favour. For example, the quiet acquisition of a troublesome young adventurer."

"How reliable is this man?"

"I can assure you, Mr Silva, that he is a man of exquisite caution."

Silva did not respond for a long time, still staring at the wall without turning to face Killian.

"Very well," Silva said. "Set up a meeting; I want to talk to this man. Also, find out exactly what he will want before the meeting happens."

70
DOMINEERING, TERRITORIAL AND ROBUST

For those who could afford them, personal transport in Jayapura consisted of platter-sized discs that floated in the air, underfoot, the rider directing them by shifting their weight. Hester brought a number of them out onto an open area of lawn for her visitors to get a handle on.

"Hoverboards!" Jason called out cheerfully.

"Their actually called personal float discs," Clive corrected him.

"Hoverboards!"

"That's not—"

"Hoverboards!" Jason asserted again.

Stash turned into a bird and flew onto Jason's head, echoing his cry.

"Hoverboards!"

"Good boy," Jason said, giving bird Stash a biscuit.

Smaller float discs, like those Hester had brought out, were for standing on. She explained that there were larger ones, each of which had a seat on them. Use of those by anyone other than the physically infirm were looked down on, however.

Humphrey and Clive had used them before, and Sophie and Jason found their balance quickly. Neil and Belinda had more trouble; they struggled to get their disc to even move, only for it to shoot out from under them as it did. While they continued to practice, Jason skimmed around the edges of the yard, giggling like a madman.

"Hoverboards," he said happily, pulling up next to Clive. "Why do we not have these in Greenstone?"

"The magical density is too low," Clive said. "It's why all the magical vehicles need someone like me to drive them."

"Doesn't that make your ability kind of useless here?" Jason asked.

Clive grinned.

"You need someone like me to drive that," Clive said, pointing up.

Jason looked into the air, where what looked like a zeppelin was floating gracefully through the sky. Instead of an inflated envelope of air, it had what looked like the wire frame of an air envelope, visibly glowing with magic.

"Awesome."

Eventually Hester judged Neil and Belinda ready for strictly supervised use of the float discs and they started down the hill and into the city, carefully for the benefit of Belinda and Neil.

"Did we have to start off downhill?" Neil asked nervously as he controlled his disc.

"Not to say I don't agree with the sentiment," Belinda said, likewise moving with caution. "It might be a bit much to ask Hester to move her house somewhere flatter for our benefit, though."

Hester led them into the city, passing through older and older sections as they moved closer to the centre. Their destination was the Mystic Quarter, where the city's main temples were located, along with the Magic and Adventure Society campuses.

"The Adventure Society trade hall should be the place to find most of what you're after," Hester told them. "You may need the Magic Society for some of the ritual components. In any case, the trade hall brokers will take all the loot off your hands you'd care to trade."

The Adventure Society campus dwarfed that of Greenstone's, although it lacked the open simplicity. Instead, it was a warren of tight alleys and narrow streets, with buildings hugging together like goods bundled in a crate. It was more like a town, the trade hall alone the size of a village.

"You should enjoy this, Humphrey," Jason said as they moved through the crowds of the main trade hall. "Unlike in Greenstone, there's no one to recognise you. You can just be some guy here."

After visiting the brokers, they spent some time shopping around. Jason's group chat allowed them to stay in contact when they split up. The moved through the crowded trade hall, the maelstrom of voices all around them, hawking and haggling.

"Does anyone have any crystal wash?" they heard a voice calling out. "Everywhere seems to be sold out, all of a sudden."

Jason looked a little shifty on hearing that and did his best to continue shopping nonchalantly. The team regrouped outside the trade hall to compare purchases. They had only bought a few things, as their main purpose was to hand over their awakening stones and essences to the brokers for auction. There was market enough that auctions took place daily, so they would be able to collect their earnings in the morning.

"I got a line on a magical tattooist with the skills I need," Jason said. "Someone who can apply the immortal crest."

The immortal crest was an item Jason obtained during the trials that was unusual in nature. Using it required the services of a specialist magic craftsperson, none of whom resided in Greenstone. Humphrey had used one himself, while travelling with his mother.

Item: [Immortal Crest] (iron rank, rare)

An object that allows the soul to mark the body **(consumable, tattoo).**

Effect: When applied by a mystical tattooist, this item will draw out a soul crest. This item can only be used on an iron rank essence user.

After acquiring the item, Jason had asked Clive about it. Clive, in turn, roped in Humphrey, who already had a soul crest. A soul crest, they explained, was a magical tattoo printed not on the body, but on the soul. That imprint would appear on the body in turn, in a form that resisted design. The form of the crest was a visible reflection of the bearer's true nature.

The crest was used as a form of identification. The unique imprint on the aura remained the same, even if the aura itself changed and the visible form of the crest with it. Impossible to track or falsify through even the strongest magic, so long as there was a record of the imprint, it was a guaranteed proof of identity.

Immortal crests were difficult and expensive to make, especially for an iron-rank item, but many wealthy adventurers commissioned one nonetheless. Once the Adventure Society had a record of the imprint, it was an ironclad proof of identity that could be verified at any branch in the world.

The visible form of the crest could not be chosen. Instead it reflected the soul that produced it. This had famously mixed results.

"If we're going to see a magical tattooist," Humphrey said, "then you should all get one. I already did, when I used my immortal crest."

As a group, they decided to make that their next stop. Clive explained magical tattoos as they traversed the city on their hover-discs.

"It will only last as long as your current rank," Clive told them. "It gets purged from your body as you rank up, along with any other magical waste that doesn't hold up to your new rank. That leaves you free to get a new tattoo at your new rank."

"What do they do?" Belinda asked. "I've heard of magic tattoos, but never seen one."

"We can change that," Humphrey said. He pulled back his sleeve to show an intricate sigil on his upper arm, confident enough in his skill with the floating disc to do so without falling off. The tattoo's colour was a brilliant shade of blue that shimmered like sunlight on the ocean.

"Different tattoos do different things," Clive said. "That looks like a mana-accumulating one."

"That's right," Humphrey said. "It slowly accumulates mana, which I can absorb when I need it. It's basically a mana potion that takes a few hours to refill itself."

"The functions of iron-rank tattoos are quite basic," Clive explained, "so most people go for some variant on health or mana recovery, be that a moderate increase to natural recovery, or an on-demand burst like Humphrey has there. There are other options, though. A short burst of damage reduction, or reducing the cooldown of an ability. Effects like that are single-use and take an amount of time to recover before being used again."

"How many can you get?" Sophie asked.

"Just the one," Clive said. "Usually, anyway. There are essence abilities that can increase that. My rune essence, for example, will frequently produce that type of ability. I didn't get one of those, though."

Following the directions Jason had obtained, Hester guided them away from the main areas of the Mystic Quarter, the streets growing narrower and the buildings older as they went.

"Are you sure this place we're going is legitimate?" Neil asked Jason.

"Are you kidding?" Jason asked. "Mysterious shopkeepers in dilapidated parts of the city where most would never tread are always better."

"According to whom?" Neil asked.

"Eighties movies."

"Eighty what?"

"I'll assess the place for myself," Hester said.

They found the tattoo shop, and while the dingy exterior was not confidence-inducing, the interior was a stark contrast. They walked into a room with polished wood, shining tiles and glass as pristine as a cloudless winter sky. Hung on the walls were pictures of various tattoos, some artistic, others with descriptions of their effects.

"If the craftsmanship we can expect is a match for what's on display here," Clive said, examining the pictures, "then I don't foresee any problems."

"Agreed," Hester said, likewise looking over the displays. She turned to Jason. "Who told you about this place?"

"I was asking around at the trade hall," Jason said. "I couldn't much tell good advice from the bad, so I tried something else. They don't differentiate the trade hall by rank like they do back in Greenstone; it's all mixed together here. So I started looking for places that seemed a bit less impressive than you'd expect at the trade hall. Eventually I found a place that didn't look like much and everyone seemed to ignore, but every person I saw go in was clearly a top-flight adventurer. It was all silver and gold rankers, the kind who have plain-looking gear that you can tell is actually the good stuff if you pay attention. So, I went in, had a little chat with the guy running it and he gave me a tip."

"Just like that?" Sophie asked.

"Well… I did have to promise to send Neil in for a special visit."

"What?" Neil asked.

"It'll be fine," Jason said. "They really liked the sound of a chunky elf. We should start looking for a sailor suit soon, though, because finding one in your size might be tricky."

"They?"

"I think he had some mates he wanted to bring along. The more, the merrier, right?"

"You know that someone is going to tie you to a boulder and drop you in the ocean one day," Neil said.

"That's fine," Jason said. "It turns out that I don't need to breathe."

A wiry woman emerged from a back room. She looked older, but hale and weathered like a tree that had survived storm after storm. Jason was unable to detect any aura from her at all.

"I was wondering who was making a commotion in my shop," she said, looking them over. "Not a lot of boisterous youths darken my door. Accompanied by Hester Maharala, no less. The lady with the house on the hill. Are you still following that Bahadir boy around?"

"You know Emir?" Hester asked.

"Know might be a strong word," the woman said. "We crossed paths when he was still a precocious boy. Good to hear he took up treasure hunting, because he was only a so-so adventurer. That couple he ran around with, now they knew their business. The sneaky one, too."

"Gabriel and Arabella Remore," Jason said. "We'll be seeing them soon, if you'd like us to pass on a greeting."

"Oh, they don't want to hear from some old shopkeeper," she said. "Who is it that sent you my way?"

"The man selling magic lamps in the trade hall."

"And you were the one who got it out of him?" she asked. "He probably saw you were an outworlder and got all excitable, the damn coot."

"I'm Jason Asano. May I have your name?"

"Tilly is good enough. You didn't come here just for tattoos, Jason Asano. You could get them plenty of places, cheaper and easier."

Jason took out a plain metal plate and handed it over.

"Immortal crest," Tilly said, turning it over in her hands. "Who made this?"

"Me, kind of," Jason said. "A looting ability. Of sorts."

"Of weird sorts, to produce something like this. Alright, I can get you sorted out. Once we've settled the matter of price."

"And that is?" Jason asked.

"Is the chunky elf with the sailor suit on the table?"

Jason blinked in surprise, then burst out laughing.

"Gods damn you, Asano," Neil said.

"The price is money, of course," Tilly said with a twinkle in her eye. "It's a tattoo shop. It'll be a wheelbarrow full of coins for an immortal crest and a day or two to get things ready."

"Once today's auctions have gone through, we'll have wheelbarrows of cash to spare," Jason said. "In the meantime, we'll get some enchanted tattoos."

Tilly took them back into a workroom with a big chair that looked like it came from the office of a really scary dentist. On a table next to it were laid out a series of very large needles, pots of oils, unguents and powders. More jars and pots were crammed together on shelves lining the walls with no visible organisation system. Light poured from the large skylight over their heads.

"You first," Tilly said to Humphrey. "Shirt off."

"I already have a tattoo," Humphrey said.

"I don't care," she said. "I want a look at that soul crest. The price of me doing one for your friend."

Humphrey tugged off his shirt, revealing his impressive physique.

"Damn, Humphrey," Jason said. "I didn't realise you waxed your chest."

"I don't wax my chest."

"You do seem oddly hairless," Belinda said. "Do you get that hair-removal cream from Jory?"

"No!"

"I think he has some kind of magic crystal he uses for shaving," Jason said.

"Would you please stop talking about my chest hair."

"You don't have any chest hair," Belinda said. "That's kind of the whole point."

"Stop gabbing and turn around," Tilly told Humphrey, who was clearly relieved to do so.

Humphrey revealed a startling image on his back: a rainbow-coloured dragon on a great, sand-coloured shield. The dragon's scales glimmered in the light, making it seem like a living thing.

"Whoever drew this out knew their business," Tilly assessed. "This is the Vitesse style. Was it Klimpsen?"

"You can tell that just from looking at it?" Humphrey asked. "I though the image was determined by the soul."

"It is," Tilly said. "It's shaped by the artist that drew it out of your soul, though. Klimpsen was a good choice but he doesn't work for just anyone. You must have some good family connections."

"His mum is kind of a big deal," Jason said.

"Lucky for some," Tilly said. "You next, Asano. I need to know what I'm dealing with to make the right preparations. Shirt off."

Jason looked at Humphrey and self-consciously removed his shirt. Jason's body was as fit as it had ever been but still looked flabby and meagre next to Humphrey.

"How is that fair?" Jason said. "You look like some famous sculpture brought to life by a witch to steal my girlfriend."

"You don't have a girlfriend," Humphrey said.

"Rub it in, why don't you?"

Tilly shoved Jason around and prodded at his back with her wizened fingers.

"You shouldn't get anything too embarrassing as a crest. You wouldn't believe the number of sheltered young idiots that get an immortal crest and aren't happy when it reveals who they really are. Which yours will too, make no mistake. If you don't think you can handle seeing your true nature then I'd stop here."

"It is what it is," Jason said. "Worst case, shirts are a thing."

"Interesting aura," Tilly said, continuing to ply Jason's back. "Domineering and territorial. Robust, especially for your rank. Something else, too. Are you some kind of priest?"

The whole team laughed at that.

"He's definitely not," Neil said. "If anything, he's the exact opposite."

"It's a little odd to find a touch of the divine on you, then."

"I've been touched by gods, alright," Jason said. "They're quite handsy, once you get to know them."

71

MORE SHADY AS WE GO ALONG

Tilly provided the group with catalogues that took the form of recording crystals, allowing them to look through projections of the available magic tattoos.

"I'm going to take the burst healing rune," Sophie said. She was soon in the big chair in her undershirt as Tilly pricked needles into her arm.

"You want privacy for this?" Jason asked her.

"You've never seen a woman's shoulder before? I feel sorry for that Cassandra girl now."

By the time Tilly had completed drawing the red rune onto Sophie's arm, the others had picked out their own tattoos. Belinda chose one that would allow her to ignore the delay before she could use an ability again. This would allow her to use her cooldown reduction power twice in a row, which would, in turn, let someone else use a powerful ability three times in quick succession. That tattoo was a small one printed on the back of the neck.

Clive took the same one, while Jason took one that made his afflictions slightly harder to resist. Jason's was imprinted on his chest, right over his heart.

"You have an impressively broad repertoire," Humphrey complimented Tilly. "The place I received my tattoo had a more restrictive selection."

"Klimpsen does quality work," Tilly said, not looking up from where she was putting needles into Jason's chest. "He's not what you'd call an innovator, though. He's the guy you go to for reliability, rather than originality."

Neil was originally going to take a tattoo that gave a general increase to his mana recovery speed, but had his mind changed by Tilly. She was able to do a burst mana-recovery tattoo, essentially a free mana potion, with a recharge time affected by his mana recovery rate. Given that Sophie and Clive both enhanced team mana recovery, he would be able to use the tattoo with enviable frequency.

Like Jason, Neil's tattoo went on the chest, but when Neil took his shirt off, he got loud reactions from the team.

"Wow," Belinda said.

"Yep," Sophie agreed, both women tilting their heads as they ran their eyes over Neil's muscular body.

"What?" Neil asked.

"Uh, we all thought you were fat," Clive said.

"Wait, you really did think I was fat?"

"I didn't," Jason said, at which Neil wheeled on him.

"You're the one responsible for this and you didn't even think I was fat?"

"I'm not going to mock an actual fat guy," Jason said. "That's just punching down. Also, your tailor is the one responsible, not me."

"Your outfits really aren't flattering," Humphrey agreed. "Is there padding in them?"

"No, there isn't padding in them."

"They drape very poorly," Jason said. "You should try Gilbert's in the trade hall back in Greenstone. He sadly doesn't sell short pants or floral print, but if you want to look good, he's your guy."

"You go to Gilbert's too?" Humphrey asked Jason.

"I do," Jason said. "I think he makes you look better than me though. You've got those powerful shoulders."

Once all the tattoos were done, they made arrangements to return the day after next for Jason's crest. After all their shopping, they sky was growing dark and they returned to Hester's house.

Hester's extended family had gathered for her return, and welcomed the team into their home for an evening of food and family. Jason quickly found his way to the kitchen. Everyone else gathered on an entertaining deck underground where colourful lights lit up the grotto as they watched the sun go down over the sea through a west-facing cave that looked out along the coast.

Belinda retired early, in anticipation of using a sobering sixteen awakening stones the next day, plus summoning at least one familiar. Late in the evening, Sophie spotted Jason in his conjured cloak, walking over the water in the grotto and out through the cave entrance. She quietly dropped over the railing, using her slow-fall power to alight on the surface of the water herself. She followed him out, to where the ocean water was eerily still and the light of two moons shone down on it. The hood of Jason's cloak was pushed back, his head tilted back and looking at the night sky.

"Clive gave you a telling off the other day," he said without looking.

He had apparently sensed her in spite of her moving in silence. Her perception powers enhanced her ability to sense auras, yet she could barely sense his. Those same abilities had allowed her to sense Jason's aura control as it become increasingly precise in the time they had known one another. She knew the dead friend she had never met had taught Jason the techniques he was passing on to her. Fastidious practice seemed to be his way of connecting with his absent mentor.

"I probably shouldn't have hit you so much," she said.

"I understand," Jason said, keeping his gaze on the stars. "I know you were holding back and I wasn't hurt. You should probably be looking for healthier expressions of freedom, though."

"Am I free?" she asked.

"If you want to leave and never come back, just talk to Hester," Jason said. "I told you that from the start."

"I've come a long way since then," Sophie said. "You've put a good amount of capital into making me an adventurer, both monetary and political."

Jason turned his gaze from the sky to her, frowning.

"I'm tired of having this conversation. I'm tired of justifying myself, as if I'm somehow not good enough to have done something just because it was right. As far as I'm concerned, I don't have an indentured servant. I have a teammate who keeps talking about leaving. If you're going to go, do us a favour and go now, because we'll need to find new people."

"Belinda and I aren't going anywhere."

"Good," he said testily, "because I am done talking about this."

Jason vanished into the shadow of his cloak, which drifted emptily before disappearing as well.

Sophie stared at the spot he had been standing.

"Good job, Wexler," she admonished herself.

In the morning the team left without the guidance of Hester, leaving her to catch up with her family. They had seen enough of the city to muddle through, as they had already visited the Mystic Quarter. It wasn't hard to get directions to the Magic Society campus and Belinda and Neil's increasing proficiency with the floating discs compensated for the time they lost while lacking a guide.

Clive took the lead at the Magic Society, his understanding of the society's workings getting them prompt consideration. They decided the order of the day would be to hire a ritual room and conduct all Belinda's remaining awakening rituals. Afterwards, they would purchase the materials Jason and Belinda would need to summon familiars. Belinda already had one such power and, with sixteen powers to be awakened, had a good chance of getting more.

"A companion specialist would be interesting," Humphrey said. "My sister's abilities are like that. It would make for some interesting potential, on top of the familiars and summons we already have."

"I think a support specialist is more likely," Clive said, "based on the power's we've seen so far. Only four powers in, though. It could be anything, really."

"Either works for me," Belinda said. "As long as I'm not in front of someone, swinging a great big sword."

"We have Humphrey for that," Jason said.

As they awakened Belinda's powers one by one, her abilities fell broadly into three categories. As expected, her trap essence produced area control powers. One was an ability Clive had from the rune essence, called rune trap. Another conjured a dimensional-space pit trap under the feet of enemies, while the final two powers used magical tethers to affect enemies in different ways.

From the magic essence she gained abilities with effects predicated on the powers of others. She had a curse that caused enemy power use to lock them out from another of their abilities. An ability called power thief was a special ranged attack that would lock out an enemy's power, giving Belinda the power to use instead. She had a spell that let her mimic spells recently used by allies, while her final ability was another summoned familiar, called an astral lantern.

"Lantern-type familiars are quite good," Humphrey said. "Judging by my sister's, at least."

"They tend to be ranged attackers," Clive said.

The adept essence started out well, with a perception power that let her see magic, like Clive. It got better with an aura that caused allied abilities to come off cooldown faster, followed by a power, usable once per day, that reset every cooldown a person had.

It was when she awakened her the last adept ability that things started going off the rails, at least from Belinda's perspective.

You have awakened the adept essence ability [Instant Adept]. You have awakened 5 of 5 adept essence abilities.

You have awakened all adept essence abilities. Linked attribute [Speed] will advance in conjunction with lowest-rank adept essence ability.

Ability: [Instant Adept] (Adept)
Special ability.
Cost: Very high mana.
Cooldown: 6 hours.

Current rank: Iron 0 (00%).

Effect (iron): Gain a significant increase to the [Speed] attribute and temporary proficiency with acrobatics, small blades and ranged weapons.

Your maximum stamina increases and you gain an ongoing stamina recovery effect.

"What kind of ability is this?" she asked as she read the power.

"I've seen these before," Clive said. "They bestow a particular set of skills, much like a skill book, but only temporarily. It lets you fill archetypal roles, not as well as a specialist, obviously, but if that's what you need at the time then it's very useful."

"It says ranged weapons," Jason said. "It might be good. Get yourself a good magic bow, fire some arrows down range and then escape with those acrobatic skills it mentions."

"I suppose that isn't too bad," Belinda said grudgingly before they moved onto the next power.

By that stage, she only had two powers from the charlatan essence left to awaken, which had already produced two unusual powers. Beside myself was a power that rendered her invisible while an illusion mimicked her nearby. Unexpected allies was a power that used illusions to make allies look like enemies, but the allies could see through it. The spell then randomly switch-teleported all the allies and enemies in the area with each other.

"It has to be better than that stupid learning archery power," Belinda said as Clive completed the ritual.

You have awakened the charlatan essence ability [Counterfeit Combatant].
You have awakened 4 of 5 charlatan essence abilities.

Ability: [Counterfeit Combatant] (Charlatan)
Special ability (shape-change).
Cost: Very high mana.
Cooldown: 6 hours.

Current rank: Iron 0 (00%).

Effect (iron): Gain a significant increase to the [Power] attribute and temporary proficiency with armour and melee weaponry. Your physique enlarges, your maximum stamina increases and you gain an ongoing stamina recovery effect.

"Oh, gods damn it."

"It does bring some versatility to the team," Humphrey offered.

"I don't want versatility! The team's already thick with versatility! I want to stand at the back, being all clever and disruptive. What's clever about braining some guy with a scimitar?"

"It doesn't have to be clever," Humphrey said. "It just has to be useful."

"You think putting me up front to hit people will be useful?"

"It'll be unexpected," Jason offered. "Who expects a small, adorable person to whack them upside the head with a big hammer?"

"I think I understand the specific dimensional space you awakened now," Clive said. "As you'll no doubt recall, its unique nuance was the ability to directly equip or unequip gear. Given your new abilities to take on specific roles, that now becomes very useful."

"Are you telling me that my next ability might be another one of these idiotic powers to hit people with weapons, like a thug?"

"I wouldn't think so," Clive said. "You already have powers to turn you into a fast attacker and a strong attacker."

"Maybe you'll be able to turn into a healer," Neil said. "The ability to have another in a pinch would be amazing."

"That's true," Belinda acknowledged, calming down.

Clive conducted her final ritual of awakening.

You have awakened the charlatan essence ability [Specious Sorcerer]. You have awakened 5 of 5 charlatan essence abilities.

You have awakened all charlatan essence abilities. Linked attribute [Recovery] will advance in conjunction with lowest-rank adept essence ability.

Ability: [Specious Sorcerer] (Charlatan)
Special ability.
Cost: Very high mana.
Cooldown: 6 hours.

Current rank: Iron 0 (00%).

Effect (iron): Gain a significant increase to the [Spirit] attribute and the ability to use magical tools. Your maximum mana increases and you gain an ongoing mana recovery effect.

Belinda groaned.

"Is it just me," she asked, "or are these ability names becoming more shady as we go along?"

"These abilities may seem underwhelming now," Clive said, "but remember this is only the beginning. Powers like these usually offer up extra powers to use while they are active. Your adept power will most likely give utility abilities, while the strength and magic based ones will probably give you special attacks and spells, respectively. You could even consider them to be a means to get more abilities than everyone else."

"Yeah?" Belinda asked thoughtfully. "I do like the idea of having more things."

"That's everyone's powers complete," Humphrey said. "Summoning familiars aside, we're ready to get down to the real work."

"The real work?" Neil asked.

"Training," Jason said. Humphrey nodded his agreement.

"Between us, we have an adventurer-and-a-half's worth of abilities to learn. The next few weeks will be strategising, testing, training and then doing it all over again. We won't just be learning how to use our powers but how to use them as a team. It's going to take weeks, maybe months to get where we need to be."

"Months?" Sophie asked.

"It won't be as tedious as he makes it sound," Jason said. "We should all be ready to work hard, though."

"I had an idea to inspire us a little," Humphrey said. "There's a public mirage area in this city. I asked Hester to reserve us a viewing room for this evening. I think seeing what the best of a large city like this can do will show you how far we have to go. If I have anything to say about it, we'll become better than anyone we see tonight."

72
MAGNIFICENT ENTITY

"Moment of truth," Jason said.

He had drawn out the summoning circle himself, rather than let Clive draw it with his ritual diagram power. All the materials were laid out: spirit coins, quintessence gems and other magical objects. After sprinkling some powdered lesser magic cores to double check everything was correct, he stood up, preparing to chant the incantation.

"When Gary heard Jason would be getting new familiars," Humphrey whispered, "he tried to bet me the incantation would be really evil."

"You didn't take that bet, did you?" Sophie asked him.

"Gods, no."

"Do you mind?" Jason asked. "I'm trying to summon an awesome British shadow creature."

"Sorry," Humphrey said. "You go ahead."

"Well, I'm self-conscious now," Jason said. "You're all going to interpret the incantation as evil, even when it's just a normal, harmless incantation."

"It'll be fine," Humphrey said. "We promise to keep an open mind."

"I don't," Neil said.

"Just do it," Sophie said. "It's not going to seem any less evil for all the build-up."

Jason groaned, but turned back to his ritual circle and started chanting.

"*I call to the realm beyond cold and darkness, where death has no meaning for life has no place. Let mine be the dark beyond darkness, falling on the final road to the end of all things. Let mine be the shadow of death.*"

As Jason chanted, dark energy boiled up to submerge the ritual circle.

"I don't know what we were worried about," Neil said. "That didn't seem at all like he was calling up some all-consuming darkness and that we should kill him to keep it from entering the world."

"I don't know that I'd say evil," Humphrey said with very little conviction.

"You wish you'd taken that bet then?" Sophie asked.

"No, I do not," Humphrey said.

Jason dropped to his knees, then rolled onto his back. He took out a mana potion and chugged it to assuage the low mana headache suddenly pounding the inside of his skull.

"That was a lot easier than last time," he said. "Summoning Colin didn't just drain just my mana, but my health and stamina, too."

Everyone's gaze turned to the ritual circle where darkness rose up like fire's dark twin, consuming light instead of shedding it. The room seemed to grow dim in spite of the magical glow-stones.

"That's odd," Clive said. "These stones are shielded so as to not affect the ambient magic in the room. Nothing in here should be able to affect them."

From the dark circle of black flame, a figure slowly rose. Nothing more than a silhouette, it seemed ephemeral, yet at the same time imposing. It had the rough shape of a man draped in a cloak. Jason's teammates couldn't help but think of Jason himself, as he looked with his magical cloak completely dimmed.

Suddenly the oppressive feeling drained away. The room lit back up and the black flames vanished, leaving only the figure who looked to be made from darkness itself, his edges blurry, even when standing in the light.

"Hello again, Jason Asano."

"Shade," Jason said, a huge grin spreading across his face. "I was hoping it would be you."

"It has been some time since I walked the worlds," Shade said. "You seem likely to see more than most. I should warn you, that the vessels I inhabit now are far less capable than those I was bound to in the astral space."

"Vessels, plural?" Jason asked.

He reached out a hand to touch Shade.

Shade (Shadow of the Reaper).
Familiar (iron rank).

Incorporeal.

Can occupy up to three shadow bodies.

Highly visible in well-lit areas but can move rapidly.

Shadow bodies can hide within the shadows of other people. When there is

not at least one shadow body attached to the summoner, the summoner has no shadow.

Can drain mana by touch. Drained mana can be passed onto anyone with a shadow body hidden within their shadow.

While at least one shadow body is hidden within the summoner's shadow, summoner can see and hear through other shadow bodies.

Shadow bodies hidden in the summoner's shadow can contain traces of the summoner's presence, with one body containing each detectable factor.

"Shade," Jason said, "I think that will do just fine. Speaking of the astral space, though, did you happen to notice anyone who stayed behind when everyone else left?"

"Yes," Shade said. "When the trial period ended, the vessels I was inhabiting were dissolved, returning me to the astral. This was the moment the gates closed, therefore those who had not used them remain there still. I am aware of which people they are."

"You know who stayed behind?" Jason asked. "Actual names?"

"Yes. The powers afforded me by the vessels I inhabited were powerful. All that was said, I heard."

"That's pretty amazing," Jason said and turned to his team. "I'm going to hire one of the Magic Society's water communication chambers and get that list of names back to Greenstone. In the meantime, you summon up your familiars, Belinda. I'm pretty tired, anyway, after doing mine. I can finish up when you're done."

Shade sidled into Jason's shadow and Jason left without any indication of his new passenger's presence. The rest of the group cleared away the remnants of his summoning circle and Belinda started setting up her own. Like Jason, she was drawing her own magic diagram, with advice, but not assistance, from Clive.

Belinda's first summon had a more mystical and less sinister chant than Jason's. Its appearance was heralded by silver-blue light that filled the room before coalescing over the ritual circle, compressing down until a silver lantern appeared around it. The lantern floated around the room, bathing it in a cool light.

"It's pretty," she said. "I like this much more than some death shadow."

"Shade was good to us in the astral space," Sophie said. "He was presumably good to everyone, but I like him."

Belinda was drained from the summoning, following Jason's example and drinking a potion to relieve the mental exhaustion. Her familiar bobbed in the air around her like a puppy seeking attention and she reached out to touch it.

Unnamed (astral lantern).
Familiar (iron rank).

Reveals nearby hidden enemies.
Makes ranged attacks with bolts of disruptive force, consuming small amounts of core energy.
Can intercept and negate magical projectiles. Negating powerful projectiles consumes core energy.
Core energy naturally replenishes over time. Summoner can use mana to restore core energy.
Familiar can be subsumed into the caster's eyes. When it has done so, the summoner can see hidden enemies and consume mana to make disruptive-force beam attacks from her eyes.

"You need a need a name, little guy," Belinda said. "Floaty? Sparkles?"

"That's terrible," Sophie said.

"You have a better idea?" Belinda asked.

Sophie thought it over as she looked at the silver lantern with the silver-blue light.

"How about Shimmer?" she said.

"I like that," Humphrey said.

"That is pretty good," Belinda said, then turned to her familiar. "What do you think? Do you like Shimmer?"

The lantern waggled side to side in the air.

"Does anyone know if that means yes?" Belinda asked.

Jason only returned once Belinda had recovered and had mostly laid out her next ritual circle.

"Since it wasn't a scheduled message," Jason said, "I had to wait for them to go get someone. I wasn't just going to drop that information to anyone, so I spoke to Rufus."

"That extra time would have been expensive."

"Rufus said he'd get the Adventure Society to pony up for it."

"Pony?"

"It's like a small horse."

"Those are the one-headed heidels, right?"

"Yeah, except with silky hair instead of creepy reptile scales."

"And what do they have to do with paying for things?"

"Nothing."

"Then why did you say it?"

"Because language is weird."

"You know, you could make more of an effort to be understood through your translation power."

"Your mum understands me."

"What does that have to do with anything?" Humphrey asked.

Jason groaned.

"Sometimes trying to aggravate people in this world only aggravates me," he complained, then levelled a suspicious gaze at Humphrey. "Were you being deliberately obtuse just to get under my skin?"

A grin teased the corners of Humphrey's mouth.

"You shouldn't be talking about my mother."

"That's true," Jason said. "That is not wrath I'd be looking to suffer."

Belinda completed her ritual and summoned her other familiar. Unlike the previous two, it was not foreshadowed by phenomena, but suddenly appeared out of nowhere. It was a strange, flickering entity, skipping around the room without passing through the intervening space. Its form constantly shifted, changing with each flickering teleport. It first appeared with Belinda's form, then Humphrey's, then Clive's. Then it was a strange amalgam of Sophie and Neil, but only for a moment as the changes continued. Sometimes it would replicate a member of the group, other times, melding two or more forms together in a bizarre gestalt. It never took any kind of form of its own.

It stilled slightly, holding in place as Belinda approached it but still flickering, like a television with bad reception. She reached out and touched it.

Unnamed (echo spirit).
Familiar (iron rank).

Incorporeal.
Can mimic the form of enemies or allies.
Can switch-teleport with mimicked allies.
Can mirror the mimicked ally's movements and attacks, but inflicts no damage or other effects.
When subsumed into the summoner's aura, the summoner can manipulate their own aura, projecting false traits or mimicking the aura of others.

"It's deception based," she said. "It works like Humphrey's new power to make an illusionary double."

"It'll be interesting to see if it doubles Humphrey's illusionary double," Jason said. "That would make him almost impossible to defend against, short of running away."

Once again Belinda needed to pick out a name. She ultimately accepted Jason's suggestion of Gemini.

"It means twins in a language from my world," he explained.

That left Jason's final familiar, which he started setting up for.

"That last incantation was pretty bad," Neil said. "This one is called an avatar of doom, though. Who's going to bet which incantation is more evil?"

"Seriously?" Jason asked, not looking up from his task.

"I'll take avatar of doom," Sophie said. "It has to be worse."

"I don't know," Belinda said. "That whole bit about the end of all things in the last one was pretty bad. I'll bet on the shadow incantation."

"Yes, I'll take the shadow familiar as well," Clive said.

"Oh, come on, Clive," Jason said. "You too?"

"What about you, Humphrey?" Belinda asked.

"No, he's the judge," Neil said. "He has to be objective, so I'll round out the numbers and pick the new one as worse."

"I should kick you all out and do this alone."

Belinda and Sophie immediately booed him, with Neil joining in. He turned to glare at them as Humphrey and Clive shrugged their shoulders, helplessly. Jason shook his head and ignored them until he was done.

"We didn't decide what we were betting for," Belinda said.

"The losers buy everyone's snacks at the mirage chamber tonight," Neil said.

"That's reasonable," Clive said.

"Really, Clive?" Jason asked.

"You don't get to complain," Neil said. "Your snacks get bought for you either way."

"My issues aren't snack-related," Jason said.

"Maybe just get it done and out of the way?" Humphrey suggested.

"You're just in it because your snacks are guaranteed, too."

Scowling, Jason turned back to his ritual circle and started chanting.

"*When worlds end, you are the arbiter. When gods fall, you are the instrument. Herald of annihilation, come forth and be my harbinger. I have doom to bring.*"

At first, it seemed like nothing was happening. Neil had just opened his mouth to accuse Jason of getting it wrong when the glow-stones lighting the room started flickering.

"That really shouldn't be happening," Clive said.

The glow-stones went out, one by one, until the room was plunged into darkness. Then they all flared up at once, flooding the room with glare before they started shattering, stone fragments falling into the crystal that should have shielded them from anything in the room.

After the blinding brightness, the dark seemed especially deep. As they looked around, a speck of orange light appeared, floating over the circle. It expanded, swirling in the dark like a nebula in the void of space. The orange was joined by blue and soon they could see the expanding colours take the shape of an orange eye with a vibrant blue iris.

The darkness around the nebula eye started to coalesce, taking on physical substance the way Jason's conjured cloak did. It even took on the form of a cloak, draping around the nebula eye, which floated where the torso would be. Two orbs manifested around the cloak, themselves smaller versions of the eye. One was blue in orange, the other, orange in blue. They drifted through the air, slowly circling the cloak like guardians.

Jason's teammates had been poised to mock the incantation but were transfixed by the beauty of the familiar. In the darkness left from the shattered glowstones, the eye nebula and the floating orbs were the only sources of light.

"Ah, crap," Jason said. "I'm going to be a chuuni forever."

"Hey, Clive," Neil said.

"Uh, yeah?"

"I'm guessing that wasn't meant to happen either."

"No, it was not," Clive said, his normal inquisitiveness reasserting itself.

He moved next to Jason to look at the new familiar.

"It's curious that the familiars are both reflective of your appearance," Clive observed. "Your appearance while wearing your cloak, anyway. I did notice that Shade looks somewhat different than he did in the astral space. There, his silhouette was closer to a person's form, instead of the cloak shape he inhabits now."

"Can you speak?" Jason asked the familiar.

The shadowy cowl shook its empty non-head slowly, an ominous gesture in the light coming from its own body. Its cloak shape was dominated by the eye, but the rest of the space in the cloak was slowly being occupied by what looked like a less formed nebula, with shades of red, green purple and other colours that shifted like a rainbow tide.

"You can understand me, though, that's good," Jason said. "Let's try this: Make the orb that's blue on the outside glow slightly brighter for yes and the one that's orange on the outside for no. Can you do that?"

The blue orb glowed brighter.

"Nice. This will work out just fine."

He reached out to touch the avatar, his hand getting a strange tingle as it met the light of the nebula eye.

Unnamed (avatar of doom).
Familiar (iron rank).

Incorporeal.
Each orb can make sustained beam attacks. One orb inflicts disruptive-force damage, the other, resonating-force damage.
Enemies damaged by the avatar are afflicted with [Vulnerable]. Sustained beam damage will cause additional instances to be accrued.
The avatar's normal movement is slow but it can make rapid energy dashes, inflicting disruptive-force damage on enemies in the path of the dash. Orbs do not attack during the dash.

Can be subsumed into the summoner's aura, making the summoner's aura much harder to detect and read.

[Vulnerable] (affliction, unholy, stacking): All resistances are reduced. Additional instances have a cumulative effect. Consumed to cleanse instances of [Resistant] on a one-to-one basis.

"No name, then?"

Orange orb.

"Do you want one?"

Blue orb.

"Yeah, you should have one. I can't be all, 'hey, Avatar of Doom, do you want a sausage?' That would be absurd."

"It doesn't look like it's big on sausages," Belinda said.

"You have to give it a majestic name," Neil said. "Even I'm willing to acknowledge that is a magnificent entity."

Jason rubbed his chin thoughtfully. "I'm going to call you… Gordon."

"What?"

"No!"

"You can't call it that!"

"What do you say, Gordon?" Jason asked. "Want to go take a look at the mirage arena?"

Blue orb.

73

I TRY TO FIND THE TRUTH, BUT THAT'S YOUR HIDING PLACE

The city of Jayapura featured a vast mirage chamber complex that was larger and more sophisticated than the Geller family's private chamber in Greenstone. The higher magical density of Jayapura meant that more advanced magical effects could be used and supported. This included potent dimensional magic that allowed the replication of vast spaces, as well as multiple, concurrently operating chambers in the same complex.

In addition to hiring out spaces for training, it was the premier entertainment space in the city. Essence users would pit themselves against one another or illusionary challenges, all for the entertainment of a paying audience. This produced more than enough funding for the frequent upgrades and regular maintenance required of a top-tier facility.

The organisation that owned and operated the chamber had close ties with the Magic Society, Adventure Society and local government. As it was important for both the amenities and the revenue it provided the city, the Mirage Chamber Association enjoyed significant power and influence within Jayapura.

Rather than a dome, the mirage chamber was a flat, circular building at the edge of the Mystic Quarter. Very large, it spilled into the adjacent theatre district, appropriately enough. Most people came looking for entertainment, rather than to use the facilities for themselves.

"There are whole essence user teams who never become adventurers," Hester explained as they arrived. She had met up with the team after they were done at the Magic Society, leading them to the site of their evening's entertainment. They joined the crowd heading in through the large public entrances.

"They make all their money here in the arena, and use monster cores to rank up."

"They can make enough money for that?" Belinda asked.

"They have competition leagues here at the arena," Hester explained. "Teams facing off against one another all year, leading up to the grand championships. There are two leagues a year, in silver, bronze and iron divisions. Obviously, silver is the big draw, with the largest following and the biggest prizes."

"No gold division?" Neil asked.

"Even with the money running through here, getting to gold rank using monster cores is a tough ask," Hester said. "They just don't have the numbers to make a gold division, which is why the handful of professionals successful enough stop using cores before they hit gold. Being at the peak of silver keeps them at the top of their game."

"And because they used monster cores to get there," Jason realised, "they're well-past their abilities being able to advance through regular use and training."

"Exactly," Hester said. "They keep going until silver-rank longevity is no longer enough, at which point they retire and make their way to gold for the extended life span. This whole place is run by former participants who are all gold rank now."

"Is this common practice in big cities?" Jason asked.

"It is," Humphrey said. "I've travelled to a number of large cities and seen the same thing in each."

"Is it all PvP, or do they mix it up?" Jason asked.

"PvP?" Hester asked.

"Hot adventurer-on-adventurer action," Jason clarified.

"There are three events, but the big one is the team-against-team arena battles," Hester said. "They're fast and exciting, with plenty of powers flying around. There's also monster hunts, but they aren't as popular. That tends to bring in competitors who are also active adventurers, but most spectators prefer to see people go up against one another. Lastly is team conflict again, but in larger, more complex environments, with roaming monsters. It's a slower, more complicated event that doesn't interest the public as much. It mostly gets attention from the professional adventurer crowd."

They went inside with the crowd but instead of the large viewing rooms for the general public, a member of the staff took them upstairs to a private viewing box. It was a large lounge, with a front wall made of dark, impenetrable glass. Luxurious chairs and couches were arrayed in front of it and several low tables were filled with food and drinks.

"Aside from the more comfortable environs," the staff member explained, "these private rooms differ from the public areas in that you can choose what you want to be looking at any given time. Any event, any division, any match, at your leisure. The projector is controlled from the tablet on the table there. The same tablet is used to order any food or drink you might want from our comprehensive selection and it will be brought right up."

"Who do we pay for the snacks?" Neil asked her.

"All costs are included with the room," the attendant told him.

"Then how are Clive and Belinda going to pay for them?"

"Us?" Belinda asked.

"Clearly you lost the bet," Neil said.

"No way," Belinda argued. "'Mine is the shadow of death' is way worse than the other chant."

"You're clearly wrong. The other one talked about killing gods. Gods!"

"It didn't mention doing it personally. Don't forget about that 'final road to the end of all things' bit."

Clive went up to reassure the attendant, who was starting to look a little nervous.

"Don't worry," Clive assured her. "They're just talking about our friend's new familiars. We'll be fine here; you can go."

"Honestly," Sophie said as she left, "The blood-drinking apocalypse beast is more sinister than either of them. I bet that incantation was the worst of the lot…"

The attendant hurried out, closing the door behind her.

"Am I mistaken," Neil said, his eyes glued to the viewing screen, "or are these people really good? As in, really, really good."

"They're good," Humphrey confirmed.

They were watching one of the iron-rank monster-hunt events, where teams would take turns hunting identical monsters in identical circumstances and be judged on their performance.

"How do you think we would stack-up against teams like this?" Clive asked.

"Poorly," Jason said. "These people are at the top of their game in a city with a lot of game to climb over to get there. They're obviously practised and work effectively together. My guess would be that they're all closing in on bronze rank."

"They are," Hester said. "These are the best Jayapura has to offer and they are, indeed, closing in on bronze rank."

"We'll get there," Humphrey said. "Training and experience, that's all it is."

"The only people on our team operating at this level right now," Jason said, "are Humphrey and Neil. The rest of us have our strengths, but also critical flaws. Clive has been out of the game a long time and his power set is all about judging the circumstances and picking his moments. It's the kind of thing only experience can improve. The same goes for Belinda but even more so, given she's been an essence user for about an hour. She isn't even ready for the Adventure Society field test."

"We'll get you there, Lindy," Sophie assured her friend.

"Yes, we will," Jason said. "Wexler has skills to match anyone out there but has too many abilities she hasn't had a chance to get a handle on, yet. The same is true for all of us, to a degree. As for me, my power set doesn't give me the margin of error Humphrey's or Neil's do, with armour and self-shields. I can be dropped in one hit if I get blind-sided and I've only been in this world half a year. I still have a lot of blind spots where the rest of you would see danger coming."

"So, all those people who went into the astral space with us," Clive said. "They were all this good?"

"No," Hester said. "These people we're watching today have already fulfilled whatever potential they had. When I was selecting people for the Reaper trials, Emir had me looking at unfulfilled potential. These people here are good, but the people who went through the trials have at least the potential to be as good or better."

"And we beat them all," Sophie said with satisfaction.

"That was luck," Jason said. "Sigrid was almost as fast, and she wasn't the only one to jump through that final ring."

"You never told us what you saw, there at the end," Clive said.

"Nor should he," Hester said, her voice full of warning. "I checked in with Emir today and there has been an unusual development. One of the others who reached that final stage has gone missing, along with everyone who accompanied them to Greenstone. Gone without a trace, leaving all their possessions behind."

"Some secrets are best left dead and buried," Jason said, "lest you be buried with them. I imagine that some of you will speculate as to the meaning of what happened. Keep that speculation to yourself, for all our sakes."

"That mirrors the advice Emir asked me to impart," Hester said. "I was going to wait until after we returned for the evening to tell you, but since the topic came up it seemed appropriate."

Jason was frustrated at having no one to discuss it with, if only to act as a sounding board. As the others continued to watch the viewing screen, his mind was consumed with possibilities. If the Order of the Reaper wanted to remain secret, why would they act so blatantly? Were they preparing for a grand reappearance or were they not involved at all? If Jason wanted to kill someone who had also reached that secret last stage, the Order of the Reaper would make an intimidating, if risky, patsy.

He reflected again on how, in this world, the answer to every question and the solution to every problem was the same: get stronger. He had been putting off his final awakening stones for the Reaper trials and while he couldn't be sure if the legendary stones he acquired were worth the delay, he suspected his new familiars were formidable.

He could feel them in his shadow and his aura, much as he could feel his first familiar inside his blood. They felt like power waiting to be unleashed, and it was only the beginning. While Jason was iron-rank, he still felt within the realms of a normal human, whatever Clive said about the strange inner workings of his body. Bronze-rank was the threshold beyond which the ordinary was left behind, surpassing even the most exceptional normal person.

The very concept of reaching those levels was bizarre and exciting. Stronger than an Olympic powerlifter and more agile than an Olympic gymnast at the same time. His perception was linked to his spirit attribute, which left him wondering what that would mean. Telescopic vision? Seeing the infrared spectrum, or hearing ultrasonic sounds?

In a world of monsters, magic, adventurers and cultists, it somehow was all acceptable. When considered within the context of his own world, it suddenly became impossible and absurd. Was there really a place for him there anymore? Did he want it? Absently he took out the world-phoenix token, turning it over in his hands.

Knowledge told him it would take him home, but could he trust the words of the goddess? It looked much like the Reaper token he had already used. Would it trigger another gift evolution? How was he meant to use it? The goddess told him that he lacked the faith in magic. Jason was no longer an atheist but that did not mean he was willing to jump into faith. He liked believing in things for good reason.

Sophie got up from her chair to grab some food and spotted Jason, uncharacteristically quiet as he looked at something in his hands. She crashed down next to him on the couch.

"What's that?" she asked.

"I'm not sure," Jason said, putting the tablet away. "The future, maybe."

The next day, the team made their way through the streets of Jayapura, back towards Tilly's nondescript tattoo parlour. As they floated along on their discs, the topic of discussion was the nature of Jason's personal crest.

"I bet it's just a picture of him with an idiotic grin and a sandwich," Neil said.

"I think it'll be something intimidating," Clive said. "Look at his familiars. It'll be all dark and spooky."

"How is Jason in any way intimidating?" Neil asked.

"Try fighting him," Sophie said. "I'm the only one here who's done it for real. I had a well-executed plan, meticulous preparation and, as it turned out, a silver-ranker intervening on my behalf. Even then, it took a priest of the god of healing and an alchemist healer working together to keep me alive and he wasn't even trying to kill me. He makes people like you think he's an idiot because, otherwise, they'd run for the hills."

"She exaggerates," Jason said. "I'm with Neil. I think it's going to be sandwich-related."

"What about you, Humphrey?" Clive asked. "You've known him longer than the rest of us."

"I don't know what his crest will be," Humphrey said. "I suppose I can say what I want it to be."

The others looked over at Humphrey, their interest piqued. Neil turned his eyes back to where he was going, though, when he almost drove his disc into a wall.

"What do you mean?" Sophie asked, looking between Humphrey and Jason.

Humphrey's expression was sober and thoughtful, Jason's blank and unreadable. He had mostly stayed quiet during their guessing game.

"Jason is good at putting on masks to get what he wants," Humphrey said. "He becomes what he needs to be to provoke the response he's looking for, whether it's absurd buffoon, or callous killer. I've seen him be friendly and approachable with ordinary people, sharp and provoking towards aristocrats. He'll stare down silver-rankers and capitulate to his landlady. I'd like to see who he is under all that. Which parts of what he shows us is really who he is."

The others all looked at Jason, who remained impassively silent.

"Damn," Neil said. "That got heavy fast."

The rest of the trip took place in awkward silence. When they reached the tattoo shop, Tilly took in the strange air over them and nodded towards the back room without saying anything.

Jason stripped off his shirt as Tilly adjusted the chair so she could work on his back. She took out a series of pots, some of which were faintly glowing, and set them out on a table with a set of brushes.

"You have the crest?"

Jason took the immortal crest out from his inventory. Tilly took a stick of chalk from her pocket, scrawling some symbols on it as Jason held it in place. Then she ushered him onto the chair, telling him to hold it to his chest. He did so, placing it over the sigil of his magic tattoo.

Tilly began drawing an intricate magical diagram on Jason's back, using the brushes and paint she had set out. She would stop frequently, her face caught up in thought as if pondering what to do next. Sometimes she would make slow progress, a minute or more passing between strokes of the brush. Other times would be a fury of activity as she wildly applied paint to whole sections. Her haste seemed to have no ill-effect on her precision.

Her brushes dipped into one pot after another as every part of Jason's back was filled with tiny, precise lines and sigils. The diagram was drawn out in ordinary black, vibrant blue, shimmering silver and bright gold. Finally, she put down her brush and wheeled the table away, before pulling up another one. She took out a rolled-up cloth and unfurled it on the table, revealing a dazzling array of needles. Some were silver, others, black, green, red and gold. She started poking them into Jason's back, one after another. By the time she was done, Jason's back was a forest of metal, the elaborate diagram completely obscured.

She moved away from the chair, then took out a tarp and set it on the workshop floor.

"Get up and go stand on that," she instructed.

Jason did so.

"Now we wait," she said.

They all stood in silence, Jason's eyes glued to the floor. Sophie and Humphrey had their gazes locked on Jason while the others shared awkward glances. Just as the silence grew so heavy it felt like someone had to say something, there was a dull sound as a needle fell from Jason's back and onto the tarp. It was followed by a second, third, rapidly increasing until they started cascading from his back to form a pile around his feet.

No one said anything for a moment.

"Well?" Neil asked, breaking the silence. "Turn around and let us see."

"He sees first," Tilly said, her tone brooking no dissent. She took a sheet of dark glass the size of a large book, and held it behind Jason's back for a moment. She passed it to Jason to look at. He held the glass in his hands, staring for a long time at the image it had recorded from his back. Finally he nodded, handing the glass back to Tilly.

"It's a good one," she said, "but you don't have to show them. You don't have to show anyone, if you don't want."

"It's fine," Jason said, stepping carefully out of the needles at his feet. Then he turned around, allowing the others to see.

On his back was the image of a dark, empty cloak, not unlike his new familiar, Gordon. Around the cloak was a dark sky full of silver stars. Inside the cloak was an open blue sky, with a golden sun right where Gordon's nebula eye was located, right in the middle of the chest.

"Is it shining?" Clive asked, squinting his eyes.

Tilly walked over to the wall, tapping a crystal. Shutters came down over the windows and the glow-stones in the workshop dimmed to nothing. In the darkness, the only light was the faint flow of the sun and stars on Jason's back. They softly illuminated his new crest, the silver stars highlighting the dark sky and the gold light of the sun lighting up the bright portion in the middle.

"It looks like the day, hidden in the night," Humphrey said.

"Yep," Sophie said. "That's going to get you laid, alright."

74

THE LAST REWARD

In the early morning, Jason stood at the edge of a platform in the underground grotto, looking out to the cave entrance and the ocean beyond. Daylight was yet to penetrate the west-facing cave and the illumination was still provided by the colourful glow-stones shining from beneath the water.

"It's only been a couple of days, but I'm going to miss this," Jason said.

"It definitely beats hiding out in the back of a disused boat warehouse," Sophie said, emerging from her own room to join him in leaning on the rail.

"Still," Jason said, pushing himself off the railing. "There's a world of wonders waiting out there for us. Shall we go see if we can find it?"

"Sure," Sophie said, giving him a smile.

As the made their way up the spiral staircase, Jason happily reflected on Sophie finally not viewing any approach as some kind of attack. Reaching the top, an open terrace looking out over the cliff face to the ocean, they found Humphrey and Clive were already waiting for them.

"Ever since we haven't been actively hunted," Sophie said, "Lindy has taken to sleeping in."

"Very sensible," Neil said, emerging from the main house. "I know Humphrey has been planning dawn to dusk training for when we get back, so this might be our last lazy morning for a while."

"Night training as well," Humphrey said, not denying it. "We can't be ready for every circumstance, but we can try."

Belinda and Hester appeared together.

"Thank you for the generous hospitality," Jason said. "Especially for those of us who hadn't left Greenstone before, this was a great experience."

The time they had spent awakening abilities, summoning familiars and getting tattoos had only been a portion of their several days in Jayapura. They had also taken in the city, visiting markets and the city's various places of interest. New customs, new food. New sights and sounds, tastes and smells.

Jason had always wanted to travel, until circumstances derailed his life plans. Instead of finishing university, he had taken a job in retail and barely travelled beyond a few city blocks. More and more, his new life had him reflecting on his old one.

Hester opened up a portal and they stepped through, arriving at the district of the Island called Marina North. Jason knew it quite well, as he had travelled through it frequently. It contained the bridge he most often used to cross between Old City and the Island, and was the place he first met—and was kicked in the face by—Sophie.

They were at one of the marinas for which the district was named. The entire east side of the Island was lined with marinas holding the private watercraft of the city's elite. Trade shipping was restricted to the sprawling port on the Old City side, with the Island serving as a vast breakwater.

Emir was waiting for them, along with Constance. They were in an open area beside the main marina building, the area pleasantly laid out with subdued green and yellow pavers.

"Excellent," he greeted as they arrived. "I hope you had a nice trip home, Hester. I need to put my logistics coordinator to work."

"Of course," Hester said amenably.

"Constance has the details," Emir said. "She can fill you in while I attend to Jason. Are you ready for your cloud…well, not palace, yet."

"I definitely am," Jason said.

"My cloud palace is still at the lake, since my people are now largely concerned with studying the underwater complex. I've taken the liberty of renting marina space for you to use—by which I mean I had Constance do it. She has all the paperwork, so see her about all that after. It's nothing you can't afford."

Emir reached into his jacket and pulled a large flask from the dimensional space within. It was round, with a cylindrical neck, identical to the one that Emir used for his own cloud palace. Through the glass they could see energy swirling inside, a vortex of blue and white. He handed the bottle to Jason, who immediately dropped what turned out to be the profoundly heavy object.

"Oh, right," Emir said. "I forgot how weak iron-rankers are."

"Did I break it?" Jason asked in horror, looking down at the bottle laying on the stone pavers.

"Don't worry about that," Emir said, gesturing to the stone, three-storey building beside them. "You could drop this building on that bottle and it wouldn't get so much as a scratch."

He took out a notebook, thumbing through pages until he found what he was after and passed it over to Clive.

"Can you knock that one out for me?" Emir asked. "It might be a little tricky."

Clive only spent a moment glancing over notes before he started drawing out a ritual circle using his power. Passers-by looked over in curiosity as golden light traced out a magic diagram. When he was done, Emir picked up the bottle and carried it into the middle of the circle, directing Jason to join him.

"You won't need to enact the ritual, Clive," Emir said. "Jason just needs to drop a little blood into the bottle. Just a few drops will do it."

Emir took the glass stopper out of the bottle and Jason nicked a finger with the blade under his wristband. He kept it there even when not wearing his combat gear in case he needed to call out Colin in a pinch.

The droplets of blood fell into the bottle. Emir stoppered it again as the contents swirled about wildly. Despite only losing a few drops of blood, Jason felt suddenly drained. The mana and stamina bars at the periphery of his vision emptied and he staggered before righting himself.

You have bound [Cloud Flask] to you.
[Cloud Flask] is currently iron rank.
You can summon, dismiss and alter the iron-rank options of your [Cloud Flask].

After Jason tipped mana and stamina potions down his throat, Emir held out the flask for Jason to take.

"That didn't go so well last time," Jason said, but took the proffered bottle, nonetheless.

To his surprise, the bottle now was so light as to be almost weightless. He could feel a connection to the energy inside it, not dissimilar to the sense of his familiars he had while they were subsumed within his body.

Item: [Cloud Flask] (iron rank [growth], legendary)

This item is bound to you and cannot be used by anyone else.
Use the energies within the cloud flask to create buildings and vehicles made of clouds. Available forms are restricted by rank.
Items contained within the cloud construct when it is returned to the flask are stored in a dimensional space and cannot be recovered until another cloud construct is formed.

Available forms (iron rank): Cloud house (grand), cloud house (adaptive).

"Soul-bound items are rare, even compared to other growth items," Clive said.

"Ten years in the Magic Society and this is only the third one I've seen. The advancement requirements are usually quite prohibitive."

Jason looked over the growth requirements.

1000 [Air Quintessence (bronze)].
1000 [Water Quintessence (bronze)].
200 [Dimension Quintessence (bronze)].
10,000 [Bronze Spirit Coins]

"Oh, that's a lot," Jason said. "Really, a lot."

"Not to worry," Emir said. "I have everything you need to upgrade it to bronze. You can grab it all next time you're in the cloud palace. After that, you're in charge of your own supplies, though."

"Thank you," Jason said gratefully. "That's very generous."

"I think it's time to try it out," Emir said. He led the group to find the right pier, where he had leased three adjacent berths to make sure Jason had the room he needed.

"So, how does it work?" Jason asked. "Do I just open the bottle?"

"That's the first step," Emir said. "Do that now."

Jason opened the bottle and mist flowed out, shifting in colour as it formed a small image of a house in the air. It looked like a small manor, in the sunset colours they recognised from the cloud palace.

"Here you can choose which configuration of house you want to use," Emir told him. "What you're looking at now is the grand form. Put your hand into the image and turn it."

Jason did as instructed, and the image changed, from a manor to a large house boat.

"That's the adaptive form," Emir explained. "It won't be as large as the grand form but it will fit into its surroundings much better, even camouflaging itself. Good for unusual environments or when you don't want to make a spectacle. Once I used the adaptive form of the palace in a forest and got a series of treehouses connected by swinging bridges. It was amazing."

"How do I set it off?" Jason asked.

"Once you've picked your form," Emir said, "concentrate on where you want it to go and just give it a push."

Jason left the small image in the form of a houseboat and shoved it with his hand. The image broke apart as fog started pouring out of the bottle and into the empty space along the marina dock. They watched as the fog slowly took the form of a large houseboat, with three imposing storeys and clearly too ponderous to move. It took some ten minutes to achieve its final shape, after which the cloud-stuff from which it was constructed started taking on the look of painted wood until it was indistinguishable from an actual wooden houseboat.

"I would have picked you for going with the grand version," Emir said. "What's the point of having a cloud palace if no one knows about it?"

"Enjoying it for yourself," Jason said. "I'm not gold rank, Emir. I have to be judicious about how and when I make a spectacle of myself."

"You do?" Clive asked.

"It seems more like you're making it up as you go along," Neil said.

"Of course I am," Jason said. "But when it works out, you have to tell everyone that you planned it all along."

Emir burst out laughing. "Exactly right."

They went aboard, discovering that the houseboat's facade was just that; the interior had been constructed from the familiar cloud-stuff. They toured around, discovering several bedrooms, two entertaining decks and a formidable kitchen.

"Every cloud building has certain similarities," Emir explained as they explored. "They all have their own nuances, however, reflective of their owners. My houses, for example, never have kitchens in them."

"That's actually common with soul-bound items," Clive said. "No magic item can match the potential contained within a soul, so items connected to one tend to take on its properties. This becomes more pronounced with growth items as they advance in rank."

"So, you could use a person's soul-bound items to judge their true nature?" Humphrey said.

"Oh, yes," Clive said. "If you meet someone who seems like a good person but has a hideous and twisted soul-bound item, stay clear. Compare that to Emir's cloud palace, which is so obviously a reflection of him. Outrageously grandiose, yet welcoming and beautiful."

"Clive," Emir said warmly. "That may be the nicest thing anyone has ever said about me. Speaking of revealing the true nature, though, Hester said you were getting a personal crest, Jason. I have to admit to being curious."

"It's just me eating a sandwich with a big stupid grin," Jason said. "It's kind of embarrassing, to be honest."

Emir gave Jason a sceptical look but didn't challenge his assertion.

"You should be careful not to rely on the security of this cloud house," Emir warned, turning the subject back to Jason's new abode. "Yours is only iron rank, so a bronze-ranker could force their way in given enough time. With the right skill set, someone could even sneak their way inside. I imagine that Clive and Belinda could do just that, if they put their heads together. As it ranks up, you'll find it becomes increasingly more resistant to all forms of trespass."

Jason discovered, as they roamed around, that he was quickly gaining a sense for the houseboat, even able to sense the people inside. Emir walked Jason through the various functions, such as taking aura imprints to allow others to have various permissions.

"There are some other things that I've figured out from using my own cloud flask," Emir said, giving Jason the notebook he had handed to Clive earlier. "Everything I've learned is collected here. I direct your attention especially to the section on plants, which is the product of many years of trial and error."

"Thank you, Emir," Jason said, taking the notebook.

"I'm glad it was you," Emir said, "although, I will admit to being a little surprised. You had some impressive competition, who you apparently made friends with. The boats have left already, but several notable groups stayed behind and will have to make their own arrangements. They've been waiting for you to get back."

"It sounds like a housewarming party is in order," Jason said. 'I'll have to get some supplies."

"Nothing too raucous," Humphrey said. "Tomorrow, we start training in earnest."

"We also have to sort out living arrangements," Jason said. "With the cloud palace off at Sky Scar Lake, you and Lindy, Wexler, should probably shack up here. Unless you want to make your own arrangements."

"And give up cloud beds?" Belinda said. "No chance."

"There's about eight bedrooms in here," Jason said. "Any of the rest of you are welcome to join them. It could be good for team building."

"I'll take you up on that," Clive said. "I've been living in the Magic Society dorm for years."

"That's a great idea," Humphrey said. "We can regulate our training so much better if we're all together."

Neil groaned. "You're really going to let Humphrey push us through training every waking minute?"

"You say that," Jason said, "but you train as hard as anyone. You can act as disaffected all you like, but we all know how driven you are."

"And what happens when Humphrey starts planning the meals for maximum effectiveness?" Neil asked.

Jason's eyes went wide.

"Now that I think about it," he said, "maintaining a respectful separation may be what's best for the team."

75
IMPOSSIBLE WASN'T ENOUGH

In a training hall within the Adventure Society campus, Prince Valdis was squaring off against Rufus. Both held training swords that would leave a painful sting but not inflict any permanent damage.

Valdis moved swiftly, rushing around Rufus while delivering a flurry of rapid but precise strikes. Rufus was more languid, moving with slow, consistent steps as he deflected every attack with almost dismissive ease. He remained on the defensive yet never seemed pressured, casually throwing out the occasional attack to disrupt Valdis's rhythm.

By the time their practice session was done, Valdis was lying in a sweating heap as Rufus wiped down the swords and returned them to the rack on the wall.

"You're not too bad," Rufus said. "Once you stop trying to be my grandfather and start fighting your own way, you might actually become good."

"Thank you for doing this," Valdis said, pushing himself to his feet.

"Of course," Rufus said. "I spoke to my grandfather the other day and he expressed his respect for your father. Have you seen the water speaking chambers they have here?"

"Yes, I used one to tell my mother that my team would be staying in Greenstone for a while. They have impressive chambers here for such an out-of-the-way city."

"I've found this city to be full of surprises," Rufus said.

"I should have suspected as much from the place that produced the Geller family," Valdis said. "Is it true your academy is establishing an annex here?"

"It is," Rufus said. "It's my personal project, but my attention has been drawn away by other matters."

"This business with the astral spaces is certainly concerning," Valdis said. "Do you think this cult used the Reaper trials to place people inside the astral space?"

"Almost certainly," Rufus said. "Emir's people are seeing if getting inside is any more feasible now the trials are completed."

Valdis walked to the side of the room, taking a stamina potion from his dimensional bag and drinking it.

"Jason Asano is a friend of yours, right?" Valdis asked. "Did you imagine he would be the one who succeeded in the trials?"

"Yes," Rufus said.

"Really? I never saw him in action during the trials but I've seen some recordings since. He's coming along with his skills and mastering his power set, but there were dozens of people participating with better training, superior skills and greater mastery of their abilities."

Rufus chuckled.

"The day I met Jason I learned that something being impossible wasn't enough to stop him. My grandfather has a lot of sayings about adventurers and I find Jason tends to remind me of them. I'm guessing your father has a few sayings of his own."

Valdis laughed. "More than a few."

"Well," Rufus said, "you wondered how someone with less skill and less training could beat out all these people like you. What would your father say?"

Valdis thought Rufus question over for a moment.

"One of my father's sayings," he said, finally, "is that mastering your powers can make you good adventurer, but only a good one. To be a great adventurer, you have to master destiny."

"That's a little overdramatic, but a good enough point. Around half a year ago, I was in as bad a situation as I've ever been in. I thought of this place as an isolated backwater and underestimated the dangers. I let my team get ambushed and we were caged up with suppression collars, waiting to be killed. I was certain we were going to die."

"Obviously that didn't happen," Valdis said.

"No," Rufus said. "That was when I met Jason. He was in a worse situation than we were. He had only been in our world a matter of hours and had no idea of what was going on. He came from a world with no magic, no monsters, no essences. I had to tell him what a spirit coin was. He was caged up with us, no suppression collar but his only essence abilities were falling slowly and seeing in the dark."

"He helped you escape?"

"Helped? He broke out and released us. Of course, that was only for us to confront the bronze-rankers who caught us and get punished because we still had the suppression collars. So Jason stepped in. Two essence abilities against two bronze-rankers, but they're dead and we're here."

"How?"

"Exactly how you'd expect: by talking a lot of nonsense. Great adventurers are the ones who find their skills and powers aren't enough and they win anyway. That's why I wasn't surprised when Jason was the one who grabbed the scythe."

"You know, someone from my team almost beat him to it."

"Then make sure they stay on your team."

Valdis thanked Rufus again and went for the shower room, while Rufus left. On his way out of the building, a voice came from a shadow.

"A word, please, Mr Remore?"

Rufus moved closer.

"Mr Dorgan," Rufus said. "I was beginning to wonder if I would hear from you again."

"I think we both know the kind of risks involved in what you've asked of me," Dorgan said. "I don't even trust messengers with this information."

Rufus's gaze grew sharp. "You have something?"

"Yes."

"Should we be talking here?"

"Don't forget who my daughter is," Dorgan said. "This seems like a casual conversation, but no small effort has been made to keep it and my presence here private. The closest set of ears is your young prince friend, who is being watched."

"What do you have?" Rufus asked.

"I told you last time we met that someone was covering up every trace. You told me who, which gave me something to work with, but looking into a church's activities is delicate business. Normally bribes and blackmail are reliable tools, but people get real committed when religion gets involved. You never know when zeal is going to throw good sense out the window, especially with the church of Purity."

"I understand."

"Once the Mercers went crazy and started rooting everything out, it all changed. These cultist pricks started pulling everything out of the city and mistakes were made. Making the most of others' mistakes is what I do best. I managed to track some supplies that were taken out of the city in a rush, without the usual careful cut-outs."

"And?"

"There's an island," Dorgan said. "All those materials you had me tracking that passed through the city before mysteriously vanishing? That's where they've been going."

"You have a location?"

Dorgan handed Rufus a large, thick envelope.

"Everything I have is in there."

"Who knows about this?"

"I've been keeping the people I'm using apart from one another," Dorgan said.

"None of them know enough to put anything together and all of them know enough not to try and find out more. All they know is that I've been running this thing personally, which I never do. Even my daughter doesn't know any more than that I'm doing something for you."

"What about the people keeping this meeting private?" Rufus asked.

"She made sure they can't listen in, and they're all people she brought into the Adventure Society herself. They're loyal."

Rufus looked at the envelope in his hands, nodding gravely.

"Thank you, Dorgan."

"You aren't the only one concerned about these people, you know," Dorgan said. "You might look down on me but I'm part of this community. The people of Old City are my people."

Rufus nodded, offering his hand for Dorgan to shake.

"I'll remember that," Rufus said. "Your daughter will have my support in her position, for what it's worth."

Dorgan accepted Rufus's handshake.

"I thought you might hold a grudge," Dorgan said. "I know you lost a friend on that expedition."

"There's plenty of blame to go around," Rufus said. "I know who the enemy is."

"Rufus isn't here?" Valdis asked. "I was training with him just this morning."

Jason was hosting a small gathering on his cloud houseboat, largely of adventurers who had been through the Reaper trials. A number of teams had stayed behind, deciding to use Greenstone's lower-ranked monsters for some experience operating independently. This included Valdis's team and Padma's, both of whom were present at Jason's party.

"Probably best not to talk about that," Humphrey said quietly. "He took off out of the city with my parents and some other silver rankers late this morning."

Rick Geller and his team were also present. Rick and his sister Phoebe had both reached bronze rank during the trials and would soon be returning to their home city. Going with them would be Dustin, Neil's friend who had once suffered with him as Thadwick's lackey.

Humphrey's sister, Henrietta, was also in attendance. She had been bronze-rank for almost two years, now returned to Greenstone with their father in readiness for the monster surge. They originally hadn't intended to, but with the increasing delay, they took the chance to visit home.

"Henri has agreed to help us train," Humphrey enthusiastically explained to his teammates. "She has the full set of familiars and summons, which is an area we really need to work on. We've really been underutilising the ones we have and now we have even more."

Jason looked at Henrietta, who was looking them over in turn. She was statuesque, like her brother, with strong, handsome features and hair cropped practical and short. Jason had now met Humphrey's father, and noticed that the siblings both favoured the burly man in physique, compared to their slender mother.

Jason smiled to himself. It was plain that Henrietta was less interested in helping them train than in making sure the ragtag group Humphrey had assembled was good enough for her little brother.

"You find something funny?" she asked Jason.

"Invariably," Jason said with a laugh.

With so many new abilities, Jason and his team had immense amounts of work to do. Humphrey was as good as his promise at driving the team's training, from the basics on up. Physical training, movement training and meditation took up the mornings, then more individualised work to master their abilities in the afternoons.

Jason's training fell into two areas. Along with his new familiars, he started incorporating his new shadow arm power into his combat style. What at first seemed like a simple addition to his repertoire turned out to be a highly flexible power, both literally and figuratively. More than just being a much-welcomed source of necrotic afflictions, it offered incredible utility when incorporated into his parkour and martial arts.

It was while learning to use the shadow arm that he began to understand just how comprehensive the Way of the Reaper fighting style truly was. It had technique for incorporating various powers into movement and even martial technique. This included reach and teleport powers, such as Jason's, as well as movement powers like Sophie's.

Sophie was undergoing a similar revelation, even more so with her larger number of new powers. They practiced the same style but her techniques didn't come from a skill book. This gave her a stronger foundation than Jason but meant she didn't already have the techniques she required and had to turn to the books they brought back from the Reaper trials to advance her knowledge.

Humphrey had gifted her his set of the Way of the Reaper books; he had his own fighting style and no intention to switch. Shade had once demonstrated the ability of the books to create a projection that offered guidance on the content of the books. Shade himself, however, was a far superior guide. Once the familiar to one of the old Order of the Reaper's leaders, Shade was well versed in their techniques. His active assistance was better than anything to be found in a book, even a skill book.

Each of Jason's three familiars brought something different to the table. Colin had proven his value time and again as an affliction bulk-delivery system that was incredibly hard to dislodge because of his swarm nature. The remaining two familiars, despite both being intangible cloak-shaped entities, were very different.

Shade offered little in the way of direct combat impact, as he was only able to drain mana. His function was primarily one of utility. In addition to being an effective spy, Jason could teleport in and out of his shadowy figure. Placed judiciously around a battlefield, he made Jason all the more mobile. He could also be deposited in the shadow of enemies, almost impossible to detect, turning them into beacons from which Jason could discreetly spy while remaining hidden.

Gordon, by contrast, was the most directly combative aspect of Jason's arsenal, including Jason himself. The twin orbs floating around Gordon each blasted out sustained, destructive beams. One beam was orange, inflicting resonating-force damage that penetrated armour. The other was blue, delivering disruptive-force damage that was effective against magical protection and incorporeal enemies. The beams weren't wildly powerful, but they were too strong to ignore, tracked their targets and never relented.

Gordon was an incorporeal entity himself, barely affected by most forms of attack. Magic had a limited effect, but only disruptive-force attacks posed him a real threat. Part of the team's versatile nature was that many of them had such attacks, from Sophie's unarmed strikes to Clive's legendary weapons and Humphrey's new special attack, spirit reaper. During mock battles in the Geller mirage chamber, they would frequently go after Gordon to put a stop to his unrelenting attacks. He had the power to rapidly evade, however, transforming into a blue-orange cloud that could dash across the battlefield before he reformed to resume his attacks. The best deterrent turned out to be Belinda's lantern familiar, which had disruptive-force attacks of its own.

On top of their damage, Gordon's beam attacks doled out a stacking affliction that made enemies more susceptible to further afflictions by diminishing their resistances. It quickly became evident that the affliction or even the damage was not what made Gordon such an effective tool for Jason. It was the fact that Gordon's attacks, while not overwhelming, were both powerful enough to require a response and completely unrelenting.

To a mindless monster, Gordon's continual attacks would be a constant source of threat, at least one of the beams effective against almost any kind of defence. To a more intelligent enemy they would recognise the threat Gordon would pose if left unchecked. Many healers and ranged magic users, like Clive and Neil, possessed magical shields that would protect them long enough for a guardian to intervene. A constant barrage of disruptive force would quickly penetrate that barrier and no team of essence users was stupid enough to leave the healer exposed.

Gordon's presence on the battlefield was not overpowering but it did require an answer, forcing the enemy out of their own pace and right into Jason's. A distracted enemy, reacting instead of acting, was exactly the scenario in which his hit-and-run style thrived. The fires of chaos were fed as he appeared and disappeared, loading up the enemy with afflictions.

Jason thought back to his fight against Rick's team. He no longer had the need to resort to extravagant theatrics to keep enemies off balance. With Gordon to force an enemy's hand and Shade for stealth and mobility, Jason wouldn't have to work so hard to crack a team's formation. Even in an open environment he could jump from one of Shade's duplicates to another, swift and elusive as the enemy still had Gordon to deal with. While his opponents scrambled to pin him down, he would be baiting them into the perfect place to unleash Colin, showering them in apocalypse beast.

All of that was when he was operating alone. Working with the team, there were several strategies open to him. For extremely tough opponents he would be the main damage dealer. He could be to his team what Gordon was to him: a distraction the enemy couldn't ignore lest it ruin them all. They could also flip that role, with the team engaging the enemy as Jason went around afflicting them all.

They devised a wide array of strategies for all manner of situations, varied enough to apply broadly and flexible enough to adapt to specifics. As they developed and refined their strategies, it became evident that rather than any individual strength, the team's greatest asset was flexibility. The versatility of their potential strategies made their defining trait the power to dictate the pacing of a battle.

Their efforts were excessive for fighting iron-rank monsters but they had their sights set higher. Monsters would become more intelligent at higher ranks, their powers more exotic. In the short term, there was no telling when they might find themselves in battle with Builder cultists. They worked up specific strategies for what they knew about the cult and their tactics, Jason focusing on the controllers as the team contained the constructs.

Each evening, the team would wind down after their training on the deck of the houseboat, frequently joined by another team. Some, like Beth's team, were mirroring Jason's in pouring themselves into training. Foreign teams like Valdis's and Padma's were enjoying the freedom of undertaking contracts without supervision. Padma's team mostly stayed around for Rufus who, with Gary, had claimed the two empty bedrooms on the houseboat while the cloud palace was still off at the lake.

Beth put the idea of some more contests in the mirage arena to Humphrey. Humphrey begged off each time, seeing only how far the team had to go. Finally, Jason weighed in on the other side.

"It's time we had some pressure on us," Jason told him. "We have to put the team in the fire to see if we cook."

76
ECLIPSE

The strike force had been small, to restrict information: three gold-rankers, six silver-rankers and a dozen bronze-rankers. Rufus's parents, Gabriel and Arabelle, along with their teammate, Callum, were the golds. The silvers were Danielle Geller, Thalia Mercer, Elspeth Arella, Emir's chief of staff, Constance, and two more silver-rankers under Emir's employ. The bronze were Rufus, Gary and ten more of Emir's people, under Constance's command.

They arrived on the island in the dead of night. To avoid sharp senses they used no abilities, magical items or even magically propelled vessels, instead sailing on ordinary ships and rowing ashore in dinghies. Only once they had eyes on the island's inhabitants were they sure that the enemy had not been forewarned. As expected, the cultists outnumbered them, even discounting the small army of construct creatures standing idle in rows.

To their good fortune, the island the cultists were occupying was not inhabited for a reason. Off the coast, a good way north of Greenstone, the terrain was harsh, with the few flat, usable areas isolated from one another by ridges and gorges. There was very little plant life, mostly barren rocks, but the wild landscape of cliffs and rises gave them plenty of places to hide away.

The harsh topography forced the cultists to segment themselves into a series of camps and outposts, scattered around the island. Some were clearly well-established, with buildings of hewn brick or stone warped through essence abilities. For most, however, they were stuck with tents pitched onto rock or, for the lucky ones, hard-packed earth.

The best scout they had was Callum, the gold-ranked assassination specialist.

He set out to reconnoitre while the others waited, quiet and hidden amongst the boulders on ridge top, for his return.

Gabriel looked at his son, whose schooled expression couldn't quite hide the rage behind his eyes. Rufus's mind seared with the memory of Farrah's death. With the panicked, unexpected battle and every mistake he made along the way. If he'd fought the way he should, the way he'd been taught, then maybe he could have bought those fleeting few seconds he hadn't known he needed before Danielle's intervention.

Rufus reflected again on his lack of experience. His whole life he had been told of the amazing adventurer he was going to be, all the while shielding him from ever truly being responsible for himself. He had become sloppy and complacent, which became evident once he arrived in Greenstone and fell into the hands of the blood cultists.

For all his superbly trained, bronze-ranked might, the reality was that he was wildly inexperienced. The value of the Geller family's approach of raising their members with the most potential in a place where they could be responsible for themselves proved more and more true. He didn't realise just how great a deficit he faced until he was standing over Farrah's fallen body.

Since Farrah's death, Rufus's mind had been consumed with the next fight. He put aside luxuries and rest, spending every moment he could spare preparing for the next time he would face the cultists. If his father didn't have time to train with him then Emir, his mother, Danielle, or anyone stronger than him would do. If he couldn't find someone stronger, then he trained others. Growing up in an academy he knew that teaching others could be a learning experience for yourself. Only when his parents, Gary or Jason forced him to take a break would he stop to rest or engage in some social activity. Even then, the fight to come was a fire in his mind.

Rufus had always been hailed as a prodigy, even amongst his family who trained the best adventurers in the world. Since coming to Greenstone he had failed to live up to that, time and again. No more. He was going to bring every bit of training, every bit of experience to the fight. They would suffer for every lesson he had learned, from every mistake he had made.

"Son," Gabriel said.

"I know," Rufus said. "Put the rage in a box and only take it out when I need it."

"Easier said than done," his mother, Arabelle, told him.

"The anger doesn't help me," Rufus said, his voice cold. "Last time I didn't fight the way I know I can. I was on the back foot, letting myself be caught up instead of making the battle my own. My eyes are clear."

Gabriel and Arabelle shared a look but didn't say any more. Shortly after, Callum returned.

"We have confirmation," he told them. "Priests of Purity are here. In full colours, no less. They're clearly confident we don't know about this place."

"Did you get a recording for proof?" Arella asked.

Callum shook his head. "There's a gold-rank priest down there. Too much chance he would have sensed it."

"We'll use recording crystals when we attack," Danielle said. "Just the one gold ranker?"

Callum nodded.

"What kind of numbers are we looking at, Cal?" Gabriel asked.

Callum took them through the numbers and dispositions of the priests and cultists on the island. There were more than a dozen different camps. They strategised a plan of attack, the low numbers that had given them this chance was now their biggest weakness

"We aren't going to get them all, whichever way we go," Callum said. "The portal devices set up at various points around the camp will probably serve as escape points once they realise things are going wrong. They may even run straight for them. Destroy them if you can but don't take any undue risks. We have trouble enough with the numbers."

"If they have as many portal devices as you described," Danielle said, "then they really do have better astral magic than we do."

"How do you get that from just a lot of portals?" Gary asked.

"The cost," Danielle said. "If they had the resources it would take to make that many portal devices with our knowledge, they could have mounted a very different operation."

Ultimately, they decided to break into task-focused teams, trying to sweep through the camps as quickly as possible. They could take on such a larger force because the disparity in rank made up for the disparity in numbers. Three goldrankers to one was more than enough to even the odds, so long as they could bring that power to bear effectively. They hadn't been expecting even one gold-ranker, so they had to put him down fast.

That was the task of team one. Their objective was to eliminate the leadership, the gold-rank priest, his silver-rank followers and the silver-rankers from the cult. Team one was the smallest but most powerful, consisting of all the gold-rankers and most of the silver. The goal was to finish their task quickly and move to support the others. The enemy only had one gold-ranker to their three, and their three were all top-tier by any measure.

Elspeth Arella would lead a second team to engage the construct monsters, wiping them out before they could be brought to bear elsewhere. The largest contingent of constructs was gathered in the largest camp, which was where they would strike first.

The third team, led by Constance, would seek to sweep the bulk of the cultist forces of bronze-rank and below. The leadership was gathered in the least awful of the island's outposts, while the remainder of their forces was scattered around the various camps.

The bulk of their own bronze-rankers would be split between teams two and three. They would both face superior numbers, but again, they were relying on quality over quantity.

"We don't have a way of taking cultists prisoner without them killing themselves, so don't even try," Gabriel said as they prepared to move. "We're outnumbered, so remember that you might be stronger than any of your enemies, but you aren't stronger than all of them. Reserve your strength as best you can. Staying alive until team one comes in to mop up is your top priority. The entire point of splitting up is so that they can't consolidate. Hitting multiple points will hopefully get them thinking our numbers are greater than they seem until our gold-rankers are brought fully to bear and it's too late."

"What about the priests?" Gary asked. "Do we take them prisoner?"

"We don't have the numbers," Gabriel said. "If they aren't one of us, put them down. Any that live to be taken as prisoners at the end is a bonus."

"Assuming we win," Arabelle added. "You all know your withdrawal points; a fighting retreat early is better than a rout later. The withdrawal points are defensive enough to hold until we come for you."

The three teams struck under cover of darkness. Team one came down like the hammer of god, three gold-rankers erupting like an explosion. Gabriel blasted out waves of fire and wind with sweeps of his sword, turning everything they passed through to tumbling cinders. He moved swiftly, every move devastating as he crashed through the battlefield like the embodiment of wrath, delivering annihilation left and right as he bore down on the gold-rank priest.

Arabelle moved through like a breeze, the enemies she touched with her hand collapsing to withered husks. With each one, an urn, glowing red with life force appeared around her, ready to fuel her other powers. As the priests and cultists fought back, she used that life force to fuel potent healing magic and devastating attacks. Trailed behind her husband, however, she went unnoticed by few beyond her victims.

Gabriele, Arabelle and Callum had been companions for decades, falling into one another's rhythms like dancers. Gabriel enacted his attention-grabbing onslaught with Arabelle to cover his flanks and heal his injuries. Callum used that opportunity to hone in on the true objective. As the gold-rank priest prepared for the oncoming threat of Gabriel, Callum appeared behind him to strike.

Callum was an expert assassin and his abilities landed strong and true on the priest, to devastating effect. No gold-ranker would die easily, however, and even Callum's prowess was not enough to secure the kill immediately. The priest was already healing as he responded to Callum's assault, even as Gabriel and Arabelle moved closer.

The silver-rankers were not as overwhelming as they clashed with their cultist counterparts and the rapidly awakening construct monsters. Nonetheless, they more than held their own. Every member of the small force they had brought along was a powerhouse for their rank.

Team two struck the largest collection of constructs first, rows upon rows of them arrayed like soldiers on parade. Elspeth Arella had not been chosen at random to lead, the reasons for which were obvious as she made devastating headway. Her telekinetic powers were constrained against people, requiring that she first penetrate their auras. Since the constructs had little more aura than an inert rock, she could wield her powers against them to full and spectacular effect.

She raised her arms out in front of her and entire clusters of the constructs floated into the air. Waving her arms like a conductor, she smashed them into each other again and again until all that remained was a floating cloud of debris. She then flung her arms back down, sending the debris cloud crashing into the panicking cultists trying to send more of the constructs to their defence.

As Arella started the whole process over, the rest of team two surged forwards with Gary at the lead. In his hand was a hammer he had forged himself, specifically to fight such enemies. The heavy head came down on the first construct he could reach, shattering it like glass. The others surged around him; he had been picked out as most effective against their artificial enemies.

Team three had the largest number of actual cultists to deal with and Constance didn't have the kind of powers Arella did to make such a potent opening salvo. Worse was an unpleasant surprise, hidden amongst the cultists: three silver rankers to their one. Callum had scouted out all the silver-rankers but apparently they had moved camps while the team was plotting their attack.

The initial assault went well, with most of the cultists asleep in their tents. The attackers still didn't know of the silver rank surprise waiting in store, though. The first sign was a defence that was organised much more quickly than anticipated. The cultists were forming squads and awakening constructs in a swift and organised manner under the tyrannical control of the silver-rankers.

The element of surprise was soon overwhelmed by the numerical superiority as the cultists organised a counterattack. Constance tried to curb the troubling response, which was when the silver-rankers revealed themselves. All three launched themselves at Constance, although her habitual caution prevented her from suffering. She responded with a careful and defensive withdrawal. The moment she sensed three silver-rank auras, she loudly called for all her people to retreat.

The call almost came too late, however, with team three scattered by the cultist counteroffensive. It was a near thing, but the team was saved by a swift and destructive force passing through the enemy, leaving death in its wake. Golden light of the sun and silver light of the moon alternated bright flashes as Rufus moved through the cultist ranks, untouchable and unstoppable.

Rufus's movements were swift and smooth, except when he flickered with a flash of sun or moonlight, vanishing from one spot to appear in another, one of his two swords securing a kill. In one hand he held a searing, golden sword. It passed through cultist and construct alike, as if his enemies were a soft cheese platter. In his other hand was a silver sword, almost impossible to see in motion. Unable to read its trajectory, it found a critical joint or soft throat before the enemy realised they were dead.

Those few who managed to survive the kiss of Rufus's blades were left with malign reminders. Those injured by the golden sword had a small orb of fire, a miniature golden sun, float around them, scorching them with the heat it put out. Those touched by the silver sword had a tiny moon instead. It soaked up heat instead of delivering it, chilling to the bone and sapping strength.

Rufus's path of death was marked by beautiful light. The tiny suns and moons shone brightly in the night. With his power to speed up so quickly, the world seemed to freeze and he left a trail of light where he moved. Cut-apart constructs and severed chunks of armour glowed red-hot where his golden sword had passed through.

With Constance fending off the silver-rankers, it was Rufus and his whirlwind efforts that extracted the bulk of team three, reducing their losses from near-total to only a few. A trail of death was left in his wake. Frustration squirmed through his mind as what was meant to be a vindicating attack became another fighting retreat, just like the last time.

His people were getting away. It was time to withdraw. But anger blazed through him as this battle and the last merged together in his mind. He saw Constance fighting back against the silver-rankers the way he, Gary and Farrah had fought back the cultists and their creations in the astral place.

Looking at Constance's battle in glances as he continued to massacre his way through the lower-ranked enemy, he first thought he was imagining what he saw, that his mind was projecting. Then he looked again and saw he was right. One of the trio Constance was barely holding off was the man who had killed Farrah. It was the same macabre mixture of flesh and steel.

Their people were on the retreat and he had to leave, Rufus knew that. The last time he had faced the monstrosity it had bested him in moments. He knew that. It was time for him to go back. He knew that.

He went forwards.

In the midst of the chaos, the cultist, Timos, hurried in the direction of the closest portal device. There was yelling and screaming, constructs lumbering into motion and cultists running back and forth. He had no idea how anyone had found them; they had been so careful. He realised, logically, that the flaw in their veil of secrecy most likely came from their church of Purity allies. His instincts, however, wanted to blame the man at his side.

"What are we going to do?" Thadwick asked in a panicked half-squeal.

"Shut up," Timos snarled.

Against Timos's emphatic recommendation, his superiors had not only decided to keep Thadwick alive in case there was some use for him, but made Timos responsible for the idiot. While others around him were running, wild with panic, he made purposeful strides for the portal as his mind silently piled a litany of hatred on Thadwick.

Everything had started to go wrong the moment Thadwick joined them, like a curse somehow sent from their enemies. Timos knew Thadwick wasn't truly the engineer of their troubles, yet couldn't dislodge the idea from his mind.

He saw the portal flare to life up ahead, shining silver-blue in the darkness. He considered leaving Thadwick behind and claiming he was lost in the chaos. The consequences of disobedience if the lie was discovered, however, still outweighed his hatred for Thadwick. He grabbed the fool by the front of his shirt and yanked him in the direction of the portal.

There was a trap in Rufus's powers that he had been warned time and again not to fall into. It was a trap that many essences users had. Synergistic powers were potent, but one could easily spend so much time setting up the perfect moment that they died for missing the good one.

Now, Rufus was diving into the trap he had been drilled for years to avoid. Willing Constance to hold out, he didn't make directly for the place the silver-rankers were fighting. Instead, he continued moving through the crowd of enemies, disappearing from one spot and appearing in another, accompanied by flashes of light.

Unlike Jason, Rufus didn't have a teleport power he could use over and over again. Instead, he had a slew of powers that blended movement, teleportation, illusionary after-images and attacks. It took skill and practice to chain them all together in a dynamic environment. Rufus did exactly that with absolute confidence. By the time he worked through his powers, they became available all over again and he became an unstoppable dervish of light.

Now, Rufus was no longer going for the kill. With grazing wounds and minor cuts, his twin blades left a swarm of tiny suns and miniature moons behind as his swords flashed with absolute precision. He kept moving, kept slicing, cutting and moving forwards, desperately urging Constance to hold out. Every time he caught a glimpse of the silver-rank battle, she was being pressed harder and harder.

Gradually, a sea of tiny suns and tiny moons orbited amongst the crowd of enemies, construct and cultist alike. The enemy milled, their earlier coordination turning to confusion. Their leadership was caught up battling Constance, too busy to give the earlier direction. The enemy had retreated, leaving only

Constance and the elusive dervish of light moving through them like a poltergeist.

Constance's voice cried out in a scream as a powerful attack penetrated the magical bubble shielding her. It had been key to withstanding the barrage of attacks she was subjected to but it was close to collapsing entirely. Rufus knew the time had come to act, and, in any case, he had pushed himself to near collapse. His body and mind ached with the depletion of his stamina and mana. Turning finally towards the silver-rank battle, he tossed away his conjured swords and threw back the strongest recovery potion he had. He felt the fresh infusion of mana and stamina flush through his body like dipping into cool water. He activated his speed ability one more time.

Time seemed to freeze around him. Ahead, the three silver-rank abominations and Constance stood motionless before him like a painting of the battle. He did not use his fleeting moment of acceleration to attack. Instead, he stopped and chanted a spell without suffering an attack from the enemies surrounding him.

"*Darkness and light, sun and moon; be mine to awaken and move at my command. Mine is the realm and mine is the power; bring forth the kingdom of eclipse.*"

Rufus's speed power came to an end just as he completed his chant. Darkness, like some great explosion, swept over the battlefield. The stars in the sky were gone, as were the twin moons that had lit up the battle. Every glow-stone embedded in a construct or floating around a cultist went dim, leaving only the tiny suns and moon to cast light. The crowd of cultists cried out in shock and even the silver-rankers were startled into giving pause. The halt in their attacks gave Constance a much-needed reprieve.

The suns and moons floated up, into the air. The people they left behind were suddenly drained of colour, leaving only dark silhouettes. Flames of silver and gold lit up, limning the dark silhouettes as they began to scream.

Above them, the suns and the moons merged together, growing and melding as they formed an enormous orb of darkness, shrouded in light to form an eclipse, floating over their heads. It loomed over the battlefield, potent and domineering in the magical darkness that filled the air. The shrieking cries of those burning in fire of silver and gold below made a horrifying accompaniment to the ominous eclipse.

The silver rankers had strong magical senses and felt the connection between the darkness that had enveloped them, the orb floating above them and the person who had called it into being. They turned as one, their gazes falling on Rufus. He was finally standing still but the cultists around him were either burning with fire or wild with panic, too busy to recognise the enemy in their midst. A construct lunged at him but he raised a hand without even looking at it, a stream of sun fire launching out and melting the steel monstrosity on the spot.

One of the three silver-rankers sneered with recognition as he locked eyes with

Rufus. Rufus's face was impassive as he rose an arm to point at him, the cultist who had taken Farrah's life. From the orb above, a terrifying beam blasted down at the abomination, a bright beam with a dark core, pouring transcendent damage into the cultist.

Rufus has never before come anywhere close to building up so much power with which to use this attack. Under this power, anything short of silver rank would have been instantly annihilated and even most silver-rankers would have died in moments. The cultist upon whom Rufus poured all his rage and all his power was no ordinary silver-ranker, however. Standing at the peak of his rank, on the cusp of obtaining gold, and with the fullness of power bestowed by its other-worldly master, the cultist was still standing when the beam was spent, the power gathered in the eclipse exhausted. It vanished, the oppressive field of darkness vanishing with it.

Across the battlefield, dozens of cultists and constructs were dead. The fires had taken their toll. The enemy that had taken the brunt of that power still stood, although anyone looking at his state might assume he wished he hadn't. The cultist had conjured one steel wall after another to endure the transcendent blast but it stormed through them, one after another. The cultist suffered much the same treatment, the flesh and steel of his body fused together like a candle melted by sunlight through a window.

There was an odd stillness throughout the battlefield, all eyes on the ruined cultist. He moved, just a little, then a little more. He flexed his warped limbs and melted muscles roaring in wordless pain and rage.

Rufus was as spent as his power, everything he had and more burned through to set up and deliver one grand attack. The last thing he saw before passing out, surrounded by enemies, was the hideously injured cultist, more an abomination than ever, moving in his direction.

THANK YOU FOR READING HE WHO FIGHTS WITH MONSTERS, BOOK TWO.

We hope you enjoyed it as much as we enjoyed bringing it to you. We just wanted to take a moment to encourage you to review the book. Follow this link: He Who Fights With Monsters 2 to be directed to the book's Amazon product page to leave your review.

Every review helps further the author's reach and, ultimately, helps them continue writing fantastic books for us all to enjoy.

Want to discuss our books with other readers and even the authors? Join our Discord server today and be a part of the Aethon community.

Facebook

Instagram

Twitter

Website

You can also join our non-spam mailing list by visiting www.subscribepage.com/AethonReadersGroup and never miss out on future releases. You'll also receive three full books completely Free as our thanks to you.

ALSO IN SERIES

HE WHO FIGHTS WITH MONSTERS

BOOK ONE

BOOK TWO

BOOK THREE

Looking for more great LitRPG?

Jeff Driscoll becomes the only active Game Master for the VRMMORPG Infinite Worlds after a rogue patch turns the game into a buggy, dangerous mess. Can he fix it on his own and save the players?

GET MANUFACTURING MAGIC NOW!

When Hall is trapped inside of Sky Realms Online, he loses everything. His level, his stats, his real world life. Even worse, nobody knows the new rules. What's next, permadeath?

GET GRAYHOLD TODAY!

When lifelong gamer Dave is portaled into a game-world called Eloria with no way out, he thinks all his dreams have come true. However, in none of those dreams did his wife and daughter ever accompany him. Can he keep them safe in this strange new world?

GET WATCHER'S TEST NOW!

When there's no way to win, cheat, and cheat BIG. Howard, desperate to save his friends and countless innocents, hatches a plan to fix things. Using his deep knowledge of game mechanics, he'll start again as a level 0 necromancer and exploit his way to power.

GET UNDERPOWERED HOWARD NOW!

I was in my garage when the space elves addressed the whole world.

They didn't call themselves space elves, of course. Most humans struggled to pronounce Khjurhnalva, so we opted for the easier version. They had a message for us: forces that had eradicated their species' males were now heading for Earth.

Hungry for our resources, the alien hordes annihilate everything that stands in their way. The space elves offered us access to the System and asked for very little in return. After all, cooperation was vital to the survival of both our species.

I, Mathew Alexander Dunphy, know all of the above is bullshit. I saw the truth with my own eyes and heard it from their beautiful, delicate, deceitful mouths. No one believes me, though. They call me mad.

What reason could the space elves have to lie?

Planet-wide survival reality show?

Ridiculous.

For all our LitRPG books, visit our website.